THE PENGUIN CLASSICS

FOUNDER EDITOR (1944–64): E. V. RIEU

EDITORS

Robert Baldick (1964-72)   *Betty Radice*

COUNT LEO NIKOLAYEVICH TOLSTOY was born in 1828 at Yas-
naya Polyana in the Tula province, and educated privately. He studied
Oriental languages and law at the University of Kazan then led a life
of pleasure until 1851 when he joined an artillery regiment in the
Caucasus. He took part in the Crimean war and after the defence of
Sevastopol he wrote *The Sevastopol Stories*, which established his reputation. After a period in St Petersburg and abroad, where he studied
educational methods for use in his school for peasant children in Yas-
naya, he married Sophie Andreyevna Behrs in 1862. The next fifteen
years was a period of great happiness; they had thirteen children, and
Tolstoy managed his vast estates in the Volga Steppes, continued his
educational projects, cared for his peasants and wrote *War and Peace*
(1865–68) and *Anna Karenin* (1874–76). *A Confession* (1879–82) marked
an outward change in his life and works; he became an extreme rationalist and moralist, and in a series of pamphlets after 1880 he expressed
theories such as rejection of the state and church, indictment of the
demands of the flesh, and denunciation of private property. His teach-
ings earned him numerous followers in Russia and abroad, but also
much opposition and in 1901 he was excommunicated by the Russian
holy synod. He died in 1910, in the course of a dramatic flight from
home, at the small railway station of Astapovo.

ROSEMARY EDMONDS was born in London and studied English,
Russian, French, Italian and Old Church Slavonic at universities in
England, France and Italy. During the war she was translator to General
de Gaulle at Fighting France Headquarters in London and, after the
liberation, in Paris. She went on to study Russian Orthodox Spiritu-
ality, and has translated Archimandrite Sophrony's *The Undistorted
Image*. She has also translated Tolstoy's *War and Peace*, *The Cossacks*,
Anna Karenin and *Childhood, Boyhood and Youth; The Queen of Spades* by
Pushkin, and Turgenev's *Fathers and Sons*, all for the Penguin Classics.
Her other translations include works by Gogol and Leskov. She is at
present working in Spanish, and researching into Old Church Slavonic
texts.

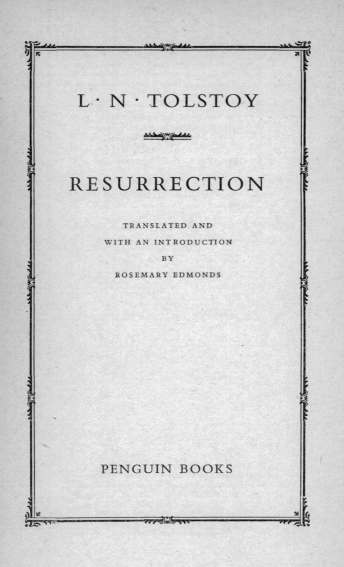

L · N · TOLSTOY

RESURRECTION

TRANSLATED AND
WITH AN INTRODUCTION
BY
ROSEMARY EDMONDS

PENGUIN BOOKS

Penguin Books Ltd, Harmondsworth, Middlesex, England
Penguin Books Inc., 7110 Ambassador Road, Baltimore, Maryland 21207, U.S.A.
Penguin Books Australia Ltd, Ringwood, Victoria, Australia
Penguin Books Canada Ltd, 41 Steelcase Road West, Markham, Ontario, Canada
Penguin Books (N.Z.) Ltd, 182–190 Wairau Road, Auckland 10, New Zealand

—

This translation first published 1966
Reprinted 1969, 1970, 1971, 1973, 1974

—

Copyright © Rosemary Edmonds, 1966

—

Made and printed in Great Britain
by Richard Clay (The Chaucer Press) Ltd,
Bungay, Suffolk
Set in Monotype Bembo

INTRODUCTION

'I SHOULD like to live long, very long; and the thought of death fills me with a childlike, poetic alarm.'

So wrote Tolstoy in his youth. But when he was verging on the age of fifty and, like Job before the time of testing, had nothing left to wish for, the poetic alarm turned all at once to panic fear as he stared into the black void – the *gouffre* which Pascal called the eternal framework of our transitory existence. 'Life stood still and grew sinister' is how he formulated the onslaught of his spiritual crisis.

The next three decades were devoted to a Titanic struggle for truth. This anguished search for a meaning that death would not destroy, estranged him from his wife, and made him indifferent to his children and his friends and no longer interested in the universe of his novels that had brought him wealth and fame. Suddenly he yearned for an art 'which would awaken higher and better feelings'; and ceased to be satisfied with describing the futilities of life to amuse idle readers, which was what he considered he had done in *War and Peace* and *Anna Karenina*. Art must not be an end in itself but have an overriding ethical purpose. And so Tolstoy the artist became subservient to Tolstoy the preacher and prophet.

Tolstoy chose 'Resist not evil' as the text for his 'message' to mankind, and proceeded to repudiate the State and withdraw from the Church. The next twenty years were dedicated entirely to polemic writing on religious, social and educational themes (which the authorities vainly tried to suppress), until, as an old man of seventy-one, the plight of the Doukhobors moved him to look through his portfolio of unfinished literary works and complete something in aid of the Doukhobor Fund.

The 'Doukhobors' was the name given to a fundamentalist peasant sect whose precepts had much in common with Tolstoy's own teaching. Numbering between fifteen and sixteen thousand, they preached chastity, teetotalism, vegetarianism, the sharing of all goods and property and, above all, non-resistance to evil by force. Etymologically, the word signifies 'spirit-fighters', being originally intended by the Orthodox clergy to imply that the Doukhobors fought against the Spirit of God; but the Doukhobors themselves accepted the term as denoting that they fought not against but for and with the Spirit. The community was first heard of in the middle of the eighteenth century. Their doctrine became so clearly defined, and the number of their adherents increased so steadily, that by 1891 the Russian Government and the Church were seriously alarmed and started an energetic campaign to suppress the sect, whose refusal to have any part in military service was regarded as open rebellion. Hundreds died in the persecutions that followed, and some four thousand were scattered in remote mountain villages in the Caucasus, where they fell victim to hunger and disease. Tolstoy was deeply shocked, identified himself with the agitation in their favour and sent an article, *The Persecution of Christians in Russia in 1895* (the year he came in contact with them personally), to the London *Times*. As a result, the Society of Friends in England petitioned Emperor Nicholas II for permission for the Doukhobors to leave Russia. By 1898 this request to migrate abroad was granted, provided the sect agreed never to return and the Government was not called upon to finance their departure. A first party sailed for Cyprus, which was originally chosen for their settlement because at that time funds were not sufficient for transferring them to any other British territory. But as contributions swelled it was found possible to send a number of Doukhobor emigrants to Canada, where they were offered asylum and hospitality, and where they were joined early in 1899 by the party from Cyprus.

If it had not been for the Doukhobors and the necessity to raise money for their mass exodus Tolstoy might never have finished *Resurrection*, the idea for which had been suggested to him ten years previously by a report confided to him of a nobleman serving on a jury and recognizing the prostitute on trial for theft as a girl he had seduced when he was a young man.

Tolstoy was soon so absorbed in his first full-length novel for over twenty years (*Anna Karenina* had appeared in 1877) that distractions of any kind were almost painful. Since *War and Peace*, he told his wife, he had never been so powerfully gripped by the creative urge. *Resurrection* was the last of his great novels, and no contemporary literary work was so eagerly awaited, in Russia or abroad. It was at once translated into many languages and the proceeds handed over to the Friends' Doukhobor Committee. But in October 1901 the clerk of the Committee, John Bellows, declared that the Society of Friends ought not to have accepted 'money coming from a smutty book'. 'It arouses lust,' he wrote, 'and after a careful thinking it over . . . I must refund the money out of my own pocket, rather than let it remain as it is.'

To this Tolstoy replied a couple of months later (in English):

When I read a book the chief interest for me is the *Weltanschau-[u]ng des Autors*, what he likes and what he hates. And I hope that the reader, which will read my book with the same view will find out what the author likes or dislikes and will be influenced with the sentiment of the author. And I can say that when I wrote the book I abhorred with all my heart the lust and to express this abhorrence was one of the chief aims of the book.

He might have added 'The whole truth can never be immoral', his verdict on the fiction of de Maupassant.

If, as Tolstoy himself most firmly believed, the criterion of a work of art is that it should convey the author's feelings, *Resurrection* is art of a high order. Its chief themes are the basic themes of art – love, passion, death – but they are treated with such burning sincerity, such Evangelical simplicity and vitality, that they seem almost new to art. The reader's heart is infected by pity, his conscience by a compulsive need to crusade against cruelty and injustice; and Tolstoy's heroic search to discover the purpose of life becomes our striving, too. Tolstoy had now determined that the fictional form should be the means of propagating the stern message he was bent on delivering.

Like a clown at a country fair grimacing in front of the ticket-booth in order to lure the public inside the tent where the real play is being performed, so my imaginative work must serve to attract the attention of the public to my philosophic teaching [he wrote in a letter at the turn of the century].

Resurrection is the great imaginative synthesis of Tolstoyism, gravid with the fruits of a lifetime's agony. 'It is a kind of shrapnel shell of a novel,' declared one contemporary critic. 'The novel is but the containing case. The genius of the author is the explosive force, which scatters its doctrines like the closely packed bullets among the enemy' – the enemy on this occasion being the whole fabric of society, the Law Courts, the prison system and, in particular, the Church.

Resurrection is a panorama of Russia, of humanity in general, depicted on a canvas almost as vast as that of *Anna Karenina*; but in contrast to the aristocratic *ambiance* of *Anna Karenina* it is the underworld that we *experience* in *Resurrection*. And since Tolstoy could not work independently of nature, since his genius lay, not in invention but in a meticulous and sensitive reflecting – in the transmutation of actual persons – in the central figure of Nekhlyudov we have the last of Tolstoy's great self-portraits. In Nekhlyudov Tolstoy expresses his own deepest aspirations, his own views on every aspect of human existence. Nekhlyudov affixes the seal, as it were, to Tolstoy's own life. By the end of the book he has rendered accounts to himself and to the world. 'That night,' the novel concludes, 'an entirely new life began for Nekhlyudov, not so much because he had entered into new conditions of life, but because everything that happened to him from that time on was endowed with an entirely different meaning for him. How this new chapter of his life will end, the future will show.' This hints at a sequel that will tell the story of Nekhlyudov in his new life, and indeed, six months after he finished the work, Tolstoy notes in his diary: 'I terribly want to write an artistic, not a dramatic but an epic continuation of *Resurrection*: the peasant life of Nekhlyudov.'

Tolstoy set himself to reproduce in artistic form the resurrection of fallen man. But he does not recognize the Christian conception of resurrection, and therefore it is the process of regeneration that he describes. Nekhlyudov does not rise from the dead: he is merely re-born to lead a (supposedly) better life. And we are not sure that he will even achieve this. Has not his whole career been one 'resurrection' after another? Inherited wealth enables him to change his form of life whenever one set of ideas is supplanted by another. As a university student, under the influence of Herbert Spencer he refused the property inherited from his father and gave it to the peasants. But as an officer in the Guards he finds his monthly allowance inadequate, and there are unpleasant interviews with his mother over money matters. He goes abroad to visit the picture galleries of Europe, and immediately sees himself as a painter; though of course the picture he starts never gets finished. A liaison with the wife of a marshal of the nobility begets an interest in schools, public works and liberalism, which, like the unfinished painting, palls in its turn; so that when he recognizes Maslova in the witness-box he is ripe for still another 'purging of the soul', as he terms his periodic reappraisals. And, as always, it will be carried out in his 'usual conscientious way' as he 'considers it right to do'. (Each time there are 'tears of tender emotion at his own goodness', and each time the new course is the one and only true direction, which he marvels that everybody else does not recognize, too.) On the face of things it would appear that the Nekhlyudovs of this world are concerned with their

9

fellow men, grieve with them, would right their wrongs. They confess their own guilt and are eager to atone – but all because at the given moment they like the idea and find 'something pleasurable and soothing' in the recognition of their own baseness. A sacrifice to the demands of conscience affords them 'the highest spiritual enjoyment'. But when the impulse falters and the mood changes, to be replaced by a new inspiration, everything with which they lately sympathized to the point of self-abnegation is forgotten in a flash and no longer affects them. When Maslova refuses to take advantage of the 'pardon' obtained for her, in order to marry Simonson and follow him to the mines, Nekhlyudov is so immediately preoccupied with the search for a new life to take the place of the one that has just collapsed like a pack of cards that the spectacle of several hundred prisoners stifling in their stinking prison cells, where typhus is rife, his visit to the mortuary, where among others he sees the dead body of a consumptive whom only the day before he had been talking to and of whom he had grown 'particularly fond' – these dreadful scenes from Dante's *Inferno* hardly register in his mind and it never occurs to him to do anything to alleviate the suffering all around him. He does not ever wonder how Maslova will survive punishment which she does not deserve and of which he is the main cause.

From the outset Maslova senses the false note in Nekhlyudov's repentance. And anyway, what good could his repentance do her? It could not rehabilitate her. Nor can she bring herself to compromise and make use of him as her companions urge. She will intercede only for an old woman wrongly imprisoned for arson. Ten years of prostitution have not extinguished the Divine spark in her. (The decision she and two prostitute friends took one night in Carnival week, the merchant's trust in her, the story behind the poisoning she was accused of, her 'Madam's' regard for her; her behaviour at the trial towards the real culprits, the attitude of her fellow prisoners, her reactions to Nekhlyudov and Simonson –

are all abundant proof of this.) Nekhlyudov interprets her refusal to marry him as a sign that she loves him and therefore does not want to spoil his life. But in fact she has so little respect for him, so little belief in him, that she is always on her guard, never discussing her position with him, as she does with her companions in prison, never telling him of her thoughts, feelings or hopes. She behaves to him as a grown-up person to a child, allowing him to amuse himself with his new sensations – until she can bear it no longer and in an outburst of wounded pride tells him that she is not going to serve a second time as an object for his selfish experimenting. 'You want to save yourself through me. You had your pleasure from me in this world, and now you want to get your salvation through me in the world to come.' Except right at the beginning, when she had loved him and for a while continued to love him even after he got her with child before discarding her, their relationship did not ring true to her – any more than it did to Countess Tolstoy, who described it as 'utterly false'. (Indeed, the Countess found the book 'repulsive', although she admitted and paid tribute to the genius of the descriptive passages. She was troubled by the likeness she could not help noticing between Nekhlyudov and her husband, who had portrayed his hero as progressing from degradation to regeneration. 'He thinks this way about himself,' she remarked in her Journal, no doubt for Tolstoy to read – they always read each other's journals. 'He has described all these regenerations in books very well, but he has never practised them in life . . .')

In technique *Resurrection* equals the great epics of Tolstoy's prime; but it covers more ground than any of his other novels. The essence of all that Tolstoy had thought and suffered since his spiritual change is crammed into its pages. There is no place for the lies which would cheat us into the belief that wrong may sometimes be right through passion, or genius, or heroism. Tolstoy's concern is with the 'grave, noble face of truth' – he will compel us to recognize what is bad and infect us with an urgent desire for improvement. *Resurrection* is written with all the old sustained exuberance. He has lost nothing of the creative compass of *War and Peace*, written over thirty years earlier when his powers were at their zenith. But the architectural lines are different. Whereas in his previous novels attention is continually shifted from one hero to another, in *Resurrection* Tolstoy follows Nekhlyudov step by step, hardly letting him out of sight for an instant. Other characters and incidents appear only in so far as they affect Nekhlyudov; otherwise they are allowed little validity beyond the seeming irrelevance of much that happens in 'real' life. It is psychologically exquisite. If Tolstoy is to know a man's thoughts and feelings he must first of all study every aspect of his physical being. He builds up his *dramatis personae* line upon line, like Holbein, until we have – not a photograph but the accumulated life of a personality. He is the most clear-seeing of all artists and can paint a colossal fresco with all the grandeur and economy which such a style demands, and at the same time give the marvellous detail almost of a miniature. With true artistic genius he senses the great and the eternal in the most apparently unimportant manifestations of everyday life: the curve of a mother's arms as she cradles her child; the awkward walk of someone who is embarrassed; a peasant's clumsy clothes, crooked legs or squinting eye. He sees beyond the historical reality of the given moment because his business is with the transcendental.

There could be no title more significant for a Russian than *Resurrection*. All down the centuries the Russian Christian has been preoccupied with the idea of, with the search for, immortality. The earthly history of mankind could not be an end in itself, could not be merely temporal. But victory over time – over death – postulates Resurrection, in the Gospel sense. For the Orthodox believer Christ is the manifestation of God in history, and the resurrection of Christ lies at the heart of all mystical striving. Tolstoy belongs far more to the Western world with its emphasis on the 'moral' and 'ethical' teaching of Christ and a consequent enthusiasm for *l'activité utile*. But for the Russian mystic morals can *only* be the result of faith in eternal life. Kant's ethical teleology holds no attraction whatsoever for him. He is not interested in the 'utilitarian' aspect of morality as a means to the better organization of human society; but he has no difficulty in understanding and accepting the proposition: 'If I die, then the whole world dies in me, with me. If I am resurrected, then all mankind is resurrected in me, with me.'

Tolstoy's humanism antagonized his own class, whom he accused of doing violence to the little man. With the exception of a brief period after the Russo–Japanese war freedom of speech has never been realized in Russia, and *Resurrection* was ruthlessly cut by the official Censorship. In Part One the whole of Chapter 13 describing the effect of army life disappeared; and of Chapters 39 and 40 only the words 'The service began' were left. Nekhlyudov's visit to Toporov – a portrait of Pobedonostsev who presided over the Holy Synod from 1880 to 1905 – had, of course, to be struck out of Chapter 27 of Part Two; and Chapter 19 introducing the aged general in charge of the prison in Petersburg, Chapter 30 analysing the various categories into which so-called criminals fell and Chapter 38 describing the departure of the convict train from Moscow all suffered badly. But naturally it was Part Three, telling of the treatment of the prisoners on their way to Siberia, and conditions in Siberia, that suffered most. The first complete Russian text of *Resurrection* was published in England, where Vladimir Tchertkov, Tolstoy's disciple, had settled at Maldon in Essex after being banished from Russia, together with a number of other progressives. Tchertkov's wife discovered an old compositor who prided himself on being able to set Russian type, and in the year 1900 the firm of 'Headley Brothers, Printers, 14, Bishopgate Without, London, E.C.' printed a Russian text 'not mutilated by the Censor', as the title-page roundly informs us.

Tolstoy's attempts to rouse the oppressed against their

oppressors and his clamour for a moral reconstruction of all the institutions of contemporary society provoked opposition from the Church, for the reason that the Orthodox Church disclaims revolution brought about by force, seeing in any such violent change merely the substitution of one form of coercion for another. The Russian religious consciousness looks to Transfiguration, rather than revolution. It is impossible to establish justice on earth if people themselves do not suffer a sea-change and become 'different' by surmounting their narrow egoism, which is practicable only by considering meaning in relation to eternity, in contact with the Creator. But Tolstoy could never quite accept the fact that 'the law made nothing perfect' – that no law will turn bad people into good society. His hero does not see visions to send him winging his way to God: he must climb the laborious path of expiation, painful step after painful step, inspired only by an inner, 'moral' *desire* to atone.

In *Resurrection* Tolstoy voices this conflict with the Church, the bitterest of all the conflicts forced upon him by his unflinching search for absolute truth. To the end of his life he persisted in confining his quest to the ethical plane, until even his intrepid 'purgings of the soul' could advance him no farther and he found himself at a full stop – confronted by the cataclysmic choice between resurrection or – death.

It was Tolstoy's tragedy – and ours – that, like Selyenin, the assistant public prosecutor, he 'knew so little' of the teaching of the Church. In every description he gives of church services, ritual, traditions, texts, he disfigures and caricatures with such obvious tendentiousness and vehemence that art goes by the board. ('I wish you more spiritual freedom,' Turgenyev wrote to him in a brilliant flash of insight.) Everything that, as a rationalist, he could not accept, everything in which he could not BELIEVE, Tolstoy rejected with the intransigence of a man who knows himself to be right. Interpreting the essence of religious feeling as a consciousness of the 'equality and brotherhood of man', he plunged into the ideological fray with the aim of helping the people 'to struggle out of their dark ignorance', indignant with those who used their enlightenment only 'to plunge them still deeper into it'.

The attack on the Church in *Resurrection* led to Tolstoy's formal excommunication by a decree dated 22 February 1901. An examination of the conflict, to which he himself attached enormous significance, can do much to explain the course of Russian history. The Russian is endowed by nature with a strong sense of the other world, and his concern with the primary source, the First Principle, places him on the boundary between the two worlds, where he lives two realities, the historical and the meta-historical, at one and the same time. Because of the importance of the eternal, the temporal is held to be of small account, and so there is little inclination to fight for temporal 'rights' and privileges – the Russian consciously or unconsciously looks to another judgement, on another plane. And so Tolstoy fought in vain when he strove to establish the kingdom of heaven by reforming the institutions of this globe. Moved as he could be by the dying of an ordinary unlettered peasant, he never perceived what lay at the root of nobility and peace in the face of death, so preoccupied and grieved was he by the injustices suffered by man in the course of his earthly existence. And yet in the person of the little old man whom Nekhlyudov met on the ferry, and saw in prison later the same day, Tolstoy has drawn perhaps the most striking portrait of Melchizedek in all literature – Melchizedek 'without father, without mother, without descent, having neither beginning of days, nor end of life; but made like unto the Son of God'.

At the beginning of October 1899, just as Tolstoy was finishing the third part of *Resurrection*, an unknown correspondent wrote to him from Baku, giving an account of himself and his principles which Tolstoy inserted almost word for word. 'They' hadn't been able to do anything to him because he was 'a free man', above every sort of insult or injury. He did not have a name because he had renounced every name, place, country. He knew no name to answer to but the name of – Man. Nor did he reckon how old he was: he could not count the years, since he always was, and always would be. Like Melchizedek he had neither father nor mother; his Father was God, and his mother – the Earth. But even here Tolstoy proved unable to overcome the limitations of his rational moralism – although he did counsel his correspondent not to concentrate on the exposure of lies and deception to the exclusion of the love one owes to an erring fellow being. (As Maxim Gorky said, 'Tolstoy was a human-kindly man.') In an interview with a reporter of a Moscow newspaper Tolstoy said that in *Resurrection* he had 'tried to portray various forms of love: exalted love, sensual love, and love of a still loftier kind, the love that ennobles man, and in this form of love lies resurrection'.

This work of Tolstoy's goes farther than being a literary masterpiece: it steps outside the framework of pure art. (Those who disparage it, complaining of the philosophical digressions, are those in whom 'the word that leaves behind the murk of passion and desire awakens no response'.) *Resurrection* is an expression of an integral contemplation of the world; a propagation of Tolstoy's faith and moral ideals, portraying Russia as he saw her, within the bounds in which he was capable of experiencing her. There is never any indifference in Tolstoy, never an instant's sparing of himself. His preoccupation was with mankind's eternal problem, and nothing short of a whole solution would satisfy him. When he was brought to death 'Earth felt the wound'.

ROSEMARY EDMONDS, London, 1965

Except on page 437 and page 468 the footnotes have been added by the translator.

PART ONE

'Then came Peter to him, and said,
Lord, how oft shall my brother
sin against me, and I forgive
him? till seven times?
'Jesus saith unto him, I say not
unto thee, Until seven times:
but, Until seventy times seven.'

(Matt. xviii, 21-2)

'And why beholdest thou the mote
that is in thy brother's eye,
but considerest not the beam that
is in thine own eye?'

(Matt. vii, 3)

'He that is without sin among
you, let him first cast a
stone at her.'

(John viii, 7)

'The disciple is not above his
master: but every one that
is perfect shall be as his
master.'

(Luke vi, 40)

1

THOUGH men in their hundreds of thousands had tried their
hardest to disfigure that little corner of the earth where they
had crowded themselves together, paving the ground with
stones so that nothing could grow, weeding out every blade of
vegetation, filling the air with the fumes of coal and gas, cutting down the trees and driving away every beast and every
bird – spring, however, was still spring, even in the town. The
sun shone warm, the grass, wherever it had not been scraped
away, revived and showed green not only on the narrow strips
of lawn on the boulevards but between the paving-stones as
well, and the birches, the poplars and the wild cherry-trees
were unfolding their sticky, fragrant leaves, and the swelling
buds were bursting on the lime-trees; the jackdaws, the
sparrows and the pigeons were cheerfully getting their nests
ready for the spring, and the flies, warmed by the sunshine,
buzzed gaily along the walls. All were happy – plants, birds,
insects and children. But grown-up people – adult men and
women – never left off cheating and tormenting themselves
and one another. It was not this spring morning which they
considered sacred and important, not the beauty of God's
world, given to all creatures to enjoy – a beauty which in-
clines the heart to peace, to harmony and to love. No, what
they considered sacred and important were their own devices
for wielding power over each other.

Thus, in the office of the provincial prison, what they regarded as sacred and important was not the fact that the grace
and gladness of spring had been given to every animal and
human creature, but the fact that a numbered document, bearing a seal and a superscription, had been received on the previous day, ordering that on this, the 28th day of April, at nine

o'clock in the morning three prisoners at present detained in the prison, two women and one man, should be brought to the court-house. One of these women, as the most important prisoner, was to have a special escort. So now, in conformity with this order, on the 28th day of April, at eight o'clock in the morning, the head warder entered the dark, foul-smelling corridor of the women's section of the prison. He was followed by a haggard-looking female with curly grey hair, wearing a jacket with braided sleeves and a belt edged with blue piping. She was the prison matron.

'It is Maslova you want?' she inquired, as she and the warder on duty went towards the door of one of the cells that led from the corridor.

The warder, rattling his iron keys, turned the lock and, opening the door of the cell, which emitted a whiff of air still more offensive than that in the corridor, shouted:

'Maslova to the court-house!' and closed the door again while he waited.

The fresh, bracing air of the fields had even penetrated into the prison yard, wafted to the city by the wind. But in the corridor the air was heavy with the germs of typhoid and the smell of sewage, tar and putrefaction, which instantly made everyone who came in feel depressed and melancholy. Though she was used to the bad air the prison matron, who had just come in from the yard, was affected by it. The moment she entered the corridor she felt languid and wanted to go to sleep.

A commotion could be heard inside the cell: there were women's voices and the sound of bare feet on the floor.

'Now then, Maslova, hurry up there, I tell you!' shouted the head warder through the cell door.

A couple of minutes later a short full-bosomed young woman in a grey cloak over a white jacket and skirt came briskly out of the door, swung round and stood beside him. She was wearing calico stockings and prison shoes, and round her head she had tied a white kerchief, from beneath which a few ringlets of curling black hair had with evident intent been allowed to escape. Her face was pale with the pallor peculiar to people who have been shut in for a long time and which puts one in mind of the shoots which sprout from potatoes kept in a cellar. Her small broad hands and as much of the plump neck as could be seen beneath the big collar of her prison cloak were the same colour. Her sparkling jet-black eyes, though they were somewhat puffy and one of them had a slight cast, were very lively and offered a striking contrast to the dull pallor of her face. She held herself absolutely erect, her full bosom well forward. Emerging into the corridor, head thrown back a little, she looked the warder straight in the eye and stood ready to obey his orders, whatever they might be. The warder was just about to lock the door of the cell when a wrinkled old woman with straight grey hair thrust out a pale austere face. She started to say something to Maslova, but the warder slammed the door on her and the head disappeared. Inside the cell a woman roared with laughter. Maslova smiled too, and turned towards the little barred window in the cell door. The old woman on the other side clung to the opening and said in a hoarse voice:

'Mind now, don't say a word more than you need, stick to your story and stay mum.'

'If only they would settle it one way or the other, it couldn't be worse than it is now,' said Maslova, with a shake of her head.

'Of course they'll settle it, and in one way, not the other,' said the head warder, with the self-assured wit of a superior. 'After me, quick march!'

The old woman's eye vanished from the opening, and Maslova advanced into the middle of the corridor and with rapid mincing steps followed the head warder. They went down a stone staircase, passed the still fouler and noisier cells in the men's section, pursued by many eyes peering at them through the grated windows, and entered the office, where two armed soldiers were waiting to escort her. A clerk sitting in the office handed one of the soldiers a document reeking of tobacco, and pointing to the prisoner said, 'Take her.'

The soldier, a peasant from Nizhni Novgorod with a red pock-marked face, stuck the document into the cuff of his greatcoat and with a glance towards the prisoner winked slyly at his companion, a broad-cheeked Chuvash. The soldiers, with the prisoner between them, descended the stairs and walked over to the main exit. Here a small gate was opened for them, and passing through it they proceeded to the other side of the town, keeping to the middle of the cobbled streets.

Cabbies, tradespeople, cooks, labourers, clerks in government service stopped and looked with curiosity at the prisoner; some shook their heads and thought to themselves: 'This is what evil conduct – conduct not like ours – leads to.' Children stared terror-stricken at the criminal, until they saw that she was guarded by soldiers and could not do any more harm. A peasant from the country, who had sold his charcoal and been drinking tea in the tavern, went up to her, crossed himself and gave her a kopeck. The prisoner blushed, bowed her head and murmured something. Aware of the looks directed towards her, without turning her head she glanced out of the corner of her eye at those who were gazing at her, and enjoyed the attention she was attracting. She was cheered, too, by the spring air, so pure in comparison with that in the gaol, but she had become unused to walking, and the cobblestones and her clumsy prison shoes hurt her feet; and so she looked down at them and tried to step as lightly as possible. Passing a corn-chandler's, her foot almost touched one of the pigeons strutting about unmolested in front of the shop. The blue-grey bird fluttered up and flew past her ear, fanning her with its wings. The prisoner smiled, then heaved a deep sigh as she recalled her present circumstances.

2

THE story of the prisoner Maslova was nothing out of the ordinary. Her mother had never been married and was the daughter of a serf-woman who worked in the farm-yard of two maiden ladies living in the country. Every year this un-married girl had given birth to a child and, as generally hap-pens in the country, the baby was baptized but afterwards the mother did not suckle the unwelcome useless little stranger, who hindered her in her work, and the child was soon dead of starvation.

Five children died in this way. Each was baptized, starved and allowed to expire. The sixth, begotten by an itinerant gipsy, was a girl who would have shared the fate of the others had it not so chanced that one of the two maiden ladies went to the farm-yard to reprimand the dairymaids for sending up cream that smelt of the cow. Lying in the cowshed was the mother with a fine healthy new-born baby. The mistress up-braided them on account of the cream and also for allowing a woman who had just given birth to lie in the cowshed, and was about to leave when she caught sight of the new baby. Her heart was touched and she offered to be godmother to the child. This she duly did and then, out of compassion for her godchild, gave the mother milk and money, and so the girl lived. And for ever afterwards the old ladies called her 'the rescued one'.

The child was three years old when her mother fell ill and died. The grandmother, the old cow-woman, found the infant a burden and so the maiden ladies took her into the house with them. The little black-eyed baby grew into an extremely lively and attractive girl and was a great comfort to the old ladies.

The younger of the two, Sophia Ivanovna, had the kindlier nature – it was she who had stood godmother to the child – and the elder, Marya Ivanovna, was rather stern. Sophia Ivanovna dressed the little girl in pretty clothes, taught her to read and wanted to bring her up like a lady. Marya Ivanovna thought the child should be trained to work and be a good servant; so she was exacting with her and punished and even beat her when she was in a bad temper. Thus, be-tween these two influences, the girl grew up half servant, half

23

young lady. They called her Katusha, a sort of compromise between Katka and Katenka.[1] She sewed, kept the house tidy, polished the metalwork of the ikons with chalk, roasted, ground and served the coffee, did light laundry work and sometimes sat and read aloud to the ladies.

Though she had more than one offer for her hand she would not marry: she felt that life as the wife of any of the working-men who courted her would be too hard, spoilt as she was by the comforts of the manor.

Thus she lived until her sixteenth year. Just after her six-teenth birthday the student nephew of the old ladies, a rich young prince, came on a visit to his aunts, and Katusha, though she did not dare to acknowledge the fact to him or even to herself, fell in love with him. Then two years later this same nephew stayed four days with his aunts on the way to join his regiment, and the night before he left he seduced Katusha and, thrusting a hundred-rouble note into her hand, departed. Five months after his departure she knew for certain that she was pregnant.

From that moment everything became hateful and her one thought was of how to escape the disgrace which awaited her, and she not only went about her duties in a listless, negligent fashion but one day, without knowing how it happened, she burst out. Repenting bitterly afterwards, she spoke in-solently to her mistresses and asked to be allowed to leave.

And the ladies, seriously displeased with her, let her go. From them she went as a housemaid in the family of the dis-trict police-officer, but only stayed three months because the police-officer, a man of fifty, began to pester her with his attentions, and once when he was being particularly insistent she lost her temper, called him a fool and an old devil, and gave him such a push in the chest that he fell. She was dis-missed for her rudeness. It was useless to look for another place – the time of her confinement was drawing near – and she took lodgings with the village midwife, a widow who also

1. Not so rough as the one, but less affectionate than the other.

24

trafficked in liquor. It was an easy birth; but the midwife, who was looking after a sick woman in the village, infected Katusha with puerperal fever, and the child, a boy, was sent to the foundling hospital, where, according to the old woman who took him there, he died at once.

When Katusha came to the midwife's she possessed in all a hundred and twenty-seven roubles – twenty-seven which she had earned and the hundred given her by her seducer. When she left, six roubles was all that remained. She did not know how to save money, and spent on herself and gave to anyone who asked her. The midwife charged her forty roubles for two months' board and lodging, including the tea she drank; twenty-five went for the child to be taken away; and forty the midwife borrowed to buy a cow; and nearly twenty roubles disappeared on clothes and sweetmeats; so that when Katusha recovered she had no money and had to look for a place. She found one at a forester's. The forester was a married man, but like the police-officer before him he, too, from the very first day began badgering her. She detested him and tried to avoid him. But he was a man of experience and too crafty for Katusha – besides, he was her master and could send her wherever he liked and, having waited his moment, he seized her. His wife found out and, catching her husband alone with Katusha one day, rushed and started hitting the girl. Katusha defended herself and there was a fight, which ended in her being turned out of the house without her wages. Then Katusha went to her aunt in the city. The aunt's husband was a bookbinder and had once been comfortably off, but now he had lost all his customers and taken to drink, squandering at the tavern every kopeck he could lay hands on.

The aunt kept a small laundry and managed to support herself, her children and her good-for-nothing husband. She offered Maslova a place in her laundry. But seeing the hard life of her aunt's laundresses Maslova hesitated, and went to the employment offices in search of domestic employment. She found a place with a lady who had two sons at the high-school. A week after she entered her service the elder boy, who was in the sixth form and already had a moustache, abandoned his studies and started following Maslova about everywhere, giving her no peace. His mother laid all the blame on Maslova and paid her off. She could not find another situation, but it so happened that in the employment office she met a lady with bracelets on her plump bare arms and rings on her fingers. Hearing that Maslova was looking for a place, this lady gave the girl her address and asked her to call. Maslova went. The lady received her very kindly, offered her cakes and sweet wine, and sent her maid somewhere with a note. In the evening a tall man with long greying hair and a grey beard came into the room; this old man at once sat down beside Maslova and with flashing eyes, and smiling, began to look her over and joke with her in a familiar sort of way. The mistress of the house called him into another room and Maslova heard her say, 'A fresh one, straight from the country.' Then she took Maslova aside and told her that the man was a writer with a lot of money who would not grudge her anything if he found her to his liking. She was to his liking and the writer gave her twenty-five roubles, promising to see her often. The money very soon went in paying her aunt for her board and buying a new dress, ribbons and a bonnet. A few days later the writer sent for her again. She went. He gave her another twenty-five roubles and offered her an apartment of her own.

While living in the apartments which the writer had rented for her Maslova fell in love with a jolly young shop assistant who lived in the same house. She told the writer, and moved to other, smaller lodgings. But the shop assistant, after promising marriage, left without a word and went to Nizhni, evidently throwing her over, and Maslova found herself alone. She would have liked to continue in the apartment by herself, but this was not allowed. The inspector of police said she could only live there like that if she got a yellow licence[1]

1. Prostitute's card.

and submitted herself to regular medical examinations. So she went back to her aunt. Her aunt, seeing her fine dress, the mantle and bonnet, received her with respect and no longer dared to offer her laundry work: as she understood things, her niece had risen above that. Nor did it occur now to Maslova to wonder whether or not to become a laundress. She now looked with pity at the back-breaking lives led in the front rooms by the pale laundresses – some of them already consumptive – with their thin arms washing and ironing in a temperature of nearly 90°, the atmosphere full of soapy steam, and windows open summer and winter. She looked at them and shuddered at the thought that she, too, might have accepted such drudgery.

And it was just about this time, when Maslova was in very dire straits, no new protector having made his appearance, that she was approached by a procuress who provided girls for brothels.

Maslova had long ago acquired the habit of smoking, but it was only during her liaison with the shop assistant, and especially after he left her, that she began to drink. She liked wine not only for its flavour but most of all because it made her forget all the misery she had suffered, and gave her abandon and confidence in her own worth, which she never felt except under the influence of drink. Without wine she felt depressed and ashamed.

The procuress regaled her aunt and then, having plied Maslova with drink, offered to place her in the best establishment in the town, picturing to her all the advantages and benefits of such a life. Maslova had the choice either of going into service, to be humiliated, subjected to the unwelcome attentions of men and forced into a series of secret, casual adulteries; or of entering upon a secure, quiet life, sanctioned by law, with open, legitimate, well-paid and regular adultery – and she chose the latter. Besides, she thought that in this way she could be revenged on her first betrayer, and the shop assistant, and all the other people who had wronged her.

27

Another thing that tempted her and greatly influenced her decision was the woman's promise that she could order any dresses she liked – velvet, *poult-de-soie*, silk – ball-gowns with low necks and bare arms. The mental picture of herself arrayed in bright yellow silk trimmed with black velvet – *décolletée* – was irresistible, and she handed over her identity papers. That same evening the procuress called a cab and took her to the notorious establishment kept by Madame Kitayeva.

And from that moment there began for Maslova that life of chronic violation of every commandment, divine and human, a life which hundreds of thousands of women lead, not only with the consent but under the patronage of a government concerned for the welfare of its subjects: a life which for nine out of ten women ends in painful disease, premature old age and death.

Heavy sleep until late in the afternoon followed the orgies of the night. At three or four o'clock a weary rising from a dirty bed, seltzer water to counteract the effects of too much drink, coffee, listless pacing up and down the rooms in peignoirs, bed-jackets or dressing-gowns, gazing out of the windows from behind the drawn curtains, half-hearted squabbling with one another; then ablutions, pomading, perfuming of body and hair, trying on dresses, disputes about them with the proprietress, contemplation of oneself in the looking-glass, the painting of face and eyebrows; fatty, sweet food; then dressing in gaudy silks cut to expose the body, and coming down into the much ornamented, brilliantly lit parlour. Then the guests arrive, there is music, dancing, sweetmeats, wine, smoking and debauchery with young men, middle-aged men, men half children and decrepit old men, unmarried and married, merchants, clerks, Armenians, Jews, Tartars; with rich and poor, healthy and diseased, tipsy and sober, men rough and men gentle, military men and civilians, students and schoolboys – with men of all classes, ages and characters. And cries and jests, brawls and music, and tobacco and wine, and wine and tobacco, and music from evening to daybreak. And only in the morning release and heavy slumber. And so on every day throughout the week. At the end of the week the drive to the government offices -- to the police-station where doctors in government service subject these women to a medical examination, sometimes with dignified gravity, sometimes with playful levity, doing away with the modesty nature bestows on man and also on beast to protect them against transgression, and then hand them a licence for the continuation of the transgressions which they and their partners have been committing all the week. And another week starts. And so it goes on, day after day, summer and winter, weekdays and holidays.

Thus Maslova spent seven years. During this time she changed houses twice, and once went to hospital. It was in the seventh year of her life in the brothel and the eighth dating from her first fall, and when she was twenty-six years old, that the incident occurred for which she was arrested and was now being brought to the court-house after six months in gaol with murderers and thieves.

3

AT the time Maslova, exhausted after the long walk with her guards, was nearing the court-house, Prince Dmitri Ivanovich Nekhlyudov, the nephew of her patronesses and the man who had seduced her, was still lying on his high crumpled bed with its springs and down mattress. He had unbuttoned the collar of his fine white linen night-shirt with the well-pressed pleats over the chest, and was smoking. His eyes gazed vacantly into space while he considered what he had to do that day and what had happened the day before.

He sighed as he thought of the previous evening spent at the Korchagins – people of some wealth and social importance whose daughter everyone expected he would marry – and throwing away the butt of his cigarette was about to take another from his silver case but changed his mind, put down his smooth white legs, felt for his slippers with his feet, threw his silk dressing-gown over his broad shoulders and, stepping heavily, hurried into his dressing-room, where the air was oppressive with the artificial odours of elixirs, eau de Cologne, pomatum and perfumes. There, with a special powder, he cleaned his teeth, many of which had gold fillings, rinsed his mouth with scented water and then began to wash his body all over, drying himself with various different towels. Having washed his hands with scented soap, he carefully cleaned his long nails with a nail-brush and rinsed his face and stout neck at the large marble wash-stand. Then he walked into a third room off the bedroom where a shower-bath awaited him. Here he bathed his muscular, plump white body in cold water and dried it with a rough bath-sheet, put on clean freshly ironed linen and boots which shone like glass, and finally seated himself at the dressing-table with a brush in each hand to brush his short curly black beard and the curling hair on his head which was beginning to thin at the temples.

Everything he used – all the appurtenances of his toilet – his linen, his clothes, boots, neckties, tie-pins, cuff-links were of the best and most expensive kind: unobtrusive, simple, durable and costly.

Picking up from among a dozen neckties and tie-pins the first that came to hand – at one time choosing what to wear had been novel and amusing but now it was a matter of complete indifference to him – Nekhlyudov put on the carefully brushed clothes lying ready on a chair, and, clean now and perfumed if not feeling altogether refreshed, he proceeded to the long dining-room, where three men had laboured the day before to polish the parquetry. The room was furnished with a huge oak sideboard and an equally large extension-table to which widely spaced legs carved in the shape of lions' paws gave an imposing air. On this table, which was covered with a fine starched cloth with large monograms, stood a silver coffee-pot of fragrant coffee, a silver sugar-bowl, a cream-jug with hot cream, and a bread-basket filled with freshly baked rolls, rusks and biscuits. Beside his plate lay the morning post – letters, newspapers and the latest number of the *Revue des Deux Mondes*. Nekhlyudov was on the point of taking up his letters when the door from the dining-room to the passage outside opened and a stout middle-aged woman in mourning, a lace cap over the widening parting of her hair, glided into the room. This was Agrafena Petrovna, formerly lady's maid to Nekhlyudov's mother, who had died quite recently in this very apartment: she had stayed on with the son as his house-keeper.

Agrafena Petrovna had at different times spent some ten years abroad with Nekhlyudov's mother, and had the appearance and manners of a lady. She had lived with the Nekhlyudovs ever since she was a child and had known Dmitri Ivanovich when he was a little boy and they called him Mitenka.

'Good morning, Dmitri Ivanovich.'

'Good morning, Agrafena Petrovna. What's the latest news?' asked Nekhlyudov jocularly.

'A letter from the princess – or from the young lady, may-be. A maid brought it some time ago and is waiting in my room,' said Agrafena Petrovna, handing him the letter with a significant smile.

'Very well, I will attend to it,' said Nekhlyudov, taking the letter and frowning as he noticed Agrafena Petrovna's smile.

Agrafena Petrovna's smile meant that the letter was from the young Princess Korchagina whom Agrafena Petrovna believed he had made up his mind to marry. This supposition of hers expressed by a smile annoyed Nekhlyudov.

'Then I will tell her to wait,' and Agrafena Petrovna restored to its proper place a crumb-brush, and sailed out of the dining-room.

Nekhlyudov broke the seal of the perfumed note which Agrafena Petrovna had given him, and began to read.

Having taken it upon myself to be your memory –

so ran the letter which was written on thick grey deckle-edged paper in a pointed but sprawling hand –

I remind you that today, the 28th of April, you have to appear at the court-house to serve on a jury and therefore you can on no account accompany Kolossov and us to the picture-gallery as in your usual reckless fashion you promised last night; *à moins que vous ne soyez disposé à payer à la cour d'assises les 300 roubles d'amende, que vous vous refusez pour votre cheval,*[1] for not appearing at the appointed time. I thought of it yesterday, the moment you left. So now don't forget.

Princess M. Korchagina

On the other side was a postscript:

Maman vous fait dire que votre couvert vous attendra jusqu'à la nuit. Venez absolument à quelle heure que cela soit.[2]

Nekhlyudov frowned. The note was a continuation of the skilful campaign which the young princess had been waging for the past two months now, designed to bind him ever more tightly to her with invisible threads. But apart from the usual hesitation of men past their first youth about marrying when they are not passionately in love, there was another important reason to prevent Nekhlyudov from making an immediate offer of marriage, even if he did decide to do so. It was not that ten years previously he had seduced Katusha and deserted her – he had forgotten all about that, and he would not have regarded it as any impediment to marriage. The reason was a liaison with a married woman. So far as he was concerned the affair was at an end, but the lady had not yet recognized the fact.

Nekhlyudov was very shy with women, and it was this very shyness of his which had tempted the married woman to try and win him. She was the wife of the Marshal of the

1. Unless you feel disposed to pay the Assize Court a fine of 300 roubles, the price of the horse you deny yourself.
2. *Maman* asks me to tell you that dinner will be kept for you until late at night. Come whatever the time.

Nobility of the district where Nekhlyudov went for the elections. And she had drawn him into an intimacy which entangled him further every day and every day grew more distasteful. At first Nekhlyudov had not been able to resist the temptation; then, feeling guilty towards her, he could not bring himself to force a break against her will. And this was why he did not consider he had a right to propose to the young Princess Korchagina, even had he been so inclined.

There on the table at this moment lay a letter from the lady's husband. Seeing the handwriting and the postmark, Nekhlyudov flushed and immediately felt an upsurge of energy, as always happened at the approach of danger. But his excitement was uncalled for: the husband, the Marshal of the Nobility of the district where Nekhlyudov's largest estates were situated, wrote to inform him that a special assembly of the *Zemstvo*[1] was to be held at the end of May, and asked him to be sure to come *pour donner un coup d'épaule*[2] at the important debates on schools and local railways, as strong opposition from the reactionary party was expected at the meeting.

The Marshal was a liberal-minded man, and with others who shared his views struggled to oppose the current of reaction that ran so strongly under Alexander III; absorbed heart and soul in the struggle, he was quite unaware of his domestic misfortune.

Nekhlyudov remembered all the painful moments he had experienced in connexion with this man: he remembered how one day he had thought that her husband had found out, and how he had made arrangements for a duel with him and decided how he would fire in the air; and the terrible scene with her when she had rushed distraught into the garden to drown herself in the pond, and he had run out to look for her. 'I can't go and I can't do anything until I hear from her,' thought Nekhlyudov. A week ago he had written her a firm letter in which he acknowledged his guilt and declared

1. Elective district council.   2. To lend support.

himself ready to atone for it in any and every way, but at the same time, 'for her own good', he regarded their relations as ended for ever. It was to this letter that he was awaiting, and had not received, a reply. The fact that there was no answer was a good sign in a way. If she did not agree to break off their friendship she would have written days ago, or even come herself, as she had on previous occasions. Nekhlyudov had heard that a certain officer in the country was paying court to her now, and though this gave him twinges of jealousy, at the same time it filled him with hope of release from the deceit that oppressed him.

The other letter was from his chief steward, who wrote that it was essential for Nekhlyudov to visit his estates in order to take formal possession and also to decide on future policy: were they to continue to run the estates as they had been run during the lifetime of the late princess or were they to do as he had suggested to the deceased and now suggested to the young prince – increase the stock and themselves farm all the land now let out to the peasants? The steward wrote that this would be a far more profitable way of working the estate. He also apologized for being late with the three thousand roubles income due on the first of the month. These monies would be sent by the next post. The reason for the delay was that he had been quite unable to collect from the peasants, who had grown so irresponsible and unscrupulous that he had been obliged to appeal to the authorities. This letter Nekhlyudov found partly disagreeable and partly pleasant. It was gratifying to feel himself master of so large a property, but the letter made disagreeable reading because in the first flush of youth he had been an ardent admirer of Herbert Spencer, being particularly struck, as a large landed proprietor, by Spencer's theory (in *Social Statics*) that the private ownership of land was wrong. With the unswerving determination of youth he had then not only argued that land could not form the object of private ownership, and written a thesis on the subject while at the university, but had actually surrendered to the peasants a small piece of land (which did not belong to his mother – he had inherited it personally from his father) since he did not wish to go against his convictions and own land. Now that he had become a great landed proprietor he had to choose one of two things: either to renounce his property, as he had done ten years before with the five hundred acres that had come to him from his father, or by tacit acceptance admit the error and falsity of his early ideas.

He could not do the former because the land was his sole means of existence. He did not want to go back into government service, and, moreover, he had acquired luxurious habits which he felt unable to give up. Nor was there any inducement to: the strong convictions, the determination, the ambition and the desire to startle people of his young days were gone. As to the second course – that of repudiating those clear and irrefutable arguments against the private ownership of land, which he had first discovered in Spencer's *Social Statics* and the brilliant confirmation of which he had found later, much later, in the works of Henry George – it was out of the question.

And this was why the steward's letter made disagreeable reading.

4

AFTER he had finished his coffee Nekhlyudov went to his study to look up the summons and see at what hour he was to appear at the court-house, and to answer the princess's note. In order to reach the study he had to pass through the studio. On an easel in the studio there was an unfinished painting with its back to the room, and various sketches hung on the walls. The sight of the picture, over which he had laboured for two years, and the sketches and the whole studio renewed a suspicion, which had come over him more and more of late, that he could progress no farther in painting. He told himself that this was because his aesthetic taste was too highly developed, but still the feeling was a most unpleasant one.

Seven years before this he had given up his government position, having decided that he had a talent for painting, and from the heights of his artistic activity had looked down somewhat contemptuously on all other occupations. Now it seemed that he had no right to do so. And thus every reminder of this was disagreeable. He surveyed all the luxurious appointments of the studio with a heavy heart, and it was in no cheerful mood that he entered his study, a large lofty room designed with a view to elegant appearance, comfort and convenience.

He found the summons at once in the pigeon-hole of the huge writing-table marked *Immediate*: it said that he had to be at the court-house at eleven o'clock. He sat down to write a note to the young princess, thanking her for the invitation and promising to come to dinner if he could. But he had no sooner written than he tore it up: it seemed too intimate. He wrote another – it was cold, almost rude. He tore this one up too and pressed a button on the wall. His servant, an elderly morose-looking man, clean-shaven except for side-whiskers, wearing a grey calico apron, entered the room.

'Send for a cab, please.'

'Certainly, sir.'

'And tell the person waiting from the Korchagins that I am much obliged and will try to come.'

'Yes, sir.'

'It's not very civil but I can't write. No matter, I shall see her tonight,' thought Nekhlyudov, and went to get his overcoat.

When, dressed and ready, he came out on to the porch a familiar cab with rubber tyres was at the door waiting for him.

'You 'ad 'ardly left the Korchagins yesterday,' said the cabby, half turning towards him a strong, powerful, sunburnt neck in a white shirt collar, 'when I drove up and the 'all-porter at the door says, "Just gone, 'e 'as." '

'Even the cabmen know about my visits to the Korchagins,' thought Nekhlyudov, and the unsettled question, which had of late constantly preoccupied him – should he, or should he not marry the young Princess Korchagina? – presented itself to him, and he could not decide either way, any more than he could decide most of the other questions that came to his mind.

In favour of marriage in general, besides the comforts of hearth and home, was, firstly, the consideration that by removing the irregularities of his sexual life marriage would make it possible for him to lead a moral existence; and secondly, and most important of all, a family – children – would give a meaning, so Nekhlyudov hoped, to his now empty life. This much for marriage in general. But against marriage in general was, in the first place, the fear, common to bachelors past their first youth, of losing his freedom, and in the second, an unconscious awe of that mysterious being, woman.

In favour of marrying Missy in particular (Princess Korchagina's name was Marya, but, as is usual among a certain set, she had a nickname) was, to begin with, that she came of good family, and in everything – dress, carriage, manner of speaking and laughing – stood out from the common people, not by anything exceptional but by her 'good breeding': he could find no other term for this quality and he esteemed it very highly; and secondly, there was the fact that she thought more highly of him than of any other man she knew, which, as he saw things, meant that she understood him. And this understanding of him, that is, her recognition of his superior worth, was proof to Nekhlyudov of her good sense and sound judgement. But against marrying Missy in particular was, first, the consideration that he might quite likely find a girl possessed of an even greater number of desirable qualities than Missy had, and who consequently would be worthier of him; and secondly, she was already twenty-seven years old, and therefore he could hardly be her first love – and this was a painful idea for Nekhlyudov. His pride revolted against the thought that she could have loved anybody but him, even in the past. Of course she could not have known that she would meet him, but the very notion that she could have been in love with someone else offended him.

Thus there were as many arguments for as against; at any rate they weighed equally with Nekhlyudov, who laughed at himself and called himself the ass of the fable, unable to decide which bundle of hay to turn to.

'All the same, until I get an answer from Marya Vassilyevna' (the wife of the Marshal of the Nobility) 'and that affair is wound up, I can't do anything,' he said to himself.

And the knowledge that he could and should delay taking a decision was welcome to him.

'However, I will go into all this later,' he said to himself as the cab drew up noiselessly on the asphalt outside the entrance to the court-house. 'Now I must fulfil a public duty in my usual conscientious way, as I consider it right to do. Besides, these cases are frequently quite interesting,' he said to himself, and made his way past the doorkeeper into the hall of the court-house.

5

THE corridors of the court-house were already bustling with activity. Janitors walked briskly, even ran, backwards and forwards, not lifting their feet from the floor but sliding along, breathlessly delivering messages and papers. Ushers, lawyers and judges went hither and thither; plaintiffs, or defendants who were not in custody, wandered dejectedly along by the walls or sat about waiting.

'Where is the court-room?' Nekhlyudov asked one of the janitors.

'Which one do you want? There is a Civil Division and there is a Criminal Court.'

'I am one of the jury.'

38

'Criminal Court. You should have said so. Here to the right, then left and it's the second door.'

Nekhlyudov followed the directions. At the door indicated two men stood waiting: one, a tall fat merchant, a kindly-looking fellow, had clearly wined and eaten well and was in the best of spirits. The other was a shop assistant with Jewish blood in him. They were chatting about the price of wool when Nekhlyudov approached them and inquired if this was the jury-room.

'This way, sir, this way. You one of the jury, too?' asked the cheery merchant with a jovial wink. 'That's good, we shall be working together,' he continued, after Nekhlyudov had answered in the affirmative. 'My name's Baklashov, merchant of the Second Guild,' he said, holding out a soft, broad, flexible hand. 'One can't avoid work. With whom have I the honour?'

Nekhlyudov gave his name and passed into the jury-room.

There were about ten men in the small room, of all sorts and descriptions. They had only just assembled, and some were seated while others walked about, eyeing one another and getting acquainted. There was a retired colonel in uniform, others wore frock-coats or ordinary suits; only one was clad in the sleeveless coat of the peasant.

Though a good many of them were protesting and complaining about the interruption to their work their faces all bore a certain look of satisfaction at the prospect of fulfilling an important public duty.

The jurors, those who had become acquainted with each other and those who were still guessing who was who, were talking among themselves, discussing the weather, the early spring and the matter before them. Those who did not know Nekhlyudov made haste to get introduced, evidently regarding this as a special honour. And Nekhlyudov took it as his due, as he always did when among strangers. If he had been asked why he considered himself superior to the majority of mankind he would have been unable to find an answer, no facet of his life being distinguished for any particular qualities. The fact that he spoke English, French and German with a good accent, and that his linen, his suits, his ties and his cuff-links came from the very best outfitters could in no way justify an assumption of superiority – he realized that himself. And yet he was undoubtedly conscious of being superior, and accepted as his due the respect paid to him, and was hurt when he did not get it. In the jury-room he had occasion to experience this disagreeable sensation of being treated with a want of respect. Among the jury there happened to be a man whom he knew, a former tutor of his sister's children, one Piotr Gerassimovich. (Nekhlyudov had never known his surname, and even prided himself a little on the fact.) This Piotr Gerassimovich had finished his studies and was now a master at a high-school. Nekhlyudov could never endure him on account of his free and easy manner, his self-satisfied laugh – in short, his 'commonness', as Nekhlyudov's sister used to call it.

'Aha! So you've been caught, too, have you?' Piotr Gerassimovich greeted Nekhlyudov with a guffaw. 'You didn't manage to wriggle out of it?'

'I never thought of wriggling out of it,' replied Nekhlyudov in a languid, forbidding tone.

'There's public spirit for you! But just you wait till you're hungry and tired, then you'll sing a different tune,' proclaimed Piotr Gerassimovich, laughing still more loudly.

'This confounded son of a priest will be slapping me on the back next,' thought Nekhlyudov, and walked away with such a funereal expression on his face that he might just have received the news of the death of every member of his family, to join a group gathered round a tall clean-shaven man of imposing appearance, who was talking with great animation about the trial now going on in the Civil Court. He seemed to be well up in the affair, referring to the judges and the famous lawyers by their Christian names and patronymics.

He was expatiating on the remarkable way a celebrated lawyer had handled his case, whereby one of the parties, an old lady who was entirely in the right, would have to pay a huge sum to the other side.

'A brilliant lawyer!' he said.

His hearers listened respectfully. Some of them tried to put in a word of their own, but he interrupted them all with the air of one who is much better informed than the rest of the world.

Though Nekhlyudov had been late in arriving he had to wait a long time. The hearing was being held up because one of the judges had still not appeared.

6

THE president of the court, a tall, stout man with long grey side-whiskers, had come early. He was a married man but led a very dissolute life, and his wife did the same. They did not stand in each other's way. That morning he had received a note from the Swiss governess who had been in their employ the summer before and was now on her way from South Russia to Petersburg, telling him that she would be in the town that day and would expect him between three and six o'clock at the Hotel Italia. He was therefore anxious to begin the sitting and get through with it as early as possible, in time to call before six o'clock on the red-haired little Klara Vassilyevna, with whom he had begun a romance in the country last summer.

Going into the judges' room, he latched the door, took a pair of dumb-bells from the lowest shelf of the cupboard with the documents, and stretched twenty times up, forward, sideways and down, and then, holding the dumb-bells above his head, squatted lightly three times.

'Nothing keeps one going so much as a cold shower and exercises,' he thought, feeling with his left hand, on the fourth finger of which he wore a gold ring, the biceps of his right arm. He had still to do the *moulinet* exercise (he always went through these two exercises before a long session), when someone shook the door, trying to open it. The president hastily put away the dumb-bells and opened the door.

'I beg your pardon,' he said.

One of the members of the court, a small man with hunched shoulders and a frowning face, who wore gold-rimmed spectacles, entered the room.

'Matvey Nikitich isn't here again,' said he in an irritated tone of voice.

'Not yet,' responded the president, putting on his uniform. 'He's always late.'

'I wonder he isn't ashamed of himself,' said the other angrily, sitting down and taking out a cigarette.

This member of the court, a very precise man, had had an unpleasant scene with his wife that morning: she had spent the money which should have lasted till the end of the month and had asked him to advance her some more, but he had refused to give way. A quarrel ensued. His wife had said that if that were the case he need not expect any dinner at home, there wouldn't be any. Whereupon he had departed, very much afraid that she would carry out her threat, for she was capable of anything. 'So this is what you get for leading a good virtuous life,' he reflected, looking at the beaming healthy face of the jolly good-natured president who, elbows wide apart, with his beautiful hands was smoothing his luxurious grey whiskers on either side of the embroidered collar of his uniform. 'He is always contented and cheerful, while I am a martyr.'

A secretary came in, bringing some documents.

'Thanks very much,' said the president, lighting a cigarette. 'Which case shall we hear first?'

'The poisoning affair, I suppose,' replied the secretary, apparently with indifference.

'Very well, the poisoning affair let it be,' said the president, thinking that he could get this case over by four o'clock and then leave. 'But what about Matvey Nikitich – not come yet?'

'Not yet.'

'Is Breve here?'

'He is,' replied the secretary.

'Then if you see him tell him that we begin with the poisoning case.'

Breve was the assistant public prosecutor who was to prosecute at the present sitting.

Going out into the corridor the secretary met Breve. With shoulders hunched high and uniform unbuttoned he was hurrying along the corridor, heels tapping, almost at a run. He had a portfolio under one arm and was sawing the air with his free arm, keeping the palm of his hand perpendicular to the direction of his walk.

'The president wants to know if you are ready,' the secretary asked him.

'Ready? I am always ready,' said the assistant prosecutor. 'What are we taking first?'

'The poisoning case.'

'Excellent,' said the assistant prosecutor, although in his own mind he thought it anything but excellent: he had not been to bed all night. There had been a farewell party for a friend, they had drunk and played cards until two in the morning and then called on the women in the very house where Maslova had been until six months ago, so there had been no time to read up the poisoning case, which he had meant to glance through that morning. The secretary, who knew that he had not read up the poisoning case, had purposely advised the president of the court to begin with it. The secretary was a man of liberal, even radical views, while Breve was a conservative and, like all Germans in Russian government service, a devout member of the Orthodox Church; and the secretary disliked him and envied him his position.

'And how about the *Skoptzi*?'[1] asked the secretary.

'I have already said that I can't do it without witnesses,' replied the assistant prosecutor, 'and I shall tell the court so.'

'Dear me, does it matter? . . .'

'I cannot do it,' said the assistant prosecutor and, waving his arms as before, went into his private room.

He was delaying the case of the *Skoptzi* in the absence of a quite unimportant and unnecessary witness simply because if it were tried in a court where the jury was composed of educated men the accused might be acquitted. So by agreement with the president this case was to be transferred to a provincial town where most of the jury would be peasants and therefore there would be more chance of securing a conviction.

The commotion in the corridor was increasing. Most people crowded round the doors of the Civil Division, where the case was on that the juror of imposing appearance who knew all about lawsuits had been talking about. During a recess the old lady came out whose property that genius of a lawyer had succeeded in getting hold of for his sharp-witted client, who had not the slightest right to it – which the judges knew, and the plaintiff and his counsel knew even better; but the case had been so presented that there was nothing for it but to take the old lady's property and hand it over to the sharp dealer. The old lady was a stout woman in her best clothes with enormous flowers in her bonnet. Coming through the door she stopped in the corridor and, making a helpless gesture with her hands, kept repeating, 'But what will happen? I beg of you, what does it mean?' as she turned to her lawyer. The lawyer was looking at the flowers on her bonnet and not listening to her, preoccupied with something else.

Following the old lady out of the door of the Civil Court, starched shirt-front resplendent under his low-cut waistcoat, a self-satisfied look on his face, hurried the famous advocate who had fixed matters in such a way that the old lady with the

1. A sect practising castration.

flowers lost all she had, while the smart fellow, his client, for a fee of ten thousand roubles, had got his hands on over a hundred thousand. Aware that all eyes were directed upon him, his whole bearing seemed to say: 'Please, I don't need any acts of homage,' and quickly made his way through the crowd.

7

FINALLY Matvey Nikitich arrived, and the usher, a thin man with a long neck and sidling gait, and a lower lip that protruded sideways too, came into the jury-room.

The usher was an honest fellow who had had a university education but could never keep a position for any length of time because of his periodical bouts of drunkenness. Three months before, a certain countess who took an interest in his wife had obtained his present post for him, and he had so far been able to hold it, which made him feel happy.

'Well, gentlemen, are you all here?' he said, fitting his pince-nez on his nose and looking over them.

'Yes, I think so,' said the jovial merchant.

'All right, we'll soon see,' said the usher, and, taking a list from his pocket, he began to call out the names, looking at those he called sometimes through and sometimes over his pince-nez.

'Councillor of State[1] I. M. Nikiforov.'

'Present,' said the imposing-looking gentleman who knew all about legal matters.

'Ivan Semyonovich Ivanov, retired colonel?'

'Here,' answered the thin man in the uniform of a retired officer.

'Merchant of the Second Guild Piotr Baklashov.'

'Ay, ay,' said the good-humoured merchant, grinning. 'All ready!'

'Guards' lieutenant, Prince Dmitri Nekhlyudov.'

1. Civil Service post in Tsarist Russia.

'Present,' replied Nekhlyudov.

The usher looked at him over his pince-nez and welcomed him with a particularly polite bow, as though wishing to honour him above the rest.

'Captain Yuri Dmitriyevich Danchenko, Grigori Yefimovich Kuloshov, merchant!' etc., etc. All but two were present.

'Now, gentlemen, please proceed to the court,' said the usher, pointing to the door with an amiable wave of his hand.

They all moved towards the door, where they paused to make way for each other to pass into the corridor and thence into the court-room.

The court-room was a large, long room. One end was occupied by a platform with three steps leading up to it. In the middle of the platform stood a table covered with a green cloth having a fringe of darker green. Behind the table were three arm-chairs with very high carved oak backs; and on the wall behind hung a striking full-length portrait in a gilt frame of a general in uniform and sash, one foot advanced, grasping a sword. In the right-hand corner of the hall hung a case with an ikon of Christ crowned with thorns; a lectern stood beneath the ikon and to the right of the lectern was the public prosecutor's desk. On the left, opposite the desk and well back, was the secretary's little table, while nearer to the public was a railing of turned oak, with the prisoner's bench, as yet unoccupied, behind it. On the platform towards the right there were two rows of high-backed chairs for the jurors and on the floor below were the tables for the lawyers. All this was in the front part of the court, which was divided from the rear by a railing. The back was all taken up by benches, rising tier upon tier till they reached the wall. Sitting on the front benches were four women – factory girls or chambermaids – and a couple of working-class men, all evidently overawed by the grandeur of the court-room and therefore not venturing to speak above a whisper.

Soon after the jury had entered the usher stepped into the

middle of the court-room with his sidling gait, and in a loud voice calculated to inspire dread in those present proclaimed:

'The Court approaches!'

Everybody rose, and the judges walked on to the platform: the president with his muscles and fine side-whiskers came first; next, the gloomy member of the court in his gold-rimmed spectacles, now more gloomy than ever, having a moment before the sessions opened run into his brother-in-law, a candidate for some position in the government legal department, who informed him that he had just called in to see his sister (the member's wife), and she had told him there would be no dinner at home that day.

'So it looks as if we shall have to go to some pot-house,' the brother-in-law had added, laughing.

'I don't see anything funny in that,' said the gloomy member of the court, and grew gloomier still.

And, finally, the third member of the court, that same Matvey Nikitich who was always late – he was a bearded man with large, bulging, kindly eyes. He suffered from gastric catarrh and on his doctor's advice had that very morning begun a new treatment, which had delayed him at home even longer than usual. Now, as he ascended the steps to the platform, his face wore an expression of deep concentration, resulting from a habit he had of using various curious means to decide the answers to questions which he put to himself. Just now he was counting the number of steps from the door of his study to his chair: if they would divide by three the new treatment would cure his catarrh. If not, the treatment would be a failure. There were twenty-six steps, but he managed to get in an extra short one and reached his chair exactly at the twenty-seventh.

The presiding judge and the members of the court in their uniforms with collars embroidered in gold lace made an impressive sight. They felt this themselves and as though embarrassed by their own grandeur kept their eyes lowered and hurriedly sat down in their carved chairs behind the table with the green cloth, on which stood a three-cornered object surmounted by an eagle, some glass jars like those used to hold sweetmeats that one sees in refreshment rooms, an inkstand, pens, lovely new paper and freshly sharpened pencils of various sizes. The assistant public prosecutor came in with the judges. Still hurrying, with his portfolio under one arm and swinging the other as before, he crossed to his place near the window and was instantly absorbed in reading and looking through the papers of the case, not wasting a moment to prepare himself for the business in hand. This was only the fourth occasion he had prosecuted. He was very ambitious and firmly determined to make a career, and so considered it essential to secure a conviction every time he prosecuted. He knew the general outline of the poisoning case and had already decided on the main points of his speech, but he still needed a few more facts and these he was hastily copying out.

The secretary sat at the opposite end of the platform and, having arranged all the documents that might be required, was looking through a newspaper article suppressed by the censor, which he had obtained and read the day before. He was anxious to discuss this article with the bearded member of the court, who shared his views, and wanted to become thoroughly familiar with it first.

8

THE president examined some papers, put a few questions to the usher and the secretary, and receiving answers in the affirmative ordered the accused to be brought in. The door behind the railing was instantly thrown open and two gendarmes appeared with their caps on their heads and holding naked swords in their hands. They were followed by the first defendant, a red-haired freckled man, and two women. The man wore a prison cloak which was too wide and too long for him. Entering the court-room, he stuck his thumbs out and held his arms close to his sides, thus keeping the sleeves,

48

which were also too long, from slipping over his hands. Without looking at the judges or the spectators he gazed steadfastly at the bench which he walked round. Having got to the other end he sat down carefully on the very edge, leaving plenty of room for the others. Fixing his gaze on the president he began twitching the muscles of his cheeks as if he were muttering something. After him came a middle-aged woman, also dressed in a prison cloak. Her head was wrapped in a prison kerchief, her face was grey, she had neither eyebrows nor eyelashes but her eyes were red. She seemed perfectly composed. As she was going to her seat her cloak caught on something: she detached it carefully, without haste, and sat down.

The third defendant was Maslova.

The moment she entered, the eyes of all the men in the court-room turned her way and stayed for a long time riveted on her white face with her lustrous, brilliant black eyes and the swelling bosom under the prison cloak. Even the gendarme, as she passed him, gazed after her until she was seated, and then with a guilty air swung round and, giving himself a shake, stared at the window in front of him.

The president waited until the defendants had taken their seats and as soon as Maslova was in her place he turned to the secretary.

Then began the usual procedure: the roll-call of the jury, remarks about those who had not come, the imposition of fines, the decisions concerning those who claimed exemption, and the filling of vacancies on the jury from the reserve list. Next the presiding judge folded up some slips of paper, put them in one of the glass jars, rolled back the embroidered sleeves of his uniform a little, baring his hairy wrists, and like a conjuror picked out one slip at a time, smoothed it out and read it. Then, having pulled down his cuffs, the president requested the priest to swear in the jury.

The little old priest, with his puffy sallow face, his brown cassock, his gold cross hanging round his neck and some trifling decoration pinned on one side of his vestment, laboriously moving his stiff legs beneath his cassock, went up to the lectern beneath the ikon.

The jurymen got up and crowded towards the lectern.

'Come forward,' he said, fingering the cross at his breast with his pudgy fingers and waiting until all the jurors had come close.

This priest had taken orders forty-seven years ago and in three years' time would be celebrating the fiftieth anniversary of his ordination, just as the archpriest at the cathedral had recently celebrated his. He had served in the court ever since it was opened, and was very proud of having sworn in some tens of thousands of men, and that at his advanced age he still continued to labour for the good of the Church, of his country and of his family, to whom he expected to leave a capital sum of quite thirty thousand roubles in interest-bearing securities, not to mention the house they lived in. The fact that his work in the court-room, which consisted in having men swear on the Gospel in which all oaths are expressly forbidden, was not a good occupation never occurred to him, and far from being irked by it – he liked this familiar employment of his: it often brought him in contact with nice people. Not without a certain satisfaction he had just made the acquaintance of the famous lawyer who had won his respect for getting ten thousand roubles for that one case against the old lady with the enormous flowers on her bonnet.

When the jury had all mounted the platform the priest, bending his bald grey head to one side, wormed it through the greasy opening of his stole and, arranging his scanty hair, addressed the jurors.

'Raise your right hand and put your fingers together thus,' he said in his tremulous old voice, lifting his pudgy hand with dimples on every finger and putting the thumb and first two fingers together as if taking a pinch of something. 'Now repeat after me,' he said, and began: 'I promise and swear by Almighty God, before His holy Gospels and the life-giving

Cross of the Lord, that in this matter which . . .' he said, pausing after every comma – 'Don't drop your arm, keep it like this,' he remarked to a young man who had lowered his arm – 'that in this work which . . .'

The stately gentleman with the side-whiskers, the colonel, the merchant and a few more held their arms and arranged their fingers as the priest required of them, high and very precisely, and seemed really to enjoy doing so; others were reluctant and vague. Some repeated the words over loudly, almost defiantly, as much as to say: 'All the same, I will and shall speak.' Others again whispered very low and lagged behind the priest until they suddenly took fright and caught up with him at the wrong moment; one or two in a challenging way kept their fingers tightly together, as if fearing to drop the pinch of invisible something they were holding; others let their fingers go slack, then suddenly compressed them again. Everyone save the old priest felt awkward, but he was firmly convinced that he was fulfilling a most useful and important function. After the swearing in the presiding judge requested the jury to choose a foreman. They rose and, jostling one another, went into the jury-room, where most of them immediately took out cigarettes and began to smoke. Someone proposed that the stately gentleman should be foreman, and he was unanimously accepted. Then the jurymen put out their cigarettes and threw away the stubs, and returned to the court-room. The elected foreman informed the president that he had been chosen, and stepping over each other's feet they all seated themselves once more on the chairs with the high backs.

Everything went without a hitch, swiftly and with a certain solemnity, and this decorum, this order and solemnity evidently pleased the participants, confirming them in the belief that they were performing a serious and important public duty. Nekhlyudov, too, felt this.

When the jury were seated the president judge made a speech to them about their rights, duties and responsibilities.

While delivering his address the presiding judge kept shifting about; now he leaned on his left elbow, now on his right; now he flung himself against the back of his chair or rested on the arms; he straightened the papers in front of him, stroked the paper-knife, fingered his pencil.

They had the right, he told them, of interrogating the prisoners through the president himself. They were allowed paper and pencils, and could inspect the exhibits. Their duty was to find a true, not a false verdict. Concerning their responsibilities – if the secrecy of their deliberations were violated or any communication were established with the outside world they would be liable to punishment.

Everybody listened with respectful attention. The merchant, diffusing a smell of brandy around him and trying to restrain loud hiccups, nodded his head in approval at every sentence.

9

WHEN he had finished his speech the president turned to the prisoners.

'Simon Kartinkin, stand up,' he said.

Simon sprang to his feet, the muscles of his cheeks twitching more violently still.

'Your name?'

'Simon Petrov Kartinkin,' he said quickly, in a ringing voice, as if he had prepared for the questions and had his answers ready.

'Class?'

'Peasant.'

'What province and district do you come from?'

'Province of Tula, Krapivensk district, rural parish of Kupyansk, village of Borki.'

'Your age?'

'Thirty-three, born in 18— . . .'

'Religion?'

'We are of the Russian religion, Orthodox.'

'Married?'

'Oh no, sir.'

'Your occupation?'

'I was a cleaner in the Hotel Mavritania.'

'Ever been in court before?'

'Never, because like I used to live . . .'

'You have not been in court before?'

'God forbid! Never.'

'Have you received a copy of the indictment?'

'I 'ave.'

'Sit down. Euphemia Ivanovna Botchkova,' said the presiding judge, turning to the next prisoner.

But Simon remained standing and so hid Botchkova from view.

'Kartinkin, sit down!'

But Kartinkin went on standing.

'Kartinkin, sit down!'

But Kartinkin still stood and only sat down when the usher, his head on one side and eyes preternaturally wide open, ran up and said in a tragic whisper: 'You must sit down, you must sit down!'

Kartinkin then sat down as fast as he had shot to his feet before, wrapped his prison cloak round him and began silently twitching his cheeks again.

'Your name?' the president asked the second defendant with a weary sigh, not looking at her and consulting a document lying before him. All this was so much a matter of routine for the president that to expedite matters he was able to do two things at once.

Botchkova was forty-three years old, came from the town of Kalomna and had been a chambermaid in the same Hotel Mavritania. She had never been in court before, she had a copy of the indictment. She answered insolently, in a tone of voice which seemed to say: 'Yes, my Christian name is Euphemia and my surname is Botchkova, I have received the indictment, and don't care who knows it, and people had better think twice before they make fun of me.' Botchkova did not wait to be told but sat down the moment the last question was answered.

'Your name?' the presiding judge asked the third defendant most affably: he was always the ladies' man. 'You should stand up,' he added, softly and gently, seeing that Maslova still kept her seat.

Maslova got up quickly and with an expression of readiness, thrusting her bosom forward, without answering, looked the judge straight in the face with her smiling black eyes that had a slight squint.

'What is your name?'

'Lyubov,' she said quickly.

Nekhlyudov meanwhile had put on his pince-nez and was watching the defendants as the questions were put to them. 'No, it can't be,' he thought, not taking his eyes off the prisoner. 'But how could it be Lyubov?' he thought, hearing the name.

The president was just going on to the next question when the member of the court in spectacles, angrily whispering something under his breath, stopped him. The president nodded and turned to the defendant.

'Lyubov?' he said. 'That is not the name entered here.'

The defendant was silent.

'I am asking for your real name.'

'What were you christened?' asked the bad-tempered member.

'I used to be called Katerina.'

'No, it can't be,' Nekhlyudov kept saying to himself, yet he had no doubt at all now that it was she, the same girl, half ward, half servant, with whom he had once been in love, really in love, and whom in a moment of thoughtless passion he had seduced, and deserted, and then never thought of again because the memory would have been too painful and would have condemned him out of hand: it would have proved that he who was so proud of his 'good breeding' not only was not a gentleman but had treated this woman disgracefully.

Yes, it was she. There was no mistaking that especial, mysterious individuality which distinguishes every face from all others, giving it something peculiar, all its own, and making it different from every other face in the world. In spite of the unhealthy pallor and the plumpness of her face, it was there – that sweet characteristic individuality: there on those lips, in the slightly squinting eyes and, above all, in the naïve smile and the look of readiness not only of face but of figure, too.

'You should have said so at once.' The president's voice was very gentle again. 'What is your father's name?'

'I am illegitimate,' said Maslova.

'Well then, were you not called after your godfather?'

'Yes, Mikhailovna.'

'What crime can she possibly have committed?' Nekhlyudov was thinking. He had difficulty in breathing.

'Your family name – your surname, I mean?' the president went on.

'They called me by my mother's surname, Maslova.'

'Class?'

'Working class.'

'Religion – Orthodox?'

'Orthodox.'

'Occupation? What was your occupation?'

Maslova was silent.

'What was your employment?' repeated the president.

'I was in an establishment.'

'What sort of establishment?' the member in spectacles asked severely.

'You know yourself what sort it was,' said Maslova, and smiled. And with a hurried look round she again fixed her eyes on the presiding judge.

There was something so unusual in the expression of her

face, something so dreadful and pitiful in the meaning of the words she had uttered, in the smile and in the quick glance she had cast round the court-room, that the president looked down and for a moment there was absolute silence in the court. The silence was broken by a laugh from someone in the public seats. Somebody else said, 'Ssh!' The president raised his head and continued his questioning.

'Have you ever been on trial before?'

'No,' answered Maslova softly, and sighed.

'Have you received a copy of the indictment?'

'I have.'

'Take your seat,' said the president.

The defendant leaned backwards to pick up her skirt with the same movement a fine lady makes when she adjusts her train, and sat down, folding her small white hands in the sleeves of her cloak, her eyes still fixed on the president.

Then began the roll-call of the witnesses, who were sent out of court; the doctor who was to give expert medical evidence was called. Next, the secretary rose and started reading the indictment. He read distinctly (though he mispronounced his *l*'s and *r*'s) in a loud voice, but so rapidly that the words ran into one another and formed a long uninterrupted soporific drone. The judges leaned now on one, now on the other arm of their chairs, now on the table or back in their seats; they closed their eyes and opened them again, and whispered among themselves. Several times one of the gendarmes repressed a yawn.

Of the defendants, Kartinkin never stopped twitching his cheeks. Botchkova sat quite still and erect, occasionally scratching her head with a finger under her kerchief.

Maslova sat motionless, listening to the secretary reading, and gazing at him; now and again she gave a slight start, as though she wanted to object, blushed and then sighed heavily, shifted the position of her hands, looked round her and again let her eyes rest on the secretary.

Nekhlyudov sat in his high-backed chair, the second from

the end in the front row. Without removing his pince-nez he stared at Maslova, while a complex, painful process took place in his soul.

10

THE indictment ran as follows:

'On the seventeenth day of January 188– at the Hotel Mavritania the sudden death occurred of a merchant of the Second Guild from Kurgan, one Ferapont Emilianovich Smelkov.

'The local police doctor of the fourth district certified that death was due to rupture of the heart caused by excessive use of alcoholic liquor. The body of the said Smelkov was interred.

'A few days later a fellow countryman and friend of Smelkov, the merchant Timokhin, returning from Petersburg and learning of Smelkov's death and the attendant circumstances, expressed his suspicion that Smelkov had been poisoned with the object of stealing the money which he had on him.

'This suspicion was confirmed at a preliminary investigation, which established:

'1. That not long before his death Smelkov had received three thousand eight hundred roubles in silver from the bank. Whereas an inventory, made as a precautionary measure, of the deceased's effects showed an amount of only three hundred and twelve roubles, sixteen kopecks.

'2. The whole day and night preceding his death Smelkov had spent with the prostitute Lyubov (Katerina Maslova) in the brothel and at the Hotel Mavritania, where at Smelkov's behest and in his absence Katerina Maslova had gone to collect money, which she got from Smelkov's portmanteau, unlocking it (with the key Smelkov had given her) in the presence of the chambermaid of the Hotel Mavritania, Euphemia Botchkova, and the cleaner, Simon Kartinkin.

57

When Maslova unlocked Smelkov's portmanteau Botchkova and Kartinkin, who were present, saw some bundles of hundred-rouble bank-notes.

'3. When Smelkov returned from the brothel to the Hotel Mavritania, accompanied by the prostitute Maslova, the latter, on the advice of the cleaner Kartinkin, put a white powder, which she received from Kartinkin, into Smelkov's brandy-glass.

'4. The following morning the prostitute Lyubov (Katerina Maslova) sold to her mistress, the proprietor of the brothel, the witness Kitayeva, a diamond ring of Smelkov's, which Smelkov had allegedly given her as a present.

'5. On the day following Smelkov's demise the chamber-maid of the Hotel Mavritania, Euphemia Botchkova, had deposited in her current account at the local commercial bank the sum of one thousand eight hundred roubles in silver.

'A post-mortem examination of Smelkov's internal organs which had revealed the undoubted presence of poison in the organism of the deceased gave grounds for concluding that death was caused by poisoning.

'Maslova, Botchkova and Kartinkin, brought to court and accused of the crime, pleaded not guilty and declared: Maslova – that she really had been sent by Smelkov from the brothel where she "works" (as she expressed it) to the Hotel Mavritania to fetch some money for the merchant, and that, having unlocked the portmanteau with the key given her by the merchant, she had taken out forty silver roubles, as she had been told to, but that she had not taken any more money, to which Botchkova and Kartinkin could be her witnesses, for she had opened and closed the portmanteau and taken out the money in their presence. She further testified that on her second visit to the merchant Smelkov's room she did, at the instigation of Simon Kartinkin, put into the brandy some kind of powder which she thought was a soporific, in the hope that the merchant would fall asleep and let her go quicker. The ring Smelkov himself had given her as a present after he had beaten her and she had cried and wanted to leave him.

'Euphemia Botchkova testified that she knew nothing about the missing money, and had not even gone into the merchant's room, but that Lyubov had been busy there all by herself, and if anything had been stolen from the merchant, then it must have been stolen by Lyubov when she came with the merchant's key to get his money.'

At this point Maslova gave a start and gazed at Botchkova open-mouthed.

'When Euphemia Botchkova was confronted with the receipt for the eighteen hundred roubles at the bank' – the secretary continued reading – 'and was asked how she had come by such a sum, she said that it was what she and Simon Kartinkin had saved over twelve years, and she was going to marry him.

'At his first examination Simon Kartinkin confessed that he and Botchkova together had stolen the money, at the instigation of Maslova who had come from the brothel with the key, and had shared it out between the three of them.' Here Maslova gave another start and even jumped up from her seat, flushed purple and began saying something, but the usher stopped her. 'Finally,' the secretary went on, 'Kartinkin confessed, too, that he had supplied Maslova with the powder to send the merchant to sleep; but when he was examined the second time he denied having had anything to do either with the stealing of the money or giving Maslova the powder, and accused her of having done everything all by herself. Concerning the money which Botchkova had deposited at the bank, he said the same as she did, that it was money they had earned in tips during twelve years' service at the hotel.'

Then followed an account of the confrontation of the accused, the depositions of the witnesses, the opinion of the experts and so on.

The indictment concluded as follows:

'In consequence of the aforesaid, the peasant of the village

Borki, Simon Petrov Kartinkin, thirty-three years of age; the citizens Euphemia Ivanovna Botchkova, forty-three years of age, and Katerina Mikhailovna Maslova, twenty-seven years of age, are charged with having on the 17th day of January 188– jointly conspired and stolen from the merchant Smelkov money to the value of two thousand five hundred roubles in silver, and a finger-ring, and of having administered poison to the said Smelkov with intent to deprive him of life, and thereby in fact causing Smelkov's death.

'This crime is specified in paragraphs 4 and 5 of Article 1453 of the Penal Code. Therefore, in pursuance of Article 202 of the Statutes of Criminal Procedure, the peasant Simon Kartinkin and the women Euphemia Botchkova and Katerina Maslova stand committed for trial by jury at the District Court.'

Thus the secretary ended his reading of the lengthy act of indictment and, having collected up his documents, he resumed his seat, smoothing his long hair with both hands. Everybody drew a sigh of relief in the pleasant knowledge that now the trial had begun, and everything would be made clear and justice be satisfied. Nekhlyudov was the only one not to experience this feeling: he was overwhelmed with horror at the thought of what Maslova, the innocent and charming girl he had known ten years ago, might have done.

11

WHEN the reading of the indictment was over the president, after consulting with the members of the court, turned to Kartinkin with an expression that said plainly: 'Now we are going to get to the truth of the matter, down to the last detail.'

'Peasant Simon Kartinkin,' he said, inclining over to the left.

Simon Kartinkin rose to his feet, stretching his arms down by his sides and continuing to move his cheeks inaudibly.

'You are charged with having, on the 17th day of January 188–, conspired with Euphemia Botchkova and Katerina Maslova to steal money from a portmanteau belonging to the merchant Smelkov, and of having procured arsenic and incited Katerina Maslova to administer the said poison to the merchant Smelkov in his wine, thus causing Smelkov's death. Do you plead guilty?' said the president, inclining to the right.

'Course I don't, 'cause our business is to attend to the guests and . . .'

'You will have a chance to tell us about that later. Do you plead guilty?'

'Oh no, sir, I only –'

'You shall say that later. Do you plead guilty?' the president repeated quietly but firmly.

' 'Ow can I do that, knowin' . . .'

Here the usher again rushed to Simon Kartinkin and stopped him in a tragical whisper.

With an expression on his face that said, 'That's settled,' the president shifted the elbow of the hand in which he held the paper, and turned to Euphemia Botchkova.

'Euphemia Botchkova, you are charged with having, on the 17th day of January 188–, in the Hotel Mavritania, together with Simon Kartinkin and Katerina Maslova, stolen money and a finger-ring from the merchant Smelkov's portmanteau, and, after dividing the stolen property among yourselves, of having tried to conceal your crime by administering poison to the merchant Smelkov, thereby causing his death. Do you plead guilty?'

'I am not guilty of anything,' boldly and firmly replied the defendant. 'I never went near the room . . . but when that hussy went in she did the whole business.'

'You may say that later,' repeated the president, as quietly and firmly as before. 'So you do not plead guilty?'

'It wasn't me took the money, and it wasn't me that give him any drink, I wasn't even in the room. If I'd been there I'd have chucked the creature out.'

'You do not plead guilty?'

'Never.'

'Very well.'

'Katerina Maslova,' began the presiding judge, addressing the third defendant, 'the charge against you is that, having come from the brothel to the Hotel Mavritania with the key of the merchant Smelkov's portmanteau, you stole from that portmanteau a sum of money and a finger-ring,' he said, as though reciting a lesson learned by heart, meanwhile leaning his ear towards the member on his left, who was telling him that a phial listed among the material exhibits was missing. 'You stole from that portmanteau a sum of money and a finger-ring,' he repeated, 'and shared it out; then, returning to the Hotel Mavritania with the merchant Smelkov, you gave the said Smelkov poison in his drink, thereby causing his death. Do you plead guilty?'

'I am not guilty of anything,' she began rapidly. 'As I said in the beginning, I say again now: I did not take anything, I did not, I did not: I did not take anything, and the ring he gave me himself . . .'

'You do not plead guilty to having stolen two thousand five hundred roubles?' said the president.

'I've said I took nothing but the forty roubles.'

'Well, what about having given the merchant Smelkov a powder in his drink – do you plead guilty to that?'

'I do. Only I believed what they told me, that it was a sleeping powder, that it wouldn't do him any harm. I never thought, I never wanted to kill him. God is my witness, I never wanted that,' she said.

'So you do not plead guilty to the charge of stealing money and a finger-ring from the merchant Smelkov,' said the presiding judge. 'But you do plead guilty to the charge of having administered the powders?'

'Well, yes, I plead guilty to that, only I thought they were sleeping powders. I only gave them to send him to sleep. I never meant, I never thought anything else.'

'Very well,' said the president, evidently satisfied with the results attained. 'Then tell us how it all happened,' he said, leaning back in his chair and putting his folded hands on the table. 'Tell us all about it. A frank confession will be to your advantage.'

Maslova was silent, but she continued to look straight at the presiding judge.

'Tell us what happened.'

'What happened?' Maslova suddenly began, speaking very fast. 'I arrived at the hotel, they took me to the room where he was, and he was already drunk.' She pronounced the word *he* with a peculiar expression of horror, opening her eyes wide. 'I tried to go, but he would not let me.'

She stopped, as if she had lost the thread or was thinking of something else.

'Well, and then?'

'What do you mean, and then? Then I stayed a bit, and afterwards went home.'

At this point the assistant prosecutor half raised himself, leaning awkwardly on one elbow.

'Do you wish to interrogate?' asked the president, and receiving an answer in the affirmative he indicated by a gesture that he was at liberty to do so.

'I should like to ask if the defendant had any previous acquaintance with Simon Kartinkin?' said the assistant prosecutor, without looking at Maslova.

Having put the question, he compressed his lips and frowned.

The president repeated the question. Maslova stared at the assistant prosecutor in alarm.

'With Simon? Yes, I knew him before,' she said.

'I should like to know the nature of the acquaintance between the defendant and Kartinkin. Did they often see each other?'

'The nature of the acquaintance? He used to send for me for the hotel guests. There wasn't an acquaintance,' replied

Maslova, glancing uneasily from the assistant prosecutor to the judge, and back again.

'I should like to know why Kartinkin always sent for Maslova in preference to the other women,' said the assistant prosecutor, with a cunning Mephistophelian smile, his eyes half closed.

'I don't know. How should I know?' answered Maslova, casting a frightened look round her and for a moment resting her eyes on Nekhlyudov. 'He asked for whoever he wanted.'

'Is it possible she recognized me?' thought Nekhlyudov in terror, feeling the blood rushing to his face; but Maslova immediately turned away, without distinguishing him from the others, and again fixed her eyes anxiously on the assistant prosecutor.

'The defendant, then, denies having had any close relations with Kartinkin? Very well, I have nothing further to ask.'

And the assistant prosecutor immediately removed his elbow from the desk and began writing something. As a matter of fact he was not noting anything down – he was just running his pen over the letters of his brief – but he had seen attorneys and lawyers, after putting a clever question, enter a remark in their notes which should subsequently confound their opponents.

The presiding judge did not at once turn to the prisoner, because he was asking the member with the spectacles whether he agreed with the interrogation (though all the questions had been prepared and written out beforehand).

'Well, what happened next?' he continued his inquiry.

'I went home,' Maslova resumed, with a little more assurance, looking only at the president, 'gave the money to Madam and went to bed. I had just fallen asleep when Bertha, one of our girls, woke me up and said: "Get up, your merchant has come back again." I did not want to go down but Madam made me. He' – again she articulated the word with obvious horror – 'he was treating the girls with wine and

64

wanted to send for more but his money was all gone. Madam would not trust him. So he sent me to his room in the hotel. And he told me where the money was and how much to take. So I went.'

The president happened to be whispering just then to the member on his left and did not hear what Maslova was saying, but in order to appear as if he had heard it all he repeated her last words.

'You went. Well, and then what happened?'

'I went and did like he told me to – I went to his room. I didn't go in alone, I called Simon Mikhailovich and her,' she said, pointing to Botchkova.

'That's a lie: I never set foot in the room . . .' Botchkova began, but was stopped.

'With them there I took out four notes,' continued Maslova, frowning, and without looking at Botchkova.

'Well, and didn't the defendant notice how much money was there while she was taking the forty roubles?' the prosecuting attorney asked again.

Maslova flinched when the prosecuting attorney spoke to her. She did not know why it was but she felt that he wished her evil.

'I did not count it; I only saw there were some one hundred-rouble notes.'

'The defendant saw hundred-rouble notes – I have no more to ask.'

'Well, so you brought back the money?' the presiding judge went on to ask, looking at the clock.

'I did.'

'Well, and then?' inquired the presiding judge.

'And then *he* took me to the hotel with him again,' said Maslova.

'Well, and how was it you gave him the powder? In his wine?'

'How? I poured it into the wine, and gave it to him.'

'But what did you do it for?'

She did not answer at once, but heaved a deep and heavy sigh.

'He wouldn't let me go,' she said, after a moment's silence. 'I was dead tired with him. I went into the corridor and said to Simon Mikhailovich: "I wish he'd let me go. I'm tired." And Simon Mikhailovich said: "We're sick of him, too. We are thinking of giving him a sleeping draught; that will send him off, and then you can get away." I said, "All right." I thought it was some harmless powder. So he gave me the powder. I went back, and *he* was lying on the other side of the partition and at once he told me to give him some cognac. I took a bottle of *fine champagne* from the table, poured out two glasses – one for myself and one for him, and put the powder into his glass and gave it to him. Would I have given it if I'd known?'

'Well, and how did the finger-ring come into your possession?' asked the president.

'He gave me the ring himself.'

'When did he give it to you?'

'That was when we came back to his room. I wanted to leave, and he struck me on the head and broke my comb. I got angry and said I was going. He took the ring off his finger and gave it to me, to persuade me to stay,' she said.

Here the assistant prosecutor again slightly raised himself and with the same feigned air of simplicity asked for permission to put a few questions. His request being granted, he bent his head over his embroidered collar and asked:

'I should like to know how long the defendant remained in the merchant Smelkov's room.'

Again Maslova seemed frightened, and looking anxiously from the assistant prosecutor to the president said hurriedly:

'I don't remember how long it was.'

'And does the defendant also forget whether she went anywhere else in the hotel after she left the merchant Smelkov?'

Maslova reflected.

66

'Yes, I went into an empty room next door,' she said.

'And what did you go in there for?' asked the assistant prosecutor, carried away and addressing the question directly to her.

'I went in to arrange my dress and wait for a cab.'

'And was Kartinkin in the room with the defendant, or not?'

'He came in too.'

'And why did he come in?'

'There was some of the merchant's cognac left, and we finished it together.'

'Ah, you finished it together. Excellent. And did the defendant have any conversation with Kartinkin, and if so, what was it about?'

Maslova suddenly frowned, flushed crimson and said quickly:

'What about? I did not talk about anything. I have told you all that happened, and I don't know any more. Do what you like with me. I am not guilty, and that's all.'

'I have nothing more to ask,' the prosecuting attorney said to the judge, and shrugging his shoulders in an unnatural manner he began swiftly noting down in the brief for his speech that, on the defendant's own admission, she had gone into the empty room with Kartinkin.

There was a silence.

'You have nothing more to say?'

'I have told you everything,' she said with a sigh, and sat down.

The president then made a note of something and, after hearing a whispered communication from the member on his left, announced a ten-minute adjournment, rose hurriedly and left the court-room. The deliberation between the president and the member on his left, a tall bearded man with large kindly eyes, concerned the fact that the latter's stomach felt slightly out of order and he wanted to do a little massage and take some drops. It was this that he told the presiding judge, and at his request the proceedings were interrupted.

When the judges had risen, jury, lawyers and witnesses all got up and, with the pleasurable sensation that part of this important business was already over, walked about the court-room.

Nekhlyudov went into the jurymen's room and sat down by the window.

12

YES, it was Katusha.

The relations between Nekhlyudov and Katusha had been as follows:

The first time Nekhlyudov saw Katusha was as a third-year student at the university when he stayed for the summer with his aunts, working on his thesis about the ownership of land. Usually he spent the summer vacation with his mother and sister on his mother's large estate near Moscow. But that year his sister had married and his mother had gone to a watering-place abroad; so, having his thesis to prepare, he decided to spend the summer with his aunts. It was very quiet with them in the depths of the country, there were no distractions, his aunts had a very soft spot for their nephew and heir, and he was fond of them and of their simple old-fashioned way of living.

During that summer at his aunts' Nekhlyudov experienced that rapturous state of exaltation when a young man discovers for himself, without any outside recommendation, all the beauty and significance of life, and the importance of the task allotted in life to every man; when he sees the endless per-fectibility of himself and the whole universe; and devotes himself not only hopefully but in complete confidence to attaining the perfection he dreams of. That year at the uni-versity he had read Spencer's *Social Statics*, and Spencer's theory of land tenure had made a strong impression on him, all the more so because he was himself heir to large estates. His father had not been rich but his mother had received over twenty-five thousand acres of land for her dowry. It was then that he realized for the first time all the cruelty and injustice of private ownership of land, and, being one of those to whom a sacrifice to the demands of conscience affords the highest spiritual enjoyment, he had resolved to relinquish his property rights and had given away to the peasants the land he had inherited from his father. And it was on this subject that he was writing his thesis.

His life that year with his aunts in the country ran on these lines: He would get up very early, sometimes as early as three o'clock, and before sunrise go to bathe in the river at the foot of a hill; often the morning mists had not yet lifted, and he would return while the dew still lay on the grass and flowers. Sometimes after his coffee he would sit down to work on this thesis, or look up references for his thesis, but very often instead of reading or writing he would leave the house again and wander through the fields and woods. Before dinner he took a nap somewhere in the garden; at table he amused and entertained his aunts with his gaiety; then he went riding or for a row on the river, and in the evening he read again or sat with his aunts, playing patience. Often at night, on a moonlight night especially, he could not sleep, simply because he was filled to overflowing with the joy of life, and instead of going to bed he would roam the garden, sometimes till daybreak, with his dreams and thoughts.

Thus, happy and tranquil, he spent the first month at his aunts', never noticing their half ward, half servant, the black-eyed, swift-footed Katusha.

Brought up under his mother's wing, Nekhlyudov at nineteen was still an innocent boy. If a woman figured in his dreams at all it was only as a wife. All the women who, according to his ideas, could not be his wife, were not women but just people. But on Ascension day of that summer a neighbour happened to call with her children – two young daughters and a high-school boy – together with a young artist of peasant stock who was staying with them.

After tea they went to play catch in the newly mown meadow in front of the house. They took Katusha with them. Presently Nekhlyudov found himself paired off with Katusha. He always enjoyed looking at Katusha, but it never entered his head that there could be any special friendship between them.

'I'll never catch those two unless they slip and fall,' said the jolly young painter, whose turn it was to catch the others and who could run very fast on his short, bandy but strong peasant legs.

'You – of course you won't catch us!'

'One, two, three!'

They clapped hands three times. Hardly suppressing her laughter, Katusha quickly changed places with Nekhlyudov, and with her strong, rough little hand pressing his large one, she started running to the left, her starched skirts rustling.

Nekhlyudov could run fast, and not wanting to be caught by the artist he raced as fast as he could. When he looked round he saw the artist chasing Katusha but she kept well ahead, her lithe young legs moving rapidly. In front was a clump of lilac bushes, behind which nobody was running, and Katusha, looking back at Nekhlyudov, made a sign with her head for him to join her there. He understood and ran behind the bushes. But he did not know that there was a narrow ditch there, overgrown with nettles; he stumbled and fell in, stinging his hands in the nettles and getting them wet with the evening dew; but he picked himself up at once, laughing at himself, and ran on to an open space.

Katusha, radiant with happiness, her shining eyes black as sloes, was flying towards him. They met and caught hold of each other's hands.

'I bet you got stung,' she said, adjusting her straying hair with her free hand. She was panting and smiling, looking straight up at him.

'I didn't know there was a ditch there,' he said, smiling too and not letting go of her hand.

She drew nearer and without knowing how it happened he bent his face towards her; she did not draw back, he pressed her hand tighter and kissed her on the lips.

'Well I declare!' she said, and freeing her hand with a quick movement she ran away from him.

Running up to a lilac bush, she broke off two branches of white lilac which was already beginning to drop, and tapping her burning face with them and looking round at him she went to rejoin the other players, swinging her arms briskly in front of her.

From that moment relations between Nekhlyudov and Katusha were changed and the sort of connexion was established which often exists between an innocent young man and an equally innocent young girl, who are attracted to one another.

The instant Katya entered the room, or if he saw her white apron from a distance, it was as if the sun had come out: everything seemed more interesting, gayer, and life held more meaning and was happier. And she felt the same. But it was not only Katusha's presence or the fact that she was near that had this effect on Nekhlyudov: the mere thought that Katusha existed, and for her that Nekhlyudov existed, produced the same effect. If Nekhlyudov received an unpleasant letter from his mother, or could not get on with his thesis, or if he felt sad for no reason, the way young people do – he had only to think that there was a Katusha and he would be seeing her, and all his troubles would vanish.

Katusha had much to do about the house but she managed to get through it, and her spare time she would spend reading. Nekhlyudov gave her Dostoyevsky and Turgenyev, whom he had just finished reading himself. She liked Turgenyev's *A Quiet Nook* best. They talked in snatches, when they met in a passage, on the veranda or in the yard, and occasionally in the room which Katusha shared with his aunts' old maid, Matriona

Pavlovna, and where Nekhlyudov sometimes went to drink unsweetened tea and suck bits of sugar. And it was these talks in Matriona Pavlovna's presence which were the most enjoyable. When they were alone it was worse. Their eyes at once began to say something very different and far more important than what their lips were saying; their mouths seemed shuttered, and a strange unaccountable fear made them part hurriedly.

Such were the relations between Nekhlyudov and Katusha right to the end of his first visit to his aunts. The aunts noticed, took alarm and even wrote abroad to Princess Helena Ivanovna, Nekhlyudov's mother. Aunt Marya Ivanovna was afraid lest Nekhlyudov should form an illicit liaison with Katusha. But there was no danger of that. Though he did not know it, Nekhlyudov loved Katusha with an innocent love, and his love was his main shield against his downfall and against hers. He not only had no desire to possess her physically but the very thought of such a possibility filled him with horror. There was much more foundation for the fears of the romantic Sophia Ivanovna that Dmitri, with his uncompromising, determined character, having fallen in love with the girl, might take it into his head to marry her without ever considering her birth or station in life.

Had Nekhlyudov at that time clearly understood his feelings for Katusha, and especially had they tried to argue and tell him that he could not and must not link his destiny with a girl in her position, it might very easily have happened that, being entirely straightforward, he would have come to the conclusion that there could be no possible reason against his marrying a girl, no matter who she was, so long as he loved her. But his aunts did not mention their fears to him, and so he left, still unaware of his love for Katusha.

He was sure that his feeling for Katusha was simply one of the manifestations of the joy of life that filled his whole being and was shared by that sweet, light-hearted girl. Yet for all that, when he was going away and Katusha, standing on the porch with his aunts, saw him off with her black eyes that had a slight cast full of tears, he was conscious of leaving behind him something beautiful and precious, which could never be repeated. And he grew very sad.

'Good-bye, Dmitri Ivanovich,' she said in her agreeable, caressing voice, and, keeping back the tears which filled her eyes, ran into the hall, where she could cry her fill.

13

AFTER that Nekhlyudov did not see Katusha for three years. When he did see her again he had just been given his commission and was about to join his regiment. On the way he stopped to spend a few days with his aunts; but he was now a very different person from the one who had spent the summer with them three years before.

Then he had been an honest unselfish lad, ready to devote himself to any good cause; now he was a dissolute accomplished egoist, caring only for his own enjoyment. Then he had seen God's world as a mystery which with excitement and delight he strove to penetrate; now everything in life was simple and clear and depended on the circumstances in which he happened to be. Then he had felt the necessity and importance of communion with nature, and with men who had lived, thought and felt before his time (philosophers and poets); now worldly affairs and social intercourse with his comrades were the necessary and important things. Then women had seemed mysterious and enchanting creatures – enchanting because of their very mystery; now his idea of a woman, of any woman except such as were of his own family or the wives of his friends, was precisely defined: women were a familiar means of enjoyment. Then he had not required money and less than a third of what his mother gave him would have sufficed, and it was possible to refuse the property inherited from his father and give it to the peasants; but now his monthly allowance of fifteen hundred roubles was not enough, and there had been some unpleasant interviews with his mother over money matters. Then he had regarded his spiritual being as his real self; now his healthy virile animal self was the real *I*.

And all this terrible change had come about simply because he had ceased to put his faith in his own conscience and had taken to trusting in others. And he had ceased to trust himself and begun to believe in others because life was too difficult if one believed one's own conscience: believing in oneself, every question had to be decided, never to the advantage of one's animal self, which seeks easy gratifications, but in almost every case against it. But to believe in others meant that there was nothing to decide: everything had been decided already, and always in favour of the animal *I* and against the spiritual. Moreover, when he trusted his own conscience he was always laying himself open to criticism, whereas now, trusting others, he received the approval of those around him.

Thus, when Nekhlyudov used to think, read and speak about God, about truth, about wealth and poverty, everyone round him had considered it out of place and in a way ridiculous, and his mother and aunt had called him, with kindly irony, *notre cher philosophe*. But when he read novels, told *risqué* stories, drove to the French theatre to see absurd vaudevilles and gaily repeated the jokes – everybody admired and encouraged him. When he considered it his duty to moderate his needs, and wore an old overcoat and abstained from wine, they had all thought it odd, as if he were being eccentric in order to show off; but when he spent large sums on hunting, or on the appointments of a special and luxurious study for himself, everybody praised his taste and gave him expensive presents. While he had been chaste and had meant to remain so till he married, his family had been afraid for his health, and even his mother was not distressed but rather pleased when she found out that he had become a real man and had taken a certain French lady away from one of his comrades. But so far as the episode with Katusha was concerned, the princess could not think without a shudder that it might have occurred to him to marry the girl.

It was the same when Nekhlyudov came of age and gave to the peasants the small estate he had inherited from his father, because he considered the private ownership of land wrong – the action had filled his mother and family with dismay and provided all his relatives with matter for reproaching and making fun of him. They never stopped telling him that the peasants when they had got the land were not only no better off but, on the contrary, were the poorer for it, having set up drinking-houses on the estate and completely left off doing any work. But when Nekhlyudov entered the Guards and gambled away so much money in the company of his aristocratic companions that Helena Ivanovna, his mother, had to draw on her capital, she was hardly upset at all: it was natural and even a good thing that wild oats should be sown at an early age and in good society.

At first Nekhlyudov made a fight for his principles but the struggle was too hard, since everything he had considered right when he put his faith in his own conscience was wrong according to other people, and, vice versa, everything which he, believing himself, regarded as bad, was held to be good by all the people round him. And at last Nekhlyudov gave in: that is, he left off believing in his own ideals and began to believe in those of other people. At first this renunciation of his true self was unpleasant but the disagreeable sensation lasted a very short while and very soon Nekhlyudov, who in the meantime had begun to smoke and drink wine, forgot the uncomfortable feeling and even experienced great relief.

And Nekhlyudov, with his passionate nature, surrendered himself unreservedly to this new way of life which commanded the world's approval, and completely stifled the voice in him which cried out for something different. This transformation began after he moved to Petersburg, and received its finishing touch in the army.

Military service always corrupts a man, placing him in conditions of complete idleness, that is, absence of all intelligent and useful work, and liberating him from the common obligations of humanity, for which it substitutes conventional considerations like the honour of the regiment, the uniform and the flag, and, on the one hand, investing him with unlimited power over other men, and, on the other, demanding slavish subjection to superior officers.

But when, to the general debasement resulting from life in the army with its glorification of the uniform and the flag, and its authorized violence and murder, is added the seduction of wealth and intimacy with the Imperial family, as is the case with select regiments of the Guards, in which only rich and aristocratic officers serve – then this demoralization develops into a perfect madness of selfishness. And Nekhlyudov had been in this state of mad selfishness ever since he entered the army and began living as his companions lived.

He had nothing whatever to do except don a fine uniform, made and kept brushed, not by himself but by others, with helmet and weapons likewise forged and polished and handed to him by others, and ride a beautiful charger broken in, exercised and fed by somebody else, to take part in parades and reviews with other men like himself, and gallop about, and wave swords, shoot off guns and teach others to do the same. There was no other occupation, and highly placed dignitaries, young and old, the Tsar and his suite, not only approved of this occupation but extolled and rewarded it. In addition to this, it was regarded excellent and important to gather together in order to eat – and particularly to drink – in officers' clubs and the most expensive restaurants, squandering money received from some invisible source; then theatres, balls, women and riding out on horseback again, swordplay, gallops and back to flinging money about, and wine, cards, women.

Such a life has a peculiarly corrupting influence upon the military because, where a civilian would not be able to help being secretly ashamed of such conduct, a soldier thinks it the proper way to live, brags and is proud of it, especially in time of war, as was the case with Nekhlyudov, who entered the army just after the declaration of war with Turkey. 'We are ready to sacrifice our lives in war, and therefore a gay carefree existence is not only pardonable but absolutely necessary for us – and so we live that life.'

In some such confused fashion Nekhlyudov thought at this period of his life; and all this time he felt the delight of being liberated from the moral restraint he had formerly accepted for himself, and lived in a continuous mad state of chronic selfishness.

That was the condition he was in when after an absence of three years he came to visit his aunts again.

14

NEKHLYUDOV decided to drop in on his aunts because their estate was on the road he had to take to catch up with his regiment, and because they had begged him to come, but chiefly he went in order to see Katusha. Perhaps in his inmost heart he had already formed those evil designs against Katusha which the brute beast in him suggested, but he was not conscious of this intention: he simply wanted to revisit the spot where he had been so happy and see his rather comic but dear kind-hearted aunts, who always, without his noticing it, surrounded him with an atmosphere of love and admiration, and dear Katusha, of whom he had such an agreeable recollection.

He arrived at the end of March, on Good Friday, after the thaw had set in, in a downpour of rain, so that he was wet to the skin and chilled, but excited and full of spirits as always at that time. 'I wonder whether she is still here,' he thought as he drove into the familiar courtyard of his aunts' old manor-house surrounded by a low brick wall. The ground was thick with snow which had fallen from the roof. He expected her to come running out on the porch when she heard his sleigh-bells, but only two bare-footed old women with buckets and their skirts tucked up, who had evidently been scrubbing floors, came out of the side door. She was not at the front door either; only Tikhon, the man-servant, in an apron – very likely he, too, had been busy cleaning – came out on to the porch. His aunt Sophia Ivanovna, wearing a silk gown and a cap, met him in the hall.

'How nice that you have come!' said Sophia Ivanovna, kissing him. 'My Marya is not feeling very well: she got tired standing in church. We have been to Communion.'[1]

'My congratulations, Aunt Sophia,'[2] said Nekhlyudov, kissing Sophia Ivanovna's hand. 'Forgive me, I have made you wet.'

'You must go straight to your room. You are soaked through. Dear me, you've grown a moustache . . . Katusha! Katusha! Quick now, bring him some coffee.'

'Coming!' he heard the familiar pleasant voice from the corridor.

And Nekhlyudov's heart cried out, 'She's here!' And he felt as though the sun had come out from behind the clouds. Nekhlyudov gaily followed Tikhon to his old room to change his clothes.

Nekhlyudov wanted to ask Tikhon about Katusha, how she was, what she was doing, was she going to be married? But Tikhon was so respectful and at the same time so stern, so firmly insistent about pouring the water out of the basin on to his hands for him that Nehklyudov could not bring himself to ask about Katusha and inquired only after his grand-children, the old stallion and the mongrel-dog Polkan. All were alive and well except Polkan, who had died of rabies the year before.

1. In fact, Good Friday in the Eastern Orthodox Church is a day of total fasting, and there is no celebration of the Liturgy or Communion.
2. It is usual in the Orthodox Church to congratulate those who have received Communion.

He had just taken off his wet clothes and was dressing again when he heard hurried steps and somebody knocked at the door. Nekhlyudov recognized the footsteps and the knock. Nobody but she walked and knocked that way.

He threw his wet greatcoat over his shoulders and went to the door.

'Come in!'

It was she, Katusha. The same Katusha, only more enchanting than before. The naïve black eyes with the slight cast smiled up in the same old way. Now, as then, she had on a clean white apron. His aunts had sent her with a cake of scented soap, fresh from the wrapper, and two towels, one a long Russian embroidered one, the other a bath towel. The new cake of soap with its raised lettering, the towels and she herself were all equally clean, fresh, unblemished and pleasant. Her sweet firm red lips puckered as of old into a smile of irrepressible happiness at the sight of him.

'Welcome to you, Dmitri Ivanovich,' she brought out with difficulty, her face suffused with a rosy blush.

'Hullo, my . . . Hullo,' he did not know what to say to her, and blushed, too. 'Alive and well?'

'Yes, the Lord be thanked. . . . Here is your favourite pink soap which your aunt sent me with,' she said, putting the soap on the table and the towels over the arms of an easy chair.

'He has his own,' said Tikhon, speaking up in defence of the dignity and independence of the visitor and pointing proudly at Nekhlyudov's large open dressing-case with its huge collection of silver-topped bottles, brushes, pomades, perfumes and toilet articles of all kinds.

'Give my thanks to my aunt. Oh, how glad I am to be here,' said Nekhlyudov, feeling all of a sudden as light-hearted and tender as of old.

She only smiled in answer to these words, and went out.

The aunts, who had always been devoted to Nekhlyudov, made more of a fuss of him this time than ever. Their Dmitri was off to the war, where he might be wounded or killed, and this affected the old ladies.

Nekhlyudov had arranged to stay only twenty-four hours with his aunts but after he had seen Katusha he agreed to remain another two days, over Easter, with them, and telegraphed to his friend and comrade Schönbock, whom he had promised to join in Odessa, to come and stay at his aunts' house.

No sooner had Nekhlyudov seen Katusha again than he felt the old feeling towards her. As it had been in the past, so it was now: he could not see her white apron without emotion; the sound of her footstep, her voice, her laugh filled him with delight; he could not look at her eyes, which were black as sloes with the dew on them, without his heart melting, especially when she smiled; and above all he could not remain indifferent when he noticed that she blushed every time she encountered him. He knew he was in love, but not in the same way as before when love was a mysterious thing and he would not acknowledge, even to himself, that he was in love, and he had been convinced that love came only once. Now he knew he was in love and was glad of it; and although he refused to admit it he vaguely recognized the nature of his emotion and its probable outcome.

In Nekhlyudov, as in all of us, there were two men. One was the spiritual being, seeking for himself only the kind of happiness that meant happiness for other people too; but there was also the animal man out only for his own happiness, at the expense, if need be, of the good of the rest of the world. At this period of insane egoism, engendered by life in Petersburg and in the army, the animal nature prevailed, completely suppressing the spiritual man in him. But when Nekhlyudov saw Katusha again and experienced the same feelings which he had had for her before, the spiritual man in him raised his head once more and began to assert his rights. And throughout the two days to Easter a ceaseless struggle was waged within him, though he did not realize what was happening.

He knew in the depths of his soul that he ought to go away, that there was no sound reason for staying on at his aunts', knew that no good could come of it; and yet it was so pleasant, so delightful, that he shut his eyes to the facts, and stayed.

On Easter eve the priest with his deacon and subdeacon arrived to sing matins, their sleigh having had great difficulty, they said, in journeying through puddles and across the bare earth for the couple of miles that separated the church from the old ladies' house.

Nekhlyudov attended the service with his aunts and the servants, never taking his eyes off Katusha, who stood near the door and brought in the censers. After exchanging the Easter greeting with the priest and his aunts he was on the point of retiring to bed when he heard Matriona Pavlovna, his aunts' elderly maid, and Katusha in the corridor outside, getting ready to go to church for the blessing of the Easter cakes and sweet curds. 'I'll go too,' he thought.

The road to the church was impassable either in a sleigh or on wheels, so Nekhlyudov, who gave orders in his aunts' house as if he were at home, told them to saddle the old horse for him, and instead of going to bed put on his gorgeous uniform with the tight-fitting riding breeches, threw his greatcoat over his shoulders and, mounting the stout overfed old stallion, that never stopped neighing, he rode in the darkness through the puddles and snow to the church.

15

THIS midnight service remained for ever after one of the happiest and most vivid memories of Nekhlyudov's life.

The service had already begun when he rode into the churchyard out of the black night, relieved only here and there by patches of white snow, his horse splashing through the water and pricking its ears at the sight of the little lights round the church.

Some peasants, recognizing Marya Ivanovna's nephew, led

him to a dry place to dismount, tied his horse up and conducted him into the church, which was full of people.

On the right stood the men: old men in home-spun caftans, bast shoes and clean white leg-bands; the younger ones in new cloth tunics with bright-coloured belts round their waists, and top-boots. On the left were the women, with red silk kerchiefs on their heads, sleeveless velveteen jackets, bright red blouses and gay-coloured skirts of blue, green and red, and boots with steel heel-plates. The more staid, older women with white kerchiefs, grey jackets and old-fashioned linen petticoats, and leather or new bast shoes on their feet, stood behind; between them and the others were the children, their hair greased, and dressed in their best clothes. The men were crossing themselves and bowing, shaking back their hair when they brought their heads up; the women, especially the old women, riveting their faded eyes upon one of the many ikons, each with lighted candles burning before it, made the sign of the cross, firmly pressing their bent fingers to the kerchief on their foreheads, to each shoulder and their stomachs, moving their lips all the while, and bowed or fell to their knees. The children imitated their elders and prayed earnestly whenever anyone was looking at them. The golden ikonostasis shone in the light of the tapers round the big candles decorated with golden spirals. The candelabra was bright with tapers, and from the choir came the cheerful singing of amateur choristers with bellowing basses and the boys' thin treble.

Nekhlyudov passed up to the front. In the middle of the church stood the local gentry: a landed proprietor with his wife and son, the latter wearing a blouse, the district police-officer, the telegraph operator, a tradesman in top-boots, the village elder with a medal on his chest; and to the right of the reading desk, behind the wife of the landowner, stood Matriona Pavlovna in a shot-silk lilac gown and fringed white shawl, and Katusha in a white dress with a tucked bodice and blue sash, and a little red bow in her black hair.

Everything was festive, solemn, happy and beautiful: the clergy in their silver cloth vestments with gold crosses; the deacon and the subdeacon in their gala silver and gold surplices; the choir singers in their best clothes, with their hair well oiled; the gay dancing melodies of the Easter hymns; the continual blessing of the people by the clergy with their triple flower-bedecked candles; and the ever-repeated salutation: 'Christ is risen! Christ is risen!' It was all lovely, but best of all was Katusha in her white dress and blue sash, with the little red bow on her dark head, and her sparkling rapturous eyes.

Nekhlyudov felt that she saw him, though she did not turn her head. He noticed it as he passed close to her on his way to the chancel. He had nothing to tell her but he made up something and whispered as he went by:

'My aunt told me that she would break her fast after the service.'

The young blood rushed to Katusha's sweet face, as it always did when she looked at him, and her black eyes, laughing and full of joy, gazed naïvely up and rested on Nekhlyudov.

'I know,' she said with a smile.

Just then a subdeacon with a brass coffee-pot[1] in his hand, making his way through the crowd and not noticing Katusha, brushed her with his surplice. The subdeacon, apparently wishing to leave a respectful distance between himself and Nekhlyudov, had brushed against Katusha. But Nekhlyudov wondered how it was that he, this subdeacon, did not understand that everything here – here, and in the whole wide world, too – existed solely for Katusha, and that one might be careless about everything else in the world but not about her, because she was the centre of the universe. For her glittered the gold of the ikonostasis; for her burned all the candles in the candelabrum and the candle-stands; for her the joyful chant rang out: 'The Passover of the Lord, Rejoice, O ye

1. Coffee-pots were often used for holding holy water in Russian churches.

people!' All – all that was good on earth was for her. And it seemed to him that Katusha knew that it was all for her. So it seemed to Nekhlyudov when he looked at her slender form in the white dress with the tucked bodice, and the happy rapt face whose expression told him that the song that his own heart was singing was echoed word-for-word in hers.

During the pause between the first and second service Nekhlyudov went out of the church. The people stood aside to let him pass, and bowed. Some recognized him; others asked who he was. He stopped on the steps. The beggars instantly clamoured round him and he gave them all the change he had in his purse, and walked down the steps.

It was light enough to see but the sun had not yet risen. People were sitting on the graves in the churchyard. Katusha had remained in the church, and Nekhlyudov stopped, waiting for her.

The congregation was still coming out and, clattering with their nailed boots on the flagstones, walked down the steps and scattered in the churchyard and the graveyard.

A very old man with shaking head, his aunts' pastry-cook, stopped Nekhlyudov in order to give him the Easter kiss, and his wife, an old woman with a wrinkled Adam's apple showing under her silk neckerchief, took a saffron-yellow egg from her pocket-handkerchief and gave it to him. At the same time a smiling muscular young peasant in a new sleeveless coat and green belt came up.

'Christ is risen!' he said, with laughing eyes, and coming close to Nekhlyudov enveloped him in his peculiar agreeable peasant odour, and, tickling him with his curly beard, kissed him three times squarely on the mouth with his firm fresh lips.

While Nekhlyudov was exchanging kisses with the peasant and receiving from him an egg dyed dark brown, Matriona Pavlovna's shot-silk gown and the dear black head with the little red bow appeared.

She caught sight of him at once over the heads of those who were walking in front of her, and he saw her face light up.

She had come out into the porch with Matriona Pavlovna and stopped, distributing alms to the beggars. A beggar with a red scar in place of a nose went up to Katusha. She took something from her pocket-handkerchief, gave it to him and then drew nearer to him and without showing the least disgust – on the contrary, her eyes shone with joy as brightly as ever – kissed him three times. And while she was exchanging kisses with the beggar her eyes met Nekhlyudov's with a look as if she were asking, 'Am I doing right?'

'Yes, yes, dear, everything is right, everything is just as it should be, and I love you.'

They came down the steps of the porch and he walked over to her. He did not mean to exchange the Easter kiss with her, he only wanted to be nearer to her.

'Christ is risen!' said Matriona Pavlovna, bowing her head and smiling, her tone implying, 'On this night we are all equal,' and wiping her mouth with her handkerchief rolled into a ball offered him her lips.

'He is risen indeed!' responded Nekhlyudov, exchanging kisses with her.

He looked round at Katusha. She blushed and at once went up to him.

'Christ is risen, Dmitri Ivanovich!'

'He is risen indeed!' he said. They kissed twice, then paused, as though considering whether a third kiss was necessary, and, having decided that it was, kissed a third time and smiled.

'You aren't going up to the priest?' asked Nekhlyudov.

'No, we shall sit out here a bit, Dmitri Ivanovich,' said Katusha with an effort, as if she had accomplished some joyous task, breathing a deep sigh and looking him straight in the face with her submissive, chaste, loving eyes with their very slight cast.

In the love between a man and a woman there is always a

moment when that love reaches its zenith – a moment when their love is unconscious, unreasoning and with nothing sensual about it. Such a moment came to Nekhlyudov on this joyful Easter night. Now when he thought of Katusha, this was the occasion which effaced all others. The smooth glossy black head, the white dress with the tucked bodice chastely enveloping her graceful figure and small bosom, the blushing cheeks, the tender sparkling black eyes with their faint suspicion of a squint because she had not slept that night, and her whole being stamped with two main characteristics: the purity of virginal love – love not only for him (he knew that) but for everybody and everything; love not only for the good there was in the world but even for the beggar whom she had kissed.

He knew she had that love in her because that night and morning he was conscious of it in himself, and conscious that in this love he became one with her.

Ah, if it had all stopped there, at the feeling which he had experienced that night! 'Yes, all that dreadful business began only after that Easter night!' he thought, as he sat by the window in the jury-room.

16

RETURNING from church, Nekhlyudov broke the fast with his aunts and, to fortify himself, took a glass of spirits and some wine, a habit he had acquired in the regiment, and then went to his room, where he immediately fell asleep without undressing. He was awakened by a knock at the door. He knew by the knock that it was she, and sat up, rubbing his eyes and stretching himself.

'Katusha, is it you? Come in,' he said, getting to his feet.

She half opened the door.

'Dinner is ready,' she said.

She was wearing the same white dress but the knot of

ribbon in her hair was missing. Glancing into his eyes, she beamed, as if she had communicated some extraordinary good news to him.

'Just coming,' he said, picking up a comb to comb his hair.

She lingered for a minute longer than was necessary. He noticed it and dropping the comb moved towards her. But at that very moment she turned quickly and walked with her customary swift light steps along the strip of carpet down the centre of the corridor.

'Dear me, what a fool I am!' Nekhlyudov said to himself. 'Why ever didn't I make her stay?'

And he ran into the corridor and caught her up.

What he wanted her for, he did not know himself. But it seemed to him that when she came into his room there was something he ought to have done, something that everyone does on such occasions and he had failed to do.

'Katusha, wait,' he said.

She looked round.

'What is it?' she said, stopping.

'Nothing, only . . .'

And with an effort, calling to mind how men generally behave in such circumstances, he put his arm round her waist.

She stood still and looked into his eyes.

'Don't, Dmitri Ivanovich, don't,' she said, blushing to the point of tears and pushing his arm away with her strong rough little hand.

Nekhlyudov let her go, and for a moment he felt not only uncomfortable and ashamed but disgusted with himself. He ought to have listened to the voice of his conscience but he did not realize that this uneasiness and shame were the finest qualities of his soul begging for recognition, whereas, on the contrary, he thought it was only his stupidity, and that he ought to behave as everybody else did.

He caught up with her a second time, put his arm round her

again and kissed her on the neck. This kiss was very different from the other two – the first innocent kiss behind the lilac bush, and the Easter kiss after church that morning. This was a terrible kiss, and she felt it so.

'Oh, what are you doing?' she cried, in a voice as though he had smashed a priceless treasure, and ran away from him as fast as she could.

He went into the dining-room. His aunts, elegantly attired, the doctor and a lady from the neighbourhood were standing at a table where the appetizers were set out. Everything was as usual but in Nekhlyudov's soul a storm was raging. He did not understand a word of what was said to him and answered at random, thinking only of Katusha and recalling the sensation of that last kiss when he caught up with her in the passage. He could think of nothing else. Whenever she entered the room, although he did not even glance in her direction his whole being was conscious of her presence and he had to force himself not to look at her.

After dinner he at once went to his room and for a long time paced up and down in the greatest agitation, listening to all the sounds in the house and waiting for her step. The animal man in him had now not only lifted his head but had trampled underfoot the spiritual man he had been at the time of his first visit and even that very morning in church, and now that dreadful animal man in him ruled supreme. Though he watched for her all that day he never once succeeded in seeing her alone. She was probably trying to avoid him. Towards evening, however, she was obliged to go into the room next to his. The doctor was to stay the night, and Katusha had to make up the bed for the visitor. Hearing her footsteps, Nekhlyudov, treading softly and holding his breath as though he were about to commit a crime, followed her in.

She was putting a clean pillow-case on the pillow, holding it by two of its corners with her arms inside the pillow-case. She looked round at him and smiled, not her former gay happy smile but a frightened pitiful smile. This smile seemed to be telling him that what he was doing was wrong. For a moment he paused. There was still the possibility of making a struggle. Though feebly, the voice of his real love for her was still audible, speaking to him of *her*, of *her* feelings, *her* life. But another voice kept saying: 'Mind, or you'll miss the opportunity for *your* enjoyment, *your* happiness.' And this second voice stifled the first. He walked up to her resolutely. And a terrible, ungovernable animal passion took possession of him.

Without letting her out of his embrace he forced her down on to the bed, and feeling that more remained to be done sat down beside her.

'Dear Dmitri Ivanovich, please let me go,' she said in a piteous voice. 'Matriona Pavlovna is coming!' she cried, tearing herself away, and indeed someone was coming to the door.

'Well then, I will come to you in the night,' whispered Nekhlyudov. 'You'll be alone, won't you?'

'What are you saying? On no account! No, no!' she said but only with her lips: the tremulous confusion of her whole being said something quite different.

It really was Matriona Pavlovna who had come to the door. She came into the room with a blanket over her arm and with a reproachful glance at Nekhlyudov began angrily scolding Katusha for having taken the wrong blanket.

Nekhlyudov left the room without a word. He did not even feel any shame. He could see by Matriona Pavlovna's expression that she disapproved of him, and knew that she was right in disapproving of him, just as he knew that what he was doing was bad – but the animal feeling which had worked itself free from his former feeling of true love for Katusha was now dominant, to the exclusion of everything else. He now knew what he had to do in order to gratify his passion and sought only the opportunity.

All that evening he was restless: now going into his aunts' room, now leaving them for his own room or the porch, thinking of one thing only – how to see her alone; but she herself avoided him and Matriona Pavlovna did not let her out of her sight.

17

AND so the evening passed and night came. The doctor went to bed. The aunts had also retired. Nekhlyudov knew that Matriona Pavlovna was now with them in their bedroom and that Katusha would be in the maids' room – alone. He went out on to the porch again. It was dark out of doors, and damp and warm, and the white mist of spring which drives away the last snow, or is born of the last melting snow, filled the air. From the river below the slope, about a hundred yards from the front door, there were strange sounds: it was the ice breaking up.

Nekhlyudov descended the steps from the porch and, using patches of frozen snow as stepping-stones, made his way across the puddles to the window of the maids' room. His heart beat so fiercely in his breast that he could hear it; his breath now stopped, now burst out in a heavy gasp. In the maids' room a small lamp was burning. Katusha sat alone by the table, looking thoughtfully in front of her. Nekhlyudov watched her for a long time without moving, wanting to see what she would do, believing herself unobserved. For a minute or two she sat quite still; then she lifted her eyes, smiled and shook her head as if chiding herself, and, changing her position, abruptly placed both her hands on the table and fell to gazing before her.

He stood and looked at her, involuntarily listening to the beating of his own heart and the strange noises from the river. There on the river, in the mist, a slow and tireless labour was going on, and he could hear sounds as of something wheezing, cracking, showering down, and thin bits of ice tinkling like glass.

He stood looking at Katusha's pensive worried face which

betrayed the inner struggle of her soul, and he felt pity for her but, oddly enough, this pity only intensified his desire.

Desire took entire possession of him.

He knocked on the window. She started as though she had received an electric shock, her whole body trembled and a look of terror came into her face. Then she sprang up, went to the window and put her face close to the pane. The look of terror did not leave her face even when, putting both palms to her eyes like blinkers, she recognized him. Her face was unusually grave – he had never seen it like that before. She smiled only when he smiled – smiled as it were in submission to him: there was no smile in her heart, only fear. He beckoned to her to come outside to him. But she shook her head and remained at the window. He brought his face close to the pane again and was going to call out to her to come, but at that moment she turned to the door – evidently someone had called her. Nekhlyudov moved away from the window. The mist was so thick that five steps from the house the windows could not be seen: there was only a black shapeless mass from which the light of the lamp shone red and huge. And all the while on the river the mysterious sobbing, rustling, crackle and tinkle went on. Somewhere in the mist not far off a cock crowed; others answered near by, and far away in the village the village cocks took up the cry, at first interrupting each other and finally joining into one sound of crowing. But everything else around, except for the river, was hushed and silent. It was already the second cockcrow.

After walking a couple of times backwards and forwards round the corner of the house and stumbling into an occasional pool of water, Nekhlyudov went back to the window of the maids' room. The lamp was still burning and Katusha was again sitting alone at the table with the look of indecision on her face. He had hardly approached the window when she glanced up at him. He knocked. And without looking to see who it was that had knocked she ran out of the room and he heard the outside door loosen and creak. He was waiting for her by the side-porch and put his arms round her without saying a word. She clung to him, raised her head and met his kiss with her lips. They were standing behind the corner of the porch on a spot where the snow had melted away and the ground was dry, and he was filled with a tormenting, unsatisfied desire. Suddenly the back door gave the same sort of smack and creak, and Matriona Pavlovna's angry voice was heard:

'Katusha!'

She tore herself away from him and returned to the maids' room. He heard the latch being fastened with a snap. Then all was quiet. The red eye of the window disappeared and nothing was left but the mist and the noise on the river.

Nekhlyudov went up to the window – no one was to be seen. He knocked – nobody answered him. He went back into the house by the front door but could not sleep. He took off his boots and went barefooted along the passage to her door, next to Matriona Pavlovna's room. At first he heard Matriona Pavlovna's quiet snoring and was on the point of going in when suddenly she began to cough and turn over on her creaking bed. His heart stopped and he stood motionless for about five minutes. When all was quiet once more and the peaceful snoring was heard again he went on, trying to step on the boards that did not creak. Now he was at Katusha's door. There was no sound. Evidently she was not asleep or he would have heard her breathing. And indeed the moment he whispered 'Katusha!' she jumped up, went to the door and angrily, so he thought, began trying to persuade him to go away.

'This is shameful! How can you? Your aunts will hear,' said her lips, but her whole being cried, 'I am yours,' and it was only this that Nekhlyudov understood.

'Open the door, just for a moment. I implore you!' He scarcely knew what he was saying.

She was silent. Then he heard her hand fumbling for the

latch. The latch clicked and he slipped through the opened door.

He caught hold of her just as she was, in her stiff unbleached nightshirt with bare arms, lifted her up and carried her away.

'Oh, what are you doing?' she whispered.

But he paid no heed to her words, carrying her to his room.

'Oh, you mustn't. . . . Let me go,' she said, clinging closer and closer to him.

*

When she left him, trembling and silent, giving no answer to his words, he stepped out on to the porch and stood there trying to realize the significance of what had happened.

It was lighter now; down below on the river the crackling and tinkling and sighing had grown louder and a gurgling noise was added to the other sounds. The mist had begun to settle lower and the last quarter of the moon sailed out from behind the wall of fog, shedding a sombre light on something black and menacing.

'What is the meaning of it all? Has a great happiness or a great misfortune befallen me?' he wondered. 'It happens to everybody, everybody does it,' he said to himself, and went to bed.

18

NEXT day Schönbock, brilliant and gay, came to fetch Nekhlyudov from his aunts' and quite won their hearts by his elegance and amiable manner, his high spirits, his liberality and his affection for Dmitri. But though the old ladies very much admired his generosity it rather perplexed them by its exaggeration. He gave a rouble to some blind beggars who came to the gate, and fifteen roubles in tips to the servants; and when Sophia Ivanovna's lap-dog, Suzetka, hurt its paw and it bled, without a moment's hesitation he tore into strips his hem-stitched cambric handkerchief (Sophia Ivanovna knew that such handkerchiefs cost at least fifteen roubles a dozen) and made bandages of it for Suzetka. The aunts had never met anyone like this before and did not know that this Schönbock owed something like two hundred thousand roubles, which, he knew full well, would never be paid, and that therefore twenty-five roubles more or less did not matter a bit to him.

Schönbock stayed only one day, and on the following night drove off with Nekhlyudov. They could not stay any longer, their leave of absence having expired.

During this last day of Nekhlyudov's visit to his aunts, when the events of the past night were still fresh in his mind, two emotions struggled in his heart. One was the burning sensual recollection of voluptuous love (whose realization, however, had fallen far short of its promise) accompanied by a certain satisfaction at having accomplished his object; the other was a consciousness of having done something very wrong, which had to be put right, not for her sake but for his own.

In his present condition of selfish madness Nekhlyudov could think of nothing but himself – of whether he would be censured, and how much he would be censured, if it were found out how he had acted towards her; but he did not consider Katusha's feelings now and what would become of her.

He thought that Schönbock guessed his relations with her, and this flattered his vanity.

'No wonder you grew so fond of your aunts all of a sudden that you had to stay a whole week,' Schönbock remarked after seeing Katusha. 'In your place I wouldn't have left either. She's charming!'

Nekhlyudov was also thinking that, though it was a pity to go away without having fully gratified his passion, the peremptory need for departure had its advantages in that it put an immediate stop to relations which would have been difficult to sustain. He was thinking, too, that he must give her some money, not for herself, not because she might need money but because it was the thing to do and it would be regarded as dishonourable on his part if, having taken advantage of her, he did not pay her. And so he gave her a sum of money – as much as he thought proper according to their respective stations.

On the day of his departure, after dinner, he lingered in the vestibule waiting for her. She flushed when she saw him and was about to pass on, indicating with her eyes the open door into the maids' room, but he stopped her.

'I wanted to say good-bye,' he said, crumpling in his hand an envelope containing a hundred-rouble note. 'Here, I . . .'

She guessed what it was, frowned, shook her head and pushed his hand away.

'No, you must take it,' he stammered, and thrust the envelope into her bodice and ran back to his room, frowning and groaning as though he had burnt his fingers.

And for a long time after that he strode up and down the room writhing and even stamping and groaning aloud as if in pain as he thought of this last scene.

'But what else could I have done? It is always that way. It was like that with Schönbock and the governess he was telling me about, and Uncle Grisha, and father when he was living in the country and had that illegitimate son Mitenka by a peasant woman. Mitenka is still alive. And if everybody does it, it must be all right.' Thus he tried to find comfort for himself but with no success. The memory of what he had done seared his conscience.

In his heart, in the very depths of his heart, he knew that he had behaved so meanly, so contemptibly, so cruelly that the knowledge of this act of his must prevent him, not only from criticizing anyone else but even from looking straight into other people's eyes, not to mention the impossibility of regarding himself as the splendid, noble, high-minded young fellow he considered himself to be. And yet he had to continue in that opinion of himself if he wished to carry on his old free, happy life. There was only one thing to do: not think about it. And this was the course he adopted.

The life which he was now entering upon – the new surroundings, new friends, the war – all helped. And the longer he lived the more he forgot, until in the end he really did forget entirely.

Only once, after the war, when he visited his aunts in the hope of seeing Katusha again and learned that she was no longer there – soon after his previous visit she had left to give birth to a child, and his aunts had heard that she had been confined somewhere or other and had quite gone to the bad – his heart gave him a painful twinge. Judging by the time of its birth, the child might have been his, and yet it might not have been his. His aunts said that she was a bad girl, and depraved by nature, just like her mother. And this opinion of his aunts' afforded him satisfaction because it seemed to acquit him. At first he did think of trying to find her and the child, but then, precisely because in the depths of his soul the thought of it all was too mortifying and painful, he never made the necessary effort to look for her, and still further lost sight of his sin and ceased to think of it.

But now this strange coincidence brought everything back and demanded that he should acknowledge the heartless cruelty and baseness which had made it possible for him to live peacefully for ten years with such a sin on his conscience. But he was still very far from making such acknowledgement and was only thinking now of how at any moment the affair might be discovered and she or her lawyer might recount the facts and put him to shame before everyone.

19

IN this state of mind Nekhlyudov left the court and went into the jury-room. He sat by the window, listening to what was being said around him, and smoking incessantly.

The cheerful merchant was evidently in sympathy with Smelkov's way of spending his time.

'There, sir, he had his fling in true Siberian fashion, that's what I say. He knew what he was about when it came to choosing a girl.'

The foreman was expatiating on the importance of the experts' testimony. Piotr Gerassimovich was joking with the Jewish clerk and they burst out laughing about something. Nekhlyudov answered in a monosyllable to all the questions addressed to him, and longed for only one thing – to be left in peace.

When the usher came with his sidling gait to call the jurors back to the court-room Nekhlyudov was panic-stricken, as though he were going, not to give a verdict but to be tried himself. In the depths of his soul he now felt that he was a scoundrel, who ought to be ashamed to look people in the face, and yet by sheer force of habit he stepped on to the platform in his usual self-possessed manner and took his seat, next but one to the foreman, crossing his legs and toying with his pince-nez.

The defendants, who had also been taken out of the court-room, were now brought in again.

There were some new faces in the court – witnesses – and Nekhlyudov noticed that Maslova seemed unable to take her eyes off a fat woman who sat in the first row by the railing, very showily dressed in silk and velvet, a high-crowned hat trimmed with a large bow, and an elegant reticule on her arm, which was bare to the elbow. This was, as he subsequently found out, one of the witnesses, the mistress of the establishment in which Maslova had lived.

The examination of the witnesses began: name, religion and so on. Then, after consultation with both parties as to whether the witnesses should give evidence on oath or not, the old priest came in again, dragging his legs with difficulty, and, again fingering the gold cross on his silk vestment, administered the oath to the witnesses and the expert with the same tranquil assurance that he was performing an exceedingly useful and important function. The witnesses having been sworn, all but Kitayeva, the keeper of the brothel, were led out under escort. She was asked what she knew about the case. With an affected smile and speaking in a strong German accent, but clearly and at length, she gave her evidence as follows, nodding her head under her hat at every sentence:

First of all the hotel servant Simon, whom she knew, had come to her establishment to get a girl for a rich Siberian merchant. She had sent Lyubov. After a time Lyubov came back with the merchant.

'The merchant vass already a bit "elevated",' Kitayeva said with a slight smile. He had gone on drinking and treating the girls; but as his money gave out he sent this same Lyubov, to whom he had taken a 'predilection', back to his room at the hotel, she told them, with a glance at the defendant.

Nekhlyudov thought he saw Maslova smile at this, and the smile filled him with disgust. A strange indefinable feeling of loathing mingled with compassion arose in him.

'And what was your opinion of Maslova?' timidly asked the blushing applicant for a judicial post who had been appointed by the court to be Maslova's counsel.

'A ferry goot one,' replied Kitayeva. 'She iss an etucated girl with plenty of style about her. She was prought up in a goot family and can reat French. She tid haf a trop too much sometimes put nefer forcot herself. A ferry goot girl.'

Katusha looked at the woman, then suddenly transferred her eyes to the jury and fixed them on Nekhlyudov, and her face grew serious and even stern. One of her stern eyes looked asquint. For quite a while those two strange eyes gazed at Nekhlyudov, and in spite of the terror that seized him he could not turn away from these squinting eyes with their bright clear whites. He relived that dreadful night with the ice breaking, and the mist, and, more especially, that waning moon with the upturned horns which had risen towards morning and shed its light on something black and terrible.

Those two dark eyes gazing at him and at the same time beyond him reminded him of that black and awful something. 'She has recognized me,' he thought. And Nekhlyudov shrank back as if expecting a blow. But she had not recognized him. She sighed quietly and began to look at the presiding judge again. Nekhlyudov sighed too. 'If only it could be over,' he thought. He experienced the same feeling he had when he was out hunting and had to put a wounded bird out of its misery: a mixture of loathing, pity and vexation. The wounded bird struggles in the game-bag: one is disgusted and yet feels pity, and is in a hurry to put an end to its suffering and forget it.

Such were the mingled emotions that filled Nekhlyudov's breast as he sat listening to the examination of the witnesses.

20

BUT, as if to spite him, the case dragged on for a long time: after each witness had been examined separately, and the expert last of all, and after the assistant prosecuting counsel and the lawyers for the defence with their customary air of importance had put a number of irrelevant questions, the presiding judge invited the jurors to inspect the exhibits brought into court as material evidence. They consisted of an enormous ring with a cluster of diamonds, which had evidently been worn on a very fat forefinger, and a test-tube containing the poison which had been analysed. These things had seals and labels attached to them.

Just as the jurors were about to look at these objects the assistant prosecutor rose again and demanded that the medical examiner's report should be read before passing to the inspection of the exhibits.

The presiding judge, who was hustling the business through as fast as he could in order to get to his Swiss girl, though he knew very well that the reading of the document could be nothing but a bore and delay the luncheon recess, and that the assistant prosecutor only wanted it read because he knew he had the right to demand it, could not refuse however, and expressed his consent. The secretary got out the report and again began to read in his doleful voice, slurring all the *l*'s and *r*'s.

'The external examination showed that:

'1. Ferapont Smelkov was six feet five inches tall.'

('I say – what a strapping fellow!' whispered the merchant, impressed, into Nekhlyudov's ear.)

'2. Judging from outward appearances his age could be determined as, roughly, forty years.

'3. The body had a swollen appearance.

'4. The flesh was of a greenish hue and showed dark spots in places.

'5. The skin was variously blistered and in places had peeled off and in places hung in large strips.

'6. The hair was dark brown and easily detached from the skin.

'7. The eyeballs protruded from their sockets and the cornea looked dull.

'8. Frothy serous fluid oozed from the nostrils, both ears and the mouth cavity; the mouth was half open.

'9. The face and chest were swollen to such an extent that practically no neck was to be seen.'

And so on, and so on.

This description of the terrible, enormous, fat, swollen and decomposing body of the merchant who had been making merry in the city continued on through twenty-seven paragraphs and occupied four pages of medical report. The indefinable disgust which Nekhlyudov felt was intensified by this description of the condition of the corpse. Katusha's life, the serum oozing from the nostrils of the dead body, the eyes protruding from their sockets and his own treatment of her – all seemed to belong to the same order of things, and he was surrounded and engulfed by things of this nature. When, at last, the reading of the external examination was over, the

...residing judge heaved a sigh and raised his head, hoping that ...was the end. But the secretary immediately proceeded to read ...he report concerning the internal organs.

The president's head again dropped into his hand and he closed his eyes. The merchant who sat beside Nekhlyudov could hardly keep awake, and now and then swayed to and fro; the defendants and the gendarmes behind them sat perfectly still.

'Examination of the internal organs revealed that:

'1. The skin over the skull was easily separated from the cranial bones, and there was no sign of bruising.

'2. The bones of the skull were of average thickness and in sound condition.

'3. Two small pigmented patches about four inches long showed on the hard cerebral membrane, the membrane itself being mat and pallid.'

And so on, and so on, for another thirteen paragraphs.

Then came the names and signatures of the coroner's jury, and the doctor's conclusion showing that the changes observed ... at the post-mortem examination and described in the official report, lent *great probability* to the conclusion that Smelkov's death was caused by poison which had found its way into the stomach with the wine. To determine from the state of the stomach and intestines exactly what kind of poison it was that had been introduced was difficult; but that the poison entered the stomach with the wine must be surmised from the fact that a large quantity of wine was found in Smelkov's stomach.

'He knew how to drink, and no mistake,' whispered the merchant again, having just woken up.

But even the reading of this report, which took nearly an hour, did not satisfy the assistant prosecutor. When it was over the president turned to him and said:

'I presume it will not be necessary to read the documents referring to the investigation of the internal organs.'

'I must request to have them read,' said the assistant prosecutor severely, without looking at the president. He drew himself up sideways in his chair and showed by his tone of voice that he had a right to have the report read and would insist on this right, and that if it were not granted there would be grounds for an appeal.

The member of the court with the big beard and kindly drooping eyes, who suffered from catarrh, feeling quite done up, turned to the president:

'What is the use of reading all this? You only drag the business out. These new brooms don't sweep any cleaner, they take longer about it, that's all.'

The member with the gold spectacles said nothing but stared gloomily in front of him, expecting no good either from his wife or from life in general.

The reading of the document began:

'On the fifteenth of February in the year 188– I, the undersigned, on instructions from the Medical Department, reference No. 638–,' the secretary started off in ringing tones, raising the pitch of his voice as if to ———— dispelling the sleepiness that had overtaken all present – 'in the presence of the assistant medical inspector made an examination of the following internal organs:

'1. The right lung and heart (contained in a 6 lb. glass jar).
'2. The contents of the stomach (in a 6 lb. glass jar).
'3. The stomach itself (in a 6 lb. glass jar).
'4. The liver, the spleen and the kidneys (in a 3 lb. glass jar).
'5. The intestines (in a 6 lb. earthenware jar).'

As the reading began the presiding judge leaned over to one of the members and whispered something to him; then he leaned over to another and, having received their consent, at this point interrupted the secretary.

'The Court finds the reading of this document to be superfluous,' he said.

The secretary stopped and gathered up his papers. The assistant prosecutor angrily made a note of something.

'The gentlemen of the jury may now examine the material evidence,' said the presiding judge.

The foreman and a few of the jurymen rose and went to the table, not quite knowing what to do with their hands. In turn they looked at the ring, the glass jars and the test-tube. The merchant even tried the ring on his finger.

'That was something like a finger,' he said, returning to his seat. 'As big as a cucumber,' he added, obviously enjoying the Hercules image he had formed in his mind of the poisoned merchant.

21

WHEN the examination of the exhibits was finished the presiding judge announced that the investigation was not concluded, and, eager to get through as quickly as possible, took no recess but called on the prosecutor to proceed, hoping that he too, being human, might want to smoke and have some dinner himself, and therefore show a little mercy to the rest of them. But the assistant prosecutor had no mercy either for himself or them. Besides being very stupid by nature the assistant prosecutor had had the misfortune to finish high-school with a gold medal, and receive a prize for his thesis on slavery when reading Roman Law at the university, all of which made him exceedingly self-assured and conceited (to which his success with the ladies contributed still further), and in consequence he was quite monumentally stupid. When called on to speak he rose slowly to his feet, displaying his graceful figure full length in his gold-laced uniform, placed both hands on the desk and, slightly inclining his head, looked round the room, avoiding the eyes of the defendants, and began:

'Gentlemen of the jury, the case now before you concerns, if I may so express myself, a crime of a typical nature.' (He had prepared his speech while the reports were being read.)

In his view the speech of the assistant prosecutor should

always have great public significance, like the famous speeches delivered by counsel who had become famous. True, he only had an audience of three women – a sempstress, a cook and Kartinkin's sister – and a coachman; but this did not matter. Those other celebrated lawyers had begun in the same way. The assistant prosecutor made it a rule always to be at the height of his calling – that is, to penetrate into the depths of the psychological significance of crime and lay bare the ulcers of society.

'You see before you, gentlemen of the jury, a crime characteristic, if I may so express myself, of the end of the century, bearing, so to speak, the specific features of that melancholy phenomenon, the decay to which those elements of our present-day society – which are, so to say, particularly exposed to the scorching rays of this process – are subject . . .'

The assistant prosecutor spoke at great length, trying on the one hand to remember all the clever things he had thought of and, on the other – this was most important – not to stop for a moment but make his speech flow smoothly on for an hour and a quarter.

Only once did he pause, taking a considerable time to swallow saliva, but he soon recovered and made up for the interruption by heightened eloquence. He spoke, now in a gentle persuasive voice, putting his weight first on one leg, then on the other, and looking at the jury; now in quiet, businesslike tones, glancing into his notebook; now with a loud accusing voice, addressing the public and the jury in turn. But he never once looked at the defendants, all three of whom had their eyes riveted on him. All the latest catchphrases then in vogue in his set, everything that then was and still is accepted as the last word in scientific wisdom was included in his speech – heredity and congenital criminality, Lombroso and Tarde, evolution and the struggle for existence, hypnotism and hypnotic suggestion, Charcot and decadence.

The merchant Smelkov, according to the definition of the assistant prosecutor, was a type of the genuine, physically powerful, munificent Russian, whose trusting generous nature made him an easy prey to the deeply degraded individuals into whose hands he had chanced to fall.

Simon Kartinkin was the atavistic product of serfdom, downtrodden, illiterate, without principles, without religion even. Euphemia was his mistress and a victim of heredity. She showed all the signs of a degenerate personality. But the chief instigator of the crime was Maslova, an example of the very lowest type of degenerate.

'This woman,' the assistant prosecutor went on, not looking at her, 'is educated – as we have heard in court today from the mistress of her establishment. Not only can she read and write but she knows French. She is an orphan, and in all likelihood carries in her the germs of criminality. Brought up in a cultured family of gentlefolk, she might have earned her living by honest work; but deserting her benefactors she gave herself up to her passions, to satisfy which she entered a house of prostitution, where she was distinguished from her companions by her education and chiefly, gentlemen of the jury, as you have heard from her mistress, by her ability to gain influence over her visitors by that mysterious faculty lately investigated by science, by the school of Charcot in particular, known as the power of hypnotic suggestion. This is the means by which she gains control over Smelkov – the kind, trusting Russian hero, Sadko – and takes advantage of his trust, first to steal his money, and then pitilessly to deprive him of life.'

'Running away with himself, isn't he?' said the presiding judge with a smile, bending towards the austere member of the court.

'A fearful dunderhead!' said the austere member.

'Gentlemen of the jury,' the assistant prosecutor continued meanwhile, gracefully swaying his lithe form from side to side, 'in your hands rests not only the fate of these persons but also, to a certain extent, the fate of society, which will be influenced by your verdict. You will consider the significance of this crime, the danger to society from such pathological individuals, if I may be permitted so to term them, like this Maslova, and guard it from infection. Protect the innocent healthy elements of this society from infection and, in many cases, from actual destruction.'

And as though overcome by the importance of the verdict about to be returned the assistant prosecutor fell back into his chair, evidently highly delighted with his speech.

The gist of his argument, shorn of the flowers of rhetoric, was that Maslova, having insinuated herself into the merchant's confidence, hypnotized him and went to his room intending to take all the money herself, but, surprised by Simon and Euphemia, had been obliged to share it with them. Then, in order to conceal the traces of her crime, she had returned to the hotel with the merchant and there poisoned him.

After the assistant prosecutor had spoken a middle-aged man in swallow-tail coat and low-cut waistcoat showing a broad semicircle of starched white shirt-front, rose from the counsels' bench and made a glib speech in defence of Kartinkin and Botchkova. This was the barrister they had engaged for three hundred roubles. He did his best to clear both and lay all the blame on Maslova.

He rejected Maslova's evidence that Botchkova and Kartinkin were with her when she took the money, insisting that the testimony of a poisoner could have no weight. The two thousand five hundred roubles, said the counsel, could easily have been earned by two hard-working and honest persons getting as much as three and five roubles a day in gratuities. The merchant's money had been stolen by Maslova and transmitted by her to some third party or even lost, since she was not in a normal state. The poisoning was the work of Maslova alone.

He therefore asked the jury to acquit Kartinkin and Botchkova of the theft of the money; or, if they found them guilty of theft, he demanded their acquittal of all participation with intent in the poisoning affair.

In conclusion, with a thrust at the assistant prosecutor, he remarked that the brilliant observations of his learned friend on the subject of heredity, though they might throw light on the scientific problems of heredity, were inapplicable in this case, since Botchkova was the child of unknown parents.

The assistant prosecutor, showing his teeth, as it were, made a note on a piece of paper and shrugged his shoulders in contemptuous surprise.

Then Maslova's counsel rose, and timidly and with hesitation began his speech in her defence. Without denying the fact that she had taken part in the theft of the money he insisted only that she had had no intention of poisoning Smelkov, and had given him the powder merely to make him fall asleep. He tried to indulge in a little eloquence, describing how Maslova had been led into a life of debauchery by a man who had gone unpunished while she had had to bear the whole brunt of her fall, but this excursion into the domain of psychology was so unsuccessful that everybody felt uncomfortable. When he meandered on about the cruelty of men and the helplessness of women the president, wishing to help him out, requested him to keep closer to the points of the case.

After this defence the prosecuting counsel rose again to argue, against the first defence counsel, that even if Botchkova were of unknown parentage this in no way invalidated the doctrine of heredity. Science had so far established the law of heredity that we could not only deduce the crime from heredity but heredity from the crime. As to the hypothesis of the defence that Maslova had been corrupted by an imaginary (he uttered the word 'imaginary' with particular venom) seducer, the facts rather tended to suggest that she had played the part of temptress to many and many a victim who had passed through her hands. With this, he sat down, triumphant.

Then the defendants were told that they could speak in their own defence.

Euphemia Botchkova repeated once more that she knew nothing and had taken part in nothing, and stubbornly laid all the blame on Maslova. Simon Kartinkin merely repeated several times:

'Say what you like, I didn't do it, you got it all wrong.'

But Maslova never opened her mouth. When the presiding judge invited her to speak in her own defence she only looked up at him, cast her eyes round the room like a hunted animal and immediately put her head down and burst into tears, sobbing loudly.

'What's the matter?' asked the merchant who sat next to Nekhlyudov, hearing him utter a strange sound. The sound was a strangled sob.

Nekhlyudov still had not grasped the full significance of his present position and attributed the sobs he could hardly keep back and the tears that welled into his eyes to the weak state of his nerves. He put on his pince-nez in order to hide the tears, then got out his pocket handkerchief and began blowing his nose.

Fear of the disgace which would befall him if all these people here in the court-room were to learn of his conduct stifled the inner working of his soul. This fear was, during this first period, stronger than anything else.

22

AFTER the last words of the prisoners had been heard, and both sides had been consulted as to the way the questions should be stated, which also took some considerable time, the presiding judge began his summing up.

Before putting the case to the jury he explained to them at great length in a pleasant homely tone of voice that burglary was burglary and theft was theft, and that stealing from a place which was under lock and key was stealing from a place under lock and key, and stealing from a place not under lock and key was stealing from a place not under lock and key.

While offering these explanations he very frequently glanced over to Nekhlyudov, as though particularly anxious to impress on him these important points, in the hope that if he understood he would make his fellow jurymen understand them too. Then, surmising that the jury were now sufficiently imbued with these truths, he proceeded to expatiate on another truth – namely, that murder was an action which has, as its consequence, the death of a human being, and that poisoning, therefore, was also murder. When this truth, too, had in his opinion been imbibed by the jury he explained to them that when theft and murder are committed at the same time, then the crime constitutes theft with murder.

Although he was himself anxious to finish as quickly as possible and his Swiss girl was even now waiting for him, he had grown so used to his work that, having once begun to speak, he could not stop, and went on to instruct the jury in much detail that if they found the defendants guilty they had a right to give a verdict of guilty; and if they found them not guilty, to give a verdict of not guilty; and if they found them guilty of one of the crimes and not of the other, they might pronounce them guilty on the one count and not guilty on the other. Then he explained to them that though they had this right they must use it with discretion. He was also about to explain that if they gave an affirmative answer to a given question, they would thereby affirm everything included in the question; so that if they did not wish to affirm the whole of the question they should mention the part of the question they wished to be excepted. But glancing at the clock and seeing that it was already five minutes to three he decided to proceed to his summary.

'The facts of the case are as follows . . .' he began, and repeated all that had already been said several times by the defence and the assistant prosecutor and the witnesses.

The president spoke and the members of the court on either side of him listened with an air of profound attention and occasionally looked at the clock, and although they approved of his speech or, in other words, considered it such as it ought to be, they found it somewhat lengthy. So did the assistant prosecutor and all the judicial personages generally, and everyone else in the court-room. The president finished the summing up.

It seemed there could be nothing left to say. But the president could not let go of his right to speak – it gave him such pleasure to listen to the inspiring tones of his own voice – and he found it necessary to add a few words concerning the importance of the rights appertaining to the jury: how attentively and carefully they should use those rights and beware of abusing them. He reminded them that they were on their oath, that they were the conscience of society and that the secrecy of their deliberations in the jury-room should be held sacred, and so on, and so on.

From the moment the presiding judge began to speak Maslova never took her eyes off his face, as though fearful of losing a single word; so that Nekhlyudov was not afraid of meeting her glance and he therefore gazed at her intently. And his mind's eye suffered the familiar sequence in which at first we only notice the changes in a face that we have not seen for a long time, and then gradually the beloved face begins to look exactly as it was those many years ago: the changes all disappear until our spiritual eyes see only the one unique inimitable spiritual personality.

This was what happened with Nekhlyudov.

Yes, in spite of the prison cloak, the plumper body and full bosom, in spite of the thickened lower jaw, the lines on the forehead and around the temples, and the swollen eyelids, there was no doubt that this was the Katusha who on that Easter morning had so innocently gazed up at him, the man she loved, her adoring laughing eyes full of joy and life.

'And what an extraordinary coincidence! That I should be on the jury in this particular case! I have not seen her for ten years, and now I come across her here, in the prisoners' dock! And how will it all end? Oh, if it would only end soon!'

He still would not give in to the feelings of repentance which were beginning to stir in him. He tried to think of it as a coincidence which would pass without upsetting his life. He felt like a puppy when its master seizes it by the neck and rubs its nose in the mess it has made. The puppy squeals and draws back, trying to get as far away as possible from the effects of its misdeed and forget it; but the implacable master will not let it go. So Nekhlyudov, now appreciating the baseness of what he had done, felt the mighty hand of the Master; but he still did not realize the significance of what he had done, or recognize the Master's hand. He did not want to believe that what he saw now was his doing. But the inexorable, invisible hand held him and he already had a presentiment that he would never wriggle free. He still put on a bold face as he sat there in the second chair of the first row with his usual air of careless ease, by force of habit crossing one leg over the other and toying with his pince-nez. Yet all the while in the depths of his soul he was conscious of all the cruelty, cowardice and baseness, not only of this particular action of his but of his whole idle, dissolute, cruel and complacent life; and that dreadful veil which had all this time, for ten years, in some unaccountable manner concealed from him this sin of his, and the whole of his life since, was beginning to wobble, and now and again he caught a glimpse of what was hidden behind it.

23

A T last the presiding judge finished his speech and, picking up the list of questions with a graceful movement, he handed it to the foreman, who came forward to take it. The jury rose, glad to be able to get away, and one after another went to the jury-room, looking ashamed somehow and not knowing what to do with their hands. As soon as the door had closed behind them a gendarme went up to it and, pulling his sword out of the scabbard and raising it to his shoulder, took up his position there. The judges rose and left the court. The defendants were also led out.

Again the first thing the jury did when they reached their room was to get out their cigarettes and start smoking. The unnaturalness and falseness of their situation, which to a greater or less degree they had all been conscious of, sitting in their places in the court, passed as soon as they entered the jury-room and lit their cigarettes, and with a feeling of relief they settled down and immediately started an animated conversation.

'The girl's not guilty, she didn't know what she was doing,' said the kind-hearted merchant. 'We must let her down easy.'

'That's just what we have to consider,' said the foreman. 'We must not be misled by our personal impressions.'

'That was a good summing up the president made,' remarked the colonel.

'Good, you call it? It nearly sent me to sleep.'

'The chief point is that the servants couldn't have known about the money if Maslova had not been in league with them,' said the Jewish-looking clerk.

'So you think she stole it?' asked one of the jury.

'You'll never make me believe that,' cried the kind-hearted merchant, 'it was all that red-eyed old witch!'

'A nice lot, all of them,' said the colonel.

'But she says she never went into the room.'

'Take her word for it if you like. I wouldn't for the world believe a slut like that.'

'Whether you would believe her or not doesn't settle the matter,' said the clerk.

'She was the one who had the key.'

'What if she did?' retorted the merchant.

'And the ring?'

'She told us about that, didn't she?' cried the merchant again. 'The fellow had a temper, and he'd been drinking, and walloped the girl. Well then, naturally, he was sorry. "Here, don't cry," he says, "have this." From what they said he was a strapping fellow, six foot five tall – must have weighed all of twenty stone.'

'That's not the point,' interrupted Piotr Gerassimovich. 'The question is, was she the chief instigator of the whole affair, or was it the servant-woman?'

'The servant-woman couldn't have done it alone. The other one had the key.'

This random talk went on for some time. At last the foreman said: 'Please, gentlemen, I propose that we seat ourselves round the table and discuss the case. Come, please.' And he took the chair.

'Those girls are a bad lot,' said the clerk, and as a confirmation of his opinion that Maslova must have been the chief culprit he related how a friend of his had had his watch stolen on the boulevard by one of her sort.

This gave the colonel the opportunity to narrate a still more startling story about the theft of a silver samovar.

'Gentlemen, I beg you to give your attention to the questions,' said the foreman, tapping the table with his pencil.

All were silent. The questions had been framed as follows:

1. Is the peasant of the village of Borki in the district of Krapivensk, Simon Petrov Kartinkin, thirty-three years of age, guilty of having conspired on the seventeenth day of January 188– in the city of —— to deprive the merchant Smelkov of his life, for the purpose of robbing him, in company with others, by administering to him poisoned brandy, thereby causing the death of the said Smelkov, and of having stolen from him some two thousand five hundred roubles and a diamond finger-ring?

2. Is Euphemia Botchkova, forty-three years of age, working class, guilty of the crimes described above?

3. Is Katerina Mikhailovna Maslova, twenty-seven years of age, working class, guilty of the crimes described in the first question?

4. If the defendant Euphemia Botchkova is not guilty of the crimes set down in the first question, is she guilty of having, on the seventeenth day of January 188–, in the city of ——, while in the service of the Hotel Mavritania, stolen from a locked portmanteau belonging to the merchant Smelkov, a guest at the said hotel, and which was in

the room occupied by him, the sum of two thousand five hundred roubles, for which purpose she unlocked the portmanteau with a key which she brought and fitted to the lock?

The foreman read out the first question.

'Well, gentlemen, what do you say?'

This question was quickly answered. All agreed to say 'Guilty', finding him guilty of participation in both the poisoning and the robbery. The only one who refused to find Kartinkin guilty was an old artisan who voted for an acquittal on all counts.

The foreman thought he did not understand, and explained to him that there was no possible doubt that Kartinkin and Botchkova were guilty, but the old man replied that he understood all right but that it would be better to exercise mercy. 'We're not saints ourselves,' he said, and stuck to his opinion.

The second question, concerning Botchkova, was answered after much talk and discussion by 'Not guilty', there being no clear proof that she had taken part in the poisoning – a point upon which her counsel had dwelt most emphatically.

The merchant, anxious to acquit Maslova, kept insisting that Botchkova was the chief instigator of the whole thing. Many of the jurors sided with him, but the foreman, trying to remain within strictly legal bounds, said that there were no grounds for considering her an accomplice in the poisoning. After much argument the foreman won the day.

To the fourth question, concerning Botchkova, the answer was 'Guilty' – but at the old artisan's insistence they added a recommendation to mercy.

But the third question, relating to Maslova, raised a fierce dispute. The foreman insisted that she was guilty both of the poisoning and of the robbery, but the merchant disagreed and was supported by the colonel, the clerk and the old artisan – the rest seemed to be wavering, but the opinion of the foreman began to gain ground, especially since all the jurymen were tired and therefore the more ready to support the opinion which promised the sooner to unite and so release them all.

From all that had come out at the judicial investigation, and from his former knowledge of Maslova, Nekhlyudov felt sure that she was innocent of both the robbery and the poisoning, and at first he was confident that all of them would recognize this; but when he saw how the merchant's clumsy defence (obviously based on his personal fancy for the girl, of which he made no secret) had aroused the opposition of the foreman, and how their general fatigue was inclining them to find a verdict of guilty, he wanted to object, but he was afraid to speak up for Maslova – it seemed to him that at any moment they would all discover his relations with her. Yet at the same time he felt he could not leave things as they were, and must protest. He blushed and grew pale by turns, and was on the point of opening his mouth to speak when Piotr Gerassimovich, who up to then had been silent but was now evidently irritated by the foreman's authoritative manner, suddenly began to argue with him and said in so many words precisely what Nekhlyudov was about to say.

'One moment, please,' he said. 'You say she must have committed the theft because she had the key. But could not the hotel servants have unlocked the portmanteau with some key of their own after she had gone?'

'Hear, hear!' the merchant seconded.

'She just couldn't have taken the money, because in her situation she couldn't dispose of it.'

'That's exactly what I say,' confirmed the merchant.

'It is more likely that her going to the room put the idea into the servants' heads and they seized the opportunity and then shifted all the blame on her.'

Piotr Gerassimovich spoke irritably. And his irritation infected the foreman, who consequently began more obstinately still to urge the opposite view; but Piotr Gerassimovich spoke so convincingly that the majority agreed with him in believing that Maslova had taken no part in stealing the money, and that the finger-ring had been a present to her. And when they went on to discuss her complicity in the poisoning her ardent champion, the merchant, declared that she must be acquitted because she could have no motive for poisoning. The foreman, however, said that it was impossible to acquit her of that, since she herself had pleaded guilty to giving him the powder.

'Yes, but she thought it was opium,' said the merchant.

'Opium can also deprive one of life,' said the colonel, who was fond of wandering from the subject; and thereupon he began to tell them how his brother-in-law's wife had taken an overdose of opium and poisoned herself, and would certainly have died had there not been a doctor at hand to take the proper measures in time. The colonel told his story so impressively, and with such self-assurance and dignity, that no one had the courage to interrupt him. Only the clerk, infected by his example, decided to break in with a tale of his own.

'Some people get so used to it,' he began, 'that they can take forty drops at a time. A relative of mine –'

But the colonel would tolerate no interruption, and continued to relate the effects of the opium on his brother-in-law's wife.

'Why, it's gone four o'clock, gentlemen,' said one of the jurors.

'Well, gentlemen, what do you say then?' the foreman addressed them. 'Let us find her guilty without intent to rob, and without stealing any property. Will that do?'

Piotr Gerassimovich, satisfied with his victory, assented.

'But we must recommend her to mercy,' added the merchant.

They all agreed to this. The old artisan was the only one to hold out for a verdict of 'Not guilty'.

'That's really what it amounts to,' explained the foreman. 'Without intent to rob, and without stealing any property. That makes her not guilty.'

'Go on, that'll do. And we recommend her to mercy. That should see the end of it,' cried the merchant gaily.

They were all so worn out and so muddled with arguing that nobody thought of adding the clause, '*but without intent to take life*'.

Nekhlyudov was in such a state of agitation that he did not notice the omission. And so the answers were written down in the form agreed upon, and taken back to the court-room.

Rabelais tells of a lawyer to whom people had come about a lawsuit who, after quoting all sorts of laws and reading twenty pages of meaningless judicial Latin, invited the contending parties to throw dice: odds or even. If an even number turned up, the plaintiff was right; if odd – it was the defendant.

It was much the same in this case. This, instead of another verdict was returned, not because all were agreed but because, first, the presiding judge, who had summed up at such length, this time omitted to say what he always said, namely, that they could find a verdict of 'Guilty – *but without intent to take life*'; secondly, because the colonel had told such a long and tedious story about his brother-in-law's wife; and thirdly, because Nekhlyudov had been so agitated that he did not notice the omission of the proviso 'without intent to take life' and thought that the words 'without intent to rob' nullified the charge; and fourthly, because Piotr Gerassimovich happened to leave the room just as the foreman was reading over the questions and replies; and – chiefly – because everybody was tired and they all wanted to get away as soon as possible and were therefore ready to agree to the verdict which would bring matters to an end soonest.

The jury rang the bell. The gendarme standing at the door with drawn sword put it back into the scabbard and stepped aside. The judges took their seats and the jury filed in.

The foreman carried the sheet of paper with a portentous air. He went up to the president and presented it to him. The president read it and, obviously surprised, shrugged his shoulders and turned to consult his colleagues. The president was surprised that the jury, having put in the first proviso, 'without intent to rob', should have omitted the second, 'without intent to take life'. It followed, according to the jury's findings, that Maslova has not stolen, had not robbed, but had poisoned a man without any apparent object.

'Just look at this absurd verdict,' he said to the member on his left. 'This means penal servitude, and she is innocent.'

'What do you mean, innocent?' said the surly member.

'Simply not guilty. In my view this comes under Article 818.' (Article 818 states that if the Court finds the charge unjust it may set aside the jury's verdict.)

'What do you think?' the judge asked the kind-hearted member.

The kind-hearted member did not immediately reply. He looked at the number on a paper before him and added up the figures: it would not divide by three. He had settled in his mind that if the number did divide by three he would agree with the president; but though it would not divide, in the kindness of his heart he agreed with him.

'I think so too,' he said.

'And you?' said the president, turning to the irritable member.

'On no account,' he replied emphatically. 'As it is, the papers are saying that juries acquit criminals. What will they say if the Court does the same thing? I shall not consent in any circumstances.'

The president looked at the clock.

'Well, I am sorry,' he said. 'Then nothing can be done,' and he handed the questions to the foreman to read out.

Everyone rose, and the foreman, shifting his weight from one foot to the other, cleared his throat and read out the questions and the answers. The whole court – secretary, lawyers, even the prosecuting counsel – showed surprise.

The defendants sat impassive, apparently not understanding what the answers meant. Everybody sat down again, and the president asked the prosecutor what sentences he suggested for the defendants.

The prosecutor, elated over his unexpected success in obtaining Maslova's conviction, and ascribing this success to his own eloquence, consulted some papers, stood up and said:

'Simon Kartinkin should be dealt with in accordance with Article 1452 and paragraph 4 of Article 1453; Euphemia Botchkova in accordance with Article 1659; and Katerina Maslova in accordance with Article 1454.'

All these punishments were the heaviest that could be inflicted.

'The Court will adjourn to consider sentence,' said the president, rising.

Everybody rose after him, and with the relief and the pleasant feeling of a task well done began to leave the room or walk about.

'I say, my dear fellow, we have made a shameful hash of it,' said Piotr Gerassimovich, going up to Nekhlyudov, to whom the foreman was relating something. 'Why, we've dispatched her to Siberia.'

'What's that?' cried Nekhlyudov, this time oblivious of the teacher's familiarity.

'Of course we have. We didn't put "Guilty, but without intent to take life" in our answer. The secretary's just told me that the prosecutor is for sentencing her to fifteen years' penal servitude.'

'But that's the way we decided,' said the foreman.

Piotr Gerassimovich began to argue, saying that it was self-evident that if she did not take the money she could not have had any intention of committing murder.

'But I read the answers to you before we came out,' said the foreman, trying to justify himself. 'No one raised any objection.'

'I wasn't in the room at that moment,' said Piotr Gerassimovich. 'But how was it you were caught napping?' he asked Nekhlyudov.

'I never thought –'

'It's obvious you didn't.'

'But we can get it put right,' said Nekhlyudov.

'Oh no, it's too late for that now.'

Nekhlyudov looked at the prisoners. Their fate about to be decided, they still sat motionless behind the railing, in front of the soldiers. Maslova was smiling at something. Up to now, expecting her acquittal and that she would remain in the town, he had not made up his mind how he would act towards her. Any kind of relation with her would be difficult. But penal servitude and Siberia at once destroyed every possibility of any relations with her: the wounded bird would stop fluttering in the game-bag and would remind him of its existence no longer.

24

PIOTR GERASSIMOVICH'S assumption was correct.

The president returned from the judges' room with a paper, and read as follows:

'April the 28th, 188–, by order of His Imperial Majesty, the District Criminal Court, by virtue of the verdict of the jury, in accordance with paragraph 3 of Article 771, paragraph 3 of Article 776 and Article 777 of the Penal Code, decrees that the peasant Simon Kartinkin, thirty-three years of age, and the burgess Katerina Maslova, twenty-seven years of age, be deprived of all civil rights and be sent to penal servitude in Siberia: Kartinkin for a term of eight years, Maslova for a term of four years, with the consequences stated in Article 25 of the said Code. The burgess Euphemia Botchkova, forty-three years of age, shall be deprived of all particular individual and acquired rights and privileges, and be imprisoned for a term of three years with consequences in accord with Article 49 of the said Code. The costs of the case to be borne equally by the prisoners, but in the event of their inability to pay the same shall be defrayed by the Crown. The exhibits presented in the case to be sold, the finger-ring to be returned and the glass jars to be destroyed.'

Kartinkin stood, body stretched taut as before, arms pressed close to his sides and fingers splayed out, his cheeks twitching. Botchkova was apparently quite calm. When Maslova heard her sentence she flushed a crimson shade. 'I am not guilty, I am not guilty!' she shrieked suddenly, in a voice that resounded through the court-room. 'It's wicked. I am not guilty. I didn't mean – I never dreamed. It's the truth I'm saying. The truth!' And dropping down on the bench she sobbed aloud.

When Kartinkin and Botchkova went out she still sat there weeping, so that a gendarme was obliged to touch the sleeve of her cloak.

'No, it can't be left like this,' Nekhlyudov said to himself, entirely forgetful of his selfish thoughts, and, without knowing why, he hurried out into the corridor to get another glimpse of her. An animated crowd of jurors and lawyers, pleased to have dispatched the case, jostled in the doorway, so that he was held back for several moments. When at last he got out into the corridor she was already some way off. He rushed along the corridor after her, regardless of the attention he was attracting, caught her up, went beyond and stopped. She had ceased crying now, and only sobbed fitfully, wiping her blotched face with the corner of her kerchief. She passed by him without looking round. After she was gone he turned hurriedly back to find the president, but the president had already left the court-room.

Nekhlyudov ran after him and caught him in the vestibule.

'Sir, may I have a word with you concerning the case that has just been tried?' Nekhlyudov said, going up to the president just as he had donned his light-grey overcoat and was taking his silver-mounted walking-stick from an attendant. 'I was a member of the jury.'

'Oh, certainly. Prince Nekhlyudov, I believe? Delighted, I think we have met before,' said the president, pressing

Nekhlyudov's hand and recalling with satisfaction how well and gaily he had danced – better than all the youngsters – that evening when he first met Nekhlyudov. 'What can I do for you?'

'There was a mistake in the answer in regard to Maslova. She was not guilty of the poisoning and yet she has been sentenced to penal servitude,' said Nekhlyudov with an anxious frown.

'The Court gave its decision in accordance with the answers you yourselves brought in,' said the president, moving towards the entrance door, 'although the answers did seem to the Court to be inconsistent with the facts.'

He remembered that he had intended to explain to the jury that to answer 'guilty' and omit to add 'without intent to take life' meant guilty of murder with intention, but, in his hurry to get the business over, had not done so.

'Yes, but cannot the error be rectified?'

'Grounds for appeal can always be found. You must speak to a lawyer,' said the president, putting his hat on a fraction to one side and continuing to move towards the door.

'But this is terrible.'

'You see, in Maslova's case there were just two alternatives,' said the president, evidently wishing to be as agreeable and polite to Nekhlyudov as he could. Then, having arranged his whiskers over his coat collar, he put his hand lightly under Nekhlyudov's elbow and walking him towards the front entrance he continued: 'You are leaving too, are you not?'

'Yes,' said Nekhlyudov, quickly putting on his coat and going out with him.

They went out into the bright cheerful sunlight and at once had to raise their voices to be heard above the rattling of wheels on the roadway.

'The situation is a curious one, you see,' the president went on, raising his voice, 'in that one of two things could have happened to her, this Maslova, I mean: either almost a complete acquittal with only a brief prison sentence – or, taking the preliminary confinement into consideration, perhaps none at all – or else . . . Siberia. There is no other course. If you had added the words "without intent to cause death" she would have been acquitted.'

'It was an unpardonable omission on my part,' said Nekhlyudov.

'That's where the trouble lies,' said the president with a smile, looking at his watch.

He had only three-quarters of an hour in which to see Klara.

'I should advise you to consult a lawyer. You'll have to find grounds for an appeal. That can always be done.' Then, replying to a cabman, 'Dvoryanskaya Street. Thirty kopecks – I never give more.'

'This way, your excellency.'

'Good day. If I can be of any use, my address is Dvoryanskaya Street, Dvornikov House. It's easy to remember.' And with a friendly bow he drove off.

25

THE talk with the president of the court, and the fresh air, somewhat calmed Nekhlyudov. He began to think that perhaps he had been overwrought by a morning spent in such unusual circumstances.

'Of course, it is a remarkable and striking coincidence! And I must do everything possible to ease her lot, and do it quickly. This very moment. Yes, I must find out from the court here Fanarin's address, or Mikishin's.' He remembered the names of two well-known lawyers.

He returned to the court-house, took off his overcoat and went upstairs. Actually in the first corridor he met Fanarin. He stopped him and told him he was just going to look him up on a matter of business. Fanarin knew Nekhlyudov by sight and by name, and said he would be very glad to be of service.

'Though I am rather tired . . . but if it will not take long, perhaps you might tell me what it is now. Let us go in here.'

And Fanarin led Nekhlyudov into a room, probably the private room of one of the judges. They sat down by the table.

'Well now, what is it about?'

'First of all I must ask you to treat this as strictly confidential. I do not want it known that I am taking an interest in the affair.'

'Oh, that goes without saying. Well?'

'I served on the jury today and we condemned a woman to penal servitude – an innocent woman. This troubles me very much.'

Nekhlyudov, to his own surprise, blushed and hesitated.

Fanarin glanced at him sharply, and looked down again, listening.

'Well now,' was all he said.

'We have condemned an innocent woman, and I should like to appeal to a higher court.'

'To the Senate, you mean,' Fanarin corrected him.

'And so I want you to take the case.'

Nekhlyudov, in haste to get over the worst, went on hurriedly, the colour again rising to his face:

'I will bear the fees and other expenses, whatever they may be.'

'Oh, we can settle that later,' replied the lawyer, with a smile of condescension at Nekhlyudov's inexperience.

'What are the facts of the case now?'

Nekhlyudov told him.

'Very well. Tomorrow I'll take it up and look into the matter. And the day after tomorrow – no, on Thursday afternoon – come and see me at six o'clock, and I will give you my answer. Is that all right? And now, if you will excuse me, I have a few inquiries to make here.'

Nekhlyudov said good-bye and left him.

The conversation with the lawyer and the fact that he had

taken measures for Maslova's defence still further relieved his mind. He went out into the street. The weather was lovely and he drew in a joyous breath of spring air. Cabmen offered their services but he chose to walk, and immediately a whole swarm of thoughts and memories of Katusha and the way he had treated her began whirling in his brain. Depression overcame him and everything looked gloomy. 'No, I will think about that later,' he said to himself. 'Now I must try to throw off these disagreeable reflections.'

He remembered the Korchagins' dinner and glanced at his watch. It was not too late and he could get there in time. A horsetram was tinkling past him. He ran and caught it. At the square he jumped off and took a good cab, and ten minutes later he was at the entrance of the Korchagins' big house.

26

'COME in, your excellency,' said the fat friendly doorkeeper of the Korchagins' big house, opening the oak door which swung noiselessly on its English hinges. 'They are at dinner, but my orders are to ask you in.'

The man went to the staircase and rang a bell.

'Any visitors?' asked Nekhlyudov, taking off his overcoat.

'Monsieur Kolossov and Mikhail Sergeyevich; otherwise only the family.'

A handsome footman in a swallow-tail coat and white gloves looked down over the balusters.

'Please to come up, sir. Your excellency is expected,' he said.

Nekhlyudov mounted the stairs and walked through the splendid, familiar large ballroom into the dining-room. Here the whole Korchagin family – except the mother, Princess Sophia Vassilyevna, who never left her own rooms – was sitting round the table. At the head of the table sat old Korchagin; next to him, on his left, the doctor, and on his right, a visitor, Ivan Ivanovich Kolossov, a former Marshal of the

Nobility, now a bank director, Korchagin's friend and a liberal. Next to the doctor was Miss Rayder, the governess of Missy's little sister, and the four-year-old child herself; opposite them, Missy's brother, Petya, the Korchagins' only son, a high-school boy in the sixth form, on whose account the whole family was still in town, waiting for his examinations; next came the university student who was coaching him. Farther down on the left, Katerina Alexeyevna, a maiden lady of forty, a rabid Slavophile. Opposite her sat Missy's cousin, Mikhail Sergeyevich Telegin, generally called Misha; and at the foot of the table sat Missy herself, with an empty place next to her.

'Ah, that's right. Sit down – we are still only at the fish course,' said old Korchagin, carefully and with difficulty chewing with his false teeth and looking up at Nekhlyudov with bloodshot, apparently lidless eyes.

'Stepan,' he called, with his mouth full, addressing the stout dignified butler and indicating with a glance the empty place.

Although Nekhlyudov knew old Korchagin quite well and had seen him many a time at the dinner-table, today the red face with the sensual smacking lips above the napkin tucked into his waistcoat, and the thick neck and the whole pampered military figure, struck him very disagreeably. Nekhlyudov could not help remembering what he had heard of the cruelty of this man, who – heavens knows why, for he was wealthy and eminent, and had no need to curry favour – had had men flogged and even hanged when he was a provincial governor.

'Immediately, your excellency,' said Stepan, getting a large soup-ladle out of the sideboard loaded with silver. And he made a sign with his head to the handsome whiskered footman, who at once began to arrange the untouched knives and forks and the elaborately folded starched napkin with the family crest uppermost at the empty place next to Missy.

Nekhlyudov went round shaking hands with everyone. Except old Korchagin and the ladies, they all got up when he approached them. And this walk round the table, this shaking the hands of everyone in the room, though with the majority of them he had never exchanged a word, today seemed particularly disagreeable and absurd. He apologized for being late, and was on the point of seating himself in the empty place at the end of the table between Missy and Katerina Alexeyevna, when old Korchagin insisted that if he would not take a glass of vodka he must at least whet his appetite with a bit of something from the side table, on which were small dishes of lobster, caviar, cheese and salt herring. Nekhlyudov did not know he was so hungry but, having started with some bread and cheese, could not stop and ate voraciously.

'Well, have you been undermining the foundations of society?' said Kolossov, ironically quoting the words used by a reactionary newspaper in its campaign against trial by jury. 'I suppose you've been acquitting the guilty and condemning the innocent, eh?'

'Undermining the foundations . . . Undermining the foundations . . .' repeated Prince Korchagin, chuckling. He had unbounded confidence in the wit and learning of his liberal friend.

At the risk of seeming uncivil Nekhlyudov did not answer Kolossov and, sitting down to his steaming soup, continued to munch.

'Do let him eat,' said Missy with a smile. She used the pronoun 'him' to remind them all of her intimacy with Nekhlyudov.

Meanwhile Kolossov went on to give a loud and lively account of the contents of the article against trial by jury which had aroused his indignation. Missy's cousin, Mikhail Sergeyevich, agreed with all he said and repeated the gist of another article from the same newspaper.

Missy was very *distinguée* as usual, and well, unostentatiously well, dressed.

'You must be dreadfully tired and hungry,' she said to Nekhlyudov, waiting until he had swallowed what was in his mouth.

'No, not particularly. What about you? Did you go to the picture gallery?'

'No, we put it off and went to play lawn tennis at the Salamatovs'. Really, Mr Crooks plays a marvellous game.'

Nekhlyudov had come here to divert his mind, for he used to like being in this house, not only because its air of luxury and good taste appealed to him but also because of the atmosphere of tender flattery and deference with which they unobtrusively surrounded him. But, strange to say, today everything in the house jarred – everything, beginning with the doorkeeper, the wide staircase, the flowers, the footmen, the table decorations, even Missy herself, who now seemed unattractive and affected. Nor did he care for Kolossov's self-satisfied, commonplace Liberalism; he did not like the ox-like, conceited, sensual appearance of old Korchagin, or the French phrases of the Slavophile Katerina Alexeyevna, or the diffident faces of the governess and the student-tutor; and, above all, he disliked that pronoun 'him' applied to himself. . . . Nekhlyudov had always wavered in his attitude to Missy: sometimes he looked at her as it were through half-closed eyes, or by moonlight, and saw her all beautiful – pure, lovely, clever and natural. . . . And then suddenly it was as if the sun came out and he saw – could not help seeing – her imperfections. Today was just such a day for him. Today he noticed all the wrinkles on her face; he knew – he saw – how her hair was fluffed out; saw her sharp elbows and, worst of all, how large her thumbnail was, exactly like her father's.

'I call it deadly dull,' said Kolossov, speaking of tennis. 'The ball game we used to play in our childhood was much more fun.'

'Oh, but you haven't tried. It's awfully exciting,' retorted Missy, pronouncing the word 'awfully' in a particularly affected way, Nekhlyudov thought.

And a general discussion started in which Mikhail Sergeyevich and Katerina Alexeyevna joined. Only the governess, the tutor and the children sat silent and looked bored.

'Oh, these everlasting arguments!' said old Korchagin, bursting into a guffaw; and he pulled the napkin from his waistcoat, noisily pushed back his chair (which the footman instantly caught hold of) and rose from the table. Everybody got up after him and went to a small table where there were finger-bowls of warm scented water, and, rinsing their mouths, they continued the conversation which did not interest anyone.

'Don't you think so?' Missy turned to Nekhlyudov, appealing to him for confirmation of her opinion that nothing shows up a person's character so much as a game. She had noticed that preoccupied and what seemed to her condemnatory look on his face which made her afraid of him, and she wanted to find out the cause of it.

'I really couldn't say. I have never thought about it,' Nekhlyudov answered.

'Shall we go to mamma?' asked Missy.

'Yes, all right,' he said, in a tone which plainly showed that he did not want to go, and took out a cigarette.

She glanced at him in silence, with a questioning look, and he felt ashamed. 'It's not very nice of me to call on people and make them feel depressed,' he thought to himself, and trying to be amiable he said he would go with pleasure if the princess would see him.

'Oh yes, mamma will be pleased. You can smoke there, too. And Ivan Ivanovich is there.'

The mistress of the house, Princess Sophia Vassilyevna, was an invalid. For eight years her visitors had seen her only in a reclining position, all lace and ribbon, surrounded with velvet, gilding, ivory, bronzes, lacquer and flowers, never going out and only receiving, as she put it, her 'own' friends, that is all those who according to her idea stood out from the common herd. Nekhlyudov counted among these friends because he was considered a clever young man, because his mother had been an intimate friend of the family, and because it would be a good thing if Missy were to marry him.

Princess Sophia Vassilyevna's room was beyond the large and the small drawing-rooms. In the large drawing-room Missy, who was walking in front of Nekhlyudov, deliberately stopped and, resting her hand on the back of a little gilt chair, faced him.

Missy was very anxious to get married, and Nekhlyudov was a good match. Besides, she liked him and had accustomed herself to the idea that he would be hers (not that she would belong to him, but he to her), and she pursued her goal with the unconscious but persistent cunning so often to be seen in the mentally unbalanced. She said something now to persuade him to tell her what was wrong.

'I see something has happened,' she said. 'What is the matter?'

He thought of the encounter in the law-courts, frowned and changed colour.

'Yes, something has happened,' he said, trying to be truthful. 'Something strange and serious and out of the ordinary.'

'What is it? Can't you tell me what it is?'

'Not now. Please do not ask me to speak. I haven't had time to reflect upon it properly myself yet,' he said, his face going even redder.

'Then you won't tell me?' A muscle twitched in her face and she pushed back the chair she was holding.

'No, I cannot,' he answered, feeling that in answering her thus he was answering himself and acknowledging that really something important had happened to him.

'Well, come along, then.'

She shook her head as if to drive away useless thoughts, and went on in front with a quicker step than usual.

He fancied that she pressed her lips together to hold back her tears. He was sorry and ashamed at having hurt her feelings, but he knew that if he showed the smallest signs of weakness it would be the end of him, that is, would bind him to her. And today he feared that more than anything, so he followed her in silence to the princess's boudoir.

Princess Sophia Vassilyevna had just finished an exquisite and very nourishing dinner. She always took her meals in private so that no one should see her performing such an unpoetical function. By her couch stood a small table with her coffee, and she was smoking a special kind of cigarette. Princess Sophia Vassilyevna was a long thin woman with dark hair, large black eyes and long teeth, still trying to look younger than her age.

People talked of her intimacy with her doctor. On previous occasions Nekhlyudov had not thought about the rumours, but this evening when he saw the doctor sitting by her couch, with his oily shining beard parted in the middle, he not only remembered but was filled with disgust.

Kolossov was sitting in a soft, low easy chair near Sophia Vassilyevna, with a little table beside him, stirring his coffee. A glass of liqueur stood on the table.

Missy came in with Nekhlyudov, but did not stay.

'When mamma gets tired and sends you away, come to me,' she said, turning to Kolossov and Nekhlyudov, and speaking as if nothing had happened between them. And with a gay smile she moved noiselessly over the heavy carpet and went out of the room.

'Well, how are you, my friend? Sit down and tell me all about it,' said Princess Sophia Vassilyevna with an artificial, feigned smile, remarkably like a real smile, which showed her fine long teeth – a splendid imitation of those she had once been endowed with. 'I hear that you have come from the courts in a very gloomy mood. I think it must be an ordeal for people of sensibility,' she added in French.

'Yes, that is so,' said Nekhlyudov. 'One frequently feels one's own lack of . . . that one has no right to sit in judgement . . .'

'*Comme c'est vrai,*'[1] she cried, as though struck by the truth of his observation. She always artfully flattered those with whom she conversed.

'Well, and what of the picture you are painting? It does interest me so,' she went on. 'If I were not such a poor invalid I should have been to see it long ago.'

'Oh, I have quite given that up,' Nekhlyudov replied dryly. Today her flattery was as obvious as her age which she was trying to conceal, and he could not bring himself to be amiable.

'Oh, that *is* a pity! You know, Repin himself told me he has real talent,' she said, turning to Kolossov.

'I wonder she isn't ashamed to tell such lies,' Nekhlyudov thought, and frowned.

When she had come to the conclusion that Nekhlyudov was in an ill humour and there was no inveigling him into an agreeable and clever conversation Sophia Vassilyevna turned to Kolossov, asking his opinion of a new play, using a tone of voice which said that Kolossov's opinion must be the final word on the subject and every syllable he uttered deserved to be immortalized. Kolossov found fault with the play and took the opportunity to air his views on art in general. Princess Sophia Vassilyevna appeared to be impressed by the truth of his arguments, tried to defend the author of the play, but then immediately surrendered or looked for some compromise. Nekhlyudov watched and listened, and he saw and heard something quite different from what was going on in front of him.

Listening now to Sophia Vassilyevna, now to Kolossov, Nekhlyudov saw, first, that neither of them cared anything about the play or each other, and that if they talked it was only to satisfy the physical need to exercise the muscles of the throat and tongue after eating; secondly, that Kolossov, having drunk vodka, wine and liqueur, was a little tipsy – not tipsy like the peasants, who drink seldom, but like people who are in

1. How true that is!

the habit of drinking wine. He did not reel about or talk nonsense, but he was in an abnormal condition – excited and self-satisfied; and thirdly, Nekhlyudov noticed that during the conversation Princess Sophia Vassilyevna kept casting uneasy glances at the window through which a slanting sunbeam was beginning to creep towards her, which might cast too strong a light on her ageing face.

'How true that is,' she said in reply to some remark of Kolossov's, and pressed the button of an electric bell in the wall by her couch.

Whereupon the doctor rose and, like one at home in the house, left the room without saying anything. Sophia Vassilyevna followed him with her eyes as she continued the conversation.

'Please draw that curtain, Philip,' she said, indicating the curtain at the window when the handsome footman came in answer to the bell.

'No, whatever you say, there is something mystical in him, and without the mystic element there is no poetry,' she said, one black eye angrily following the footman's movements as he drew the curtain.

'Mysticism without poetry is superstition, and poetry without mysticism is prose,' she said with a sad smile, watching the footman straightening the curtain.

'Philip, not that curtain – the one at the large window,' she exclaimed in a long-suffering tone, evidently regretting the effort she had to make in order to pronounce these words, and immediately, to soothe her nerves, she raised the scented, smoking cigarette to her lips with her jewel-bedecked fingers.

The muscular, broad-chested, handsome Philip made a slight inclination of the head, as though begging her pardon, and stepping softly over the carpet with his strong legs with their well-developed calves, silently and obediently went to the other window and, carefully looking at the princess, began to arrange the curtain so that not a single ray should dare fall on her. But again he did not do it properly, and again the exhausted Sophia Vassilyevna was obliged to interrupt her conversation about mysticism, and correct that idiotic Philip who harassed her so pitilessly. For an instant Philip's eyes flashed.

'"The devil alone knows what you want," was probably what he was saying to himself,' thought Nekhlyudov, watching the whole comedy. But the strong handsome Philip at once concealed his twitch of impatience and quietly went on doing what the feeble, emaciated, artificial creature, Princess Sophia Vassilyevna, commanded of him.

'Of course there is a good deal of truth in Darwin's theory,' said Kolossov, lolling back in the low arm-chair and looking at Sophia Vassilyevna with sleepy eyes, 'but he oversteps the mark. Yes.'

'And do you believe in heredity?' asked Princess Sophia Vassilyevna, turning to Nekhlyudov, whose silence annoyed her.

'In heredity?' Nekhlyudov repeated her question. 'No, I don't,' he said. At that moment his whole mind was taken up by strange images that for some unaccountable reason were rising in his imagination. By the side of the strong handsome Philip, whom he saw as an artist's model, he seemed to see the naked figure of Kolossov, with a stomach like a melon, bald head and thin whip-like arms. In the same dim way he thought of Sophia Vassilyevna's shoulders, which were now covered with silk and velvet: he imagined them in their natural state but this picture was so hideous that he made haste to banish it from his mind.

Sophia Vassilyevna looked at him appraisingly.

'Well, Missy is waiting for you,' she said. 'Go and find her. She wants to play you a new piece by Schumann . . . it is most interesting.'

'She doesn't want to play me anything. For some reason or other this woman never speaks the truth,' thought Nekhlyudov, rising and pressing Sophia Vassilyevna's transparent, bony, jewelled fingers.

In the drawing-room Katerina Alexeyevna met him and at once began, in French as usual –

'I see the duties of a juryman have had a melancholy effect upon you.'

'Yes, forgive me, I am in low spirits tonight. I ought not to be here depressing other people.'

'Why are you in low spirits?'

'I must ask you to excuse me from explaining,' he said, looking round for his hat.

'Don't you remember how you used to say that one must always tell the truth? And what cruel truths you used to tell us all! But why won't you speak out now? . . . Don't you remember, Missy?' she said, turning to Missy, who had just come into the room.

'Because that was a game then,' replied Nekhlyudov gravely. 'One may tell the truth in a game. But in real life we are so wicked . . . I mean, I am so wicked that I at least cannot tell the truth.'

'Oh, don't correct yourself – better tell us why we are so wicked,' said Katerina Alexeyevna in a bantering tone and pretending not to notice that Nekhlyudov was serious.

'There is nothing worse than to confess being in low spirits,' said Missy. 'I never do, and so I am always in good spirits. Well, shall we go to my room and try to dispel your *mauvaise humeur?*'

Nekhlyudov understood how a horse must feel when it is being coaxed into its bridle and harness. And never had he felt less inclined to draw his load than now. He excused himself, declaring that he really must go home, and began to say good-bye. Missy kept his hand longer than usual.

'Remember that what is important to you is important to your friends,' she said. 'Will you be here tomorrow?'

'I don't think so,' said Nekhlyudov, and, feeling ashamed (he did not know whether for himself or for her), he blushed and left.

'What is the matter? *Comme cela m'intrigue*,'[1] said Katerina Alexeyevna when Nekhlyudov had gone. 'I must find out. I suppose it is some *affaire d'amour propre: il est très susceptible, notre cher Mitya.*'[2]

'*Plutôt une affaire d'amour sale*,'[3] Missy was going to say, but she stopped and looked in front of her with a face from which all the light had gone, quite different from the one with which she had looked at him. She could not utter the vulgar little pun, even to Katerina Alexeyevna, but merely remarked: 'We all have our good and bad days.'

'Is it possible that he, too, will disappoint me?' she thought. 'After all that has happened it would be very bad of him.'

If Missy had been asked to explain what she meant by 'all that has happened' she could not have said anything definite, and yet she knew beyond doubt that he had not only raised her hopes but had almost given her a promise. It had not been done by any definite words – only looks, smiles, hints, silences – but still she regarded him as hers, and to lose him would be very hard.

28

'DISGRACEFUL and disgusting, disgusting and disgraceful,' Nekhlyudov was thinking meanwhile, as he walked home through familiar streets. The depression he had felt while talking to Missy would not leave him. He felt that formally, so to speak, he had not wronged her: he had said nothing to her that could be considered binding, had made no proposal to her; but he knew that in reality he had bound himself to her, had promised to be hers. And yet today he felt with his whole being that he could not marry her. 'Disgraceful and disgusting, disgusting and disgraceful,' he kept repeating to himself, not only about his relations with Missy but about everything.

1. I must say that intrigues me.
2. A question of *amour propre*: our dear Mitya is very susceptible.
3. More likely an improper love affair.

'Everything is disgusting and shameful,' he repeated, as he entered the porch of his house.

'I don't want any supper,' he said to Korney, who followed him into the dining-room where the table was laid ready for him. 'You may go.'

'Yes, sir,' said Korney, but instead of going he began to clear the table. Nekhlyudov looked at Korney with a feeling of ill-will. He wanted to be left alone and it seemed to him that everybody was being intentionally annoying in order to spite him. When Korney had gone with the supper things Nekhlyudov went up to the samovar and was going to make himself some tea, but hearing Agrafena Petrovna's footsteps he hurried into the drawing-room to avoid her, and shut the door after him. This room – the drawing-room – was the one his mother had died in three months before. Now, going into the room, which was lit by two lamps with reflectors, one near his father's portrait and the other near his mother's, he recalled how he had felt about her at the last, and their relations seemed to him unnatural and repulsive. They, too, were disgraceful and disgusting. He remembered how, towards the end of her illness, he had positively wanted her to die. He had told himself he wanted her to die for her sake, that she might be released from her suffering, whereas in actual fact he had wanted it for his own sake, to be released from the sight of her sufferings.

Anxious to recall a pleasant memory of her he glanced up at her portrait, which had been painted by a famous artist for five thousand roubles. She was wearing a low-cut gown of black velvet. The artist had evidently taken great pains over the modelling of the bosom, and the shadow between the breasts, and the dazzlingly beautiful shoulders and neck. This was absolutely disgraceful and disgusting. There was something revolting and profane in this representation of his mother as a half-naked beauty. It was all the more disgusting because three months ago, in this very room, this same woman had been lying there, dried up like a mummy but still filling not only the whole room but the whole house with a heavy sickening smell which nothing could smother. He thought he could smell it even now. And he remembered how the day before she died she had taken his strong white hand in her bony discoloured fingers, looked him in the eyes and said: 'Do not judge me, Mitya, if I have not done what I should,' and how the tears had come into her eyes, grown dull with suffering. 'How disgusting!' he said to himself again, looking up at the half-naked woman with her superb marble shoulders and arms, and the triumphant smile on her lips. The half-bared bosom of the portrait reminded him of another young woman whom he had seen *décolletée* a few days before. It was Missy, who had devised an excuse for calling him into her room one evening just as she was ready to start for a ball, so that he might see her in her ball dress. He thought with disgust now of her beautiful shoulders and arms. And that coarse animal father of hers, with his evil past and his cruelties, and that *bel esprit*, her mother, with her doubtful reputation. All of it disgusted him and at the same time made him feel ashamed. 'Disgraceful and disgusting, disgusting and disgraceful.'

'No, no,' he thought. 'I must break away: I must break away from my false relationship with the Korchagins and Marya Vassilyevna and the inheritance and all the rest. . . . Oh, to breathe freely – to go abroad, to Rome, and work at my picture. . . .' He remembered his doubts as to his talent for art. 'Well, anyway, just to breathe freely. First to Constantinople, then Rome. Anything to be through with this jury business. And have the matter arranged with the lawyer.'

And suddenly there flashed into his mind an extraordinarily vivid picture of the prisoner with her black eyes and their slight cast. How she had wept when the prisoners had been allowed to say their last words! He hurriedly stabbed the butt of his cigarette in the ashtray, lit another and started pacing up and down the room. And one after another scenes from the times he had spent with her rose in his imagination. He remembered that last meeting with her, the animal passion that had seized him, and the sense of disappointment he had experienced when his passion had been satisfied. He remembered the white dress with the pale-blue ribbon, remembered the Easter service. 'I really did love her, truly loved her with a good, pure love that night – loved her even before that. Yes, I loved her the first time when I was staying with the aunts and writing my thesis!' And he remembered himself as he had been then. A breath of that early freshness, youth and fullness of life blew over him, and he felt painfully sad.

The difference between what he had been then and what he was now was enormous: as great, if not greater, than the difference between Katusha in church that night and the prostitute who had caroused with the merchant and whom they had tried this very morning. Then he had been free and fearless, with endless possibilities ready to open before him; now he felt caught in the meshes of a stupid, empty, purposeless, insignificant life from which he could see no means of extricating himself – indeed, for the most part he did not want to extricate himself. He remembered how proud he used to be of his straightforwardness; how he had made it a rule always to speak the truth, and really had been truthful; and now he was entangled in lies – in the most dreadful lies, lies which all the people who surrounded him accepted as the truth. And there was no way out of these lies, at least so far as he could see. And he was sunk deep in them, was used to them, revelled in them.

How was he to break off his relations with Marya Vassil-yevna and her husband in such a way as to be able to look him and his children in the eyes? How disentangle himself from Missy without lying? How escape the contradiction between his recognition that the private ownership of land was not right and his retention of the land inherited from his mother? How atone for his sin against Katusha? This last, at any rate, could not be left as it was. 'I cannot abandon a woman I have loved, and be satisfied with paying a lawyer to save her from hard labour in Siberia which she does not even deserve – I can't atone for my fault with money, in the way I did years ago when I gave her money and thought I had done what was required of me.'

And he vividly remembered the moment when he had caught up with her in the passage, thrust some money into the bib of her apron and run away. 'Oh, that money!' he thought with the same horror and disgust as he had felt at the time. 'Oh, dear, oh dear, how contemptible!' he said aloud, just as he had done at the time. 'Only a blackguard could have done that! And I – I am just such a blackguard!' he went on aloud. 'But am I really' – he stopped and stood still – 'am I really such a scoundrel? – Well, am I not?' he answered himself. 'And is this all?' he continued to accuse himself. 'Are not my relations with Marya Vassilyevna and her husband mean and contemptible? And my position with regard to riches? To make use of wealth which I believe in my heart to be morally wrong, on the excuse that it was inherited from my mother? And the whole of my idle, bad life. And to crown it all, my conduct towards Katusha. Scoundrel, blackguard! They (people) can judge me as they like: they are easily deceived, but I cannot deceive myself.'

And suddenly he realized that the aversion he had lately, and particularly today, felt for people – for the prince, and Sophia Vassilyevna, and Missy, and Korney – was aversion for himself. And strange to say, in this recognition of his own baseness there was something painful, and at the same time something pleasurable and soothing.

More than once in Nekhlyudov's life there had been what he called a 'purging of the soul'. This was the name he gave to a state of mind in which, sometimes after a long interval, he would suddenly recognize the slothfulness of his inner life, or even the total cessation of activity, and set to work to clean up all the dirt which had clogged his soul to the point of inaction.

After such awakenings Nekhlyudov would make rules for himself which he meant to follow for ever after: he would keep a diary and begin a new life, which he hoped never to go back on – turning over a new leaf, he called it to himself in English. But time after time the temptations of the world ensnared him, and before he knew it he had fallen – often lower than before.

Several times in his life he had thus purified and raised himself. The first time was during the summer he spent with his aunts. That had been his most vital, most rapturous awakening. And its effects had lasted for a considerable while. There was another such awakening when he gave up the civil service and entered the army during the war, with the idea of sacrificing his life for his country. But here the choking-up process occurred very quickly. Then there was the awakening when he resigned from the army and went abroad, devoting himself to painting.

From that day to this a long period had passed without any moral purging, and consequently he had never before sunk to such depths, and never had there been such discord between what his conscience called for and the life he was leading, and he was horrified when he saw the distance separating the two.

The distance was so great, the defilement so complete, that at first he despaired of the possibility of being cleansed. 'Haven't you tried before to improve and be better, and nothing came of it?' whispered the voice of the tempter within. 'So what is the use of trying any more? You are not the only one – everyone's the same – life is like that,' whispered the voice. But the free spiritual being, which alone is true, alone powerful, alone eternal, had already awakened in Nekhlyudov. And he could not but trust it. However vast the disparity between what he was and what he wished to be, everything appeared possible to this newly awakened spiritual being.

'Whatever it costs me, I will shatter the lie which is binding me, and admit everything, and tell the truth to everybody, and act truthfully,' he said aloud with resolution. 'I will tell Missy the truth, that I am a libertine and cannot marry her, and have upset her life for nothing. I will tell Marya

Vassilyevna' – this was the wife of the Marshal of the Nobility – 'no, there is nothing to tell her: I will tell her husband that I, blackguard that I am, have been deceiving him. I will dispose of the estate in such a way as to be consistent with the truth. I will tell her, Katusha, that I am a blackguard, that I have wronged her and will do all I can to ease her lot. Yes, I will see her and ask her to forgive me. Yes, I will beg her pardon, as children do.' He stopped. 'I will marry her if necessary.'

He stopped, crossed his hands over his breast as he used to do when he was a child, lifted his eyes and said, addressing someone:

'O Lord, help me, instruct me, come and take Thine abode in me and cleanse me from all impurity.'

He prayed, asking God to help him, to enter into him and cleanse him; and in the meantime that which he asked had already happened. The God who dwelt within him had awakened in his conscience. He felt himself one with Him, and therefore he was conscious not only of the freedom, the courage and joy of life, but of all the power of righteousness. All, all the best a man could do, he now felt himself capable of doing.

His eyes filled with tears as he was saying all this to himself, good and bad tears: good because they were tears of joy at the awakening of the spiritual being within him, the being that had slumbered all these years; and bad tears of tender emotion at his own goodness.

He felt hot. He went to the window – the double winter glazing had been removed – and opened it. The window looked on to the garden. It was a still, fresh moonlight night. Wheels rattled past in the street, and then all was silent. The shadow of a tall leafless poplar fell on the ground immediately beneath the window, the outline of its forked branches sharply defined on the newly swept gravel. On the left, the roof of the coach-house shone white in the bright moonlight. In front, the black shadow of the garden wall was visible through the interlacing branches of the trees. Nekhlyudov gazed at the moonlit garden, the roof and the shadow of the poplar, and drank in the fresh invigorating air.

'How good, how good, O Lord, how good!' he said of what was in his soul.

29

IT was six o'clock in the evening before Maslova was back in her cell, tired and footsore after trudging nearly nine miles over the cobblestones, when she was not used to walking. She was crushed by the unexpectedly severe sentence, and on top of everything else she was hungry.

Her mouth had watered and she realized that she was hungry when the guards ate bread and hard-boiled eggs during one of the recesses, but she considered it beneath her dignity to ask them for food. Three hours later, however, the desire to eat had passed and she only felt weak. It was in this state that she heard the unexpected sentence. At first she thought she had not heard right: she could not believe her ears, could not think of herself as a convict. But when she saw the calm businesslike faces of judges and jury, who took the sentence as a matter of course, she rebelled and cried aloud that she was innocent. But seeing that her scream, too, was taken as something natural, something to be expected that could not affect the case, she burst into tears, feeling that submission to the cruel and amazing injustice was all that remained to her. What astonished her most was that men, young men, not old men – the very ones in whose eyes she had always found favour – should condemn her so cruelly. One of them – the assistant prosecutor – she had seen in quite a different humour. Sitting in the prisoners' room before the trial and during the recesses she had seen these men, pretending that they were on other business, pass by the door or come into the room to have a look at her. And then suddenly for some reason these same men had sentenced her to hard labour although she was innocent of the charge against her. At first she wept in the prisoners' room, but then calmed down and sat quietly, completely stunned, waiting to be taken back. She only wanted one thing now – to smoke. This was the condition Botchkova and Kartinkin found her in when they were brought to the same room after the sentence. Botchkova immediately began to rail at her and call her a 'convict'.

'Copped it, haven't you? Gettin' off, was you? I don't think – no fear, you wasn't, you slut! Got what you deserved. Out in Siberia you'll have to give up your airs and graces, I can tell you.'

Maslova sat with bowed head, her hands in the sleeves of her prison cloak, staring in front of her at the dirty floor.

'I don't bother you, so you leave me alone. I don't bother you, do I?' she repeated several times, then relapsed into silence. It was only after Kartinkin and Botchkova had been led away and the guard brought her three roubles that she brightened up a little.

'You Maslova?' he inquired. 'Here – lady sent you this,' he said, giving her the money.

'What lady?'

'You just take it. I don't want no talk with you.'

The money had been sent by the brothel-keeper. As she was leaving the court-room Kitayeva had turned to the usher and asked whether she might give Maslova a little money. The usher said she could. Having received this permission, she pulled the three-button suède glove from her plump white hand, drew a stylish note-case from the back folds of her silk skirt, and selecting from a fairly large bundle of coupons,[1] just cut off from some interest-bearing papers she had earned in her establishment, one worth two roubles and fifty kopecks, she added two twenty- and one ten-kopeck coins, and handed the sum to the usher. The usher called one of the guards and in the presence of the donor handed him the money.

'Be sure you gif it to her,' Karolina Albertovna Kitayeva said to the guard.

1. Coupons cut off interest-bearing papers were often used as money in pre-Revolution Russia.

The guard was annoyed by her lack of confidence, and this made him surly with Maslova.

Maslova was glad to have the money because it could give her the only thing she now desired.

'If only I could get hold of some cigarettes and have a smoke!' she said to herself, and all her thoughts centred on the one longing to smoke. So frantic was she that she greedily inhaled the air whenever a whiff of tobacco smoke drifted through the door of one of the offices that opened on to the corridor. But she had to wait for quite a time because the secretary whose business it was to give the order for her return forgot all about the prisoners, so engrossed was he in a discussion – indeed, it was quite an argument – with one of the lawyers about the censored newspaper article. A number of people, both young and old, dropped in, too, after the trial, to have a look at her, saying something to each other in whispers. But now she did not even notice them.

At last, just after four, she was allowed to go, and her escort – the man from Nizhni-Novgorod and the Chuvash – led her away from the court-house by a back door. While still in the vestibule of the court-house she gave them twenty kopecks, asking them to buy two rings of white bread and some cigarettes. The Chuvash laughed, took the money and said:

'Right you are, we'll get 'em,' and did in fact buy both cigarettes and rolls, and gave her back the right change.

But she could not smoke in the street, so that she reached the prison with her craving unsatisfied. As they approached the entrance about a hundred prisoners who had arrived by rail were being brought in. She ran into them in the passageway.

The convicts – bearded, clean-shaven, old, young, Russians, foreigners, some with half their heads shaved – clanking the shackles on their legs, filled the ante-room with dust, noise and the acrid smell of sweat. All of them stared hungrily at Maslova, and some, their faces distorted with lust, came up to her and brushed against her in passing.

'Here's a good-looking wench,' said one.

'My respects, missy,' said another, winking at her.

A swarthy fellow, the back of his head showing blue where it had been shaved, with a moustache on his beardless face, stumbled over his rattling chains as he sprang towards her and embraced her.

'Don't you know a friend when you see him? Come on, none of your airs, now!' he shouted, showing his teeth and flashing his eyes when she pushed him away.

'What d'you think you're up to, you bastard?' shouted the assistant chief officer, coming up from behind.

The convict shrank back and quickly jumped away. The assistant chief officer turned to Maslova.

'What are you doing here?'

Maslova wanted to tell him that she had been brought back from the court-house but she was so tired she could not be bothered to speak.

'She has come from the Court, sir,' said the senior of her escort party, stepping forward with his fingers to his cap.

'Well, hand her over to the head warder. I won't have this sort of thing!'

'Yes, sir.'

'Sokolov, see to her!' shouted the assistant chief officer.

The head warder came up and giving Maslova an angry push on the shoulder, and making a sign with his head that she must follow, led her to the women's section. There she was searched and as nothing prohibited was found on her (she had hidden her packet of cigarettes inside one of the rings of bread) she was readmitted to the cell she had left that morning.

30

MASLOVA'S cell was a long room, some sixteen feet wide and twenty-one in length; it had two windows and a dilapidated stove which stuck out into the room. Two-thirds of the space was taken up by sleeping-benches made of warped planks. In the middle, opposite the door, hung a dark ikon with a wax candle stuck to it and a dusty bunch of everlasting flowers hanging underneath. To the left, on a blackened part of the floor behind the door, stood a vile-smelling tub. The roll had just been called and the women were locked in for the night.

In all fifteen people occupied this cell – twelve women and three children.

It was still quite light, and only two of the women were lying on their plank-beds: one, an imbecile arrested for having no identity papers, who spent most of the time asleep with her head wrapped in her prison cloak; and the other, a consumptive serving a sentence for theft. She was not asleep but lay with wide-open eyes, the prison-cloak folded under her head, trying to keep back the phlegm that filled and tickled her throat, so as not to cough. The other women, all of them bareheaded and with nothing on but coarse brown holland chemises, were either sitting on bunks sewing or standing at the window watching the convicts crossing the yard. Of the three who were sewing, one was the old woman who had seen Maslova off in the morning, Korablyova by name – a tall, powerful, sullen-looking woman with knitted brows, wrinkled skin hanging in a loose bag under her chin, a short plait of fair hair turning grey at the temples and a hairy wart on her cheek. She had been sentenced to penal servitude for killing her husband with an axe. She had murdered him because he had been badgering her daughter. She was the cell monitor and carried on a small trade in drink. She wore spectacles to sew, and held the needle in her large rough hands the way peasant women do, with three fingers and the point towards her. Next to her, also sewing bags of sail-cloth, sat a snub-nosed, dark-skinned little woman with small black eyes, good-hearted and talkative. She was a signal-woman on the railway, sentenced to three months' imprisonment for not having come out of her hut with a flag to meet the train, so that an accident had occurred in consequence. Fedosya –

Fenichka, her companions called her – the third of the trio who were sewing, was quite a young woman, very pretty with a white skin and rosy cheeks, clear blue eyes like a child's and a couple of long fair plaits, which she wore twisted round her small head. She was in prison for an attempt to poison her husband. She had tried to poison him immediately after their marriage, which had taken place when she was barely sixteen years old. In the eight months during which she had been on bail awaiting her trial she not only made it up with her husband but became so fond of him that she was found to be living with him in the greatest harmony. Although her husband, her father-in-law and especially her mother-in-law, who had grown devoted to the girl, moved heaven and earth to get her acquitted she was sentenced to hard labour in Siberia. This good-natured, cheerful Fedosya, whose face was often wreathed in smiles, had her plank-bed next to Maslova's, and not only liked her very much but regarded it as her responsibility to look after her and help her. Two other women were sitting on their plank-beds doing nothing; one, a woman of about forty with a pale thin face, had evidently once been very handsome but was now thin and pale. She had a child in her arms and was suckling it at her white long breast. This was her crime: one day a recruiting party arrived at her village to take away a lad who, so the peasants thought, was being wrongfully conscripted; the people stopped the police-officer and got the conscript from him; and this woman – an aunt of the lad who was being wrongfully conscripted – was the first to seize the bridle of the horse on which they were taking him away. The other woman who sat doing nothing was a short wrinkled kindly old thing with grey hair and a hump-back. She sat on a plank-bed by the stove, pretending to catch a pot-bellied little boy of four with hair cropped close to his head, who ran backwards and forwards in front of her, laughing gaily. The little lad had nothing on but a shirt, and every time he ran past her he cried out: 'There, you didn't catch me!' This old woman, who with her son was accused of arson, bore her imprisonment with the utmost good temper, troubled only about her son, who was also in gaol, and still more about her old man: she was sure he was being eaten up by vermin, since her daughter-in-law had gone off and there was no one to keep him clean.

In addition to these seven women four others were standing at one of the open windows, holding on to the iron grating, and making signs and shouting to the convicts who were passing to and fro in the yard and whom Maslova had met at the entrance to the prison. One of these women was serving a sentence for theft, a large heavy creature with a flabby body, red hair and freckles all over her sallow face, her arms and her thick neck, which stuck out over an unbuttoned open collar. She kept calling through the window, shouting obscenities in a loud raucous voice. By her side stood a clumsy swarthy prisoner no bigger than a child of ten, with a long body and very short legs. Her face was red and blotchy, she had wide-set black eyes and short thick lips which failed to hide her protruding white teeth. By snatches she broke into screeching laughter at what was going on in the yard. Nicknamed Beauty for her love of finery, she was being tried for theft and arson. Behind them, in a very dirty grey chemise, stood a stringy, haggard, miserable-looking pregnant woman with a huge abdomen, who was accused of receiving stolen property. This woman stood there without speaking but all the time smiled with pleasure and approval at what was happening below. The fourth woman at the window – in for selling spirits without a licence – was a short thick-set peasant with very bulging eyes and an amiable face. She was the mother of the little boy who was playing with the old woman, and of a seven-year-old girl, who were with her in prison because she had no one to leave them with. Like the others she was looking out of the window, but she went on knitting a stocking, and frowned and closed her eyes disapprovingly at what the prisoners in the yard were saying. Her seven-year-old daughter, though, in nothing but her little chemise, her fair hair flowing loose, clutching the red-haired woman's skirt with her thin little hand, eyes wide open stood drinking in the words of abuse the women and the convicts flung at each other, repeating them softly to herself as if she were learning them by heart. The twelfth prisoner was the daughter of a subdeacon who had drowned her baby in a well. She was a tall stately girl with dishevelled fair hair escaping from her short thick plait, and staring, protruding eyes. She took no notice of anything that was going on around her but, bare-foot and wearing only a dirty chemise, paced up and down the free space in the cell, turning abruptly on reaching the wall.

31

WHEN the lock clanked and Maslova was let into the cell every eye turned to her. Even the subdeacon's daughter stopped for a moment and looked at the newcomer with lifted brows, but without saying anything immediately resumed her dogged striding up and down. Korablyova stuck her needle into the coarse sacking and peered questioningly at Maslova over her spectacles.

'Oh dear, oh dear! You back again. I thought you'd be acquitted, I must say,' she exclaimed in her hoarse, deep, almost masculine voice. 'So they've settled your 'ash.'

She took off her spectacles and laid her sewing down beside her on the plank-bed.

'And 'ere me and old Aunty 'ave been talking about you, dearie. Likely you'd be let free at once, we said. It 'appens that way, we said. And if you strike it right, you get a 'eap of money into the bargain,' the signal-woman began at once in her melodious voice. 'Oh well, so it's turned out like this. Seems we guessed wrong. The Lord willed otherwise, my dearie,' she went on in her caressing musical voice.

''Ave they really convicted you?' asked Fedosya with tender concern, looking at Maslova with childlike light blue eyes; and her bright young face changed entirely, as if she were going to cry.

Maslova did not answer, and silently crossed to her place, which was the second from the end, next to Korablyova, and sat on the boards of her bed.

'I don't suppose you've 'ad anything to eat?' said Fedosya, getting up and walking over to Maslova.

Without answering, Maslova put the rings of bread at the head of the bed and started to undress: she took off her dusty cloak, and the kerchief from her curly black hair, and sat down.

The hunchbacked old woman who had been playing with the little boy at the other end of the row of beds also came up and stood in front of Maslova.

'Tst, tst, tst!' she clicked with her tongue, shaking her head sympathetically.

The little boy approached too, behind the old woman, and sticking out a corner of his upper lip stared wide-eyed at the rolls Maslova had brought. The sight of all these sympathetic faces after all she had gone through that day made Maslova want to cry, and her mouth trembled. But she tried to control herself, and succeeded until the old woman and the little boy came up. But when she heard the kindly compassionate clicking of the old woman's tongue and met the boy's serious eyes turned from the rolls to her face she could bear it no longer. Her whole face quivered and she burst into sobs.

'Didn't I keep telling you to get a proper lawyer,' said Korablyova. 'Well, what is it? Siberia?' she asked.

Maslova wanted to answer but could not and, still sobbing, she drew the packet of cigarettes out of the bread – it was decorated with a picture of a pink-cheeked lady with hair done up very high and a gown with a V-necked bodice – and handed it to Korablyova. Korablyova glanced at the picture, shook her head disapprovingly (mainly at the foolish way Maslova had spent her money), took out a cigarette and, lighting it by the flame of the lamp, drew a puff herself and thrust it back at Maslova. Maslova, crying all the while, began to inhale avidly.

'Penal servitude,' she said with a convulsive sob.

'They don't know what the fear of God is, the damned fiends,' muttered Korablyova. 'Sentencing an innocent girl like that.'

At this moment a peal of laughter burst from the women who were still at the window. The little girl laughed too, her thin childish laughter mingling with the raucous screeching of the other three. A convict in the yard had done something which had this effect on those watching at the window.

'Just look at the shaved son of a bitch, what 'e's doing!' cried the red-haired woman, and swaying her whole fat body and pressing her face against the grating she shouted meaningless obscenities.

'Shut up, you cackling fool! What's she yelling about?' said Korablyova, shaking her head at the red-haired woman. Then, turning to Maslova again: 'Time?'

'Four years,' said Maslova, and the tears flowed so copiously from her eyes that one fell on the cigarette. She crumpled it up angrily and took another.

The signal-woman, though she did not smoke, immediately picked up the stub and began to straighten it out as she went on talking.

'Truth 'as gorn to the dogs, my dearies, and no mistake,' she said. 'They do what they likes. Matveyevna was sayin' they'd let you off, but "No," I sez, "I've a feelin' they'll give it 'er," I sez. And so it's turned out,' she concluded, evidently liking the sound of her own voice.

By now all the convicts had passed through the yard, and the women who had been exchanging remarks with them left the window and also came up to Maslova. The first to come over was the goggle-eyed woman imprisoned for selling spirits without a licence, with her little girl.

'Crool with you, was they?' she asked, sitting down beside Maslova and continuing with her knitting.

'They was rotten on 'er because there weren't no money. If she'd 'ad money to get a lawyer who was up to their tricks she'd 'ave been acquitted all right,' said Korablyova. 'That fellow – what's 'is name? The one with the shaggy 'air and big nose. 'E'd bring you dry out of the ocean, 'e would. She ought to 'ave 'ad him.'

''Im, oh yes,' grinned Beauty, sitting down near them. 'Why, 'e won't even spit at you for less than a thousand.'

'Seems you, too, was born under an unlucky star,' put in the old woman imprisoned for arson. 'Just think – entice the boy's wife away from 'im and then 'ave 'im locked up to feed the lice, and me, too, in me old age,' and she began for the hundredth time to tell her story. 'If it isn't prison it's the beggar's sack, you can't get away from it. One or t'other.'

'Yes, that's the way of it,' said the woman who had sold spirits, and looking closely at her daughter's head she put the stocking down beside her, drew the child between her knees and began with practised fingers to search her scalp.

'"What you doin', sellin' drink?" they asks. 'Ow 'm I goin' to feed the kids if I don't?' she said, resuming her knitting.

These words made Maslova think of vodka.

'I wish I could have a drink,' she said to Korablyova, wiping her tears away with her sleeve and sobbing less frequently.

'All right, cough up,' said Korablyova.

32

MASLOVA got out the money which she had concealed in the bread and handed it to Korablyova. Korablyova took it, looked at it and, though she could not read, trusted Beauty, who knew everything, that the slip of paper was worth two roubles fifty kopecks, and then climbed up to the ventilator, where she had hidden a small flask of vodka. Seeing this, the women whose bunks were not near Maslova's moved away, while Maslova shook the dust out of her kerchief and cloak, and getting on to her bed she began to eat the bread.

'I saved some tea for you, but I'm afraid it's cold now,' said Fedosya, taking down from the shelf a mug and a tin teapot wrapped in a rag.

The tea was stone cold and tasted more of tin than tea, but Maslova filled the mug and began to drink as she ate her roll.

'Here, Finashka, here's a bit for you,' she called, breaking off a piece of bread and giving it to the boy, whose eyes were fixed on her mouth.

Korablyova in the meantime handed her the flask of vodka and a mug. Maslova offered some to Korablyova and Beauty. These three were regarded as the aristocracy of the cell because they had money and shared what they had.

A few minutes later Maslova had brightened up and was giving them a lively description of the court, mimicking the public prosecutor and telling them what had struck her most. In the court-house they had all looked at her with obvious pleasure, she said, and had kept on coming into the prisoners' room on purpose.

'The guard said to me himself: "All they come in here for is to look at you." One would come in, pretending he wanted a paper or something, but I could see he didn't want any paper: he was just eating me up with his eyes all the while,' she said, smiling and shaking her head in wonder. 'Like actors in the theatre.'

'Oh yes,' chimed in the signal-woman, and her melodious voice immediately flowed on. 'They're like flies round a jam jar. Whatever else they don't know, and that's plenty, where a woman's concerned they're all there. They'd sooner go without food than . . .'

'Everywhere it was just the same' Maslova interrupted her. 'The same thing happened here, too. They had just brought me back when a party came up from the railway-station. They pestered me so, I didn't know how to shake them off. If it hadn't been for the chief officer. . . . One held on so I could hardly get rid of him.'

'What kind of a fellow was 'e?' asked Beauty.

'A dark chap, with moustaches.'

'It must be 'im.'

'Him – who?'

'Shcheglov. 'Im that just went past.

'Who's Shcheglov?'

'She don't know who Shcheglov is! 'E escaped twice from Siberia. Now they've caught 'im, but 'e'll get away again. Even the warders are afraid of 'im,' said Beauty, who managed to exchange notes with the male prisoners and knew all that went on in the gaol. ''E'll run away, you bet your life.'

'Well, if 'e does, 'e won't take us with 'im,' remarked Korablyova. 'You'd better tell us what the lawyer said about your appeal,' she said, turning to Maslova. 'Is it now you're to send it in?'

Maslova said she didn't know anything about it.

Just then the red-haired woman, with both her freckled hands in her thick red hair, scratching her head with her nails, walked up to the 'aristocracy' drinking their vodka.

'I'll tell you all about it, Katerina,' she began. 'First of all you must write it down on paper that you're not satisfied with the sentence, and then send that to the prosecutor.'

'What call 'ave you got to come interferin'?' Korablyova turned to her angrily, speaking in her bass voice. 'Smell vodka, don't you? There's no need for you to stick your nose in. We don't 'ave to ask you what to do.'

'No one's speaking to you. Don't get so excited.'

'It's the drink you're after, isn't it? That's why you come wriggling up.'

'All right, give her some,' said Maslova, who always gave away everything she had.

'I'll give 'er something . . .'

'Let's see you try,' said the red-haired woman, advancing towards Korablyova. 'I'm not afraid of you.'

'Prison scum!'

''Ark who's talking!'

'Boiled tripe!'

'Me tripe? You convict, you – murderer!' shouted the red-haired woman.

'Get out, d'you 'ear,' said Korablyova darkly.

But the red-haired woman only moved up closer, and Korablyova hit her on her bare heavy breasts. This apparently was what the red-haired woman was waiting for. Out flew one hand and grabbed Korablyova by the hair, while the other made to hit her in the face, but Korablyova grabbed the hand. Maslova and Beauty caught the red-haired woman by the arms, trying to drag her away, but she had a firm hold of Korablyova's plait and would not let go. Only for an instant did she relax her grip, and then it was to twist the hair more tightly round her fist. Korablyova, with her head bent to one side, punched the red-haired woman's body with one hand and tried to bite her arm. The other women crowded round the pair who were fighting, screaming and doing their best to separate them. Even the consumptive one came up and, coughing, watched the fight. The children cried and huddled together. The noise brought the warder and the female-warder in. The fighting women were separated, and Korablyova undid her grey plait and picked out the tufts of hair that had been torn from her head, while the red-haired woman held her ripped chemise over her yellow chest; both of them were loud with their explanations and complaints.

'It's vodka at the bottom of all this, I know that,' said the wardress. 'Tomorrow I shall report you to the head warder: he'll give it you. I can smell it. You'll get rid of it if you know what's good for you. I've no time to listen to your stories now. Get back to your places and keep quiet!'

But it was a long time before silence was established. The women went on quarrelling, telling each other how it had all begun and whose fault it was. Finally the warder and the female-warder went away, and the women slowly quietened down and began going to bed. The old woman stood before the ikon and said her prayers.

'Two gaol-birds got together,' the red-haired woman suddenly called out in a hoarse voice from the other end of the room, accompanying each word with extraordinarily complicated oaths.

'You'd better watch out or you'll catch it again,' Korablyova replied immediately, with a train of similar abuse. And both relapsed into silence.

'If they 'adn't stopped me I'd have scratched your wall-eyes out . . .' the red-haired woman began again, and again Korablyova was not behind with a retort in kind.

There followed another interval of silence, longer than the first, and then more abuse. But the intervals grew longer and longer, until finally everything was quiet.

All of them were lying on their beds, and some were snoring. Only the old woman (who always took a long time over her prayers) was still bowing before the ikon, and the deacon's daughter, who got up the moment the wardress had left, was pacing up and down the room again.

Maslova did not sleep. She kept thinking that she was now a convict condemned to hard labour, and that she had already twice been reminded of the fact – once by Botchkova and once by the red-haired woman – and she could not get used to the idea. Korablyova, who was lying with her back towards her, turned over.

'I never thought – I never dreamed it would come to this,' said Maslova in a low voice. 'Other people do far worse things and nothing happens to them, while I have to suffer for a crime I never committed.'

'Never mind, girl. Siberia isn't the end – people manage to live there, too. You'll get over it,' Korablyova tried to comfort her.

'I know I'll survive. But it's still not fair. I ought to have had a different fate – I'm used to a comfortable life.'

'You can't go against Providence,' said Korablyova with a sigh. 'You can't go against Providence.'

'I know, old girl, but it's hard all the same.'

They were silent for a while.

'Do you hear that blubberer?' said Korablyova, drawing Maslova's attention to the strange sounds coming from the other end of the room.

It was the smothered sobbing of the red-haired woman. She was crying because they had called her names and hit her, and not given her any of the vodka she wanted so badly. She was crying too because all her life she had had nothing but abuse, jeers, insults and blows. She tried to console herself by thinking of her first sweetheart, a factory hand whose name was Fedka Molodenkov, but when she thought of this first love of hers she also remembered how it had ended. It had ended one day when this Molodenkov was drunk and for a joke had dabbed vitriol on the most sensitive spot of her body and then roared with laughter with his mates while she writhed in agony. She remembered this and felt so full of pity for herself that, thinking no one could hear her, she burst into tears and wept as children do, moaning and snuffling and swallowing the salt tears.

'You can't help feeling sorry for her,' said Maslova.

'A course you can't. But she shouldn't come poking her nose in.'

33

NEKHLYUDOV's first sensation when he awoke the next morning was that something had happened to him, and even before he recalled what it was that had happened to him he knew that something important and good had happened. 'Katusha . . . the trial.' Yes, he must stop lying and tell the whole truth. And, by a singular coincidence, that very morning the long-awaited letter arrived from Marya Vassilyevna, the Marshal of the Nobility's wife, the letter which he now needed particularly. She gave him full freedom and wished him happiness in his intended marriage.

'Marriage!' he muttered ironically. 'I am a long way from that now!'

And he remembered his determination of the night before to tell her husband everything, ask his forgiveness and declare his readiness to give him any kind of satisfaction. But this morning this did not seem so easy as it had yesterday. 'Besides, why make a man unhappy, if he does not know? If he asks, then I'll tell him. But why go and tell him deliberately? No, that was unnecessary.'

And telling the whole truth to Missy seemed just as difficult this morning. Again, he couldn't begin it – it would be too hurtful. As in so many everyday matters something had to be left merely implied. Only one thing he was firm about this morning: not to visit there, and he would tell the truth if they asked him.

But there was to be nothing unsaid in his relations with Katusha.

'I shall go to the prison and tell her everything, and ask her to forgive me. And if need be . . . yes, if need be, I will marry her,' he thought.

This idea that, on moral grounds, he was ready to sacrifice everything and marry her made him feel very warm and tender towards himself that morning.

It was a long time since he had met the coming day with so much energy. When Agrafena Petrovna came in he announced with more firmness than he thought himself capable of that he would no longer be requiring these apartments or her services. There had been a tacit understanding that he was keeping up so spacious and expensive an establishment because he was thinking of getting married. Consequently, giving up the house had a special significance. Agrafena Petrovna looked at him in surprise.

'I am very much obliged to you, Agrafena Petrovna, for all your care of me, but I no longer have any use for such a large place and all the servants. If you want to help me, be so good as to see to all the things, put them away for the time being, as was done in mamma's lifetime. And when Natasha arrives, she will arrange about everything.' (Natasha was Nekhlyudov's sister.)

Agrafena Petrovna shook her head.

'See to things? Why, they'll be required again,' she said.

'No, they won't, Agrafena Petrovna. They certainly won't,' said Nekhlyudov, answering the thought she was expressing by the shake of her head. 'Please, also, tell Korney that I will pay him two months' wages, but shall have no further need of him.'

'You are making a mistake, Dmitri Ivanovich,' she said. 'Supposing you do go abroad, you'll still need a place.'

'You are wrong, Agrafena Petrovna. I am not going abroad; if I go anywhere, it will be in quite a different direction.'

He suddenly flushed scarlet.

'Yes, I shall have to tell her,' he thought. 'Nothing must be kept back, I must tell everybody everything.'

'A very strange and important thing happened to me yesterday. I expect you remember Katusha at Aunt Marya Ivanovna's?'

'To be sure I do, I taught her to sew.'

'Well, Katusha was tried in court yesterday, and I was one of the jury.'

'Merciful heavens, what a dreadful thing!' cried Agrafena Petrovna. 'What was she being tried for?'

'Murder, and it was all my doing.'

'How was it your doing? That's a very funny way of talking,' said Agrafena Petrovna, with a flash in her old eyes.

She knew of the affair with Katusha.

'Yes, I am the cause of it all. And it is this that has altered all my plans.'

'But what difference can it make to you?' said Agrafena Petrovna, keeping back a smile.

'This difference: I started her along that path, and so I must do everything I can to help her.'

'Of course you do as you like, but I can't see as how you are particularly to blame. Such things can happen to everybody, and if people use their common sense, affairs like that are soon smoothed over and forgotten, and life goes on,' Agrafena Petrovna said, speaking sternly and gravely, 'and there's no reason why you should shoulder it. I heard that she had gone to the bad, but who's to blame for that?'

'I am. And that's why I want to put it right.'

'Well, it won't be no easy matter.'

'That is my business. But if you are thinking about yourself, then let me say that mamma expressed the wish . . .'

'I am not thinking about myself. The late princess provided for me so generously that I want for nothing. Lisanka' (this was her married niece) 'has invited me to live with her, and I shall go there when I'm no longer required here. Only it's a pity you're taking this so much to heart; it happens to everybody.'

'Well, I don't think so. But I still ask you, help me to let the house and put away the things. And don't be angry with me. I am very, very grateful to you for all you have done.'

It was a strange thing – ever since Nekhlyudov had begun to realize his own faults and to be disgusted with himself he ceased to be disgusted with other people: on the contrary, he felt a kindly respect for Agrafena Petrovna and Korney. He would have liked to go and confess himself to Korney too, but Korney's manner was so impressively respectful that he could not bring himself to do so.

On his way to the court-house, driving through the same streets in the same cab, Nekhlyudov marvelled at himself, for he felt such an entirely different being today.

The marriage to Missy, which only yesterday had seemed so probable, now appeared quite impossible. The day before, he had felt so sure of his position that there could be no doubt that she would be glad to marry him; today he felt unworthy even to offer her friendship, let alone marriage. 'If she only knew what I am, nothing would induce her to see me again. And I was reproaching her for flirting with another man! Besides, even if she consented to marry me now, how could I enjoy happiness or peace of mind, knowing that the other was in prison, and tomorrow or the next day would be trudging off to Siberia? How could I receive congratulations and go paying calls with my young bride while the woman I ruined was on her way to hard labour? Or how could I count votes for and against proposals for inspecting schools, and so on, with the Marshal of Nobility, whom I have so shamefully deceived, all the while making assignations with his wife (horrible thought!); or continue to work at my picture, which will certainly never get finished, for I have no business to waste time on such trifles, and anyhow I can't do anything of that kind now,' he said to himself, incessantly rejoicing at the change he felt within himself.

'The first thing now is to see the lawyer and find out what he has decided to do,' he thought, 'and then – then go and see her in prison, her, yesterday's prisoner, and tell her everything.'

And when he pictured himself seeing her and telling her everything, confessing his guilt to her, telling her he would do everything in his power to atone for it by marrying her, an extraordinary feeling of elation seized him, and tears came into his eyes.

34

ARRIVING at the court-house Nekhlyudov met the usher of the day before in the passage again and asked him where the prisoners were held after sentence, and to whom one had to apply for permission to visit them. The usher explained that the prisoners were held in different places, and that, until their sentence was announced in its final form, permission to visit them depended on the public prosecutor.

'I'll come and call you myself, after the sitting, and take you to him. He isn't even here yet. But after the session you can see him. And now please go in – they're just starting.'

Nekhlyudov thanked the usher (who today seemed to him much to be pitied) for his kindness, and went to the jury-room.

As he approached, the other jurymen were just leaving it to go into the court. The merchant was as jolly, and had eaten and drunk as liberally as on the day before, and greeted Nekhlyudov like an old friend. And Piotr Gerassimovich did not excite any aversion in Nekhlyudov today by his familiarity and loud laughter.

Nekhlyudov felt like telling all the jurymen, too, about his relations to yesterday's defendant. 'By rights,' he thought to himself, 'I ought to have got up during the trial yesterday and made a public acknowledgement of my guilt.' But when he entered the court with the other jurymen, and the procedure of the day before was repeated – again 'The Court approaches!', again three men on the platform in their embroidered collars, the same silence, the same settling of the jury in their high-backed chairs, the gendarmes, the portrait, the priest – he felt that though he ought to have done so he could not have brought himself yesterday either to disturb this solemnity.

The preparations for the trial were the same as on the day before, except that the swearing in of the jury and the president's address were omitted.

Today the case was one of burglary. The defendant, guarded by two gendarmes with drawn swords, was a thin narrow-chested lad of twenty, in a grey prison cloak and with a grey bloodless face. He sat all alone in the dock, peering from under his eyebrows at everyone who entered the court. The lad was accused of having, together with a companion, broken into a shed and stolen some old mats valued at three roubles and sixty-seven kopecks. It appeared from the indictment that a policeman had stopped the boy as he was walking away with his companion, who was carrying the mats on his shoulder.

The pair at once confessed and both were locked up. The lad's companion, a locksmith, had died in prison, so the boy was to be tried alone. The old mats lay on the table as material evidence.

The case was conducted in exactly the same way as on the previous day, with all the ritual of argument, evidence, witnesses, their swearing-in, questioning, experts and cross-examinations. To each and every question put to him by the president, the prosecutor and the counsel for the defence the policeman called as a witness answered with complete lack of interest: 'Exactly, sir' . . . 'I couldn't say, sir' . . . 'Exactly' . . . But in spite of the fact that he had been drilled into stupidity and had become a mere machine he was clearly sorry for the lad and reluctant to testify about his arrest.

The other witness, the proprietor of the house and owner of the mats, evidently a splenetic old man, when asked whether he identified the mats, very unwillingly answered that he did; but when the assistant prosecutor began to ask him what he had intended doing with the mats, and were they of much use to him, he waxed angry and replied:

'The devil take the mats – I don't want them. Had I known there'd be all this fuss I'd never have gone looking for them. I'd have thrown in a ten-rouble note with them – a couple of ten-rouble notes, even – not to be dragged here and pestered with questions. I have spent something like five roubles on cabs alone. And I'm not in good health. I suffer from hernia and rheumatism.'

So testified the witnesses, but the accused himself confessed everything and, looking unseeingly around like a trapped animal, related in a halting voice how it had all happened.

It was a clear case, but the assistant prosecutor kept shrugging his shoulders as he had the day before, and putting artful questions calculated to entrap a wily criminal.

In his speech he argued that the theft had been from occupied premises and accompanied by forcible entry, and therefore the lad must be most severely punished.

The lawyer briefed for the defence maintained that the theft had not been from occupied premises and that therefore, although the crime could not be denied, the criminal was not yet the menace to society that the assistant prosecutor asserted.

The president, as on the previous day, personified impartiality and justice, and in detail explained to the jury, and impressed on them, what they already knew and could not help knowing. As on the day before, there were adjournments, again they smoked, again the usher proclaimed 'The Court approaches!' and again, trying not to fall asleep, the two gendarmes sat with their drawn swords threatening the prisoner.

The proceedings revealed that the lad's father had apprenticed him to a tobacco factory, where he had remained five years. This year he had been discharged after some trouble between the master and the men, and, being out of work, he had wandered about the town, spending his last kopeck on drink. In an inn he fell in with another like himself, a locksmith by trade and a heavy drinker, who had lost his job before the prisoner had, and that night the pair of them, drunk, had broken the lock of a shed and taken the first thing they happened to lay hands on. They were caught. They made a full confession. They were held in prison, where the locksmith died while awaiting trial. And now the boy was being tried as a dangerous character against whom society must be protected.

'Just as dangerous a creature as yesterday's criminal,' thought Nekhlyudov, listening to all that was going on. '*They* are dangerous – but aren't we dangerous? . . . I am a rake, a fornicator, a liar – and all of us, all those who know me for what I am, not only do not despise me but respect me. But even supposing this lad were more dangerous to society than anyone in this room what in common sense ought to be done when he gets caught?

'It's quite obvious that this lad is no extraordinary villain, but just an ordinary person – anyone can see that – and that he became what he is simply because he found himself in circumstances which create such people. And so it seems obvious that if we don't want lads like this we must try to wipe out the conditions that produce such unfortunate individuals.

'But what do we do? By chance we get hold of just one such unfortunate lad, knowing quite well that a thousand others remain at liberty, and shut him up in prison, in conditions of complete idleness or work of the most unhealthy, senseless kind, in company with fellow beings like himself, debilitated and confused by life, and then deport him at public expense to Irkutsk in company with the most depraved characters from Moscow and surrounding places.

'We do not merely do nothing to get rid of the conditions in which such people are born – we actually encourage the institutions which produce them. We all know what these institutions are: the mills, the factories, the workshops, the inns, the pot-houses, the brothels. And far from wiping out establishments of this sort – considering them necessary, we encourage and regulate them.

'We rear not one but millions of such people, and then arrest one and imagine that we have done something, protected ourselves, and that nothing more can be required of us, now we have transported him from Moscow to Irkutsk,' reflected Nekhlyudov with unusual verve and clarity, sitting in his chair next to the colonel and listening to the different tones of voice of the defending counsel, the assistant prosecutor and the president, and watching their self-confident gestures. 'And how much effort, what strenuous efforts, this pretence costs,' Nekhlyudov went on thinking to himself as he looked round the huge court-room, seeing the portraits, the lamps, the arm-chairs, the uniforms, the thick walls, the windows, and remembering the great size of the building and the still more enormous size of the establishment, the whole army of officials, clerks, warders, messengers, not only here but throughout Russia, who received salaries for performing this farce that nobody needed. 'Supposing we spent even a hundredth part of all this effort on helping these derelict creatures whom we now look upon merely as so many arms and bodies vitally necessary for our comfort and tranquillity? It only needed one person,' thought Nekhlyudov, looking at the sickly scared face of the lad, 'to take pity on him when poverty made his father send him from the village to the town, and lend a helping hand; or later, after he had come to town – if there had been someone to say, "I wouldn't do that, Vanya, it isn't right," when at the end of twelve hours' work in the factory the older men were tempting him to go to the pot-house – the boy wouldn't have gone, or got into bad ways, and would not have done anything wrong.

'But no one was found to take pity on him – not one single person – during all those years of his apprenticeship, when this poor chap was living in the city like some wild animal, with his hair cropped short against lice, running errands for his masters; on the contrary, all he heard from his masters and his companions after he came to live in town, was that the man who cheats, drinks, swears, brawls and leads a generally dissolute life is a fine fellow.

'Then, when he is ill and vitiated by unhealthy work, drink and debauchery, and knocking aimlessly about town in a bewildered stupor gets into some sort of shed and takes some old mats which nobody needs – then we, all of us well-to-do, educated people in easy circumstances, instead of trying to get rid of the causes which had led the boy to his present condition, think to mend matters by punishing him!

'Terrible! And which is worse – the cruelty of it or the absurdity? Anyway, both seem to have been brought to their ultimate limit.'

Nekhlyudov was thinking all this and no longer listening to what was going on. And he was horrified by what he was discovering. He could not understand why he hadn't been able to see it before, and how it was others could not see it.

35

A T the first adjournment Nekhlyudov got up and went into the corridor, having made up his mind not to return to the court-room again. Let them do what they liked with him, he was not taking any further part in that awful, horrible tomfoolery.

Having inquired for the office of the public prosecutor, he went straight to him. The attendant did not want to admit him, explaining that the prosecutor was busy now. But Nekhlyudov, paying no heed, walked through the door, requesting the clerk who came forward to announce his name to the prosecutor and say that he was on the jury and had very important business with him. Nekhlyudov's title and good clothes helped. The official announced him to the prosecutor, and Nekhlyudov was admitted. The prosecutor met him standing, obviously annoyed at Nekhlyudov's persistence.

'What is it you want?' asked the prosecutor sternly.

'I am on the jury, my name is Nekhlyudov, and I must see the prisoner Maslova,' said Nekhlyudov quickly and with determination, blushing and feeling that he was taking a step which would have a decisive influence on his whole life.

The public prosecutor was a short dark man with short grizzled hair, quick flashing eyes and a thick clipped beard on his protruding lower jaw.

'Maslova? Oh yes, I know. Accused of poisoning,' the prosecutor said quietly. 'But why must you see her?'

And then, as though wishing to soften the acerbity of his question, he added: 'I cannot give you permission until I know your reason for wanting it.'

'I require it for a particularly important reason,' Nekhlyudov began, reddening.

'Indeed,' said the prosecutor, and lifting his eyes gazed attentively at Nekhlyudov. 'Has her case been heard or not?'

'She was tried yesterday and quite irregularly sentenced to four years' hard labour. She is innocent.'

'Yes? If she was sentenced only yesterday,' said the prosecutor, ignoring Nekhlyudov's declaration concerning Maslova's innocence, 'she must still be in the preliminary detention prison until the sentence is promulgated in its final form. Visiting is allowed there on certain days only. I should advise you to inquire there.'

'But I must see her as soon as possible,' said Nekhlyudov, his jaw trembling as he felt the decisive moment approaching.

'Why must you?' asked the prosecutor, somewhat uneasily raising his eyebrows.

'Because she is innocent and has been sentenced to hard labour. But it is I who am the guilty one,' said Nekhlyudov in a voice shaking with emotion, feeling that he was saying what need not be said.

'How is that?' asked the public prosecutor.

'Because I seduced her and brought her to her present pass. If she were not what I helped to make her she would not now have been subjected to such an accusation.'

'All the same, I fail to see what that has to do with your visiting her.'

'This: I want to follow her to Siberia and . . . marry her,' Nekhlyudov brought out, and, as always, immediately he spoke of it, the tears started to his eyes.

'Really? Dear me!' said the prosecutor. 'This is certainly a very exceptional case. You are, I believe, a member of the Krasnopersk Rural Council?' he asked, apparently recalling having heard before of this Nekhlyudov who was now expressing such a strange decision.

'I beg your pardon, but I do not think that has any connexion with my request,' retorted Nekhlyudov, flaring angrily.

'Of course not,' said the prosecutor, with a scarcely perceptible smile and not in the least abashed, 'only your wish is so unusual and so out of the common . . .'

'Then may I have the permit?'

'The permit? Certainly, I will give you an order of admittance at once. Please take a seat.'

He went up to the table, sat down and began to write.

'Please be seated.'

Nekhlyudov remained standing.

Having written the order and handed it to Nekhlyudov, the prosecutor looked at him curiously.

'I must also inform you,' said Nekhlyudov, 'that I can no longer take part in the sessions.'

'For that you will have to lay valid reasons before the Court, as you know.'

'My reasons are that I consider all law-courts not only useless but immoral.'

'Do you?' said the public prosecutor with the same barely perceptible smile, the smile implying that he had heard that sort of thing before and found it rather amusing. 'That may be, but I am sure you will understand that I, as public prosecutor, cannot agree with you on this point. Therefore I should advise you to state your case to the Court, and the Court will consider your application and find it valid or not valid, and in the latter instance will impose a fine. Apply, then, to the Court.'

'I have declared myself and am not going anywhere else,' Nekhlyudov said angrily.

'Then, good day, sir,' said the public prosecutor, with a bow, evidently anxious to be rid of this strange visitor.

'Who was that?' asked a member of the Court entering the room just as Nekhlyudov was going out.

'Nekhlyudov; you know, the one who used to make all sorts of strange proposals at the Krasnopersk Rural Council meetings. Just fancy! He is serving on the jury, and among the defendants there was some woman or girl sentenced to penal servitude whom he says he seduced, and now he wants to marry her.'

'Impossible!'

'That's what he told me . . . he's in a very excited state.'

'There's something abnormal about young people these days.'

'But he is not so very young.'

'No? Oh, I must tell you, my dear fellow, how your famous Ivashenkov bored us to tears. He carries the day by wearing one out: talks and talks, there's no end to it.'

'People of that kind should simply be stopped; otherwise they become real obstructionists . . .'

36

FROM the public prosecutor Nekhlyudov went straight to the preliminary detention prison. But it turned out there was no Maslova there, and the chief warder explained to him that she must be in the old deportation prison. Nekhlyudov drove there.

Maslova was there all right. The public prosecutor had forgotten that six months previously some political incident had been exaggerated to the utmost limits by the gendarmery, with the result, it would seem, that all the preliminary detention centres had been swamped by students, doctors, labourers, girl-students and doctors' assistants.

There was a huge distance between the two prisons, and it was almost nightfall before Nekhlyudov reached the deportation prison. He was about to go up to the door of the vast gloomy building when the sentry stopped him, and he only rang. A gaoler came in answer to the bell. Nekhlyudov showed him his order of admittance but the gaoler said he could not let him in without the superintendent's permission. Nekhlyudov went to the superintendent's quarters. As he was going up the stairs he heard through a door the sounds of an elaborate bravura being played on the piano. When a sulky servant-girl with a bandage over one eye opened the door to him, the sounds seemed to burst out of the room and strike his ears. It was the well-known *Rhapsody* of Liszt that everybody was tired of, splendidly played but only up to a certain point. When this passage was reached the pianist went back over it again. Nekhlyudov asked the maid with the bandaged eye if the superintendent was in. She replied that he was not.

'Will he be back soon?'

The *Rhapsody* again stopped, and was again repeated loudly and brilliantly up to the bewitched passage.

'I will go and ask.'

And the servant went away.

The *Rhapsody* was in full swing once more but suddenly, before reaching the charmed place, broke off and a woman's voice came from the other side of the door.

'Tell him he is not in and won't be today. He is out visiting. What do they come bothering for?'

The *Rhapsody* began again but stopped, and there was the sound of a chair being pushed back. Evidently the irritated performer wanted to give a piece of her mind to the tiresome caller who had come out of hours.

'Papa is not in,' expostulated a pale, ill-looking girl with crimped hair and dark circles round her dull eyes, as she came out into the ante-room; but the sight of a young man in a well-cut coat mollified her. 'Won't you come in? What is it you want?'

'I should like to see one of the prisoners here.'

'A political prisoner, I suppose?'

'No, not a political prisoner. I have a permit from the public prosecutor.'

'Well, I don't know, papa is out. But do come in, please,' she invited him in again from the little ante-room. 'Or you could speak to his assistant. He is in the office now. What is your name?'

'Thank you,' said Nekhlyudov, without answering her question, and went out.

The door had hardly closed upon him when the same gay lively strains were heard again, so ill-suited both to the surroundings they came from and to the appearance of the sickly girl so resolutely practising them. In the courtyard Nekhlyudov met a young officer with bristly dyed moustaches, and asked for the assistant superintendent. It was the assistant himself. He took the permit, looked at it and said that he could not admit him on a pass for the preliminary detention prison. Besides, it was too late . . .

'Come back tomorrow. Tomorrow at ten o'clock everybody is allowed in. You come then, and you will find the superintendent himself here. You could see the prisoner in the common room, or, if the superintendent allows it, in the office.'

And so, not having succeeded in obtaining an interview that day, Nekhlyudov set off for home. Agitated at the idea of seeing her, Nekhlyudov walked through the streets, thinking now not of the court but of his conversation with the public prosecutor and the prison superintendents. The fact that he had been seeking an interview with her and had told the public prosecutor of his intention, and had been to two prisons in order to see her excited him to such an extent that it was a long time before he could compose himself. When he got home he immediately fetched out his long-neglected diaries, read a few passages out of them, and entered the following:

'For two years I have not kept my diary, and I thought I should never return to such childishness. Yet it was not childishness but converse with my own self, the true divine self which lives in every man. All this time I was asleep and there was no one for me to converse with. This self of mine was awakened by an extraordinary event on the 28th of April, in the law-court, where I was one of the jury. I saw her in the prisoners' dock, the Katusha I seduced, in a prison cloak. Through a strange mistake, for which I blame myself, she was sentenced to penal servitude. I have just come back from the public prosecutor and the prison. They would not let me see her but I am determined to do all in my power to see her, confess to her and atone for my sin – by marriage if need be. O Lord, do Thou help me! My soul is at peace and I am full of joy.'

37

MASLOVA could not get to sleep for a long time that night but lay with wide-open eyes looking at the door, which the sub-deacon's daughter hid from view every time she paced to and fro, and listening to the red-haired woman's sniffling.

She was thinking that not for anything would she marry a convict at Sakhalin but arrange matters differently somehow – with one of the prison officials, a clerk, even a warder, even an assistant warder. All men were susceptible to a woman. 'Only I mustn't get thin. That would be the end of me.' And she remembered how her lawyer had looked at her, and also the judge, and the people she met at the court who had walked past her on purpose. She remembered what Berta, who paid her a visit at the gaol, had told her about the student she had been so fond of while she was at Madame Kitayeva's. He had gone to them and inquired about her, and said he was very sorry for her. She thought of the fight with the red-haired woman and felt sorry for her; she thought of the baker, who had sent out an extra roll. She thought of many people but not Nekhlyudov. She never recalled to mind her childhood and youth, and least of all her love for Nekhlyudov. That would have been too painful. Those memories lay untouched somewhere deep in her soul. She never even dreamed about Nekhlyudov. She had not recognized him that day in the court, not so much because when she last saw him he was a beardless man in uniform, with a small moustache and hair which, though it was short, was thick and curly, whereas now he was approaching middle age and had a beard – it was simply because she never thought of him. She had buried all her memories of him on that terrible dark night when he had passed through the town on his way from the army without stopping to see his aunts.

Until that night, as long as she could hope that he would come, she did not feel oppressed by the child she carried beneath her heart – indeed, she was often moved to wonder by the gentle but sometimes sudden stirring inside her body. But with that night everything changed and the unborn child became nothing but an encumbrance.

His aunts had expected Nekhlyudov, and had asked him to come and see them in passing, but he had telegraphed that he could not because he had to be in Petersburg at a certain time. When Katusha heard this she decided to go to the station and see him. The train was due to pass through at two o'clock in the morning. After helping the old ladies to bed she put on a pair of old boots, threw a shawl over her head and, persuading the cook's daughter, Masha, to come with her, gathered up her skirts and ran to the station.

It was a dark, rainy, windy night in autumn. The rain now splashed down in warm, heavy drops, now stopped again. In the field they could not see the path beneath their feet but in the wood it was black as pitch, and Katusha, though she knew the way, lost it in the woods and reached the little station where the train stopped for three minutes, not ahead of time, as she had hoped, but after the second bell. Hurrying on to the platform, Katusha saw him at once at the window of a first-class carriage. This carriage had a particularly bright light. Two officers without their tunics were sitting opposite each other on the velvet seats, playing cards. On the small table near the window two stout dripping candles were burning. In close-fitting breeches and a white shirt he sat on the arm of a seat, leaning against the back and laughing at something. As soon as she saw him she tapped at the carriage window with her benumbed hand. But at that very instant the last bell rang and the train, after a backward jerk, slowly began to move, and then one after another the carriages jolted forward. One of the players rose with the cards in his hand and looked out. She tapped again and pressed her face to the window. At that moment the carriage where she was standing gave a jerk and began to move. She went with it, looking through the window. The officer tried to lower the window but could not. Nekhlyudov got up and pushing the officer aside began lowering it himself. The train gathered speed. She quickened her step, keeping up with it, but the train went faster and faster, and just when the window was down the guard pushed her aside and jumped in. Katusha was left behind but she went on running along the wet boards of the platform; then the platform came to an end and it was all she could do to save herself from falling as she ran down the steps. She kept on running but the first-class carriage was far away in front. Now the second-class carriages were racing past her, then, faster still, those of the third class, but still she ran. When the last carriage with the lamp at the back had gone by she was beyond the water tank which fed the engines, out in the open with no protection, and the wind pounced on her, snatching her shawl from her head and making her skirts cling to her legs. The wind carried off her shawl but still she ran.

'Auntie Mikhailovna!' screamed the little girl, barely keeping up with her. 'You've lost your shawl!'

Katusha stopped, threw back her head and clasping it with both hands sobbed aloud. 'There he sits on a velvet chair in a lighted carriage, joking and drinking,' she thought, 'and I stand here in the mud and dark, in the rain and the wind, weeping.'

'Gone!' she cried.

The little girl was frightened and put her arms round Katusha's wet dress.

'Auntie, let's go home.'

'A train will come – I'll throw myself under the wheels, and it'll all be over,' Katusha was thinking, not answering the little girl.

Yes, that was what she would do. But just then, as always happens in the first moment of quiet after great agitation, the child within her, his child, suddenly jerked, gave a push, softly stretched itself and again pushed with something thin, delicate and sharp. And suddenly all that a moment before had tortured her so, until it seemed impossible to go on living, all her bitterness against him and the desire to be revenged upon him if only by her own death – all this suddenly faded. She pulled herself together, smoothed her dress, put the shawl on her head and went home.

Exhausted, wet and muddy, she returned home, and that day saw the beginning of the change in her which had made her what she was now. After that dreadful night she ceased to believe in God and goodness. Before that she had believed in God and believed that other people did, too, but after that night she was convinced that no one believed in Him and that all they said about God and goodness was just in order to cheat people. He, the man she had loved and who had loved her – she knew he had – had deserted her, having had his pleasure of her and outraging her feelings. Yet he was the best man she had ever known. All the others were worse still. And everything which happened afterwards, at every turn, confirmed this. His aunts, who were pious old women, turned her out of the house when she could no longer serve them as she used to. The women she came in contact with all tried to make money out of her, and the men, from the old district police-officer to the prison warders, looked upon her as an instrument for pleasure. And no one in the world cared for anything else but pleasure, just this pleasure. The old writer with whom she lived during the second year of her life of independence had confirmed her still more in this belief. He used to tell her in so many words that all the happiness of life consisted in this – he called it poetry and aesthetics.

Everybody lived for himself only, for his own pleasure, and all the talk about God and righteousness was an illusion. And if sometimes doubts arose in her mind and she wondered why everything was so badly arranged in the world that everyone was so wicked to each other and hurt each other, it was better not to think of it. When you feel depressed – have a cigarette or a drink or, best of all, make love, and it will pass.

38

THE next day was Sunday and at five o'clock in the morning when the customary whistle sounded in the women's section of the prison Korablyova, who was already awake, roused Maslova.

'I am a convict,' thought Maslova with horror, rubbing her eyes and involuntarily breathing in the air that had become terribly fetid towards morning. She would have liked to go to sleep again, into the realm of oblivion, but the habit of fear was stronger than sleepiness, and she roused herself and sat up, drawing her feet under her and looking about the room. The women were all awake, only the children still slept. The vodka-seller with the bulging eyes was pulling a prison cloak from beneath the children, gently, so as not to wake them. The woman who had attacked the recruiting party was at the stove, hanging up to dry the rags that served the baby as swaddling clothes, while the baby screamed desperately in the arms of blue-eyed Fedosya, who was swaying to and fro with it and trying to hush it with a tender lullaby. The consumptive was coughing, clutching her chest, the blood rushing to her face, breathing heavily, almost with a scream, in the intervals of coughing. The red-haired woman was lying on her back with her fat knees drawn up, loudly and gaily relating the dream she had had. The old woman accused of arson was standing in front of the ikon again, crossing herself and bowing, and repeating the same words over and over in a whisper. The subdeacon's daughter sat motionless on her bunk, still half asleep, gazing before her with vacant eyes. Beauty was curling her coarse greasy black hair round her finger.

Footsteps were heard shuffling along the corridor, the lock rattled and two convict scavengers, in jackets and grey trousers that did not reach anywhere near their ankles, came in. With earnest cross faces they lifted the stinking tub on to a yoke and carried it away. The women went out to the taps in the corridor to wash. There a quarrel broke out between the red-haired woman and a woman from another cell. Again abuse, screams and complaints . . .

'Is it the punishment cell you want?' shouted the warder, giving the red-headed woman a slap on her fat bare back that was heard from one end of the corridor to the other. 'Don't let me hear your voice again!'

'Lawks, the old boy's a bit frolicsome today,' said the red-haired woman, taking his action for a caress.

'Look lively now! Get ready for church.'

Maslova had not finished combing her hair when the chief warder entered with his retinue.

'Roll-call!' shouted the warder.

Other prisoners came out from other cells and they all formed two rows along the corridor, the women in the rear placing their hands on the shoulders of those in front. They were all counted.

After the roll-call a female warder led the prisoners into church. Maslova and Fedosya were in the middle of a column of over a hundred women from the different cells. All of them wore white kerchiefs, jackets and skirts, except for a few here and there in their own coloured garments. These were wives who, with their children, were following their convict husbands to Siberia. The entire stairway was filled with this procession. The soft patter of feet in prison slippers mingled with voices and occasional laughter. At the bend on the stairs Maslova caught sight of her enemy, Botchkova, who was walking in front, and pointed out her spiteful face to Fedosya. When they reached the foot of the stairs the women were silent and, crossing themselves and bowing, they passed through the open doors into the as yet empty church, all glittering with gold. Their places were on the right and they crowded in, jostling and pushing one another. Immediately after the women the men came in in their grey prison cloaks: convicts on their way to Siberia, men serving a term of imprisonment and others banished from their village communes.

Coughing noisily, they formed themselves into a solid crowd on the left and in the centre of the church. Up above in the choir gallery were those who had been brought in earlier: on one side hard-labour convicts with half-shaven heads, whose presence was indicated by the clanking of the chains on their feet; on the other, prisoners awaiting trial (these wore no chains and their heads were not shaven).

The prison church had been newly erected and decorated by a wealthy merchant who had spent some tens of thousands of roubles on it, and it fairly glittered with bright colours and gold.

For a time the silence in the church was broken only by coughing, the blowing of noses, babies crying and an occasional rattle of chains. Presently the prisoners standing in the middle shifted and pressed against each other to make a passage down the centre for the superintendent, who walked to the front of them all and stationed himself in the middle of the church.

39 ·

THE service began.

The service went like this: the priest, having robed in a peculiar, strange and very inconvenient garment of gold cloth, cut and arranged little bits of bread on a saucer and then put most of them into a cup of wine, at the same time repeating various names and prayers. Meanwhile the subdeacon steadily went on, first reading various prayers and then singing them turn and turn about with the choir of convicts. These prayers were in old Slavonic – difficult enough to understand at any time but made still more incomprehensible by the rapidity with which they were read and sung. They consisted mainly of supplications for the well-being of the Emperor and his family. These petitions were repeated in prayer after prayer, sometimes separately, sometimes in conjunction with other prayers, the congregation kneeling. In addition to this the subdeacon read several verses from the Acts of the Apostles in such a strange tense voice that it was impossible to understand a thing, and the priest read very distinctly the passage from the Gospel according to St Mark wherein we are told how Christ, being risen from the dead, before flying up to heaven to sit on the right hand of His Father, appeared first to Mary Magdalene, out of whom he had cast seven devils, and then to the eleven disciples, and ordered them to preach the gospel to every creature, at the same time declaring that he that believeth not shall be damned but he that believeth and is baptized shall be saved and shall, moreover, cast out devils, heal people of their sickness by laying his hands on them, speak with new tongues, take up serpents and not die if he drink any deadly thing but remain unharmed.[1]

The essence of the service consisted in the supposition that the bits of bread cut up by the priest and put into the wine, when manipulated and prayed over in a certain way are transformed into the body and blood of God. These manipulations consisted in the priest uniformly raising his arms and holding them aloft, hampered though he was by the gold cloth sack he had on, then sinking to his knees and kissing the table and the objects on it. But the most important operation was when the priest picked up a napkin in both hands and rhythmically and smoothly waved it over the saucer and the golden cup. This was supposed to be the moment when the bread and wine turned into flesh and blood, and therefore this part of the service was performed with the utmost solemnity.

'More especially for our most holy and undefiled, most blessed Mother of God,' the priest cried loudly after this from behind the screen, and the choir sang out solemnly that it was a very good thing to glorify the Virgin Mary who had given birth to Christ without impairing her virginity and so was worthy of greater honour than some kind of cherubim and

1. Passages on the Resurrection are read during Matins – not during the Liturgy, which Tolstoy thinks to describe here.

greater glory than some kind of seraphim. After this the transformation was considered accomplished, and the priest, having
taken the napkin from the saucer, cut the middle piece of
bread in four and put it, first into the wine and then into his
mouth. The idea was that he had eaten a piece of God's flesh
and swallowed a sip of His blood. Next the priest drew aside a
curtain, opened the doors in the middle and taking the golden
cup in his hands came out with it into the centre of the doors
and invited those who also wished to partake of the body and
blood of God contained in the cup to come and do so.

A few children appeared to want to.

After having asked the children their names the priest carefully took a bit of bread soaked in wine out of the cup with a
spoon and thrust it far into the mouth of each child in turn,
while the subdeacon, wiping the children's mouths, in a gay
voice sang a song about the children eating God's flesh and
drinking His blood. After that the priest carried the cup back
behind the partition, and drinking up all the blood left in the
cup and eating all the remaining bits of God's body, and pains-
takingly licking round his moustaches and wiping his mouth
and the cup, briskly marched out from behind the partition,
in the most cheerful frame of mind, the thin soles of his calf-
skin boots creaking slightly as he walked.

The most important part of this Christian service was now
over. But the priest, anxious to console the unfortunate
prisoners, added another service to the ordinary one. This
special service consisted in the priest taking his stance in front
of an image in gilt (with a black face and black hands)
illuminated by a dozen wax candles, of the very same God he
had been eating, and proceeding to recite the following words,
not exactly singing and not exactly speaking, in a strange
artificial voice:

'Jesu, most sweet, O glory of the apostles, O Jesu mine,
lauded by the martyrs, Almighty ruler, Jesu save me; Jesu
my Saviour, Jesu most beautiful, have mercy upon me, who
dost turn to Thee, Jesu my Saviour, by the prayers of her who

didst bear Thee, and of all Thy saints, O Jesu, and of all the prophets, Jesu my Saviour; and make me worthy of the joys of heaven, O Jesu, lover of mankind.'

Here he paused, drew breath, crossed himself, bowed to the ground, and everyone else did likewise. The superintendent bowed, so did the warders and the prisoners, and above in the gallery shackles clanked very frequently indeed.

'Creator of the angels and Lord of hosts,' he continued, 'Jesu most wondrous, marvel of the angels; Jesu most powerful, redeemer of our forefathers; Jesu most sweet, exaltation of patriarchs; Jesu most glorious, the support of kings; Jesu most blessed, the fulfilment of prophets; Jesu most wonderful, of martyrs the strength; Jesu most gentle, of monks the joy; Jesu most merciful, of priests the sweetness; Jesu most charitable, the continence of those that fast; Jesu most sweet, the delight of the just; Jesu most pure, the chastity of virgins; Jesu before all ages, of sinners the salvation; Jesu, Son of God, have mercy upon me,' he reached a halt at last, his voice more wheezy every time he repeated the word 'Jesu'. Holding up his silk-lined vestment with his hand and letting himself down on one knee he bowed to the ground, and the choir sang the last words 'Jesu, Son of God, have mercy upon me', while the prisoners fell to their knees and rose again, tossing back the hair that was left on the unshaven half of their heads and rattling the chains that chafed their thin legs.

This continued for a very long time. First came the praises which ended with the words 'Have mercy upon me', and then fresh praises ending with the word 'Alleluia'. And the prisoners crossed themselves, bowed and fell to the ground. At first the prisoners bowed at every clause, then they started to bow after every two, and then it was after every three, and they were all very glad when the glorification ended and the priest, with a sigh of relief, shut the book and retired behind the partition. One last act remained: the priest picked up from a large table a gilt cross with enamelled medallions at the ends, and came out into the centre of the church with it.

First the superintendent approached and kissed the cross, then his assistant and the warders; and lastly the convicts, pushing and jostling and abusing each other in whispers, came forward. Chatting with the superintendent, the priest stuck the cross and his hand at the mouths, and sometimes the noses of the convicts coming up to him, who were anxious to kiss both the cross and the priest's hand. Thus ended the Christian divine service, performed for the comfort and edification of our brethren who had erred and gone astray.

40

AND to not one of those present, from the priest and the superintendent down to Maslova, did it occur that this Jesus Whose name the priest repeated in wheezy tones such an endless number of times, praising Him with outlandish words, had expressly forbidden everything that was being done there; that He had not only prohibited the senseless chatter and the blasphemous incantation over the bread and wine but had also, in the most emphatic manner, forbidden men to call other men their master or to pray in temples, and had commanded each to pray in solitude; had forbidden temples themselves, saying that He came to destroy them and that one should worship not in temples but in spirit and in truth; and above everything else He had forbidden not only sitting in judgement on people and imprisoning, humiliating, torturing and executing them, as was done here, but had even prohibited any kind of violence, saying that He came to set at liberty those that were captive.

It did not occur to any one of those present that everything that was going on there was the greatest blasphemy, and a mockery of the same Christ in Whose name it was all being done. No one seemed to realize that the gilt cross with the enamel medallions at the ends, which the priest held out to the people to kiss, was nothing else but the emblem of the gallows on which Christ had been executed for denouncing the very things now being performed here in His name. It did not occur to anyone that the priests, who imagined they were eating the body and drinking the blood of Christ in the form of bread and wine, were indeed eating His body and drinking His blood – but not in little bits of bread and in the wine, but first by misleading 'these little ones' with whom Christ identified Himself and then by depriving them of their greatest blessing and subjecting them to the most cruel torments, by concealing from them the good things that He had brought them.

The priest performed his functions with an easy conscience because he had been brought up from childhood to believe that this was the one true faith which had been held by all the saints that had ever lived and was held now by the spiritual and temporal authorities. He did not believe that the bread became flesh, or that it was good for the soul to pronounce a great number of words, or that he had really devoured a bit of God – no one could believe that – but he believed that one ought to believe it. But the main thing that confirmed him in this faith was the fact that, in return for fulfilling the demands of this faith, for eighteen years now he had been drawing an income which enabled him to support his family, and send his son to a high-school and his daughter to a school for the daughters of clergy. The subdeacon believed in these things even more firmly than the priest, since he had entirely forgotten the substance of the dogmas of this faith, and only knew that the warm water for the wine, prayers for the dead, the Hours, a simple thanksgiving service and a choral thanksgiving service – everything had its fixed price which devout Christians gladly paid, and therefore he called out his 'Have mercy, Have mercy', and sang and read what he had to sing and read as a matter of course, just as another man sells wood or flour or potatoes. The prison superintendent and the warders, though they had never either known or tried to find out what the dogmas of the faith consisted in, and what all that went on in the church meant, believed that one must believe in this faith because the higher authorities and the Tsar himself believed in it. Besides, they felt dimly (they could never have explained why) that this creed was a justification of their cruel duties. But for this creed it would have been harder for them – impossible, even – to employ all their energies tormenting people, as they did now with a perfectly easy conscience. The superintendent was such a kind-hearted man that he could never live as he was now living, if he had not been sustained by his religion. And so he stood motionless and straight, assiduously bowed and crossed himself, tried to feel deeply moved when 'The Cherubim' was being sung, and when the priest began to administer the Sacrament to the children he stepped forward and lifted one of them up to the priest with his own hands.

The majority of the prisoners (with the exception of a few who saw through the deception practised on those who adhered to this faith, and laughed at it in their hearts) – the majority of them believed that these gilded ikons, candles, chalices, vestments, crosses, repetitions of incomprehensible words, 'Jesu most sweet' and 'Have mercy', possessed a mystic power by means of which a great many comforts might be obtained, in this life and in the life to come. Though most of them had made several attempts – by means of prayers, special services, candles – to get the goods of this life, and their prayers had remained unanswered, each of them was firmly convinced that their lack of success was accidental and that the establishment, approved by learned men and by archbishops, must be a thing of the greatest importance, and indispensable, if not for this life, at any rate for the hereafter.

Maslova believed the same way. Like the others she felt a mixed feeling during the service of devotion and boredom. At first she stood in the middle of the crowd behind a railing and could see no one except her companions; but when the communicants began to move forward she and Fedosya moved forward too, and then she saw the superintendent, and behind the superintendent and between the warders she espied a little peasant with a very light beard and fair hair – – Fedosya's husband, who never took his eyes off his wife. All through the anthem Maslova busied herself in scrutinizing him and exchanging whispers with Fedosya, and only crossed herself and bowed when everyone else did.

41

NEKHLYUDOV left home early. There was still a peasant from the country driving along a side street and calling out 'Milk-o, milk-o, milk-o!' in the voice peculiar to his trade.

The first warm spring rain had fallen the day before, and now, wherever the ground was not paved, green grass sprouted. The birch-trees in the gardens looked as if they were covered with green fluff; the wild cherry and the poplars were unfolding their long fragrant leaves, and in shops and houses the double window-frames were being removed and the windows cleaned. In the second-hand market, which Nekhlyudov had to pass on his way, a dense crowd was surging along the row of booths, and tattered men walked about with boots under their arms and smoothly ironed trousers and waistcoats hanging over their shoulders.

Men in clean coats and shining boots, having the Sunday off from their factories, and women with bright silk kerchiefs on their heads and jackets embroidered with glass beads, were already crowding round the doors of the taverns. Policemen, with the yellow cords of their pistols, stood on their beats, on the look-out for a scrimmage which might help to dispel the boredom that oppressed them. Along the paths of the boulevard and on the fresh green grass children and dogs ran about playing, while the old women sat on the benches gossiping happily to each other.

In the streets, still cool and damp on the shady side on the left, and dried up in the middle, heavy carts rumbled over the carriageway, cabs rattled and tramcars rang their bells. On all sides the air vibrated with the pealing and clanging of church bells calling people to a service like the one that was now taking place in the prison. And the people, dressed in their Sunday best, were making their way to their different parish churches.

The cabby drove Nekhlyudov not up to the prison itself but to the turning that led to the prison.

A number of people, men and women, most of them with small bundles, stood at this turning, about a hundred yards from the prison. On the right there were some low wooden buildings; and on the left a two-storied house with some sort of sign outside. The huge brick building, the prison proper, was just in front, but the visitors were not allowed to go near it. An armed sentry paced backwards and forwards, shouting roughly at anyone who tried to pass him.

At the gate to the wooden buildings on the right, opposite the sentry, a warder in a uniform with gold lace was sitting on a bench, a notebook in his hand. The visitors went up to him and said whom they wanted to see, and he wrote the names down. Nekhlyudov also went up, and gave the name of Katerina Maslova. The warder with the gold lace made a note of it.

'Why are we not allowed in?' asked Nekhlyudov.

'The service is still going on. When the service is over you'll be let in.'

Nekhlyudov went over and joined the waiting crowd. A man in ragged clothes and a battered hat, with tattered shoes on his bare feet and red streaks all over his face, detached himself from the crowd and started towards the prison.

'Where d'you think you're going?' the soldier with the gun shouted at him.

'Shut your mouth,' answered the tramp, not in the least intimidated, and turned back. 'If you won't let me in, I can wait. To 'ear 'im shout, anyone'd think 'e was a general.'

The crowd laughed approvingly. The visitors were mostly poorly clad people, some in rags even, but there were some to outward appearances respectable men and women. Next to

Nekhlyudov stood a stout well-dressed man with a clean-shaven red face, carrying a bundle which looked as if it might contain underclothing. Nekhlyudov asked him if this was his first visit. The man with the bundle replied that he came every Sunday, and they got into conversation. He was a commissionaire at a bank; he came to see his brother, who was to be tried for forgery. The amiable fellow told Nekhlyudov the whole story of his life, and was on the point of asking him for his when their attention was distracted by the arrival of a student and a veiled lady, who drove up in a trap with rubber tyres drawn by a big black thoroughbred. The student held a large bundle in his hands. He went up to Nekhlyudov and asked him whether it was permitted, and what must he do, to give the prisoners alms – rolls of bread – he had brought.

'I am doing it at the request of my betrothed. This is my betrothed. Her parents advised us to bring the bread to the convicts.'

'Myself I am here for the first time and I don't know,' said Nekhlyudov, 'but I think you had better ask that man,' and he indicated the warder with the gold lace and the notebook, sitting on the right.

While Nekhlyudov was talking with the student the heavy iron prison doors with a little window in the middle were opened and a uniformed officer accompanied by another warder came out, and the warder with the notebook announced that visitors would now be admitted. The sentry moved aside and all the visitors hurried to the doors, some walking briskly, others actually running as if afraid of being too late. One of the warders stood at the door and as the visitors passed him counted them in a loud voice: 'Sixteen, seventeen,' and so on. Another warder, inside the building, touching each one with his hand, counted them all over again as they went through the second door, so that when the time came for them to leave the numbers should tally, no visitors being left in the prison and no prisoner allowed to escape. This teller, not looking to see who it was filing past, slapped

Nekhlyudov on the back, and for a moment Nekhlyudov felt outraged at the touch of the warder's hand, but he immediately remembered the reason that brought him here and was ashamed of his feeling of annoyance and affront.

Immediately beyond the doors was a large vaulted hall with iron bars to the small windows. In this room, which was called the assembly hall, Nekhlyudov was startled to see a large picture of the Crucifixion, hanging in an alcove.

'What's that here for?' he wondered, his mind involuntarily connecting the image of Christ with liberation and not with captivity.

Nekhlyudov walked slowly, allowing the hurrying visitors to go before him, with mixed feelings of horror at the evildoers who were locked up in this building; of compassion for the innocent, like Katusha and the lad he had seen yesterday; and of shyness and tender emotion at the thought of the meeting before him. As he was leaving the first room he heard the warder at the other end saying something. But, absorbed in his thoughts, Nekhlyudov paid no attention and continued to go where the main stream of visitors were going – that is, to the men's section instead of the women's, where he should have gone.

Having let those who were in a hurry pass him, he was the last to enter the visiting-room. The first thing that struck him as he opened the door and went in was the deafening noise of a hundred voices merging into one roar. It was only when he drew nearer to the people who were clinging, like flies settled on sugar, to the wire-netting that divided the room into two, that he understood what it meant. The room with windows in the wall at the back, opposite the door, was divided not by one but by two screens of wire-netting reaching from the floor to the ceiling. In the space between the wire-netting warders patrolled up and down. Behind the nets on one side were the prisoners, and on the other side the visitors. Separating them were two sets of wire-netting and a distance of fully seven feet, so that not only was it impossible to pass anything over – it was almost out of the question, especially for a short-sighted person, to distinguish a face even. It was also difficult to talk – one had to shout at the top of one's voice in order to be heard. On both sides wives, husbands, fathers, mothers, children pressed their faces against the nets, trying to see each other and to say what they wanted. But as each one tried to speak so as to be heard by the one he was talking to, and his neighbours did the same, and their voices interfered with other voices, they ended by trying to out-shout one another. This was the cause of the din, broken by shouts, which so struck Nekhlyudov when he first entered the room. It was quite impossible to make out what was being said. It was only by the faces that one could guess what they were saying and the relations between the speakers. Next to Nekhlyudov was an old woman with a kerchief on her head. She stood pressed to the wire, her chin trembling, and was shouting something to a pale young man, half of whose head was shaven. The prisoner, raising his eyebrows and puckering his forehead, was listening to her carefully. Next to the old woman was a young fellow in a peasant coat, listening with his hands to his ears and shaking his head to what a prisoner with a grizzled beard and a haggard face, who resembled him, was saying. A little farther off a man in rags was waving his arms, shouting something and laughing. And beside him a woman with a good woollen shawl on her shoulders sat on the floor with a baby in her lap, sobbing bitterly: apparently this was the first time she had seen the grey-haired man on the other side in prison clothes, in chains and with his head shaven. Beyond this woman was the commissionaire Nekhlyudov had talked to outside: he was shouting for all he was worth to a bald-headed convict with very bright eyes on the other side. When Nekhlyudov realized that he would have to talk in these conditions a feeling of indignation against the people who could invent and enforce such a system arose in him. He was astonished that such a dreadful state of affairs, this outrage to human feelings, should apparently offend no one. The soldiers, the warder, the visitors and the prisoners acted as though they thought all this was as it should be.

Nekhlyudov stayed in this room for about five minutes, conscious of a curious sort of depression, aware of how powerless he was, how at odds with the whole world. A moral sensation of nausea seized him, like sea-sickness on board ship.

42

'WELL, I must do what I came here for,' he said, trying to bolster up his resolution. 'But how shall I set about it?'

He began to look round for someone in authority and catching sight of a short thin man with a moustache, wearing the straps of a prison officer, walking up and down behind the visitors, he approached him.

'Could you possibly tell me, sir,' he said with the most elaborate politeness, 'where the women prisoners are, and where one is allowed to see them?'

'Is it the women's section you want?'

'Yes, I should like to see one of the women prisoners,' Nekhlyudov replied, with the same strained civility.

'You ought to have said so when you were in the hall. Who is it then, that you want to see?'

'Katerina Maslova.'

'Is she a political prisoner?' asked the assistant superintendent.

'No, she's just a –'

'Has she already been sentenced then?'

'Yes, she was sentenced the day before yesterday,' answered Nekhlyudov meekly, fearing to upset the good temper of the warder, who seemed well disposed towards him.

'If you want the women's section, please come this way,' said the warder, having decided from Nekhlyudov's appearance that he was worthy of attention. 'Sidorov,' he called out to a moustached under-officer with medals on his breast, 'take this gentleman to the women's section.'

'Yes, sir.'

At this moment heart-rending sobs were heard coming from someone near the wire-netting.

Everything seemed strange to Nekhlyudov, but strangest of all was that he should have to thank, and feel himself under an obligation to, the warder and the senior warder – people who were doing all the cruel things that were done in this building.

The warder took Nekhlyudov out of the men's visiting-room into the corridor, and, opening a door immediately opposite, led him into the women's visiting-room.

This room, like that of the men, was divided into three by two rows of wire-netting but it was much smaller and there were fewer visitors and prisoners; yet the din and the noise were the same as in the men's room. Here, too, a prison officer walked up and down between the netting but this time authority was represented by a female warder dressed in a uniform with gold cord on the sleeves and dark-blue piping, and the same sort of belt. And just as in the men's room people were pressing close to the wire-netting: behind one wire screen the visitors from outside in all sorts of clothes, behind the other the prisoners, some in white prison dress, others in their own garments. The whole length of the net was taken up with people. Some rose on tiptoe to be heard across the heads of others; some talked sitting on the floor.

Most noticeable of all the prisoners, both by her piercing voice and her appearance, was a thin dishevelled gipsy-woman, with her kerchief slipping from her curly hair. She was standing by a post in the middle of the wire-netting on the prisoners' side, shouting something, accompanied by quick gestures, to a gipsy in a blue coat girdled tightly below the waist. Next to the gipsy-man a soldier squatted on the ground talking to a prisoner; next to him, face pressed close to the wire, was a young peasant in bast shoes with a fair beard and a flushed face, struggling to keep back his tears. He was talking to a pretty fair-haired prisoner who gazed at him with bright blue eyes. This was Fedosya and her husband. Next to them a tramp was talking to a slatternly broad-faced woman; then a couple of women, a man, another woman – each with a woman prisoner opposite. Maslova was not among them. But at the back of the prisoners on the far side there was one more woman and Nekhlyudov knew at once that it was she, and at once he felt his heart beating faster and his breath stopping. The decisive moment was at hand. He went up to the wire-netting and recognized her. She was standing behind the blue-eyed Fedosya and smiled as she listened to what Fedosya was saying. She was not wearing the prison cloak now, as she had been two days ago, but a white jacket, tightly belted and straining over her very full chest. As they had in the court-room, her black curls peeped out from under her kerchief.

'In a moment now, it will be decided,' he thought. 'How am I to call her? Or will she come up herself?'

But she did not come. She was expecting Klara and it never entered her head that this visitor was for her.

'Who do you want?' the woman warder who was walking up and down between the wire partitioning asked Nekhlyudov.

'Katerina Maslova,' said Nekhlyudov with difficulty.

'Maslova, someone to see you!' the wardress shouted.

43

MASLOVA looked round and with head erect and her bosom thrust forward walked up to the wire with that expression of willingness which Nekhlyudov knew so well, pushing in between two prisoners and looking at Nekhlyudov in a surprised, inquiring way, not recognizing him.

Concluding, however, from his clothing that he was a man of wealth, she smiled.

'Is it me you want?' she said, putting her smiling face with the slightly squinting eyes nearer to the wire.

'I wanted to see –' Nekhlyudov hesitated, wondering whether to speak in the old intimate way and deciding to be more formal. He did not raise his voice any louder than usual. 'I wanted to see you . . . I . . .'

'Don't try pulling the wool over my eyes!' cried the tramp next to him. 'Did you take it or didn't you?'

'I tell you he's dying, what more d'you want?' somebody shouted from the other side.

Maslova could not hear what Nekhlyudov was saying, but the expression of his face while he was talking suddenly reminded her of him. But she did not believe it possible. Nevertheless the smile vanished from her face and a deep line of suffering appeared on her brow.

'I can't hear what you say,' she called out, screwing up her eyes and wrinkling her forehead more and more.

'I came . . .'

'Yes, I am doing what I ought to do, I am showing that I'm sorry,' thought Nekhlyudov; whereupon the tears welled to his eyes and he felt a choking sensation in his throat. Clutching the wire-netting with his fingers, he was silent for a moment, trying to repress a sob.

'I say, why stick your nose in where you have no business . . .' someone shouted from the other side.

'I know nothing about it, so help me God,' screamed a prisoner from another direction.

When she saw his agitation Maslova recognized him.

'You look like – but no, I don't know you,' she shouted, without looking at him, and her flushed face went darker still.

'I have come to ask you to forgive me,' he shouted in a loud expressionless voice, like a lesson learned by heart.

Having called out these words, he was covered with shame and looked round. But immediately it occurred to him that if he felt ashamed, so much the better – he had to bear this shame. And he continued at the top of his voice:

'Forgive me, I wronged you terribly . . .' he shouted again.

She stood motionless, not taking her squinting eyes off him.

He could not go on and turned away from the wire, trying to check the sobs that shook his chest.

The warder, the one who had directed Nekhlyudov to the women's side and whose interest he seemed to have aroused, came into the room and seeing Nekhlyudov not at the wire-netting asked him why he was not talking with the prisoner he wanted to see.

Nekhlyudov blew his nose, pulled himself together and made an effort to appear calm.

'I cannot speak through that wire,' he answered. 'It is impossible to hear anything.'

The warder considered for a moment.

'All right then, she can be brought out here for a short time.'

'Marya Karlovna!' he addressed the female warder. 'Bring Maslova out here.'

A minute later Maslova came out by the door at the side. Stepping lightly she walked up close to Nekhlyudov and stopped, looking up at him from under her brows. Her black hair escaped to frame her face as it had done two days before; her face, ill, puffy and white, was comely and serene, though the lustrous dark eyes with their slight squint glittered strangely from beneath the swollen lids.

'You may talk here,' said the warder, and moved away.

Maslova cast a questioning look at the warder and then, shrugging her shoulders in surprise, followed Nekhlyudov to a bench and sat down at his side, arranging her skirt.

'I know it is hard for you to forgive me,' Nekhlyudov began, but stopped again, feeling the tears impeding him, 'but if it is too late now to put the past right I will do all I can. Tell me . . .'

'How did you find me?' she asked, without answering his question and neither looking away from him nor quite at him with her squinting eyes.

'O God, help me. Show me what to do!' Nekhlyudov prayed in his heart, looking at her face now so changed for the worse.

'I was on the jury the day before yesterday,' he said, 'when you were being tried. Didn't you recognize me?'

'No, I didn't. I had no time for recognizing people. And what's more, I didn't look,' she said.

'There was a child, wasn't there?' he asked, and felt himself blushing.

'It died at the time, thank God,' she replied curtly and spitefully, turning away from him.

'How was that? What did it die of?'

'I was so ill, I nearly died myself,' she said, without raising her eyes.

'How could my aunts have sent you away?'

'Who's going to keep a servant that has a baby? As soon as they noticed, they turned me out. But what's the use of talking? I don't remember a thing, I have forgotten all about it. It is all over now.'

'No, it is not all over. I cannot leave matters as they are. Late as it is, I want to atone for my sin.'

'There is nothing to atone for; it's all over and done with,' she said, and – to his great surprise – she suddenly gave him a smile that was both disagreeable, insinuating and sad.

Maslova had never expected to see him again, and certainly not at this time and not here, and so his reappearance startled her into remembering things she never thought of now. The first moment brought back to her dimly that new wonderful world of emotions and thoughts which had been revealed to her by the charming young man who had loved her and whom she had loved; and then she remembered his incomprehensible cruelty and the whole long chain of degradation and suffering which had followed that enchanted happiness and been its direct consequence. And she felt sick at heart. But not being strong enough to analyse it all, she did what she always did: she rid herself of her memories, flinging over them the veil of a dissolute life; this was exactly what she did now. In the first moment she associated the man sitting beside her with the young man she had once loved, but then, finding that this was too painful, she stopped connecting him with that youth. Now this well-dressed, well-groomed gentleman with the perfumed beard was no longer the Nekhlyudov she had loved, but only one of those men who made use of creatures like herself when they needed them, and whom creatures like herself had to make use of in their turn as profitably as they could. And that was why she gave him that alluring smile. She was silent, reflecting how she could best make use of him.

'So it's all over,' she said. 'Now I'm condemned to Siberia.'

And her lips trembled as she pronounced the dreaded word.

'I knew, I was certain you were not guilty,' said Nekhlyudov.

'Guilty! Of course not. As if I could be a thief or a robber! They say here, everything depends on the lawyer,' she continued. 'They say I ought to put in an appeal. Only lawyers cost a lot of money, they say . . .'

'Yes, by all means,' said Nekhlyudov. 'I have already spoken to a lawyer.'

'No money ought to be spared: he must be a good one,' she said.

'I will do everything in my power.'

Both were silent.

She smiled at him again in the same way.

'But I'd like to ask you . . . for a little money, if you can spare it. Not much . . . ten roubles would do,' she said suddenly.

'Why, yes, certainly,' Nekhlyudov replied, embarrassed, and fumbled for his pocket-book.

She threw a quick glance at the warder, who was walking up and down the room.

'Don't give it to me in front of him. Wait until he's not looking, or they'll take it away from me.'

Nekhlyudov took out his pocket-book as soon as the warder had turned his back but before he had time to give her the ten-rouble note the warder was facing them again. He crumpled it in his hand.

'This woman is dead,' he thought, looking at the once sweet face, now defiled and bloated, and seeing the evil gleam in her black, slightly squinting eyes as they turned from watching the warder's movements to his hand that held the crumpled note. And for a moment he hesitated.

The tempter that had been speaking to him in the night again raised his voice, as always trying to lead him away from the question of what he ought to do to the question of what the consequences would be and what would be most expedient.

'You won't be able to do anything with this woman,' said the voice. 'You will only be tying a stone round your neck, which will drown you and prevent you from being of any use to the rest of the world. Wouldn't it be better to give her some money, all you have, say good-bye to her and make an end of it once and for all?' whispered the voice.

And yet he felt that now, at this very moment, something of the utmost importance was taking place in his soul, that his inner life was, as it were, wavering in the balance, and that the slightest effort would tip the scale to one side or the other. And he made the effort, calling to the God Whose presence he had felt in his soul the day before, and that God instantly responded. He resolved to tell her everything now – at once.

'Katusha, dear Katusha, I came to ask you to forgive me, but you have not told me – have you forgiven me? Will you ever forgive me?' he said, using the loving tone of voice of the old days.

She was not listening to him but looking first at his hand, then at the warder. The moment the warder turned away she hastily stretched out her hand to him, grabbed the note and tucked it into her belt.

'Funny things you're saying,' she said, with what seemed to him a sarcastic smile.

Nekhlyudov felt that there was some spirit in her actively hostile to him, propping up the person she was now and preventing him from reaching her heart.

But, strange to say, this did not repel him but drew him to her all the more, with a new special sort of force. He felt that he must awaken her soul, that this would be dreadfully difficult; but the very difficulty attracted him. He now felt towards her as he had never before felt towards her or anyone else. It was a feeling that had nothing personal in it: he did not want anything from her for himself. All he wanted was that she should cease being what she was now, that she should awaken and become what she had been before.

'Katusha, why do you speak like that? You see, I know you, I remember you as you were in the old days at Panovo –'

'What's the use of recalling the past?' she remarked dryly.

'I recall it so as to make amends and atone for my sin, Katusha,' he began, and was on the point of saying that he wanted to marry her but he met her eyes and read in them something so terrible, so coarse and revolting, that he could not go on.

At this moment the visitors began to leave. The warder came towards Nekhlyudov and said that their time was up. Maslova got to her feet, waiting meekly to be dismissed.

'Good-bye – I still have much more to say to you, but as you see I cannot do so now,' Nekhlyudov said, and held out his hand. 'I will come again.'

'I think you've said all there is to say . . .'

She gave him her hand but did not press his.

'No, I shall try to see you again, somewhere where we can talk, and then I shall tell you something very important – something I have to say to you,' said Nekhlyudov.

'Well then, come. Why not?' she answered, smiling the smile she gave to men whom she wished to please.

'You are dearer to me than a sister,' said Nekhlyudov.

'How funny!' she said again, and shaking her head went behind the wire-netting.

44

BEFORE this meeting between them Nekhlyudov was expecting that when she saw him and heard that he had repented and meant to do everything he could for her Katusha would be touched and happy, and would again become the Katusha of old, but to his horror he found that Katusha existed no more – there was only Maslova. This shocked and horrified him.

What surprised him most was that she showed no sign of shame, except of being a convict – she was ashamed of that, but not of being a prostitute. On the contrary, she seemed rather pleased, almost proud of it. And yet, how could it be otherwise? Nobody can wholeheartedly do anything unless he believes that his activity is important and good. Therefore, whatever a man's position may be, he is bound to take that view of human life in general that will make his own activity seem important and good. People usually imagine that a thief, a murderer, a spy, a prostitute, knowing their occupation to be evil, must be ashamed of it. But the very opposite is true. Men who have been placed by fate and their own sins or mistakes in a certain position, however irregular that position may be, adopt a view of life as a whole which makes their position appear to them good and respectable. In order to back up their view of life they instinctively mix only with those who accept their ideas of life and of their place in it. This surprises us when it is a case of thieves bragging of their skill, prostitutes flaunting their depravity or murderers boasting of their cruelty. But it surprises us only because their numbers are limited and – this is the point – we live in a different atmosphere. But can we not observe the same phenomenon when the rich boast of their wealth, i.e. of robbery; when commanders of armies pride themselves on their victories, i.e. on murder; and when those in high places vaunt their power – their brute force? We do not see that their ideas of life and of good and evil are corrupt and inspired by a necessity to justify their position, only because the circle of people with such corrupt ideas is a larger one and we belong to it ourselves.

It was after this fashion that Maslova had formed her view of life and of her position in the world. She was a prostitute, condemned to penal servitude, yet she had formed a conception of life which allowed her to think well of herself and even take pride in her position.

According to her philosophy the highest good for all men without exception – old and young, schoolboys and generals, educated and uneducated – consisted in sexual intercourse with attractive women, and therefore all men, though they pretended to be occupied with other things, in reality cared for nothing else. She, now, was an attractive woman who had it in her power to satisfy, or not to satisfy, their desires, and this made her an important and necessary person. All her past and present life confirmed the truth of this attitude.

For the last ten years, wherever she had been, she had seen that men – starting with Nekhlyudov and the old police-officer down to the warders in the prison – needed her; she did not see and did not remark the men who had no need of her. Consequently, the whole world seemed to her to be made up of people possessed by lust, who watched her on all sides, trying by every means in their power – deception, violence, purchase, cunning – to get hold of her.

This, then, was how Maslova understood life, and with such a conception of the world it was natural that she should consider herself not the lowest but a very important person. And Maslova prized this view of life more than anything else on earth; nor could she help prizing it, because if she were to change her ideas of life she would lose the importance it accorded her. And in order not to lose her significance in life she instinctively clung to the kind of people who looked upon life in the same way as she did. Sensing that Nekhlyudov wanted to draw her into another world, she resisted him, foreseeing that in the world into which he would take her she would have to lose her place in life with the confidence and self-respect it gave her. It was for this reason that she warded off every recollection of both her girlhood and her early relations with Nekhlyudov. Those recollections did not go with her present conception of living and so they had been entirely obliterated from her memory, or, to be more accurate, they lay somewhere buried and untouched, closed up and plastered over, so that there should be no access to them, just as to protect the results of their labour, bees sometimes plaster up a nest of wax-worms. Therefore the present Nekhlyudov was for her not the man she had once loved with a pure love but only a rich gentleman who could and must be made use of, and with whom she might have only the same relations as with all other men.

'No, I could not tell her the most important thing,' thought Nekhlyudov, moving towards the exit with the rest of the visitors. 'I did not tell her I would marry her. I did not say that, but I will,' he thought.

The warders at the door let the visitors out, counting them over again, so that no extra person left and no one remained inside. This time the slap on the shoulder did not offend Nekhlyudov: he did not even notice it.

45

NEKHLYUDOV had meant to change the circumstances of his life: to let his large house, send away the servants and move into a hotel. But Agrafena Petrovna pointed out that there was no sense in making any change before the winter; no one would take over a town house in summer, and anyhow he would have to live and keep his furniture and things somewhere. Thus all his efforts to change his manner of life (he felt he wanted to live in a simple fashion, like a student) came to naught. Not only did things remain as they were but the house was suddenly filled with new activity: everything made of wool or fur was taken out to be aired and beaten, a performance in which the house-porter, the boy, the cook and Korney himself took part. First various uniforms and strange garments of fur which no one ever wore were brought out and hung on the line; then it was the turn of the carpets and furniture, and the house-porter and the boy, shirt-sleeves rolled up over muscular arms, vigorously started to beat everything, keeping strict time, and the smell of camphor balls spread through all the rooms. When Nekhlyudov crossed the courtyard or looked out of the window he marvelled what a terrible lot of things there were, and how utterly useless they were. Their only use and purpose, Nekhlyudov thought, was to provide exercise for Agrafena Petrovna, Korney, the house-porter, the boy and the cook.

'It's not worth while altering my mode of life now until Maslova's case is settled,' he reflected. 'Besides, it is too difficult. The change will come of its own accord when she is released or exiled and I follow her.'

On the appointed day Nekhlyudov drove up to the lawyer's private house. Entering Fanarin's magnificent apartments with their huge plants and wonderful curtains at the windows and all the expensive furnishings generally which indicate the possession of much easy money – that is, money which has not had to be earned – such as are only to be seen in the homes of people who have grown rich suddenly, Nekhlyudov found in the reception-room, as at a doctor's, a number of clients waiting their turn, sitting gloomily by little tables on which lay illustrated magazines intended to help them while away their time. The lawyer's assistant was also sitting in the room, at a high desk, and recognizing Nekhlyudov came up to greet him and say he would announce him at once. But he had barely reached the door of the office when it opened and the loud animated voices were heard of a middle-aged, stocky man with a red face and thick moustaches, wearing brand-new clothes, and of Fanarin himself. The expression on both faces was that of men who have just concluded a profitable but not quite honest transaction.

'That's your own fault, my dear fellow,' said Fanarin, smiling.

'We'd all git to 'eaven if it wasn't for our sins.'

'Oh yes, we know all about that.'

And both men laughed awkwardly.

'Oh, Prince Nekhlyudov, please come in,' said Fanarin, catching sight of Nekhlyudov, and nodding once more to the departing merchant he led Nekhlyudov into his office, which was furnished with rigid simplicity. 'Have a cigarette, will you?' said the lawyer, seating himself opposite Nekhlyudov and trying to repress a smile evidently due to the success of the transaction just completed.

'Thank you. I have come about Maslova's case.'

'Yes, yes, I know. Ugh, what rascals these fat money-bags are!' he said. 'You saw that fellow? He's worth about twelve million. But he says "'eaven" and "git". And he'd tear a tenner off you with his teeth if he saw the chance.'

'He says "'eaven" and "git", and you talk about a "tenner",' Nekhlyudov was thinking with an insurmountable feeling of disgust for this man with his free and easy tone which was meant to show that he belonged to the same class as Nekhlyudov and that the clients who came to him, and the rest of mankind, were in another, alien camp.

'He has given me no end of trouble, the scoundrel. I felt I had to unburden my heart,' said the lawyer, as if to excuse himself for not talking business with Nekhlyudov. 'Well, about your case . . . I have gone through it carefully and "disapprove of the contents thereof", as Turgenyev says. I mean to say, that wretched little lawyer missed just about every point which could have been grounds for an appeal.'

'What have you decided, then?'

'Excuse me. Tell him,' he said to his assistant who had just come in, 'that I stick to what I said: if he can, well and good; if he can't, it doesn't matter.'

'But he won't agree.'

'Well then, let him go,' replied the lawyer, and his cheerful self-satisfied expression became sullen and spiteful.

'And they say we lawyers get our money for doing nothing,' he said, bringing the former pleasant amiability back into his face. 'I saved a bankrupt debtor from a totally false charge and now they all flock to me. But every such case means an enormous amount of work. As some author or other said, we, too, "write with our heart's blood". Now about your case, or rather, the case you are interested in,' he went on. 'It has been abominably mishandled. There are no good grounds for an appeal, still we can have a try, and here are the notes I have made.'

He took up a sheet of paper covered with writing and began to read rapidly, slurring over the uninteresting legal terms and laying particular stress on other words. '"To the Court of Appeal, Criminal Department, etc., etc. The Petition of So-and-so. By the decision, etc., etc., and according to the verdict, etc., one Maslova was found guilty of having caused the death by poisoning of the merchant Smelkov, and, by virtue of Article 1454 of the Penal Code, has been sentenced to hard labour, etc."'

He paused. Evidently, in spite of being so used to it, he still found pleasure in listening to his own compositions.

'"This sentence,"' he continued impressively, '"is the direct consequence of judicial infringements and errors so serious as to make it subject to rescission. In the first place, the reading of the report of the post-mortem examination of Smelkov's intestines was interrupted by the President at the very beginning." That is point one.'

'But it was the prosecution who demanded the reading,' Nekhlyudov said in surprise.

'Makes no difference. The defence might have had cause to ask for it, too.'

'But there was no earthly need for it.'

'It is a ground for appeal, though. To continue: "In the second place, when the counsel for the defence, trying to describe Maslova's personality, was referring to some of the causes of his client's fall, the President stopped him and called him to order for introducing irrelevant material. Now it is recognized that in criminal cases (and this has been repeatedly pointed out by the Senate) the elucidation of the moral character and personality of the defendant is of prime importance, even if only as a guide in determining the correct degree of responsibility." That is point number two,' he said, glancing at Nekhlyudov.

'But he spoke so wretchedly that it was impossible to understand him,' said Nekhlyudov, more and more astonished.

'The fellow's a complete fool, he couldn't be expected to say anything sensible,' Fanarin said, laughing; 'but all the same it will do as a cause for appeal. Well, to go on: "Thirdly, in his summing-up the President violated the categorical demand of Par. 1, Article 801 of the Penal Code by omitting to inform the jury exactly what is required by law for the conviction of an alleged criminal, and did not tell them that although they were agreed on the fact that Maslova had administered the poison to Smelkov, nevertheless, since proofs of wilful intent to deprive Smelkov of life were absent, they had the right to bring in a verdict, not of murder but of the misdemeanour of carelessness resulting in the merchant's death, which she did not desire." And that is the really important point.'

'But we ought to have understood that ourselves. That was our mistake.'

'"And, finally, in the fourth place,"' continued the lawyer, '"the answer of the jury to the question of Maslova's guilt was couched in language which contained a palpable contradiction. Maslova was accused of the wilful poisoning of Smelkov solely for mercenary motives – there being no other motive for murder; yet the jury in their verdict acquitted her of any intent to rob and of participation in the theft of the valuables – from which it is manifest that they also intended to acquit her of the intent to murder and only through a misunderstanding, which arose from the incompleteness of the President's summing up, omitted to express this in proper form in their findings; in consideration whereof this verdict of the jury calls for the application of Articles 816 and 808 of the Penal Code – that is, an explanation by the President to the jury of their mistake, to be followed by their retirement to reconsider their verdict concerning the defendant's guilt,'" read Fanarin.

'Then why ever did the President not do this?'

'That's what I'd like to know,' replied Fanarin, with a laugh.

'So you think the Senate will rectify the error?'

'That will depend on which of the old men are present at the time.'

'What do you mean – old men?'

'Old men who ought to be in the work-house. So there you are. Further I say: "Such a verdict did not entitle the Court to sentence Maslova for a criminal offence,'" he continued rapidly, '"and the application in her case of Par. 3, Article 771 of the Penal Code constitutes a direct and flagrant violation of the fundamental principles of our criminal law. On the grounds stated above I have the honour to appeal, and so on and so forth, that this verdict be set aside in conformity with Articles 909, 910, Par. 2 of 912, and 928 of the Penal Code, etc., etc. . . . and that the case be transferred to another division of the said Court for a retrial." There! All that can be done is done but, to be frank, I have little hope of success. Still, it all depends on what members are present in the Senate. If you have any influence, see what you can do.'

'I do know some of them.'

'All right; only be quick about it or they'll all be off to cure their piles, and then you'll have three months to wait. . . . Then, if that's no good, we can fall back on a petition to His Majesty. That depends, too, on wire-pulling behind the scenes. In that case I am also at your service – not with the wire-pulling, I mean, but in drawing up the petition.'

'I thank you. And your fee –'

'My assistant will give you a clean copy of the appeal, and he will tell you.'

'There is another thing I wanted to ask you: the public prosecutor gave me a pass to visit this person in prison, but at the prison they told me that I must obtain permission from the governor if I wished to see her other than at the regular time and place. Is that necessary?'

'Yes, I think so. But the governor is not here just now, and the deputy governor is in charge. But he's such a hopeless fool, I doubt whether you'll do anything with him.'

'Is that Maslennikov?'

'Yes.'

'I know him,' said Nekhlyudov, and got up to go.

At this moment a fearfully ugly, skinny, snub-nosed, yellow-faced little woman flew into the room. It was the lawyer's wife, who did not seem to be the least bit dejected by her ugliness. Not only was she dressed in the most extravagantly original manner in some garment made of velvet and silk in bright yellow and green but her thin hair was crimped and curled, and she made a triumphal entry into the room accompanied by a lank, smiling man with a greenish complexion, wearing a coat with silk lapels, and a white tie. This was a writer; Nekhlyudov knew him by sight.

'Anatole,' she said, opening the door. 'Come in here a moment. Semeon Ivanovich has promised to read his poem, and you absolutely must come and read to us about Garshin.'

Nekhlyudov was rising to leave, but the lawyer's wife whispered something to her husband and immediately turned towards him.

'I beg your pardon, prince – I know who you are, so I think we may dispense with an introduction. Do come to our literary matinée. It will be very interesting. Anatole reads delightfully.'

'You see what a variety of occupations I have,' said Anatole, making a helpless gesture with his hands and smilingly indicating his wife, as much as to say, who could resist such a bewitching creature?

With a grave and melancholy air, and with the greatest politeness, Nekhlyudov thanked the lawyer's wife for the honour she did him in inviting him but excused himself for lack of time, and went out into the waiting-room.

'What affectation!' remarked the lawyer's wife when he was gone.

In the waiting-room the assistant handed Nekhlyudov the prepared petition, and, to his inquiry about the fee, said that Monsieur Fanarin had fixed it at a thousand roubles, adding that Monsieur Fanarin did not usually take cases of that sort but had made an exception for Nekhlyudov.

'And about the petition, who signs it?' asked Nekhlyudov.

'The defendant herself may, or if that presents a difficulty Monsieur Fanarin could if he gets a power of attorney from her.'

'Oh no. I will take it along and get her signature,' said Nekhlyudov, glad of an excuse for seeing her before the regular day.

46

AT the usual hour the warders' whistles sounded along the prison corridor, the iron doors of the cells rattled open, bare feet pattered, heels clattered, and the prisoners who acted as scavengers went by, filling the air with a nauseating stench. After they had washed and dressed, the prisoners filed out into the corridors for roll-call, and after roll-call went to fetch boiling water for their tea.

The one subject of conversation in all the cells as the prisoners drank their tea that morning was the impending punishment of two prisoners who were to be flogged that day. One, Vassilyev, was a young man of some education, a clerk, who had killed his mistress in a fit of jealousy. His fellow prisoners liked him because he was cheerful and generous with them and firm in his behaviour with the prison authorities. He knew the regulations and insisted on their being carried out. For this reason the authorities disliked him. Three weeks before, a warder had struck one of the scavengers for splashing soup over his new uniform. Vassilyev stood up for the man, declaring that it was against the law to strike a prisoner.

'I'll teach you the law,' said the warder, calling Vassilyev all sorts of names. Vassilyev replied in kind. The warder was about to hit him but Vassilyev caught hold of his arms, holding them fast for two or three minutes, then turned him round and pushed him out of the door. The warder entered a complaint and the superintendent ordered Vassilyev to be put in solitary confinement.

The solitary confinement cells were a row of dark closets locked with bolts on the outside. In these dark cold cells there were neither beds, tables nor chairs, so that the person confined in them had to sit or lie on the dirty floor, where the rats, of which there were a great many, ran over him, and were so bold that it was impossible to keep them from getting at the prisoner's bread. They would snatch the bread from his hands and even attack him if he stopped moving. Vassilyev said he wasn't going into solitary because he hadn't done anything. He was taken by force. He began struggling, and two other prisoners helped him to free himself from the warders. Then all the warders, including one, Petrov, who was renowned for his strength, got together. The prisoners were overpowered and pushed into the solitary cells. The governor was hastily informed that something very like a mutiny had taken place. He sent back a written order for the flogging of the two ring-leaders, Vassilyev and the tramp Nepomnyashchy, thirty strokes of the birch each.

The punishment was to take place in the women's visiting-room.

The whole prison had known about this since the night before, and now the forthcoming punishment was the subject of animated discussion in all the cells.

Korablyova, Beauty, Fedosya and Maslova sat together in their corner, all of them flushed and excited by the vodka they had drunk, for Maslova, who now had a constant supply, treated her companions freely. They were drinking their tea and discussing the flogging.

''E never made no disturbance nor nothing,' Korablyova said about Vassilyev, nibbling tiny bits off a lump of sugar with her strong teeth. ''E only stood up for 'is mate, because it ain't allowed to strike a prisoner these days.'

'They say 'e's a decent fellow,' added Fedosya, who sat, with her long plaits uncovered, on a log of wood by the plank-bed on which the teapot stood.

'You ought to tell ''im about it,' the signal-woman said to Maslova, by 'him' meaning Nekhlyudov.

'I will. He'll do anything for me,' replied Maslova, tossing her head and smiling.

'Yes, when 'e comes; but they've gone to fetch the poor fellows already,' said Fedosya. 'It's really terrible,' she went on, and sighed.

'I once see 'em floggin' a man at the police-station. Father-in-law, 'e sent me to the village elder, and when I got there, there 'e was, being . . .' and the signal-woman began a long story. It was interrupted by the sound of voices and steps in the corridor above them.

The women stopped talking and listened.

'There they are, 'auling 'im along, the devils!' said Beauty. 'They'll do 'im in, they will. The warders are that mad with 'im because 'e gives 'em no peace.'

All was quiet again overhead and the signal-woman finished her story of how frightened she had been when she went into the barn by the police-station and saw them flogging the peasant; her inside turned over at the sight. Next Beauty told how Shcheglov had been flogged and had never uttered a sound. Then Fedosya put away the tea-things and Korablyova and the signal-woman took up their sewing, while Maslova sat down on the bedstead with her arms round her knees, feeling bored and depressed. She was just thinking she would lie down and have a nap when the female warder called her to come to her office to see a visitor.

'Mind you tell 'im all about us,' said old Granny Menshova while Maslova was arranging her kerchief before the looking-glass that had half its quicksilver worn off. 'It wasn't us set the place on fire, 'e did it 'isself, the rotter, and 'is man saw 'im do it – 'e'd not damn 'is soul by denying it. You tell 'im to ask to see my Mitri. Mitri'll tell 'im all about it, as plain as the palm of your 'and. Just think of us locked up in prison when we never knew a thing about it, while that old bastard sits in the pot-'ouse carrying on with another man's wife.'

'That's not the law,' Korablyova confirmed her.

'I'll tell him, I'll certainly tell him,' answered Maslova. 'Suppose I have one more drop, to keep up my courage,' she added, with a wink.

Korablyova poured her out half a cupful. Maslova drained it, wiped her mouth, and repeating the words 'to keep up my courage', followed the wardress along the corridor, tossing her head and smiling cheerfully.

47

NEKHLYUDOV had been waiting in the hall for some time.

When he arrived at the prison he rang at the main door and handed the warder on duty the pass he had received from the public prosecutor.

'Who do you want to see?'

'The prisoner Maslova.'

'You can't now: the superintendent's busy.'

'Is he in his office?' asked Nekhlyudov.

'No, he's here in the visiting-room,' the warder replied, and Nekhlyudov thought he seemed embarrassed.

'Why, this isn't a visiting day, is it?'

'No, it's special business.'

'When can I see him then?'

'When he comes out, you can speak to him then. Wait a bit.'

At this point a sergeant-major with a smooth shiny face, and moustaches impregnated with tobacco smoke, came in through a side door, the gold stripes on his uniform glistening, and sharply addressed the warder.

'What do you mean by letting anyone in here?... The office –'

'I was told the superintendent was here,' said Nekhlyudov, wondering at the signs of uneasiness noticeable in the sergeant-major too.

Just then the inner door opened and Petrov came out, hot and perspiring.

'He'll not forget that in a hurry,' he said to the sergeant-major.

The sergeant-major indicated Nekhlyudov with a glance, and Petrov said no more but frowned and went out through a door at the back.

'Who will not forget in a hurry? Why are you all so embarrassed? Why did the sergeant-major make that sign to him?' wondered Nekhlyudov.

'You cannot wait here. Please step across to the office,' said the sergeant-major, addressing Nekhlyudov again, and Nekhlyudov was about to go when the superintendent came through the door at the back, looking even more agitated than his subordinates. He was sighing all the time. When he saw Nekhlyudov he turned to the gaoler.

'Fedotov, have Maslova, cell 5, Women's Section, brought to the office.'

'Will you come this way, please,' he said to Nekhlyudov. They climbed up a steep staircase into a small room with one window, a writing-table and a few chairs. The superintendent sat down.

'Mine is a heavy responsibility, very heavy,' he remarked, taking out a fat cigarette and turning to Nekhlyudov.

'I can see you are tired,' said Nekhlyudov.

'Tired of the whole business – my duties are very trying. You endeavour to alleviate their lot and only make it worse. My one thought now is how to get away. The responsibilities are very, very heavy.'

Nekhlyudov did not know what the superintendent's particular difficulty was, but he saw that today he was in a singularly dejected, hopeless mood, which evoked his sympathy.

'Yes, I should think they are very heavy,' he said, 'but why do you stay here?'

'I have a family, and no other means.'

'But if you find it so painful . . .'

'Well, still, you know – in a way I do some good. I make things easier whenever I can. Another man in my place would do quite differently. Why, we have over two thousand people here. And what people! One has to know how to deal with them. It is easier said than done, you know. And after all, they're human beings, you can't help feeling sorry for them. And yet you can't be too lenient.'

The superintendent began telling Nekhlyudov about a recent brawl among the prisoners, which had ended in one man being killed.

His story was interrupted by the arrival of Maslova preceded by a warder.

Nekhlyudov saw her in the doorway before she noticed the superintendent. Her face was flushed and she walked briskly behind the warder, smiling and tossing her head. When she saw the superintendent she gazed at him with a frightened face, but immediately recovered herself and addressed Nekhlyudov boldly and gaily.

'How d'you do?' she said in a drawling voice, smiling as she spoke, and grasped his hand firmly, not like the first time.

'I have brought you a petition to sign,' said Nekhlyudov, somewhat surprised at the bolder manner with which she greeted him today. 'The lawyer has drawn up this petition which you must sign, and then we will send it to Petersburg.'

'All right, I don't mind signing. Anything you like,' she said, screwing up one eye and smiling.

Nekhlyudov drew a folded paper from his pocket and went up to the table.

'May she sign it here?' asked Nekhlyudov, turning to the superintendent. 'Here's a pen for you. Can you write?'

'Come here and sit down,' said the superintendent.

'I could once upon a time,' she said, and smiling and arranging her skirt and the sleeves of her jacket she sat down at the table, took the pen awkwardly in her small energetic hand, and glanced up at Nekhlyudov with a laugh.

He showed her where and what to write.

Carefully dipping her pen into the ink and shaking off a drop or two, she signed her name.

'Is that all you want?' she asked, looking from Nekhlyudov to the superintendent and putting the pen first into the ink-well, then on to some sheets of paper.

'I have something to say to you,' said Nekhlyudov, taking the pen from her hand.

'All right, tell me,' she said; and suddenly, as if remembering something or feeling sleepy, she began to look serious.

The superintendent rose and went out of the room, and Nekhlyudov was left face to face with her.

48

THE gaoler who had brought Maslova in sat down on the window-sill, at some distance from the table. For Nekhlyudov the decisive moment had arrived. He had never ceased to reproach himself for not having told her the main thing at their first interview – namely, that he intended to marry her – and was firmly determined to tell her now. She was sitting on one side of the table, and Nekhlyudov sat down opposite her, on the other side. The room was light, and Nekhlyudov for the first time saw her face clearly, close to – he saw the wrinkles round her eyes and mouth, and the swollen eyelids. And he felt more pity for her than ever.

Leaning across the table so as not to be heard by the gaoler sitting at the window (a man of Jewish appearance with grizzled side-whiskers) but only by her, he said:

'If this petition fails, we shall appeal to the Emperor. Everything possible will be done.'

'If I'd had a decent lawyer from the first –' she interrupted him. 'As it was, the lawyer I had was nothing but an old fool. He did nothing but pay me compliments,' she said, and burst into a laugh. 'If they'd known you and I were old acquaintances it would have been another matter. Now they all think I am a thief.'

'How strange she is today,' thought Nekhlyudov, and was on the point of saying what he had in mind when she began again:

'There's something I want to say. There's an old woman here with us, a good old thing, you know, everyone's really surprised she's here. She's a marvellous old woman, and in prison for nothing, her and her son; and everyone knows they're not guilty, but they were convicted for arson, and now they're inside. When she heard I knew you,' said Maslova, twisting her head round to glance at him, '"Tell him to ask to see my son," she says. "He'll tell him all about it." Menshov is their name. Well, will you do it? Such a fine old thing she is; you can see at once she's innocent. Be a dear and take up their case,' she said, looking up at him and then lowering her eyes and smiling.

'Very well, I will find out about them,' said Nekhlyudov, marvelling more and more at her free-and-easy manner. 'But I want to speak to you on matters which concern me. You remember what I told you last time?' he said.

'You said a lot of things. What was it?' she said, continuing to smile and turning her head from side to side.

'I said I had come to ask your forgiveness,' he said.

'What's the use of keeping on about forgiveness? You'd do better to . . .'

'I told you I wanted to atone for my guilt,' continued Nekhlyudov, 'and atone not in words but in deeds. I have made up my mind to marry you.'

Her face suddenly expressed fear. Her squinting eyes remained fixed on him and yet did not seem to be looking at him.

'Why should that be necessary?' she said, scowling angrily.

'I feel I must do so before God.'

'What has God got to do with it? You're talking nonsense. God? What God? You ought to have thought of God when you –' she said, and stopped with her mouth open.

It was only now that Nekhlyudov noticed that her breath smelt of spirits and realized the cause of her excitement.

'Calm yourself,' he said.

'I'm calm enough. You think I'm tipsy? So I am, but I know what I'm saying.' She began speaking fast, her face scarlet. 'I'm a convict, a whore . . . but you are a gentleman, a prince, and you've no business soiling yourself with me. You go to your princesses: my price is a ten-rouble bank-note.'

'Say all the cruel things you like, you can never say all that I feel myself,' Nekhlyudov said softly, trembling all over. 'You cannot imagine how deeply I feel my guilt towards you. . .!'

'Feel your guilt!' she mocked him spitefully. 'You didn't feel any guilt then, but shoved a hundred roubles at me. "Here's your price . . ."'

'I know, I know, but what can we do about it now?' said Nekhlyudov. 'I am determined not to forsake you,' he repeated, 'and I shall do what I have said.'

'And I tell you you shan't!' she cried, and laughed aloud.

'Katusha!' he began, touching her hand.

'Go away from me! I am a convict and you are a prince, and you've no business here,' she cried, her whole face distorted with anger, snatching her hand from him. 'You want to save yourself through me,' she continued, hurrying to pour out every feeling in her heart. 'You had your pleasure from me in this world, and now you want to get your salvation through me in the world to come! You disgust me – with your spectacles and your fat ugly mug. Go away, go away!' she screamed, springing to her feet.

The gaoler came up to them.

'What are you kicking up this row for? That won't –'

'Let her alone, please,' said Nekhlyudov.

'I just wanted her not to forget herself,' said the gaoler.

'No, just wait a bit, if you please,' said Nekhlyudov.

The warder went back to the window.

Maslova sat down again, with eyes lowered and tightly clasping her small hands, fingers interlaced.

Nekhlyudov was standing over her, not knowing what to do.

'You do not believe me?' he said.

'That you mean to marry me? That will never be. I'd rather hang myself. So there!'

'Well, still I shall devote myself to you.'

'That's your affair. Only I don't want anything from you. That's the truth I'm telling you,' she said. 'Oh, why didn't I die then?' she added, and began to cry piteously.

Nekhlyudov could not speak: her tears communicated themselves to him.

She raised her eyes, looked at him in surprise and with the corner of her kerchief began to wipe away the tears running down her cheeks.

The warder came over again and reminded them that their time was up. Maslova rose.

'You are upset now. If it is possible I will come tomorrow. And in the meantime, you think it over,' said Nekhlyudov.

She made no answer and, without giving him another glance, followed the gaoler out of the room.

'Well, girl, you'll be all right now,' Korablyova said when Maslova returned to the cell. ''E must be quite smitten with you. Make the most of things while you 'ave 'im in tow. 'E'll get you out. Rich people can do anything.'

'That's so,' remarked the signal-woman in her sing-song voice. 'A poor man 'as to think twice before 'e gets married, but a rich man need only make up 'is mind what 'e wants, and it's done. We 'ad a gentleman up our way once, birdie, and what do you think 'e did? . . .'

'Well, did you tell 'im about me?' asked the old woman.

But Maslova did not answer her cronies but lay down on her plank-bedstead, her squinting eyes fixed on a corner of the room, and stayed thus until the evening. An agonizing process was going on in her. What Nekhlyudov had said took her back into the world where she had suffered, which she had left without understanding it, and hating it. Now she had been wakened from the trance in which she had been living, but to live with a clear memory of what had been was too painful. So in the evening she bought some more vodka and got drunk with her companions.

49

'So this is what it means – this,' thought Nekhlyudov as he left the prison, only now fully understanding his crime. Had he not tried to expiate, to atone for his guilt he would never have felt the extent of his crime; moreover, neither would she have become conscious of just how much she had been wronged. Only now was all the horror of it made plain. Only now did he see what he had done to the soul of this woman; only now did she see and realize what had been done to her. Up to now Nekhlyudov had been dallying with his feelings of remorse, delighting in himself: now he was quite simply filled with horror. To cast her off – that, he felt, he could never do now, and yet he could not imagine what would come of his relations to her.

As he was leaving the prison a warder with crosses and medals on his breast approached him and with an air of mystery handed him a note. He had a disagreeable ingratiating face.

'Here is a note from a certain person, your excellency,' he said, giving Nekhlyudov an envelope.

'What person?'

'Read it, and you will see. A woman political prisoner. I am in charge of her ward, so she asked me. And though it's against the regulations, still, feelings of humanity . . .' The gaoler spoke in an unnatural manner.

Nekhlyudov was surprised that a gaoler of the ward where the political prisoners were kept should pass notes, inside the very prison walls and almost within sight of everyone; he did not know then that the man was both a gaoler and a spy, but he took the note and read it as he came out of the prison. The note was written in pencil, in a bold hand, in the new orthography, and ran as follows:

Having heard that you visit the prison and are interested in one of the convicts, I thought I should like to talk to you. Ask for a permit to see me. It will be granted to you, and I can tell you much of importance both for your *protégée* and our group.

Yours gratefully,
Vera Bogodoukhovskaya.

Vera Bogodoukhovskaya had been a teacher in an out-of-the-way part of the province of Novgorod, where Nekhlyudov and some friends of his had once gone bear-hunting. She had come to him to ask if he would give her some money so that she could attend a course of studies. Nekhlyudov gave her money and forgot about her. Now it appeared that the lady was a political offender and in prison, where, no doubt, she had heard about him, and was now offering her services. How simple and easy everything had been then. And how difficult and complicated it all was now. Nekhlyudov vividly and with pleasure recalled the old days and his acquaintance with Bogodoukhovskaya. It was just before Lent, in a remote spot about forty miles from the railway. The hunt had been successful – they had killed two bears and were having dinner before starting back, when the owner of the cottage in which they were stopping came in to say that the deacon's daughter wanted to speak to Prince Nekhlyudov.

'Is she pretty?' somebody asked.

'That will do!' said Nekhlyudov, putting on a serious look and rising from the table, wiping his mouth and wondering what the deacon's daughter could want with him, as he went into the landlord's private hut.

There he found a girl in a felt hat and a warm cloak – a wiry girl with a thin plain face in which only the eyes with their arched brows were beautiful.

'Here, miss, you can speak to him now,' said the old woman of the hut. 'It's the prince himself. I'll leave you with him.'

'What can I do for you?' Nekhlyudov asked.

'I . . . I . . . . You see, you are a rich man, you squander money on trifles, on hunting, I know,' the girl began, in great embarrassment, 'and I have only one desire in the world – I want to be of use to people, and I can do nothing because I am ignorant.'

Her eyes were so truthful, so kind, and her whole expression, which was both resolute and yet shy, was so touching that Nekhlyudov, as often happened with him, suddenly put himself in her place, and understood and felt sorry for her.

'What can I do?'

'I am a schoolteacher, but I should like to take a university course, and they won't take me. That is to say, they would take me, but I have no money. Give me the money, and I will pay you back when I have finished the course. I think it's wrong that rich people bait bears and give the peasants drink. Why shouldn't they do some good? I only need eighty roubles. But if you don't want to, I don't care,' she added angrily.

'On the contrary, I am very much obliged to you for the opportunity. . . . I will bring it this minute,' said Nekhlyudov.

He went out into the passage and there met one of his companions who had overheard the conversation. Paying no heed to his comrades' chaffing, he took the money out of his pouch and brought it to her.

'Oh, please, do not thank me: it is I who should be thanking you.'

It was pleasant for Nekhlyudov to remember all this now: pleasant to remember how he had nearly had a quarrel with an officer who tried to make the whole thing an objectionable joke; how another of his comrades had taken his part and how that had led to a closer friendship between them; how successful and happy the whole expedition had been, and how content he had felt as they returned by night to the railway-station. The line of two-horse sleighs glided swiftly and silently along the narrow road through the forest, fringed here with tall pine-trees, there with low firs, all weighed down by the snow caked in heavy lumps on their branches. There is a red glow in the dark as someone lights a fragrant cigarette. Ossip, the game-keeper, runs from sledge to sledge, up to his knees in snow, arranging a strap here, a rug there, and telling them about the elks now going about in the deep snow and gnawing the bark off the aspen-trees, and about bears lying asleep in their hidden dens, their warm breath puffing out from the air-holes.

Nekhlyudov remembered all this, but more than anything else he remembered the blissful awareness of his own health and strength, and freedom from care. His lungs breathe in the frosty air so deeply that his sheepskin coat is drawn tight across his chest; the fine snow spatters down on to his face every time the shaft-bow touches the branches overhead; his body feels warm, his face fresh, and his soul knows neither care, nor regret, nor fear, nor desires. What a good time it was! And now? O God, what torment, what trouble! . . .

Evidently Vera Bogodoukhovskaya was a revolutionary, and now in prison for her activities. He must see her, especially as she promised to advise him how to make things easier for Maslova.

50

WAKING early next morning, Nekhlyudov recalled everything that had happened the day before, and shuddered.

But in spite of his fear he was more determined than ever
to continue what he had begun.

With this feeling of a sense of duty he left home and drove
to Maslennikov, to ask for his permission to visit in the prison,
not only Maslova but the old woman Menshova and her son,
for whom Maslova had interceded. He also wanted a pass to
see Bogodoukhovskaya, who might be able to help Maslova.

Nekhlyudov had known Maslennikov a long time ago in
the regiment. At that time Maslennikov had been the regi-
mental paymaster. He was a kind-hearted, punctilious officer,
knowing nothing and wishing to know nothing in the world
beyond the regiment and the Imperial family. Now Nekhlyudov found him a government official, who had exchanged the
regiment for an administrative post. He had married a wealthy
and spirited woman who had forced him to leave the army for
the civil service.

She made fun of him and caressed him as if he were a pet
animal. Nekhlyudov had been to see them once during the
previous winter and found the couple so uninteresting that
he had not gone again.

Maslennikov beamed all over his face when he saw
Nekhlyudov. His face was just as fat and red, his figure just
as corpulent, and he was just as splendidly turned out as in his
military days. Then it had been an unfailingly immaculate
uniform cut in the latest style, tightly fitting his chest and
shoulders, or else a double-breasted jacket; now he wore a
civil service uniform of the latest fashion, which fitted his
well-fed body just as snugly and showed off his broad chest.
This was his undress-uniform. In spite of the difference in
their years (Maslennikov was getting on for forty) there was
no ceremony between them.

'Hello, my boy! How good of you to come! Let us go and see my wife. I have just ten minutes to spare before a meeting. My chief is away, you know, so I'm at the head of the administration,' he said, unable to disguise his satisfaction.

'I have come to see you on business.'

'What is it?' asked Maslennikov, in an apprehensive and somewhat severe tone, instantly putting himself on his guard, as it were.

'In the prison there is a person I am very much interested in' (at the word 'prison' Maslennikov's face became sterner still), 'and whom I should like to see, not in the general visiting-room but in the office, and not only at the usual visiting hours but oftener. I am told it depends on you.'

'Of course, *mon cher*, I am ready to do anything I can for you,' said Maslennikov, touching Nekhlyudov's knees with both hands, as though to mitigate his grandeur; 'but remember, I am monarch only for an hour.'

'So you will give me a permit to see her?'

'It's a woman?'

'Yes.'

'What is she there for?'

'Poisoning. But she was unjustly convicted.'

'Yes, there's your just jury system for you, *ils n'en font point d'autres*,'[1] he said, for some reason in French. 'I know you don't agree with me, nevertheless, *c'est mon opinion bien arrêtée*,'[2] voicing an opinion he had been reading in one form or another for the last twelve months in a reactionary conservative paper. 'I know you're a liberal.'

'I don't know whether I am a liberal or not,' Nekhlyudov said, smiling; he was always surprised to find that he was supposed to belong to some party and be called a liberal just because he maintained that a man should be heard before he was judged, that all men are equal before the law, that nobody ought to be ill-treated and beaten, especially if they had not been tried and found guilty. 'I don't know whether I am a

1. That's just like them.   2. It's my firm opinion.

liberal or not; but I do know one thing – however bad the present jury system is, it is better than the old tribunals.'

'And who is your lawyer?'

'I have spoken to Fanarin.'

'Oh, Fanarin!' said Maslennikov with a grimace, recalling how at a trial the year before this Fanarin had cross-examined him as a witness and, in the politest manner, held him up to ridicule for a full half-hour. 'I should advise you to have nothing to do with him. Fanarin – *est un homme taré*.'[1]

'I have one more request to make,' said Nekhlyudov, without answering him. 'A long time ago I knew a girl, a school-teacher – a pitiable little creature. She's in prison, too, now, and wants to see me. Can you give me a pass to see her as well?'

Maslennikov bent his head on one side and considered.

'Is she a political?'

'Yes, so I have been told.'

'Well, you see, only relatives get permission to visit political prisoners. Still, I'll give you an open order. *Je sais que vous n'abuserez pas.*[2] What is the name of your protégée? Bogodoukhovskaya? *Elle est jolie?*'[3]

'*Hideuse.*'[4]

Maslennikov shook his head disapprovingly, went over to the table and briskly wrote on a sheet of paper with a printed heading, 'The bearer, Prince Dmitri Ivanovich Nekhlyudov, is hereby permitted to interview in the prison office the woman prisoner Maslova, likewise the medical assistant Bogodoukhovskaya,' and he finished with an elaborate flourish.

'Now you'll be able to see how well-regulated the place is. And it is very difficult to maintain order in a prison like that because it is so crowded, especially with convicts on their way to deportation: but I keep a strict eye on things and like the work. You will find them very comfortable and con-

1. Has a bad reputation.   2. I know you won't abuse it.
3. Is she pretty?   4. Hideous.

tented. Only one must know how to treat them. Now the other day there was trouble – a case of insubordination. Another man in my place might have called it mutiny and made no end of wretched victims. But with us it all passed off quietly. It takes care – and a firm hand,' he said, and clenched his plump white fist with a turquoise ring on one finger, that emerged from the gold-linked stiffly starched white cuff of his shirt-sleeve. 'Yes, care and a firm hand.'

'Well, I don't know about that,' said Nekhlyudov. 'I was there twice, and found it dreadfully depressing.'

'Do you know what? You ought to meet Countess Passek,' continued Maslennikov, warming to the conversation. 'She has devoted herself entirely to this sort of work. *Elle fait beaucoup de bien.*[1] It is thanks to her – and perhaps I may add without false modesty, to me – that all these changes have come about: changes that mean that the horrors of the old days no longer exist, and the prisoners are really quite comfortable there. You will see for yourself. As to Fanarin, I do not know him personally – my position keeps our ways apart – but he is most certainly a bad character; and then he takes the liberty of saying such things in court, such things that –'

'Well, I am much obliged,' said Nekhlyudov, picking up the paper, and without listening further he bade his former comrade good-bye.

'Won't you go in and see my wife?'

'No, you must excuse me. I am pressed for time just now.'

'How is that? She will never forgive me,' said Maslennikov, accompanying his old acquaintance down to the first landing, as he accompanied people not of the first but of secondary importance, in which category he classed Nekhlyudov. 'Do go in, if only for a moment.'

But Nekhlyudov remained firm, and while the footman and the porter rushed to give him his overcoat and stick and open the door, outside which stood a policeman, he said again that he really could not stay now.

1. She does a great deal of good.

'Well, come on Thursday, then. It's her at home day. I will tell her,' Maslennikov called to him from the stairs.

51

NEKHLYUDOV drove straight from Maslennikov's to the prison and went to the superintendent's apartments which were now familiar to him. Again, as on the previous occasion, he heard sounds coming from an inferior piano but this time it was not a rhapsody that was being played but exercises by Clementi, with the same unusual vigour, distinctness and rapidity. The servant with the bandaged eye, who opened the door, said that the superintendent was in, and showed Nekhlyudov into a small drawing-room, where there was a sofa and, on the table in front of it, a large lamp with a pink paper shade scorched on one side, standing on a crochet mat of wool. The superintendent entered with a careworn gloomy face.

'Please take a seat. What can I do for you?' he said, buttoning the middle button of his uniform.

'I have just come from the deputy-governor, and have this order from him,' said Nekhlyudov, handing him the paper. 'I should like to see the prisoner Maslova.'

'Markova?' queried the superintendent, not catching what he said because of the music.

'Maslova.'

'Oh yes! Oh yes!'

The superintendent got up and went to the door whence proceeded Clementi's roulades.

'Marusya, can't you stop just a minute?' he said, in a voice that showed that her music was the bane of his life. 'We can't hear ourselves speak.'

The piano was silenced; peevish steps were heard and someone looked in at the door.

The superintendent, apparently relieved now that the music had stopped, lit a fat cigarette of mild tobacco and offered one to Nekhlyudov. Nekhlyudov declined it.

'So, as I say, I should like to see Maslova.'

'It is not convenient for you to see Maslova today,' said the superintendent.

'How's that?'

'Well, I'm afraid it's your own fault,' said the superintendent with a slight smile. 'Prince, don't give her money. If you wish, give it to me. I will keep it for her. But no doubt you gave her money yesterday, and she got hold of some vodka (it is an evil we cannot manage to root out) and today she is quite tipsy, even violent.'

'Is it possible?'

'Indeed it is. I was even obliged to use severe measures, and transfer her to another cell. In the ordinary way she's a quiet woman, but I beg you, don't give her money. These people are like that . . .'

Nekhlyudov instantly recalled what had happened the day before, and again a feeling of horror came over him.

'What about Bogodoukhovskaya, a political prisoner – may I see her?' he asked after a moment's pause.

'Certainly. That's all right,' said the superintendent. 'Well, what do you want here?' he added, turning to a little girl, five or six years old, who had come into the room and was walking towards her father, twisting her head round so as to keep her eyes fixed on Nekhlyudov. 'Mind, you'll fall,' cried the superintendent, smiling as the little girl, not looking where she was going, caught her foot in a rug and ran up to him.

'Well, then, if I may, I should like to go straightaway.'

'Oh yes,' said the superintendent, putting his arms round the child, who was still gazing at Nekhlyudov. Then he got up, gently removed the little girl, and went into the ante-room.

The superintendent had hardly got into his overcoat, which the servant with the bandaged eye handed to him, and gone through the door before Clementi's precise roulades began again.

'She was at the Conservatoire, but it's such a muddle there. She has great talent, though,' said the superintendent, as they went down the stairs. 'She hopes to be a concert pianist.'

The superintendent and Nekhlyudov walked over to the prison. The wicket gate flew open at the superintendent's approach. The warders, their fingers lifted to their caps, followed him with their eyes. In the corridor four men, with half-shaven heads, who were carrying tubs filled with something, shrank back when they saw him. One of them crouched down in a peculiar way and scowled darkly, his black eyes glaring.

'Of course, talent like that must be developed, it would be wrong to bury it, but in a small house, you know, it can be pretty hard,' the superintendent continued the conversation, taking no notice of the prisoners, and, dragging weary feet, accompanied by Nekhlyudov, he walked into the assembly hall.

'Who is it you want to see?'

'Bogodoukhovskaya.'

'Oh, she's in the tower. You'll have to wait a little,' he turned to Nekhlyudov.

'Then in the meantime couldn't I see the Menshovs, mother and son, who are accused of arson?'

'That's cell twenty-one. Yes, they can be sent for.'

'But mayn't I see Menshov in his cell?'

'Oh, it'll be pleasanter for you in the visiting-room.'

'No, I should be interested to see the cell.'

'Well, you have found something to be interested in!'

Just then a foppish young officer, the assistant superintendent, came in from a side-door.

'Here, escort the prince to Menshov's cell. Number twenty-one,' the superintendent said to his assistant. 'And then take him to the office. While I summon the woman – what's her name?'

'Vera Bogodoukhovskaya,' said Nekhlyudov.

The superintendent's assistant was a fair-haired young man with dyed moustaches, who diffused the scent of eau-de-cologne.

'This way, sir,' he said to Nekhlyudov with a pleasant smile. 'Our establishment interests you?'

'Yes, and I am interested in this man, who, I am told, is here through no fault of his own.'

The assistant shrugged his shoulders.

'Yes, that does happen,' he said quietly, politely allowing the visitor to pass before him into the foul-smelling corridor. 'But you can't believe all they say, either. This way, please.'

The cell doors were open and some of the prisoners were in the corridor. With a slight nod to the warders, and a rapid side-glance at the prisoners, who went back to their cells, keeping close to the wall, or else, with hands pressed to their sides like soldiers, stood gazing after them, the assistant guided Nekhlyudov along the corridor into another on the left, separated from the first by an iron door.

This corridor was narrower, darker and smelt even worse than the first. On both sides were padlocked doors, each having a little hole in it about an inch in diameter, called a peep-hole. There was no one in this corridor except an old gaoler with a melancholy wrinkled face.

'Which is Menshov's cell?' asked the superintendent's assistant.

'The eighth on the left.'

52

'MAY I take a look?'

'Certainly, if you wish,' said the assistant with his pleasant smile, and turned to ask the gaoler something. Nekhlyudov looked through one of the peep-holes and saw a tall young man with a stubby black beard striding up and down, wearing nothing but an undergarment. Hearing a noise at the door, he looked up, frowned and continued pacing the cell.

Nekhlyudov looked through another peep-hole: his eye met a big frightened eye looking through the hole at him, and he hurried away. In a third cell he saw a man of diminutive size curled up and asleep on the bed, his prison cloak over his head. In the fourth a man with a broad pale face was sitting with his elbows on his knees and head bowed. At the sound of footsteps he lifted his head and looked up. His whole face, especially the large eyes, bore an expression of hopeless dejection. He was clearly not interested to know who was looking into his cell. Whoever it might be looking at him, the prisoner obviously did not expect anything good from any man. It was terrible and Nekhlyudov stopped looking through any more peep-holes and went on to number twenty-one, Menshov's cell. The gaoler turned the key and opened the door. A muscular young fellow with a long neck, kindly round eyes and a small beard was standing beside the cot, hastily putting on his prison cloak and looking at the new-comers with a frightened face. Nekhlyudov was particularly struck by the kindly round eyes that darted scared inquiring looks from him to the gaoler, the assistant superintendent and back again.

'Here is a gentleman who wants to ask you about your case.'

'Thank you, sir.'

'Yes, I was told about your case,' Nekhlyudov said, crossing the cell to the dirty barred window, 'but I should like to hear about it from you yourself.'

Menshov also walked over to the window and at once began telling his story, at first looking timidly at the superintendent's assistant but gradually growing bolder. When the assistant went into the corridor to give some orders he became quite confident. In accent and manner the story was that of a good, very ordinary peasant lad, and Nekhlyudov found it singularly strange to hear it told in a prison cell by a man wearing degrading prison clothes. Nekhlyudov listened and at the same time looked round him at the low bunk with its straw mattress, the window with the thick iron grating, the dirty damp besmeared walls, and at the pitiful face and form of this unfortunate disfigured peasant in his prison cloak and shoes; and he felt sadder and sadder. He wished he could believe that what this good-hearted fellow was telling him was not true, for it was dreadful to think that people could seize such a lad, without any reason except that he himself had suffered wrong, dress him in convict clothes and shut him up in this horrible place. On the other hand, it was still more distressing to suspect that this straightforward story and the kindly face might be a fraud and a deception. According to the story, soon after the young fellow's marriage the village innkeeper had enticed his wife away. He tried everywhere to get justice. Everywhere the innkeeper bribed the officials and was always acquitted. Once he took his wife back by force, but she ran away again the next day. Then he went to demand her back. The innkeeper told him his wife was not there (though he had seen her as he came in), and ordered him to go away. He refused. The innkeeper and his servants beat him until they drew blood, and the next day the innkeeper's house was burnt down. He and his mother were accused of having set fire to it, but he had not done it – he had gone to see a friend at the time.

'And you really did not set the place on fire?'

'I never thought of such a thing, sir. That old scoundrel must have done it himself. I heard he had insured it just before. They said me and mother went and threatened him. It's true I did call him names that day, I couldn't stand it any longer. But as to setting the house on fire, I didn't do it. And I wasn't there when the fire started. He planned it on purpose for that day because mother and me had been there. He started the fire himself to get the insurance, and said we done it.'

'Can this be true?'

'It's God's truth, sir. Oh, sir, be so good . . .' and Nekhlyudov had difficulty in preventing him from falling at his feet.

'Help me to get out, I'm dying here, and I've done nothing,' he continued.

And suddenly his cheeks began to twitch and he burst into tears, and rolling up the sleeve of his cloak began to wipe his eyes with the sleeve of his grimy shirt.

'Are you ready?' asked the assistant superintendent.

'Yes. Don't lose heart now, we will do what we can,' said Nekhlyudov, and he went out. Menshov was standing by the door so that the gaoler knocked him with it when he closed it. While the gaoler was locking the door Menshov remained looking out through the peep-hole.

53

WALKING back along the wide corridor (it was dinner-time and the cells were open) past the men dressed in light yellow cloaks, short wide trousers and prison shoes who looked avidly at him, Nekhlyudov felt a strange mixture of sympathy for them, and horror and perplexity at the conduct of those who had thrown them into prison and kept them there, and shame on his own account, though he did not know why, for calmly investigating it all.

In one corridor a man ran to a cell, his shoes clattering, and some men came out and barred Nekhlyudov's way, bowing to him.

'Please, your honour – we don't know what to call you – get our case settled somehow.'

'I am not an official. I know nothing about it.'

'It doesn't matter, tell somebody, you can tell the authorities,' said an indignant voice. 'We haven't done anything, and here we've been up against it for nearly two months.'

'How is that? Why?' asked Nekhlyudov.

'They just locked us up. This is the second month we're in gaol, and we don't know why.'

'That is so, it was a kind of accident,' said the superintendent's assistant. 'These people were arrested because they had no identity papers, and they ought to have been sent back to their own province, but the prison there was burnt down and the local authorities appealed to us not to send them on. We dispatched all the others to their respective provinces, but these we are keeping.'

'What, is that the only reason?' Nekhlyudov exclaimed, stopping at the door.

A crowd of some forty men, all in prison clothes, surrounded Nekhlyudov and the assistant. Several voices began to speak at the same time. The assistant checked them.

'Let one of you speak.'

A tall good-looking peasant of about fifty stood out from the rest. He explained to Nekhlyudov that they had all been ordered back to their homes and were now in prison for not having passports. But they had passports all right, only they had expired about two weeks before they were arrested. It happened every year, passports expired and nobody had ever said anything, but this year they had been arrested and held in prison over a month now, as if they were criminals.

'We are all stonemasons, and belong to the same *artel*.[1] They say the prison in our province is burnt down. But that is not our fault. For God's sake help us.'

Nekhlyudov listened but he hardly took in what the handsome old man was saying, his attention being riveted by a large, dark grey, many-legged louse crawling through the hair on the nice-looking stonemason's cheek.

'Is it possible? Can there be no other reason?' Nekhlyudov said, turning to the assistant.

'Yes, the authorities have mismanaged it: they should have been sent off back to their homes,' said the assistant.

Before the officer had finished speaking a little man, also in a prison cloak, detached himself from the crowd and with strange contortions of his mouth began to say that they were being treated rough and they'd done nothing.

'Worse than dogs . . .' he began.

1. Guild.

'Now then, enough of that. Hold your tongue, or you know . . .'

'What do I know?' the little man cried desperately. 'We've done nothing wrong, have we?'

'Shut up!' shouted the assistant superintendent, and the little man was silent.

'What does all this mean?' Nekhlyudov thought to himself as he left the cells, while he ran the gauntlet of a hundred eyes – eyes which watched him through the peep-holes in the doors, eyes which met his as he passed prisoners in the corridor.

'Is it possible entirely innocent people are kept here?' Nekhlyudov exclaimed when they left the corridor.

'What would you have us do? Of course, they don't all speak the truth. To hear them talk, they are all of them innocent,' said the superintendent's assistant.

'But surely those men have done nothing wrong.'

'Maybe not. But they are all a pretty bad lot. You have to be strict with them. There are some dare-devils among them, one has to be on one's guard all the time. Only yesterday we were compelled to punish two of them.'

'Punish them? In what way?'

'Flog them, by order.'

'But corporal punishment has been abolished.'

'Not for those who have been deprived of civil rights. They are still liable.'

Nekhlyudov remembered what he had seen the day before while waiting in the hall, and realized that the punishment was being inflicted even then, at the very time he was there; and he was swept to an especially overwhelming degree by a mixed feeling of curiosity, depression, bewilderment and moral – and very nearly physical – nausea, such as he had experienced before, but never so strongly as now.

No longer listening to the assistant superintendent, he walked as fast as he could, looking neither right nor left, until the corridors were behind him and he reached the office.

The superintendent, still in the corridor attending to some other business, had forgotten to summon Vera Bogodou-khovskaya. Only when Nekhlyudov entered the office did he remember to send for her.

'I am having her brought at once. Please sit down,' he said.

54

THE office consisted of two rooms. The first was lighted by a couple of dirty windows and had a very large dilapidated stove which jutted out into the room. In one corner there was a black yard-stick for measuring a prisoner's height, while in another hung the customary appurtenances of all places of barbarity – a large image of Christ, as it were in mockery of His teaching. In this first room several warders were standing. But in the other room some twenty people, men and women in groups and in pairs, sat along the walls, talking in under-tones. By the window there was a writing-table.

The superintendent sat down at the writing-table and offered Nekhlyudov a chair beside him. Nekhlyudov sat down and became absorbed in watching the people in the room.

The first person to attract his attention was a pleasant-faced young man wearing a short jacket who was standing in front of a middle-aged woman with black eyebrows and talking to her excitedly, and gesticulating with his hands. Near them sat an old man in blue spectacles, holding the hand of a young woman in prison clothes and listening, perfectly still, to what she was telling him. A high-school boy with a fixed scared expression on his face was gazing at the old man, never taking his eyes off him. Not far from them, in a corner, sat a pair of lovers: she was very young and pretty, with short fair hair and an energetic face, and was fashionably dressed; he was a handsome youth with delicate features and wavy hair, wearing a waterproof jacket. They sat in their corner whisper-ing to one another, obviously melting with love. Nearest to the table sat a grey-haired woman in black, evidently the mother of a consumptive-looking young man, who also wore a waterproof jacket. Her eyes were riveted on him and she was trying to say something, but could not speak for tears: several times she began, but had to stop. The young man held a slip of paper in his hand, and, apparently not knowing what to do, kept folding and crumpling it, with an angry look on his face. Beside them sat a plump rosy-cheeked comely girl with very bulging eyes, wearing a grey dress and pelerine. She was sitting next to the weeping mother, tenderly stroking her shoulder. Everything about this girl was beautiful: her large white hands, her short wavy hair, her firmly modelled nose and lips; but the supreme charm of her face lay in the kindly, truthful hazel eyes like those of a sheep. When Nekhlyudov came in the beautiful eyes turned away from the mother for a moment and met his. But she looked away at once and began to say something to the mother. Not far from the lovers a swarthy dishevelled man with a gloomy face sat talking angrily to a beardless visitor who looked like a *skopetz*.[1]

Nekhlyudov seated himself beside the warder and looked around with tense curiosity. His attention was diverted by a little boy with closely cropped hair who came up and addressed him in a shrill voice:

'And who are you waiting for?'

Nekhlyudov was taken aback by the question, but looking at the boy and seeing the serious intelligent little face with its bright intent eyes he replied gravely that he was waiting to see a woman he knew.

'Is she your sister, then?' asked the boy.

'No, she's not my sister,' Nekhlyudov answered, wondering. 'And who are you with?' he asked the boy.

'I am with mamma. She's a political,' said the boy proudly.

'Marya Pavlovna, look after Kolya,' said the warder, no doubt considering Nekhlyudov's conversation with the boy as a breach of the regulations.

1. The *skoptsy* were a religious sect who practised castration.

Marya Pavlovna, the handsome girl with eyes like a sheep who had attracted Nekhlyudov's attention, rose tall and erect, and with a powerful, almost masculine step walked over to Nekhlyudov and the boy.

'I suppose he has been asking you who you are?' she inquired, with a slight smile, gazing confidently and so simply into his eyes, and seeming to suggest that, of course, she always was and must be on natural, friendly terms with all the world. 'He has to know everything,' she said, giving the boy such a wide, sweet, kind smile that both the boy and Nekhlyudov found themselves smiling back.

'Yes, he asked me who I came to see.'

'Marya Pavlovna, it is against the rules to talk to strangers. You know that,' said the warder.

'Very well, very well,' she said, and taking Kolya's little hand in her own large white one, she went back to the consumptive man's mother, Kolya looking up at her all the time.

'Whose child is he?' Nekhlyudov asked the warder.

'His mother is one of the political prisoners, he was born here in the prison,' said the warder, with a certain satisfaction in pointing out how exceptional his establishment was.

'Is that really so?'

'Yes, and now he is going to Siberia with his mother.'

'And that young girl?'

'I cannot tell you about her,' said the warder, shrugging his shoulders. 'Ah, here comes Bogodoukhovskaya.'

55

VERA YEFREMOVNA BOGODOUKHOVSKAYA walked fussily in through a door at the back of the room. She was thin and sallow, with short hair and huge kind eyes.

'Thank you so much for coming,' she said, pressing Nekhlyudov's hand. 'Do you remember me? Let us sit down.'

'I did not expect to find you in a place like this.'

'Oh, I am happy, perfectly happy! I couldn't ask for

anything better,' said Vera Yefremovna, with a startled glance of her enormous kindly round eyes – they always looked startled – and twisting her terribly thin, stringy, sallow neck which stuck out from the shabby, crumpled, soiled collar of her blouse.

Nekhlyudov asked her how she came to be in prison. Speaking animatedly in reply, she began to tell him about herself, interspersing her story with foreign words like *propaganda*, *disorganization*, *groups*, *sections* and *subsections*, which she was apparently quite sure everybody knew but which Nekhlyudov had never heard of.

She poured it all out, obviously quite convinced that he would be very interested and pleased to hear about the secrets of the People's Freedom Movement. But Nekhlyudov was looking at her miserable neck and thin unkempt hair, and wondering why she had been doing such astonishing things and was now telling him all about it. He felt sorry for her, but not at all in the same way as he was sorry for the peasant fellow, Menshov, who was locked up in this stinking prison for no fault of his own. She was to be pitied mainly for the manifest jumble that filled her mind. It was plain that she considered herself a heroine ready to lay down her life for the success of her cause, and yet she would have found it hard to explain what her cause consisted in and wherein lay its success.

The case which Vera Yefremovna wanted to see Nekhlyudov about was this: a friend of hers, a girl named Shustova, who did not even belong to their 'subsection', as she called it, had been arrested with her five months before and confined in the St Peter and St Paul fortress, merely because certain books and papers (which had been given to her for safe-keeping) had been found in her possession. Vera Yefremovna considered herself partly responsible for Shustova's arrest and implored Nekhlyudov, as a man with influence, to do everything in his power to obtain her release. The next thing she asked was that he should get permission for another friend of hers, one Gourkevich (also imprisoned in the fortress), to see his parents and to be allowed certain scientific books which he needed for his studies.

Nekhlyudov promised to do what he could when he went to Petersburg.

As to her own story, this is what Vera Yefremovna said: After completing her course in midwifery she had fallen in with a group from the People's Freedom Movement, and begun to work with them. At first everything went well: they wrote proclamations and did propaganda work in the factories, but then a prominent member was arrested, their papers were seized and widespread arrests followed.

'They arrested me, too, and now I am to be deported,' she concluded her story. 'But it doesn't matter. I feel splendid – in Olympian spirits,' she said, with a pitiful smile.

Nekhlyudov asked her about the girl with the eyes like a sheep's. Vera Yefremovna told him that she was the daughter of a general and had been a member of the revolutionary party for a long time, and was in prison after declaring that it was she who had shot a policeman. She had been living at a secret address where there was a printing-press. One night, when the police came to search the house, the occupants decided to defend themselves: they put the lights out and began to destroy incriminating evidence. The police forced their way in and one of the conspirators fired, mortally wounding a gendarme. When they were questioned as to who had fired the shot this girl said that she had done it, although she had never held a pistol in her hand and would not kill a fly. The matter was left at that, and now she was being deported to hard labour in Siberia.

'An altruist, a fine character,' said Vera Yefremovna approvingly.

The third matter she wanted to discuss concerned Maslova. She knew – everything gets known in prison – Maslova's history and Nekhlyudov's connexion with her, and advised him to take steps to get her transferred to the political ward, or else sent to help in the hospital, where there were a great many patients just then and workers were needed.

Nekhlyudov thanked her for her advice and said he would try to act upon it.

<h1 style="text-align:center">56</h1>

THEIR conversation was interrupted by the warder, who rose and announced that the visiting hour was over and they must leave. Nekhlyudov got to his feet, said good-bye to Vera Yefremovna and walked to the door, where he stopped to survey the scene.

'Gentlemen, time's up, time's up!' repeated the warder, now rising, now sitting down again.

The warder's demand only heightened the animation of all in the room, prisoners and visitors alike, but no one even thought of leaving. Some rose and continued to talk standing. Others kept their seats and went on chatting. A few began tearfully saying farewell. The mother and her consumptive son were especially pathetic. The young man kept twisting his bit of paper, and his face looked blacker than ever, so great were his efforts not to follow his mother's example: when she heard that it was time to go she laid her head on his shoulder and sobbed and sniffed. The girl with the gentle eyes like a sheep – Nekhlyudov could not help watching her – was standing before the sobbing mother and trying to comfort her. The old man with the blue spectacles was standing holding his daughter's hand and nodding his head to what she was saying. The young lovers rose and held hands, gazing silently into each other's eyes.

'Those two are the only happy ones here,' said a young man in a short coat, pointing to the lovers: he was standing beside Nekhlyudov and, like him, watching the general leave-taking.

Conscious that Nekhlyudov and the young man at his side were watching them, the young man in the waterproof jacket and his fair-haired, sweet-faced girl stretched out their arms and clasping one another's hands leaned back and whirled round, laughing.

'They are to be married here in the prison this evening, and she will follow him to Siberia,' said the young man.

'Who is he?'

'A convict sentenced to penal servitude. Just as well they have the heart to be gay – it's too distressing to listen to that,' the young man went on, hearing the sobs of the consumptive's mother.

'Now, my good people, please, please! Don't compel me to resort to severe measures,' said the warder, repeating the same words again and again. 'Do please go, I beg of you!' he said in a weak, hesitating voice. 'What do you mean by it? It's high time you were gone. This really is intolerable. I am telling you for the last time,' he kept saying wearily, now puffing, now putting down his Maryland cigarette.

It was plain that, in spite of the artful, old and time-worn arguments men use to enable them to ill-treat others without feeling any personal responsibility for the evil they do, this warder could not help realizing that he was partly the cause of the sorrow which filled the room; and this obviously troubled him sorely.

At last prisoners and visitors began to separate, the former through the inner, the latter by the outer door. The man in the waterproof jacket, the consumptive and the swarthy-skinned, shaggy-haired man departed, and then Marya Pavlovna with the boy who had been born in the prison.

The visitors began to leave, too. The old man in the blue spectacles went out, moving heavily, and after him Nekhlyudov.

'Yes, it's a wonderful system they have here,' said the loquacious young man as if continuing a conversation that had been interrupted, as he descended the stairs side by side with Nekhlyudov. 'All thanks to the governor, a kind-hearted chap who doesn't stick too closely to the regulations.

It does them good to be able to talk and unburden their hearts.'

'Don't other prisons have this sort of visiting?'

'M'mm! Good gracious no! It's one at a time, and then through a grille.'

Thus chatting with the talkative young man who introduced himself as Medyntsev, Nekhlyudov reached the hall, where the warder came up to him with a weary face.

'So if you would like to see Maslova, please come tomorrow,' he said, evidently wanting to be obliging.

'Very well,' said Nekhlyudov, and hurried away.

The sufferings of the evidently innocent Menshov seemed terrible – and not so much his physical suffering as the bewilderment, the distrust of goodness and of God which he was bound to feel, seeing the cruelty of the men who made his existence wretched without cause. Terrible were the disgrace and misery inflicted on hundreds of innocent people simply because their papers were not properly made out. Terrible were those besotted gaolers, convinced that they were performing a useful and important task by tormenting their fellow men. But most terrible of all, he thought, was that kind-hearted warder in poor health and getting on in years, whose duty it was to part mother and son, father and daughter – human beings just like himself and his own children.

'Why should these things be?' Nekhlyudov wondered, aware this time more than ever of the moral nausea which turned into a physical sickness that he experienced whenever he visited a prison; and found no answer to the question he had asked himself.

57

THE next day Nekhlyudov went to his lawyer and told him about the Menshovs, requesting him to undertake their defence, too. The lawyer, after hearing all he had to say, promised to look into the case and if it turned out to be as

Nekhlyudov said, which was very probable, to undertake their defence without a fee. Nekhlyudov also told him about the hundred and thirty men being held in prison through a misunderstanding, and asked him who was responsible, who was to blame. The lawyer was silent for a moment, evidently anxious to give a correct answer.

'Whose fault? No one's,' he said decidedly. 'Ask the public prosecutor, he'll say it's the governor's fault; ask the governor, he'll blame the public prosecutor. No one is to blame.'

'I am on my way to see Maslennikov. I will tell him.'

'Oh, that's no good,' said the lawyer with a smile. 'He is such a – not a relation or a friend of yours, is he? – such a blackguard, if I may say so, and at the same time a cunning brute!'

Recalling what Maslennikov had said about the lawyer, Nekhlyudov did not reply, and taking his leave drove to Maslennikov's. He had two requests to make: he wanted Maslova transferred to the prison hospital and redress for the hundred and thirty men without identity papers. It went very much against the grain to ask favours of a man whom he did not respect, but there was no other way and he must go through with it.

As he drew near the house Nekhlyudov saw various carriages by the front door and remembered that it was Madame Maslennikov's at home day, to which he had been invited. As he drove up there was a barouche at the entrance, and a footman in livery with a cockade in his hat was helping a lady from the step of the porch into the carriage. She was holding up the train of her gown and showing her slippered feet and thin ankles in black stockings. Among the waiting carriages he recognized the Korchagins' closed landau. Their grey-haired, ruddy-faced coachman took off his hat and bowed in a respectful and friendly manner, as to a gentleman he knew well. Before Nekhlyudov had time to ask the door-keeper for Mikhail Ivanovich (Maslennikov), Maslennikov himself appeared on the carpeted stairs, escorting a very important guest not only to the first landing but all the way down. This very important visitor, a military man, was talking in French about a lottery for the benefit of some children's homes which were being founded in the city, and expressing his opinion that this was a good occupation for the ladies. 'It amuses them, and brings in the money.

'*Qu'elles s'amusent et que le bon Dieu les bénisse . . .*'[1] Ah, Nekhlyudov, how are you? Where do you hide yourself nowadays?' he greeted Nekhlyudov. '*Allez présenter vos devoirs à madame.*[2] The Korchagins are here, too. And Nadine Bukshevden. *Toutes les jolies femmes de la ville*,'[3] he said, slightly hunching his uniformed shoulders as his own footman in magnificent gold-braided livery helped him on with his greatcoat. '*Au revoir, mon cher!*' And he pressed Maslennikov's hand again.

'Now let us go up. I am so glad to see you,' said Maslennikov enthusiastically, taking Nekhlyudov by the arm and, in spite of his own bulk, hurrying him quickly up the stairs.

Maslennikov was in extremely good spirits as the result of the attention bestowed on him by the important personage. Maslennikov ought to have been used by now to meeting the Imperial family, but obviously the commonplace thrives on repetition and every such attention produced in Maslennikov the same rapture that an affectionate little dog feels whenever his master strokes it, pats it on the head or scratches it behind the ear. The dog wags its tail, crouches on the ground, wriggles, lays back its ears and rushes madly round in circles. Maslennikov was ready to do the same. He did not notice the serious expression on Nekhlyudov's face, did not listen to him and impetuously dragged him along to the drawing-room, so that Nekhlyudov could not but follow.

'We'll talk business later. I will do anything in the world for

1. Let them enjoy themselves and may God bless them.
2. Go and pay your respects to Madame.
3. All the pretty women in the town.

you,' said Maslennikov as they were crossing the ballroom. 'Announce Prince Nekhlyudov,' he told a footman, without stopping. The footman ambled off ahead of them. '*Vous n'avez qu'à ordonner.*[1] But first you absolutely must see my wife. I got into trouble last time for not bringing you in.'

By the time they reached the drawing-room the footman had already announced Nekhlyudov, and Anna Ignatyevna, the deputy-governor's lady (*Madame la générale*, as she styled herself) turned a beaming smile on him from behind the heads and bonnets that surrounded her sofa. At the other end of the drawing-room several ladies were seated at a tea-table, while men, some in military, some in civil attire, stood round them. The hubbub of men's and women's voices never slackened.

'*Enfin!*[2] We thought you had quite forgotten us. How have we offended?' With these words, suggesting an intimacy between them which had never existed, Anna Ignatyevna greeted Nekhlyudov.

'Do you know each other? Have you met? Madame Byelyavskaya, Mikhail Ivanovich Chernov. Come and sit near us. Missy, *venez donc à notre table. On vous apportera votre thé. . . .*[3] And you, too,' she said to an officer who was talking to Missy, having apparently forgotten his name, 'please come over here. . . . A cup of tea, prince?'

'No, I shall never agree with you, never: she simply did not love him,' a feminine voice was heard to say.

'But she did love cakes.'

'Oh, you and your silly jokes!' laughingly put in another lady, resplendent in silks, gold and jewels, and a tall bonnet.

'*C'est excellent*, this wafer biscuit, and it's so light. I'd like another.'

'Are you leaving soon?'

'Yes, today is our last day. That's why we are here.'

1. You have only to say the word.
2. At last!
3. Missy, do come over to our table. Your tea shall be brought to you. . . .

'Such a delightful spring, it must be lovely now in the country.'

Missy looked beautiful in a hat and a sort of dark striped gown that fitted her slender waist like a glove – she might have been born in it. She blushed when she saw Nekhlyudov.

'Why, I thought you had gone,' she said to him.

'I should have gone,' he replied, 'but business detained me. I am really here on business today.'

'Do go and see mamma. She would be so pleased,' she said, and knowing that it was not true, and that he knew it wasn't, she blushed still more.

'I shall hardly have time,' replied Nekhlyudov sullenly, trying to appear as if he had not noticed her blushing.

Missy frowned angrily, shrugged her shoulders and turned to an elegant young officer who seized the empty cup from her hands and manfully carried it across the room to another table, his sword knocking against every chair on the way.

'You, too, must contribute something towards the orphanage.'

'I am not refusing, but I want to keep all my largess for the lottery. There I shall show up in all my glory.'

'Well, see that you do!' exclaimed a voice, followed by a noticeably artificial laugh.

Her at home was being a brilliant success and Anna Ignatyevna was beside herself with delight.

'Mika tells me that you are interested in prison work. I understand you so well,' she said to Nekhlyudov. 'Mika' (this was her fat husband) 'may have his faults, but you know how kind-hearted he is. All those unfortunate prisoners – they're his children That is exactly the way he feels about them. *Il est d'une bonté . . .*'[1]

She stopped, finding no words to do justice to the *bonté* of her husband, by whose orders men were flogged, and immediately turned with a smile to welcome a wrinkled old woman in lilac ribbons, who was just coming in.

1. His kindness is . . .

When he had made as many remarks as were necessary, and had as little meaning as was necessary in order not to flout the conventions, Nekhlyudov rose and walked over to Maslennikov.

'Can you give me a few minutes now?'

'Oh yes, of course. What is it? Let us go in here.'

They entered a small room furnished in Japanese style, and sat down by the window.

58

'Well, sir, *je suis à vous.*[1] Will you smoke? But wait a moment, we mustn't make a mess here,' he said, and brought out an ashtray. 'Well now?'

'There are two things I want to ask you about.'

'Dear me!'

Maslennikov's face clouded and he looked despondent. All trace of the excitement of the little dog whose master has scratched it behind the ears vanished absolutely. The sound of voices reached them from the drawing-room. One, a woman's, was saying: '*Jamais, jamais je ne croirais,*'[2] and from the other end of the room a masculine voice kept repeating: 'La comtesse Vorontsov and Victor Aprakhsin.' From another direction came only the confused hum of voices and laughter. Maslennikov tried at one and the same time to hear what was going on in the drawing-room and to listen to what Nekhlyudov was saying.

'I have come again about the same woman,' said Nekhlyudov.

'Yes, the one who was unjustly convicted. I remember, I remember.'

'I should like to ask you to have her transferred to work in the prison hospital. They tell me it can be done.'

1. I am at your disposal.
2. Never, never would I believe it.

Maslennikov compressed his lips and considered.

'Hardly,' he said. 'But I will inquire into it and telegraph you tomorrow.'

'I was told there are a lot of patients and more help is wanted.'

'Well, it may be so. In any case, I will let you know.'

'Please do,' said Nekhlyudov.

A general burst of laughter came from the drawing-room, and even sounded genuine.

'That must be Victor,' said Maslennikov, smiling. 'He can be astonishingly witty when he's in good form.'

'The other thing,' said Nekhlyudov, 'is that you have a hundred and thirty people being kept in gaol simply because their passports have run out. They have been there over a month.'

And he related the circumstances of their case.

'How did you find that out?' asked Maslennikov, and his face suddenly expressed uneasiness and annoyance.

'I was walking along the corridor to see one of the prisoners when I was surrounded by these men, and they asked me . . .'

'Which prisoner were you visiting?'

'A peasant who is being unjustly accused. I have put his case into the hands of a lawyer. But that is not the point. Is it possible that people who have done nothing wrong are kept in prison for no other reason than that their passports have run out . . .?'

'That's the public prosecutor's business,' Maslennikov interrupted irritably. 'You were telling me the other day that the new courts are so much better and fairer than the old ones! It is the duty of the assistant prosecutor to visit the gaols and find out whether the prisoners are detained there lawfully. But they don't do a thing except play cards.'

'Then there is nothing you can do?' Nekhlyudov said dejectedly, remembering what the lawyer had said about the governor shifting responsibility on to the public prosecutor.

'Oh yes, I can. I will investigate at once.'

'So much the worse for her. *C'est un souffre-douleur,*'[1] a woman's voice was heard from the drawing-room, evidently quite indifferent to what she was saying.

'All right, then, I shall take this instead,' a man said jocosely on the other side of the room and a woman laughed playfully, evidently refusing to give him something he wanted.

'No, no, not for anything in the world,' said the woman's voice.

'Very well, then, I'll do all you ask,' Maslennikov repeated, putting out the cigarette he held in his white hand with the turquoise finger-ring. 'And now let us join the ladies.'

'One thing more,' said Nekhlyudov, stopping at the drawing-room door and not going in. 'I was told that some of the men received corporal punishment in the prison yesterday. Is that true?'

Maslennikov went red.

'Good heavens, my dear fellow, what will you ask next! No, *mon cher*, it positively doesn't do to let you in there, you're too inquisitive. Come along now, Annette is calling us,' he said, taking Nekhlyudov by the arm and becoming as worked up as he had been after the attention accorded him by the important personage, but this time it was not joyful excitement but a state of anxious perturbation.

Nekhlyudov pulled his arm away and without taking leave of anyone or saying a word crossed the drawing-room and the ballroom, and strode past the footmen, who sprang towards him, through the vestibule and out into the street, a black expression on his face.

'What is the matter with him? What have you done to him?' Annette asked her husband.

'That's *à la française,*'[2] somebody remarked.

'*À la française*, indeed – I call it *à la zoulou.*'[3]

'Oh, but he's always been like that.'

Someone got up, someone else came in, and the twittering

---

1. She's a doormat.   2. Taking French leave.
3. Taking Zulu leave.

continued its normal course: the Nekhlyudov incident furnished the company with a convenient topic of conversation for the rest of the at home.

The day after his visit to Maslennikov Nekhlyudov received a letter from him written in a magnificent bold hand on thick glazed paper with a crest and seals, informing him that he had written to the doctor concerning Maslova's transfer to work in the prison hospital, and that in all likelihood his request would be granted The letter ended: 'Your affectionate old comrade', and beneath the signature 'Maslennikov' there was a large, firm and wonderfully elaborate flourish.

'Fool!' Nekhlyudov could not help saying – 'comrade' savoured too much of condescension. Maslennikov seemed to think that holding an office, whose duties from a moral point of view were as base and contemptible as they could be, gave him the right to consider himself a man of much importance; and he wished, if not exactly to flatter Nekhlyudov, at least to show him that he was not too proud to call him comrade.

59

ONE of the commonest and most generally accepted delusions is that every man can be qualified in some particular way – said to be kind, wicked, stupid, energetic, apathetic and so on. People are not like that. We may say of a man that he is more often kind than cruel, more often wise than stupid, more often energetic than apathetic or vice versa; but it could never be true to say of one man that he is kind or wise, and of another that he is wicked or stupid. Yet we are always classifying mankind in this way. And it is wrong. Human beings are like rivers: the water is one and the same in all of them but every river is narrow in some places, flows swifter in others; here it is broad, there still, or clear, or cold, or muddy or warm. It is the same with men. Every man bears within him the germs of every human quality, and now manifests one, now another, and frequently is quite unlike himself, while still remaining the same man. In some people the volte-face is particularly abrupt. And to this category belonged Nekhlyudov. His shifts of mood were due both to physical and spiritual causes. And just such a change took place in him now.

The feeling of solemnity and joyful regeneration which he had experienced after the trial, and after his first meeting with Katusha, had vanished completely, to be replaced – after their last interview – by dread, and even disgust of her. He was determined not to leave her, not to abandon his decision to marry her if she wished; but it seemed grievously hard.

The day after his visit to Maslennikov he went to the prison to see her again.

The superintendent consented to the interview, but not in the office, and not in the lawyers' room, but in the women's visiting-hall. For all his kind heart, the superintendent was more reserved with Nekhlyudov than previously: apparently his talks with Maslennikov had resulted in an order for greater reticence towards this visitor.

'You may see her,' said the superintendent, 'only please do as I asked you with regard to money. . . . As to her transfer to the hospital, that his excellency wrote about, it could be done, and the medical officer would agree. Only she herself does not want to go. She says she doesn't care to "empty slops for that scabby lot". You don't know these people, prince,' he added.

Nekhlyudov made no reply, and asked to see her. The superintendent called a warder, and Nekhlyudov followed him into the women's visiting-hall, empty save for Maslova. She came out from behind the netting, quiet and timid. She went up close to Nekhlyudov and said, looking past him:

'Forgive me, Dmitri Ivanovich, I said wicked things to you the day before yesterday.'

'It is not for me to forgive you,' Nekhlyudov began.

'But all the same, you must leave me alone,' she continued, and in the dreadfully squinting eyes she turned on him Nekhlyudov read the old strained and spiteful expression.

'Why should I leave you?'

'Just because –'

'Because why?'

She glanced at him again with, as he thought, the same malicious look.

'Well, that's how it is,' she said. 'You leave me alone – I'm telling you the truth. I can't. You must give up the idea,' she said with trembling lips, and was silent for a moment. 'It's true. I'd rather hang myself.'

Nekhlyudov felt hatred for himself, and resentment for an unforgiven injury, in her refusal, but there was something else, too – something good and significant. Uttered quite calmly, this corroboration of her previous rejection immediately did away with all Nekhlyudov's doubts and uncertainty and restored him to his former solemn and exalted mood of tender emotion.

'Katusha, I said it before, and I say it again,' he articulated very earnestly. 'I ask you to be my wife. But if you don't want to marry me, and for as long as you do not want to, I shall stay with you, and be where you are, and go wherever they take you.'

'That's your affair, I've nothing more to say,' she said, and her lips began to tremble again.

He, too, was silent, unable to speak.

'I am going to the country, and afterwards to Petersburg,' he said when he had regained his composure. 'I shall do all I can about your – about our – case, and, God willing, get the sentence revoked.'

'And if it isn't, never mind. If I don't deserve it for this, I do for other things,' she said, and he saw what an effort she had to make to keep back her tears.

'Well, did you see Menshov?' she asked suddenly, to hide her emotion. 'It's true, isn't it, that they are innocent?'

'Yes, I think it is.'

'She is such a wonderful old woman,' she said.

He repeated to her what Menshov had told him, and asked whether she needed anything for herself. She replied that she did not want anything.

Again they were silent.

'About the hospital,' she said suddenly, glancing at him with squinting eyes. 'I will go if you like, and I won't touch any more drink either . . .'

Nekhlyudov looked silently into her eyes. They were smiling.

'That's very good,' was all he could answer, and then he said good-bye to her.

'Yes, yes, she is an entirely different person,' Nekhlyudov thought, experiencing after all his former doubts a feeling he had never known before – the certainty that love is invincible.

★

When Maslova returned to her stinking cell after this interview she took off her cloak and sat down in her place on the plank-bedstead, with her hands folded in her lap. The only other prisoners in the cell were the consumptive girl from Vladimir with her baby, Menshov's old mother and the signal-woman with the two children. The subdeacon's daughter had been pronounced insane the day before and removed to the hospital. And all the other women were away, washing clothes. The old woman was asleep on her bunk; the children were in the corridor, the door into which was open. The girl from Vladimir with the baby in her arms and the signal-woman with the stocking she was knitting with swift fingers came up to Maslova.

'Well, did you see 'im?' they asked.

Maslova sat silent on the high bunk, swinging her legs which did not reach to the floor.

'Mopin' ain't no use,' said the signal-woman. 'You gotter keep yer end up, that's the main thing. Come on now,

Katusha, cheer up!' she went on, her fingers moving like lightning.

Maslova did not answer.

'Our folks are all out washing their clothes,' said the Vladimir woman. 'You can't think what almsgiving there is today. A tidy bit been brought in, they say.'

'Finashka!' the signal-woman cried through the door. 'Where's the little imp got to?'

And she stuck a knitting needle through the ball and the stocking, and went out into the corridor.

Just then the sound of footsteps and women's voices was heard from the corridor, and the other occupants of the cell entered, wearing prison shoes but no stockings, each of them carrying a bread roll – some of them even had two. Fedosya at once went up to Maslova.

'What's the matter? Anything wrong?' she asked, her clear blue eyes looking affectionately at her friend. 'These are for our tea,' she added, putting the fancy loaves on the shelf.

'Changed 'is mind about marrying you, 'as 'e?' said Korablyova.

'No, he hasn't, but I don't want to,' said Maslova. 'And I told him so.'

'More fool you!' said Korablyova in her deep bass.

'If you can't live together, what's the use of marrying?' said Fedosya.

'There's your 'usban' – 'e's goin' along with you, ain't 'e?' said the signal-woman.

'Yes, but we're already married,' said Fedosya. 'But what's the point of 'im tying 'imself up if 'e can't live with 'er afterwards?'

'What for? Don't be a fool! If 'e marries 'er she'll be rollin' in money.'

'He says: "No matter where they take you, I'll follow," ' said Maslova. 'But I don't care whether he does or not. I'm not going to ask him to. He's going to Petersburg now.

to see about my case. All the ministers there are relations of his,' she continued. 'But I've no use for him all the same.'

'Of course not!' Korablyova agreed suddenly, rummaging in her bag and evidently thinking about something else. 'Let's 'ave a drop, shall we?'

'You have a drop,' replied Maslova. 'I won't.'

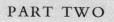

PART TWO

CHAPTER TWO

1

MASLOVA'S case was likely to come before the Senate in a fortnight's time, and Nekhlyudov meant to be in Petersburg by then, so that if matters went wrong he would be able to petition the Emperor, as the lawyer who had drawn up the appeal had advised him to do. Should the appeal prove fruitless – and according to the lawyer it was best to be prepared for that, since the grounds for appeal were so slight – the party of convicts which included Maslova might start off early in June. Therefore, in order to be ready to follow her to Siberia, which was Nekhlyudov's firm intention, it was necessary for him to visit his estates and settle matters there.

Nekhlyudov went first to the nearest, Kuzminskoye, a large estate in the black soil belt, from which he derived the bulk of his income. He had lived on this estate in his childhood and youth, and had been there twice since. On one occasion, at his mother's request, he had taken a German bailiff with him and gone over the whole property, so that he was familiar with the condition of the estate and knew the relations the peasants bore to the 'office' (that is, to the landlord). These relations were such that the peasants were – to put it nicely – entirely dependent on his management, or – to speak plainly – in a state of servitude to the office. It was not active serfdom such as had been abolished in the year 1861 (the thraldom of certain persons to their master) but a general state of serfdom among persons owning no land, or very little, *vis-à-vis* the great landlords in general and primarily, and sometimes solely, those among whom the peasants lived. Nekhlyudov knew this, he could not be ignorant of it, since the economy of his estates was based on this serfdom, and he had assisted in the setting up of this economy. But not only was this known to Nekhlyudov – he knew, too, that it was unjust and cruel, and had known it since he was a university student, when he had accepted and advocated the teaching of Henry George and, in accordance with that teaching, had given to the peasants the land left to him by his father, considering the ownership of land just such a sin in our time as the ownership of serfs had been fifty years ago. It is true that when he left the army, where he got into the habit of spending some twenty thousand roubles a year, he ceased to regard his former views as binding, and they were forgotten, and he not only entirely left off inquiring into his attitude to property and where the money came from that his mother allowed him but tried not to think about it. But his mother's death, his own subsequent inheritance and the necessity of managing his estate, that is, the land, brought up again the question of his attitude to the private ownership of land. A month ago Nekhlyudov would have told himself that he could not change the existing order of things, that it was not he who was managing the estate; and one way or another would have eased his conscience, living as he did at a distance from his estates and having the money sent to him. But now he decided that he could not leave matters as they stood, even though he had the journey to Siberia before him, as well as a complicated and difficult relationship with the prison world, which would require money: he must make a change, though he would be the loser by it. Therefore he decided not to farm the land himself but to let it out to the peasants at a low rent, thus giving them a chance to become independent of the land-owner in general. Many a time, comparing the position of a landowner with that of an owner of serfs, Nekhlyudov had equated the renting of land to the peasants (instead of culti-vating it with hired labour) with the old system of making serfs pay quit-rent in lieu of their labour. This was not a solu-tion to the problem, but it was a step in that direction: it was a change from a harsh to a less harsh form of tyranny. And this was what he meant to do.

Nekhlyudov arrived at Kuzminskoye around noon. Trying to simplify his life in every respect, he did not telegraph but at the station hired a peasant trap with two horses. The driver was a young fellow in a long-waisted, full-skirted nankeen coat, belted low. He sat sideways on the box, like a country driver, and was glad to talk to the gentleman since while they were talking his jaded, lame white wheeler and the emaciated, broken-winded trace-horse could go at a foot-pace, which was what they always liked.

The driver spoke about the bailiff at Kuzminskoye, not knowing that he was driving 'the master'. Nekhlyudov had purposely not told him who he was.

'A proper swell, that German fellow,' said the driver, who had lived in the town and read novels. He was sitting sideways, half turned towards his fare, grasping his long whip now at the top, now at the bottom, and obviously showing off his education. 'Got 'isself a troika of light bays, an' when 'e drives out with 'is lady – oh my!' he went on. 'At Christmas 'e 'ad a tree up at the big 'ouse. I drove some of the company. It 'ad 'lectric lights. There wasn't the like of it in the 'ole countryside. The money 'e 'as raked in – you wouldn't believe! 'E can 'ave any mortal thing 'e wants. They say 'e's bought 'isself a fine estate.'

Nekhlyudov had imagined that he was quite indifferent to the way the German managed and made use of his estate. But the long-waisted driver's story was disagreeable hearing. He enjoyed the beautiful day; the heavy darkening clouds that every now and again obscured the sun; the fields of spring grain where the peasants were walking behind their ploughs, hoeing the young oats; the thickly sprouting verdure with the larks soaring overhead; the woods with the trees – except for the tardy oak – all covered with young foliage; the meadows dotted with grazing cattle and horses; and the fields and the ploughmen in the distance – but no, no, it suddenly came back to him that something disagreeable had happened, and when he asked himself what it was he remembered the driver's story about the way his German bailiff had been managing his Kuzminskoye estate.

But once he reached Kuzminskoye and set to work Nekhlyudov forgot about the unpleasant feeling he had had.

An examination of the account books and a talk with the bailiff, who artlessly pointed out the advantages deriving from the fact that the peasants had very little land of their own, and what they had was surrounded by the landlord's fields, made Nekhlyudov all the more determined to give up farming and let all the land to the peasants. From the ledgers and discussion with the bailiff he discovered that, as before, two-thirds of the finest arable land was being worked by hired labour and improved machinery, while the remaining third was tilled by peasants who were paid five roubles a *desyatina*[1] – that is to say, for five roubles a peasant had to plough each *desyatina* three times, harrow it three times, sow and reap the corn, tie it into sheaves or scythe and deliver it to the thresh-ing-floor: in other words, perform work which at the cheapest hired rate would cost at least ten roubles. Moreover, the peasants paid with their labour – and dearly, too – for everything they got from the estate. They paid with their labour for the use of meadow-land, for wood and potato tops, and nearly all of them were in debt to the office. Thus the peasants paid four times as much for the land which they rented beyond the cultivated fields as the owner could have got by selling it and investing the proceeds at five per cent.

Nekhlyudov had known all this before, but it now struck him as something fresh, and he only marvelled how it was that he and others in his position could help seeing the abnormity of such a state of affairs. The bailiff's arguments that if the land were let to the peasants the agricultural imple-ments would fetch next to nothing – they could not be sold for a quarter of their value; the peasants would ruin the land; and in general Nekhlyudov would lose a great deal through the transfer, only strengthened Nekhlyudov's conviction that

1. About two and three-quarter acres.

he was doing the right thing in giving the land to the peasants and depriving himself of a large part of his income. He decided to settle the business on the spot, while he was there. The harvesting, the selling of the crops and agricultural implements and of the useless out-buildings, he would leave to the bailiff after his departure. But now he asked the bailiff to call a meeting for the next day of the peasants from the three villages lying in the midst of his Kuzminskoye estate, so that he could tell them what he meant to do and arrange the terms at which they were to rent the land.

Pleased with himself for the firmness he had shown in face of the bailiff's arguments and for his readiness to make a sacrifice, Nekhlyudov left the office and, thinking over the business before him, strolled round the outside of the house through the neglected flower-garden (this year flowers had been planted only in front of the bailiff's house), across the tennis court, now overgrown with succory, and along the avenue of lime-trees where he used to go to smoke his cigar and where he had flirted with the pretty Kirimova girl when she had been staying with his mother three years ago. After he had planned the speech he would make to the peasants next day he went back to the bailiff and over tea discussed with him again how to wind up the whole estate. Then he withdrew, quite calm and contented, to the bedroom prepared for him in the big house which had always been used for guests.

A clean bed with a spring mattress had been placed in this neat little room, with views of Venice on the walls, a looking-glass between the two windows and a small table on which stood a decanter of water, some matches and a candle-snuffer. On a large table by the looking-glass lay his open portmanteau, showing his dressing-case and some books he had brought with him: one in Russian, dealing with research into the laws of criminality, another in German and a third in English on the same subject, which he meant to read during his leisure moments while travelling to and fro between his estates, but it was too late today, and he prepared to go to bed so as to be able to get up early and be ready for the meeting with the peasants.

An old-fashioned inlaid mahogany arm-chair stood in one corner of the room, and the sight of this chair, which Nekhlyudov remembered as having been in his mother's bedroom, suddenly evoked a totally unexpected emotion in his heart. All at once he felt sorry for the house that would tumble to ruin, the garden that would run wild, the forest that would be cut down, and all the barns, stables, tool-sheds, the machinery, the horses and the cows, which he knew had cost so much effort – though not to himself – to acquire and to maintain. He had thought it would be easy to give it all up, but now he regretted not only all this but the land, too, and the loss of half his income, which he might so well have need of now. And instantly arguments to show that it would not be proper to give the land to the peasants and destroy his estate came to his aid.

'I have no right to own land. And if I don't I can't keep up the house and the farm. Besides, I shall very soon be going to Siberia, and then I shall have no need of either the house or the farm,' said one voice. 'All that is true,' said another, 'but, to begin with, you are not going to spend all your life in Siberia. And if you marry, there may be children, and just as you received the estate in good condition, so you must hand it over to them. There is a duty to the land, too. It is easy enough to give it all up and let it go to ruin, but acquiring it was far from easy. But most important of all – you ought to take time for reflection and consider what it is you intend to do with your life, and arrange for your property accordingly. But are you sure of yourself? Then again – are you acting sincerely, as your conscience dictates, or are you posing for effect, to win people's applause?' Nekhlyudov asked himself, and was forced to admit that he was influenced by the thought of what people would say about him. And the longer he pondered, the more questions presented themselves and the more unsolvable they became. To escape from his thoughts he got into his spotless bed and tried to go to sleep, in the hope of waking with a clear head which would find the answer to the problems that were now such an enigma to him. But he could not sleep for a long time. Together with the crisp air and the moonlight, the croaking of frogs poured in through the open windows, broken by the clicking and trilling of the nightingales far away in the park – and one close to the window, in a lilac bush in bloom. Listening to the nightingales and the frogs, Nekhlyudov remembered the playing of the superintendent's daughter; then he thought of the superintendent; that brought him to Maslova, whose lips had quivered, like the croaking of the frogs, when she said, 'You leave me alone.' Then the German bailiff began going down to the frogs, and had to be held back, but he not only got right down but turned into Maslova, saying with reproach: 'You are a prince, and I am a convict.'

'No, I won't give up,' thought Nekhlyudov, waking, and he asked himself: 'Well, am I doing right or wrong? I don't know, and anyway it makes no difference to me. No difference at all. The thing is to get to sleep.' And now he himself started to slip slowly down where the bailiff and Maslova had gone, and there he knew no more.

2

NEKHLYUDOV woke at nine o'clock in the morning. The young clerk who waited on 'the master' heard him stir and brought him his boots, shining as they had never shone before, and some cold, beautifully clear spring water, and informed him that the peasants were beginning to assemble. Nekhlyudov jumped out of bed, collecting his thoughts. Not a trace remained of yesterday's regret at the idea of surrendering the land and breaking up the estate. He was surprised that he had ever felt any regret. Now he looked forward happily to what lay before him, and was involuntarily proud of it. Through the window he could see the tennis court, overgrown with succory, where the peasants were gathering in obedience to the orders of the bailiff. No wonder the frogs had been croaking the night before: it was a cloudy morning. There was no wind. A soft warm rain had been falling since early in the day and hung in drops on leaves, twigs and grass. Through the window came the smell of earth crying for more rain, as well as the fragrance of fresh vegetation. While dressing, Nekhlyudov several times looked out of the window to watch the peasants gathering on the tennis court. One by one they arrived, took off their caps as they bowed to one another, and placed themselves in a circle, leaning on their sticks. The bailiff, a stout, muscular strong young man in short pea-jacket with a green stand-up collar and enormous buttons, came in to tell Nekhlyudov that they were all assembled but that they could wait until Nekhlyudov had had his breakfast – tea or coffee, whichever he pleased, both were ready.

'No, I would rather go and see them at once,' said Nekhlyudov, feeling quite unexpectedly shy and ill at ease at the thought of the talk he was going to have with the peasants.

He was about to fulfil their dearest wish – one they never dared dream of even: to let the land to them at a low price; that is, he was going to do them a great kindness, and yet he felt ashamed of something. When he went out to them and the brown heads and grey heads, curly heads and bald heads were bared before him he was so embarrassed that he could say nothing. The rain continued to fall in a fine drizzle, leaving drops clinging to their hair, their beards and the nap of their long tunics. The peasants looked at 'the master', waiting to hear what he had to say to them, but he was too abashed to speak. The awkward silence was broken by the quiet, self-possessed German bailiff, who considered that what he didn't know about the Russian peasant wasn't worth knowing, and who spoke Russian like a native. This overfed Hercules of a man, like Nekhlyudov himself, presented a striking contrast to the peasants with their thin wrinkled faces and lean shoulder-blades sticking out under their tunics.

'The prince here wishes to do you a good turn – he is thinking of letting the land to you, only you don't deserve it,' said the bailiff.

'Why don't we deserve it, Vassily Karlovich? Haven't we worked well for you? The late mistress – the Kingdom of Heaven to her! – was very good to us, and the young prince, God be thanked, doesn't abandon us,' began a red-haired peasant who had the gift of the gab.

'I have called you here because I want you to have all the land, if you would like it,' Nekhlyudov brought out.

The peasants were silent; either they did not understand him or they could not believe their ears.

'How do you mean – let us have the land?' asked a middle-aged peasant in a long-waisted coat.

'To let you have it to farm for yourselves, and charge you a very small rent.'

'I say, that's something like,' said an old man.

'If only the rent won't be more than us can afford,' said another.

'Why shouldn't we take the land?'

'We know how to farm – we make our living off the land!'

'All the better for him, it'll be,' several voices were heard saying. 'Nothing to do but sit and let the money come in. But think of the worry and trouble there is now!'

'It's you who cause the worry and trouble,' said the German. 'If only you did your work properly and behaved yourselves . . .'

'That's easy said, Vassily Karlovich,' put in a thin sharp-nosed little old man. 'You say to me, "Why did you let your 'orse get into the wheat?" but let me ask you 'ose fault it was. All day long likely I was swinging a scythe or something, till the day seems as long as a year, or I drops off to sleep while I'm watching the 'orses at night, and before I knows it me 'orse is in your wheat. Then you flay me alive.'

'Well, you should be more careful.'

'It's all very well for you to say that, but it just ain't in us,' objected a tall, shaggy, dark-haired man, who was not very old.

'Then why don't you give us the timber,' protested a short ill-favoured little peasant from the back. 'I was goin' to put up a fence this 'ere summer, and cut down a sapling, when you stuck me in the lock-up to be eaten by vermin for three months. That was the end of that fence.'

'What is he talking about?' Nekhlyudov asked the bailiff.

'*Der erste Dieb im Dorfe*,'[1] answered the bailiff in German. 'Every year he's caught stealing wood from the forest. You'd better learn to respect other people's property,' he said.

'Don't we show you respect enough?' said an old man. 'We can't not show you respect because we're in your power: you do what you like with us.'

'Oh, there's no getting the better of you, my fine fellow: all I ask is that you shouldn't get the better of us.'

'Is that so, indeed! Didn't you smash my jaw for me last summer, and did I get any damages? You know yourself it's no good goin' to law with the rich.'

'And you see to it you don't break the law.'

Obviously this was a tournament of words, with the participants not understanding too clearly what they were arguing about or why. But it was not difficult to discern bitterness held in check by fear on the one side, and on the other a consciousness of superiority and power. Nekhlyudov found it distressing to listen to, and he tried to return to the matter about the rent and dates of payment.

'Well now, about the land. Do you want it? And what rent do you suggest if I let you have it all?'

'It's your land, you say what you want.'

Nekhlyudov named a figure. As always, though it was much lower than other rents paid in the neighbourhood, the peasants began to haggle and to find the figure too high. Nekhlyudov had expected that his offer would be welcomed with delight, but no signs of pleasure were visible. Only one

1. The biggest thief in the countryside.

thing showed Nekhlyudov that his offer was to the peasants' advantage, and that was the bitter disputes which broke out when the question of who should rent the land was discussed: should it be the whole commune or a representative body from each village? The peasants in favour of keeping out the feeble and the poor payers argued fiercely with those they wanted to exclude. At last, thanks to the bailiff, the amount of rent and dates of payment were settled, and the peasants, talking noisily, started down the hill in the direction of their villages, while Nekhlyudov and the bailiff went into the office to draw up the terms of the agreement.

Everything was arranged in the way Nekhlyudov wanted and expected it to be: the peasants were to receive the land at about thirty per cent less than was asked in the neighbourhood; his income from the land was cut to almost half, but was more than enough for Nekhlyudov, especially with the addition of the sum he received for a forest he sold, and another which he would get from the sale of his livestock and farm machinery. Everything, it would seem, was going splendidly, yet all the time Nekhlyudov felt restless and ill at ease with himself. He saw that the peasants, though they spoke words of gratitude to him, were dissatisfied and had expected something more. It turned out that he had made a serious sacrifice and yet not fulfilled the peasants' expectations.

On the following day the agreement was signed between them, and Nekhlyudov, escorted by a deputation of elderly peasants who had come to see him off, stepped into the bailiff's 'swell' troika (as the driver from the station had called it) and drove off to catch the train, with the unpleasant feeling of something left unfinished. He said good-bye to the peasants, who stood puzzled and discontentedly shaking their heads. Nekhlyudov was dissatisfied with himself. What made him dissatisfied, he did not know, but he felt all the time depressed for some reason, and for some reason ashamed.

3

FROM Kuzminskoye Nekhlyudov drove to the estate he had inherited from his aunts – the one where he first met Katusha. He meant to make the same arrangement about the land there as he had at Kuzminskoye; he also wanted to find out everything he could about Katusha and their child: whether it was true that it had died, and how it had died. He got to Panovo early in the morning and the first thing that struck him as he drove into the courtyard was the air of decay and neglect that hung over all the buildings, and particularly the house itself. The sheet-iron roof, which had once been green but had not been painted for a long time, was now red with rust, and several sheets were bent back, probably after a storm; some of the weather-boarding had been torn away wherever it could be easily got at by loosening the rusty nails. Both porches, especially the one at the back which he remembered so well, were rotten and broken down: only the joists remained. Some of the windows were boarded up where the glass had been broken, and the wing occupied by the bailiff, and the kitchen and the stables, were all dilapidated and grey. Only the garden had not fallen into decay but, on the contrary, had grown lush and was in full bloom; on the other side of the fence he could see flowering cherry-, apple- and plum-trees looking like white clouds. The lilac hedge was in blossom, too, just as it had been fourteen years ago when Nekhlyudov had played catch with the eighteen-year-old Katusha and had fallen and stung himself in the nettles behind one of those same lilac bushes. The larch his Aunt Sophia Ivanovna had planted near the house – he remembered it as a slender sapling – was now a tall tree with a trunk fit for a good solid beam and its branches were covered with soft yellow-green needles like down. The river, now within its banks, rushed noisily over the mill dam. All kinds of cattle belonging to the peasants were grazing in the meadow across the river.

The bailiff, a student who had left the seminary without finishing the course, met Nekhlyudov in the courtyard with a smile on his face, still smiling invited him into the office and, smiling again and seeming to promise something especially pleasant, went behind the partition. Here there was some whispering, and then silence. The driver who had brought Nekhlyudov from the station, having received his tip, drove away with tinkling bells, and all was quiet. Then a barefooted girl in an embroidered peasant blouse and fluffy ear-rings[1] ran past the window, followed quickly by a peasant, clattering with his nailed boots on the hard-trodden path.

Nekhlyudov sat down by the window, looking out into the garden and listening. A fresh spring breeze wafted the scent of newly turned soil through the little casement window, lightly stirring the hair on his damp forehead and the papers lying on the window-sill, which had been hacked all over by a knife. From the river came the *tra-pa-tap*, *tra-pa-tap* of the wooden paddles with which the women beat the clothes they were washing, the sounds echoing over the glittering sunlit surface of the mill pool; and he could hear the rhythmical fall of the water over the wheel, and the loud buzzing of a startled fly close to his ear.

And suddenly Nekhlyudov remembered how, in just the same way, long ago, when he was young and innocent, he had heard, above the rhythmical sound of the mill, the women's wooden paddles beating the wet clothes, how in just the same manner the spring breeze had blown the hair about on his damp forehead and stirred the papers on the knife-scarred window-sill, and another startled fly had flown past his ear; and it was not exactly that he remembered himself as the lad of eighteen he had been then, but he seemed to feel himself the same as he was then, possessed of the same freshness and purity, and a future full of great possibilities, and at the same time, as happens in a dream, he knew that all this could be no more, and he felt terribly sad.

1. Home-made drop ear-rings of down or fur.

'When would you like something to eat?' asked the bailiff, with a smile.

'Oh, any time – I am not hungry. I'm going to take a turn down to the village.'

'Wouldn't you like to come into the house? I keep everything in good order indoors, even though outside it may look . . . Won't you please look in . . .'

'Not now, thank you; later on. I wonder if you know of a woman here by the name of Matriona Kharina?' (This was Katusha's aunt.)

'Oh yes, in the village. I can't do anything with her. She keeps a pot-house. I know it perfectly well, and I've told her so over and over again, and threatened her, but when it comes to taking her up, I haven't the heart to: she's an old woman, and has grandchildren with her,' said the bailiff with his everlasting smile, which expressed both his desire to please 'the master' and his conviction that Nekhlyudov looked upon these matters in the same way as himself.

'Where does she live? I should like to walk over and see her.'

'At the end of the village, on the other side of the street, the third cottage from the end. On the left there is a brick cottage and her hovel is beyond that. But I'd better take you,' said the bailiff, smiling happily.

'No, thanks, I shall find it all right. And in the meantime please call a meeting of the peasants, and say that I want to speak to them about the land,' Nekhlyudov ordered, intending to make the same sort of agreement with the peasants as he had at Kuzminskoye, and, if possible, that very evening.

4

As Nekhlyudov was leaving the gate he met the peasant girl with the tassel ear-rings, who was returning along the hard-trodden path across the pasture ground overgrown with plantain and wild rosemary. She was wearing a gay-coloured apron and trotted briskly along on her plump bare legs. Her left arm swung vigorously across her path, while with her right hand she clutched a red rooster to her stomach. The rooster, his scarlet comb quivering, seemed perfectly quiet, although his eyes rolled and occasionally he thrust out a black foot to claw at the girl's apron. As she drew near 'the master' she slowed down and then her run changed to a walk. When they drew level she stopped and with a backward jerk of her head bobbed to him, and only when he had passed did she continue on with the fowl. Going down towards the well, Nekhlyudov met an old woman in a coarse dirty blouse, carrying two heavy pails of water slung on a yoke across her bent back. The old woman carefully set the pails on the ground and then she, too, bowed to him with the same backward jerk of the head.

Beyond the well began the village. It was a bright hot day and already sultry, though only ten o'clock in the morning. Gathering clouds now and then obscured the sun. The whole length of the street was filled with a pungent and not un-pleasant smell of dung, coming partly from the carts rumbling along the smooth shining road up the hillside, but chiefly from the heaps of manure lately forked over in the yards, by the open gates of which Nekhlyudov had to pass. The peasants walking barefooted up the hill beside their carts, their shirts and drawers smeared with dung, turned round to look at the tall stout gentleman with grey hat and silk hatband shining in the sun, walking up the village street, at every other step touching the ground with a gleaming silver-headed cane. The peasants returning from the field, jogging along in their empty carts, took off their hats and gazed in astonishment at this extraordinary person walking up their street. Women came out of their gates or stood in the porches of their huts and pointed him out to each other, following him with their eyes.

When Nekhlyudov was passing the fourth gate he was stopped by a cart driving out of the yard, its wheels creaking.

It was loaded high with manure, smacked flat on top, where there was a piece of matting to sit on. A barefooted, six-year-old boy, excited at the prospect of a ride, followed the cart. A young peasant striding along in bast shoes was leading the horse out of the yard. A long-legged bluish-grey colt leaped out of the gate, but, startled at the sight of Nekhlyudov, pressed close to the cart and, scraping its legs against the wheels, slipped through ahead of the mare, who showed her uneasiness by a gentle whinny as she drew the heavy load through the gate. The next horse was being led out by a thin active old man, also barefooted, with protruding shoulder-blades, dressed in a grimy shirt and striped drawers.

When the horses were out on the hard road, strewn with bits of dry ash-coloured dung, the old man went back to the gate and bowed to Nekhlyudov.

'Would you be the nephew of our mistresses?'

'Yes, I'm their nephew.'

'Welcome 'ere. Come to look us up, eh?' said the garrulous old man.

'Yes, that's it. Well, and how are you getting along?' asked Nekhlyudov, not knowing what to say.

' 'Ow are we gettin' along! As bad as can be,' the old man drawled, as if it gave him pleasure to say so.

'Why so badly?' Nekhlyudov inquired, stepping inside the gate.

'What sort of a life is it – you can 'ardly call it livin',' said the old man, following Nekhlyudov to the part of the yard that was roofed over.

Nekhlyudov stepped after the old man into the lean-to.

'There look, I 'ave twelve mouths to feed,' continued the old man, pointing towards a couple of women who stood, pitchforks in hand, sweating on the last pile of manure. Their kerchiefs were awry and their skirts were tucked up showing bare calves splashed half-way to the knee with manure. 'Not a month passes but what I 'ave to buy more'n fifteen stone o' rye, and where's the money to come from?'

'Doesn't your own rye see you through?'

'Me own?' echoed the old man, with a scornful smile. 'Why, I've only land enough for three, and last year we only 'arvested eight stooks that didn't last till Christmas.'

'What do you do then?'

'What do we do? Well, I 'ired one son out as a labourer, and then I borrowed some money from your honour. Spent it all before Shrovetide, and the taxes ain't paid yet.'

'And how much do you have to pay?'

'Oh, it's seventeen roubles for my 'ouse'old. I tell you, 'tis a 'ard life. Sometimes I wonders 'ow we manage at all!'

'May I go into your cottage?' asked Nekhlyudov, walking across the yard over the ill-smelling, saffron-coloured layers of manure that had been raked up here and there.

'To be sure! Come in,' said the old man, and with rapid strides of his bare feet, the liquid manure oozing between his toes, he ran ahead of Nekhlyudov and opened the door for him. The women straightened their kerchiefs and let down their skirts, gazing with inquisitive awe at the clean gentle-man with gold cuff-links who was entering their house.

Two little girls with nothing on but coarse chemises rushed out of the hut. Taking off his hat and stooping to get through the low door, Nekhlyudov made his way into the passage and thence into the dirty cramped hut which smelled of sour food and where two looms took up most of the space. An old woman was standing by the stove, her sleeves rolled up over her thin stringy sunburnt arms.

' 'Ere's the master come to see us,' said the old man.

'You're welcome, sir, I'm sure,' said the old woman kindly, pulling down her sleeves.

'I wanted to see how you live,' said Nekhlyudov.

'Well, we lives just as you see. The 'ut is ready to tumble down at any moment, it'll be the death of somebody yet. But my old man says it's a good one as 'uts go, so 'ere we lives like kings,' said the lively old woman, jerking her head nervously. 'I be just gettin' the dinner ready now, to feed the men.'

'And what are you going to have for dinner?'

'What are we goin' to 'ave? Good food, we 'ave. First course bread with *kvass*,[1] and t'other course, *kvass* with bread,' said the old woman with a grin that revealed teeth worn away to stumps.

'No, seriously, let me see what you are having today.'

'What we are 'aving – it won't take long to show you that,' said the old man, laughing. 'Show 'im, wife.'

The old woman shook her head.

'So you want to see our peasant fare, do you? You are a one, I must say. Wants to know everything. I told you – bread and *kvass*, and then soup – one of the women brought us some gout-wort last night, that's what the soup's made of – and after that, 'taties.'

'Is that all?'

'What more d'you want? We'll wash it down with milk,' said the old woman, laughing and looking towards the door.

The door was open and the passage outside was crowded with people – boys, girls, women with babies in their arms – all staring at the strange gentleman who wanted to see the food the peasants ate. The old woman was evidently proud of herself for knowing how to behave with the gentry.

'Yes, sir, ours is a wretched life, ours is, there's no saying it ain't,' declared the old man. ' 'Ere, you get out of 'ere!' he shouted to the crowd by the door.

'Well, good-bye,' said Nekhlyudov, feeling awkward and ashamed, though he could not account for his feelings.

'Thank you kindly for comin' to see us,' said the old man.

The peasants outside in the passage pressed close together to let Nekhlyudov pass, and he went into the street and walked on. Two barefooted boys who had been in the passage followed him out. One, the elder, was wearing a shirt that had once been white and was now very dirty; the other had on a

1. A drink made of rye and malt.

worn and faded pink one. Nekhlyudov looked round at them.

'And now where are you goin'?' asked the boy in the white shirt.

'To Matriona Kharina's. Do you know her?'

The little boy in the pink shirt for some reason broke into a laugh, but the elder boy inquired in a serious tone:

'Which Matriona is that? Is she old?'

'Yes, she is.'

'O-oh,' he drawled. 'He means Semeonikha. She lives the other end of the village. We'll take you. Come on, Fedka, let's go with 'im.'

'But what about the 'orses?'

'Never mind about them. I daresay they'll be all right.'

Fedka agreed, and the three of them walked up the village street together.

5

NEKHLYUDOV felt more at ease with the boys than with the older folk, and chatted to them as they went along. The little boy in the pink shirt stopped laughing and talked as intelligently and sensibly as the older child.

'Who are the poorest people in your village?' Nekhlyudov asked them.

'The poorest? Mikhail is poor. So is Simeon Makarov. And Marfa's mighty poor.'

'What about Anisya – she's poorer 'n any of 'em. Anisya ain't even got a cow. They 'ave to go beggin' for their livin',' said little Fedka.

'She ain't got no cow but there's only three of 'em; but Marfa's got five mouths to feed,' objected the elder boy.

'But the other one's a widow,' said the little pink-shirted boy, standing up for Anisya.

'You say Anisya's a widow, but Marfa's just the same as a widow,' continued the elder boy. 'She ain't got no 'usband either.'

'Where is her husband, then?' asked Nekhlyudov.

'In gaol, feedin' lice,' said the elder boy, using the expression common among the peasants.

'Last summer 'cos 'e cut down a couple of little birch-trees in the forest, they shut 'im up in prison – 'cos the forest belongs to the gentry, you see,' the little boy in pink hastened to explain. ' 'E's been there six months now, an' 'is wife 'as to go beggin'. She's got three children an' a poor old grandmother,' he added circumstantially.

'Where does she live?' asked Nekhlyudov.

'Over there – that's their 'ome,' said the boy, pointing to a hut in front of which, on the footpath where Nekhlyudov was walking, a tiny tow-haired child stood balancing itself with difficulty on its rickety legs.

'Vasska! Where's the little scamp got to?' shouted a woman in a dirty grey blouse (it looked as if it had been dusted with ashes) who came running out of the hut. She rushed forward in front of Nekhlyudov, seized the child and carried it into the hut, her frightened face implying a fear that Nekhlyudov might do the baby some harm.

This was the woman whose husband was in gaol for cutting down Nekhlyudov's birch-trees.

'Well, and what about Matriona – is she poor?' Nekhlyudov asked as they approached Matriona's door.

'She poor? Not likely. She sells spirits,' the thin little boy in the pink shirt answered decidedly.

When they reached Matriona's hut Nekhlyudov left the boys outside and went through the passage into the hut. Old Matriona's hovel was just fourteen feet long and the bed which stood behind the stove would have been too short for a tall man to stretch out in. 'On that very bed,' Nekhlyudov thought, 'Katusha bore her baby and then lay so ill.' Most of the hut was taken up by a loom on which the old woman and her eldest grand-daughter were arranging the warp when Nekhlyudov entered, hitting his head against the low doorway. Two other grandchildren rushed headlong in after

Nekhlyudov and stopped behind him in the doorway, clinging to the lintel.

'Who is it you want?' the old woman asked crossly, in a bad temper because the loom was giving trouble. Besides, as she carried on an illicit trade in spirits, she was afraid of all strangers.

'I am the owner of the estate. I should like to speak to you.'

The old woman was silent, regarding him intently; then she was suddenly transformed.

'Why it's you, me dearie! What an old fool I am, not to recognize you. I thought it was someone passing by,' she said in dulcet tones that did not ring true. 'So it's you, me blessed lamb . . .'

'I should like a word with you alone,' said Nekhlyudov, with a glance towards the open door where the children were standing, and behind them an emaciated woman holding a pale sickly baby, though it smiled all the time, wearing a little patchwork cap.

'What are you staring at? I'll give it to you! Just let me have me crutch!' the old woman shouted at them. 'Go on, shut that door!'

The children ran off, and the woman with the baby closed the door.

'Thinks I to meself, now who can that be? And it's the master himself, me jewel, me treasure!' said the old woman. 'To think that he should condescend to come here! Sit down, sweetheart, sit down, your honour, sit on the bench here,' she said, dusting the bench with her apron. 'And I was thinking who the devil was it coming in, and it's your honour himself, our good master, our benefactor and protector. Forgive me, the old fool that I am – I must be going blind.'

Nekhlyudov sat down; the old woman stood in front of him, leaning her cheek on her right hand, her left hand supporting her bony elbow, and went on in a sing-song voice:

'Dear me, your honour's aged all right. Why, you used to

be as fair as a daisy, and look at you now! I can see you have cares, too.'

'I came to ask you something: do you remember Katusha Maslova?'

'Katerina! I should think I do! She's me own niece . . . I'm not likely to forget her, after all the tears I shed because of her. I know all about it. Eh, sir, show me the man who hasn't sinned before God, who hasn't offended against the Tsar. You were both young in those days, you used to drink tea and coffee together, so the devil got hold of you. He's a strong one, he is! Well, there was no help for it. Now if you had thrown her out, but no, you did honest and fair by her, paid her a hundred roubles. And what did she do? She wouldn't be reasonable. If she had listened to me, she'd have been all right. I must call a spade a spade, though she is my niece – that girl's no good. I got a fine place for her, but she wouldn't knuckle down, she was high and mighty with the master. Is it for the likes of us to put on airs with the gentry? Of course she lost the place. Then there was the forester's: she might have stayed there, but she wouldn't.'

'I wanted to ask you about the child she had. She was confined here, wasn't she? Where is the child?'

'The child, sir, I thought a lot about the child at the time. She was mighty bad, I never expected her to get up again. So I christened the baby, proper like, and sent it to the Foundlings'.[1] Why leave a little angel to suffer because the mother is dying? I know plenty of them just leave the baby, don't feed it and it dies. But no, thinks I, I'd rather take some trouble, and send it to the Foundlings'. We had the money, so we could send it away.'

'Did he have a registration number?'

'Yes, there was a number, but the child went and died straight off. She said she'd hardly got there before it snuffed out.'

1. A large foundling hospital in Moscow, where most of the children died soon after admission.

'Who is *she*?'

'The woman who used to live in Skorodnoye. She made a business of it. Malanya was her name, she's dead now. She was a clever one. What do you think she used to do? They'd bring her a baby, and she'd keep it and feed it till she had enough of them to take to the Foundlings'. And when she'd collected three or four of the little things, she'd take 'em off all together. Arranged it all so clever – she had a large cradle, a sort of double one, so she could put them in this way and that. And there was a handle to it. She would place four of 'em with their heads at each end and feet together in the middle, so they shouldn't kick each other, and that way she'd carry four at a time. She'd stick a rag dummy in their little mouths to keep 'em quiet, the pets.'

'Well, go on.'

'Well, she took Katerina's baby, too. Kept it a couple of weeks or so first, I believe. It got worms while it was still with her.'

'Was it a healthy child?' asked Nekhlyudov.

'A finer child as you'd find nowhere. The image of its father,' the old woman added with a wink.

'Then why did it sicken? I suppose it wasn't fed properly?'

'Fed properly? It only got a lick and a promise. It wasn't her child. All she cared about was to get him there alive. She told us it snuffed out just as they reached Moscow. She brought back a certificate and everything. A clever one, she was.'

And that was all Nekhlyudov could find out about his child.

6

HAVING again banged his head against the top of both doors – into the hut and in the passage – Nekhlyudov emerged into the street. The boy in the grimy white shirt and the other in the pink one were waiting for him. A few newcomers had joined them. There were some women, too, with babies at the breast, and Nekhlyudov recognized the emaciated woman holding her bloodless infant in its patchwork cap as if it weighed no more than a feather. The baby had a strange fixed smile on its little wizened face and kept wriggling its bent and twisted big toes in a strained sort of way. Nekhlyudov knew the smile to be one of suffering. He asked who the woman was.

'It's that Anisya I told you about,' said the elder boy.

Nekhlyudov turned to Anisya.

'How are you getting along?' he asked. 'What do you live on?'

'What do I live on? I beg,' said Anisya, and began to cry.

The wizened baby grinned all over its face and wriggled its skinny little legs which were hardly thicker than worms.

Nekhlyudov took out his pocket-book and gave the woman ten roubles. Before he had gone two steps another woman with a baby caught him up, then an old woman, then another young one. All spoke of their poverty and asked him for help. Nekhlyudov distributed the sixty roubles in small notes that he had in his pocket-book and, terribly sick at heart, returned home, that is, to the bailiff's house. The bailiff met Nekhlyudov with a smile and told him that the peasants would be coming that evening. Nekhlyudov thanked him, and without going indoors made straight for the garden to stroll along the overgrown paths now white with the petals of apple blossom, thinking over everything he had seen.

At first all was quiet near the house but presently Nekhlyudov heard the voices of two angry women interrupting each other, with the calm voice of the ever-smiling bailiff breaking in from time to time. Nekhlyudov listened.

'I can't stand no more of it, why you'd drag the very cross from round me neck!' cried one furious female voice.

'But she only got in for a moment,' said the other voice. 'Give her back, I tell you. It's only tormenting the poor beast, and the kids 'aving to go without their milk.'

'Pay up, then, or work out the fine,' said the calm voice of the bailiff.

Nekhlyudov left the garden and walked up to the porch, where two dishevelled women were standing, one of them pregnant and evidently near her time. On the steps of the porch, his hands in the pockets of his holland coat, stood the bailiff. Seeing the master, the women fell silent and began straightening the kerchiefs which had slipped from their heads, while the bailiff took his hands out of his pockets and began smiling.

The trouble was this, the bailiff explained: the peasants purposely let their calves and even their cows into the meadow belonging to the estate. Thus two cows belonging to these women had been caught in the meadow and driven into the yard. The bailiff demanded from the women thirty kopecks for each cow, or two days' work. The women, however, maintained, to begin with, that the cows had only just strayed in; that, secondly, they had no money; and, thirdly, they wanted the cows, which had stood in the blazing sun without food ever since morning, lowing pitifully, to be returned to them at once, even if it had to be on the understanding that the fine should be worked off later on.

'How often have I begged of you, if you drive your cattle home at noon to keep an eye on them,' said the smiling bailiff, looking round at Nekhlyudov as if calling on him to be a witness.

'I only ran for a moment to see to the baby, and they were gone.'

'Then don't go away when it's your business to watch them.'

'And 'oo's going to feed the child? *You* won't give 'im the breast.'

'If she'd really cropped the meadow 'er belly wouldn't be empty and paining 'er now, but she barely got in,' said the other woman.

'They are ruining all the meadows,' the bailiff addressed

Nekhlyudov. 'If I don't exact a penalty there will be no hay.'

'Don't tell such wicked lies! My cows ain't never gone there before,' cried the pregnant woman.

'Well, they've been caught there now, so either you pay the fine or work it off.'

'All right, I'll work it off, then, but let the cow go and don't starve it to death,' she exclaimed angrily. 'I don't get a moment's peace, day or night. Mother-in-law ailing, 'usband always drunk. I'm all alone to do everything, and I've no strength left. I 'ope the work you screws out of me chokes you!'

Nekhlyudov asked the bailiff to release the cows, and went back into the garden to continue brooding over his thoughts, but there was nothing more to think about. It was all so clear to him now that he could not marvel enough that others did not see it, and that he himself had taken so long to realize what was so obvious and plain.

'The people perish, they are accustomed to the process of perishing, customs and attitudes to life have appeared which accord with the process – the way children are allowed to die and women made to overwork, and the widespread under-nourishment, especially of the aged. And this state of affairs has come about so gradually that the peasants themselves do not see the full horror of it, and do not raise their voices in complaint. For this reason we, too, regard the situation as natural and proper.' Now it was as clear as daylight to him that – just as the peasants always recognized and pointed out – it was the landlords who were mainly responsible for their poverty, the landlords who deprived them of the land which was their only means of support. And was it not perfectly plain that the children and old people died because they had no milk, and there was no milk because there was no land on which to pasture the cows and harvest grain and hay. It was perfectly obvious that all the misery of the people, or at least the chief and most immediate cause of the people's suffering, sprang from the fact that the land which should feed them did not belong to them but was in the hands of men who take advantage of their ownership to live by the labours of the people. And the land, which was so vital to them – they starve for want of enough land to support them – is toiled over by these same peasants on the verge of starvation, to the end that the grain might be sold abroad and the owners of the land might buy themselves hats, canes, carriages, *objets d'art* and so on. This was now as clear to him as that horses, shut up in an enclosure where they have eaten every blade of grass under their feet, will grow thin and starve unless they are put on to other land where they can find food for themselves. And this was a terrible state of affairs which could not and must not continue. And means must be found to stop it, or at least to have no part in it. 'And I am certainly going to find a way,' he thought, walking up and down the path in the avenue of birch-trees near the house. 'In learned societies, in government institutions, in the newspapers we are always discussing the causes of poverty among the people and ways of improving their circumstances, but there is never a word on the one sure method of raising their standard of living – which is not to deprive them of the land they need so badly.' And the fundamental doctrine of Henry George came vividly to mind, and he remembered his former enthusiasm and wondered how he could ever have forgotten it all. 'Land ought not to be an object of private ownership, it ought not to be bought and sold, any more than water, air or sunshine. Everyone has an equal right to land and to all the benefits that can be derived from it.' And now he understood why he felt ashamed to remember the transaction he had made at Kuzminskoye. He had been deceiving himself. Knowing that no man could have any right to own land, he had assumed such a right for himself and had given the peasants a part of something which, in the depths of his heart, he knew he had no right to. He would not do that here, and he would alter the arrangement at Kuzminskoye. And he sketched out a mental plan for letting the land to the peasants, and the rents he received he would recognize as belonging to them, to be used to pay taxes and help the community generally. This was not the single-tax system but the nearest approach to it possible in the existing circumstances. His chief consideration now was to renounce his right to the private ownership of land.

When he returned to the house the bailiff, with a particularly happy smile, announced that dinner was ready but he was afraid that the food his wife had prepared with the help of the girl with the fluffy ear-rings might be overdone.

The table was covered with a rough cloth; an embroidered towel served as a napkin, and on the table stood a Dresden china tureen with a broken handle full of potato soup in which floated fragments of the very same cockerel which had stuck out first one, then the other black leg and was now chopped – even hacked – into small bits, many of them covered with hairs. After the soup there was more of the same fowl with its hairs singed, and pancakes of cottage cheese with a large quantity of butter and sugar. Unappetizing as it all was, Nekhlyudov ate without noticing what he was eating, so absorbed was he by the idea that had in a moment dispelled the gloom he had brought with him from the village.

The bailiff's wife kept peeping through the door while the frightened girl with the ear-rings brought in the dishes, and the bailiff himself grinned from ear to ear with pride at his wife's skill.

After dinner, insisting that the bailiff should sit down with him, in order to check up on his own thoughts and tell them to someone, he explained his project of letting the land to the peasants, and asked the bailiff's opinion. The bailiff smiled as if he had thought all this himself long ago and was delighted to hear it expressed, but in reality he did not understand a word – not because Nekhlyudov was not making himself clear but because the plan apparently meant that Nekhlyudov would be sacrificing his own interests for the good of others; and the conviction that everybody in the world was concerned to benefit himself at other people's expense was so deeply rooted in the bailiff that he imagined there was something he had not understood when Nekhlyudov said that all the income from the estate should go to form the communal capital of the peasants.

'I see,' he said, brightening up. 'So the income from the capital will belong to you?'

'No, of course not. Don't you understand that land cannot be an object of private ownership?'

'That's true.'

'And therefore all that the land brings forth belongs to each and everyone.'

'Then you will have no income at all?' asked the bailiff, smiling no longer.

'No, I am renouncing it.'

The bailiff sighed heavily, and then began smiling again. Now he understood. He understood that the master was not quite right in the head, and he immediately set out to discover in Nekhlyudov's plan to give up his land some means of making a profit for himself, and tried to get the hang of the scheme so as to avail himself of the land being given away.

But when he saw that even this was not possible he felt aggrieved, lost interest in the affair and continued to smile only to please the master. Realizing that the bailiff did not understand him, Nekhlyudov dismissed him and seating himself at the scarred, ink-stained table began to sketch out his project on paper.

The sun had already set behind the newly budded lime-trees, and the mosquitoes swarmed into the room and stung him. Just as he finished his notes he heard the lowing of cattle and the creaking of gates opening in the village, and the voices of the peasants gathering together for the meeting. He told the bailiff not to call them to the office, saying that he would go along to the village himself and see the men in the yard where they were assembling. Hastily swallowing a tumbler of tea offered him by the bailiff, Nekhlyudov departed for the village.

7

THE crowd assembled in the yard of the village elder's house were talking noisily but as soon as Nekhlyudov came up they fell silent, and just as at Kuzminskoye one after another they all took off their caps. They looked far more wretched than the Kuzminskoye people; just as the women and girls wore fluff-rings in their ears, so nearly all the men were wearing bast shoes and homespun coats. A few of them were barefoot and in their shirt-sleeves, having come straight from the fields.

Nekhlyudov, after a struggle with himself, began his speech by telling the peasants of his intention to make the land entirely over to them. The men were silent and the expression on their faces underwent no change.

'Because I consider,' said Nekhlyudov, flushing, 'that land shouldn't belong to someone who does not work on it, and that everybody has a right to enjoy the benefits of the land.'

'That's true. That's a fact,' said several voices in the crowd.

Nekhlyudov went on to tell them that the revenue from the land must be distributed equally, and that he therefore proposed that they should take the land and pay a rent – which they would agree upon among themselves – into a common fund which would be for their own use. There were more murmurs of approval and assent, but the grave faces of the peasants became graver and graver, and the eyes which had been fixed on the master were now cast down, as if to spare him the shame of knowing that they all saw through his stratagems and he was deceiving no one.

Nekhlyudov spoke plainly enough, and his listeners were intelligent men, but they did not and could not understand him, for the same reason that the bailiff had taken so long in understanding him. They were firmly convinced that it is natural for every man to look out for his own interest. Had not generations of experience proved to them that the land-owner always watched his own interest at the expense of the peasants? Therefore, if a landlord calls them together and makes this unheard-of offer it could only be in order to swindle them more cunningly still.

'Well, then, what rent will you fix for the land?' asked Nekhlyudov.

' 'Ow can us fix rents? We can't do it. The land's yours, and you're the master,' voices from the crowd answered him.

'But no, you will be using the money for communal purposes.'

'We can't do it. The commune's one thing, and this is another.'

'Don't you understand,' said the bailiff with a smile, in an attempt to throw more light on the matter (he had followed Nekhlyudov to the meeting), 'the prince is letting the land to you for money, and that money goes back to you as your own capital, for your common good.'

'Oh, we understand all right,' said an irritable, toothless old man, without raising his eyes. 'It's same as puttin' money in a bank, on'y we should 'ave to pay in at special times. We don't want it: things are 'ard enough for us as it is, and that'd fair put the stopper on us.'

'It's no good. We're better off the old way,' cried several voices, some sulky, others downright hostile.

The opposition grew more and more determined when Nekhlyudov mentioned that he would draw up a contract which he would sign and would expect them to sign also.

'What's the use of signing anything? We've worked all along, and we'll go on working. What's the good of all this? We're ignorant people. We can't agree to it, it's not what we're used to. Leave things as they are. But it would be a good thing to make another arrangement about the seed,' voices cried variously from the crowd.

Under the old system the peasants had to provide the seed

for the crops from which they paid their dues to the land-owner, so this was a request that he should provide it.

'Then you mean that you refuse to take the land?' Nekhlyudov asked, addressing a middle-aged, bare-footed peasant with a beaming countenance, in a torn tunic, who was holding his tattered cap stiffly in his bent left hand, the way soldiers do when ordered to uncover.

'Yes, sir,' replied the man, who had evidently not yet shaken off the hypnotic influence of a soldier's training.

'Then you have all the land you want?' said Nekhlyudov.

'Oh no, sir,' answered the ex-soldier, with an artificially cheerful air, carefully holding his tattered cap in front of him, as if offering it to anyone who might like to make use of it.

'Well, anyhow, you had better think over what I have said.' Nekhlyudov spoke with surprise and again repeated his offer.

'Nothin' to think over. We 'old by what we've said,' muttered the morose, toothless old man angrily.

'I shall be here all day tomorrow – if you change your minds, come and let me know.'

The peasants did not reply.

So Nekhlyudov could make no headway at all, and he went back to the office.

'If you will permit me to say so, prince,' remarked the bailiff when they got home, 'it's a waste of time trying to explain anything to them, they're a pig-headed lot. The minute you get them all together they turn as stubborn as mules and there's no moving them after that. It's because they're suspicious of everything. And yet there are some intelligent men among them – that grey-haired fellow, for example, or the swarthy one who kept raising objections. If they come to the office and I sit them down to a tumbler of tea,' continued the smiling bailiff, 'we get talking and you'd be surprised – wise as Solomon, they are: they can thrash the matter out and get the right answer every time. But let the same man come to a meeting and he's a different person altogether, and just goes on repeating the same thing over and over again . . .'

'Then couldn't we send for a few of the more intelligent ones to come here?' said Nekhlyudov. 'I could go through the plan with them in detail.'

'Yes, that can be done,' answered the smiling bailiff.

'Then please have them come tomorrow.'

'Very well,' said the bailiff, and smiled more cheerfully still, 'I'll call them for tomorrow.'

*

'There's an artful dodger for you!' a black-haired peasant with an unkempt beard, who sat swaying on his well-fed mare, said to a lean old man in a torn tunic riding by his side, his horse's iron hobbles clanking.

The pair were on their way to pasture their horses for the night by the roadside, or, if they got a chance, in the forest belonging to the estate.

' "I'll let you have the land for nothing if you'll just sign!" Haven't they fooled the likes of us often enough? No, my friend, you won't catch us, nowadays we know a thing or two ourselves,' he added, and began calling a colt that had fallen behind. He stopped and looked back, but the colt had not remained behind – it had gone into the meadow by the roadside.

'Curse the little devil! Taken a liking to the master's fields,' said the black-haired peasant with the unkempt beard, hearing the snapping of sorrel stalks as the whinnying colt galloped across the sweet-smelling, swampy meadow.

'Just listen to that – the meadow's all overgrown. We shall have to send the women out one Sunday to do a bit of weeding,' said the thin peasant in the torn tunic. 'Else we'll be ruining our scythes.'

' "Just sign," he says,' the peasant with the shaggy beard continued on the subject of his master's address. 'Sign, indeed, and let 'im swaller yer alive!'

'That's sure,' replied the old man.

And they said no more. The only sound was the clopping of the horses' hooves on the hard road.

8

WHEN Nekhlyudov returned he found in the office which had been arranged as a bedroom for him a high bedstead with a feather bed, two pillows and a large coverlet of crimson silk, elaborately quilted and very stiff – borrowed no doubt from the trousseau of the bailiff's wife. The bailiff offered Nekhlyudov what had been left over from dinner and, when Nekhlyudov declined, apologized for the poor hospitality and uncomfortable quarters, and went away, leaving Nekhlyudov to himself.

The peasants' rejection of his offer had not upset Nekhlyudov. On the contrary, although at Kuzminskoye it had been accepted gratefully, whereas here it had met with suspicion and even hostility, he felt calm and happy. It was stuffy in the office and not very clean. Nekhlyudov went outside and was making for the garden when he remembered that other night, the window in the maids' room, and the porch at the back of the house – and he did not like the idea of strolling about in places defiled by guilty memories. He sat down again on a seat in the front porch and, breathing in the warm air heavy with the sharp scent of young birch leaves, remained for a long time looking into the dark garden and listening to the mill-wheel, the nightingales and some other bird that whistled monotonously in a bush close by. The light disappeared from the bailiff's window; over in the east, beyond the barn, appeared the first glow of the rising moon; summer lightning flashed brighter and brighter, lighting up the lush, blooming garden and the dilapidated house; there was a distant roll of thunder, and a black cloud overspread a third of the sky. The nightingales and the other birds were silent. The cackling of geese sounded above the noise of the mill waters, and then the first cocks in the village began to call to their fellows in the bailiff's yard, crowing early, as cocks generally do on hot thundery nights. There is a saying that cocks crow early on a gay night. This was more than a gay night for Nekhlyudov – it was a joyous, happy night. His imagination took him back to the happy summer he had spent in this place as an innocent youth, and he felt now that he was again the sort of person he had been – not only then but at all the best moments of his life. He did not just remember but actually felt like the boy of fourteen praying to God to reveal His truth; again he was the child who had cried in his mother's lap when they had to part, promising always to be good and never grieve her; he felt as he had felt in the days when he and Nikolenka Irtenyev made resolutions to help each other to lead good lives and try to make everybody happy.

He thought how at Kuzminskoye he was tempted to regret the house, the forest, the estate, the land, and he asked himself whether he still regretted them – but it seemed strange now that he could ever have felt any regret. He went over everything he had seen that day: the woman with the children whose husband was in prison for cutting down trees in his, Nekhlyudov's, forest, and that horrible creature, Matriona, who thought (or at least talked as if she thought) that the best thing for women of their class was to become a gentleman's paramour; he recalled her attitude about babies and the way they were hurried off to the Foundling Hospital; and that wretched, wizened, smiling little mite in the patchwork cap, dying of starvation. He recalled the tired pregnant woman obliged to work for him because, overburdened as she was, she had not kept an eye on her hungry cow. And then he suddenly remembered the prison – the shaven heads, the cells, the disgusting smell, the chains – and, side by side with it, the senseless luxury of his own life and the lives of the aristocracy in a great metropolis. Everything was now quite clear and unambiguous.

The bright, almost full moon rose from behind the barn:

dark shadows fell across the yard, and the iron roof of the dilapidated house glittered.

And, as though reluctant to waste this light, the nightingales, which had fallen silent, began singing and trilling in the garden again.

Nekhlyudov called to mind how at Kuzminskoye he had started to reflect over his life, trying to decide what he should do and how he should do it, and remembered how tangled up he had become, unable to arrive at any decision because there were so many considerations connected with each problem. He now put the same problems to himself and was surprised how easy they were. Everything was simple now because he was not thinking of what would be the result for himself – he was not even interested in that – but only of what he ought to do. And, strange to say, he had no idea what to do for his own needs, but knew beyond any doubt what he had to do for others. He knew beyond all doubt now that the peasants must have the land because to keep it would be wrong. He knew beyond all doubt that he must never abandon Katusha but try to help her as best he could, in order to expiate his guilt towards her. He knew beyond all doubt that he must study, examine, elucidate to himself and comprehend the whole system of trial and punishment, in which he was conscious of seeing something that nobody else saw. What the result would be of all this he did not know, but he knew for certain that this, that and the other he had to do. And this firm conviction gave him joy.

The black cloud had spread until the whole sky was dark. Now it was not sheet- but fork-lightning that flashed vivid, lighting up the yard and outlining the crumbling house with its tumble-down porches, while thunder growled overhead. The birds were all silent but the leaves began to rustle and the wind reached the porch where Nekhlyudov sat, and blew his hair about. One drop fell, then another; then the rain began to drum on the dock-leaves and the iron roof, and there was a sudden blaze of light; all was still, and before Nekhlyudov

296

could count three a fearful crash sounded immediately above his head and went rolling across the heavens.

Nekhlyudov went into the house.

'No, no,' he thought, 'the reason for what happens in our lives, all that we do, the meaning of it, is incomprehensible and must remain incomprehensible to me. Why did I have aunts? Why did Nikolenka Irtenyev die, while I am still alive? Why should there be a Katusha? What about my lunacy? Why that war? Why my reckless life afterwards? To understand all that, to understand the Master's purpose is beyond me. But to do His will, inscribed in my conscience – is in my power, and this I know unquestioningly. And when I am obeying His will, there is no doubt that my soul is at peace.'

The rain was coming down in torrents, splashing from the roofs into the rain-water barrel; the lightning less often lit up the yard and house. Nekhlyudov returned to his room, undressed and got into bed, not without some apprehension – the dirty, torn wall-paper made him suspect the presence of bugs.

'Yes, to feel oneself not the master but a servant,' he said to himself, and rejoiced at the thought.

His misgivings were justified. No sooner had he put out the candle than the bugs began to settle on him and bite.

'To give up the land and go to Siberia – the fleas, the bugs, the dirt. . . . Well, what of it? If I have to bear it, I will bear it.' But in spite of his good intentions he could not endure it and got up and sat by the window, feasting his eyes on the fleeting clouds and the reappearing moon.

9

IT was almost daybreak before Nekhlyudov fell asleep and so he awoke late the next day.

At noon the seven peasants who had been chosen and summoned by the bailiff assembled in the orchard under the apple-trees, where the bailiff had arranged a table and benches over posts driven into the ground. It was some time before the peasants could be persuaded to put on their caps and sit down on the benches. The ex-soldier especially, who today was wearing clean leg-rags and bast shoes, persisted in holding his torn cap in front of him, in the way laid down in army regulations for funerals. But when one of them, a venerable, broad-shouldered old man with a curly grey beard like Michelangelo's *Moses* and thick grey hair waving round his bald sunburnt forehead, put on his large cap, wrapped his homespun coat round him, climbed over the bench and sat down, the others followed his example.

As soon as they were all seated Nekhlyudov sat down opposite them and, leaning with his elbows over the paper on which he had drawn up his project, he began to expound it to them.

Whether it was because there were fewer peasants present, or because he was occupied not with himself but with the business in hand, this time Nekhlyudov felt perfectly at ease. Without meaning to, he addressed himself mainly to the broad-shouldered old man with the curly white beard, looking to him for approval or opposition. But Nekhlyudov had mistaken his man. The venerable old patriarch, though he nodded his handsome head approvingly, or shook it and frowned when the others raised objections, obviously had great difficulty in understanding what Nekhlyudov was saying, even after the other peasants had explained it to him in their own words. A little old fellow, practically beardless and blind in one eye, in a patched nankeen coat and old boots worn down on one side, who was sitting next to the patriarch – he was a stove-maker, Nekhlyudov found out later – understood him much better. He kept moving his eyebrows in an effort to take in everything, and immediately repeated what Nekhlyudov said in his own words. Equally quick at seizing his meaning was a short, stocky old man with a white beard and bright intelligent eyes, who never missed an opportunity to interject ironical jokes, which he evidently prided himself on. The ex-soldier, too, might have understood were his wits not blunted by army life, and if he would not confuse himself with the inane language he had adopted. Most serious of all in regard to the matter in hand was a tall man with a long nose and a small beard, who spoke in a deep bass voice and was wearing clean home-spun clothes and new bast shoes. He took in everything, and spoke only when it was necessary. The remaining two – one of them, the toothless old man who the day before had shouted a flat refusal to every suggestion Nekhlyudov made, and a lame old chap with a kindly face, tall and pale, his thin legs tightly wrapped round with strips of linen – were almost entirely silent, though they listened attentively.

First of all Nekhlyudov explained his ideas about the private ownership of land.

'To my mind land ought neither to be bought nor sold, because if it can be sold people with money can buy it all up and then exact anything they like for the use of it from those who have none. They will take money for the right to stand on the earth,' he added, making use of an argument of Spencer's.

'The on'y thing left would be to tie on a pair of wings and fly,' said the old man with the white beard and laughing eyes.

'That's right,' said the long-nosed man in his deep bass.

'All correct,' said the ex-soldier.

'A woman picks a 'andful of grass for 'er cow, she's caught – an' to the lock-up with 'er,' remarked the lame old man with the kindly face.

'Our land is three or four miles from 'ere, an' as to rentin' any, it's not to be thought of: they've put the price so 'igh we'd never make it pay,' added the toothless, cross-grained old man. 'They twist us round their little fingers, it's worse than when we was serfs.'

'That is what I think myself,' said Nekhlyudov, 'and I consider it a sin to own land. So I want to give it away.'

'Well, that would be a good thing,' said the patriarchal old man with the curly beard like Michelangelo's *Moses*, apparently thinking that Nekhlyudov meant to let the land.

'I have come here for this reason: I no longer wish to own any land, and now we must consider how I am to get rid of it.'

'Why, jus' give it to the peasants, that's all you 'ave to do,' said the toothless, cross-grained old man.

Nekhlyudov hesitated for a moment, feeling that these words implied a doubt as to the sincerity of his intentions. But he quickly recovered his composure and took advantage of the remark to express what was in his mind.

'I should be glad to do that,' he said, 'but to whom, and how? To which peasants? Why should I give it to you rather than to the peasants at Deminskoye?' (This was a neighbouring village with very little land.)

No one spoke, except the ex-soldier who exclaimed, 'All correct!'

'Now tell me,' Nekhlyudov went on, 'if the Tsar said that the land was to be taken from the landowners and divided among the peasants . . .'

'Why, is there talk of that?' asked the same old man.

'No, the Tsar doesn't come into it. I was simply saying that if the Tsar were to say, "Take the land from the landowners and give it to the peasants," how would you set about it?'

' 'Ow would we set about it? Divide it equally, a course, so much for every man, gentry and peasant alike,' said the stove-maker, rapidly raising and lowering his eyebrows.

'How else? Equal shares,' confirmed the kindly lame man with the white strips of linen round his legs.

Everybody agreed that this solution would be satisfactory.

'What do you mean, so much per man?' asked Nekhlyudov. 'Would that include the indoor servants, too?'

'Oh no,' said the ex-soldier, trying to look amused.

But the thoughtful, tall peasant did not agree with him.

'If it's a question of dividin', then everyone must 'ave equal shares,' he said in his deep bass voice, after reflection.

'It can't be done,' said Nekhlyudov, having prepared his objection in advance. 'If we are all to share alike, those who do no work themselves – the gentry, footmen, cooks, officials in offices, clerks, all the people who live in towns and have never used a plough – will take their shares and sell them to the rich. And again the land will get into the hands of the rich, while those who live by working their own holding will multiply, and there will be no land left for them. Again the rich will gain control of those who need land.'

'All correct,' the ex-soldier hurriedly confirmed.

'Make it against the law to sell land, and only let them 'ave it 'oo ploughs it theirselves,' said the stove-maker, angrily interrupting the ex-soldier.

To this Nekhlyudov replied by asking how anyone could tell whether a man was ploughing his own land for himself or was doing it for someone else.

Here the tall, thoughtful man suggested a partnership arrangement whereby those who ploughed shared the produce. And those who did not got nothing, he argued in his imperative bass.

Nekhlyudov had his answers ready against this communistic project too, and said that this would mean every man having his own plough and horses as good as his neighbours', and that nobody should lag behind, or else that everything – horses, ploughs, threshing-machines and all farming implements – should be held in common, and to put that into practice everybody would have to be of one mind.

'You're never goin' to make our people agree, not in a 'ole lifetime,' said the cross-grained old man.

'They'd never stop fighting,' said the old man with the white beard and laughing eyes. 'The women would be at each other's throats.'

'And how about the kind of land?' said Nekhlyudov

'Why should one man get black loam, and another clay and sand?'

'Divide it up into small lots, so as everyone gets the same,' said the stove-maker.

To this Nekhlyudov answered that it was not only a question of sharing out the land in one commune but a general division of land in different provinces. If the land were to be given away free, why should some peasants have good holdings and others bad ones? They would all want good soil.

'That's correct,' said the soldier.

The rest remained silent.

'So you see, it is not as simple as it seems,' said Nekhlyudov. 'And not only are we thinking about it – many other people are too. There is an American, Henry George, who has reasoned it out like this, and I agree with him –'

'But you're the master, you give it away as you like. What's to stop you? You're at liberty to do so,' said the cross-grained old man.

This interruption annoyed Nekhlyudov; but he was delighted to see that he was not the only one to resent it.

'Wait a moment, Uncle Simeon, let 'im tell us about it,' said the thoughtful peasant with the imposing bass voice.

This encouraged Nekhlyudov and he began to expound Henry George's single-tax system to them.

'The land is not anybody's, it belongs to God,' he began.

'That's so. That's true,' several voices put in.

'The land is common property. Everyone has an equal right to it. But there is good land and bad. And everybody wants to get the good soil. What are we to do to make things fair all round? Like this: let the man who owns good land pay the value of it to those who have none,' Nekhlyudov went on, answering his own question. 'But as it would be difficult to decide who should pay and who should be paid, and as money has to be collected for the needs of the community, it ought to be so arranged that whoever owns any land pays into the public fund what his land is worth. Then everyone would share equally. If you want land, pay for it – more for good land, less for bad land. If you don't want land, you don't pay anything and those who own land will pay the taxes and other communal expenses for you.'

'That's right,' said the stove-maker, moving his eyebrows. 'The man who has the better land must pay more.'

''E 'ad a 'ead on 'im, that 'enry George,' said the imposing old man with the curly beard.

'If on'y we ain't got to pay more'n we got the money for,' said the tall man with the bass voice, evidently beginning to make out what it was all leading to.

'The payment must be neither too high nor too low. . . . If it is too high, it won't be paid and there will be a loss, and if it is too low, everybody will start trying to buy from each other, and there will be speculation in land,' said Nekhlyudov. 'Well, now you understand what it is I want to do with you here.'

'That's right, that's fair. Yes, that ain't bad at all,' said the peasants.

'That George man 'ad a 'ead on 'im,' repeated the broad-shouldered old peasant with the curly beard. 'Thought it out clever.'

'How will it be if I want to have some land?' asked the bailiff, smiling.

'If there is a holding to spare, you may take it and work it,' said Nekhlyudov.

'What *you* want land for? You're well enough off as it is,' said the old man with the laughing eyes.

With this the conference ended.

Nekhlyudov repeated his offer again but did not ask for an immediate answer: instead, he advised them to talk things over with the whole village and then come back and tell him their decision.

The peasants said that they would discuss it with the others and bring an answer, and taking their leave went away in a great state of excitement. It was a long time before the clamour of their voices receded into the distance, and late into the night the sound of talking echoed up the river from the village.

*

Next day the peasants did not go to work but spent their time discussing the master's offer. The village was split into two factions: those who saw the offer as a profitable one which could do them no harm, and those who thought there was a catch in it, which they could not detect and therefore feared all the more. By the third day, however, they all agreed to accept the proposal made to them, and came to Nekhlyudov to announce their decision. The village had been much influenced by the opinion of an aged woman, which the old men accepted and which did away with all fear that they were being cheated, that the master was acting so because he had begun to be anxious about his soul and was doing this in the hope of salvation. This explanation was further confirmed by the generous alms which Nekhlyudov had distributed while at Panovo. His alms-giving here came about because never before had he known such a degree of poverty and misery as had overtaken the peasants: he was appalled by their poverty, and though he realized that it was unwise he could not resist giving them money, of which he happened just then to have particularly large sums available – receipts from the sale of a forest at Kuzminskoye the year before, and also certain deposits on the sale of stock and implements.

No sooner was it discovered that the master was giving money to anyone who asked for it, than crowds of peasants, chiefly women, began to come to him from all the surrounding country, begging for help. He was utterly at a loss to know how to deal with them: how to decide how much to give, and to whom. He felt that to refuse to give money, of which he had so much, to those who asked him for it and who were obviously poor, was impossible. At the same time it was not wise to give indiscriminately to all who came begging to him.

The only way out seemed to be to depart, and this he hurried to do.

During the last day of his stay at Panovo Nekhlyudov went into the house and looked over the things that were left there. Rummaging through an old mahogany chiffonier with a bow front and brass lion's-head handles with rings through them that had belonged to his aunts, he found a number of letters in a lower drawer, and among them a photograph of a group – Sophia Ivanovna and Marya Ivanovna, himself as a student, and Katusha, pure, untouched and innocent, and full of the joy of living. Of all the things in the house he took only the letters and this photograph. Everything else he left for the miller, who, at the instance of the smiling bailiff, had bought the house, to be pulled down, and all it contained – for a tenth of their real value.

Looking back at the sense of regret he had experienced at the loss of his Kuzminskoye property, Nekhlyudov wondered how it was he could have had such a feeling. Now he felt nothing but a never-ending sensation of deliverance and novelty, such as a traveller must feel when he discovers new lands.

10

THE town impressed Nekhlyudov in a strange, fresh fashion when he reached it this time. It was dusk and the street lamps were lit when he drove from the station to his house, where all the rooms still smelt of naphthaline, and Agrafena Petrovna and Korney – both tired and bad-tempered – had even had a quarrel over things which, it seemed, were never used but only brought out, aired and then put away again. His own room was not being used but it had not been done and was, indeed, so cluttered with piles of boxes and trunks that it was difficult to get inside. It was evident that his arrival interfered with the life of the house, which carried on by a curious kind of inertia. The contrast between the abject poverty of the peasants in the country and this stupid waste in which he himself had once taken part was so disagreeable to Nekhlyudov that he decided next day to move to a hotel, leaving Agrafena Petrovna to manage matters in her own way until his sister should arrive and finally dispose of everything in the house.

Nekhlyudov departed early the next morning and took a couple of rooms in one of the very modest and not over-clean lodging-houses in the vicinity of the prison. Then, giving orders for a few of his things to be fetched from the house, he went to see his lawyer.

It was chilly out of doors. After the thunder-storms and the rain a cold spell had set in, as generally happens in spring. It was so cold, and the wind so piercing, that Nekhlyudov shivered in his light overcoat and walked as fast as he could, trying to get warm.

His thoughts were full of the peasants in the country – women, children, old men – and the poverty and suffering which he seemed to have seen for the first time, especially the smiling baby like a little old man, kicking with its skinny legs that had no calves, and he could not help comparing their lot with that of the townsfolk. As he passed the butchers', fishmongers', and ready-made clothiers' he was struck again, as though he saw it for the first time, by the well-fed appearance of such an immense number of clean, fat shopkeepers, the like of whom simply did not exist in the country. These people were obviously firmly convinced that their efforts to cheat the ignorant who knew nothing about the quality of their wares was a very useful occupation, certainly not an idle one. The coachmen with their huge backsides and rows of buttons behind looked just as well-fed; so did the house-porters in their caps with gold braid; so did the chamber-maids with their curled fringes and their aprons; and so especially did the dare-devil cab-drivers with the nape of their necks clean-shaven, lolling back in their seats and staring insolently at pedestrians. In all these people Nekhlyudov could not help seeing peasants who had been driven to the town owing to lack of land. Some had adapted themselves to city life, become independent and were well-content with their situation; but others had fallen into a worse state than had been theirs in the country, and were even more pitiable. In this pitiful category were the bootmakers Nekhlyudov noticed working in basement windows; the pale dishevelled washerwomen with their thin bare arms, ironing at open windows from which the soapy steam poured out in clouds; the two house-painters he met, in aprons and with ragged footwear, bespattered with paint from top to toe. Their sleeves were rolled up above the elbows of their stringy, feeble brown arms, and they were carrying a bucket of paint, swearing at each other without interruption. Their faces looked haggard and ill-tempered. The same expression was to be seen on the dusty, swarthy draymen, jolting along in their carts. The same expression was on the swollen faces of the ragged men and women with children in their arms, who stood begging at the street corners. The faces Nekhlyudov caught sight of at the open windows of an eating-house he passed wore a like expression. Red, perspiring dull-eyed men sat shouting and chorusing at dirty tables littered with bottles and tea-things, waiters in white swaying and hurrying about between them. One man sat by the window with up-lifted eyebrows, pouting lips and a fixed stare, as if trying to remember something.

'And why are they all gathered here?' Nekhlyudov wondered, involuntarily breathing in with the dust which the cold wind blew into his face the ubiquitous smell of rancid oil and fresh paint.

In one street a procession of carts caught up with him, loaded with iron of some sort, which made such a terrific din on the uneven roadway that his ears and head started to ache. He began to walk faster in order to get ahead of the row of carts, when suddenly he heard his name called above the clatter. He stopped and saw a few steps in front of him an officer with sharp-pointed waxed moustaches and a smooth shining face, sitting in a smart *droshky* and waving his hand in greeting, his smile displaying a row of remarkably white teeth.

'Nekhlyudov! Can it be you?'

Nekhlyudov's first feeling was one of pleasure.

'Why, Schönbock!' he exclaimed with delight, but the next moment he knew that there was absolutely nothing to be delighted about.

This was the same Schönbock who had called for him at his aunts' that day. Nekhlyudov had quite lost sight of him, but had heard that in spite of his debts, leaving the regiment and staying in the cavalry reserves, he had somehow managed to keep his place in the society of the wealthy. His gay contented appearance seemed to corroborate this report.

'So glad I saw you! There isn't a soul in town,' he said, getting out of the trap and straightening his shoulders. 'But you've aged, my dear fellow! I only recognized you by your walk. Can't we dine together? Is there anywhere we can find a decent meal?'

'I don't know that I have the time,' said Nekhlyudov, trying to think of some way to escape that would not offend his old friend. 'What are you doing here?' he asked.

'Business, my dear fellow, business. A matter of a trusteeship. You see I am a trustee. I manage Samanov's affairs for him – you know, the millionaire. He's got softening of the brain – but he owns getting on for a hundred and fifty thousand acres!' he said with great pride, as if he himself had created all those acres. 'His affairs had been dreadfully neglected. The entire estate had been let out to the peasants. They were paying nothing and were over eighty thousand roubles in arrears. In a single year I changed everything and increased the revenue by seventy per cent. What do you say to that?' he asked proudly.

Nekhlyudov remembered having heard that Schönbock, for the very reason that he had run through his own fortune and piled up debts, had by some special influence been appointed trustee for the property of a rich old man who was squandering his estate; and he was now, apparently, living on the trusteeship.

'How can I get away without hurting his feelings?' wondered Nekhlyudov, looking at the sleek fat face with the waxed moustaches, and listening to his good-hearted friendly chatter about where one could get a good dinner, and his bragging over the way he managed the affairs of his trust.

'Now then, where shall we dine?'

'Really I have no time,' said Nekhlyudov, glancing at his watch.

'Well, then, look here. Tonight at the races – will you be there?'

'No, I shan't.'

'Oh, please do! I haven't any horses of my own these days but I always back Grisha's. Do you remember him? He has a first-rate stable. So come, won't you, and we'll have supper together.'

'No, I can't have supper with you either,' said Nekhlyudov with a smile.

'Well, that's too bad! Where are you going now? Let me give you a lift.'

'I am on my way to my lawyer. He's just round the corner here,' said Nekhlyudov.

'Oh yes, of course. You have got something to do with prisons – have turned prisoners' advocate, I hear,' said Schönbock, laughing. 'The Korchagins told me. They have already gone out of town. What does it all mean? Do tell me about it!'

'Yes, yes, it is quite true,' Nekhlyudov replied, 'but I can't tell you about it in the street.'

'Of course, of course, you always were a crank. But you will come to the races?'

'No, I can't, and really I don't want to. Please don't be angry with me.'

'Why should I be angry? But where is it you live?' he asked, and all at once his face grew serious, his eyes became fixed and he raised his eyebrows. He was evidently trying to recall the address, and Nekhlyudov suddenly recognized the same dull expression that had struck him on the face of the man with the raised brows and pouting lips at the window of the eating-house.

'Isn't it cold, eh?'

'Yes, it is indeed.'

Schönbock turned to the driver. 'You've got the parcels?'

'Well, good-bye, then. I am awfully glad to have met you,' he said, and pressing Nekhlyudov's hand warmly, jumped into the trap, waving his broad hand in a new white chamois-leather glove in front of his sleek face and smiling a habitual smile which showed his unusually white teeth.

'Was I really like that once?' Nekhlyudov thought, continuing on his way to the lawyer's. 'Perhaps not quite like that, but I wanted to be, and believed I should spend life in that way.'

11

THE lawyer admitted Nekhlyudov before his turn and at once began to discuss the Menshovs' case, which he had been reading over. He was indignant at the unfounded charge brought against them.

'It is a shocking affair,' he said. 'Very likely the owner started the fire himself to get the insurance money, but the point is that the Menshovs' guilt was not proved at all. In fact, there was no evidence whatever. It was all due to the especial zeal of the examining magistrate, and the assistant prosecutor's negligence. If only the case comes up here and is not heard in a provincial court, I guarantee an acquittal and I won't take a fee. Now, about this other matter – Fedosya Biryukova's appeal to the Emperor is ready. If you go to Petersburg, take it with you and hand it in in person, with a request that it be considered. Otherwise the Appeals Committee will make a few inquiries, wash their hands of it as quickly as may be – that is, turn it down – and that will be the end of it. You must try to get at someone high up.'

'The Emperor?' queried Nekhlyudov.

The lawyer laughed.

'Yes, that would be high all right – the Supreme Court. No, by high up I mean the secretary of the Appeals Committee or someone at the top. Well, that's all now, isn't it?'

'No, I have a communication here from some sectarians,' said Nekhlyudov, bringing a letter out of his pocket. 'It's an astonishing thing, if what they write is true. I'll try and see them today and find out what it's all about.'

'I see you've become a sort of funnel, a mouth-piece for the complaints of the entire prison,' said the lawyer, smiling. 'It's too much – you won't be able to cope with it.'

'But this really is a startling case,' said Nekhlyudov, and gave a brief outline of the main points: a little group in the country had been meeting in order to read the Gospels; the authorities had come along and broken up the meeting. The following Sunday they gathered together again, the village policeman was called, a report was made and they were committed for trial. The magistrate examined them, the public prosecutor drew up an indictment, the court confirmed the indictment and committed them for trial. The public prosecutor charged the accused, on the table lay the material evidence – a New Testament – and they were sentenced to deportation. 'I call that a terrible state of affairs,' said Nekhlyudov. 'Do you think it can be true?'

'What is it that surprises you?'

'Why, everything. I can understand the village constable who simply obeys orders, but the prosecutor who made out the indictment is an educated man.'

'But that is just where our mistake lies,' said the lawyer. 'We are in the habit of thinking that our prosecutors and judges are men of modern liberal views. Once upon a time that was so, but it is quite different in these days. They are simply officials, only interested in the twentieth day of the month when they get their salaries. They need more, and there their principles end. They are prepared to accuse, try and sentence anyone you like.'

'Yes, but do laws really exist that can deport a man for reading the Bible in company with others?'

'Yes, and not only to other parts of the country but to hard labour in Siberia if it can be proved that he has been expounding the Bible after a fashion critical of the Church's interpretation. To detract in public from the Orthodox Faith means, in accordance with Article 196, exile to Siberia.'

'Impossible!'

'I assure you it is so. I always tell the gentlemen of the law that I cannot set eyes on them without feeling a sense of gratitude: it is only due to their kindness that I, and you, and all of us are not in gaol. It's the easiest thing imaginable to sentence a man to loss of special privileges, and have him sent to "less remote parts",' said the lawyer.

'But if that is so and everything depends on the arbitrary will of the prosecutor and other persons who have the power to apply or not apply the law, what is the use of having law-courts at all?'

The lawyer burst into a peal of laughter.

'What questions you do ask! Well, that, my dear sir, is philosophy. But there is no reason why we shouldn't discuss philosophy. You must come along on Saturday. You will meet scholars at my house, writers, painters. And then we will discuss these "abstract problems" together,' said the lawyer, with ironical feeling on the words 'abstract problems'. 'You have met my wife? Do come if you can.'

'Thank you, I will try to,' said Nekhlyudov, conscious that he was not telling the truth and that if he tried to do anything it would be to keep away from the lawyer's literary evenings and his circle of scholars, writers and painters.

The laughter with which the advocate greeted Nekhlyudov's remark that law-courts were pointless if judges could apply or not apply the law as they liked, and his tone when he spoke of 'philosophy' and 'abstract problems', showed Nekhlyudov how very differently he and the lawyer, and the lawyer's friends too, probably, looked at things; and he felt that, great as was the gulf that now separated him from his former friends, Schönbock and the rest, he had even less affinity with the lawyer and his set.

12

THE prison was a long way off and it was growing late so Nekhlyudov took a cab. In one of the streets they drove along, the cabby, a middle-aged man with an intelligent kindly face, turned to Nekhlyudov and drew his attention to an enormous house that was being put up.

'Isn't that a huge affair?' he asked, as though he were partly responsible for the building and was proud of it.

It really was an enormous house, planned in a complicated and unusual style. A solid scaffolding of heavy pine timbers, held together by iron ties, surrounded the structure, which was separated from the street by a hoarding. Workmen bespattered with plaster scurried to and fro like ants. Some were laying bricks, some trimming them into shape, others were carrying heavy hods and buckets up and bringing them down empty.

A stout well-dressed gentleman, probably the architect, stood by the scaffolding, pointing upward as he talked to the contractor, a man from the province of Vladimir, who listened to him with respectful attention. All the while empty carts rolled out of the gates past the architect and the contractor, and full ones came in.

'How sure they all are – those who do the work as well as those who make them do it – that it is right that while their wives at home, big with child, slave away beyond their strength, and their children in patchwork caps, before their imminent death from starvation, smile like wizened old men and kick with their little legs – that it is right for them to be building a stupid useless palace for some stupid useless person, one of the very people who rob and ruin them,' thought Nekhlyudov, as he looked at the house.

'Yes, it's an idiotic house,' he said his thought aloud.

'What do you mean – an idiotic 'ouse?' the cabby protested in an offended tone. 'Thanks to it the people get work. I don't call that idiotic.'

'But it is such useless work.'

'It can't be useless, or they wouldn't be buildin' it. It means food for the people,' said the driver.

Nekhlyudov was silent, especially as it would have been difficult to talk above the clatter the wheels made. Not far from the prison the cabby branched off the cobblestones on to a macadam road, so that it was easier to talk, and he turned to Nekhlyudov again.

'And what a lot of folks come flockin' to the town nowadays, it's fair shockin',' he said, swinging round on his box and pointing to a party of country labourers approaching with saws and axes, sheepskin coats and sacks slung across their backs.

'More than in other years?' Nekhlyudov asked.

'I'll say so! It's terrible this year, everywhere's crowded. The employers just flingin' the workmen about same as they were shavin's. Not a job to be got nowhere.'

'What's the reason for it?'

'They've spawned so. There's no room for 'em.'

'But what of it? Why don't they stay in the country?'

'No work for 'em in the country. They've got no land.'

Nekhlyudov felt like a man with a bruise which always seems to be getting knocked, as if on purpose; yet it is only because the place is tender that the knock is noticed.

'I wonder, can it be the same everywhere?' he thought, and began inquiring of the cabby how much land there was in his village, how much he himself had, and why he was living in the city.

'There are three of us, sir, and we've got about two and a 'alf acres apiece,' the cabby said, eagerly getting into conversation. 'There's father and a brother at home, another brother's servin' in the army. They work the land. But there's naught to work really, so my brother thought of comin' to Moscow.'

'And can't you rent land?'

'Where's a man to rent land nowadays? The gentry, they was like that, went and squandered theirs. The merchants got their 'ands on it. You can't buy from them – they want to work it theirselves. In our parts it's a Frenchie owns the lot – bought the estate from the old master and won't rent a square yard to no one, so you might as well shut your trap.'

'Who is this Frenchman?'

'Dufar the Frenchman. Maybe you've 'eard of 'im? 'E makes wigs for the actors at the big theatre. It's a good business, so 'e's made a fortune. Bought all the estate as belonged to our mistress. Now we're in 'is power. 'E does what 'e likes with us. It's lucky for us 'e's a good man. Only 'is wife, she's a Russian, is a real bitch, God save us. Robs the people right and left. Awful, it is. Well, 'ere's the prison. Where shall I put you down, at the entrance? I reckon they won't let us inside.'

13

WITH a sinking heart, and dreading the state he might find Maslova in this time, Nekhlyudov rang the bell at the main entrance and asked the warder who came out to him for Maslova. He was dismayed by the mystery that both she and all the other people collected in the prison were to him. After making inquiries the warder said that she was in the hospital. Nekhlyudov went to the hospital. There a gentle old man, the hospital doorkeeper, let him in at once and, on being told who it was Nekhlyudov wished to see, directed him to the children's ward.

A young doctor, smelling of carbolic, came out into the passage and sternly demanded to know what he wanted. This doctor was always making things easier for the prisoners and was therefore continually coming into conflict with the prison authorities, and even with the head doctor. Fearing that Nekhlyudov would call on him to break some rule, and wishing besides to show that he made no exception for anybody, he pretended to be angry.

'There are no women here – this is the children's ward,' he said.

'I know, but there is an attendant here who was transferred from the prison.'

'Yes, there are two of them. Which one do you want?'

'I am a friend of the one named Maslova,' said Nekhlyudov, 'and I should like to see her. I am going to Petersburg to enter an appeal on her behalf, and I wanted to give her this. It is only a photograph,' Nekhlyudov said, taking an envelope out of his pocket.

'All right, you may do that,' said the doctor, relenting, and turning to an old woman in a white apron he told her to call the prison-nurse Maslova. 'Please take a seat, or would you rather go into the waiting-room?'

'Thank you,' said Nekhlyudov, and taking advantage of the favourable change in the doctor's manner he asked how they liked Maslova in the hospital.

'Pretty fair. She doesn't do too badly, considering her former life,' said the doctor. 'But here she is.'

The old nurse came in at one of the doors, followed by Maslova in a white apron over a striped dress, her hair completely hidden under a three-cornered kerchief. When she saw Nekhlyudov she flushed scarlet and paused irresolutely; then she frowned, and with downcast eyes walked quickly towards him along the strip of matting down the middle of the passage. Coming up to Nekhlyudov, at first she was not going to give him her hand but then she did hold it out, flushing redder still. Nekhlyudov had not seen her since the day when

316

she apologized for her outburst, and he was expecting to find her in the same frame of mind. But today she was quite different: there was something new in the expression of her face, something reserved and shy, and, it seemed to Nekhlyudov, something hostile towards him. He repeated to her what he had told the doctor – that he was going to Petersburg – and handed her the envelope with the photograph he had brought from Panovo.

'I found this at Panovo – it's an old photograph. I thought you might like it. Do have it.'

Raising her dark eyebrows in surprise, she looked at him with her squinting eyes, as though asking 'What is this for?' and silently took the envelope and tucked it into her apron.

'I saw your aunt while I was there,' said Nekhlyudov.

'Did you?' she said indifferently.

'Are you comfortable here?'

'Yes, quite,' she replied.

'The work is not too hard?'

'No, it's all right. I'm not used to it yet.'

'I am glad, for your sake. Anyhow, better here than there.'

'What do you mean by "there"?' she said, the colour flooding her face.

'There, in the prison,' said Nekhlyudov hastily.

'In what way?' she asked.

'I should think the people are nicer here. Not like those that were there.'

'There are plenty of good people there,' she said.

'I have been seeing about the Menshovs and am hopeful they will soon be released,' said Nekhlyudov.

'Please God! She's such a wonderful old woman,' she said, repeating her former description of the old woman and smiling slightly.

'I am going to Petersburg today. Your case will come up soon, and I hope the sentence will be quashed.'

'Whether it is or not, I don't mind now,' she said.

'Why do you say "now"?'

317

'Just because,' she said, darting a questioning glance into his eyes.

Nekhlyudov understood the words and the glance to mean that she wanted to know whether he still kept firm to his decision or had accepted her refusal.

'I do not know why you don't mind,' he said. 'But so far as I am concerned, it really doesn't make any difference whether you are cleared or not. Whatever happens, I am ready to do what I said I would,' he declared firmly.

She lifted her head, and her black squinting eyes rested on him and looked beyond him, and her whole face shone with happiness. But the words she spoke were not at all what her eyes were saying.

'It's no use you talking like that,' she said.

'I'm saying it so that you should know.'

'We've gone over it all, and there's no more to be said,' she replied, with difficulty restraining a smile.

There was a sudden noise in the ward, and the sound of a child crying.

'I think they're calling me,' she said, looking round anxiously.

'Well, good-bye, then,' he said.

She pretended not to see his outstretched hand and without taking it turned away, trying to hide the elation she felt, and walked swiftly back along the strip of matting down the passage.

'What's going on in her mind now? What is she thinking? What are her feelings? Is she testing me or can she really not forgive me? Is it that she cannot say what she thinks and feels, or doesn't she want to? Has she softened towards me, or is she still bitter?' Nekhlyudov asked himself and found no answer. He knew this much only – she had changed, and that the change was an important one for her, drawing him closer not merely to her but to Him in Whose name the transformation was being accomplished. And this union lifted him into a state of joyous exaltation and humility.

When she got back to the ward, where there were eight cots, the sister told her to make one of the beds, and bending over too far with the sheet she slipped and nearly fell. A convalescent boy with a bandage round his neck, who had been watching her, laughed, and Maslova could contain herself no longer. She sat down on the edge of the bed and burst into a loud peal of laughter so infectious that several of the children also roared with laughter, and the sister shouted at her angrily:

'What are you cackling about? Do you think you're back where you came from? Go and fetch the dinners.'

Maslova stopped laughing and taking the plates and things did as she was told, but catching the eye of the boy with the bandaged neck, who had been forbidden to laugh, she giggled again. Several times when she happened to be alone during the day Maslova slid the photograph half out of the envelope and took a delighted look at it; but it was not until the evening, when she was off duty and by herself in the room she shared with another nurse, that she pulled the photograph right out of the envelope and, sitting quite still, looked long at the faded yellow picture, her eyes caressing every detail of the faces, the clothes, the steps of the veranda, the shrubbery which served as a background for his face, and hers, and the aunts'. She could not feast her eyes enough, especially on herself, her young beautiful face with the hair curling round her forehead. She was so absorbed that she did not notice her fellow nurse come into the room.

'What's that? Did he give it to you?' asked the fat good-natured girl, leaning over the photograph. 'It can't be you?'

'Who else could it be?' said Maslova, looking into her companion's face with a smile.

'And who's that? Is it him? And is that his ma?'

'His aunt. Wouldn't you have recognized me?' asked Maslova.

'Not much! Not on me life. The face is all different. I bet it's all of ten years since them days!'

'Not years ago but a lifetime,' said Maslova, and suddenly all her animation vanished. She looked downcast and a deep line appeared between her brows.

'But you lived cushy *there*, didn't you?'

'Yes, cushy,' Maslova echoed, closing her eyes and shaking her head. 'Worse than hard labour.'

'What d'you mean?'

'I mean that from eight o'clock in the evening until four in the morning, all the year round –'

'Then why don't they chuck it?'

'They'd like to, but they can't. But what's the use of talking about it?' cried Maslova, springing to her feet and flinging the picture into the drawer of the table; and forcing back tears of rage she ran out of the room, slamming the door behind her. Looking at the photograph, she had felt herself the person she was when it was taken, and had mused on her happiness then, and thought of how happy she could be with him even now. The nurse's words had reminded her of what she was now and what she had been in the old days: reminded her of the horror of her past life, which she had recognized dimly at the time but not allowed herself to realize. Only now did she recall all those terrible nights, and especially one, in Carnival week, when she was expecting a student who had promised to buy her out. She was wearing a low-necked red silk dress with wine stains all over it, and a red ribbon in her dishevelled hair. Tired, worn out and half tipsy, having seen her visitors off – it was getting on for two o'clock in the morning – she sat down during an interval between the dances beside the bony pianist with the blotchy face who accompanied the violinist, and began complaining of her hard fate. She remembered how the pianist had said that she didn't like her occupation either and wanted to make a change, and how Klara had come up to them, and they suddenly decided all three of them to get out. They thought they had finished for the night and were just about to go upstairs when the drunken voices of new arrivals were heard in the ante-room. The violinist struck up a *ritornello* and the pianist pounded out the first figure of a quadrille, introducing the accompaniment to a hilarious Russian song. A small perspiring man hiccuping and smelling of drink, in a dress suit and a white tie, which he took off after the first figure, seized her in his arms; while another fat man with a beard, also wearing evening dress (they had come from a ball), grabbed Klara, and for ages they whirled, danced, screamed, drank. . . . And so it had gone on for a year, two years, three – how could she help changing? And it was he who had been the cause of it all.

And again all her old bitter fury against him rose inside her and she wanted to revile, to upbraid him. She was sorry she had missed the opportunity of telling him again today that she knew the sort of man he was and she wasn't going to submit to him, that she would not let him make use of her spiritually as he had done physically, nor would she allow herself to be an object for any magnanimity on his part. Pity for herself and futile condemnation of him made her so wretched that she longed for drink. Had she been in the prison instead of the hospital she would have broken her promise and drunk some vodka; here, however, she could not get any spirits except by applying to the doctor's assistant, and she dreaded approaching him because he pestered her with his attentions. She had come to hate the thought of a man. After sitting for a while on a bench in the passage she went back to her room and, making no response to her companion's talk, Maslova wept for a long time over her ruined life.

14

NEKHLYUDOV had three matters to attend to in Petersburg: Maslova's petition to the Senate; Fedosya Biryukova's case before the Appeals Committee; and Vera Bogodoukhov-skaya's requests to try – at the Office of the Gendarmery, or perhaps the Third Division[1] – to get her friend Shustova

1. Secret Police.

released from prison, and to obtain permission for a mother to see her son who was confined in the Fortress (Vera Bogo-doukhovskaya had sent him a note about this). These last two matters he considered as one. Then there was a fourth thing, the business of the sectarians, who were to be separated from their families and sent to the Caucasus for reading and expounding the Gospels. He had promised, not so much to them as to himself, to do all he could to clear up this affair.

Since his last call on Maslennikov, and especially since his visit to the country, Nekhlyudov had not exactly decided to give up, but had conceived a whole-hearted loathing for the society in which he had lived till then: a society where the suffering borne by millions of people in their efforts to ensure the convenience and comfort of a small minority was so carefully concealed that those who benefited neither saw nor could see this suffering and the consequent cruelty and wicked-ness of their own lives. Nekhlyudov could no longer move in this society without feeling ill at ease and guilty. And yet the habits of a lifetime drew him to this circle, as did his family and friends; but, above all, in order to do the one thing which concerned him now – to help Maslova and the other unfortunates he was anxious to help – he would have to call on the assistance and influence of these people for whom he had no esteem and who even aroused his indignation and contempt.

Arriving in Petersburg and staying with his aunt – his mother's sister – the Countess Tcharskaya, wife of a former Minister of State, Nekhlyudov found himself plunged into the very heart of that aristocratic society which had become so alien to him. This was disagreeable, but what else could he do? If he had gone to a hotel instead of to his aunt's she would have been offended, and besides, his aunt had important con-nexions and might be extremely useful in all the matters he had to attend to.

'Well, what are all these marvellous tales I hear about you?' asked Countess Katerina Ivanovna as she offered him coffee after his arrival. '*Vous posez pour un Howard,*[1] helping criminals, visiting prisons, putting things right.'

'Oh no, not at all.'

'Why not? It's a good thing. But haven't I heard there is some romance connected with all this? Come along, tell me all about it.'

Nekhlyudov described his relations with Maslova – told her the whole truth.

'Yes, yes, I remember. Hélène, your poor mother, talked to me about it at the time, when you were staying with those two old women. They wanted to marry you to that ward of theirs, didn't they?' (Countess Katerina Ivanovna had always looked down on Nekhlyudov's aunts on his father's side.) 'So that's the girl, is it? *Elle est encore jolie?*'[2]

Aunt Katerina Ivanovna, a jolly woman of sixty, bursting with health and energy, was tall and very stout, and had a distinctly perceptible black moustache on her upper lip. Nekhlyudov was fond of her and even as a child had found her energy and high spirits infectious.

'No, *ma tante,*[3] all that is over. I only want to help her, first because she was not guilty of the crime she was sentenced for, and I am to blame for that, and to blame, too, for the life she has led. I feel it my duty to do all I can for her.'

'But someone told me you meant to marry her.'

'So I did, but she refuses me.'

Katerina Ivanovna looked at her nephew in silent amazement, her forehead bulging and her eyes lowered. Suddenly her face altered and with a delighted expression she exclaimed:

'Well, she has more sense than you have. Oh dear, what a fool you are! And you really would have married her?'

'Most certainly.'

'After what she has been?'

'All the more, since it was all my fault.'

1. Pretending to be a Howard (John Howard, eighteenth-century prison reformer).

2. Is she pretty still?

3. Aunt.

'Yes, you're an absolute goose,' said his aunt, repressing a smile. 'A terrible goose, but that's the very reason I love you – for being such a terrible goose,' she repeated, obviously very pleased with the word, which to her mind precisely conveyed the mental and moral state of her nephew. 'You know, this is very *à propos*,' she went on. 'Aline is in charge of a wonderful home for fallen Magdalenes. I went there once. They are quite revolting. Afterwards I did nothing but wash and wash. But Aline is devoted to it, *corps et âme*,[1] so we shall send her – that girl of yours – there. If anyone can reform her, it is Aline.'

'But she has been sentenced to penal servitude. I have come on purpose to appeal about it. It's the first thing I want your help with.'

'I see! Well, where is her case to be heard?'

'In the Senate.'

'The Senate? Why, my dear cousin Levushka is in the Senate. But he's in that idiotic heraldry department. I don't know any of the senators themselves. Heavens above, aren't they all Germans of some sort – Geh, Feh, Deh, *tout l'alphabet*,[2] or else every imaginable Ivanov, Simeonov, Nikitin (or Ivanenko, Simonenko, Nikitenko, *pour varier*). *Des gens de l'autre monde*.[3] But I'll speak to my husband. He knows them. He knows all sorts of people. I'll tell him. But you had better explain to him yourself – he never understands what I tell him. Whatever I say, he always declares he can't make head or tail of it. *C'est un parti pris*.[4] Everyone else understands, but not he.'

Just then a footman in knee-breeches brought in a note on a silver tray.

'There now, it's from Aline. You'll have a chance of hearing Kiesewetter.'

'Who is Kiesewetter?'

'Kiesewetter? Come tonight and you will find out who he

1. Body and soul.   2. The whole alphabet.
3. To ring the changes. A separate species.
4. His mind is made up beforehand.

is. He speaks with such eloquence that the most hardened criminals fall on their knees and weep and repent.'

Countess Katerina Ivanovna, however strange it might seem and however little in keeping with her temperament, was a fervent adherent of the doctrine which teaches that faith in the Redemption is the essence of Christianity. She attended all the meetings where this doctrine, fashionable at the time, was preached, and held meetings of the 'faithful' in her own house. But although the doctrine rejected all ritual, ikons and even sacraments, the countess had an ikon in every room, and one at the head of her bed, also, and continued to observe all that the Church demanded, seeing no inconsistency in this.

'I wish your Magdalene could hear him: he would convert her,' said the countess. 'Now don't forget to be home to-night. You will hear him. He is a remarkable man.'

'But, *ma tante*, I am not interested.'

'But I assure you, it *is* interesting. And you certainly must come. Now, what else do you want of me? *Videz votre sac.*'[1]

'I have some business in the Fortress.'

'The Fortress! Well, I can give you a note to Baron Kriegsmuth there. *C'est un très brave homme.*[2] But you know him, don't you? He was a colleague of your father's. *Il donne dans le spiritisme.*[3] But never mind, he's a good fellow. What is it you want there?'

'I want permission for a woman to visit her son who's confined there. But I heard it depended on Tchervyansky, not Kriegsmuth.'

'I don't care for Tchervyansky, but anyway he's Mariette's husband. We can ask her. She will do it for me. *Elle est très gentille.*'[4]

'Then I want to present a petition on behalf of a woman who has been in the Fortress for several months and no one knows why.'

'Don't tell me that. She knows all right – they all know per-

---

1. Unbosom yourself.   2. He's an excellent man.
3. He goes in for spiritualism.   4. She is very nice.

fectly well. I think those suffragette women get just what they deserve.'

'We don't know whether they deserve it or not. But they suffer. You are a Christian, you believe in the Gospel, and yet you have no mercy.'

'That has nothing to do with it. The Gospel is one thing, and what is disgusting remains disgusting. It would be worse if I were to pretend to like Nihilists – and particularly those short-haired women Nihilists – when the truth is that I cannot stand them.'

'Why can't you stand them?'

'Do you ask why, after March the 1st?'[1]

'But not all of them took part in the March 1st affair.'

'It makes no difference: let them keep out of what does not concern them. Women have no business meddling with such matters.'

'What about Mariette now – you seem to think that she can take part in public affairs,' said Nekhlyudov.

'Mariette? Mariette is Mariette. But Heaven knows who these young women are, and they want to go teaching everybody.'

'Not teach, but simply help the common people.'

'We don't need them to do that. We know very well whom to help and whom not to help.'

'But the people are in want. I have just come from the country. Is it right that the peasants should toil to the last ounce of their strength and never get enough to eat, while we live in this dreadful luxury?' said Nekhlyudov, beguiled by his aunt's kindliness into confiding his thoughts to her.

'What do you want, then – that I should work and have nothing to eat?'

'No, I shouldn't like you not to eat,' replied Nekhlyudov with an involuntary smile. 'I only want us all to work and all have enough to eat.'

1. On 1 March (Old Style) 1881 the Emperor Alexander II was assassinated.

His aunt again lowered her forehead and eyes and stared at him curiously.

'*Mon cher, vous finirez mal.*'[1]

'Why is that?'

Just then a tall broad-shouldered man entered the room. It was the countess's husband, General Tcharsky, former Minister of State.

'Ah, Dmitri, how are you?' he said, presenting a freshly shaven cheek for his nephew to kiss. 'When did you arrive?'

He kissed his wife silently on the forehead.

'*Non, il est impayable,*'[2] exclaimed Countess Katerina Ivanovna, turning to her husband. 'He's ordering me to go and be a washerwoman and flap linen in the river, and live on potatoes. He is an awful fool, but all the same do what he asks you. A terrible goose,' she corrected herself. 'Have you heard about Madame Kamenskaya? She is in such a state of despair that they fear for her life,' she went on. 'You ought to call on her.'

'Yes, it's a dreadful business,' said her husband.

'You go and talk to him now,' she said, turning to Nekhlyudov. 'I have some letters to write.'

Nekhlyudov had hardly gone into the room next to the drawing-room when she called after him:

'Shall I write to Mariette, then?'

'If you please, *ma tante.*'

'I'll leave a blank space for what you want to say about your short-haired woman, and she will tell her husband what to do. And he'll do it. You mustn't think me unkind. They're all a disgusting lot, are your protégées, but *je ne leur veux pas de mal,*[3] bother them! Run along now. But be sure you're home this evening to hear Kiesewetter. And we will have some prayers. And if only you don't resist *ça vous fera beaucoup de bien.*[4] I know very well that both Hélène and the rest of you fell behind the times in this. Good-bye for the present.'

1. My dear, you will come to a bad end.   2. Oh, he's priceless.
3. I don't wish them any harm.   4. It will do you a lot of good.

15

COUNT IVAN MIKHAILOVICH had been a minister and was a man of strong convictions.

The convictions of Count Ivan Mikhailovich had from his earliest years consisted in the belief that just as it was natural for a bird to feed on worms, be clad in feathers and down, and fly through the air, so it was natural for him to feed on the choicest and most expensive food, prepared by expensive cooks, wear the most comfortable and most expensive clothes, drive with the best and fastest horses; and therefore all these things must be to hand for him. Moreover, Count Ivan Mikhailovich considered that the more money he got out of the Treasury under various headings, the more decorations he received (up to and including the diamond-mounted insignia of something or other), and the oftener he spoke to personages of both sexes belonging to the Imperial family, the better it would be. Everything else, measured against these fundamental tenets, Count Ivan Mikhailovich found uninteresting and of no importance. Everything else might be as it was or just the reverse, for all he cared. Count Ivan Mikhailovich had lived and operated by this creed in Petersburg for forty years and at the end of that period he achieved the position of Minister of State.

The chief qualities which enabled Count Ivan Mikhailovich to attain this post were, first, his ability to comprehend documents and laws already formulated, and to draft, though clumsily, intelligible State papers, and spell them correctly; secondly, his commanding appearance by which he could, when necessary, give an impression not only of haughtiness but of unapproachable dignity, while at other times, if need arose, he could be abjectly, even passionately servile; and thirdly, having no general principles or rules of morality, either public or private, made it possible for him to agree or disagree with anybody as best suited the moment. In thus ordering his life and work, his one endeavour was always to behave with good form and avoid being too obviously inconsistent. Whether his actions were in themselves moral or immoral, whether great good or great harm would result from them for the Russian Empire or the world as a whole, was a matter of supreme indifference to him.

When he became a Minister of State not only those dependent on him (and he had a considerable entourage of people and friends dependent on him), but all those outside his immediate circle were positive, as he was himself, that he was a very clever statesman. But as time went by and he accomplished nothing, showed no ability, and when, in accordance with the rules of the struggle for existence, others like himself, imposing and unscrupulous officials who had learned how to draft and understand documents, pushed him aside and he was compelled to retire, it became plain to everybody that, far from being exceptionally clever, he was, in fact, a shallow ill-educated man of limited capacities, though extremely conceited, whose ideas scarcely reached the level of the leading articles in the conservative newspapers. It became evident that there was nothing to distinguish him from the other half-educated, self-confident officials who had elbowed him out, and he realized it himself, but this in no way shook his conviction that he was entitled to large sums of money every year from the Treasury and new decorations for his dress-clothes. This conviction was so strong that no one had the courage to dispute it, and every year he received, partly in the form of a pension, partly in the form of remuneration for being a member of a Government institution and chairman of various commissions and committees, several tens of thousands of roubles, besides the right – highly prized by him – of adding additional bits of gold lace every year to his epaulets and trousers and attaching new ribbons and enamelled stars to his dress-clothes. In consequence of this Count Ivan Mikhailovich had very high connexions.

Count Ivan Mikhailovich now heard Nekhlyudov out in

the same way as he would listen to the reports of the permanent secretaries of his department, and, having listened to the end, said he would give him two notes – one of them to Senator Wolf in the Appeals Department.

'They say all sorts of things about him, but *dans tous les cas c'est un homme très comme il faut*.[1] And he is under an obligation to me and will do what he can.'

The other note Count Ivan Mikhailovich gave him was to an influential member of the Appeals Committee. The case of Fedosya Biryukova, as related to him by Nekhlyudov, interested him very much. When Nekhlyudov said that he was thinking of writing to the Empress about it he said that it really was a very touching story and he himself would mention it at court if an occasion arose, but he could not promise. The petition had better be sent in in the ordinary way. But should there be an opportunity – if he were invited to the *petit comité*[2] on Thursday he might refer to it, he said.

In possession of both these letters and a note from his aunt to Mariette, Nekhlyudov set out to deliver them.

He went first to Mariette. He remembered her as a girl in her 'teens, the daughter of a poor but aristocratic family, and he knew that she had married a man who had made a career for himself but who did not enjoy a good reputation – Nekhlyudov had heard reports especially of his callousness towards hundreds and thousands of political offenders, whose martyrdom was his primary responsibility – and Nekhlyudov always found it horribly disagreeable, when he wanted to help the oppressed, to have to rank himself with the oppressors and seem, by his appeal to them to refrain, if only where certain individuals were concerned, from their habitual cruelties (which they were probably unaware of themselves), to recognize their activities as lawful. When this happened he always felt at odds and dissatisfied with himself, and wavered whether to ask the favour or not, but inevitably decided in

1. At all events he is very *comme il faut*.
2. Informal evening at the Palace.

the end that he must ask it. This time, on the one hand there was the fact that he would feel uncomfortable, ashamed and in an unpleasant situation with this Mariette and her husband; but, on the other, it could mean that a wretched unhappy woman in solitary confinement might be released and an end put to her and her family's sufferings. Besides the falsity and insincerity of seeking aid in a set which he no longer considered his own but which looked upon him as one of themselves, he felt in these circles that he was stepping back into the old ruts and, in spite of himself, yielding to the frivolous and immoral tone which held sway there. He had experienced this that very morning at his aunt's when they were discussing most serious matters and he dropped into a light bantering tone.

Altogether Petersburg, where he had not been for a long time, had its usual physically invigorating and morally blunting effect on him: everything was so clean and comfortable, so well ordered – and, above all, the people were so easy-going – that life seemed particularly smooth.

A fine, clean, polite cabman drove him past fine, polite, clean policemen along fine, clean, watered streets, past fine, clean houses to the house on the canal where Mariette lived.

At the entrance stood a pair of English horses with blinkers, and an English-looking coachman in livery, with whiskers half-way up his cheeks, sat on the box, proudly holding a whip.

A doorkeeper in an uncommonly clean uniform opened the door into the hall, where in still cleaner braided livery stood the carriage footman with superbly combed side-whiskers, and an orderly on duty, also in a new clean uniform.

'The General is not at home to visitors. Nor is her Excellency. They are driving out directly.'

Nekhlyudov handed over Countess Katerina Ivanovna's letter and taking out a visiting-card went up to a small table where the visitors' book lay, to write a few words of regret that he had not found anyone at home, when the footman moved to the staircase, the doorkeeper went out and shouted 'Now!' to the coachman, while the orderly sprang to attention, his arms pressed to his sides, looking towards and following with his eyes a small slender lady who was hurrying down the stairs at a pace inconsistent with her dignity and importance.

Mariette was wearing a large hat with a plume, a black gown and mantle, and new black gloves. Her face was hidden by a veil.

Catching sight of Nekhlyudov, she raised the veil, revealing a very pretty face with brilliant eyes that looked at him inquiringly.

'Ah, Prince Dmitri Ivanovich!' she exclaimed in a gay pleasant voice. 'I should have recognized . . .'

'Why, you even remember my name?'

'Of course I do! My sister and I used to be in love with you once upon a time,' she said in French. 'But how you have altered! I wish I weren't going out. But let us go back,' she added, and paused irresolutely.

She looked up at the clock on the wall.

'No, I mustn't. I am going to a requiem at Madame Kamenskaya's. She is in a dreadful state.'

'What has happened to her?'

'Haven't you heard? Her son was killed in a duel. He fought with Pozen. An only son. It is terrible. The mother is prostrated.'

'Oh yes, I did hear.'

'No, I had better go – but do come tomorrow, or this evening,' she said, walking to the door with swift light steps.

'I cannot come this evening,' he replied, escorting her to the front steps. 'But I have a request to make to you,' he went on, glancing at the pair of bays drawing up at the entrance.

'What is it?'

'Here is a note about it from my aunt,' said Nekhlyudov, handing her a narrow envelope with a large crest. 'You will find it all there.'

'I know Countess Katerina Ivanovna thinks I can influence my husband in official matters. She's quite mistaken. I can do nothing of the sort and I don't like interfering. But, of course, for the countess and yourself I am ready to depart from my rule. What is it about?' she said, vainly searching her pocket with her small black-gloved hand.

'There is a girl confined in the Fortress: she is ill and not guilty.'

'What is her name?'

'Shustova. Lydia Shustova. It's in the note.'

'Very well. I will do everything I can,' she said, stepping lightly into the softly upholstered barouche, its brightly varnished splash-boards glistening in the sunshine. She opened her parasol. The footman got on to the box and signalled to the coachman to drive off. Just as the barouche started she touched the coachman's back with her parasol, and the beautiful pair of thoroughbreds, bay mares, halted, their lovely heads arched and pulled back by the curb bits, their slender legs quivering.

'Mind you come and see me, but *disinterestedly*, please,' she said, smiling a smile, the power of which she well knew; and then, the performance, so to speak, being over, she let down the curtain – that is, she drew the veil over her face again. 'All right, let us go now,' and she touched the coachman a second time with her parasol.

Nekhlyudov raised his hat and the thoroughbred bays, snorting a little, clattered their hooves on the cobblestones, and the carriage rolled rapidly away, its new rubber tyres bouncing gently over the uneven places in the road.

16

REMEMBERING the smile he had exchanged with Mariette, Nekhlyudov shook his head at himself. 'I shall be drawn back into that life before I've had time to look round,' he thought, aware of the schism in himself which always oppressed him when he was obliged to invoke the aid of people whom he did not respect. After considering where to go next, to avoid retracing his steps, Nekhlyudov made first for the Senate. He was shown into the chancery, a magnificent apartment, where he found a multitude of exceedingly polite and neatly attired officials.

They informed Nekhlyudov that Maslova's petition had been received and passed on for consideration and report to that same Senator Wolf to whom his uncle had given Nekhlyudov a letter.

'The Senate meets this week,' one of the officials said to Nekhlyudov, 'and Maslova's case will hardly come up then. But by special request it might possibly be taken this week, on Wednesday.'

While Nekhlyudov stood waiting in the office for this information he heard more discussion about the duel, and a detailed account of how young Kamensky had been killed. Here for the first time he learned the circumstances of the affair, which was the talk of all Petersburg. It appeared that a party of officers had been eating oysters in a shop and, as usual, drinking freely. One of them made an uncomplimentary remark about Kamensky's regiment. Kamensky called him a liar. The other struck Kamensky. The next day they fought, and Kamensky fell with a bullet in the stomach and in two hours was dead. The murderer and the seconds were arrested and confined in the guard-house, but it was said that they would be released in a couple of weeks.

From the Senate Nekhlyudov drove to the Appeals Committee, to see the influential Baron Vorobyov, who occupied splendid apartments in a house belonging to the Crown. Here the doorkeeper and a footman informed him in severe tones that the Baron could only be seen on reception days: at present he was with His Majesty, and would again have to deliver a report on the following day. Nekhlyudov left his letter and went to Senator Wolf.

Wolf had just finished luncheon and in his customary

manner was assisting his digestion by smoking a cigar and pacing up and down the room, when Nekhlyudov was shown in. Vladimir Vassilyevich Wolf really was *un homme très comme il faut*, and placed this attribute higher than any other. From this sublime altitude he looked down on the rest of the world. Indeed, he could not but esteem the quality very highly since thanks to it alone he had made a brilliant career – the very one he desired – that is, through marriage he had acquired a fortune which brought him in a revenue of eighteen thousand roubles a year, and by his own exertions had secured the post of senator. He regarded himself not only as *un homme très comme il faut* but also as a man of chivalrous honour. By honour he meant not taking bribes on the quiet from private individuals. But he did not consider it dishonourable to claim from the Government all sorts of travelling and other expenses, postage money and so on, in return for which he was ready to perform any servile task the Government might require of him. To ruin and destroy, to cause hundreds of innocent people to be exiled and imprisoned for their devotion to their country and the religion of their fathers, as he had done when Governor of one of the Polish provinces, was not dishonourable in his eyes but a patriotic exploit of courage and nobility. Nor did he consider it dishonourable to fleece his wife, who was in love with him, and his sister-in-law. On the contrary, he thought it a wise arrangement of his family affairs.

Wolf's household consisted of his nonentity of a wife, her sister, whose fortune he had appropriated by selling her estate and depositing the proceeds in his own name, and a meek, nervous, plain daughter, who led a lonely unhappy life, from which she had lately found distraction in the evangelical meetings at Aline's and the Countess Katerina Ivanovna's.

Wolf's son was a happy-go-lucky fellow who at the age of fifteen had grown a beard and started to drink and lead a fast life, which he continued to do until, when he was twenty, he was turned out of the house for not completing any of his studies and, by frequenting low company and running up debts, compromising his father. On one occasion his father had paid a bill of two hundred and thirty roubles for him, and on another, six hundred roubles, when he told him that this was the last time, and warned him that unless he reformed he would turn him out of the house and have no more to do with him. Far from reforming, the boy ran into debt to the tune of a thousand roubles, and took the liberty of telling his father that life at home was a pain, anyway. Whereupon Wolf informed his son that he could go where he pleased, that he was no son of his. After that Wolf had affected not to have a son, and no one at home ventured to mention his name, and Wolf was quite sure that his domestic life could not have been more satisfactorily arranged.

Wolf stopped short in the middle of his promenade about the room and greeted Nekhlyudov with a gracious and somewhat ironical smile – this was his manner and the involuntary expression of his consciousness of his *comme il faut* superiority over the majority of mortals. He read the note.

'Please take a seat, and excuse me if, with your permission, I go on walking up and down,' he said, putting his hands in the pockets of his jacket and continuing to pace with light delicate steps diagonally across his large, severely furnished study. 'Very pleased to make your acquaintance, and, of course, very glad to be of service to Count Ivan Mikhailovich,' he said, emitting a puff of fragrant bluish smoke and cautiously removing the cigar from his mouth so as not to drop any ash.

'I should only like to ask that the case be heard soon, so that if the prisoner is sent to Siberia the earlier she starts the better,' said Nekhlyudov.

'Yes, yes, I understand, by one of the first steamers from Nizhni,' said Wolf with his patronizing smile. He always knew in advance what anybody was going to say. 'What is the prisoner's name?'

'Maslova . . .'

Wolf went up to the table and glanced at a paper that was lying on a cardboard file with other documents.

'Yes, yes, Maslova. Very well, I will speak to my colleagues. We will hear the case on Wednesday.'

'May I telegraph my lawyer to that effect?'

'You have a lawyer? What for? But if you like, why not?'

'The grounds of the appeal may not be sufficient,' said Nekhlyudov, 'but I think the evidence shows that the verdict was the result of a misunderstanding.'

'Yes, yes, that may be so, but the Senate cannot decide the case on its merits,' said Wolf sternly, looking at the ash of his cigar. 'The Senate is concerned only with the correct interpretation and application of the law.'

'But this seems to me to be an exceptional case.'

'I know, I know. Every case is exceptional. We shall do our duty and that is all that can be expected.' The ash still held on, but had cracked and was in imminent danger of falling. 'Are you often in Petersburg?' said Wolf, holding his cigar in such a way that the ash should not fall. But the ash began to wobble and Wolf carefully carried it to the ashtray, into which it collapsed. 'What a shocking thing that was about Kamensky,' he said. 'Such a fine young man. The only son. Just think of the poor mother,' he went on, repeating almost word for word what everyone in Petersburg was saying that day about Kamensky.

Having spoken of Countess Katerina Ivanovna and her enthusiasm for the new religious movement, which Wolf neither condemned nor approved of but which, as one so *comme il faut*, he could obviously have no need of, he rang the bell.

Nekhlyudov took his leave.

'If you find it convenient, come and dine,' said Wolf, extending his hand. 'Say, on Wednesday. I'll be able to give you a definite answer.'

It was late now, and Nekhlyudov drove home – that is, to his aunt's house.

17

COUNTESS KATERINA IVANOVNA dined at half past seven, and dinner was served in a novel fashion that Nekhlyudov had not seen before. After they had placed the dishes on the table the footmen at once withdrew, so that the diners waited on themselves. The gentlemen would not allow the ladies to exert themselves unnecessarily but, as befitted the stronger sex, manfully bore the burden of helping the ladies and themselves to food, and poured out the wine. When one course was finished the countess pressed the button of an electric bell on the table, and the footmen came in noiselessly, quickly carried away the dishes, changed the plates and brought in the next course. The dinner was exquisite, and so were the wines. In the large light kitchens a French chef was at work, with two white-clad assistants. There were six persons at the table: the count and countess, their son (a surly officer in the Guards who sat with his elbows on the table), Nekhlyudov, a French lady's companion, and the count's head bailiff who had come up from the country.

The conversation here, too, turned on the duel and they discussed the Emperor's view of the affair. It was known that the Emperor was deeply grieved for the mother – and all were grieved for the mother. But as it was known that the Emperor, though he condoled with the mother, did not intend to be severe with the murderer, who had defended the honour of his uniform, all, therefore, were lenient towards the murderer who had defended the honour of his uniform. Countess Katerina Ivanovna with her free and easy ideas was the only one to express disapproval.

'They get drunk and go and slaughter decent young men – I should not forgive them on any account,' she declared.

'Now that is a thing I cannot understand,' said the count.

'I know that you never understand what I say,' began the countess, and went on, turning to Nekhlyudov, 'Everybody understands me except my husband. All I say is that I am sorry for the mother, and I don't want the other to kill a man and then be pleased with himself.'

Whereupon her son, who had been silent up to now, took the assassin's part and quite rudely pointed out to his mother that an officer could not behave otherwise, and if he did there would be a court-martial and he would be dismissed from the regiment. Nekhlyudov listened without joining in the conversation and, having been an officer, understood, though he did not agree with young Tcharsky's arguments; at the same time he could not help contrasting the officer who had killed Kamensky with the handsome young convict he had seen in the prison, condemned to the mines for killing a man in a brawl. Both had become murderers because they had been drinking. Yet the peasant who had killed in a moment of passion was taken away from his wife and family, and now, in chains and with shaven head, was on his way to Siberia, while the officer was confined in a pleasant room in the guard-house, eating good dinners, drinking good wine, reading books, and in a day or two would be set free to continue his career as before, the affair only having made him a more interesting person.

He said what he was thinking. At first it seemed that Countess Katerina Ivanovna agreed with her nephew but then lapsed into silence, and, like everyone else present, Nekhlyudov felt that he had committed some sort of social impropriety with his story.

In the evening, not long after dinner, the large ballroom – where rows of high-backed chairs had been arranged as in a lecture-hall, with an arm-chair behind a little table on which was a decanter of water for the speaker – began to fill with people come to hear the visiting Kiesewetter preach his sermon.

Outside, elegant carriages drove up to the entrance. Ladies in silk, velvet and lace, with false hair, tightly laced waists and padded figures, sat in the luxuriously furnished ball-room. Between the ladies were men in uniform and evening-dress, and five or six from the lower classes: two house-porters, a shopkeeper, a footman and a coachman.

Kiesewetter, a thick-set man with hair just turning grey, spoke in English, and a thin girl wearing pince-nez translated quickly and well.

He said that our sins were so great, and the punishment they deserved was so great and unavoidable, that it was impossible to live, anticipating such punishment.

'Let us only reflect, beloved sisters and brethren, on ourselves, our lives, on the things we do, the way we live, how we anger the all-loving God, how we cause Christ to suffer, and we shall see that there is no forgiveness for us, no escape, no salvation – that we are all doomed to eternal damnation. A deadful doom – everlasting torment – awaits us,' he cried, with tears in his trembling voice. 'How can we be saved? My brethren, how are we to be saved from this terrible fire? The house is already in flames, and there is no escape.'

He paused, and real tears ran down his cheeks. For over eight years now, every time he reached this part of his address, which he was very pleased with, he felt his throat contracting, a tickling in his nose and the tears running down his cheeks. These tears further increased his emotion. Sobs were heard in the room. Countess Katerina Ivanovna sat with her elbows on an inlaid table and her head in her hands, while her fat shoulders heaved convulsively. The coachman gazed in surprise and apprehension at the foreign gentleman, as though he were bearing down on him and he would not get out of the way. Most of the company sat in attitudes like the Countess Katerina Ivanovna. Wolf's daughter, in a fashionable gown, who resembled her father, was kneeling with her face in her hands.

The orator suddenly uncovered his face and arranged on it something quite like a real smile, the sort of smile with which actors express joy, and began again in a sweet gentle voice:

'But salvation is to be found. Easy, blissful salvation is ours. Our salvation is the blood shed for us by the only-begotten

Son of God, Who gave Himself up to be tortured for our sakes. His suffering, His blood is our salvation. Oh, my brothers and sisters,' he exclaimed, again with tears in his voice, 'let us arise and give thanks to God, Who gave his only-begotten Son for the redemption of mankind. Holy is His blood . . .'

Nekhlyudov felt so profoundly disgusted that he quietly got up and, frowning and repressing a groan of shame, tip-toed out and went to his room.

18

NEXT morning, just as Nekhlyudov had finished dressing and was about to go down, the footman brought him a visiting-card from his Moscow lawyer. Fanarin had arrived in Petersburg on business of his own, and also (if it were to come up soon) to be present at the hearing of Maslova's case in the Senate. Nekhlyudov's telegram had crossed him on the way. When he heard when Maslova's case was to come up and who the senators were he smiled.

'Exactly – there you have all three types,' he said. 'Wolf, the Petersburg official; Skovorodnikov, the learned jurist; and Beh, the practical lawyer, and therefore the liveliest of them all. He is our best hope. Well, and how about the Appeals Committee?'

'I am going to call on Baron Vorobyov today. I couldn't get an appointment yesterday.'

'You know how Vorobyov comes to be a baron?' said the lawyer, observing the slightly ironical stress Nekhlyudov placed on this foreign title in connexion with so very Russian a surname. 'It was the Emperor Paul who rewarded his grandfather for something – he was a court footman, I think – and gave him the title. He managed to please him in some way. "I fancy making him a baron," said the Emperor, "and I'll have no objections!" And so there we have Baron Vorobyov. And very proud of it he is, too. A cunning old fox.'

'I am on my way to see him now,' said Nekhlyudov.

'Splendid! We can go together. Let me give you a lift.'

As they were leaving, Nekhlyudov met a footman in the ante-room with a note for him from Mariette.

Pour vous faire plaisir, j'ai agi tout à fait contre mes principes, et j'ai intercédé auprès de mon mari pour votre protégée. Il se trouve que cette personne peut être relâchée immédiatement. Mon mari a écrit au commandant. Venez donc disinterestedly. *Je vous attend.*

M.[1]

'How do you like that!' Nekhlyudov said to the lawyer. 'Why it's appalling – a woman whom they have kept in solitary confinement for seven months turns out to be quite innocent, and only a word was needed to get her released.'

'That's the way it always is. Well, anyhow, you have got what you wanted.'

'Yes, but it is my success that distresses me. Just think what must be going on there. Why were they keeping her?'

'I wouldn't probe too deeply into that, if I were you. Well, then, shall I give you a lift?' said the lawyer as they left the house and a fine carriage that he had hired drove up to the door. 'You are going to see Baron Vorobyov, aren't you?'

The lawyer gave the coachman the address, and the swift horses soon brought Nekhlyudov to the baron's house. The baron was at home. A young official in uniform with an extraordinarily long neck and a bulging Adam's apple, and a remarkably light gait, was in the first room with two ladies.

'Your name, please?' asked the young man with the Adam's apple, stepping lightly and gracefully from the ladies to Nekhlyudov.

Nekhlyudov gave his name.

'The baron has spoken about you. One moment, please.'

1. To please you I have acted quite against my principles, and interceded with my husband for your protégée. It turns out that this person can be set free immediately. My husband has written to the Governor. Come then, *disinterestedly*. I am expecting you.

The young assistant opened the door into an inner room and returned, leading a lady with a tear-stained face, dressed in mourning. With bony fingers the lady was trying to pull her tangled veil over her face, to hide her tears.

'This way, please,' the young man turned to Nekhlyudov, walking with a light step over to the door of the study and holding it open.

Entering the study, Nekhlyudov found himself in the presence of a thick-set man of medium height, with short hair and a frock-coat, who was sitting in an arm-chair at a large desk and cheerfully looking in front of him. His good-natured face, its high colour all the more striking against the white of his moustaches and beard, lit up with a friendly smile at the sight of Nekhlyudov.

'Very glad to see you. Your mother and I were old friends. I remember you as a boy, and later on as an officer. Sit down and tell me what I can do for you. . . . Yes, yes,' he kept saying, nodding his grey head with the short hair while Nekhlyudov was telling him Fedosya's story. 'Go on, go on – I understand – yes, indeed, it's a really sad case. And have you entered a petition?'

'I have one prepared,' said Nekhlyudov, taking it out of his pocket. 'But I wanted to speak to you first. I hoped that this case might receive special attention.'

'That was very sensible of you. I will most certainly make a report myself,' said the baron, vainly trying to impart a sorrowful expression to his cheerful face. 'Very touching. She seems to have been no more than a child, the husband treated her roughly, this estranged her, but as time went on they began to love each other. . . . Yes, I will make a report out.'

'Count Ivan Mikhailovich said he might ask the Empress –'

Nekhlyudov had hardly pronounced these words when the baron's face changed.

'Perhaps, after all, you had better hand in the petition at the chancery, and I will do what I can for my part,' he said to Nekhlyudov.

At this point the young official who seemed so proud of his elegant walk came into the room.

'The lady you have just seen would like another word with you.'

'Very well, show her in. Ah, *mon cher*, the tears one sees here! If only one could dry them all. One does what one can.'

The lady entered.

'I forgot to ask you not to let him give up his daughter; he's capable of . . .'

'I have already told you I will.'

'For God's sake, baron – you will be the saving of a mother.'

She seized his hand and began to kiss it.

'Everything shall be done.'

When the lady had gone, Nekhlyudov also rose to take leave.

'We will do what we can. We shall first write to the Ministry of Justice. When we get their reply we will do everything possible.'

Nekhlyudov left the study and went into the chancery. Again, as in the Senate, he found superb officials – spruce, polite, fastidiously correct and precise in dress and speech – in superb apartments.

'How many there are of them – how terribly many – and how well fed they are! And what clean shirts and hands and well-polished boots they all of them have! And who looks after all this? And how comfortable they all are compared, not just with prisoners in gaol but even with the peasants!' Nekhlyudov could not help thinking again.

19

THE man who had the power to ease the lot of prisoners confined in Petersburg was an aged general descended from a line of German barons. He possessed decorations enough to cover himself with but wore only one of them – the Order of the

White Cross – in his buttonhole He had seen many years of active service but now, so people said, was in his dotage. He had received this extremely flattering Cross in the Caucasus because under his command close-cropped Russian peasants dressed in uniforms and armed with guns and bayonets had killed more than a thousand men who were defending their liberty, their homes and their families. Later on he served in Poland, where he again compelled Russian peasants to commit all sorts of crimes, and got more orders and decorations for his uniform. Then he served somewhere else, and now, an enfeebled old man, he had been given his present post, which provided him with a good house, an income and public esteem. He was unrelenting in his obedience to orders 'from above' and was very proud of his severity. He ascribed particular importance to these instructions 'from above', believing that everything in this world might be amended, but not those instructions 'from above'. His duties consisted in keeping political prisoners of both sexes in casemates, in solitary confinement and in such conditions that half of them perished within ten years, some of them going out of their minds, some dying of consumption, others committing suicide – by starving themselves, cutting their arteries with bits of glass, hanging or setting fire to themselves.

The old general knew all this – it had all happened before his eyes – but all these things no more touched his conscience than accidents caused by thunderstorms, floods and so on. These things happened as a result of orders 'from above' issued in the name of His Majesty the Emperor. Such orders were to be scrupulously obeyed, and thus there was no point whatsoever in thinking about the consequences of such regulations. The old general therefore did not permit himself to think of such things, believing that it was his duty as a patriot and a soldier not to reason, since this might make him falter in the execution of these, to his mind, immensely important duties.

*

Once a week, in the performance of his office, the old general went the round of the cells and asked the prisoners if they had any requests to make. The prisoners put various requests to him. He heard them calmly, in impenetrable silence, and never granted a single one, because they were all contrary to regulations.

As Nekhlyudov was approaching the old general's house the treble bells of the belfry clock chimed out *How glorious is the Lord* and then struck two. Hearing the chimes, Nekhlyudov found himself remembering something he had read in the memoirs of the Decembrists[1] about the effect this sweet music repeated every hour had on prisoners who were confined for life. The old general, while Nekhlyudov drove up to the entrance of his house, was sitting in his dimly lighted drawing-room at an inlaid table, twisting a saucer on a sheet of paper with the aid of a young artist, the brother of one of his subordinates. The thin, moist, weak fingers of the artist were linked with the round, wrinkled, stiff-jointed fingers of the old general, and these joined hands were jerking about with the upturned saucer to and fro over the sheet of paper on which all the letters of the alphabet were written. The saucer was answering a question put by the old general – 'How do the souls of the departed recognize one another after death?'

The spirit of Joan of Arc was communicating with them through the saucer when an orderly acting as footman came in with Nekhlyudov's card. The spirit of Joan of Arc had already spelt out, letter by letter, 'They will recognize each other after the . . .' and this had been noted down. When the orderly entered the room the saucer had paused at the letter *c*, then at *l*, on to *e* and *a*, where it started to jerk about. This was because the general thought the next letter should be *n*, that is, he thought Joan of Arc was going to say that the souls of the departed would recognize one another after they had

1. A group who attempted to put an end to absolutism in Russia by means of a military revolt at the time of the accession of Nicholas I in December 1825.

346

been *cleansed* of all earthly dross, or something of the kind, and therefore the next letter had to be *n*, whereas the artist thought the next letter would be *r*, and that the spirit of Joan of Arc meant to say that the souls of the departed would recognize one another by the *clear* light emanating from their astral bodies. The general wrinkled bushy grey eyebrows and stared morosely at their hands on the saucer, and, imagining that the saucer was moving of its own accord, kept pulling it towards the *n*. But the pale-faced young artist, with his scant hair combed back behind his ears, his lifeless blue eyes fixed on a dark corner of the room and, nervously twitching his lips, was urging the saucer towards the letter *r*. The general frowned at the interruption but after a moment's silence he took the card, put on his pince-nez, and, groaning from a pain in the small of his broad back, rose to his full height, rubbing his numbed fingers.

'Show him into the study.'

'With your Excellency's permission I will finish this alone,' said the artist, standing up. 'I feel the presence.'

'Very well, you finish it,' said the general severely, and walked across the room to the study with a firm measured stride, keeping his feet straight and parallel with each other.

'Glad to see you,' he said to Nekhlyudov, uttering the friendly words in a gruff voice and pointing to an arm-chair beside the writing-table. 'Been in Petersburg long?'

Nekhlyudov said that he had just arrived.

'I trust the princess, your mother, is keeping well?'

'My mother is dead.'

'Oh, I beg your pardon. I am sorry to hear that. My son told me about meeting you.'

The general's son was pursuing the same sort of career as his father. After passing out from the Military Academy he had been appointed to the Intelligence Bureau and was very proud of his duties there. His duties consisted in supervising Government spies.

'Why, I served with your father. We were friends – old comrades. What about you – are you in Government service?'

'No, I am not.'

The general shook his head disapprovingly.

'I have come to make a request of you, general.'

'Ver – y pleased. What can I do for you?'

'If my request is improper, you will forgive me, I hope. But I must make it.'

'What is it?'

'You have a man, Gourkevich by name, confined in the Fortress. His mother asks for permission to visit him, or at least to be allowed to send him books.'

The general evinced neither pleasure nor displeasure at Nekhlyudov's request but bending his head on one side he screwed up his eyes as if considering. In fact, he was not considering at all, and was not even interested in what Nekhlyudov asked, knowing full well that he would answer in accordance with the regulations. He was simply resting mentally, and not thinking about anything.

'Matters of this kind, you see,' he began at last, 'do not rest with me. In regard to interviews there is a regulation confirmed by His Majesty, and whatever has been decreed there is observed. As to books – we have a library, and the books that are allowed are given to them.'

'But he needs scientific books: he wants to study.'

'Don't you believe it.' The general was silent for a moment. 'It is not study he wants. He's just restless.'

'But surely they need something to pass the time in their wretched circumstances,' said Nekhlyudov.

'They are always complaining,' objected the general. 'We know them, you see.' He spoke of them in a sweeping manner, as though they were a different and wicked race of people. 'They have comforts here that are seldom found in prisons,' he went on.

And as though to justify himself he started to describe in

detail all the conveniences provided for the prisoners, as if the chief aim of the institution was to make a pleasant home for the inmates.

'It was fairly harsh in the old days, I admit, but now they are excellently cared for. They have three courses to their meals, and one of them is always meat – mince or rissoles. On Sundays they get a fourth course, a sweet. Would to God every Russian fed as well as they do.'

Like all old people the general, having once got on to something he knew inside out, said all the things he had repeated times without number to show the unreasonableness of the prisoners' demands, and their ingratitude.

'They get books of a religious nature, and old periodicals. We have a library of suitable books. But they don't read much. At first they seem interested but very soon new books are returned with the leaves half cut, while the pages of the old ones are not even turned. We tried them out once,' said the general with a faint resemblance to a smile, 'by putting slips of paper in. They stayed just where we put them. Nor are they prohibited from writing,' he continued. 'We give them slates and slate pencils so that they can occupy themselves with writing. They can wipe off what they have written and write again and again. But they don't write either. No, they very soon quieten down. It's only at first that they are restless but as time goes on they even begin to grow fat and become quite peaceable,' said the general, never suspecting the terrible significance his words held.

Nekhlyudov listened to the hoarse old voice, looked at the stiffened limbs and the dull eyes beneath the grey eyebrows, at the senile, clean-shaven, flabby cheeks propped up by a military collar, at the White Cross which this old man was so proud of, especially since he had received it for extraordinarily cruel and wholesale murder – and knew that it would be useless to make any rejoinder or try to explain to him the meaning of his own words. However, he made an effort and inquired about another case, that of the prisoner Shustova, whose release, so he had heard that morning, had been ordered.

'Shustova? Shustova? I cannot possibly recall all their names, there are so many of them, you see,' he said, apparently blaming them for overcrowding the prison. He rang a bell and sent for his clerk.

While they were waiting for the clerk he began trying to persuade Nekhlyudov that he should enter the service, saying that 'honest and high-minded men' – he included himself in the category – were particularly needed by the Tsar. 'And the country,' he added, evidently only to round off the sentence. 'I am an old man, yet so far as my strength allows I go on serving.'

The clerk, a thin dried-up man with restless intelligent eyes, came in with the information that Shustova was held in some queer fortified place and that no papers had been received about her.

'We shall certainly discharge her the moment we get the papers. We do not keep them any longer than we can help,' said the general, with another attempt at a skittish smile which only distorted his aged features. 'We are not particularly anxious for their company.'

Nekhlyudov rose, doing his best not to show the mingled feelings of repugnance and pity which the appalling old man excited in him. For his part, the old man was likewise telling himself that he must not be too hard on the thoughtless and evidently misguided son of an old comrade, and must give him a word of advice before letting him go.

'Good-bye, my dear fellow, and don't take what I am going to say amiss. It's only because I like you. Don't have anything to do with the sort of people we have here. There's not an innocent one among them. All these people are a bad lot. We know them,' he said, in a tone admitting no possibility of doubt. And he really had no doubts – not because it was so but because if it were not so, he would be forced to see himself, not as a venerable hero honourably living out the last days of a good life but as a scoundrel, who had sold, and in his old age continued to sell, his conscience. 'Best of all, join the service,' he continued. 'The Tsar needs honest men . . . and the country,' he added. 'What do you suppose would happen if we all behaved like you and refused to serve? Who would be left? We are ready to find fault with the order of things, and yet we don't want to help the Government ourselves.'

With a deep sigh Nekhlyudov made a low bow, pressed the big bony hand condescendingly held out to him and left the room.

The general shook his head disapprovingly, and rubbing the small of his back returned to the drawing-room where the artist was waiting for him, with the answer from Joan of Arc's spirit already written down. The general put on his pince-nez and read: 'They will recognize each other by the clear light emanating from their astral bodies.'

'Ah,' said the general with approval and closed his eyes. 'But if everyone emits the same light, how are we to know one from another?' he asked, and interlacing his fingers again with the artist's he sat down at the table.

Nekhlyudov's cabby drove out through the gates.

'That's a dreary place, sir,' he said, turning to Nekhlyudov. 'I 'ad 'alf a mind to drive off without waiting for you.'

'Yes, it is a dreary place,' Nekhlyudov agreed, drawing in a deep breath and letting his eyes rest with a sense of relief on the smoky grey clouds floating across the sky, and the shimmering ripples in the way of boats and steamers on the Neva.

20

THE next day Maslova's case was to be heard at the Senate, and Nekhlyudov and the lawyer met at the grand entrance to the Senate building, where several carriages were already drawn up. Ascending the magnificent main staircase to the first floor, Fanarin, who knew all the ins and outs of the place, led the way to a door on the left which was carved with the date of the introduction of the Judicial Code. After taking off his overcoat in the first long room, and learning from the attendant that the senators were all assembled, the last one having just gone in, Fanarin, wearing a tail-coat, with a white tie on his white shirt-front, proceeded jauntily into the next room. Here there was, on the right, a large cupboard and then a table, and, on the left, a winding staircase. An elegant-looking official in uniform with a portfolio under his arm was coming down the stairs. In the room everyone's attention was on an old man of patriarchal appearance with long white hair. He was wearing a jacket and grey trousers. Two attendants stood respectfully beside him.

The little old man with white hair crossed to the cupboard and disappeared from sight. Meanwhile Fanarin, having espied a colleague in a tail-coat and white tie like himself, at once entered into an animated conversation with him, and Nekhlyudov studied the people who were in the room. The public consisted of about fifteen persons, among them two ladies. One of these was young and wore pince-nez, the other had grey hair. The case to be heard that day concerned a libel in the press, and the public were more numerous than usual – mainly from the world of journalism.

The usher, a florid handsome man in a gorgeous uniform, holding a slip of paper in his hand, came up to Fanarin to ask which case he was interested in. Hearing that it was Maslova's he made a note and departed. At this moment the cupboard door swung open and the patriarchal old man emerged. He had exchanged his short coat for a gold-laced uniform with dazzling metal discs across his chest, which made him look like a bird.

This absurd costume seemed to embarrass the old gentleman himself, and walking faster than was his wont he hurried out of the door opposite the one by which Nekhlyudov and the others had entered.

'That is Beh, a most estimable man,' Fanarin said to Nekhlyudov, and then, introducing him to his colleague, explained the case about to be heard, a most interesting case in his opinion.

After a short time the hearing began and Nekhlyudov with the rest of the public went into the Senate Chamber by a door on the left. All of them, Fanarin included, took their places in the part of the chamber railed off for the public. Only the Petersburg lawyer went up to a desk in front of the rail.

The Senate Chamber was smaller and more plainly furnished than the Criminal Court, and differed from it only in that the table where the senators sat was covered with – not green cloth but crimson velvet embroidered with gold. Otherwise, all the usual trappings of a court of judgement were there: the mirror of justice,[1] the ikon and the portrait of the Emperor. The usher announced in the same solemn manner 'The Court approaches!' Everybody rose in the same manner; the senators in their uniforms walked in in the same way, sat down in the same way in their high-backed chairs, leaning their elbows on the table in the same way, trying to appear at their ease.

There were four senators present: Nikitin, who presided, a clean-shaven man with a narrow face and steely eyes; Wolf, with significantly compressed lips and small white hands – he constantly turned over the sheets of paper in front of him; next, Skovorodnikov, the learned jurist, a heavy fat pock-marked man; and the fourth, Beh, the patriarchal old man who had been the last to arrive. The chief secretary and assistant public prosecutor, a spare beardless young man of medium height with a very dark complexion and sad black eyes, came in with the senators. In spite of the unfamiliar uniform Nekhlyudov recognized him at once, though it was six years or so since they had met: he had been one of Nekhlyudov's closest friends in their student days.

'Isn't that Selyenin – the public prosecutor?' he asked the lawyer.

1. A triangular prism with laws promulgated by Peter the Great inscribed round the edge, which was found in every court of law.

'Yes, why?'

'I know him very well, he is a fine fellow.'

'And an excellent public prosecutor, too – knows his business. We ought to have had him acting for us.'

'Well, I am sure he will be guided by his conscience,' said Nekhlyudov, remembering his former friendship with Selyenin and the latter's attractive qualities of integrity, honesty and probity, in the highest sense of the word.

'But it's too late now, anyway,' whispered Fanarin who was listening to the report of the case just beginning.

The case was an appeal against a judgement given by the Court of Appeal, which had confirmed a decision given in the District Court.

Nekhlyudov listened and tried to make out the meaning of what was going on; but, just as in the Criminal Court, so here the greatest difficulty lay in the fact that they argued over side issues and not what, to all intents and purposes, appeared to be the main issue. The case concerned an article in a newspaper which accused a company director of fraud. It would seem that the only important question was whether it was true that the director of the company had been robbing his shareholders, and what measures could be taken to stop him doing so. But of that not a word was said. Instead, they merely discussed whether the publisher had a legal right to print the article, or not, and whether by publishing it he was guilty of defamation or libel, and did defamation include libel, or libel include defamation – not to mention other matters more or less incomprehensible to the man in the street concerning various statutes and decrees drawn up by some general department.

The only thing that Nekhlyudov saw quite clearly was that Wolf (who was now making the report), who the day before had so strenuously insisted to him that the Senate could not try a case on its merits, was obviously in this instance passionately in favour of annulling the verdict of the Court of Appeal, and that Selyenin, entirely out of keeping with his customary reserve, was arguing the opposite opinion with unexpected violence. This fervour, which so astonished Nekhlyudov in the usually retiring Selyenin, sprang from the fact that he knew the company director to be shady in money matters, and that it had also accidentally come to his ears that practically the day before the hearing Wolf had been to a grand dinner-party at this man's house. Now, when Wolf reported on the case, guardedly enough but with evident bias, Selyenin became excited and expressed his opinion with greater vigour than such an everyday matter warranted. It was clear that his speech upset Wolf: he flushed, moved in his chair, made silent gestures of surprise and withdrew with the other senators to the conference-room, with an air of injured dignity.

'What case is it you have come about?' the usher asked Fanarin again, as soon as the senators had withdrawn.

'I have already told you – the Maslova case,' said Fanarin.

'That's right. The case is to be heard today. But . . .'

'But what?' asked the lawyer.

'Well, you see, we were not expecting it to be argued and the senators are not likely to come back after reaching their decision in this case. Still, I will call their attention to it . . .'

'What do you mean by that?'

'I will certainly call their attention.' And the usher made a note of something on a slip of paper.

The senators actually intended, after announcing their decision in the libel-suit, to dispose of all the other cases, Maslova's included, over tea and cigarettes, without leaving their conference-room.

21

As soon as the senators were seated round the table in the conference-room Wolf, with great animation, began to bring forward all the reasons why judgement ought to be reversed.

The president, an ill-natured man at the best of times, was

in a particularly bad temper that day. Listening to the case during the session, he had formed his opinion already and now sat paying no attention to Wolf but lost in his own thoughts. He was remembering what he had written the day before in his memoirs about the appointment of Vilyanov to an important post he had long coveted. President Nikitin honestly believed that his opinion concerning various officials in the two higher grades with whom he came in contact in the course of his service would furnish material for future historians. Having written a chapter on the day before in which certain officials of those first two grades were soundly rated for preventing him, as he expressed it, from saving Russia from the destruction into which her rulers were dragging her – but in reality for having prevented him from getting a higher salary – he was thinking now what a new light for posterity his revelations would shed on events.

'Yes, of course,' he replied to Wolf, not having heard a word of what he was saying.

Beh was listening to Wolf with a melancholy expression, drawing garlands all the while on the sheet of paper lying before him. Beh was a liberal of the very first water. He treasured the traditions of the 'sixties, and if he ever departed from his strictly neutral attitude it was always in favour of liberalism. Thus, in the present instance, apart from the fact that the company director who was appealing was a bad lot, the prosecution of a journalist for libel, tending as it did to restrict the freedom of the press, in itself inclined Beh to reject the suit. When Wolf had completed his argument Beh stopped in the middle of drawing a garland, and in a sad and gentle voice (he was sad to feel himself obliged to demonstrate such truisms) showed concisely, simply and convincingly that the appellant had no case, and, bending his white head, went on with his garland.

Skovorodnikov, who sat opposite Wolf and kept stuffing his moustaches and beard into his mouth with his fat fingers, the moment Beh paused stopped chewing his beard and in a loud grating voice said that, in spite of the fact that the company director was a frightful scoundrel, he would advocate setting the judgement aside if any legal grounds had existed, but as there were none he was of Beh's opinion, he said, pleased at the opportunity of getting a hit in at Wolf. The president sided with Skovorodnikov, and the appeal was dismissed.

Wolf was annoyed, especially since he seemed to have been caught showing dishonest partiality. Assuming an air of indifference, however, he unfolded the document dealing with Maslova's case and became engrossed in it. Meanwhile the senators rang the bell and asked for tea, and began discussing an event which together with the Kamensky duel was the talk of Petersburg.

This was the affair of the chief of a Government department who was accused of the crime covered by Article 995.

'How revolting!' said Beh with disgust.

'Why, where's the harm? I can show you a book in our literature in which a German writer openly puts forward the view that such acts ought not to be considered criminal, and that marriage between men should be sanctioned,' said Skovorodnikov, noisily and greedily inhaling the smoke from a squashed cigarette which he held between his fingers close to the palm of his hand, and he laughed boisterously.

'Impossible!' said Beh.

'I will show it to you,' said Skovorodnikov, giving the full title of the book, and even the year and place of publication.

'They say he is to be appointed governor of some place in Siberia,' remarked Nikitin.

'That's fine. The bishop will come out in procession to meet him with the cross. They ought to appoint a bishop of the same species. I could recommend one to them,' said Skovorodnikov, and throwing the stub of his cigarette into his saucer, he took into his mouth as much as he could of his beard and moustache and began to chew them.

At this point the usher came in and reported the request of

Nekhlyudov and his counsel to be present during the hearing of Maslova's case.

'Now this case,' said Wolf, 'is quite romantic,' and he told them what he knew of Nekhlyudov's relations with Maslova.

After having talked about it a little while they finished their cigarettes and drank their tea, the senators returned to the Senate Chamber, announced their decision in the libel case and proceeded to hear Maslova's appeal.

In his thin voice Wolf made a full report of Maslova's appeal, but again not without some bias and obviously hoping to get the sentence quashed.

'Have you anything to add?' the president asked Fanarin.

Fanarin rose and, standing with his broad white chest expanded, proved point by point, with remarkable persuasiveness and precision, how the Criminal Court had on six counts strayed from the exact meaning of the law. He went farther and touched, though briefly, on the facts of the case and the crying injustice of the sentence. The tone of his short but forceful address was one of apology to the senators for insisting on matters which they with their wisdom and knowledge of the law saw and understood far better than he: he spoke only because the obligation he had taken upon himself demanded that he should. After Fanarin's speech there seemed not the smallest reason to doubt that the senate must set aside the decision of the court. As he finished his pleading Fanarin smiled triumphantly. Looking at his lawyer and seeing this smile, Nekhlyudov felt sure the case was won. But when he glanced towards the senators he saw that Fanarin alone was smiling and triumphant. The senators and the assistant public prosecutor were neither smiling nor triumphant: they looked bored, as if they were thinking, 'We have heard your sort before, and what does it all amount to?' They were all manifestly glad when the lawyer finished, and stopped wasting their time. Immediately after the end of the lawyer's speech the president turned to the assistant public prosecutor. In a few brief but explicit, definite words Selyenin expressed himself against the reversal of the judgement – he had heard nothing to warrant such a course. Whereupon the senators rose and retired to consult among themselves. In the conference-room they were divided in their opinion. Wolf was in favour of allowing the appeal. Beh, having grasped the issue, also ardently favoured quashing the sentence, vividly painting for the senators the scene in the court and what he righly interpreted as the misunderstanding on the part of the jury. Nikitin, standing, as always, for severity in general and for strict formality, was against the appeal. The whole matter, therefore, depended on Skovorodnikov's vote. And he voted for rejecting the appeal, chiefly because he was outraged by Nekhlyudov's determination to marry the girl on moral grounds.

Skovorodnikov was a materialist and a Darwinian, and counted all manifestations of abstract morality or, worse still, religious feeling, not only as despicable folly but as a personal affront to himself. All this fuss about a prostitute, and the presence here in the Senate of a famous lawyer to defend her, and of Nekhlyudov himself, were in the highest degree repugnant to him. And he stuffed his beard into his mouth again, and made faces, pretending very convincingly to know nothing whatever about the case except that the reasons for the appeal were inadequate, and that, therefore, he agreed with the president in rejecting it.

The appeal was rejected.

22

'TERRIBLE!' said Nekhlyudov, walking out into the waiting-room with Fanarin, who was putting his papers into his portfolio. 'In a matter which is perfectly clear they attach importance only to form, and decline to intervene. Terrible!'

'The case was mismanaged in the Criminal Court,' said the lawyer.

'And Selyenin, too, was in favour of rejection. Terrible, terrible!' Nekhlyudov repeated again. 'What is to be done now?'

'We will petition His Imperial Majesty. Hand in the petition yourself while you are here. I will write it out for you.'

At this moment little Wolf with his decorations and uniform came out into the waiting-room and went up to Nekhlyudov.

'It could not be helped, my dear prince. Your grounds were not good enough,' he said, shrugging his narrow shoulders and closing his eyes, and then went his way.

After Wolf, Selyenin came out too, having heard from the senators that his old friend Nekhlyudov was there.

'I certainly never expected to find you here,' he said, walking up to Nekhlyudov with a smile on his lips, while his eyes remained sad. 'I had no idea you were in Petersburg.'

'And I did not know that you were public prosecutor . . .'

'Assistant,' Selyenin corrected him. 'What are you doing in the Senate?' he asked, looking at his friend with a sad, despondent air. 'I had heard that you were in Petersburg. But what brings you here?'

'Here? I hoped to find justice and to save an innocent woman.'

'What woman?'

'The one whose case has just been decided.'

'Oh, the Maslova case,' said Selyenin, remembering. 'There were absolutely no grounds for an appeal.'

'The question is not of the appeal but of an innocent woman being punished.'

Selyenin sighed.

'Perhaps, but . . .'

'There's no perhaps about it: it's a fact . . .'

'How do you know?'

'Because I was on the jury. I know how the mistake was made.'

Selyenin reflected.

'You should have made a statement at the time,' he said.

'I did.'

'It should have been added to the record of the proceedings. If it had been appended to the appeal . . .'

Always busy and rarely going out into society, Selyenin evidently had not heard of Nekhlyudov's romance; and Nekhlyudov, realizing this, decided that there was no need to speak of his relations with Maslova.

'But it was perfectly plain, as it was, that the verdict was absurd,' he said.

'The Senate has no legal right to declare such a thing. If the Senate took upon itself to revise the judgements of the law-courts according to its own view concerning their equity, trial by jury would lose all meaning, not to mention the fact that the Senate would be reduced to chaos and would run the risk of hampering rather than upholding justice,' said Selyenin, thinking of the case that had been heard first.

'All I know is that this woman is completely innocent, and the last hope has gone of saving her from unmerited punishment. The very highest court has confirmed an act of gross injustice.'

'No, it has not: the Senate did not and cannot enter into the merits of the case,' said Selyenin, screwing up his eyes. 'I suppose you are staying with your aunt,' he went on, evidently wishing to change the subject. 'She told me yesterday that you were here, and invited me to meet you in the evening at a gathering where some foreign preacher was to give an address,' said Selyenin, smiling with his lips.

'Yes, I was there, but left in disgust,' said Nekhlyudov irritably, annoyed with Selyenin for changing the subject.

'Why in disgust? After all, it's a manifestation of religious feeling, even though one-sided and sectarian,' said Selyenin.

'It's all so wildly absurd,' said Nekhlyudov.

'Not at all. The really strange thing is that we know so little of the teaching of our own Church that we see some new kind of revelation in what are, after all, our own fundamental dogmas,' declared Selyenin, apparently in a hurry to express his views, which were new to his old friend.

Nekhlyudov looked at him in surprise. Selyenin lowered his eyes, which expressed not only sadness but a certain ill-will as well.

'Do you, then, believe in the dogmas of the Church?' asked Nekhlyudov.

'Of course I do,' replied Selyenin, gazing straight into Nekhlyudov's eyes with a lifeless look.

Nekhlyudov sighed.

'I am surprised,' he said.

'However, we can discuss this later,' said Selyenin. 'I am coming,' he said to the usher who had approached him respectfully. 'We must certainly see each other,' he added with a sigh. 'But when shall I find you in? I am always at home for dinner at seven o'clock. Nadezhdenskaya Street –' and he gave the number. 'Much water has flowed since the old days,' he added, as he turned to go, again smiling with his lips only.

'I will come if I can,' said Nekhlyudov, feeling that this man, once so near and dear to him, had as a result of this brief conversation suddenly become strange, remote and incomprehensible, if not actually hostile.

23

THE Selyenin whom Nekhlyudov had known as a student was a good son, a faithful friend and, for his years, a well-educated man of the world with a great deal of tact, always well-groomed and handsome, and yet unusually truthful and honest. He was an excellent student, without making any especial effort or being bookish, and won gold medals for his essays.

Not only in words but in deeds he made the service of mankind the aim of his young life, and could see no better way of being useful to humanity than by serving the State. And so the moment he graduated from the university he systematically examined all the activities to which he might devote his energy and, deciding that he would be most useful of all in the second department of the Chancery (where the laws are drafted), he entered that branch of public service. But, in spite of the most scrupulous and exact discharge of the duties demanded of him, this service never satisfied his desire to be useful to mankind, nor did it give him the feeling that he was doing 'the right thing'. Friction with a vain and small-minded superior increased his dissatisfaction so much that he resigned from the Chancery and entered the Senate. Here he was more at ease, but even so his sense of dissatisfaction persisted.

He could not get away from the feeling that it was not at all what he had expected or what he ought to be doing. While occupying his post in the Senate his relatives succeeded in obtaining for him the appointment of *Kammer Junker* (Gentleman of the Bedchamber), and he was obliged to drive out in a closed carriage, wearing an embroidered uniform and white linen apron, to thank all sorts of people for having promoted him to the dignity of a lackey. However much he tried he could find no reasonable justification for such a post and felt, more even than in the Senate, that it was not 'the right thing'; and yet he could not refuse the appointment, on the one hand, for fear of offending those who were so certain that they were giving him great satisfaction, and, on the other, because it flattered the lower side of his nature to see himself in the looking-glass in a uniform with gold lace, and to be deferred to by a certain type of person.

The same sort of thing happened over his marriage. A very brilliant match from a worldly point of view was arranged for him, and he married, again mainly because by refusing he would have hurt both the young lady who wished to be married to him and those who had arranged the marriage, and also because marriage with a nice young girl of good family flattered his vanity and gave him pleasure. But the marriage very soon proved to be even less 'the right thing' than Government service and his Court duties. After the birth of their first child his wife refused to have any more children and plunged into a social round of high living in which he had to participate whether he liked it or not. She was not particularly pretty, was faithful to him and, though she was poisoning her husband's existence and apparently deriving nothing but an excessive expenditure of effort and weariness from the life she was leading, she still persevered intently. All his attempts to make a change were shattered, as against a stone wall, by her conviction (in which she was supported by her family and friends) that this was the proper life to lead.

The child, a little girl with long golden curls and bare legs, was like a complete stranger to her father, chiefly because she was being brought up quite otherwise than he would have wished. The usual lack of understanding developed between husband and wife, even an absence of any desire to understand each other, and then a silent warfare, concealed from outsiders and tempered by the need to preserve appearances, which made his home life a burden. Thus his domestic life proved even less 'the right thing' than his Government position or the place at Court.

But above all it was his attitude to religion that was not 'the right thing'. Like all of his set and generation he had, as his intellect developed, without the least effort shaken off the fetters of the religious superstitions in which he had been reared, and did not know himself the exact moment of his liberation. Being earnest and upright, in his youth, when he and Nekhlyudov were fellow students, he had made no secret of his rejection of the superstitions of the State religion. But as the years went by, bringing promotion with them – and particularly during the conservative reaction which set in in society about that time – his spiritual freedom began to be a handicap: not only in his private life, especially after his father's death when requiems were sung for him, and his mother (and public opinion half demanded this, too) wished him to fast and prepare himself to receive the sacrament, but also in his Government service, which required him to be present at all sorts of intercession services, consecrations, thanksgivings and the like. Hardly a day passed without some outward religious form having to be observed, which it was impossible to avoid. Attending these services, he had to do one of two things: either pretend that he believed what he did not believe (which his natural truthfulness forbade), or else, recognizing all these external forms as shams, arrange his life so as to avoid taking part in what he considered fraudulent. But this apparently trifling matter could be accomplished only at a heavy cost: besides entering into perpetual conflict with the people about him, he would have to alter his whole way of life, give up his Government position and sacrifice all his work for the good of mankind which, he thought, he had already begun and which he hoped to be able to continue with greater efficacy in the future. And in order to do this he had to be absolutely convinced of the correctness of his views. And he was firmly convinced of being right, as no educated man of our day can help being convinced of the soundness of his own common sense, if he knows a little history and knows the origin of religions in general and the origin and decay of Church Christianity. He could not help knowing that he was right in rejecting the truth of the Church's doctrines.

Yet under the stress of his daily life he, an honest and up-right man, allowed a trifling falsehood to creep in. He told himself that before proclaiming an unreasonable thing to be unreasonable one must first study the unreasonable thing. This was a trifling falsehood, but it led him to the great lie, in which he was now stuck fast.

When he put to himself the question whether the Orthodox faith was true – the faith in which he was born and bred, which everyone around him expected him to profess, and without which he would not be able to continue his work of service to mankind – he had already decided the answer. And so to find further light on the subject he did not turn to Voltaire, Schopenhauer, Spencer or Comte; instead, he read the philosophical works of Hegel and the religious books of Vinet and Khomyakov, and, naturally, found in them what he was looking for – a sort of peace of mind and a vindication of the religious teaching in which he had been brought up and which his reason had long since discarded, but without which his whole life was one continual unpleasantness that would vanish forthwith if he but accepted the teaching. So he adopted the usual sophisms, such as the incapacity of the individual intellect to grasp the truth; that the truth is only revealed to an aggregate of men; that it can only be known through revelation; that revelation is in the keeping of the Church; and so on. And from that time forth he could calmly and without being conscious of hypocrisy be present at intercessions, prayers for the dead, liturgies; he could fast and go to communion and cross himself before the ikons, and continue his Government service which gave him the feeling of being useful and brought consolation into his cheerless married life. He thought he believed, and yet he knew with his entire being that this faith of his was farther than anything else from being 'the right thing'.

And this was why his eyes always looked sad. And it was this which caused him, when he saw Nekhlyudov whom he had known before these lies had taken root in him, to remember the self he had been then; and particularly after he had hastened to hint at his present religious views he felt more acutely than ever that they were not 'the right thing', and became painfully sad. Nekhlyudov also felt this, after the first joy at meeting an old friend had passed.

And this was the reason why, after having promised to see each other again, neither of them sought the meeting, and so they did not see each other again during Nekhlyudov's stay in Petersburg.

24

On leaving the Senate Nekhlyudov walked on with the lawyer, who gave orders for his carriage to follow and began to tell Nekhlyudov about the head of a Government department whom the senators had been discussing – who had been found out and, instead of being sent to the mines (which is what should have happened to him according to the law), was to be appointed governor of a province in Siberia. Having come to the end of this story with all its unsavoury details, and also expatiated with particular relish on an account of how a number of highly placed personages had stolen money destined for the construction of the still unfinished monument they had passed that morning; and how So-and-so's mistress had made millions on the Stock Exchange; and how one man had sold and another bought a wife, the lawyer started on another tale about a swindle and all sorts of crimes committed by persons in high places, who occupied, not prison cells but presidential chairs in various official institutions. These stories, of which there seemed to be an inexhaustible supply, gave the lawyer much pleasure, showing as they did perfectly clearly that the means he, the lawyer, employed to earn money were quite lawful and innocent in comparison with the means employed for the same purpose by the highest functionaries of Petersburg. He was therefore very much surprised when Nekhlyudov, without listening to the end of his last story about crime at the top, said good-bye, hailed a cab and drove home to his aunt's house on the embankment.

Nekhlyudov's spirits were very low. He was saddened chiefly by the rejection of the appeal by the Senate, who thus confirmed the senseless torture Maslova was enduring, and also because this rejection made his unalterable decision to join his lot with hers still more difficult. The terrible tales of evil reigning triumphant which the lawyer had related with such gusto still further deepened his depression; nor could he forget for a moment the cold, hostile look that the once sweet-natured, frank, noble-minded Selyenin had given him.

When Nekhlyudov got in, the doorkeeper handed him a note, which he said rather contemptuously had been written by some woman or other in the hall. It was a note from Lydia Shustova's mother. She wrote that she had come to thank her daughter's benefactor and saviour, and to beg and implore him to call at their house on Vassilyevsky Island, Fifth Avenue, number so and so. This was extremely important for Vera Bogodoukhovskaya, she wrote. He need have no fear that they would weary him with expressions of gratitude: they would not speak of gratitude but simply be glad to see him. If possible, would he not come tomorrow morning?

There was another note from a former fellow officer, aide-de-camp to the Emperor, one Bogatyrev, whom Nekhlyudov had asked to pass in person to the Emperor the petition on behalf of the sectarians. Bogatyrev wrote in his large firm handwriting that he would put the petition into the Emperor's own hands as he had promised, but that the thought had just occurred to him – might it not be better for Nekhlyudov to go and see the person on whom the matter depended, and petition him in the first place?

After the impressions of the last few days in Petersburg Nekhlyudov felt quite hopeless about getting anything done. The plans he had formed in Moscow now appeared to him mere youthful dreams of the sort that are inevitably disappointed when it comes to facing life. Still, being now in Petersburg, he considered it his duty to do all he had set out to do, and so he resolved to call on Bogatyrev the very next day, after which he would follow his advice and see the person on whom the affair of the sectarians depended.

He took the petition of the sectarians out of his portfolio and was reading it over when there was a knock on the door and a footman came in with a message from Countess Katerina Ivanovna, inviting him upstairs to a cup of tea with her.

Nekhlyudov said that he would come at once and putting his papers back in his portfolio went upstairs to his aunt. Looking out of a window on his way, and seeing Mariette's pair of bays standing in front of the house, he suddenly brightened and felt inclined to smile again.

Mariette, wearing a hat and no longer in black but in a light gaily-coloured dress, was sitting beside the countess's easy chair, holding a cup of tea in her hand and chattering away, while her beautiful eyes sparkled with laughter. Nekhlyudov entered the room just as Mariette finished telling a funny story – funny and improper, Nekhlyudov guessed from the way they were laughing. The good-natured countess with the dark shadow of down on her upper lip was laughing helplessly, her fat body shaking, while Mariette, her smiling mouth twisted slightly to one side, her head a little bent, sat silently looking at her companion, with a peculiarly mischievous expression on her merry energetic face.

From a few words he had overheard Nekhlyudov could tell that they had been discussing the next most interesting piece of Petersburg news, the episode of the new Siberian governor, and that it was about this that Mariette had said something so funny that it was a long time before the countess could control herself.

'You will be the death of me,' she gasped, after a fit of coughing.

Nekhlyudov greeted them and drew up a chair near by. He was on the point of condemning Mariette for her frivolity when, noticing the serious and even somewhat disapproving look on his face, she suddenly, to please him, changed not only her own expression but her attitude of mind, too – which she had wanted to do the moment she saw him. In a twinkling she became grave, dissatisfied with her life, seeking something, striving after something. She was not pretending – she really had appropriated to herself the very same state of mind that Nekhlyudov was in, although she would not have been able to put into words what Nekhlyudov's state of mind actually was.

She asked him how he had got on with his various interests. He told her about his failure at the Senate and of his meeting with Selyenin.

'Ah, there's a pure creature. A real *chevalier sans peur et sans reproche*. A pure creature,' both ladies repeated, using the epithet commonly bestowed on Selyenin in society.

'What is his wife like?' asked Nekhlyudov.

'His wife? Well, I don't want to criticize her, but she does not understand him. Is it possible that he, too, was in favour of dismissing the appeal?' Mariette asked, with genuine sympathy. 'It is dreadful. How I pity her!' she added with a sigh.

He frowned, and wishing to change the subject began to speak about Lydia Shustova, who had been imprisoned in the Fortress and was now released, owing to Mariette's intervention. He thanked her for influencing her husband and was going on to say how terrible it was that this woman and all her family should have suffered merely because no one had reminded the authorities of them, but before he could finish she interrupted him to give expression to her own indignation.

'Don't talk to me about it,' she said. 'When my husband told me she could be set free the first thought that came to my mind was: Why has she been kept there, if she is innocent?' she went on, anticipating what Nekhlyudov was about to say. 'It is shocking – shocking!'

Countess Katerina Ivanovna saw that Mariette was flirting with her nephew, and this amused her.

'I tell you what,' she said, when there was a silence. 'Do come to Aline's tomorrow night. Kiesewetter will be there. And you come too,' she turned to Mariette.

'*Il vous a remarqué*,'[1] she said to her nephew. 'He told me that what you say – I repeated it all to him – is a very good sign that you will surely come to Christ. You absolutely must come over tomorrow. Tell him to, Mariette, and come yourself.'

---

1. He noticed you.

'In the first place, countess, I have no right whatever to offer any kind of advice to the prince,' said Mariette, and gave Nekhlyudov a look that somehow established a full understanding between them of their attitude in relation to the countess's words and to evangelism in general, 'and, secondly, I do not much care, as you know . . .'

'Yes, you always do everything contrariwise, according to your own ideas.'

'My own ideas? I am a believer, like the simplest peasant woman,' she said, smiling. 'And, thirdly, I am going to the French theatre tomorrow night . . .'

'Ah! And have *you* seen that – what is her name?' the countess asked Nekhlyudov.

Mariette mentioned the name of a celebrated French actress.

'Be sure and go. She is wonderful.'

'Well, whom shall I go to see first, *ma tante*, the actress or the preacher?' said Nekhlyudov, smiling.

'Don't you take me up on my own words!'

'I should think the preacher first, and then the French actress, or else the desire for a sermon might vanish altogether,' said Nekhlyudov.

'No, better start with the French theatre and do penance afterwards,' said Mariette.

'Stop making fun of me, both of you. The preacher is one thing, the theatre another. There is no need to pull a face a yard long and weep all the time, in order to be saved. One must have faith, and then one is happy.'

'You preach better than any preacher, *ma tante*.'

'Do you know what,' said Mariette thoughtfully. 'Why not come to my box tomorrow?'

'I am afraid I shan't be able . . .'

The conversation was interrupted by the footman announcing a visitor. It was the secretary of a philanthropic society of which the countess was president.

'Oh, he's a fearfully tedious person. I had better see him in the other room. I will return to you later. Mariette, give him some tea,' said the countess, and waddled briskly into the hall with her fidgety gait.

Mariette removed a glove from her firm, rather flat hand, the fourth finger of which was covered with rings.

'Will you have a cup?' she said, taking the silver teapot from the spirit stand and holding her little finger out in a curious manner.

Her face was grave and sad.

'It is always terribly painful to me to think that people whose opinion I value confuse me with the position in which I am placed.'

She seemed ready to cry as she said these last words. And though, if one were to analyse them, the words either had no meaning at all, or only a very vague meaning, they seemed to Nekhlyudov to be exceptionally profound, sincere and good, so attracted was he by the look in the shining eyes which accompanied the words of this young, beautiful and well-dressed woman.

Nekhlyudov gazed at her in silence, unable to tear his eyes from her face.

'You think I don't understand you and what is going on within you. Why, everybody knows what you have done. *C'est le secret de polichinelle.*[1] And I admire you and approve.'

'Really, there is nothing to admire. I have accomplished so little as yet.'

'That makes no difference. I understand how you feel, and I understand her – Very well, I will say no more.' She broke off, noticing displeasure on his face. 'But I can also understand that seeing all the misery, all the horror of what happens in prison,' Mariette went on, desiring only one thing – to attract him – and divining with her woman's instinct what was dear and important to him, 'you want to help those who suffer, and suffer so terribly, at the hands of other men, through indifference or cruelty. . . . I understand how one can

1. It is an open secret.

give up one's life to this, and I would give up mine. But to each his own fate . . .'

'Surely you aren't dissatisfied with your fate?'

'I?' she asked, as though struck with surprise that such a question could be put to her. 'I *have* to be content, and I am. But there is a worm that sometimes wakes up . . .'

'. . . And ought not to be allowed to fall asleep again. It is a voice that must be trusted,' Nekhlyudov said, falling into the trap.

Later, Nekhlyudov often remembered this conversation with shame. He would recall her words, which were not so much deliberate falsehoods as an unconscious echo of his own, and the expression of eager attention with which she listened when he told her of the horrors of the gaol and of his experiences in the country.

When the countess returned, they were conversing not merely like old friends but like intimate friends, two people who alone understood each other among an uncomprehending crowd.

They talked of the injustice of power, of the sufferings of the unfortunate, of the poverty of the people, but in reality their eyes, gazing at each other through the sounds of their conversation, kept asking: 'Can you love me?' and answering 'I can,' and physical desire, assuming the most unexpected and radiant forms, was drawing them together.

As she was leaving she said how willing she would always be to help him in any way she could, and asked him to be sure and come to see her in the theatre on the following evening, if only for a moment, as she had one other very important matter to discuss with him.

'For when shall I see you again?' she added with a sigh, carefully pulling a glove over her beringed hand. 'Say that you will come.'

Nekhlyudov promised.

That night, when Nekhlyudov was alone in his room and had gone to bed and put out the candle, he could not get to sleep for a long time. While he was thinking of Maslova, of the decision of the Senate, of his resolve to follow her all the same and to give up his rights to the land, suddenly, as though in response to his thoughts, Mariette's face appeared before him with her sigh, and the glance as she said: 'When shall I see you again?' and her smile – all so distinctly that he smiled back as though he saw her. 'Am I doing right in going to Siberia? And shall I be doing right in giving up my wealth?' he asked himself.

The white Petersburg night streamed in through the half-drawn window-blinds, but the answers to these questions were vague and confused. Everything was tangled in his mind. He thought back to his former mood and remembered how his ideas ran then; but now those ideas of his had lost something of their power to convince.

'What if it should all turn out to be an empty vision and I can't live up to it?' he said to himself, and, unable to arrive at any solution, he was seized with such anguish and despair as he had not known for a long time. Failing to find his way through his maze of doubts, he fell into the sort of heavy sleep that he used to sink into after losing a vast sum at cards.

25

NEKHLYUDOV's first feeling on waking next morning was of having done something nasty the day before.

He tried to remember. No, there had been nothing nasty, he had done nothing wrong, but he had had thoughts, wrong thoughts, that all his present intentions – to marry Katusha and give his land to the peasants – were all an unrealizable dream, which he would not have the strength to fulfil; that it was all artificial and unnatural, and that it was his duty to go on living as he lived before.

He was not guilty of any evil act, but there was something far worse than an evil action: there were thoughts which give birth to bad deeds. An evil act need not be repeated and can be repented of, but evil thoughts engender evil acts.

A bad act only smoothes the path for other bad acts, whereas evil thoughts drag one irresistibly along that path.

Ruminating on his thoughts of the previous night, Nekhlyudov wondered how he could have accepted them for a single minute. However difficult and unfamiliar the course might be that he intended to take, he knew that it was the only possible way of life for him now, and however easy and natural it might be to return to his former state, he knew that state to be death. Yesterday's temptation made him think of a man who wakes after a sound sleep and, though not sleepy any more, wants to wallow luxuriously in bed a little longer, in spite of knowing full well that it is time to get up and attend to the glad and important work that awaits him.

This was to be his last day in Petersburg, and in the morning he went to Vassilyevsky Island to see Lydia Shustova.

She lived on the second floor. The house porter directed him to the back entrance, and climbing a steep straight staircase he walked right into a hot kitchen smelling strongly of food. An elderly woman with her sleeves rolled up and wearing an apron and spectacles stood beside the stove, stirring something in a steaming saucepan.

'Who do you want?' she asked severely, peering at the stranger over her spectacles.

Nekhlyudov had hardly mentioned his name when an expression of alarm mingled with joy came over her face.

'Oh, prince!' she cried, wiping her hands on her apron. 'But why did you come up the back staircase? You, our benefactor! I am her mother. They came near killing my girl. You are our saviour,' she exclaimed, seizing Nekhlyudov's hand and trying to kiss it. 'I went to see you yesterday. My sister kept asking me to. She is here. This way, this way, please, after me,' said Lydia Shustova's mother, leading the way through a narrow door and down a dark passage, all the while pulling at her skirt, which was tucked up, and smoothing her hair. 'My sister's name is Kornilova. I expect you've heard of her,' she added in a whisper, pausing outside a door. 'She has been mixed up in political affairs. A very clever woman –'

Opening the door that led from the passage, she showed Nekhlyudov into a small room where a short plump girl in a striped cotton blouse was sitting on a sofa in front of a table. Fair wavy hair framed her round very pale face that resembled her mother's. Opposite her in an arm-chair, leaning forward so that he was bent almost double, sat a young man with little black moustaches and a beard, wearing a Russian blouse with an embroidered band round the neck. Both of them were evidently so absorbed in their conversation that they only turned round when Nekhlyudov was inside the room.

'Lydia, this is Prince Nekhlyudov, who, you know –'

The pale-faced girl sprang nervously to her feet, pushing an unruly strand of hair behind her ear, and stared timidly at the stranger with her large grey eyes.

'So you are the dangerous woman Vera Bogodoukhov-skaya pleaded for?' said Nekhlyudov, smiling and holding out his hand.

'Yes, that's me,' said Lydia, with a broad sweet smile like a child's, which displayed a row of beautiful teeth. 'It's my aunt who was so anxious to see you. Auntie!' she called through the door in a pleasant gentle voice.

'Vera Bogodoukhovskaya was very upset by your arrest,' said Nekhlyudov.

'Do sit down – no, you would be better here,' said Lydia, pointing to the battered arm-chair from which the young man had just risen. 'My cousin, Zakharov,' she said, noticing Nekhlyudov glance at the young man.

The young man greeted the visitor with a smile as kindly as Lydia's, and when Nekhlyudov sat down in his seat he brought himself a chair from the window and sat next to him. A fair-haired schoolboy of about sixteen also came into the room and silently perched himself on the window-sill.

'Vera Bogodoukhovskaya is a great friend of my aunt's, but I hardly know her,' said Lydia.

Just then a woman with an agreeable intelligent face, wearing a white blouse with a leather belt, came in from the next room.

'How do you do? Thank you for coming,' she began, when she had seated herself on the sofa beside Lydia. 'Well, and how is my dear Vera? Have you seen her? How is she bearing up to the trouble she is in?'

'She does not complain,' said Nekhlyudov. 'She says she is in Olympian spirits.'

'Ah, that sounds just like Vera!' said the aunt, nodding her head and smiling. 'One has to know her. She is a wonderful character. Always thinking of others, never of herself.'

'That's quite true – she didn't ask anything for herself, she was only concerned about your niece. She was particularly distressed because, she said, there was no cause for her arrest.'

'Yes, yes, it's a dreadful business. The truth of the matter is, she was really a scapegoat for me.'

'Not at all, auntie,' said Lydia. 'I should have taken care of the papers, anyway, without you.'

'Allow me to know better,' insisted the aunt. 'You see,' she went on to Nekhlyudov, 'it all happened because a certain person asked me to keep his papers for a while, and as I had no apartment of my own I brought them to Lydia. But that very night the police searched her room and took the papers away and her too, and kept her in prison all this time, demanding that she should say who it was gave them to her.'

'But I never told them,' said Lydia quickly, pulling nervously at a lock of hair that was not really in her way.

'I never said you did,' her aunt retorted.

'If they got hold of Mitin, it was certainly not through me,' said Lydia, blushing and looking about her uneasily.

'Don't talk about it, Lydia dear,' said her mother.

'Why not? I should like to tell,' said Lydia, no longer smiling or pulling at her hair but twisting a strand round her finger and reddening and all the time looking round the room.

'You know what happened yesterday when you began talking about it.'

'That's all right. . . . Leave me alone, mamma. I did not tell, I kept my mouth shut. When he interrogated me twice about auntie and Mitin, I said nothing, and told him I would not answer. Then he – that man, Petrov . . .'

'Petrov's a spy, a gendarme and a great scoundrel,' interrupted the aunt, explaining her niece's words to Nekhlyudov.

'Then,' Lydia hurried on agitatedly, 'he tried to persuade me. "Whatever you tell me," he said, "will do no harm to anyone. On the contrary, if you make a clean breast of it you will be setting innocent people free, who may be suffering here for nothing." But I still said I would not tell. Then he said: "All right, don't say anything – just don't deny what I'm going to say." And he began going through names, and he said Mitin's name.'

'Don't talk about it,' said the aunt.

'Please, auntie, don't interrupt me. . . .' And she kept pulling at the lock of hair and looking about her. 'And suddenly, think of it, next day I find out – we used to communicate to each other by tapping on the wall – that Mitin had been arrested. Well, I thought, I have betrayed him. And the idea tormented me so – it tormented me so that I nearly went out of my mind.'

'And it turned out it was not at all because of you that he was picked up,' said the aunt.

'Yes, but I didn't know that. I thought I had given him away. I walked up and down, from wall to wall, I couldn't stop thinking. "I betrayed him," I thought. I would lie down and cover my head, and a voice would keep whispering in my ear: "You betrayed him, you betrayed Mitin, Mitin was betrayed by you." I knew it was a hallucination but I could not keep from listening. I used to try and go to sleep – I couldn't. I tried not to think – I couldn't do that either. Oh, it was terrible!' said Lydia, growing more and more agitated, winding the lock of hair round her finger and unwinding it again, and looking about her all the time.

'Lydia dear, calm yourself,' repeated her mother, putting a hand on her shoulder.

But now Lydia could not stop.

'It's so terrible because . . .' she began again, but broke off with a sob. Jumping up from the sofa and bumping into a chair, she ran from the room. Her mother went after her.

'They ought to be hanged, the blackguards,' said the schoolboy sitting on the window-ledge.

'What's that?' asked his mother.

'Oh nothing . . . I was just . . .' the boy replied, and picking up a cigarette from the table he began to smoke.

26

'Yes, solitary confinement is a terrible thing for young people,' said the aunt, shaking her head and lighting a cigarette also.

'I should think for everybody,' said Nekhlyudov.

'No, not for everyone,' replied the aunt. 'I've been told it's a relief – a rest – for the real revolutionary. An outlaw lives in constant anxiety, enduring all sorts of material hardships, in a perpetual state of fear for himself, for others and for the cause; and when, finally, he is arrested, and it's all over, and all responsibility taken off his shoulders – then he can sit in prison and rest. I have been told that they actually feel glad when they're picked up. But for the young and innocent – and they always get hold of innocent creatures like Lydia first – the initial shock is terrible. It's not the loss of freedom, the rough treatment, the bad food and bad air, the deprivations in general – all that is nothing. If there were three times as many hardships, they could be endured easily if it were not for the psychological shock you receive when you're arrested for the first time.'

'Have you been through it, then?'

'Me? I have been in prison twice,' she answered with a sad, pleasant smile. 'When I was arrested the first time – and I had done nothing – I was only twenty-two. I had one child and was expecting another. To lose my freedom and be parted from my child and husband was hard enough, but it was nothing compared with what I felt when I realized that I wasn't a human being any longer, and had become a thing. I wanted to say good-bye to my little daughter – I was told to go and get into the trap. I asked where they were taking me – and was told I would find out when I got there. I asked what I was accused of – and they didn't answer. After my interrogation I was stripped and dressed in prison clothes marked with a number, and taken to a vaulted passage; a door was unlocked, I was shoved inside and the door locked after me; and they went away, leaving only a guard with a rifle who walked up and down the passage without saying a word, and every now and then peering through a crack in the door. I felt utterly wretched. What struck me most at the time, I remember, was that the gendarme officer who interrogated me offered me a cigarette. So he knew that people like to smoke and therefore he must have known, too, that they like light and liberty. He must have known that mothers love their children, and children love their mothers. Then how was it he could tear me pitilessly from all that was dear to me, and lock me up like a wild beast? Nobody can go through that with impunity. If one has believed in God and in humanity, has believed that human beings love one another, one loses all faith after such treatment. I have ceased to believe in humanity since then, and become bitter,' she concluded, and smiled.

Lydia's mother entered the room by the door through which Lydia had left, and said that poor Lydia was very much upset and would not be coming back.

'And why should her young life be ruined? I feel it all acutely since I was unwittingly responsible,' said Lydia's aunt.

'Please God, she will get better in the country air. We will send her to her father,' said her mother.

'Yes, if it hadn't been for you, she would have perished altogether,' said the aunt. 'We are indeed grateful to you. But what I wanted to see you for was to ask you to give a letter to Vera Bogodoukhovskaya,' she said, drawing a letter out of her pocket. 'It isn't sealed – you may read it and tear it up or hand it to her, as you think fit,' she said. 'There is nothing compromising in the letter.'

Nekhlyudov took the letter and, promising to transmit it, rose, said good-bye and went out into the street.

He sealed the letter unread, deciding to deliver it as he had been asked.

27

THE final matter to keep Nekhlyudov in Petersburg was the case of the sectarians whose petition to the Tsar he intended to hand to an officer of his old regiment, Bogatyrev, an aide-de-camp. He went to see him in the morning and found him at home having lunch, though about to leave the house. Bogatyrev was a short thick-set man, endowed with extra-ordinary physical strength (he could bend a horseshoe); a kindly, honest, straightforward man of liberal views even. Yet in spite of these qualities he was an intimate at Court, devoted to the Tsar and the Imperial family, and by some strange means able, while in those exalted circles, to see only the good side and to have no share in anything evil and corrupt. He never criticized people or legislative measures, but either kept silent or said whatever he had to say in a loud bold voice, almost shouting it, and often laughing in an equally boister-ous manner as he spoke. And he did this, not for diplomatic reasons but because such was his nature.

'Ah, that's splendid! I'm so glad you called. Would you like some lunch? Do sit down. Superb beefsteak! I always begin and end with something substantial. Ha! ha! ha! Have ı glass of wine, anyway,' he cried, pointing to a decanter of red wine. 'I was thinking about you. I will hand in the petition. I will give it into His Majesty's own hands. You can count on that. Only it occurred to me – hadn't you better see Toporov first?'

Nekhlyudov frowned at the mention of Toporov.

'Everything depends on him. He would be consulted in any event. And it might be he would meet your wishes himself.'

'If you advise it, I will call on him.'

'Good! Well, how does Petersburg agree with you?' shouted Bogatyrev. 'Tell me, eh?'

'I feel I am getting hypnotized,' said Nekhlyudov.

'Hypnotized?' Bogatyrev echoed, and laughed boisterously. 'Sure you won't have anything? Well, just as you please.' He wiped his moustaches with a napkin. 'So you will call on him, then? Eh? If he refuses, then let me have it and I will hand it in tomorrow as ever is,' he shouted, and getting up from the table crossed himself energetically, apparently as unconsciously as he had wiped his mouth, and began to buckle on his sword. 'Now good-bye, I must be off.'

'We can go out together,' said Nekhlyudov, and shaking Bogatyrev's broad strong hand he parted from him on the doorstep with the pleasant feeling one always has at contact with something so unselfconsciously fresh and healthy.

Although he expected no good result to come of his visit, Nekhlyudov followed Bogatyrev's advice and went to see Toporov, on whom the case of the sectarians depended.

The post occupied by Toporov involved an incongruity of purpose which only someone obtuse and lacking in moral sense could fail to notice. Toporov possessed both these negative qualities. The contradiction inherent in the post he occupied lay in this, that it was his duty to uphold and defend by secular means, not excluding violence, a Church which, by its own definition, had been established by God Himself and could not be shaken by the gates of hell or by any human agency. This divine and absolutely unshakeable, godlike institution had to be sustained and protected by a human institution,[1] over which Toporov and his officials presided. Toporov did not see (or did not want to see) this incompatibility, and was therefore very seriously concerned lest some Romish priest, Protestant minister or other sectarian destroy the Church against which the gates of hell could not prevail. Like all men who lack the fundamental religious sense which recognizes the equality and brotherhood of man, Toporov was quite certain that the common people were vastly different from himself and needed the something that he could very well do without. At the bottom of his heart he really believed in nothing, and found such a state very convenient and agreeable, but fearing that the people might some day arrive at the same state he considered it his sacred duty (as he called it) to try to save them from it.

Just as it says in a certain cookery book that lobsters like being boiled alive, so he was firmly convinced – not figuratively, as in the cookery book, but literally – and was wont to declare that the people liked to be kept in a state of superstition.

His attitude towards the religion he upheld was like that of a poultry-keeper to the offal he feeds his fowls on: offal is quite disgusting but fowls like it and eat it, therefore they must be fed on offal.

Of course, all that worship of the ikons of Iberia, Kazan and Smolensk is gross idolatry, but the people like it and believe in it, and therefore the superstition must be encouraged. This was how Toporov reasoned, not seeing that if the people like superstition, it is only because there have always been, and still are, cruel men like himself, who, being themselves enlightened, use their enlightenment, not as they should, to help others to struggle out of their dark ignorance, but to plunge them still deeper into it.

When Nekhlyudov entered the waiting-room Toporov

1. The Holy Synod.

was in his office talking with an abbess, a lively aristocrat who was spreading and supporting the Orthodox Faith in Western Russia among the Uniates who had been forcibly converted to the Orthodox Church.

A secretary in the waiting-room inquired Nekhlyudov's business and when he heard that Nekhlyudov proposed to hand in a petition from the sectarians to the Emperor asked if he might look through it. Nekhlyudov gave it to him and the official took it into the study. The nun in her tall head-dress, flowing veil and black train trailing behind her left the study and went out clasping a topaz rosary in her white hands with their well-tended nails. Nekhlyudov was still not asked to go in. Toporov was reading the petition and shaking his head. He was unpleasantly surprised by its clear and emphatic wording.

'If this should come into His Majesty's hands it might raise unpleasant questions and cause misunderstanding,' he thought as he finished reading the petition. And laying it on the table he rang and ordered Nekhlyudov to be shown in.

He remembered the case of these sectarians: he had had a petition from them before. The substance of the matter was that they were Christians who had fallen away from Orthodoxy and had first been exhorted, then tried in a court of law but finally acquitted. After that, the bishop and the governor had decided, on the plea that their marriages were illegal, to separate husbands, wives and children, and send them into exile. What these fathers and wives were now asking was that they should not be separated. Toporov remembered the first time the case had come to his notice. He had then hesitated, having half a mind to quash the sentence. But there could be no harm in confirming the arrangement to scatter the various members of these sectarian peasant families to different parts; whereas to allow them to remain where they were might have a bad effect on the rest of the population, in the sense that they, too, might defect from Orthodoxy. Moreover, the case was evidence of the bishop's zeal, and so he had decided to let things proceed on the lines laid out.

But now, with an advocate such as Nekhlyudov, who had influential connexions in Petersburg, the affair might be presented to the Emperor as an act of cruelty, or find its way into the foreign newspapers, and therefore he made a quick and unexpected decision.

'Good afternoon,' he said, with the air of a very busy man, continuing to stand after greeting Nekhlyudov, and passing at once to the business in hand.

'I am familiar with this case. As soon as I saw the names I remembered the whole unfortunate affair,' he went on, taking up the petition and showing it to Nekhlyudov. 'And I am most grateful to you for reminding me of it. The provincial authorities have been a little over-zealous –'

Nekhlyudov was silent, looking with distaste at the pale immobile mask of a face before him.

'– and I shall give orders to have this measure revoked and the families reinstated in their homes.'

'So that I need not present the petition?' said Nekhlyudov.

'Most assuredly not. *I* give you my word,' he said with especial emphasis on the 'I', evidently quite convinced that *his* honesty, *his* word were the best of guarantees. 'Better still, I will write a note at once. Please take a seat.'

He went up to the table and began to write. Nekhlyudov continued to stand, looking down on the narrow bald skull, at the hand with its thick blue veins that was swiftly moving the pen, and wondered why he was doing it, why a man who seemed to be so unfeeling in every way should be doing it with such care. What was the reason?

'There you are,' said Toporov, sealing the envelope. 'You may let your *clients* know,' he added, compressing his lips into a semblance of a smile.

'Why, then, were these people made to suffer?' Nekhlyudov asked, taking the envelope.

385

Toporov raised his head and smiled, as though gratified by Nekhlyudov's query.

'That I cannot tell you. All I can say is that the interests of the people over which we stand guard are of such great importance that excess of zeal in matters of religion is not so dangerous or harmful as the over-indifference which is now spreading.'

'But how is it that in the name of religion the fundamental conditions of morality are violated – families broken up . . .'

Toporov continued to smile patronizingly, as though finding Nekhlyudov's remarks very charming. Whatever Nekhlyudov might say, Toporov would have found charming and one-sided, from what he considered the lofty heights and long perspectives of his position as a statesman.

'That, from the point of view of the private individual, may seem to be the case,' he said, 'but to the State it appears in a rather different light. However, I must now bid you goodbye,' he added, bowing and holding out his hand.

Nekhlyudov pressed it in silence and quickly left the room, regretting that he had taken that hand.

'The interests of the people!' he repeated Toporov's words. 'Your own interests, you mean,' he thought as he left Toporov's office.

And he ran over in his mind the people he knew who were suffering from the activity of the various institutions for the re-establishment of justice, the support of religion and the education of the masses – the peasant woman punished for selling vodka without a licence, the young fellow for stealing, the tramp for vagrancy, the incendiary for arson, the banker for misappropriation of funds and that unfortunate Lydia Shustova, simply because they might have got some information out of her that they wanted, and the sectarians for violating Orthodoxy, and Gourkevich for desiring a constitution – and he saw with remarkable clarity that all these people had been arrested, locked up or exiled, not in the least because they had transgressed against justice or committed lawless acts but merely because they were an obstacle hindering the officials and the rich from enjoying the wealth they were busy amassing from the people.

And the woman who sold vodka without having a licence, the thief prowling about the town and Lydia Shustova with her proclamations, and the sectarians upsetting superstitions, and Gourkevich desiring a constitution – were all obstacles to this. It seemed perfectly clear to Nekhlyudov, therefore, that all these officials, beginning with his aunt's husband, the senators and Toporov, down to the petty, neat, orderly gentlemen sitting at desks in the various ministries, were not in the least troubled by the fact that innocent people suffered: their one concern was to get rid of dangerous elements.

Thus the commandment to forgive ten guilty men rather than let one innocent man be condemned was not merely disregarded but, on the contrary, ten who were harmless were punished for the sake of eliminating one dangerous person, just as in cutting a rotten piece out of anything some of the good has to be cut away too.

This explanation of all that took place seemed very simple and clear to Nekhlyudov but its very simplicity and explicitness made him hesitate to accept it. Was it possible that so complicated a phenomenon could have so simple and terrible an explanation? Could it really be that all the talk about justice, goodness, law, religion, God and so on, was nothing but so many words to conceal the grossest self-interest and cruelty?

28

NEKHLYUDOV would have left Petersburg that same evening but he had promised Mariette to join her at the theatre, and, though he knew that he ought not to do so, he went, stretching a point with his conscience and telling himself that he must keep his word.

'Am I able to withstand such temptations?' he asked himself, somewhat insincerely. 'I will try for the last time.'

Changing into a tail-coat, he arrived at the theatre in time for the second act of the perennial *Dame aux Camélias*, in which a foreign actress was demonstrating in a novel manner how consumptive women die.

The house was crowded and Nekhlyudov was at once, and with the deference due to anyone with such a destination, shown to Mariette's box.

A footman in livery stood in the corridor outside. He bowed to Nekhlyudov as to a familiar personage, and opened the door of the box.

All the people sitting in the rows of boxes opposite, those standing behind them, the backs of those near by, the grey, grizzled, bald, balding, pomaded and curled heads of those in the orchestra stalls – the entire audience was absorbed in watching the contortions of a thin bony actress elegantly attired in silks and lace, who was reciting her monologue in an unnatural voice. Someone called 'Sssh!' as the door opened, and two currents of air, one cool, the other hot, swept over Nekhlyudov's face.

In the box were Mariette, a lady in a red cloak and a large massive coiffure whom he did not know, and two men: Mariette's husband, the general, a tall handsome man with an aquiline nose and a severe inscrutable expression – he wore a uniform padded across the chest – and a light-complexioned balding man with a clean-shaven dimpled chin between pompous side-whiskers. Mariette, slim and graceful in a low-necked gown that exposed her firm shapely sloping shoulders and a tiny black mole on one side at the base of her neck, turned to look round the moment Nekhlyudov entered and with her fan motioned him to a chair behind her, welcoming him with gratitude and, as he thought, a significant smile. Her husband glanced at him in the quiet way in which he did everything, and bowed. His attitude, the look he exchanged with his wife, evinced the master, the owner of a beautiful woman.

When the monologue ended, the theatre resounded with

applause. Mariette rose and, holding her rustling silk skirt, went to the back of the box and introduced Nekhlyudov to her husband. Smiling all the time with his eyes, the general said that he was 'delighted' and then relapsed into his impenetrable silence.

'I ought to have left today but I promised you I would come,' said Nekhlyudov, turning to Mariette.

'If you don't want to see me, at least you will see a wonderful actress,' said Mariette, answering the implication of his words. 'Don't you think she was splendid in that last scene?' she asked, turning to her husband.

The husband nodded his head.

'This sort of thing leaves me unmoved,' said Nekhlyudov. 'I have seen so much real suffering today that –'

'Do sit down and tell us about it.'

The husband listened, his eyes smiling more and more ironically.

'I went to see that woman who has been released after being kept in prison for such a long time. She is completely crushed.'

'That was the woman I spoke to you about,' said Mariette to her husband.

'Yes, I was very glad she could be released,' he said quietly, nodding, and now smiling with open irony under his moustaches, so it seemed to Nekhlyudov. 'I am going outside for a smoke.'

Nekhlyudov sat, expecting that Mariette would tell him the 'something' which she had said she wanted to tell him, but she said nothing and did not even try to say anything, but made a joke or two and talked about the play, which she thought should have a special appeal for Nekhlyudov.

Nekhlyudov saw that she had nothing to tell him but only wished to show herself to him in all the splendour of her evening toilette, and to display her shoulders and the little mole, and he felt both pleased and disgusted at the same time.

The veil of enchantment which had lain over all this before was not exactly removed for Nekhlyudov but he now saw what was underneath it. Looking at Mariette, he admired her beauty but he knew that she was a fraud, living with a husband who was making his way in the world by means of the tears and lives of hundreds and hundreds of people, and this was a matter of complete indifference to her, and that everything she had said the day before was untrue, and that she wanted – neither he nor she knew why – to make him fall in love with her. And he felt both attracted and repelled. Several times he took up his hat, meaning to go, but still stayed on. But finally, when her husband returned to the box with a strong smell of tobacco on his thick moustaches and looked at Nekhlyudov with a patronizing contemptuous air, as though not recognizing him, Nekhlyudov walked out into the corridor before the door closed, and finding his overcoat left the theatre.

On his way home along the Nevsky Prospect he could not help noticing a tall, very well-built, conspicuously dressed woman walking slowly along the wide pavement in front of him, the consciousness of her detestable power apparent in her face and in her whole figure. Everyone who came towards her or caught up with her turned to look at her. Nekhlyudov quickened his step to pass her and he, too, involuntarily looked into her face, which, though no doubt painted, was handsome. The woman smiled at Nekhlyudov, flashing her eyes at him. And strangely enough, Nekhlyudov was immediately reminded of Mariette, because he experienced the same feeling of attraction and disgust as he had at the theatre. Walking hurriedly past her, Nekhlyudov, vexed with himself, turned into the Morskaya and then on to the embankment, where, to the surprise of a policeman, he began pacing up and down.

'The other one in the theatre smiled at me just like that when I entered the box,' he thought, 'and both smiles held the same meaning. The only difference is that this one says simply and directly: "If you want me, take me. If not, go on your way," while the other pretends that she has no such thought in her mind but lives in some lofty world of refined sentiments, whereas at bottom they're the same. This one at least is truthful: the other one lies. Besides, this woman here has been driven to these straits by necessity, while the other amuses herself playing with that enchanting, revolting and dreadful passion. This street-walker is like filthy stinking water to be offered only to those whose thirst overcomes their aversion; but the woman in the theatre is like a virus imperceptibly poisoning everything it touches.'

Nekhlyudov thought of his liaison with the wife of the Marshal of the Nobility, and shameful recollections flooded his mind.

'The animal nature of man is abominable,' he thought, 'but so long as it remains undisguised you can look down on it from the heights of your spiritual life and despise it, and whether you succumb or resist, you remain what you were before; but when this animality is concealed under a pseudo-aesthetic, poetic veil and demands adulation – then in worshipping the animal you become engulfed in it and can no longer distinguish good from evil. Then it is awful.'

Nekhlyudov saw this now as clearly as he saw the palace, the sentinels, the Fortress, the river, the boats and the Stock Exchange.

And just as on this northern summer night no soothing restful darkness hung over the land, but only a dismal dreary unnatural light coming from an invisible source, so there was no longer the comfortable darkness of ignorance in Nekhlyudov's soul. Everything was clear. It was clear that all the things which are commonly considered good and important are actually worthless or wicked, and all this glitter, all this luxury serve but to conceal old familiar crimes which not only go unpunished but rise triumphant, adorned with all the fascination the human imagination can devise.

Nekhlyudov would have liked to forget this, to close his eyes to it, but he could no longer help seeing it. Although he did not see the source of the light which revealed all this to him, any more than he could see the source of the light which lay over Petersburg that night, and although the light itself seemed dim, cheerless and unnatural, he could not help seeing what that light revealed, and he felt at one and the same time both happy and disturbed.

29

THE first thing Nekhlyudov did on his return to Moscow was to drive to the prison hospital to tell Maslova the sad news that the Senate had confirmed the decision of the court and she must prepare for the journey to Siberia.

He had little hope in the petition to the Emperor which the lawyer had drawn up for him and which he now brought to the prison for Maslova to sign. And, strangely enough, he was no longer anxious for its success. He had got used to the idea of going to Siberia and living among deportees and convicts, and he found it hard to imagine what arrangements he should make for Maslova and himself if she were to be acquitted. He remembered what the American writer Thoreau had said, at the time when slavery existed in America, that the only proper place for an honest man in a country where slavery is legalized and protected was the gaol. After his visit to Petersburg, especially, and all he had discovered there, Nekhlyudov thought the same.

'Yes, the only suitable place for an honest man in Russia at the present time is prison,' he reflected, and he even had a direct sensation of this as he drove up to the gaol and entered within its walls.

The porter at the hospital recognized Nekhlyudov and informed him at once that Maslova was no longer there.

'Where is she, then?'

'Back in the lock-up.'

'Why was she transferred?' asked Nekhlyudov.

'Ah, Your Excellency, what can you expect from people like that,' said the doorkeeper, smiling contemptuously.

'She started running after the medical assistant, so the head doctor sent her away.'

Nekhlyudov would never have believed that Maslova and the state of her affections could touch him so closely. The news stunned him. He felt as people feel when some unexpected calamity befalls them. He was painfully upset. His first sensation on hearing the news was one of mortification. It made him ridiculous in his own eyes to remember how happy he had felt at the spiritual change he had supposed was taking place in her. All that talk of hers about being unwilling to accept his sacrifice, the tears, the reproaches – they were all, he thought, simply devices of a depraved woman out to make use of him to the best possible advantage. It now seemed to him that on his last visit he had noticed signs of the incorrigible viciousness which had now come to light. All this flashed through his mind while he mechanically put on his hat and left the hospital.

'But what am I to do now?' he wondered. 'Am I still bound to her? Does not this behaviour of hers set me free?' he asked himself.

But the moment he put these questions to himself he immediately realized that to consider himself liberated and to abandon her would be to punish, not her, which is what he wished to do, but himself, and he was seized with fear.

'No, what has happened cannot alter my resolve – it can only strengthen it. Let her do what she must. If it is carrying on with the medical assistant, then let her carry on with the medical assistant: that is her affair. My business is to do what my conscience demands of me,' he said to himself. 'And my conscience demands that I should sacrifice my freedom in expiation of my sin; and my determination to marry her, even if it is a marriage in name only, and to follow her wherever she may be sent, remains unchanged,' he said to himself with bitter obstinacy, as he left the hospital and walked resolutely to the big gates of the prison.

At the gates he asked the warder on duty to tell the chief warder that he wished to see Maslova. The warder knew Nekhlyudov and speaking as to an old acquaintance told him an important piece of prison news: the old senior warder had retired and a new chief, who was very strict, had been appointed in his place.

'The severe measures here now – it's frightful,' said the keeper. 'He's in there, I'll let him know at once.'

The senior warder was indeed in the prison and came out to Nekhlyudov almost immediately. The new man was tall and angular, with projecting cheek-bones, morose, and very slow in his movements.

'Interviews are only allowed on certain days in the visiting-room,' he said, without looking at Nekhlyudov.

'But I have a petition to the Emperor which I want signed.'

'You may leave it with me.'

'I must see the prisoner myself. I was always allowed to before.'

'Yes, that was before,' said the senior warder, with a cursory glance at Nekhlyudov.

'I have the governor's permission,' insisted Nekhlyudov, taking out his pocket-book.

'Allow me,' said the senior warder, still not looking him in the eyes, and with his dry, long white fingers – there was a gold ring on the forefinger – he took the paper which Nekhlyudov handed to him, and read it slowly. 'Will you come into the office?' he said.

There was no one in the office. The senior warder sat down at a table and began looking through some papers lying on it, evidently intending to be present at the interview. When Nekhlyudov asked him whether he might also see the political prisoner Bogodoukhovskaya, the senior warder answered shortly that it was impossible.

'Interviews with political prisoners are not allowed,' he said, and again became engrossed in his papers.

Having a letter to Bogodoukhovskaya in his pocket,

Nekhlyudov felt like a guilty person whose plans have been discovered and frustrated.

When Maslova entered the office the senior warder raised his head and, without looking either at her or Nekhlyudov, remarked, 'You may talk,' and continued to busy himself with the papers.

Maslova had on the clothes she wore before: a white bodice, skirt and kerchief. When she came up to Nekhlyudov and saw his cold unfriendly face she flushed scarlet and fingering the edge of her bodice lowered her eyes. Her confusion was confirmation for Nekhlyudov of the hospital porter's story.

Nekhlyudov had meant to treat her in the same way as before but *could not* bring himself to hold out his hand, so repugnant was she to him now.

'I have brought you bad news,' he said in a flat voice, without looking at her or extending his hand. 'The Senate has rejected the appeal.'

'I knew they would,' she said with difficulty, as though gasping for breath.

Before, Nekhlyudov would have asked her why she said that she knew they would; now he only looked at her. Her eyes were filled with tears.

But this did not mollify him: on the contrary, it roused his irritation against her still further.

The senior warder rose and began to walk up and down the room.

In spite of the aversion Nekhlyudov now felt for Maslova, he still felt that he must express regret to her at the Senate's decision.

'You mustn't despair,' he said. 'The petition to His Majesty may be successful, and I hope –'

'I don't care about that,' she said, giving him a piteous look with her squinting tearful eyes.

'What is the matter then?'

'You have been to the hospital, and no doubt they told you I –'

'Well, that's your own affair,' said Nekhlyudov coldly, with a frown.

The cruel feeling of wounded pride rose to the surface again with renewed force when she mentioned the hospital. 'He, a man of the world, whom any girl from high society would consider herself lucky to marry, had offered himself as a husband to this woman, and she could not even wait but had to start an intrigue with a doctor's assistant,' he thought, and looked at her with hatred.

'Sign this petition now,' he said, taking a large envelope from his pocket and laying it on the table. She wiped away her tears with a corner of her kerchief, and sat down at the table, asking him where and what to write.

He showed her what and where to write, and she sat down, arranging the cuff of her right sleeve with her left hand, while he stood behind her, silently looking down at her back bent over the table and which every now and then was convulsed with repressed sobs; and two conflicting emotions of evil and good struggled in his breast: wounded pride and pity for the suffering girl – and it was pity that won.

He never could remember which came first – was it pity for her that first entered his heart, or did he first think back on himself, on his own sins, his own contemptible life – exactly what he condemned in her? Anyhow, all of a sudden he was conscious of his own guilt and that he pitied her.

When she had signed the petition and wiped an inky finger on her skirt she got up and looked at him.

'No matter what comes of it, and no matter what happens, nothing will alter my decision,' said Nekhlyudov.

The thought that he was forgiving her increased his sense of pity and tenderness, and he wanted to comfort her.

'I will do what I said. Wherever they send you, I shall be with you. '

'What's the use?' she interrupted him quickly, but her face was radiant.

'You had better think what you may need for the journey.'

'I don't know of anything in particular, thank you.'

The senior warder walked over to them, and Nekhlyudov, anticipating what he was going to say, bade her good-bye and went out, with such quiet joy, peace and love towards all men as he had never experienced before. The certainty that nothing Maslova might do could alter his love for her rejoiced and lifted him to heights unknown till now. Let her flirt with the medical orderly – that was her business: he loved her, not selfishly, but for her own sake and for God's.

As for the flirtation with the doctor's assistant for which Maslova was turned out of the hospital, and which Nekhlyudov believed to be true, it amounted to this: sent by the ward sister to fetch some herb-tea from the dispensary at the end of the corridor, Maslova found Ustinov, the doctor's assistant alone there, a tall fellow with a pimply face, who had been pestering her for some time. Trying to get away from him, she gave him such a violent push that he knocked against a shelf, from which two bottles fell down and smashed. The senior doctor who happened to be going along the corridor at that moment, hearing the crash of broken glass and seeing Maslova running out of the room, her face all red, shouted to her angrily:

'Look here, my good woman, unless you can behave yourself, I shall have to send you away. What's the trouble in here?' he went on to the medical orderly, looking at him sternly over his spectacles.

The assistant, smiling, began to make his excuses. The doctor lifted his head, so that he was now looking through his spectacles, and went on into the ward without waiting to hear the end; and that same day told the head warder to send him a more sedate person in Maslova's place. That was all there was to Maslova's flirtation with the medical orderly. Dismissal from the hospital for carrying on with men was particularly painful to Maslova, since after meeting Nekhlyudov again all relations with men, which had long been distasteful to her, had become especially revolting. What hurt her terribly and made her pity herself to the point of weeping, was that everybody, the pimply assistant included, knowing what her past life had been, and her present situation, considered they had a right to insult her and were surprised when she resisted. Now, going into the office to see Nekhlyudov, she had intended to clear herself of the false accusation which she knew he would hear about sooner or later. But when she began to explain she felt that he did not believe her and that her explanations would only confirm his suspicions. Tears choked her and she broke off.

Maslova still thought and continued to persuade herself that she had not forgiven him, and hated him, as she had told him at their second interview, but the truth was that she really loved him again, and so much so, that she could not help trying to do all she could to please him: she had given up drinking and smoking, she no longer flirted, and she had gone to work in the hospital. All this she had done because she knew he wished it. And if every time he referred to it, she refused so determinedly to accept his sacrifice and marry him, this was partly because she enjoyed repeating the proud words she had once used to him, but above all because she knew that a marriage with her would be a misfortune for him. She had firmly made up her mind not to accept his sacrifice, yet the thought that he despised her and believed that she was still what she had been, and that he had not noticed the change that had taken place in her, was very painful. That he might still be thinking that she had done something wrong in the hospital upset her far more than the news that her sentence was confirmed.

30

MASLOVA might be sent off with the first gang of prisoners, and so Nekhlyudov began to prepare for his own departure. But there was so much to do that he felt no amount of time would suffice. Everything was utterly different from the old days. Then he used to have to devise things to do, which always centred round one and the same person – Dmitri Ivanovich Nekhlyudov; and yet, notwithstanding the fact that all the interests of life had Dmitri Ivanovich as their pivot he was bored with all of them. Now everything he did concerned other people, and not Dmitri Ivanovich, and they were all interesting and absorbing, and there was no end to them.

Nor was this all. In the old days concern with the affairs of Dmitri Ivanovich always made him feel peevish and irritable; whereas now being busy for other people generally put him in a happy frame of mind.

The business at present occupying Nekhlyudov could be divided under three headings: this was what he did, in his usual systematic way, and he accordingly grouped his papers in three portfolios.

The first referred to Maslova and consisted at that stage in following up the petition addressed to the Emperor, and in making preparations for her probable journey to Siberia.

The second concerned the organization of his estates. In Panovo the land had been given to the peasants, on condition that they paid rent, which was to be devoted to their own communal use. But to make this transaction valid he had to draw up and sign his deed of gift and alter his will in accordance with it. In Kuzminskoye matters were left as he had arranged them, that is, he was to receive the rent for the land; but he still had to fix the dates of payment, and decide how much of the money to take for his own use and how much was to be set aside for the benefit of the peasants. Not knowing what the journey to Siberia would cost him, he hesitated to forgo this income altogether, although he had reduced it by half.

The third thing he had to deal with was help for the prisoners, who were turning to him more and more often.

In the beginning, when he first came in contact with the prisoners who asked his help, he at once began interceding for them, trying to alleviate their lot; but soon he had so many applications that he felt the impossibility of attending to all of them, and this automatically led him to take up a fourth piece of work, which occupied him of late more than any of his other tasks.

This fourth business consisted in trying to find the answers to the following questions: what was that astounding institution called 'criminal law', which occasioned the prison whose inmates he had to some extent got to know, and numbers of other places of confinement, from the St Peter and St Paul Fortress to the island of Sakhalin, where hundreds and thousands of victims of this, to him astonishing, criminal law were pining? What was its purpose and how had it originated?

From his personal relations with the prisoners, from questioning his lawyer and the prison chaplain and the head warder, and from the lists of those imprisoned, Nekhlyudov came to the conclusion that the prisoners, the so-called criminals, could be divided into five classes.

One of these, the first, consisted of entirely innocent people, victims of judicial blunders, like the alleged incendiary Menshov, like Maslova and others. This class was not numerous – about seven per cent according to the chaplain's estimate – but their condition excited particular interest.

The second category was made up of persons sentenced for crimes committed in peculiar circumstances: while drunk, for example, or in a fit of passion or jealousy, and so on – crimes which those who sat in judgement and meted out punishment would almost certainly have committed themselves in like circumstances. This class, so far as Nekhlyudov could see, accounted for over one-half of all criminals.

The third class consisted of people punished because they had done what seemed to them the most natural thing in the world, a good thing even, but which those other people, the men who made the laws, considered to be a crime. To this category belonged those who sold spirits without a licence, smugglers, and trespassers plucking grass and gathering firewood in fields and forests owned privately or by the Crown. Highland robbers[1] could be grouped in this class, and such infidels as robbed churches.

The fourth class was formed of men who were looked upon as criminals only because morally they stood head and shoulders above the common run of society. Such were the sectarians: such were the Poles and the Circassians, who rebelled in the name of freedom; such, too, were the political prisoners – socialists and strikers condemned for opposition to the authorities. According to Nekhlyudov's observations the percentage of such people, who were among the best elements of society, was very large.

Finally, the fifth category was composed of persons who were far more sinned against than sinning in their relations with society. They were the outcasts, stupefied by continual oppression and temptation – like the boy who stole the mats, and hundreds whom Nekhlyudov had seen in gaol and out of gaol: the conditions under which they lived seemed to lead on systematically to those actions which are termed crimes. A great many thieves and murderers with whom he had come in contact at that time belonged, in Nekhlyudov's estimation, to this class. Here, too, he assigned, when he came to know them better, those depraved and demoralized creatures whom the new school of criminology classifies as the criminal type and whose existence in society is regarded as the chief argument for the necessity of criminal law and punishment. This so-called depraved, criminal, abnormal type was, to Nekhlyudov's mind, exactly the same as the type which were more sinned against than sinning, only in this instance society had sinned, not directly against them but against their parents and forebears.

Among this latter class Nekhlyudov was struck particularly by one, Okhotin, an inveterate thief, the illegitimate son of a

1. The inhabitants of the Caucasus mountains who went on plundering the caravans of traders, and raiding Russian flocks and herds, long after the Caucasus was finally subdued by Russia in 1864.

prostitute, brought up in a doss-house, who until he was thirty had apparently never met anyone of a higher moral standard than a policeman, and who at an early age had joined up with a gang of thieves. He was gifted with an extraordinary sense of humour which made him very popular. He asked Nekhlyudov to intercede for him, at the same time making fun of himself, the judges, the prison and all laws, both human and divine. Another was the handsome Fedorov, who with a gang of which he was the leader had robbed and murdered an old man, a government official. Fedorov was a peasant whose father had been unlawfully deprived of his house, and who later served in the army, where he had been punished for falling in love with an officer's mistress. He had a winning passionate nature, out to enjoy life whatever the cost. Fedorov had never met anyone who would for any reason restrain themselves in their enjoyments, and had never heard a word said about there being any other aim in life save enjoyment. It was evident to Nekhlyudov that both these men were richly endowed by nature but were neglected and twisted like uncared-for plants. He also came across a tramp and a woman, both of whom repelled him by their half-witted insensibility and seeming cruelty, but even in them he failed to see the criminal type as described in the Italian school of criminology: he saw in them only people who were repulsive to him personally, like others were whom he met outside prison walls – in swallow-tail coats, wearing epaulets or bedecked with lace.

And so his investigation into the reasons why this very varied collection of people were put in prison, while others just like them were at large – and even sitting in judgement over them – was Nekhlyudov's fourth concern at that time.

At first he had hoped to find the answer in books, and bought everything he could find on the subject. He bought the works of Lombroso and Garofalo, Ferry, List, Maudsley and Tarde, and read them carefully. But as he read, he became more and more disappointed. It happened to him as it does to all who turn to science, not because they intend to take it up – to write or discuss or teach – but to get answers to straight, simple everyday problems. Science answered thousands of very subtle and ingenuous questions touching criminal law, but certainly not the one he was trying to solve. He was asking a very simple thing: Why and by what right does one class of people lock up, torture, exile, flog and kill other people, when they themselves are no better than those whom they torture, flog and kill? And for answer he got arguments as to whether human beings were possessed of free will or not. Could criminal propensities be detected by measuring the skull, and so on? What part does heredity play in crime? Is there such a thing as congenital depravity? What is morality? What is insanity? What is degeneracy? What is temperament? How does climate, food, ignorance, imitativeness, hypnotism or passion affect crime? What is society? What are its duties? And so on, and so forth.

These deliberations reminded Nekhlyudov of a small boy he had once met returning from school. Nekhlyudov asked him if he had learned how to spell. 'Yes, I can,' replied the boy. 'Well, then, how do you spell "paw"?' – 'What sort of paw – a dog's paw?' asked the little boy, with an artful expression on his face. Just such answers in the form of questions Nekhlyudov found in scientific works, in reply to his one fundamental inquiry.

The books he consulted contained a great deal that was wise, learned and interesting: but they furnished no answer to the chief point – by what right do some people punish others? Not only was this not answered, but the purpose of all the arguments brought forward was to explain and justify punishment, the necessity for which was taken as self-evident. Nekhlyudov read much, but in snatches, and, attributing his failure to this superficial way of reading, hoped to find the answer later on, and so he would not let himself believe in the truth of the answer which of late had begun to occur more and more frequently to his mind.

31

THE party that was to include Maslova was due to set off on the 5th of July, and Nekhlyudov arranged to start the same day. On the day before his departure his sister and her husband came to town to see him.

Natalia Ivanovna Rogozhinskaya was ten years older than her brother, who had grown up partly under her influence. She had been very fond of him when he was a boy, and later on, before her marriage, they had become as intimate as though they were the same age – she being a woman of twenty-five, he a lad of fifteen. At that time she had been in love with his friend Nikolenka Irtenyev, who afterwards died. They had both loved Nikolenka, loving in him and in themselves that which is good and which unites all men.

Since those days the characters of both had deteriorated: military service had corrupted him, together with a depraved life; and she had married a man whom she loved with a sensual love – a man who not only did not care for the things that she and Dmitri had once held sacred and precious but who could not even understand what such things were, and ascribed all her strivings after moral perfection and the service of mankind, which were the mainspring of her life, to ambition and a desire to show off (the only motives comprehensible to him).

Natalia's husband was a man without name or fortune but he was smart and had carved out a comparatively brilliant career for himself in the law by manoeuvring artfully between liberalism and conservatism, utilizing whichever of the two trends best suited his purpose at the given time and for the given occasion, and, above all, by exploiting some personal quality which made women like him. He was past his first youth when he met the Nekhlyudovs abroad, succeeded in getting Natalia – not very young then either – to fall in love with him, and married her, rather against the wishes of her mother, who looked on the marriage as a *mésalliance*. Nekhlyudov, though he would not admit it to himself, and fought against the feeling, detested his brother-in-law. He loathed him for the vulgarity of his sentiments, his conceit and his mediocrity – but, above all, because his sister could bring herself to love this stunted creature so passionately, so egoistically and so sensually, for his sake stifling all the good there had been in her. It was always an agony for Nekhlyudov to think that Natalia was the wife of that hairy self-satisfied man with the shiny bald patch on his head. He could not even repress a feeling of revulsion for their children. And each time he heard she was pregnant he felt like condoling with her for again having been infected with something evil by this man whose nature was so foreign to theirs.

The Rogozhinskys came without their children (they had two, a boy and a girl) and occupied the best rooms in the best hotel. Natalia Ivanovna at once went to her mother's old flat, but not finding her brother and hearing from Agrafena Petrovna that he had moved into furnished lodgings, she drove on there. A dirty servant who met her in the dark smelly passage, which required artificial light even in the day-time, told her that the prince was out.

Natalia Ivanovna asked to go to her brother's rooms in order to leave a note for him. The man showed her in.

Natalia Ivanovna surveyed the two small rooms attentively. Everywhere she saw familiar signs of scrupulous neatness – but she was struck by the simplicity of the surroundings, quite unusual for him. On the writing-table she noticed the paper weight with the bronze dog on it which she remembered; equally familiar to her was the tidy way in which his different portfolios and writing materials were arranged, and some volumes on criminal law, a book in English by Henry George, and a French book by Tarde, with the place marked by a large crooked ivory paper-knife, which she recognized.

Seating herself at the table she wrote a note asking him to be sure to come and see her that very day; then, shaking her head in surprise at what she saw, she returned to her hotel.

Two things regarding her brother interested her just then: his proposed marriage to Katusha, which she had heard discussed in the town where she lived – everyone was talking about it – and his giving away the land to the peasants, which was also widely known and appeared to many to have a political and dangerous significance. In one way his proposal to Katusha pleased her: she admired his courage, which was so like him and herself as they had both been in the happy days before her marriage, but at the same time she was appalled at the idea of her brother marrying such a dreadful woman. This was the stronger feeling of the two, and she decided to use all her influence to dissuade him from such a step, although she knew how difficult it would be.

The other matter – giving the land to the peasants – did not concern her so much but her husband was very indignant about it and insisted that she should do all she could with her brother. Rogozhinsky declared that an act of that sort was the height of inconsistency, irresponsibility and arrogance; that the only possible explanation – if one could be found at all – was the desire to attract attention, to show off and be talked about.

'What sense is there in giving land to the peasants and making them pay rent to themselves?' he said. 'If he wanted to do that, why didn't he sell to them through the Peasants' Bank? There might have been some sense in that. But taken all round what he has done verges on insanity,' said Rogozhinsky, already beginning to think about putting Nekhlyudov under legal restraint, and he demanded that his wife should have a serious talk with her brother about his eccentric plan.

32

As soon as Nekhlyudov came home that evening and found his sister's note on the table he set off to her hotel. Natalia Ivanovna met her brother alone – her husband was resting in the other room. She was wearing a tightly fitting black silk gown with a red bow on her chest, and her hair was puffed and combed in the latest fashion. It was obvious that she was trying to look younger than her age, which was the same as her husband's. When she saw her brother she jumped up from the sofa to greet him, her silk skirts rustling as she hurried towards him. They kissed and surveyed each other, smiling. There passed between them that mysterious, indescribable, meaningful exchange of looks in which all was truth, and there began an exchange of words from which that truth was absent. They had not seen each other since their mother's death.

'You have grown stouter and you look younger,' he said, and her lips puckered with delight.

'And you have got thinner.'

'Well, and how is my brother-in-law?' asked Nekhlyudov.

'He is resting. He did not sleep last night.'

There was much to say, but the words said nothing; only their eyes said that what ought to be said was not said.

'I was in your room.'

'Yes, I know. I left the old home. It was too big for me there. I was lonely and bored. I have no use for all that stuff, so you had better take it all. The furniture and things, I mean.'

'Yes, Agrafena Petrovna told me. I went there. It's very nice of you. But . . .'

At this point the hotel waiter brought in a silver tea-service; while he was setting out the tea-things they did not speak. Natalia Ivanovna moved over to an arm-chair by a little table and silently made the tea. Nekhlyudov was silent, too.

'Well, Dmitri, I know all about it,' Natalia began resolutely, looking at him.

'Good, I'm very glad you do.'

'Can you possibly hope to reform her after the life she has led?'

He was sitting bolt upright on a small chair and listening to her attentively, trying to grasp her meaning so that he could answer her properly. The mood evoked in him by his last interview with Maslova still filled his being with a quiet joy and goodwill to all men.

'I am wanting to reform myself, not her,' he replied.

Natalia Ivanovna sighed. 'There are other ways besides marriage.'

'But I believe that is the best way. What is more, it will take me into a world where I can be of use.'

'I hardly think that you will be happy.'

'It is not a question of my happiness.'

'Of course not. But if she has a heart, she cannot be happy either; she cannot even wish for the marriage.'

'She does not wish it.'

'I understand, but life . . .'

'What about life?'

'Life requires other things from us.'

'Life only requires us to do what is right,' said Nekhlyudov, looking into her face which was still beautiful in spite of the tiny wrinkles round the eyes and mouth.

'I don't understand,' she said with a sigh.

'Poor darling! How could she have changed so?' thought Nekhlyudov, remembering Natalia as she had been before her marriage, and feeling a tenderness towards her, woven of countless childhood memories.

At that moment Rogozhinsky came into the room, head high as always and broad chest expanded, walking lightly and softly. He was smiling, and his spectacles, his bald patch and his black beard all glistened.

'Good evening, good evening,' he exclaimed with unnatural self-conscious emphasis.

(At first, after the marriage, both men had tried to use the familiar 'thou' to each other, but had not succeeded.)

They shook hands, and Rogozhinsky sank softly into an arm-chair.

'I hope I am not interrupting your conversation?'

'Not at all. I do not hide what I say or do from anyone.'

The moment Nekhlyudov saw that face, those hairy hands, and heard the patronizing self-assured tone, his humility vanished in a flash.

'Yes, we were talking about his plans,' said Natalia Ivanovna. 'Shall I give you some tea?' she added, taking the tea-pot.

'Yes, please. What exactly are your plans?'

'To go to Siberia with a gang of convicts, among them the woman I consider I have wronged,' said Nekhlyudov.

'I hear that you mean to do more than just accompany her.'

'Yes, I shall marry her, if she will agree.'

'Really? But would you mind explaining your reasons to me? I do not understand.'

'My reasons are that this woman . . . that her first step on the road to a dissolute life . . .' Nekhlyudov was angry with himself for not being able to find the right words. 'I mean that I am the guilty one, but she is the one that has been punished.'

'If she has been punished, then she can't have been innocent.'

'She is absolutely innocent.'

And Nekhlyudov related the whole story, speaking with unnecessary agitation.

'Yes, it was carelessness on the part of the President of the Court that was responsible for the ill-considered verdict of the jury,' said Rogozhinsky. 'But there's the Senate for cases of that sort.'

'The Senate has disallowed the appeal.'

'Well, if the Senate has rejected it, there cannot have been sufficient grounds for appealing,' said Rogozhinsky, evidently sharing the opinion that truth is a product of legal argument. 'The Senate cannot review the case on its merits. If there really was an error by the court, you should address a petition to His Majesty.'

'That has been done, but there is no likelihood of its being successful. Inquiries will be made in the Ministry, the Ministry will consult the Senate, the Senate will repeat its decision, and as usual the innocent will be punished.'

'In the first place, the Ministry won't consult the Senate,' said Rogozhinsky, with a condescending smile, 'but get the record of the proceedings from the court and, if any error is discovered, will report accordingly. Secondly, innocent people are never punished – or, at least, with very rare exceptions. But the guilty are punished,' said Rogozhinsky in leisurely fashion and with a complacent smile.

'And I am convinced of the contrary,' said Nekhlyudov, with a feeling of animosity towards his brother-in-law. 'I have come to the conclusion that over half the people sentenced by the courts are innocent.'

'How do you mean?'

'Innocent in the literal sense of the word. As that woman is innocent of poisoning; as a peasant I have got to know recently is innocent of the murder he never committed; as a mother and her son are innocent who were pretty nearly convicted of arson committed by the owner of the place that was set on fire.'

'Well, of course, judicial errors have always occurred and will continue to occur. Human institutions can never be perfect.'

'And then there are a huge number of morally innocent people who have grown up in such circumstances that they do not regard their acts as crimes.'

'Forgive me, but that is not so: every thief knows that

stealing is wrong and that he ought not to steal – that stealing is wicked,' said Rogozhinsky, with a calm, self-assured, slightly contemptuous smile which specially irritated Nekhlyudov.

'No, he does not. You tell him: "Don't steal!" and he sees the factory owners stealing his labour by keeping back his wages; he knows that the Government, with all its officials, never stops robbing him by means of taxes.'

'This sounds like anarchism,' Rogozhinsky said, quietly defining the meaning of his brother-in-law's words.

'I don't know what it sounds like. I only know what happens,' Nekhlyudov continued. 'He knows that the Government robs him; he knows that we landed proprietors robbed him long ago when we took the land which ought to be common property. And now if he gathers a few sticks from that stolen land to light his fire we clap him in gaol and tell him he's a thief. Of course he knows that not he but the man who robbed him of the land is the thief, and that every restitution of what has been stolen from him is a duty he owes to his family.'

'I don't understand you, or if I do I cannot agree. Land must have an owner. If you were to divide it up –' Rogozhinsky began, with the full and calm conviction that Nekhlyudov was a socialist and that the theory of Socialism demands that the land should be divided equally – foolish as such a division would be, as he could easily prove – 'if you were to divide it up in equal shares today, tomorrow it would again pass into the hands of the most industrious and the most capable.'

'No one is thinking of dividing the land equally. Land should not be anybody's property. It should not be bought or sold or rented.'

'Man has an innate right to property. Without ownership there would be no incentive to cultivate the land. Take away the right of ownership, and we shall return to the primitive state,' Rogozhinsky pronounced authoritatively, repeating the usual argument in favour of the private ownership of land, supposed to be irrefutable and based on the assumption that people's desire to possess land proves their right to possess it.

'On the contrary, it is only when landowners stop their dog-in-the-manger behaviour – when they stop preventing other men from cultivating the land they don't know how to use themselves – that this land will cease to lie idle, as it does now.'

'Listen, Dmitri Ivanovich, what you are saying is sheer madness! Is it possible to abolish ownership of land in these days? I know this is an old hobby-horse of yours. But let me tell you frankly –' Rogozhinsky turned pale, and his voice shook: he obviously felt very keenly about the question. 'I should advise you to think this problem over carefully before you attempt to solve it in practice.'

'Are you speaking of my own personal affairs?'

'Yes. I assume that all of us who are placed in special circumstances must bear the responsibilities peculiar to those circumstances: we must maintain the traditions in which we were born, which we have inherited from our ancestors, and hand them on to our descendants.'

'I consider my duty to be –'

'Allow me to continue,' said Rogozhinsky, refusing to be interrupted. 'I am not thinking of myself or my children. Their future is safe. I earn enough for us to live in comfort, and I hope that my children will be fairly well-to-do also; therefore my protest against what you are doing – which, if you will allow me to say so, is ill-advised – does not spring from selfish personal motives: it is on a matter of principle that I cannot agree with you. I should advise you to think it over more, and read –'

'Kindly allow me to order my own affairs and choose for myself what to read and what not to read,' said Nekhlyudov, turning pale. And feeling his hands growing cold, and that he was losing control of himself, he broke off and began to drink his tea in silence.

33

'WELL, and how are the children?' Nekhlyudov asked his sister, when he had regained some of his composure.

She told him that they were with their grandmother, her husband's mother; and, relieved that the dispute with her husband was over, she went on to describe how they played at travelling, just as he used to do with his two dolls – the little negro and the one he called the French lady.

'Do you really remember that?' said Nekhlyudov, smiling.

'And isn't it odd that they should play the very same game?'

The disagreeable conversation had been brought to an end. Natalia felt more at ease, but she did not want to talk in her husband's presence of things which held meaning only for her brother, so, in order to make the conversation general, she introduced the news from Petersburg which had just reached Moscow about Madame Kamenskaya's grief at having lost her only son, killed in a duel.

Rogozhinsky expressed his disapproval of a system which excluded murder in a duel from the ordinary list of criminal offences.

This remark provoked a retort from Nekhlyudov, and another heated argument flared up on the same subject, in which everything was only half said, neither protagonist fully expressing what was in his mind, and each standing firm in mutual condemnation.

Rogozhinsky felt that Nekhlyudov criticized him and despised everything he did, and was anxious to prove how unfair he was in his opinion. Nekhlyudov, for his part, was, to begin with, annoyed at his brother-in-law's interference in his plans for the estates (though in his heart of hearts he knew that his brother-in-law, his sister and their children, as his heirs, had a certain right to protest); and, further, he was indignant that this narrow-minded man should so calmly and dogmatically persist in regarding as lawful and right what Nekhlyudov now considered absolutely senseless and criminal.

'What could a court of law have done?' he asked.

'It could have sentenced one of the two duellists to the mines like any ordinary murderer.'

Nekhlyudov's hands went cold again, and he said excitedly: 'And what would that have done?'

'Justice would have been done.'

'As if justice were the aim of courts of justice!' cried Nekhlyudov.

'What else?'

'The maintenance of class interests. The courts, in my opinion, are only an instrument for upholding the existing order of things, in the interests of our class.'

'Well, this really is a novel point of view,' said Rogozhinsky, with a quiet smile. 'A somewhat different purpose is generally ascribed to the courts.'

'In theory, they have, but not in practice, as I have had occasion to discover. The only function of the courts is to preserve society as it is, and that is why they persecute and pass sentence on people who stand above the average and want to raise it – the so-called political offenders – and those who are below it, the so-called criminal types.'

'I cannot agree with you. In the first place I cannot admit that all so-called political offenders are punished because they are above the average. For the most part they are the refuse of society – as depraved, though in a different way, as the criminal types whom you consider to be below the average.'

'But I happen to know people who are immensely superior to their judges: all the sectarians are good, courageous men –'

But Rogozhinsky, unaccustomed to being interrupted, did not listen to Nekhlyudov and went on talking at the same time, which particularly irritated him.

'Nor can I agree that the object of the law is to uphold the existing order. The law pursues its aims, either to reform –'

'A fine way of reforming a man, to clap him in gaol!' Nekhlyudov put in.

'– or to remove,' Rogozhinsky persisted stubbornly, 'the corrupt and bestial persons who undermine the existence of society.'

'That's just the trouble: it doesn't do one or the other. Society has not the means to do that.'

'What do you mean? I don't understand,' said Rogozhinsky with a forced smile.

'I mean there are only two really sensible forms of punishment, those that were applied in the old days: corporal punishment and capital punishment, but these, as time went on and customs relaxed, fell more and more into disuse,' said Nekhlyudov.

'There now, this is something novel and surprising, coming from your lips.'

'There is some sense in causing a man bodily pain in order to restrain him from committing a second time the crime he is being punished for; and there is good reason to chop off the head of a member of the community who is injurious or dangerous to it. Both these punishments have an intelligible meaning. But what is the sense of locking up a man already depraved by idleness or bad example, and keeping him in conditions of enforced idleness where he is provided for, in company with other men even more depraved? Or for some inscrutable reason transporting him at public expense – and it costs over five hundred roubles a time – from Tula to Irkutsk, or from Kursk to –'

'Yes, but all the same, people dread those journeys at public expense, and if it were not for such journeys and the prisons, you and I would not be sitting here so peacefully as we are now.'

'But gaols are powerless to ensure our safety, because these people are not kept there for ever but are let out again. On the contrary, in these institutions men are forced into greater and greater depravity and vice, so that the danger is increased.'

'You mean that the penal system ought to be improved?'

'It cannot be improved. An improved prison system would cost far more than is spent on popular education, and would lay a still heavier burden on the people.'

'But the shortcomings of the penal system in no wise invalidate the law itself.' Rogozhinsky resumed his speech, paying no attention to his brother-in-law.

'There is no remedy for these shortcomings,' said Nekhlyudov, raising his voice.

'What then? Are we to kill them off? Or, as a certain statesman has suggested, put their eyes out?' said Rogozhinsky, smiling triumphantly.

'That would be cruel all right, but to the point. What is done now is cruel and not only ineffective but also so stupid that it is impossible to understand how people in their right minds can take part in so absurd and barbarous a business as the Criminal Court.'

'I happen to take part in it,' said Rogozhinsky, paling.

'That is your affair. But I find it incomprehensible.'

'It seems to me there are a good many things you find incomprehensible,' said Rogozhinsky in a trembling voice.

'I have seen the assistant prosecutor, in court, doing his utmost to convict an unfortunate boy who could have inspired nothing but pity in any normal man. I heard how another prosecutor cross-examined a sectarian and managed to make the reading of the Gospel a criminal offence – in fact, the whole business of the courts consists exclusively of similar senseless and cruel achievements.'

'I should not serve in them if I thought so,' said Rogozhinsky, rising.

Nekhlyudov noticed a peculiar glitter behind his brother-in-law's spectacles. 'Can it be tears?' he thought. And indeed they were tears of injured pride. Going to the window, Rogozhinsky took out his handkerchief and, clearing his throat, began to rub his spectacles, removing them and wiping his eyes at the same time. When he returned to the sofa he lit a cigar and did not say another word. Nekhlyudov felt sorry and ashamed to have upset his brother-in-law and sister to such an extent, especially as he was going away the next day and would not see them again. He said good-bye, embarrassed, and went home.

'All I said may very well be true – anyhow, he had no answer to it. But I ought not to have spoken as I did. How little I have changed if I can be so carried away by ill-feeling as to offend him and grieve poor Natalia,' he thought.

34

THE party with Maslova was to set off from the railway-station at three o'clock in the afternoon, so that, in order to see them start from the gaol and go with her to the station, Nekhlyudov decided to arrive at the prison before noon.

The night before, packing his clothes and papers, he stopped to read some passages here and there in his diary, and also the last entry. The last entry, written before leaving for Petersburg, ran thus: 'Katusha will not accept my sacrifice, but is willing to sacrifice herself. She has won a victory, and so have I. She makes me happy by the change of heart which I think – I hardly dare believe it – is taking place in her. I am afraid to believe it, but it seems to me she is coming to life again.' Immediately after this he had written: 'I have gone through a very painful and a very joyful experience. I heard that she misbehaved badly in the hospital. And suddenly I felt terribly upset. I never thought it would hurt so much. I spoke to her with loathing and disgust, and then suddenly I remembered myself and how often I have been, and still am though only in thought, guilty of the very thing I hated her for – and immediately I loathed myself and pitied her and felt happy again. If only we could always see the beam in our own eye soon enough, how much more charitable we should be!' That day he had written: 'I have been to see Natalia, and just because I felt satisfied with myself I was unkind and spiteful, and now my heart is heavy. Well, it can't be helped. Tomorrow I begin a new life. A final good-bye to the old! Many ideas and impressions have accumulated which I cannot yet piece together.'

When he woke the next morning Nekhlyudov's first feeling was regret at what had passed between him and his brother-in-law.

'I can't go away leaving it like that,' he thought. 'I must go and make it up with them.'

But glancing at his watch he saw that there was no time and that he must hurry if he was not to miss the party as it set out. He quickly collected all his things and sent the porter and Tarass, Fedosya's husband who was travelling with him, straight to the station with his luggage, then took the first cab he could find and drove to the prison. The convicts' train was due to leave two hours before the mail train by which he was going, so he settled the bill for his rooms, not intending to come back again.

*

It was July, and the weather unbearably hot. The cobble-stones underfoot, the stone walls of the houses and their iron roofs, which a sultry night had done nothing to cool, threw their heat into the close still air. There was no wind, or if a slight breeze did rise it came like a whiff of hot foul air full of dust and the smell of paint. The streets were almost empty and the few people who were out tried to keep in the shade of the houses. Only some peasants with faces burnt black and bast shoes on their feet, who were mending the road, sat working in the sun, hammering at the stones they were setting in the burning sand; while gloomy policemen, in unbleached tunics with revolvers fastened to orange-coloured lanyards, stood sullenly in the middle of the road, shifting from one foot to the other; tramcars, bells ringing, clattered backwards and forwards with blinds pulled down on the sunny side, drawn by horses with white hoods over their heads with slits for the ears.

When Nekhlyudov reached the prison the party had not yet come out, and the strenuous business of handing over and taking delivery of the prisoners (which had begun at four o'clock in the morning) was still going on. There were six hundred and twenty-three men and sixty-four women in the party. They all had to be checked against a list; the ailing and feeble had to be segregated, and the party put under guard. The new senior warder, his two assistants, the doctor and his assistant, the officer of the convoy and the clerk were sitting outside in the courtyard at a table covered with writing materials and papers, and placed in the shade of a wall. They called the prisoners up one by one, examined and questioned them, and made notes.

The sun's rays were already half across the table. It was growing hot and even more oppressive from the absence of any breeze and the exhalations of the prisoners thronging round.

'Good heavens, will this never stop?' said the convoy officer, a tall, fat, red-faced man with high shoulders and short arms, who kept puffing cigarette-smoke through the moustaches which drooped over his mouth. 'I'm dead-beat. Where did you get such a lot of them? Are there many more?'

The clerk consulted the lists.

'Another twenty-four men, besides the women.'

'Well, what are you hanging about for? Come on!' shouted the convoy officer to the jostling prisoners who had not yet been checked.

The prisoners had been standing in line for over three hours now, waiting their turn, and not in the shade but in the sun.

While this was going on inside the prison yard, an armed sentry stood as usual outside the gate, where a couple of dozen carts were drawn up to carry the prisoners' belongings, and such prisoners as were too weak to walk, and at the corner a group of relatives and friends were waiting to see the prisoners as they came out, hoping, if possible, to exchange a few words and give them something for the journey. Nekhlyudov joined the group.

He stood there for about an hour. At the end of this time a clanking of chains, the sound of steps, of orders being shouted, of coughing and the low murmur of a large crowd were heard from behind the gates. This continued for some five minutes, during which time warders came in and out through the wicket-gate. At last the word of command was given.

The gates opened with a crash like thunder, the clanking of chains became louder, and the escort of soldiers in white tunics, armed with muskets, came out into the street and performed what was evidently a familiar and much practised manoeuvre, posting themselves in a wide perfect semicircle in front of the gates. When they were in their places another command was given and the convicts emerged in pairs, with flat pancake-shaped hats on their shaven heads and sacks slung over their shoulders, dragging their chained legs and swinging one free arm while the other supported the sack on their backs. First came the men condemned to hard labour, all of them wearing identical grey trousers and cloaks with black marks like aces on the back. All of them – young, old, thin or fat, pale, florid or dark, those with moustaches, the bearded and the beardless, Russians, Tartars, Jews – came out clanking their chains and briskly swinging their arms, as though preparing for a long walk, but after taking ten or twelve steps they halted and meekly arranged themselves in rows of four, one behind the other. They were immediately followed through the gates by another batch with shaven heads, and dressed like the first; they had no chains on their legs but were handcuffed together. These were prisoners sentenced to deportation. They strode out just as briskly, halted as suddenly, and ranged themselves four abreast. Then came those exiled by their village communes; after them the women, also in order – those condemned to hard labour in grey prison cloaks and kerchiefs, next women being deported, and those who were going voluntarily to be with their men-folk, wearing their own town or village clothing. Some of the women carried babies wrapped in the folds of their grey cloaks.

With the women came the children, boys and girls, huddling close to the prisoners like colts in a herd of horses. The men stood silent, only clearing their throats now and then or making abrupt remarks, but the women chattered without stopping. Nekhlyudov thought he caught sight of Maslova as she came out, but she was soon lost among the others and he saw only a crowd of grey beings – seemingly devoid of all that was human or at any rate of all that was feminine – with sacks on their backs and children round them, taking their places behind the men.

Although the prisoners had all been counted inside the prison, the escort counted them again, comparing the numbers with the list. This process took a long time, especially as some of the prisoners moved about and changed places, which upset the escort's reckoning. The soldiers shouted at and pushed the prisoners, who complied obediently but sullenly, and began the count all over again. After they had all been counted anew the officer of the convoy gave a command, and a commotion arose among the crowd. The invalid men, the women and the children pushed their way towards the carts and began to distribute their sacks and to climb up themselves. Women with yelling infants, children cheerfully squabbling for seats and cheerless dejected men all climbed in and sat down in the carts.

A few prisoners, taking off their caps, approached the officer of the convoy with a request of some sort. Nekhlyudov found out later that they were asking for places in the carts. He saw the officer, in silence and not looking at the man before him, take a long pull at his cigarette and then suddenly wave his podgy arm in front of him. Expecting a blow, the man ducked his shaven head between his shoulders and sprang back.

'I'll give you a lift you'll remember!' shouted the officer. 'You'll get there on foot!'

Only one tall tottery old fellow with fetters on his legs did the officer allow into a cart, and Nekhlyudov saw the old man take off his pancake-shaped cap and cross himself as he went forward towards the cart. For some time he was unable to climb in because of the chains which prevented him from raising his feeble old legs; then a woman already sitting in the cart helped him, pulling him up by the arm.

When all the sacks were in the carts and those with permission to ride were seated on the sacks the convoy officer took off his cap, wiped his forehead, his bald head and thick red neck with his handkerchief, and crossed himself.

'Forward – march!' he commanded.

The soldiers clattered with their rifles, the prisoners took off their caps and began crossing themselves, some doing so with their left hands; friends who were seeing them off called out something, the prisoners shouted in reply, some of the women set up a wail, and the party, surrounded by soldiers in white tunics, moved off, raising the dust with their fettered feet. The soldiers marched in front; behind them, four abreast, clanking their chains, the convicts sentenced to hard labour; next the deportees and those banished by their communes, handcuffed in pairs; then the women. Last of all came the carts carrying the sacks and the ailing prisoners. High on the baggage on one of the carts sat a woman, muffled up to her ears, who never stopped wailing and sobbing.

35

THE procession was so long that by the time the carts with the baggage and the feeble-bodied prisoners began to move, the men in front were already out of sight. When the carts trundled off, Nekhlyudov jumped into the cab which was waiting for him and told the driver to catch up with the prisoners in front, so that he could see if there were any of the men he knew in the gang, and then find Maslova among the women and ask her if she had received the things he had sent her. It had become very hot. There was no wind, and the cloud of dust raised by thousands of feet hovered all the time above the prisoners as they moved down the centre of the road. They were marching quickly, and the slow-trotting horse belonging to Nekhlyudov's cab took a long while getting ahead of the procession. Line after line they advanced, strange fearful creatures dressed alike, thousands of feet shod alike, all in step, swinging their arms as though to keep up their spirits. There were so many of them, they looked so exactly alike and their circumstances were so extraordinarily odd that to Nekhlyudov they no longer seemed to be men, but peculiar and dreadful creatures of some sort. This impression was dispelled only when he recognized the murderer Fedorov among the crowd of hard labour convicts, and among the exiles Okhotin, the wag, and another vagrant who had appealed to him for assistance. Almost all of the prisoners turned to take a quick sideways glance at the passing cab and the gentleman in it, who was scanning them. Fedorov gave a backward jerk of his head as a sign that he had recognized Nekhlyudov, and Okhotin winked. But neither of them bowed, thinking it was not allowed. Coming abreast of the women, Nekhlyudov saw Maslova at once. She was in the second row. On the outside walked an ugly, red-faced, black-eyed woman with short legs and her cloak tucked into her girdle: it was Beauty. Then came a pregnant woman hardly able to drag one foot after the other, and the third was Maslova. She was carrying a sack over her shoulder, and looking straight in front of her. Her face was calm and determined. The fourth in the row, stepping out briskly, was a handsome young woman in a short cape and her kerchief tied peasant-fashion. This was Fedosya. Nekhlyudov got out of the cab and went up to the moving women, meaning to ask

Maslova about the things he had sent, and inquire how she was feeling, but the convoy sergeant who was marching that side of the party noticed him at once and ran towards him.

'It's not allowed to go near the gang, sir,' he shouted as he came up. 'It's against the regulations.'

But when he reached Nekhlyudov and recognized him (everyone in the prison knew Nekhlyudov), the sergeant raised his fingers to his cap and, stopping beside him, said:

'Not now, sir. Wait till we get to the railway-station. It's not allowed here. Now then, don't lag behind there! Keep up!' he shouted to the prisoners and, trying to appear dashing, in spite of the heat he trotted smartly across to his place in his foppish new boots.

Nekhlyudov returned to the pavement and telling the cabby to follow walked on, keeping in sight of the party. Wherever the procession passed it attracted attention – half pity, half horror. People leaned out of their carriages and followed the prisoners with their eyes as long as they could see them. Passers-by stopped and gazed in wonder and alarm at the fearful spectacle. Some approached and offered alms, which were accepted for the prisoners by the escort. Some fell in behind, as though hypnotized, and then stopped, and shaking their heads followed the prisoners with their eyes only. People ran out of doors and gates, calling to each other, or hung out of windows, still and silent, watching the dreadful procession. At one crossing an elegant open carriage was held up by the party. A coachman with a shiny face and a broad seat, and two rows of buttons down his back, sat on the box. Inside the carriage a husband and wife sat facing the horses: the wife, a pale thin woman in a light-coloured bonnet, with a bright parasol, and the husband in a top hat and light, well-cut dust-coat. In front, opposite them, were their children: a little girl with loose fair hair, dressed up and fresh as a flower, also holding a bright parasol, and a boy of eight with a long thin neck and sharp collar-bones, wearing a sailor-hat trimmed with long ribbons. The father was angrily scolding the coach-man for failing to cross before the procession delayed them, while the mother screwed up her eyes and frowned in disgust, shielding herself from the dust and the sun with the silk parasol which she held close to her face. The broad-backed coachman scowled angrily at the unfair reprimands of his master – who had himself told him to take that street – and with difficulty restrained the glossy black stallions flecked with foam under their harness who were impatient to go on.

The policeman on the crossing would gladly have obliged the owner of such a fine equipage by stopping the columns of convicts and letting him pass, but he felt that there was a certain sombre solemnity about this procession which must not be violated even for such a wealthy gentleman as this. He only raised his fingers to the peak of his cap to show his respect for riches, and looked sternly at the prisoners as though promising at any rate to protect the people in the carriage from them. So the carriage had to wait until the whole procession had passed, and could only move on when the last of the carts with the sacks and the prisoners sitting on top of them had rattled by. The hysterical woman who had quietened down began to sob and shriek again when she saw the luxurious equipage. It was only then that the coachman lightly twitched the reins, and the high-stepping black horses, with a clatter of hooves against the cobbles, whirled the gently swaying carriage on its rubber tyres towards the country house where the husband, his wife, the little girl and the boy with the thin neck and projecting collar-bones were going to enjoy themselves.

Neither the father nor the mother gave either the girl or the boy any explanation of what they had seen. So the children had to find out for themselves the meaning of the spectacle.

The girl, considering the expression on the faces of her father and mother, came to the conclusion that these people were of a totally different kind from her parents and their friends, that they were wicked people and therefore had to be treated in that way. And so the little girl only felt frightened, and was glad when she could no longer see them.

But the boy with the long thin neck, who had watched the procession of prisoners without taking his eyes off them, came to a different decision. He knew without any doubt – he was quite sure, for he had the knowledge straight from God, that these people were just the same as he and everyone else was, and therefore something wicked had been done to them, something that ought not to be done, and he was sorry for them, and horrified not only at the people who were shaved and fettered but at the people who had fettered and shaved them. And that was why the boy's lips swelled up more and more, and he tried harder and harder not to cry, supposing that it was shameful to cry on such occasions.

36

NEKHLYUDOV kept up with the quick pace of the convicts, but clad even as lightly as he was, in a thin overcoat, he felt dreadfully hot and, above all, found that it was difficult to breathe, so hot and dusty was the motionless sultry air in the streets. After walking about a quarter of a mile he got into the trap and drove on ahead, but it felt hotter still in the middle of the street, in the trap. He tried to recall last night's conversation with his brother-in-law, but the recollection no longer agitated him as it had done that morning. It had been pushed into the background by the impression made on him at seeing the convict party emerge from the gaol and march off. But above all – it was intolerably hot. Two high-school boys were standing with their caps off before an ice-cream seller squatting by a fence in the shade of some trees. One of the boys was already enjoying his ice, licking a little horn spoon; the other was waiting for a tumbler to be filled to the brim with something yellow.

'Where could I get a drink?' Nekhlyudov asked his driver, overcome by irrepressible thirst.

'There's a good inn just here,' said the cabman, turning a corner and driving Nekhlyudov to a door with a large sign above it.

A plump man in shirt-sleeves stood behind the counter; the waiters, in clothes that had once been white, were sitting at the tables, there being scarcely any customers; they looked with curiosity at this unusual visitor and offered their services. Nekhlyudov asked for seltzer water, and sat down away from the window at a little table covered with a dirty cloth.

Two men were sitting at another table with a tea-tray and a frosted glass bottle in front of them, mopping the perspiration from their brows and assisting each other over some calculation. One of them was dark and bald, with a fringe of black hair at the back of his head like Rogozhinsky. This reminded Nekhlyudov again of last night's conversation with his brother-in-law and that he had wanted to see him and Natalia once more before his departure. 'I shall hardly have time before the train leaves,' he thought. 'I had better write her a letter.' And asking for a sheet of paper, an envelope and a stamp, he began to consider what he should say, while he sipped the cool effervescing water. But his thoughts wandered and he found it quite impossible to compose the letter.

'My dear Natalia,' he began, 'I cannot bear to go away with the memory of my conversation last night with your husband without –' ('What next? Am I to apologize for what I said yesterday? But I said what I thought. And he would think that I was taking it back. And besides, he was meddling in my affairs. . . . No, I can't do it.') And again there arose his hatred for the conceited individual who was so foreign to him and never understood him. Nekhlyudov put the unfinished letter in his pocket, and settling his bill went out into the street and told the driver to catch up with the party.

The heat had grown worse. The walls and stones seemed to exude hot air. The sizzling pavement scorched one's feet, and Nekhlyudov felt a burning sensation when he touched the lacquered wing of the vehicle with his bare hand

The horse jogged wearily along, hooves clicking monotonously on the dusty uneven cobblestones; the cabby kept falling into a doze. Nekhlyudov sat indifferently gazing before him, thinking of nothing in particular. Opposite the gates of a big house, where the road sloped to the gutter, stood a little crowd of people and a convoy soldier with his rifle. Nekhlyudov stopped his driver.

'What is it?' he asked a house-porter.

'Something the matter with one of the convicts.'

Nekhlyudov got down and approached the group. On the rough uneven cobblestones curving down to the gutter, with his head lower than his feet, lay a broad-shouldered elderly convict with a ginger beard, red face and snub nose, in a grey cloak and grey trousers. He was lying on his back with the palms of his freckled hands downwards; at long intervals his deep powerful chest heaved rhythmically and he sobbed, gazing up at the sky with staring bloodshot eyes. A frowning policeman stood over him, together with a pedlar, a postman, a clerk, an old woman with a sunshade and a boy with clipped hair holding an empty basket.

'They are weak. They get weak sitting locked up in gaol, and then they're brought out into a fiery furnace like this,' said the clerk, feeling someone was to blame, and addressing Nekhlyudov as he came up.

'He's dying, most likely,' said the old woman with the sunshade in a doleful voice.

'You ought to loosen his shirt,' said the postman.

The policeman with his thick trembling fingers began clumsily untying the tapes that fastened the shirt round the sinewy red neck. He was evidently agitated and confused, but still deemed it necessary to address the crowd.

'What are you standing round for? It's quite hot enough without all of you to keep off the breeze.'

'The doctor is supposed to see to it that the weak ones stay behind. Instead, they sent this one out more dead than alive,' said the clerk, showing off his knowledge of the regulations.

Having undone the tapes of the man's shirt, the policeman straightened himself and looked round.

'Move along there, I tell you! It's none of your business, and what are you gaping at, I should like to know,' he said, turning towards Nekhlyudov for sympathy, but meeting with no sympathy there he looked at the convoy soldier.

The soldier, however, was standing to one side examining the heel of his boot where it was worn away, and was quite indifferent to the policeman's difficulties.

'Those whose business it is don't care. Is it right to do a man to death like this?'

'He may be a convict, but he's a human being all the same,' different voices were heard saying in the crowd.

'Prop his head up higher and give him water,' said Nekhlyudov.

'They've gone to fetch water,' replied the policeman and, taking the convict under the arms, he managed with an effort to raise his body a little higher.

'Now then, what's this mob here for?' a firm commanding voice was heard all of a sudden, and a police-officer in an uncommonly clean and shiny uniform and still shinier top-boots strode up to the little knot of people round the convict. 'Move on! Nobody has any business here!' he shouted to the crowd, before he knew why they were there.

When he came close and saw the dying convict he nodded his head, satisfied, as though it was just what he expected. 'What happened?' he asked the policeman.

The policeman reported that while a gang of convicts was passing, this man had collapsed and the convoy officer had ordered him to be left there.

'Well, that's all right. He must be taken to the police-station. Get a cab.'

'The house-porter has gone for one,' said the policeman, with his fingers to his cap.

The clerk began saying something about the heat.

'What's it got to do with you? Move on!' said the police-officer, and gave the clerk such a severe look that he was silenced.

'He ought to have a little water,' said Nekhlyudov.

The police-officer frowned at Nekhlyudov, too, but said nothing. However, when the house-porter brought a mug of water he told the policeman to give some to the convict. The policeman raised the man's head which had fallen backwards, and tried to pour some water into his mouth, but he could not swallow, and the water ran down his beard, wetting the front of his jacket and his coarse dusty shirt.

'Pour it over his head,' ordered the officer, and the policeman, taking off the pancake-shaped cap, poured water over the red curly hair and the shaven skull.

The convict's eyes opened wider, as though in alarm, but he did not move. Little rivulets of dirt and dust ran down his face but the same regular gasps escaped from his mouth, and his whole body kept jerking convulsively.

'How about that cab there? Take that one,' the officer said to the policeman, pointing to Nekhlyudov's cab. 'Hey, you!'

'Engaged,' said the cabby gloomily, without looking up.

'This is my driver,' said Nekhlyudov, 'but you can take him. I will pay,' he added, turning to the cabman.

'Well, what are you waiting for?' shouted the officer. 'Get on.'

The policeman, the house-porter and the convoy soldier lifted the dying man and carried him to the trap, where they tried to make him sit up. But he could not support himself: his head fell back and his body slipped off the seat.

'Lay him down,' ordered the police-officer.

'It's all right, your honour. I'll get him to the police-station like this,' said the policeman, seating himself firmly beside the dying man and putting his strong right hand under the man's arm.

The convoy soldier lifted the stockingless feet in their prison shoes, and stretched them out under the box.

The police-officer looked round and noticing the convict's

pancake-shaped cap lying in the road picked it up and stuck it on the wet, backward-fallen head.

'Right – march!' he commanded.

The cabman looked round with irritation, shook his head and accompanied by the convoy soldier started slowly back towards the police-station. The policeman sitting beside the convict kept clutching at the slipping body, with its head swaying in all directions. The convoy soldier walked alongside, keeping the legs under the box. Nekhlyudov followed after.

37

PASSING by the fireman on duty at the gate of the police-station,[1] the cab with the convict drove into the police-station yard and stopped at one of the doors.

Some firemen in the yard, their sleeves rolled up, were laughing and talking loudly over a cart they were busy washing.

The moment the trap pulled up a number of policemen surrounded it, caught hold of the convict's lifeless body under the arms and by the legs, and lifted it from the vehicle, which creaked under their weight.

The policeman who had brought the body jumped out from the cab, began to swing his numbed arms about and, taking off his cap, crossed himself. The dead man was carried through the door and up the stairs. Nekhlyudov followed. There were four bunks in the dirty little room where they took the body. A couple of sick men in hospital dressing-gowns were sitting on two of them: one had a twisted mouth and bandaged neck, the other was a consumptive. The two remaining bunks were unoccupied. The body of the convict was laid on one of them. A little man with glittering eyes and quivering eyebrows, clad only in his underclothes and stockings, glided noiselessly over to the convict's body, looked at

1. The fire-brigade and the police used to share the same building in Moscow.

431

it and then at Nekhlyudov, and burst into a peal of laughter. It was a madman who was being kept in the police hospital.

'They are trying to scare me,' he said. 'Only they won't succeed.'

The policemen who had carried the corpse in were followed by a police-officer and a medical assistant.

Going up to the body, the medical assistant touched the sallow freckled hand which, although not quite stiff, already had the pallor of death, held it for a moment, then let it drop. It fell lifelessly on the dead man's stomach.

'It's all over with him,' said the medical assistant, shaking his head, but, apparently to comply with the rules, he undid the coarse wet shirt and, tossing back his curly hair from his ear, bent over the convict's yellow-skinned, motionless, high chest. Everyone was silent. The medical assistant straightened himself, shook his head again and with his finger touched first one, and then the other lid of the open, staring blue eyes.

'You won't scare me, you won't scare me,' the madman was saying, all the time spitting in the direction of the medical assistant.

'Well?' asked the police-officer.

'Well?' repeated the medical assistant. 'You'll have to take him away to the mortuary.'

'Mind, are you sure?' asked the police-officer.

'I ought to be,' said the medical assistant, for some reason drawing the shirt over the dead man's chest. 'However, I will send for Matvei Ivanych and let him have a look. Petrov, go and fetch him,' said the medical assistant, moving away from the body.

'Take him to the mortuary,' said the police-officer. 'And you come to the office and sign,' he added to the convoy soldier, who had not left the convict for a single moment.

'Very good, sir,' replied the soldier.

The policemen lifted the body and carried it downstairs again. Nekhlyudov wanted to follow them but the madman stopped him.

'You're not in the plot, so give me a cigarette,' he said.

Nekhlyudov took out his cigarette-case and gave him one. The madman, twitching his eyebrows, began talking quickly, telling Nekhlyudov how they tortured him by means of putting ideas into his head.

'They are all against me, you see, and torment and torture me with their suggestions.'

'Excuse me,' said Nekhlyudov, and without waiting for him to finish went out into the yard, anxious to see where they would take the body.

The policemen with their burden had already crossed the yard and were about to enter the door of a cellar. Nekhlyudov made to follow them but the police-officer stopped him.

'What do you want?'

'Nothing,' replied Nekhlyudov.

'Nothing, then be off with you.'

Nekhlyudov obeyed and returned to his cab. The driver was dozing. Nekhlyudov roused him and they started once more towards the railway-station.

They had barely gone a hundred yards when they met a cart – also accompanied by a convoy soldier with a gun – in which another convict lay, apparently already dead. He was on his back, and his shaven head with its black beard covered by the pancake-shaped cap, which had slipped down over his nose, jerked and swayed at every jolt of the wagon. The driver in heavy boots walked beside the cart, holding the reins in his hands. A policeman walked behind. Nekhlyudov touched his cabby's shoulder.

'See what they're doing!' said the cabby, stopping his horse.

Nekhlyudov jumped down from his cab and following the driver of the cart past the fireman on duty at the gate went into the yard of the police-station again. By this time the firemen had finished washing the cart and in their place a tall bony man, the captain of the fire-brigade, a dark blue band round his cap, stood with his hands in his pockets, dourly

433

inspecting a thick-necked bay stallion, which a fireman was leading up and down before him. The horse was slightly lame in one fore-leg and the captain was angrily saying something to the veterinary, who was standing near him.

The police-officer was also there. Seeing another corpse, he went up to the cart.

'Where did you pick him up?' he asked, shaking his head disapprovingly.

'In Old Gorbatovsky Street,' replied the policeman.

'A prisoner?' asked the captain of the fire-brigade.

'Yes, sir.'

'It's the second today,' said the police-officer.

'They have a funny way of doing things, I must say. And in this heat, too,' said the captain, and turning to the fireman who was leading the lame stallion, he shouted: 'Put him in the corner stall! I'll teach you, you son of a bitch, to go maiming a horse worth more than yourself, you bastard you!'

The second corpse, like the first, was lifted from the cart by the policemen and carried into the casualty room. Nekhlyudov followed as though hypnotized.

'What do you want?' asked one of the policemen.

Not answering, he went into the room where they carried the body.

The madman, seated on a bunk, was greedily smoking the cigarette Nekhlyudov had given him.

'So you've come back,' he said, and roared with laughter. Catching sight of the dead body, he made a wry face and said, 'Another one! I am sick of them. I'm not a child, am I?' he asked Nekhlyudov, with an inquiring smile.

Nekhlyudov was looking at the dead man: there was no one standing between them now, and the face which before had been hidden by the cap was in full view. This convict was as handsome in face and form as the other had been ugly. He was still in the full bloom of life. In spite of the disfigured, half-shaven head, the low straight forehead, that bulged slightly above the black, now lifeless eyes, was very fine, and so was the small aquiline nose above the thin black moustaches. A smile still hovered on his lips, now turning blue; a little beard only fringed the lower part of the face, and the shaven side of the skull revealed a small, firm, well-shaped ear. The expression on the face was tranquil, stern and kind. Let alone the fact that it was evident from the face what possibilities of spiritual life had been lost in this man, one could see by the fine bones of his hands and shackled feet, and the powerful muscles of the well-proportioned limbs what a fine vigorous agile human animal this had been – a far more perfect animal of its kind than the bay stallion, the laming of which had roused the captain of the fire-brigade to such fury. And yet he had been done to death, and no one regretted him as a human being – no one even regretted him as a working animal that had perished uselessly. The only feeling evoked by his death was a unanimous one of annoyance at the bother of having to dispose of this body which was threatening to decompose.

The doctor accompanied by his assistant and a police-inspector entered the room. The doctor was a stocky thick-set man in a tussore-silk jacket and narrow trousers of the same material that clung to his muscular thighs. The inspector was short and fat, with a round red face that looked rounder still from his habit of filling his cheeks with air and slowly letting it out again. The doctor sat down on the bunk by the side of the dead man, and, just as his assistant had done, touched the hands, put his ear to the heart, and rose, smoothing down his trousers.

'Couldn't be deader,' he said.

The inspector filled his mouth with air and slowly let it out again.

'Which prison is he from?' he asked the convoy soldier.

The convoy soldier told him, and drew his attention to the shackles on the dead man's feet.

'I'll have them removed; we have got smiths about, thank

the Lord,' said the captain, and went towards the door, again puffing out his cheeks and slowly allowing the air to escape.

'Why did this happen?' Nekhlyudov asked the doctor.

The doctor looked at him over his spectacles.

'What do you mean, why did it happen? Why men die of sunstroke? It is like this: they keep 'em locked up all through the winter, without exercise, without light, and suddenly bring 'em out into the sun, and on a day like this, too, *and* march 'em in a crowd so that there's not a breath of air. And the result is sunstroke.'

'Then whatever do they send them out for?'

'You ask them! But who are you, anyway?'

'I am a stranger here.'

'Ah! I wish you good day, I am busy,' said the doctor, annoyed. And giving his trousers a downward pull, he crossed over to the other bunks.

'Well, how are you feeling?' he asked the pale man with the crooked mouth and bandaged neck.

Meanwhile the madman, sitting on his bunk, had finished smoking and was now spitting towards the doctor.

Nekhlyudov went down into the yard and, past the fire-brigade's horses, and some hens, and the sentry in his brass helmet, walked through the gate, where he seated himself in his cab, the driver of which was dozing again, and was driven to the railway-station.

38

By the time Nekhlyudov reached the station the convicts were already seated in the railway-carriages behind barred windows. Some people come to see them off were standing on the platform: they were not allowed to approach the train. The convoy officers were particularly worried. On the way from the prison to the station, besides the two Nekhlyudov had seen, three other men had fallen and died of sunstroke. One had been removed, like the first two, to the nearest police-station, and the two others died at the railway-station.[1] The officers of the convoy were not concerned that five men who might have been alive died while in their charge. That did not interest them: their only worry was to carry out all that the law required of them on such occasions, which meant delivering the dead to the right place, together with their documents and possessions, and removing their names from the list of those to be conveyed to Nizhni – which was troublesome enough, especially in such heat.

It was this that was worrying the escort, and so until everything had been settled neither Nekhlyudov nor anyone else could get permission to go near the train. Nekhlyudov, however, tipped the convoy sergeant and was allowed to pass on condition that he made his leave-taking brief and would be off before the officer noticed. There were eighteen carriages all told, and, except for one for the officers, all were packed to suffocation with prisoners. As Nekhlyudov walked past the carriage windows he could hear what was going on inside – the clanking of chains, bustle and talk interspersed with foul and senseless language, but not a word was said about their comrades who had died on the way, which was what Nekhlyudov had expected to hear. The talk was chiefly about their baggage, water to drink and the choice of seats. Looking into one carriage window, Nekhlyudov saw two convoy soldiers in the passage down the middle taking the manacles off the prisoners. The prisoners held out their hands and one of the soldiers unlocked the manacles with a key and took them off. The other collected them. Passing all the men's carriages, Nekhlyudov came up to the women's. From the second of these he heard a woman's regular groaning cry: 'Oh, oh, oh! Help! Oh, oh, oh! Help!'

Nekhlyudov walked on and, directed by a convoy soldier, stopped beside the window of the third carriage. As he put his

1. Early in the eighties five convicts died of sunstroke in one day on their way from Butyrsky Prison (in Moscow) to the Nizhni railway-station. – L. N. Tolstoy.

face near the window he was assailed by waves of air that were hot and heavy with the smell of human sweat, and he heard the shrill squeal of women's voices. Every bench was packed with red-faced perspiring women dressed in prison clothes and jackets, all chattering away. Nekhlyudov's face at the window attracted their attention. Those nearest stopped talking and moved towards him. Maslova in a jacket but no cloak, and without a kerchief, was sitting by the window on the opposite side, and next to her was the white-skinned smiling Fedosya. Recognizing Nekhlyudov, she nudged Maslova and pointed to the window. Maslova rose hurriedly, threw her kerchief over her black hair, and with a smile on her flushed, animated, sweating face came up to the window and took hold of the iron bars.

'Isn't it hot?' she said with a glad smile.

'Did you get the things?'

'Yes, thank you.'

'Is there anything else you need?' asked Nekhlyudov, feeling the heat coming out from the carriage like heat from the hot slabs in a steam bath.

'Nothing, thank you.'

'A drink of water would be nice,' said Fedosya.

'Yes, a drink would be nice,' echoed Maslova.

'Why, isn't there any water?'

'They did put some, but it's all gone.'

'One moment,' said Nekhlyudov. 'I will ask the convoy men. We shall not see each other again now till we get to Nizhni.'

'Are you really coming, then?' said Maslova, as if not knowing it, and looked joyfully at Nekhlyudov.

'I am travelling by the next train.'

Maslova said nothing, and a few seconds later only heaved a deep sigh.

'Is it a fact, sir, 'bout twelve convicts bein' done to death?' said a stern-looking elderly woman in a gruff mannish voice. This was Korablyova.

'I did not hear that there were twelve. I saw two,' said Nekhlyudov.

'I 'eard there was twelve. Won't nothin' be done to them for it? The devils that they are!'

'Are all the women all right?' asked Nekhlyudov.

'Women are tougher,' a short little female prisoner remarked, laughing. 'Only there's one woman took it into her head to be delivered. Listen to her,' she said, pointing to the next car from which the groans were still proceeding.

'You ask if we want anything,' said Maslova, trying to keep her lips from curving into a happy smile. 'Couldn't that woman be left behind? She is in such pain. Now if you could speak to the officer . . .'

'Yes, I will.'

'And couldn't *she* see Tarass, her husband?' she added, indicating the smiling Fedosya with her eyes. 'He's coming with you, isn't he?'

'No conversation allowed, sir,' said the voice of a sergeant. It was not the one who had let Nekhlyudov pass.

Nekhlyudov turned and went in search of the chief officer to ask about the woman in labour and about Tarass, but he could not find him for a long time, nor get an answer out of the convoy soldiers. They were in a great state of bustle: some of them taking a convict from one place to another, others running about buying food for themselves and arranging their belongings in the carriages, still others attending to a lady who was travelling with the officer of the convoy, and they answered Nekhlyudov's inquiries reluctantly.

It was not until the second departure bell had rung that Nekhlyudov at last found the convoy officer. The officer, wiping with his short arm the moustaches that covered his mouth, and raising his shoulder, was reprimanding a corporal for something or other.

'You – what is it you want?' he asked Nekhlyudov.

'You've got a woman on the train who has begun her labour pains. I thought it would be . . .'

'Let her get on with it. We'll see to it later on,' said the officer, briskly swinging his short arms and going to his own carriage.

At that moment the guard went by with a whistle in his hand. The last departure bell was rung, the whistle blown, and from the people on the platform and the women in their carriages rose a wail of weeping and lamentation. Nekhlyudov stood beside Tarass on the platform and watched the carriages with their barred windows, and the shaven heads of the men behind them, move slowly off one after the other. Then the first of the women's carriages came abreast of them, and women's heads could be seen at the windows, some without kerchiefs, some with; the second carriage followed, and they could hear the woman moaning still; and now the third, with Maslova in it. She was standing at the window with the others and looked out at Nekhlyudov with a pitiful smile on her face.

39

NEKHLYUDOV had two hours to wait before the passenger train left on which he was to travel. At first he thought of using the interval to go and see his sister again, but the morning's experiences had agitated and upset him to such a degree that, sitting down on a settee in the first-class waiting-room, he suddenly felt so drowsy that he turned on his side and fell asleep with his cheek resting on the palm of his hand.

He was awakened by a waiter in a tail-coat, carrying a napkin on his arm.

'Sir, sir, aren't you Prince Nekhlyudov? There is a lady looking for you.'

Nekhlyudov started up and rubbed his eyes, remembering where he was and all that had happened that morning.

He saw in imagination the procession of convicts, the dead bodies, the railway carriages with barred windows and the women locked up in them, one of whom was suffering the agony of labour, without receiving any aid, while another was pathetically smiling at him through the iron bars. But the reality before his eyes was very different: a table set with decanters, vases, candelabra and plates, and agile waiters scurrying round it; at the end of the room, in front of a dresser, a bar-tender standing before an array of bottles and bowls of fruit, and the backs of passengers crowded up to the bar.

As Nekhlyudov changed his reclining position for an upright one and sat gradually collecting his thoughts he noticed everyone in the room staring with curiosity at something going on in the doorway. Looking in the same direction, he saw a procession of servants carrying a lady in a sedan chair, her head wrapped in a transparent veil. The bearer in front was a footman and seemed familiar to Nekhlyudov. The doorman behind with braid on his cap Nekhlyudov knew, too. A stylish lady's-maid with ringlets and an apron, who was carrying a parcel, some sort of round object in a leather case, and sunshades, was walking behind the chair. After her came Prince Korchagin in a travelling-cap, with his thick lips like a dog's, his apoplectic neck and his chest stuck well out; and next – Missy, her cousin Misha and an acquaintance of Nekhlyudov's, the diplomat, Osten, who had a long neck, a prominent Adam's apple, a jolly expression and a cheerful disposition. As he went along he was speaking emphatically, though jokingly, to Missy, who was smiling. The doctor, angrily puffing at a cigarette, brought up the rear.

The Korchagins were moving from their own estate near the city to an estate belonging to the princess's sister on the Nizhni railway line.

The procession with the bearers, the maid and the doctor vanished into the ladies' waiting-room, exciting the curiosity and respect of everyone present. But the old prince, seating himself at a table, immediately called a waiter and began ordering something to eat and drink. Missy and Osten also stayed in the refreshment-room and were just about to sit down when they saw an acquaintance in the doorway and went over to her. The lady was Natalia Ivanovna, Nekhlyudov's sister. Natalia Ivanovna, accompanied by Agrafena Petrovna, looked all round the room as she came in, and noticed Missy and her brother almost simultaneously. She went up to Missy first, merely nodding to her brother; but, having kissed Missy, she immediately turned to him.

'So I have found you at last,' she said.

Nekhlyudov rose, greeted Missy, Misha and Osten, and stood for a few minutes chatting with them. Missy told him of the fire at their country house, which necessitated their moving to her aunt's. Osten seized the opportunity to tell a funny story about a fire.

Nekhlyudov, not listening to Osten, turned to his sister.

'How glad I am that you came,' he said.

'I have been here for some time,' she replied. 'Agrafena Petrovna is with me.' She pointed to Agrafena Petrovna, in a bonnet and dust-coat, who with affectionate and bashful dignity was bowing to him from a distance, not wishing to intrude. 'We have been looking for you everywhere.'

'And I had fallen asleep here. How glad I am that you came,' repeated Nekhlyudov. 'I began a letter to you,' he said.

'Really?' she replied, startled. 'What about?'

Noticing that the brother and sister were about to begin a private conversation, Missy withdrew, surrounded by her cavaliers, while Nekhlyudov and his sister sat down on a velvet-covered sofa by the window, near somebody's things – travelling-rugs and band-boxes.

'After I left you last night I wanted to come back and say how sorry I was, but I did not know how he would take it,' said Nekhlyudov. 'I shouldn't have spoken to your husband like that, and it troubled me.'

'I knew – I was sure you didn't mean it,' said his sister. 'You know yourself . . .'

And the tears welled to her eyes and she put a finger on his hand. The sentence was obscure, but he understood her perfectly and was touched by what she was trying to express. Her words meant that apart from the love for her husband which possessed her whole being, her love for him, her brother, was important and precious to her, too, and every misunderstanding between them caused her great suffering.

'Thank you, thank you. . . . Oh, the things I have seen today!' he said, suddenly recalling the second of the dead convicts. 'Two of the convicts were murdered.'

'Murdered? How?'

'Murdered. They were brought out in this heat. And two of them died of sunstroke.'

'Impossible! What, today? Just now?'

'Yes, just now. I saw their dead bodies.'

'But why murdered? Who murdered them?' said Natalia Ivanovna.

'Whoever it was that forced them to go,' said Nekhlyudov, irritated by the feeling that she was looking even at this through her husband's eyes.

'Merciful heavens!' said Agrafena Petrovna, who had come up to them.

'We haven't the slightest idea of the things that are done to these unfortunate beings, and yet we ought to know,' said Nekhlyudov, glancing at old Prince Korchagin, who with a napkin under his chin was sitting at a table with a bottle before him, and at that moment looked round at Nekhlyudov.

'Nekhlyudov!' he cried. 'Won't you join me in something before you start? There's nothing better before a journey!'

Nekhlyudov declined and turned away.

'But what can you do about it?' continued Natalia Ivanovna.

'I shall do what I can. I don't know what, but I feel that I must do something, and what I can do I shall.'

'Yes, yes, I understand that. But how about them?' she said, smiling and glancing at the Korchagins. 'Is it all over between you and . . . ?'

'Absolutely, and I think without any regrets on either side.'

'A pity. I am sorry. I like her. However, supposing it is so, why do you want to bind yourself?' she added shyly. 'Why are you going?'

'Because I must,' he replied gravely and drily, by way of putting an end to the conversation.

But he at once felt ashamed of his coldness to his sister. 'Why not tell her all I am thinking, and let Agrafena Petrovna hear it, too?' he said to himself, with a glance at the old servant. Her presence urged him still more to speak of his decision to his sister again.

'You mean my resolve to marry Katusha? Well, you see, I made up my mind to do so, but she has definitely and firmly refused,' he said, and his voice shook as it always did when he spoke of this. 'She will not accept my sacrifice, but chooses to make the sacrifice herself – which in her situation means giving up a very great deal – and I cannot allow it if it is only a momentary impulse. So I am following her, to be where she is, to help her and make things as easy for her as I can.'

Natalia Ivanovna said nothing. Agrafena Petrovna looked at her questioningly and shook her head. At that moment the procession reappeared from the ladies' waiting-room. The same handsome footman, Philip, and the doorkeeper were carrying the princess Korchagina. She stopped the bearers, beckoned Nekhlyudov to her side, extending her white jewelled hand with a plaintive languishing air, fearful lest he grasp it too firmly.

'*Épouvantable!*'[1] she said, referring to the heat. 'I cannot endure it. *Ce climat me tue.*'[2] And after a few remarks about the horrors of the Russian climate she invited Nekhlyudov to visit them, and gave the men a signal to go on.

'Be sure and come,' she added, turning her long face towards Nekhlyudov as they were bearing her away.

Nekhlyudov went out on to the platform. The procession with the princess turned to the right towards the first-class

1. Dreadful!
2. This climate is killing me.

cars. Nekhlyudov with the porter who was carrying his things, and Tarass with his sack, turned to the left.

'This is my companion,' said Nekhlyudov to his sister, indicating Tarass, whose story he had told her earlier.

'Surely you are not travelling third-class?' asked Natalia Ivanovna when Nekhlyudov stopped before a third-class carriage which the porter with the things, and Tarass, had got into.

'Yes, I prefer to be with Tarass,' he said. 'Now – one thing more: I have not yet given the Kuzminskoye land to the peasants, so in the event of my death it will come to your children.'

'Dmitri, don't,' said Natalia Ivanovna.

'But even if I should give it away, I must tell you that everything else will be theirs, since it is unlikely that I shall marry, and if I should, there won't be any children . . . so that . . .'

'Dmitri, please, don't say that,' said Natalia Ivanovna, but Nekhlyudov could see that she was glad to hear what he said.

At the front of the train only a little knot of people stood outside a first-class carriage, all still staring into the compartment into which Princess Korchagina had been carried. Most of the passengers were already in their seats. Latecomers, hurrying, clattered along the wooden boards of the station platform; the guards slammed the doors, calling for the passengers to be seated and those who were seeing them off to come away.

Nekhlyudov entered the sunbaked, hot, smelly carriage, but at once went out on to the small platform at the back.

Natalia Ivanovna, in her fashionable bonnet and wrap, stood with Agrafena Petrovna outside the carriage and appeared to be trying to find something to say, but with no success. She could not even say '*Écrivez*',[1] because she and her brother had always made fun of the injunction so frequently repeated to people starting on a journey. The brief

1. Write.

talk about money matters had at once shattered the tender brotherly and sisterly feeling which had been on the point of taking hold of them; and now they felt estranged. So that Natalia Ivanovna was glad when the train started and she could only say, nodding her head with a sad and affectionate look, 'Good-bye, Dmitri, good-bye!' But no sooner had the carriage gone by than she began thinking out the best way of reporting to her husband the conversation with her brother, and her face became anxious and grave.

Nekhlyudov, too, though he had only the kindest feelings for his sister and never concealed anything from her, now felt depressed and uncomfortable with her and was thankful to escape. He felt that the Natalia who had once been so dear to him no longer existed, leaving only the slave of her husband, that unpleasant, dark, hairy, alien man. He saw this clearly because her face lit up with special animation only when he began speaking of something which interested her husband – that is, when he spoke about giving away the land to the peasants and about the inheritance. And this made him very sad.

40

THE heat in the large crowded third-class carriage, on which the sun had been beating down all day, was so suffocating that Nekhlyudov did not go inside but remained on the brake platform. But even there it was stifling, and Nekhlyudov got a deep breath of air only when the train had left the houses behind and a draught blew across the platform. 'Yes, murdered,' he said to himself, repeating the words he had used to his sister. And, of all the impressions of that day, the handsome face of the second dead convict arose in his imagination with extraordinary vividness – the smiling expression of the lips, the stern forehead and the small firm ear below the shaven bluish skull. 'And the most terrible thing of all is that the man was murdered and no one knows who murdered him. But it was murder. He was brought out, like all the rest of the convicts, on Maslennikov's instructions. Maslennikov probably made out the usual order, putting his stupid florid signature on some formal document with a printed heading, and naturally he won't consider himself responsible. Still less will the careful prison doctor who examined the convicts. He did his duty conscientiously, he picked out the ones who were not strong, and couldn't have been expected to foresee the terrific heat, or that the party would be taken out so late in the day and in such crowded ranks. The prison inspector? But the inspector was only obeying orders to send off a certain number of exiles and convicts of both sexes on a given day. Nor could the officer of the convoy be blamed either, for his business was to receive a certain number of prisoners at such and such a place and deliver the same to such and such a place. He led the party off in the usual manner and according to instructions, and couldn't possibly have guessed that such robust-looking men as the two Nekhlyudov saw would be unable to stand it and would die. Nobody is to blame, and yet the men are dead – murdered by these very men who are not to blame for their deaths.

'All this happened,' Nekhlyudov said to himself, 'because all these people – governors, inspectors, police-officers and policemen – consider that there are circumstances in this world when man owes no humanity to man. Every one of them – Maslennikov, the inspector, the officer of the escort – if he had not been a governor, an inspector, an officer, would have thought twenty times before sending people off in such heat and such a crowd; they would have stopped twenty times on the way if they had noticed a man getting faint and gasping for breath – they would have got him out of the crowd and into the shade, given him water and allowed him to rest, and then if anything had happened they would have shown some pity. They did nothing of the sort: they even prevented others from helping; because they were thinking not of human beings and their obligations towards them but of the duties and responsibilities of their office, which they placed above the demands of human relations. That is the whole truth of the matter,' thought Nekhlyudov. 'If once we admit, be it for a single hour or in a single instance, that there can be anything more important than compassion for a fellow human being, then there is no crime against man that we cannot commit with an easy conscience.'

Nekhlyudov was so absorbed in his thoughts that he did not notice the change in the weather. The sun had disappeared behind a storm-cloud, low and ragged, and advancing from the western horizon another cloud, dense and pearly grey in colour, was emptying slanting, driving rain over the fields and woods in the distance. There was a damp smell of rain in the air, from the overcast sky. From time to time flashes of lightning tore through the clouds and the rumble of thunder mingled more and more frequently with the rumble of the train. The cloud drew steadily nearer, and slanting rain-drops driven by the wind began to spot the platform and Nekhlyudov's coat. He crossed to the other side and breathing in the refreshing moisture and the newly-baked-bread smell of earth that has long been waiting for rain, he stood watching the gardens go gliding past, the woods, the yellowing fields of rye, the lines of oats, still green, and the black furrows between the dark green rows of potatoes in flower. Everything looked as if it had been varnished: the green turning greener, the yellow yellower, the black blacker.

'More, more!' said Nekhlyudov, rejoicing at the sight of fields, gardens and kitchen-gardens reviving under the beneficial rain.

But the heavy rain did not last long. The cloud partly spent itself and partly swept by, and soon the last quick fine drops were falling in straight lines to the moist earth. The sun reappeared, everything began to glisten, while to the east a rainbow with a conspicuous violet band arched over the horizon, not very high but bright and broken at one end only.

'Yes, what was I thinking about?' Nekhlyudov asked himself, when all these changes in nature had come to an end and the train rushed into a cutting with high sloping sides. 'Ah, yes, I remember – I was thinking that all those people: the inspector, the convoy soldiers and all the others in official positions, most of them gentle kindly people, have become bad only because of their office.'

He recalled Maslennikov's indifference when he told him what was going on in the prison, the severity of the inspector, the cruelty of the convoy officer when he was refusing places on the carts to the men who asked for them, and took no notice of the fact that a woman was in travail on the train. All these people were evidently immune and insensible to the simplest feelings of compassion only because they held office. 'As officials they are as impervious to any feeling of pity and humanity as this paved ground is to rain,' thought Nekhlyudov, looking at the sides of the cutting paved with multi-coloured stones down which the rain-water trickled in little streams, instead of soaking into the earth. 'It may be really necessary to pave the embankments with stones, but it is sad to see earth made barren when it might be yielding corn, grass, shrubs and trees like those on top of the cutting. And it is the same thing with men,' reflected Nekhlyudov. 'Perhaps these governors, inspectors, policemen are necessary, but it is terrible to see men devoid of the chief human attribute – love and pity for one another.

'This is what it comes to,' thought Nekhlyudov, 'these people accept as a law something which is not a law, and they do not acknowledge the eternal, immutable, pressing law that God Himself has written in man's heart. That is why I feel so depressed in their company,' thought Nekhlyudov. 'I am quite simply afraid of them. And indeed, they are terrible people – more terrible than brigands. A brigand might, after all, feel pity, but not these men: they are insured against pity as these stones are from vegetation. That is what makes them so terrible. They say Pugachev and Razin[1] were terrible.

1. Leaders of rebellion in Russia: Stenka Razin in the seventeenth century, Pugachev in the eighteenth.

These men are a thousand times worse. Suppose a problem in psychology were set to find means of making people of our time – Christians, humane, simple, kindly people – commit the most horrible crimes without having any feeling of guilt, only one solution would present itself: to do precisely what is being done now, namely, to make them governors, inspectors, officers, policemen and so forth; which means, first, that they must be convinced that there is a thing called government service which allows men to treat other men like inanimate objects, thereby banning all human brotherly relations with them; and secondly, that the people entering this "government service" must be so conjoined that the responsibility for the results of their treatment of people can never fall on any one of them individually. Without these conditions it would be impossible in our times to commit such atrocious deeds as those I have seen today. The whole trouble is that people think there are circumstances when one may deal with human beings without love, but no such circumstances ever exist. Inanimate objects may be dealt with without love: we may fell trees, bake bricks, hammer iron without love. But human beings cannot be handled without love, any more than bees can be handled without care. That is the nature of bees. If you handle bees carelessly you will harm the bees and yourself as well. And so it is with people. And it cannot be otherwise, because mutual love is the fundamental law of human life. It is true that a man cannot force himself to love in the way he can force himself to work, but it does not follow from this that men may be treated without love, especially if something is required from them. If you feel no love – leave people alone,' thought Nekhlyudov, addressing himself. 'Occupy yourself with things, with yourself, with anything you like, only not with men. Just as one can eat without harm and profitably only when one is hungry, so one can usefully and without injury deal with men only when one loves them. But once a man allows himself to treat men unlovingly, as I treated my brother-in-law yesterday, and there are no limits to the cruelty and brutality he may inflict on others – as I saw this morning – and no limits to the suffering he may bring on himself, as the whole of my life proves. Yes, yes, it is so,' thought Nekhlyudov. 'It is true, it is all right,' he repeated to himself again and again, enjoying the two-fold delight of refreshing coolness after the torturing heat and the assurance of having arrived at the clearest possible understanding of a problem that had occupied him for a long time.

<h1 style="text-align:center">41</h1>

THE carriage where Nekhlyudov had a seat was only half full. There were servants, artisans, factory hands, butchers, Jews, shop assistants, women, working-men's wives, besides a soldier and two ladies (one young, the other elderly, with bracelets on her bare arm), and a severe-looking gentleman with a cockade on his black peak-cap. All these people were sitting quietly, once the first bustle of disposing themselves and their belongings was over, some of them cracking sun-flower seeds, some smoking cigarettes, others carrying on animated conversations with their neighbours.

Tarass sat, looking very happy, to the right of the gangway, keeping a place for Nekhlyudov and chatting away in a lively fashion with a brawny man in an unbuttoned sleeveless coat of cloth who sat opposite him – a gardener on his way to a new job, as Nekhlyudov heard later. Before reaching Tarass Nekhlyudov stopped in the passage near a venerable old man with a white beard, in a nankeen coat, who was conversing with a young woman in peasant clothes. At the woman's side sat a little girl of seven in a new sarafan[1] with a braid of almost white hair. Her feet dangled well above the floor and she cracked sunflower seeds all the time. Glancing round at Nekhlyudov, the old man gathered up the folds of his coat to make room for him on the shiny bench which he had to himself, and said in a friendly voice:

1. Russian peasant costume.

'Please, won't you sit here?'

Nekhlyudov thanked him and took the seat he was offered. As soon as he had done so, the woman resumed her interrupted story. She was telling him that she had been to see her husband in the city and was now returning to her village.

'Yes, I was there all Carnival week and now I've been again, the Lord be praised, and God willing I'll go again at Christmas.'

'That's right,' said the old man, with a quick look at Nekhlyudov. 'You must go and see him sometimes else a young man easily goes astray, living in the town.'

'No, grandad, my man's not that sort. There's no nonsense about *him*. He's as clean-living as a young lass. Sends home every kopeck he earns. And he was that glad to see the girl here, I can't tell you how glad,' said the woman, smiling.

Spitting out the husks and listening to her mother, the little girl looked up with calm intelligent eyes into the faces of the old man and Nekhlyudov, as though to confirm what her mother said.

'Well, if his head's screwed on the right way, so much the better,' said the old man. 'None of that sort of thing?' he added, nodding towards a couple, man and wife, evidently factory hands, who were sitting on the other side of the compartment.

The husband with his head thrown back was pouring vodka down his throat out of a bottle, while his wife, holding a bag that had carried the bottle, was staring at him intently.

'No, my man doesn't drink and doesn't smoke either,' said the woman who was conversing with the old man, glad of the chance to speak in praise of her husband again. 'There aren't many in this world the like of him, grandad. That's the kind of man he is,' she said, turning to Nekhlyudov.

'What could be better?' said the old man, watching the factory worker drinking.

Having had his drink, the factory worker passed the bottle to his wife. The wife took the bottle, and laughing and shaking her head also raised it to her lips. Noticing Nekhlyudov and the old man looking at him, the factory worker addressed Nekhlyudov.

'What's the trouble, sir? Because we're having a bit of a drink, is it? When we're working nobody looks at us, but have a drop and everybody's watching. I earn my money, see, and I have a drink and treat the wife. And that's all about it.'

'Yes, yes, I see,' said Nekhlyudov, not knowing what answer to make.

'Isn't that right, sir? The wife here's a good steady woman. I'm thankful for my wife because she can feel for me. Ain't that right, Mavra?'

'There you are, take it, I don't want any more,' said the wife, giving back the bottle. 'And what are you nattering away like a fool for?' she added.

'That's how she is,' continued the man. 'Good as gold one minute and the next squeaking like a wheel that wants greasing. Mavra, ain't that right?'

Mavra, laughing, waved her hand tipsily.

'Oh my, there you go again . . .'

'Aye, she's all right for a time, but just let her get her tail over the reins, and there's no telling what she'll be up to. . . . It's God's truth I'm tellin' you. You must excuse me, sir. I've 'ad a drop, and can't do nothin' about it now . . .' said the factory worker, and began preparing for sleep, laying his head on the lap of his smiling wife.

Nekhlyudov sat on a little longer with the old man, who told him about himself: he was a stove-builder, he said, who had been working for fifty-three years and had built so many stoves in his life, there was no counting them, and now he was minded to take a rest, but couldn't spare the time. He had just been in the city, where he had put his lads to work, and now he was on his way to his village to see the people at home. After hearing the old man's story Nekhlyudov got up and went over to the place that Tarass was keeping for him.

'It's all right, sir; sit down, we'll put the sack here,' said the gardener who was sitting opposite Tarass, in a friendly tone, looking up into Nekhlyudov's face.

'It's a bit of a squeeze, but we'll keep smiling,' said the cheerful Tarass in his sing-song voice, and lifting the sack weighing more than five stone as if it were a feather in his powerful arms he carried it across to the window. 'Lots of room 'ere, besides there'd be no 'arm in standing, or we could have a lie-down under the seat. That's a comfortable place, I can tell you. We won't quarrel about that,' he said, beaming with good nature and affection.

Tarass used to say of himself that unless he had been drinking he could not find words, but that liquor helped him to find the right words and then he could say anything. And it was a fact that when sober Tarass was generally silent, but when he had been drinking, which happened rarely with him and only on special occasions, he became pleasantly talkative. He would then talk a great deal, and well – very simply, truthfully and, above all, with great kindliness, which shone out of his gentle blue eyes and the friendly smile that never left his lips.

He was like this today. Nekhlyudov's arrival silenced him for a moment or two. But, having got rid of the sack, he sat down in his old place and putting his strong work-worn hands on his knees, and looking straight into the gardener's eyes, went on with his story. He was telling his new friend all about his wife – what she was being sent to Siberia for, and why he was now following her.

Nekhlyudov had never heard the details of this affair, and so he listened with interest. The story, when he came in, had reached the point where the poisoning had already happened and the family had found out that it was Fedosya's doing.

'I'm telling 'im about my troubles,' said Tarass, turning to Nekhlyudov with heart-felt friendliness. 'I've fallen in with such a nice man – we got talking and now I'm telling 'im all about it.'

'Yes, of course,' said Nekhlyudov.

'Well, my boy, the thing came to light like this. My mother, she picks up the flat cake, you know, the one I told you about, and "I'm going for the village p'liceman," she says. "Wait a bit, old lady," says my dad – got his head screwed on right, dad 'as. "She's only a child, didn't know what she was doin'. 'Ave a bit of pity, an' she'll come to 'er senses, maybe." But dear me, she would not listen. "She'll poison us like cockroaches, while us keeps 'er 'ere," she says. An' off she goes to the village constable. 'E bounces in upon us 'ot-foot. . . . Starts calling for witnesses.'

'And you, what did you do?' asked the gardener.

'Me, chum, I was rolling about with the pain in me belly, puking right and left. All me innards was coming up, I couldn't so much as speak. So father goes and 'arnesses the mare, puts Fedosya into the cart, and is off to the p'lice-station and then to the magistrate's. And like she 'ad in the very beginning she went and confessed the 'ole story – where she got the arsenic from and 'ow she kneaded the cake. "What made you do it?" says 'e. "'Cos I can't stand the sight of 'im," says she. "I'd be better off in Siberia than living with 'im," she says. She meant with *me*,' said Tarass, with a smile. 'Well, so she confessed the 'ole business. A course they put 'er in gaol straight away. Dad come back alone. And 'arvest time just coming on, and us with no woman to 'elp us, 'cept mother, and she weren't much good. So we think, couldn't we get Fedosya back on bail? Dad went to see the chief, but no luck. Then 'e tried another. 'E saw five that way and was just goin' to give up when 'e stumbled on a clerk – 'e was a sharp one all right. "Give me five roubles," says 'e, "and I'll get 'er out." They settled on three. So I went and pawned the linen cloth she'd woven 'erself and give 'im the money. The second 'e'd written that there paper,' Tarass drawled out, as though he were speaking about a report from a gun, 'it was all right at once. I was up by that time and went to fetch 'er meself. So I goes to town, leaves the mare at the inn, takes the paper and goes to the prison. "What do you want?" – "This an' that," says I, "you've got my old woman locked up 'ere." – " 'Ave you got a paper?" I give 'im the paper right away. 'E 'as a look. "Wait," 'e says. I sits down on a bench. 'Twas gone noon by the sun. Out comes the 'ead man. "Are you Vargushov?" says 'e. "That's me." – "Well, take 'er," says 'e. They opened the gate, there and then, and brought 'er out in 'er own clothes, right an' proper. "Come on, let's go," says I. "Did you walk 'ere?" she says. "No, I come with the mare." So we went to the inn, I settled with the ostler and 'arnessed the mare. The 'ay what was left I shoved under some sacking for Fedosya to sit on. She sat down, wrapped 'er shawl round 'er, and we started. She says naught, and I 'old me tongue. Only when we was gettin' near 'ome, "Is mother all right?" she says. "She is," I says. "And father?" – "All right." – "Forgive me, Tarass," she says, "for that there silliness. I didn't know what I was doing." – "Don't talk so much," says I. "I forgive you long ago." She didn't say no more. When we come 'ome she throws 'erself at mother's feet. "It's over and done with," says mother. And dad welcomes 'er and says, "What's past is past. Now you be'ave yourself. We haven't time for all that now," says 'e. "There's the field to reap. Back of Skorodnoye, on the manured acre, the good Lord 'as given us such a crop of rye you can't get at it with a 'ook – 'tis all tangled up and lying flat. It must be reaped. You and Tarass 'ad better go and see to it tomorrow." Well, friend, from that moment she fair put 'er back into it. 'Twas a sight to see 'er working. In them days seven acres we rented, and the Lord gave us a rare crop both of rye and oats. I would cut with the sickle while she bound the sheaves, or the pair of us would reap. I'm a good worker, I ain't afraid of work, but she be better'n me no matter what she puts 'er 'and to. She's a stayer, and young too, in 'er prime. And as to work, chum, she'd grown that eager, there was no 'olding 'er. When we come 'ome of a night, our fingers was swollen, our arms ached, but she'd be out in the barn, without waiting for supper, to make binds for the sheaves next day. A different woman she were, I can tell you!'

'And did she treat you any better?' asked the gardener.

'I should say so! Clung to me like we was one mortal together. I thinks of something, and there – she's on it. Even mother, fair cranky as she were, even she would be saying: "Our Fedosya acts different. A changed woman, she be." Once we was after fetchin' in the sheaves. Two carts, an' me and 'er sittin' side by side in the first one. And I says to 'er: "What made you do it, Fedosya?" And she says: "I done it 'cos I didn't want to live with you. I'd rather die, I thinks, than live with you." – "And now?" I asks 'er. "Now," she says, "you be my sweet'eart."' Tarass stopped, smiling with happiness, and shook his head in amazement. 'One day we got back from the field, I took the flax to be steeped, I comes 'ome' – he paused for a moment – 'what do you think, there was a summons. *Appear in court*, it said. And we'd clean forgotten the business she were to be tried for.'

' 'Twas the doing of the Evil One,' said the gardener. 'No man of himself would ever take it into his head to go and destroy a living soul. There was a man in our village once . . .' and the gardener was about to begin on a story when the train started slowing down.

'I reckon 'tis a station,' he said. 'I'm going to get a drink of water.'

The conversation broke off, and Nekhlyudov followed the gardener out of the carriage on to the wet platform.

42

WHILE still on the train Nekhlyudov had noticed several elegant carriages in the station yard, some drawn by four, some by three well-fed horses with tinkling bells on their harness. As he stepped out on to the wet platform, which looked black from the rain, he saw a little knot of people in front of the first-class carriages; conspicuous among them were a tall stout lady wearing a waterproof coat and a hat expensively trimmed with feathers, and a lanky spindle-legged youth in a bicycling suit, with an enormous well-fed dog with an expensive collar by his side. Behind them stood footmen holding wraps and umbrellas, and a coachman, who had come to meet the train. The whole group, from the stout lady down to the coachman holding up with one hand the skirts of his long coat, was stamped with the seal of wealth and quiet self-assurance. An inquisitive and servile crowd rapidly gathered round the little party – the station-master in a red cap, a gendarme, a thin young woman in Russian peasant dress, with glass beads, of the type one sees on every railway-station during the summer, a telegraph clerk and various men and women passengers.

In the youth with the dog Nekhlyudov recognized young Korchagin, the high-school boy. The stout lady was the princess's sister, to whose estate the Korchagins were now on their way. The guard, in gold braid and shiny top-boots, opened the door of the railway carriage and, in token of respect, stood holding it open, while Philip and a porter with a white apron carefully lifted out the long-faced princess in her folding chair. The sisters greeted each other and then, after some talk in French as to whether the princess should go in a closed or an open carriage, the procession started towards the exit, the lady's maid with her ringlets, parasols and the band-box bringing up the rear.

Not wishing to meet them and have to say good-bye all over again, Nekhlyudov stopped a short distance from the door, waiting for the procession to pass. The princess, her son, Missy, the doctor and the maid went first, while the old prince lingered to talk to his sister-in-law, and Nekhlyudov was too far off to catch more than one or two disconnected sentences of their conversation, which was in French. As often happens, one sentence spoken by the prince for some unaccountable reason remained in his memory, with every tone and inflection of the voice.

'Oh, *il est du vrai grand monde, du vrai grand monde,*'[1] the prince was saying of someone, in his loud self-confident voice, as he walked through the station door with his sister-in-law, followed by the respectful railway guards and porters.

Just at that moment, from round a corner of the station a gang of workmen in bast shoes appeared on the platform, carrying sheepskin coats and sacks over their shoulders. With quiet but determined steps they went up to the nearest carriage and were about to climb in when a guard immediately drove them off. Without stopping they passed on to the next carriage, hurrying and treading on each other's heels, and began getting in, their sacks catching against the corners and door of the carriage; but another guard noticed them from the station exit and shouted at them angrily. The men, who by now were already inside, hurried out again and went on with the same silent firm steps to the next carriage – the one where Nekhlyudov had his seat. The guard stopped them again. They were on the point of leaving, meaning to continue farther along, but Nekhlyudov told them there was room in the carriage and invited them in. They did as he said, and Nekhlyudov followed them. The workmen were about to find places for themselves, but the gentleman with the cockade and the two ladies, taking the attempt to settle in their carriage as a personal affront, protested indignantly and wanted to turn them out. The men – there were about twenty of them, some elderly, some quite young, all of them with haggard, sunburnt, weather-beaten faces – began at once to push their way down the centre of the coach, catching against the seats, partitions and doors with their sacks. They evidently felt they were in the wrong and seemed ready to go on to the world's end and sit wherever anyone told them to, even on a bed of nails.

'Where are you devils shoving to? Sit down where you are!' shouted another guard, coming towards them from the opposite direction.

1. Oh, he is of the best society, the best society.

'*Voilà encore des nouvelles!*'[1] exclaimed the younger of the two ladies, quite sure that she would attract Nekhlyudov's attention with her excellent French. But the lady with the bracelets only sniffed and made a face, and said something about the delights of sitting in the same carriage with smelly peasants.

The workmen, experiencing the joy and relief of people who have escaped great danger, stopped and began to settle themselves, releasing the heavy sacks from their backs with a jerk of their shoulders, and stowing them away under the seats.

The gardener, who had left his own seat to talk to Tarass, now went back, which left three empty places – two opposite and one next to him. Three of the workmen took them, but when Nekhlyudov came up, the sight of his fine clothes made them feel so uncomfortable that they got to their feet as if to go; Nekhlyudov, though, asked them to stay, and himself sat on the arm of the seat next to the passage.

One of the workmen, a man of about fifty, exchanged a surprised and even dismayed look with a younger man. It perplexed and astonished them that Nekhlyudov, instead of abusing them and driving them away, the natural thing for a gentleman to do, should give up his seat to them. They were even afraid that this might have some evil consequences. But when they saw there was nothing sinister behind it, and heard Nekhlyudov chatting in a simple manner with Tarass, they ceased to worry, told a youngster to sit on his sack, and insisted on Nekhlyudov having his place back. At first the elderly workman opposite Nekhlyudov made himself as small as possible, tucking back his feet in their bast shoes for fear of touching the gentleman, but after a while he entered into such a friendly chat with Nekhlyudov and Tarass that he went so far as to slap Nekhlyudov on the knee with the back of his hand whenever he reached a point in his story to which he was especially eager to draw his attention. He told them

1. This is something new!

all about himself and his work in the peat bogs, whence he and his comrades were now returning, having worked there for two and a half months. They were taking home their wages, ten roubles a head, since part had been paid in advance when they were engaged. They worked up to their knees in water, he told them, from sunrise to sunset, with two hours off for dinner.

'For them as ain't used to it, it's 'ard, of course,' he said. 'But if you stick it, it ain't too bad. But the grub's gotter be proper grub. At first the grub was bad. But after the chaps objected, it got better and workin' was easier.'

Then he told them how for twenty-eight years he had gone out to work and sent all his earnings home: first to his father, then to his elder brother, and now to his nephew, who looked after the family holding. On himself he spent only two or three roubles out of the fifty or sixty he earned a year: they went on luxuries – tobacco and matches.

'But I'm a sinner I am – I takes a nip of vodka now and then when I'm dead-beat,' he added, with a guilty smile.

He told them, too, how the women managed things at home; and how the contractor had stood them half a bucketful of vodka[1] that morning when they left; how one of the men had died and another was coming back ill. The sick man of whom he spoke was in a corner of the same carriage. He was a young fellow with an ashen face and blue lips, evidently spent with malaria. Nekhlyudov went over, but the lad looked up at him with such a stiff suffering face that Nekhlyudov did not like to worry him with questions but advised the elderly workman to buy him quinine, and wrote the name of the medicine down on a piece of paper. He wanted to give him some money, but the elderly workman said he would pay for it himself.

'Well, I bin about a bit, but I never come across a gentleman the likes of 'im afore,' he said to Tarass. ''Stead of a

1. About ten pints.

punch on the nut he goes and gives up 'is seat to yer. Seemingly there's gentlefolk and gentlefolk.'

'Yes, this is quite another – a new, a different world,' Nekhlyudov was thinking, looking at the spare muscular limbs, the coarse home-made clothes and the sunburnt, kindly, weary faces, and feeling himself surrounded on all sides by people who were quite novel to him, with the serious interests and the joys and sufferings of a life of labour that was real and human.

'Here it is – this is *le vrai grand monde*,' thought Nekhlyudov, remembering the words Prince Korchagin had used, and all the idle luxurious world to which the Korchagins belonged, with their paltry contemptible interests.

And he felt the joy of a traveller discovering a new, unfamiliar and beautiful world.

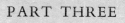

PART THREE

1

MASLOVA'S gang of prisoners travelled for about three thousand miles. As far as Perm she went by rail and steamboat with the other prisoners sentenced for criminal offences, and it was only at this town that Nekhlyudov succeeded in having her transferred to the 'political' group, as Vera Bogodoukhovskaya, herself with the politicals, had advised him to do.

The journey to Perm had been very trying for Maslova, both physically and morally: physically, because of the overcrowding, the filth and the disgusting vermin which gave her no peace; and morally, because of the no less disgusting men who, though some got out and new ones got in at every stop, swarmed round and stuck to her, giving her no peace, like the vermin. Habits of cynical debauchery were so firmly established among the women convicts, men convicts, warders and soldiers of the escort that unless a woman was willing to prostitute herself she had to be constantly on her guard, especially if she were a young woman. And this continual state of fear, and always having to fight to keep men off, was very wearing; and Maslova was one of those who suffered most from such attacks, her appearance being attractive and her past known to everyone. The determined resistance with which she met the men who pestered her was taken as a direct insult and, in addition, roused a feeling of resentment against her. In this respect her position was made a little easier by her friendship with Fedosya and Tarass, who, on learning of the molestations his wife was subject to, had got himself arrested so that he could protect her, and from Nizhni onwards had travelled as a convict with the others.

Maslova's transfer to the party of political prisoners made

her position much more bearable in every way. To say nothing of the fact that the politicals were provided with better accommodation and better food, and were less roughly treated, her condition was improved in that she no longer had to suffer annoyance from men, and could live without being reminded at every turn of that past she was so anxious to forget now. But the main advantage of the change was that she met some people whose influence on her was definitely most beneficial.

Whenever they came to a halting-place Maslova was allowed to be with the political prisoners, but as she was a strong healthy woman she had to march with the criminal convicts. Thus the whole journey from Tomsk she made on foot. Two of the politicals also marched with her, Marya Pavlovna Shchetinina, the pretty girl with the gentle eyes of a sheep who had so impressed Nekhlyudov when he visited Bogodoukhovskaya in prison, and a certain Simonson, the dishevelled dark young fellow with deep-set eyes whom Nekhlyudov had also noticed during the same visit and who was being deported to the Yakutsk region. Marya Pavlovna went on foot because she had given up her place on the cart to a woman criminal who was pregnant; and Simonson because he did not think it right to avail himself of a class privilege. These three used to set off in the early morning with the convicts, leaving the other politicals to start later in the day and follow by cart. This, then, was the arrangement at the last halting-place before they arrived at a big town where a new convoy officer took charge of the party.

It was early on a wet September morning. It snowed and it rained, and a cold wind blew in gusts. All the convicts in the party – about four hundred men and around fifty women – were already assembled in the yard of the halting-place, some of them crowding round the chief of the convoy, who was distributing money for two days' rations to orderlies chosen from among the prisoners; others were bargaining with the women-hawkers who had been admitted into the yard to sell food. The voices of the prisoners counting their money and making purchases mingled with the shrill treble of the women-vendors.

Katusha and Marya Pavlovna, both wearing knee-boots and short sheepskin coats, with shawls over their heads, came out of the building into the courtyard, where the hawkers sat sheltered from the wind, under the north wall of the yard, vying with one another in offering their goods: freshly baked pasties made of sifted flour, fish, vermicelli, buckwheat porridge, liver, beef, eggs and milk; one even had a roast pig to sell.

Simonson, in a waterproof jacket and rubber galoshes tied with string over his worsted stockings (he was a vegetarian and did not use the skin of slaughtered animals), was also in the yard waiting for the party to start. Standing by the porch, he was jotting down in his notebook a thought that had just occurred to him: 'If a bacillus were to observe and examine a human finger-nail, it would pronounce it to be inorganic matter. Similarly we, after observing the earth's crust, declare the terrestrial globe to be inorganic matter. This is not correct.'

Having bought eggs, a string of thick ring-shaped rolls, fish and fresh white bread, Maslova was packing them all into a sack while Marya Pavlovna paid the hawkers, when there was a stir among the prisoners. Everyone stopped talking and began to take their places for the march. The officer came out and gave the final orders before they started.

Everything proceeded as usual: the prisoners were counted, the chains on their legs inspected, and the men handcuffed in pairs. But suddenly the officer was heard shouting angrily. This was followed by the sound of blows falling on a human body, and the crying of a child. For a moment there was a hush, and then a hollow murmur ran through the crowd. Maslova and Marya Pavlovna went towards the spot the noise was coming from.

2

THIS is what Marya Pavlovna and Katusha saw when they reached the scene: the officer, a thick-set man with big fair moustaches, was frowning and rubbing the palm of his right hand which he had hurt in striking a convict in the face, and all the time shouting coarse words of abuse. Before him stood a tall emaciated convict in a short prison cloak and still shorter trousers, one half of whose head was shaven. He was wiping his bleeding face with one hand and holding a shrieking little girl wrapped in a shawl with the other.

'I'll teach you' – some foul words – 'to argue' – more foul words. 'Give her to the women,' shouted the officer. 'Put them on.'

The officer was insisting that one of the convicts – a man exiled by his village commune – should be manacled. He had been carrying his little daughter in his arms all the way from Tomsk, where his wife had died of typhus. His plea that he could not carry the child if he were handcuffed so irritated the officer, who happened to be in a bad temper, that he gave the convict a beating for not obeying at once.[1]

A convoy soldier stood near the prisoner who had been thrashed, together with a black-bearded man with manacles on one hand, cheerlessly looking from under his brows, now at the officer, now at the prisoner who had been beaten, and the little girl. The officer repeated his command to the soldier to take the child away. The murmur among the prisoners grew louder.

'He walked all the way from Tomsk without handcuffs,' said a hoarse voice from the back of the crowd.

'It's not a pup, it's a child.'

'What's he to do with the girl?'

'That's not the law,' said someone else.

1. An incident described by D. A. Linyev in *Transportation*. – L. N. Tolstoy.

'Who said that?' shouted the officer, rushing into the crowd as though he had been stung. 'I'll teach you the law! Who said it? You? You?'

'We all say it, because –' began a stocky broad-faced convict.

Before he could finish the officer started hitting him in the face with both hands.

'Mutiny, is it? I'll show you what mutiny means. I'll have you shot like dogs. The authorities will only thank me for it. Take the girl!'

Silence fell upon the crowd. The soldier pulled away the child, who was screaming desperately, while another manacled the prisoner, now submissively holding out his hand.

'Take her to the women,' shouted the officer, readjusting his sword-belt.

The little girl, red in the face and struggling to free her hands from under the shawl, screamed and screamed. Marya Pavlovna stepped forward from the crowd and went up to the officer.

'Let me carry the little girl, sir.'

The soldier who had the little girl halted.

'Who are you?' asked the officer.

'I am a political.'

Apparently Marya Pavlovna's pretty face with the lovely prominent eyes (he had noticed her on taking over the gang) had an effect on the officer. He looked at her in silence, as though deliberating.

'You carry her if you like; it makes no difference to me. It's all very well for you to be sorry for them, but who'd be responsible if the man escaped?'

'How could he run away with the child in his arms?' said Marya Pavlovna.

'I've no time to stay talking. Take her if you want to.'

'Shall I hand her over, sir?' asked the soldier.

'Yes, hand her over.'

'Come to me,' said Marya Pavlovna, trying to coax the child to her.

But the child in the soldier's arms went on screaming and reaching out for her father, and would not go to Marya Pavlovna.

'Wait a moment, Marya Pavlovna, she will come to me,' said Maslova, getting a bread-ring out of her sack.

The little girl knew Maslova and when she saw her face and the round ring of bread she let herself be taken.

Everything was quiet again. The gates were opened, the party walked out and drew up in rows; the soldiers counted them once more; the sacks were roped on to the carts, and the prisoners who were ill seated on top of them. Maslova with the child in her arms returned to the women and stood beside Fedosya. Simonson, who had all the time been watching what was happening, strode determinedly up to the officer just as he had finished giving his orders and was about to climb into his trap.

'That was wrong of you, sir,' said Simonson.

'Get back to your place, it is none of your business.'

'It is my business to tell you that it was wrong of you, and I have told you,' said Simonson, looking the officer full in the face from under his bushy eyebrows.

'Ready? Party – forward, march!' shouted the officer, paying no heed to Simonson; and leaning on his driver's shoulder, he climbed into the trap.

The gang of convicts moved off, spreading into a straggling column on the muddy road separated by ditches from dense forest on either side.

3

AFTER her six years of depraved, luxurious, indulgent living in the city and two months spent in prison among criminals, life with the politicals seemed very pleasant to Katusha, despite all its hardships. The daily marches of fifteen to twenty miles, with good food and a day's rest after every two days on the road, strengthened her physically; while contact with her new companions opened out a life full of interests such as she had never dreamed of. She had not only never met – she could not even have imagined – such *wonderful* people (to use her own word) as those she was now marching with.

'There now, and to think that I cried when I was sentenced!' she would say. 'Why, I must thank God for it to the end of my days. I have learned things I should never have heard of in a whole lifetime otherwise.'

The motives that guided them, she understood easily and without effort, and being of the people herself fully sympathized with them. She understood that her new friends were with the masses against the masters, and, though themselves belonging to the gentry, were sacrificing their privileges, their liberty and their lives for the people, and this made her esteem and admire them all the more.

She was delighted with all her new companions, but the one whom she particularly worshipped and loved with a peculiar, respectful and rapturous feeling was Marya Pavlovna. She was impressed by the fact that this beautiful girl, who belonged to the family of a rich general and could speak three languages, lived like an ordinary working woman and gave away everything that her wealthy brother sent her; the clothes and the shoes she wore were not just simple – they were of quite poor quality – and she devoted no thought to her appearance. This trait in her – a complete absence of coquetry – was particularly surprising and therefore attractive to Maslova. She could see that Marya Pavlovna knew and even liked knowing that she was beautiful, but far from enjoying the impression she made on men she was frightened of it, and was disgusted and horrified by affairs of the heart. Her male companions, aware of this, if they felt drawn to her dared not show their admiration but treated her as they would have treated a man. But strangers frequently pestered her with their attentions, and here, she said, her great physical strength on which she prided herself stood her in good stead.

'Once,' she told Katusha with a laugh, 'a gentleman followed me in the street, and would not leave me alone. At last I gave him such a shaking that he took fright and ran!'

She had become a revolutionary, she said, because from early childhood she had hated the way the upper classes lived, and loved the life of the common people, and was always being scolded for spending her time in the maids' room or the kitchen or the stables, instead of in the drawing-room.

'But it was fun being with the cooks and grooms, and very dull with the ladies and gentlemen,' she said. 'Then, when I began to understand things, I saw that our life was wrong. I had no mother, I wasn't fond of my father, and at nineteen I left home and went off with a friend to work in a factory.'

After the factory she had gone to live in a village, then come back to the town, to lodgings where there was a secret printing-press, and there she was arrested and sentenced to hard labour. Marya Pavlovna said nothing about it herself, but Katusha heard from the others that she had been sentenced to hard labour because she had pleaded guilty to a charge of shooting, although in fact it was one of the revolutionaries who had fired in the darkness while the police were searching the lodgings.

From the day that Katusha first met her she noticed that wherever she was, and whatever her circumstances, she never thought of herself, but was only concerned about other people and how she could help them, in big things as well as small. One of her companions of the party, Novodvorov, jestingly remarked of her that her favourite sport was charity. And this was true. Just as the hunter is bent on finding game, so the whole interest of her life lay in searching for opportunities to serve others. And this sport had become a habit, had become the business of her life. And she did it all so naturally that those who knew her had come to expect it of her and no longer appreciated it.

When Maslova joined the party Marya Pavlovna felt aversion, even disgust for her. Katusha noticed this but she also noticed that, having made an effort over herself, Marya Pavlovna became especially friendly and kind. And friendliness and kindness from such a remarkable being so touched Maslova that she surrendered her whole heart to her, unconsciously adopting Marya Pavlovna's views and involuntarily imitating her in everything. This devotion of Katusha's moved Marya Pavlovna, and she began to love Katusha, too.

The two women were also drawn together by the loathing they both felt for sexual love. One hated it because she knew all its horrors, while the other, having never experienced it, regarded it as something incomprehensible and at the same time repugnant and offensive to human dignity.

4

MARYA PAVLOVNA's influence was one of the influences to which Maslova surrendered herself. It sprang from Maslova's affection for Marya Pavlovna. The other influence was that of Simonson, which sprang from the fact that Simonson loved Maslova.

People live and act partly according to their own ideas, and partly because they are influenced by the ideas of others. The extent to which they do the one or the other is one of the chief things that differentiate men. Some people mostly only play at thinking: their minds are like a fly-wheel from which the driving-belt has been removed; their actions are determined by other people's ideas – by custom, by tradition, by laws. Others on the contrary, regarding their personal ideas as the chief motive power of all their activities, nearly always listen to the dictates of their own reason and submit to it, accepting other people's opinions only occasionally, and then only after considering them critically. Simonson belonged to the second of these types. He weighed and tested everything according to his own lights, and acted on the decisions thus arrived at.

Having come to the conclusion, while still a schoolboy, that his father's income as administrator in a government department was dishonestly earned, he told his father that he ought to give it back to the people. And when his father, far from following this advice, rated him soundly for his foolishness, he left home, refusing any longer to accept his father's assistance. Deciding that all the evil in the world arises out of ignorance, he joined up with the People's Party as soon as he left the university, became a village school-master and boldly taught and explained to his pupils and to the peasants what he considered to be just, and condemned what he considered false.

He was arrested and tried.

During his trial he came to the conclusion that his judges had no right to sit in judgement upon him, and told them so. When the judges ignored what he said and continued the trial he decided not to answer their questions, and remained resolutely silent. They exiled him to the Province of Arch-angel. There he formulated a religious teaching which governed all his activity. According to this doctrine every-thing in the world is alive; there is no inert body, but every-thing hitherto termed lifeless, 'inorganic' matter is simply part of an immense organic body which we cannot compre-hend, and that the task of man, as a particle of that huge organism, is to preserve its life and that of all its living parts. Therefore he considered it a crime to destroy life, and was opposed to war, capital punishment and killing of every sort, not only of human beings but of animals too. He also had a theory of his own in regard to marriage: to increase and multiply seemed to him only a lower function of man, the higher function being to serve all already existing life. He found a confirmation of this idea in the presence of phagocytes in the blood. Celibates, according to him, were like phago-cytes, whose mission it is to strengthen the weak, diseased parts of the organism. From the moment he came to this conclusion he lived accordingly, though as a youth he had led a dissolute life. He regarded himself now, and also Marya Pavlovna, as phagocytes in the body of the universe.

His love for Katusha did not impair this theory, since he loved her platonically, believing that such a love could not interfere with his activity as a phagocyte, but, on the contrary, would still further inspire his efforts on behalf of the weak.

But moral problems were not the only ones that he decided in this original way: he had theories of his own concerning most practical questions, too. He had a theory for every practical affair: he had rules for the number of hours a man should work and rest, the kind of food he should eat, the kind of clothes he should wear, the proper form of heating and lighting for a house, and so on.

At the same time Simonson was exceedingly shy with people, and modest. But once he made up his mind nothing could shake him.

This, then, was the man who had a decisive influence on Maslova, through his love for her. With a woman's instinct Maslova very soon divined the state of affairs, and the knowledge that she could awaken love in such an unusual man raised her in her own estimation. Nekhlyudov's offer of marriage was due to generosity and what had happened in the past, but Simonson loved her as she was now, and loved her simply because he loved her. Moreover, she felt that Simonson looked upon her as a woman out of the ordinary, different from all other women, and having certain special, high moral qualities. She did not exactly know what these qualities he attributed to her might be, but, in order to be on the safe side and not disappoint him, she tried with all her might to summon up in herself the best qualities she could think of. And this compelled her to be as good as she knew how to be.

All this had started back in the prison, on a general visiting day for the politicals, when she had become aware of the peculiarly persistent look he fixed on her with his guileless, kindly dark-blue eyes under the overhanging forehead and eyebrows. Even then she had noticed what a strange man he was and how strangely he looked at her, and had remarked the striking combination in one face of severity, emphasized by hair sticking up on end and frowning brows, with good-nature and child-like innocence. Later, at Tomsk, after she had been transferred to the politicals, she saw him again. And though not a word passed between them, the look they exchanged was an admission that they remembered each other and were important to each other. They never had any serious conversation even after that, but Maslova felt that whenever he was talking in her presence his words were meant for her, and that he spoke for her sake, trying to express himself as clearly as possible. It was when he started walking with the criminal prisoners that they began to grow specially near to one another.

5

UNTIL they left Perm Nekhlyudov succeeded only twice in seeing Katusha: once in Nizhni, before the prisoners were embarked on a barge surrounded with wire-netting, and again at Perm in the prison office. Both times he found her secretive and ill-disposed. When he asked her if she was comfortable or if she needed anything, she replied evasively, in the awkward and what seemed to him hostile, reproachful way which he had noticed in her before. Her depressed state of mind, which was only the result of the annoyance to which she was being subjected by men at that time, distressed Nekhlyudov. He feared that the exhausting and degrading circumstances in which she was placed during the journey might cause her to fall into her old state of inner conflict and despair which had made her so irritable with him and caused her to drink and smoke in the hope of forgetting her troubles. But he was unable to help her in any way during this first part of the journey, for he could never see her. It was only after her transfer to the politicals that he not only realized how unfounded his fears were but at each subsequent meeting with her noticed that inner change he so strongly desired to see in her becoming more and more marked. Indeed, the first time they met in Tomsk she was her old self again, as she had been before the departure from Moscow. She did not scowl or become embarrassed when she saw him, but greeted him happily and naturally, thanking him for what he had done, especially for having given her the chance to know the people she was now with.

After two months with the marching party the change that had taken place in her was reflected in her looks. She was thinner and sunburnt, and seemed older; little wrinkles had appeared on her temples and round her mouth, she no longer let her hair fall over her forehead but covered it with a kerchief, and neither in her dress, nor in the way she arranged her hair, nor in her manner was there any trace of her former coquetry. And this change which had taken place and was still in progress in her made Nekhlyudov exceedingly happy.

He now felt towards her something he had never felt before. The feeling had nothing in common with his early sense of romantic exaltation, still less with the sensual love which he had experienced later on, nor even with the satisfaction of a duty fulfilled (not unmixed with self-admiration) which had led him after the trial to decide to marry her. This feeling was the quite uncomplicated feeling of pity and tenderness he had felt for the first time on seeing her in prison, and later, with renewed strength, after the hospital when, curbing his disgust, he forgave her for the supposed incident with the doctor's assistant (the injustice of which had come to light afterwards). It was the same feeling, but with this difference: once it had been transitory, but now it was constant. Whatever he happened to be thinking of, whatever he was doing, his general mood now was one of pity and tenderness, not only towards Maslova but towards the whole world.

It was as if this feeling had released a spring of love in Nekhlyudov's heart, which till then had found no outlet, but now flowed out to everyone he met.

Throughout the whole journey Nekhlyudov was aware of a sort of exaltation in himself which automatically made him attentive and considerate to everybody, from coachman and convoy soldier to prison inspector and governor, with whom he came in contact.

With Maslova's transfer to the politicals Nekhlyudov naturally became acquainted with many of them, first in Ekaterinburg, where they enjoyed a good deal of freedom, being all kept together in one big cell, and later, on the road, with the five men and four women whose party she joined. Coming into contact with political exiles in this way completely altered Nekhlyudov's opinions concerning them.

From the very beginning of the revolutionary movement in Russia, and particularly after the 1st of March,[1] Nekhlyudov had regarded the revolutionaries with dislike and contempt. To begin with, he was repelled by the cruelty and secrecy of the methods they employed in their struggle against the Government, and, above all, by the brutality of the murders they committed; he also disliked the overbearing self-assurance that was common to all of them. But when he came to know them more intimately and heard what they had suffered at the hands of the Government, often for no reason, he saw that they could not be other than they were.

Terrible and senseless as were the torments inflicted on the so-called 'criminal' prisoners, there was at least some semblance of justice in the treatment they received both before and after sentence; but in respect to the political prisoners even that semblance was missing, as Nekhlyudov had seen in the case of Lydia Shustova, and was later to see in the cases of many of his new friends. These people were like

1 On 1 March 1881 the Emperor Alexander II was wounded as he rode in his carriage in Petersburg, dying in the Winter Palace the same day.

fish taken in a net: the whole catch is landed, the big fish are sorted out and the little ones left to perish unheeded on the shore. Similarly, hundreds of people, who were obviously not merely innocent but who could in no way be dangerous to the Government, were arrested and held in prison, often for years, in places where they became consumptive, went insane or took their own lives; and they were kept in prison only because there was no special reason for releasing them, whereas, safe in prison, they might possibly turn out to be useful as witnesses. The fate of these people – often innocent even from the Government point of view – depended on the whim, leisure or humour of some police-officer or spy or public prosecutor, or magistrate or governor or minister. If one of these officials happened to feel bored or was anxious to attract the limelight – he would make a number of arrests, and then, according to his fancy or that of a superior, either keep his prisoners locked up or set them free. And the higher official in his turn, depending on whether he needs to distinguish himself, or the terms he is on with his minister, either exiles them to the other end of the earth, keeps them in solitary confinement, condemns them to Siberia, to hard labour, to death, or lets them go if some lady or other asks him to.

The political offenders were treated like enemies in wartime, and they naturally used the same methods that were used against them. And just as soldiers take their tone from public opinion which not only conceals from them the guilt of their actions but represents these actions as feats of heroism, so these political offenders were likewise constantly affected by the opinions of their own circle where the cruelties they commit at the risk of liberty, life and all that is dear to man seem not wicked but glorious. This explained for Nekhlyudov the astounding fact that the mildest of men, incapable by nature of causing or even witnessing the suffering of any living creature, could calmly prepare to kill people; almost all of them considering murder lawful and just in certain circumstances: in self-defence or as a means of promoting the general welfare. As to the importance they set on their cause (and consequently on themselves), this was the natural result of the concern shown by the Government and of the cruelty of the punishments it inflicted on them. They had to have a high opinion of themselves to be able to bear what they had to bear.

When he came to know them better Nekhlyudov was satisfied that they were neither the thorough-going criminals some people imagined them to be, nor the hundred per cent heroes that others thought them, but were quite ordinary men, among whom, as anywhere else, there were good, bad and mediocre individuals. There were some among them who had turned revolutionary because they honestly considered it their duty to fight the evils of their time; but there were others who chose this activity from selfish, ambitious motives. The majority, however, had been attracted to revolutionary ideas by a thirst for danger, for risk, and the exhilaration of gambling with one's life – feelings which, as Nekhlyudov knew from his own experience in the regiment, are quite common to the most ordinary people while they are young and full of energy. The revolutionaries differed favourably from ordinary people in that their moral standards were higher. Temperance, frugal living, honesty and unselfishness were binding principles for them, and they went farther and included a readiness to sacrifice everything, even life itself, for the common cause. Those among them, therefore, who were above the average run stood very high above it and afforded rare examples of moral excellence; while those who were below the average stood far below it, many of them being untruthful, hypocritical and at the same time conceited and arrogant. So that Nekhlyudov felt not only respect but whole-hearted affection for some of his new acquaintances, while to others he remained more than indifferent.

6

NEKHLYUDOV grew particularly fond of a consumptive young man, one Kryltsov, who was being deported to hard labour and was with the party Katusha had joined. Nekhlyudov had met him for the first time at Ekaterinburg and after that had seen him on the march and had several talks with him. Once during the summer they spent nearly a whole day together at a halting-station, and Kryltsov, growing more and more communicative, told Nekhlyudov his whole story and explained why he had become a revolutionary. Up to the time of his imprisonment there was not much to tell. His father, a wealthy landowner in the southern provinces of Russia, had died when he, Kryltsov, was still a child. He was an only son, brought up by his mother. Study came very easily to him, both at school and at the university, and he graduated top in the mathematical faculty of his year. He was offered a university lectureship and the chance of travelling abroad. But he hesitated. There was a girl he was in love with and he was thinking of marriage and of taking an active part in rural administration. He wanted everything and could not make up his mind on anything in particular. At this point some fellow students asked him for a contribution to 'the cause'. He knew that this 'cause' meant the revolutionary cause, in which at that time he took no interest whatever, but, out of comradeship and pride (lest it should be thought he was afraid), he gave them money. Those who had collected the money were caught, a note was found showing that money had been given by Kryltsov; he was arrested, kept for a while at the police-station and then sent to prison.

'The discipline was not particularly strict in that prison,' Kryltsov told Nekhlyudov (he was sitting on the high sleeping bunk, with his sunken chest and his elbows on his knees, the beautiful wise kind eyes with which he looked at Nekhlyudov glittering feverishly). 'We not only tapped on the walls to each other but we could walk about the corridors and talk, share our provisions and tobacco, and in the evenings we even sang in chorus. I had a good voice. Yes, if it hadn't been for my mother, who was overcome with grief, it would have been all right in prison, even pleasant and interesting. It was there I met the famous Petrov (he later cut his throat with a piece of glass in the Fortress) and other revolutionaries, too. But I was not one myself. I also got to know my two neighbours in the cells next to mine. They had both been caught in the same affair, and arrested with Polish proclamations in their possession, and were to be tried for attempting to escape from the convoy while being taken to the railway-station. One was a Pole called Lozinski, and the other, Rozovski, was a Jew. Yes. Well, this Rozovski was quite a boy. He said he was seventeen, but he did not look more than fifteen. Small and slender, with bright black eyes, full of life, and very musical like most Jews. His voice was still breaking, but he sang beautifully. Yes. I saw them both taken to be tried. They were taken in the morning. At night they returned and told us they had been sentenced to death. No one had expected this. Their case was so unimportant: they had only tried to get away from the escort and hadn't even hurt anyone. And besides, it seemed so unnatural to execute a child like Rozovski. And all of us in the prison decided that it was only to scare them, and the sentence would never be confirmed. We were very agitated at first, but then we calmed down and prison life went on as before. Yes. Only one evening the watchman came to my door and told me mysteriously that the carpenters had come and were putting up the gallows. At first I did not understand what he meant – what gallows? But the old watchman was so upset that when I looked at him I realized it was for our two. I wanted to tap out a message to the others, but was afraid those two would hear. The other prisoners were also silent. Apparently everybody knew. There was dead silence all that evening in the corridor and in the cells. We did not tap or sing. About ten o'clock the watchman came again and said that the hangman had arrived from Moscow. He said this and went away. I began calling him back. Suddenly I heard Rozovski shout to me from his cell across the corridor: "What do you want? Why are you calling him?" I said something about his bringing me some tobacco, but he seemed to guess something was wrong and started asking me why there was no singing, why we didn't tap on the walls. I don't remember how I answered, but I stepped back quickly so as to avoid speaking to him. Yes. It was a terrible night. I listened all night long to every sound. Suddenly, towards morning, I heard doors opening and footsteps – a lot of footsteps – along the passage. I went and stood at the slit in my door. There was a lamp burning in the corridor. The chief warder went by first. He was a big fat man and usually seemed self-confident and determined. But now he looked awful: pale, his head hanging down, and sort of frightened. Behind him was his assistant – frowning, with a grim look; and after him the guard. They passed my door and halted outside the next cell, and I heard the assistant calling out in a strange voice: "Get up, Lozinski, and put on clean linen!" Yes. Then I heard the door creak as they went into the cell. Then I heard Lozinski's steps crossing to the opposite side of the corridor. I could only see the chief warder. Pale as a man could be, he stood buttoning and unbuttoning his coat and shrugging his shoulders. Yes. Suddenly he acted as though something had scared him, and stepped out of the way. It was Lozinski, who went past him and stopped at my door. A handsome young fellow he was, you know, that fine Polish type, with a straight broad forehead, a mass of fair curly hair like silk, and beautiful blue eyes. So full of vigour and health and youth. He stopped in front of the slit in my cell door, so that I could see the whole of his face – a dreadful, drawn, grey face. "Have you any cigarettes, Kryltsov?" I was just going to pass him some but the assistant, as though afraid of being late, hurriedly pulled out his own case and offered it to him. He took a cigarette and the assistant struck a match. He began to smoke and seemed to be musing. Then he seemed to remember something and began to speak. "It's both cruel and unjust. I have committed no crime. I –" Something seemed to quiver in his white young throat – I could not tear my eyes from it – and he stopped. Yes. Then I heard Rozovski shouting from the corridor in his high-pitched Jewish voice. Lozinski threw down his cigarette stub and walked away from my door. Then I could see Rozovski through the slot. His child's face with the limpid black eyes was red and running with sweat. He also had clean linen on, and his trousers were too wide, and he kept pulling them up with both hands, and was trembling all over. He put his pitiful face to my window. "Kryltsov, it's true, isn't it, that the doctor prescribed herb tea for me? I am not well. I want some more of that herb tea." No one answered, and he looked inquiringly now at me, now at the head warder. But what he wanted to say, I never understood. Yes. Then all at once the assistant assumed a stern look and called out again in a kind of squeaking voice: "What's all this nonsense? Come along!" Rozovski was apparently incapable of realizing what awaited him, and hurried along the corridor ahead of them all, almost at a run. But a moment later he stood stock-still and refused to move, and I could hear his shrill voice wailing. Then there was a general hubbub and the tramping of feet. He was uttering piercing shrieks, and sobbing. Then the sounds came fainter and fainter – the door of the passage clanged and all was quiet. . . . Yes. And so they were hanged. Both strangled with ropes. A watchman, another one, saw it done, and told me that Lozinski offered no resistance, but Rozovski struggled for a long while so that they had to drag him on to the scaffold and force his head into the noose. Yes. The watchman was a rather stupid fellow. "People told me it would be horrible, sir. But it wasn't a bit horrible. As they were hanging, their shoulders moved just twice. Like this" – and he demonstrated how the shoulders moved convulsively up and then down. "Then the hangman jerked the rope, so as to tighten the noose, and that was that: they never budged no more." No, it wasn't a bit horrible,' Kryltsov repeated the watchman's words and tried to smile, but burst into sobs instead.

For a long time after that he was silent, breathing heavily and repressing the sobs that were choking him.

'On that day I became a revolutionary. Yes,' he said, when he was quieter, and he finished his story in a few words.

He belonged to the People's Freedom party and was even head of a sabotage-group whose purpose it was to terrorize the Government into resigning and calling upon the people to assume power. To this end he went to Petersburg, journeyed abroad, went to Kiev, to Odessa, and was everywhere successful. A man in whom he had complete confidence betrayed him. He was arrested, tried, kept in prison for two years and condemned to death, though the sentence was changed to hard labour for life.

In prison he had developed consumption and in the conditions in which he now found himself it was plain that he could scarcely live more than a few months. This he knew, and had no regrets over what he had done, saying that if he had his life over again he would use it in the same way – that is, to destroy the established order of things which made possible what he had seen.

Knowing this man, and hearing his story, made a great deal intelligible to Nekhlyudov that he had not understood before.

7

ON the day of the clash between the prisoner with the child and the convoy officer at the start from the halting-station, Nekhlyudov, who had spent the night at the village inn, awoke late, and for some time wrote letters to be posted at the next town, and so he left the inn later than usual and failed to catch up with the marching party on the road, as he had on previous occasions, and it was already dusk when he reached the village where the next stop was to be made. Having dried his clothes at the inn, kept by a plump elderly widow with an extraordinarily fat white neck, he took his tea in a clean room decorated with a large number of ikons and pictures, and then hurried to the halting-place to ask the officer's permission to see Maslova.

At the last six halts the convoy officers, although several changes had been made, all without exception had refused to allow Nekhlyudov to enter the prison enclosure, so that he had not seen Katusha for over a week. This severity was due to the fact that an important prison official was expected to pass that way. Now that this official had come and gone without so much as a cursory visit to the halting-place Nekhlyudov hoped that the officer who had taken over command of the gang that morning would allow him to see the prisoners, as former officers had done.

The landlady of the inn suggested he should take her trap to the halting-place, which was at the far end of the village, but Nekhlyudov preferred to walk. A strapping broad-shouldered young fellow, a labourer wearing huge newly tarred, strongly smelling knee-boots, offered to show him the way. Dense mist was falling from the sky and it was so dark that whenever the lad strayed a couple of steps outside patches of light from windows Nekhlyudov could not see him, and only heard the squelching of his boots in the deep sticky mud.

Past the square in front of the church and down a long street of houses with brightly lit windows Nekhlyudov followed his guide to the outskirts of the village, where it was pitch dark. But here, too, light from the lanterns round the halting-place soon beamed through the mist. The reddish spots of light grew bigger and bigger. The stakes of the palisade, the black figure of the sentry moving to and fro, a post painted with black-and-white stripes, and the sentry-box became visible. The sentry called his usual, 'Who goes there?' as they approached, and finding that they were strangers would not even let them wait by the fence. But Nekhlyudov's guide was not intimidated by the severity of the sentry.

'You're in a bad temper, aren't you?' he said. 'Just shout, will you, and call the head man. We'll wait.'

The sentry made no reply but shouted something through the gates and then stood looking at the broad-shouldered young labourer scraping the mud off Nekhlyudov's boots with a chip of wood by the light of the lantern. From the other side of the fence came the hum of men's and women's voices. A couple of minutes later there was a sound of clanking iron, the wicket-gate opened and a sergeant with his cloak thrown over his shoulders stepped out of the darkness into the light of the lantern, and inquired what they wanted. Nekhlyudov handed him his previously written card, asking the officer in charge to admit him on personal business, and requested the sergeant to take it to the officer. The sergeant was not so strict as the sentry, but he made up for it by being singularly inquisitive. He insisted on knowing why Nekhlyudov had to see the officer, and who he was, evidently scenting a bribe and anxious not to miss it. Nekhlyudov said that he had some special business and would show his gratitude, and asked him to take the note to the officer. The sergeant nodded, took the note and went off. A little while after his disappearance the gate rattled again and a line of women came out, carrying baskets, round panniers made of birch-bark, earthenware jars and sacks. Their voices rang out as they chattered away in their peculiar Siberian dialect. None of them wore peasant costume, but, town-fashion, had top-coats and pelisses. Their skirts were tucked up high and their heads wrapped in shawls. They peered curiously at Nekhlyudov and his guide standing in the lamplight, and one woman, evidently pleased to see the broad-shouldered lad, affectionately broke into a shower of Siberian abuse.

'You 'orrible beast, you – you rotter – what are you doin' 'ere?' she said to him.

'I'm showin' this traveller the way,' replied the lad. 'And what did you 'ave to bring?'

'Dairy stuff, an' they want more in the morning.'

'Didn't they let yer stay the night?' asked the young fellow.

'You be damned, you puppy!' she called back, laughing. 'Eh, come along an' see us 'ome.'

The guide said something more that made the sentry laugh as well as the woman; then, turning to Nekhlyudov, he asked:

'What about it, can you find your way back alone? You won't get lost, will you?'

'No, no, I shall be all right.'

'Arter you pass the church it'll be the second 'ouse on yer right, pas' the 'ouse with two storeys. Oh, and 'ere, take my stick,' he said, handing Nekhlyudov the stick he was carrying, which was taller than himself; and splashing through the mud in his enormous boots he disappeared in the darkness, together with the women.

His voice, mingling with the voices of the women, could still be heard through the mist as the gate rattled and the sergeant came out, inviting Nekhlyudov to follow him to the officer.

8

THE halting-station, like all such stations along the Siberian road, was surrounded by a palisade of sharp-pointed stakes and consisted of three single-storey buildings standing in the middle of the enclosure. One of these, the largest, had barred windows and was for the prisoners; the second housed the soldiers of the escort, and the officers lived in the third, where the administrative work was done. Lights shone from the windows of all three houses, as always – and especially here – exciting a delusive expectation of enjoyment and comfort within their lamp-lit walls. Lanterns gleamed by the steps up to each house and a half a dozen more hung from the walls, lighting up the yard. The sergeant led Nekhlyudov along duck-boards to the steps up to the smallest house. Mounting three steps he let Nekhlyudov pass before him into the ante-room, which was lit by a small lamp and was filled with the fumes of burning charcoal. A soldier in a coarse shirt, with a neck-tie and black trousers, was standing by the stove. He had only one top-boot on – the upper part was yellow – and, bending over, was using the other boot as a bellows for the samovar.¹ Seeing Nekhlyudov, the soldier left the samovar, helped him off with his leather coat and then went into the inner room.

'He's here, your honour.'

'Well, show him in,' said an angry voice.

'Through that door,' said the soldier, and immediately busied himself with the samovar again.

In the adjacent room, which was lit by a hanging lamp, an officer was sitting at a table before two bottles and the remains of dinner; he had long fair moustaches and a very red face, and wore an Austrian jacket that fitted snugly over his massive chest and shoulders. The warm room smelled not only of tobacco smoke but also of some very strong cheap scent. When he saw Nekhlyudov the officer rose and fixed him with half ironical, half suspicious eyes.

'What can I do for you?' he said and, without waiting for a reply shouted through the door: 'Bernov, is that samovar ever going to be ready?'

'Coming at once.'

'I'll give you an "at once" you won't forget in a hurry!' shouted the officer, his eyes flashing.

'I'm bringing it right away!' called the soldier, and came in with the samovar.

Nekhlyudov waited while the soldier placed the samovar on the table. (The officer watched him with his cruel little eyes, as if he were taking aim where best to hit him.) When the

1. The soldier was holding his boot with the concertina-like sides to the chimney of the samovar and using it like a bellows to make the charcoal burn up and boil the water.

samovar was in place the officer brewed the tea. Then he got a square decanter of brandy and some Albert biscuits out of his travelling-case. Having arranged these things on the table, he turned to Nekhlyudov again.

'Well, in what way can I assist you?'

'I should like an interview with one of the women convicts,' replied Nekhlyudov, still standing.

'Is she a political? If so, it's against the regulations,' said the officer.

'This woman is not a political prisoner,' said Nekhlyudov.

'Pray take a seat,' said the officer.

Nekhlyudov sat down.

'She is not a political prisoner,' he repeated, 'but, at my request, she has been allowed by the higher authorities to march with the political prisoners –'

'Oh yes, I know,' interrupted the officer. 'The little brunette, isn't it? Well, yes, that can be managed. Will you have a cigarette?'

He moved a box of cigarettes towards Nekhlyudov, and carefully pouring out two tumblers of tea pushed one over to Nekhlyudov.

'Do have some tea,' he said.

'Thank you, but I should like to see –'

'The night is long. You'll have plenty of time. I'll send for her.'

'Why send for her? Couldn't I see her where she is?'

'Go to the political prisoners' quarters? That's against the law.'

'I have been allowed to several times. If you are afraid I might smuggle something in to them, I could do it just as well through her.'

'Oh no, she will be searched,' said the officer, with a disagreeable laugh.

'Well, then, you'd better search me.'

'I think we'll get along without that,' said the officer, opening the decanter and holding it over Nekhlyudov's tea.

'May I? No? Well, just as you like. Living as we do here in Siberia, it warms the cockles of one's heart to come across an educated man. There is no need to tell you how dreary our work is, and it's all the harder for someone who's been used to a different sort of life. People think that a convoy officer must be an uncivilized boor with no education – they never stop to consider that he may have been born for other things.'

The officer's red face, his scent, the ring on his finger and, above all, his unpleasant laugh were repulsive to Nekhlyudov, but that day, too, as during the entire journey, he was in that serious thoughtful mood which would not let him behave slightingly or disdainfully to any human being but made him feel the necessity of 'going all out' with everyone, as he defined it to himself. Having listened to what the officer had to say, and interpreting his state of mind to mean that he was weighed down by the harsh misery of the people in his power, he said gravely:

'I imagine that in your position now there might be some comfort in easing the suffering of the prisoners.'

'What do they suffer? You don't know these people.'

'They are not a special race,' said Nekhlyudov, 'different from everyone else. And some of them are innocent.'

'Of course, there are all sorts among them. Naturally, one feels sorry for them. Other officers won't overlook a thing, but I try to make it easier for them wherever I can. Better let me suffer than them. Some of our officers enforce every petty regulation, and are even ready to shoot, but I show mercy. You'll have some more tea? Please,' he said, filling his glass again. 'Who is she exactly – the woman you want to see?' he asked.

'An unfortunate woman who found her way into a brothel and there was falsely accused of poisoning, but she is really a very good woman,' said Nekhlyudov.

The officer shook his head.

'Yes, these things happen. I can tell you about one in Kazan – her name was Emma. She was a Hungarian by birth, but from her eyes you'd have taken her for a Persian,' he went on, unable to refrain from a smile at the recollection. 'And she had so much *chic* about her – Good Lord, she might have been a countess . . .'

Nekhlyudov interrupted the officer and returned to their previous topic.

'I am sure it lies in your power to ease the lives of these people while they are in your charge. I know that by doing so you will become much happier yourself,' he said, trying to speak as distinctly as possible, just as one speaks to a foreigner or a child.

The officer looked at Nekhlyudov with sparkling eyes, apparently impatient for him to stop so that he could continue with his story about the Hungarian woman with the Persian eyes, who had evidently become very vivid in his imagination and was engaging all his attention.

'Yes, I am sure, that's all quite true,' he said, 'and I do pity them. But I should like to tell you about this Emma. What do you suppose she did –?'

'It does not interest me,' said Nekhlyudov, 'and I must say frankly that though I myself was once a very different sort of man, I have come to loathe this kind of attitude to women.'

The officer gave Nekhlyudov a startled look.

'Won't you have another little glass of tea?' he said.

'No, thank you.'

'Bernov!' cried the officer. 'Take this gentleman to Vakoulov. Tell him to let him into the separate room where the politicals are. He may stay there until roll-call.'

9

ACCOMPANIED by the orderly, Nekhlyudov went out again into the dark courtyard dimly lit by the red light of the lanterns.

'Where are you going?' a soldier whom they met asked the orderly with Nekhlyudov.

'Special cell, No. 5.'

'You can't get through here, it's locked. You'll have to go round by the other steps.'

'What's it locked for?'

'The sergeant locked it and went off down to the village.'

'Well, then, come this way.'

The soldier led Nekhlyudov along the duck-boards to another entrance. Even out in the yard they could hear the din of voices and movement to and fro within, much like the sound from a good beehive when the bees are getting ready to swarm, but when Nekhlyudov came nearer and the door opened, the din grew louder and was converted into a noisy exchange of shouting, abuse and laughter. He heard the ringing sound of chains, and smelt the familiar foul stench of human excrement and disinfectant.

These two things – the din of voices mingled with the clattering of chains and the horrible smell – always merged for Nekhlyudov into one agonizing sensation of moral nausea which soon turned to a physical feeling of sickness, the one combining with and intensifying the other.

As he entered the building, which had a huge stinking tub (known in prisons as the 'close-stool') in the vestibule, the first thing Nekhlyudov saw was a woman sitting on the edge of the tub. In front of her a man was standing, his pancake-shaped cap poised sideways on his shaven head. They were talking about something. Seeing Nekhlyudov, the man winked and remarked:

'The Tsar himself can't hold back his water.'

The woman, however, pulled the skirts of her prison cloak about her and looked down in embarrassment.

A corridor ran from the entrance, with cell doors opening on to it. The first cell was for families, then a large one for unmarried men and at the end of the passage were two smaller cells reserved for the political prisoners. The building, originally intended for a hundred and fifty and now housing four hundred and fifty, was so crowded that the prisoners, unable to get into the cells, had overflowed into the passage. Some were sitting or lying on the floor; others were moving about with empty teapots in their hands or bringing them back filled with boiling water. Among the latter was Tarass. He ran up to Nekhlyudov and greeted him affectionately. Tarass' kindly face was disfigured by dark bruises on his nose and under one eye.

'What have you done to yourself?' asked Nekhlyudov.

'Oh, nothing in particular,' replied Tarass with a smile.

'They're always fighting,' remarked the guard scornfully.

'On account of a woman,' said a convict, who was walking behind them. 'He had a set-to with Blind Fedka.'

'How is Fedosya?' asked Nekhlyudov.

'She's all right. I'm taking her some hot water for tea,' said Tarass, and went into the family cell.

Nekhlyudov looked in at the door. Every inch of the room was crowded with men and women, some on, some underneath the sleeping-benches. The air was full of steam from wet clothes that were drying, and there was an incessant chatter of women's voices. The next door opened into the unmarried men's cell. This was still more crowded, and the doorway itself and the passage outside were blocked by a noisy group of convicts in wet clothes, busy sharing something out or settling a dispute. The sergeant explained that the prisoner appointed to buy provisions was paying out some of the food-money that was owing to a sharper (who had won from, or lent money to, the prisoners) and receiving back little tickets made of playing cards. When they saw the sergeant and the gentleman those who were nearest stopped talking, looking at the two with hostile eyes. Among them Nekhlyudov noticed his acquaintance, the convict Fedorov, accompanied as usual by a pale miserable youth with raised eyebrows and a swollen face, and another still more repulsive, pock-marked, noseless tramp, who was reputed to have killed a comrade while they were trying to escape in the dense marshy forest in Siberia, and then, so it was said, fed on his flesh.

The tramp stood in the passage, his wet prison cloak thrown over one shoulder, looking mockingly and boldly at Nekhlyudov, and not stepping aside for him. Nekhlyudov walked round him.

Though this spectacle was not new to Nekhlyudov, who during the last three months had seen the same four hundred convicts in many different circumstances – in the heat, enveloped in clouds of dust stirred up by the dragging of chained feet on the road, at resting-places by the way, and out in the courtyards at the halting-stations in warm weather where appalling scenes of barefaced debauchery occurred – nevertheless, every time he came among them and felt, as now, their attention fixed on him, he experienced an agonizing sensation of shame and a consciousness of his sin against them. Worst of all, to this sense of shame and guilt was added an unconquerable feeling of loathing and horror. He knew that in conditions such as theirs they could not be anything else than what they were, and yet he could not stifle his disgust.

'It's all right for them parasites,' Nekhlyudov heard a hoarse voice say, just as he approached the door of the cell where the political prisoners were. 'Whatever 'appens to them, they don't get a pain in the belly.' This was followed by some obscene abuse and a derisive burst of unfriendly laughter.

10

WHEN they had passed the cell of the unmarried prisoners the sergeant who had accompanied Nekhlyudov told him that he would come for him before roll-call, and went back. The moment the sergeant had gone a convict, stepping quickly with his bare feet and holding up his chains, came close to Nekhlyudov, enveloping him in a strong sour smell of sweat, and said in a mysterious whisper:

'Take the case in 'and, sir. They fooled the lad. Made 'im drunk. And now today at roll-call 'e answered to the name of

Karmanov. Stick up for 'im, sir. We can't – they'd murder us,' said the prisoner, looking anxiously about him and immediately walking away from Nekhlyudov.

What had happened was this. The convict Karmanov had persuaded a lad under sentence of exile, who was like him in appearance, to change names with him so that he would be exiled and the lad would go to the mines in his place.

Nekhlyudov had already heard about the affair, since this very prisoner had told him about the exchange a week before. He nodded as a sign that he understood and would do what he could, and went on without looking back.

Nekhlyudov had known the convict who spoke to him since Ekaterinburg, where he had asked him to try and get permission for his wife to join him, and he was surprised by his action. He was a man of middle height, the most ordinary peasant type, about thirty years old, condemned to hard labour for attempted robbery and murder. His name was Makar Dyevkin. His crime was a very curious one. It was not his, Makar's, doing, as he told Nekhlyudov, but the work of *him*, the devil. He said that a traveller had come to his father's house and hired a sleigh for two roubles to drive to a village twenty-five miles off. His father told Makar to take the stranger. Makar harnessed the horse, dressed himself and sat down to drink tea with the stranger. While they were drinking tea the stranger told Makar that he was going to be married and that he had with him five hundred roubles which he had earned in Moscow. When Makar heard this he went out and hid a hatchet under the straw in the sleigh.

'I don't know meself why I took the axe,' he said. 'A voice sez, "Take the 'atchet," and I took it. We got in and off we goes. We drove along, ordinary-like. I wasn't thinkin' about the axe at all. Well, there we was, gettin' near the village – only about four miles to go. The way from the cart-track to the 'igh road was up'ill. I got out and was walkin' be'ind the sleigh, and 'e whispers to me: "What's the matter with you? By the time you comes to the top of the 'ill there'll be people about, and then there's the village. 'E'll get away with 'is money. If you means to do it, now's the time: it's no good waitin'." So I stoops over the sleigh, like I wanted to shake up the straw, and without me doin' nothin' the axe seems to jump into me 'and. The man turned round. "What are you doing?" 'e says. I swung the axe ready to smash at 'im, but 'e was a nimble fellow – 'e jumped from the sleigh and seized me 'ands. "What are you up to, you villain?" 'e shouted. 'E threw me down on the snow, and I didn't even struggle but gave in at once. 'E tied me arms with 'is belt and 'urled me into the sleigh. Then 'e took me straight to the police-station. They locked me up. I was tried. The village commune give me a good character, said I never done no wrong before. The people I worked for put in a good word for me, too. But I 'ad no money to pay for a lawyer,' Makar concluded, 'and so I gets four years' 'ard.'

And now this man was trying to save a fellow country-man, though he knew that by speaking he risked his life: if the other prisoners found out that he had given away the secret to Nekhlyudov they would certainly strangle him.

11

THE political prisoners' quarters consisted of two small cells, the doors of which opened into a part of the passage partitioned off from the rest. On entering this part of the passage the first person Nekhlyudov saw was Simonson with a log of pinewood in his hand. He was squatting in his jacket in front of a stove in which the draught was so strong that it made the door of the fire vibrate.

Without getting to his feet he stretched out a hand when he saw Nekhlyudov, looking up at him from under his protruding brow.

'I am glad you have come. I want to see you,' he said, looking Nekhlyudov straight in the eyes with a significant expression.

'What is it?' asked Nekhlyudov.

'I'll tell you later on. Just now I am busy.'

And Simonson devoted himself to the stove again, which he was heating after a theory of his own, based on the minimum waste of heat energy.

Nekhlyudov was just entering the first door when Maslova came out of the other, bending over a short birch-broom with which she was pushing a pile of rubbish and dust towards the stove. She had on a white jacket, her skirt was tucked up, and she was in her stockinged feet. Her head was wrapped against the dust in a white kerchief drawn down to her eyebrows. At the sight of Nekhlyudov she straightened herself, flushing and animated, put the broom down, wiped her hands on her skirt and stood directly in front of him.

'Tidying the place up, are you?' said Nekhlyudov, giving her his hand.

'Yes, my old occupation,' she said, and smiled. 'You can't imagine how dirty it is here. We've been scrubbing and scrubbing. . . . Well, is the rug dry?' she asked, turning to Simonson.

'Almost,' said Simonson, looking at her in a peculiar way that struck Nekhlyudov.

'All right, I'll come for it, and bring the cloaks to dry. Our people are all in there,' she said to Nekhlyudov, pointing to the first door while she herself went in at the second.

Nekhlyudov opened the door and entered a small cell dimly lit by a little metal lamp standing on one of the lower bunks. The room was cold and smelled of dust which had not settled, damp and tobacco. The tin lamp threw a bright light on those near it, but the benches were in the dark and wavering shadows flickered on the walls.

Everybody was in this small room with the exception of two of the men who were in charge of the provisions and had gone to fetch boiling water and food. Here was Nekhlyudov's old acquaintance, Vera Bogodoukhovskaya, thinner and more sallow than ever, with her large frightened eyes and the vein that stood out on her forehead. Her hair was cut short and she wore a grey blouse. Spread out in front of her was a newspaper and on it lay some tobacco which she sat jerkily stuffing into little cardboard tubes to make cigarettes.

Here, too, was one of the women politicals Nekhlyudov liked best – Emilia Rantseva, who kept house for the group and managed to give an appearance of feminine order and charm to even the most trying surroundings. She was sitting near the lamp, her sleeves rolled up over her beautiful sun-burnt arms, deftly wiping and placing mugs and cups on a towel spread on a bench. Rantseva was a plain-looking young woman with an intelligent and gentle expression, and when she smiled her face had a way of suddenly being transformed and becoming gay, lively and enchanting. She now greeted Nekhlyudov with just such a smile.

'Why, we thought you must have gone back to Russia,' she said.

Here, too, in the shadows in the far corner, was Marya Pavlovna, busy with a little fair-haired girl who was prattling away in a sweet childish voice.

'How nice that you have come! Have you seen Katusha?' she asked Nekhlyudov. 'Look at the visitor we have!' And she showed him the little girl.

Here, too, was Anatoly Kryltsov. Wasted and pale, he sat in another corner at the end of the sleeping-bunks, bent and shivering, his feet in felt boots tucked under him, and his hands thrust into his coat-sleeves, watching Nekhlyudov with feverish eyes. Nekhlyudov started to go towards him, but to the right of the door a man with red curly hair, in spectacles and a rubber jacket, sat talking to a pretty smiling girl – Grabetz by name – while he sorted something out in a sack. This was the famous revolutionary, Novodvorov, and Nekhlyudov hastened to exchange greetings with him. He was particularly eager to do so because of all the political prisoners in the group Novodvorov was the only one he dis-liked. There was a glint in Novodvorov's blue eyes as he looked through his spectacles at Nekhlyudov and, frowning, held out his slim hand.

'Well, are you enjoying your journey?' he asked with evident irony.

'Yes, there is much that is interesting,' replied Nekhlyudov, pretending not to notice the irony but to take the inquiry as a polite remark, and he passed on to Kryltsov.

Outwardly Nekhlyudov appeared indifferent, but in his heart he was far from feeling indifferent to Novodvorov, whose words and obvious desire to say and do something unpleasant disturbed the benign mood which possessed him at this time, and made him feel depressed and sad.

'Well, how are you?' he said, pressing Kryltsov's cold trembling hand.

'Pretty fair, only I can't get warm. I got soaked to the skin,' said Kryltsov, hurriedly returning his hand to the sleeve of his sheepskin coat. 'And it's beastly cold here. Look at those broken windows.' He pointed to two broken panes behind the iron bars. 'What about you? Why haven't you been to see us?'

'I couldn't get in, the authorities were very strict. It was only today that I found an officer who was obliging.'

'Obliging, indeed! You ask Marya what he did this morning.'

Marya Pavlovna, from her place in the corner, related what had happened about the little girl as they were leaving the halting-station.

'I think we ought to protest in a body,' said Vera Bogodoukhovskaya in determined accents, at the same time glancing from one face to another with hesitant scared eyes. 'Simonson did make a protest, but that is not enough.'

'What protest do you want?' muttered Kryltsov with a grimace. It was obvious that Vera Bogodoukhovskaya's lack of simplicity, her artificial tone of voice and nervous manner, had been irritating him for some while. 'Are you looking for Katusha?' he asked Nekhlyudov. 'She works the whole time, cleaning up. She has done this cell – the men's cell – and now she is on the women's. Only, of course, there's no getting rid of the fleas, they're eating us alive. And what is Marya doing there?' he asked, nodding towards the corner where Marya Pavlovna was.

'Combing out her adopted daughter's hair,' said Rantseva.

'I hope she won't let the vermin loose on us?' said Kryltsov.

'No, no, I am being very careful. She's a clean little girl now,' said Marya Pavlovna. 'You have her,' she said to Rantseva, 'while I go and help Katusha. And I must fetch him the rug, too.'

Rantseva took the child on her lap, pressing the plump bare little arms to her bosom with the tenderness of a mother, and gave her a lump of sugar.

As Marya Pavlovna went out the two men came into the cell with the boiling water and the provisions.

12

ONE of the newcomers was a short thin young man in cloth-covered sheepskin coat and top-boots. He walked with a light quick step, carrying two large steaming teapots filled with hot water and holding under his arm bread wrapped in a cloth.

'Well, so our prince has put in an appearance again,' he said, setting a teapot down among the mugs and handing the bread to Maslova. 'We've bought some wonderful things,' he went on, taking off his coat and tossing it over the heads of the others on to a corner bunk. 'Markel has bought milk and eggs; why, we'll have a regular ball tonight. And I see Rantseva is still at it, radiating her aesthetic cleanliness,' he said, and looked with a smile at Rantseva. 'Now then, make the tea,' he told her.

The whole presence of this man – his movements, his voice, the expression of his face – seemed to breathe good cheer and gaiety. The other newcomer – also a short bony man with very prominent cheek-bones in a thin sallow face, beautiful greenish wide-set eyes and a finely drawn mouth – was exactly the reverse, dejected and despondent. He wore an old wadded coat and galoshes over his boots. He was carrying two earthenware pots and two round boxes made of birch-bark. Depositing his load in front of Rantseva, he nodded to Nekhlyudov, bending his neck only and keeping his eyes fixed on him all the while. Then, having reluctantly given him his clammy hand to shake, he began to take out the provisions.

Both these political prisoners were men of the people. The first, Nabatov, was a peasant; the other, Markel Kondratyev, was a factory hand. Markel had fallen in with the revolutionary movement at the ripe age of thirty-five, while Nabatov had joined when he was eighteen. Having by reason of his exceptional ability found his way from the village school to the high-school, Nabatov supported himself all the while by giving lessons. He finished his schooling with a gold medal, but did not proceed to the university because, while still in the senior class at school, he had decided to go back among the people from whom he had come, taking enlightenment to his neglected brothers. This he did, first becoming a clerk in a large village, but he was soon arrested for reading books to the peasants and organizing a consumers' and producers' association among them. The first time he was kept in prison for eight months, after which he was released and placed under secret surveillance. The moment he was free he went to another village in another province, established himself as a schoolteacher, and did the same thing again. He was picked up again, and this time imprisoned for a year and two months, which served only to strengthen his convictions.

After his second term in prison he was exiled to the province of Perm. He ran away from there. Again he was arrested and after seven months in prison deported to the province of Archangel. From there he was sentenced to exile in Yakutsk for refusing to take the oath of allegiance to the new Tsar; so that half his adult life had been spent in prison and in exile.

All these adventures had in no way embittered him, nor had they diminished his energy; if anything, they seemed to have stimulated it. He was an indomitable man with a splendid digestion, always alike active, cheerful and vigorous. He never regretted anything, and never looked far into the future, but applied all his mental powers, his cleverness and common sense to life in the present. When he was at liberty he worked towards the aim he had set himself – the enlightenment and organization of the working people, particularly of the peasants. When in prison he was just as energetic and practical in establishing contact with the outside world and in arranging life, not only for himself but for the little circle of people with him, as comfortably as circumstances would permit. First and foremost, he was a social being. He did not seem to want anything for himself and was content with very little, but for his comrades he demanded much and could do any sort of work, physical and mental, non-stop, without sleep or food. As a peasant he was industrious, quick-witted, smart at his work and naturally abstemious and polite without effort, and considerate not only of other people's feelings but of their opinions, too. His widowed mother, an illiterate superstitious old peasant woman, was still living and Nabatov helped her and went to see her whenever he was at large. During the time he was at home he entered fully into her life, assisted her with the work and always kept in touch with his old companions in the village. He smoked cheap tobacco with them in paper twisted into the shape of a dog's hind-leg, took part in their friendly bouts and tried to make them understand that they had always been cheated and that they ought to do all they could to free themselves from the state of deception in which they were being kept. When he thought or spoke of what a revolution could do to benefit the masses he always had in mind the class from which he himself had sprung, and saw them living in very nearly the same conditions as now, only possessing land and being independent of gentry and bureaucracy. The revolution, according to him, ought not to change the people's basic way of living – in this respect he differed from Novodvorov and Novodvorov's follower, Markel Kondratyev. The revolution, in his opinion, ought not to destroy the whole fabric but only alter the inner workings of the great, solid, beautiful old structure he loved so passionately.

He was also a typical peasant in his views on religion: he never thought about metaphysical problems, about the origin of all origins or life in the next world. To him, as to Arago,[1] God was a hypothesis for which, so far, he had had no use. He was not in the least concerned about the origin of the universe, and did not care whether Moses or Darwin were right, and Darwinism, which seemed so important to his associates, he took no more seriously than the story of the creation of the world in six days.

He was not interested in the question of how the world came into being, just because he was constantly occupied by the question of how best to live in this world. Nor did he ever think of the future life, having inherited from his ancestors the firm and calm belief, common to all who till the soil, that just as in the animal and vegetable kingdoms nothing ceases to exist but is continually being transformed from one thing into another – manure into grain, grain into fowl, tadpole into frog, caterpillar into butterfly, acorn into oak – so man does not perish either but only undergoes a change. This he believed, and therefore he always looked death bravely and even gaily in the eye and unflinchingly bore the suffering that leads up to it; but he did not like and did not know how to talk about these things. He was fond of work and was always busy with practical affairs, and encouraged his comrades to do the same.

The other political prisoner in this party who originated from the people, Markel Kondratyev, was a man of a different type. He started work at fifteen and took to smoking and drinking as a way of stifling a dim sense of injury. He first had the feeling when they (the village boys) were brought in

1. François Jean Dominique Arago, French physicist, 1786–1853.

to look at a Christmas-tree which the mill-owner's wife had arranged. He and his friends received a penny whistle, an apple, a gilded walnut and a fig, while the mill-owner's children were given toys which seemed to him to be presents from fairyland, and had cost, as he afterwards heard, over fifty roubles. When he was twenty a famous woman revolutionary came to work in his factory and, noticing Kondratyev's marked ability, she began to give him books and pamphlets, and to talk to him, explaining his position to him, the cause of it and how it could be improved. When the possibility of freeing himself and others from oppression became clear in his mind the injustice of their present circumstances appeared more cruel and terrible than ever, and he longed passionately not only for deliverance but for revenge on those who had established and who maintained such cruel injustice. It was knowledge, he was told, that gave this possibility, and he devoted himself feverishly to the acquisition of knowledge. He did not see how the socialist ideal was to be realized through knowledge, but he believed that, as knowledge had revealed to him the injustice of the conditions in which he lived, so it would also remedy the injustice itself. Besides, knowledge would raise him in his own estimation above other people. He therefore gave up drinking and smoking, and used all his spare time, of which he now had more, having been promoted to store-keeper, for studying.

The woman revolutionary who taught him was struck by the amazing aptitude with which, insatiable, he devoured knowledge of every sort. In two years he had mastered algebra, geometry, history (of which he was particularly fond), and had read widely in belles-lettres and critical philosophy and, above all, the works of socialist writers.

The woman revolutionary was arrested and Kondratyev with her, forbidden books having been found in his possession. He was sent to prison and afterwards exiled to Vologda. There he became acquainted with Novodvorov, read a great deal more revolutionary matter, memorized everything and became even nore confirmed in his socialist views. After his term of exile he organized a big strike which ended in the destruction of a factory and the murder of its director. He was arrested and sentenced to loss of civil rights and exile.

His views on religion were as negative as his views on the existing economic order of things. Realizing the absurdity of the faith in which he had been brought up, and having with difficulty freed himself from it – knowing terror in the process, and then rapture – as if in retribution for the deception which had been practised on his forefathers and himself, he never tired of pouring venomous and embittered ridicule on priests and religious dogmas.

By habit an ascetic, he was content with very little, and like any man who has been used since childhood to working and has a powerful physique, he was quick and skilful at all forms of manual labour; but what he valued most was the leisure in prisons and at the halting-stations, which enabled him to continue his studies. He was now poring over the first volume of Marx, which he carried about in his sack with the greatest care, like some priceless treasure. Except Novodvorov, to whom he was particularly attached and whose judgements on all subjects he accepted as irrefutable truth, he treated all his companions with reserve and indifference.

For women, whom he considered a hindrance in all useful activity, he had an insurmountable contempt. But he pitied Maslova and was kind to her, seeing in her an example of the exploitation of the lower by the upper classes. He disliked Nekhlyudov for the same reason, was taciturn with him and never pressed his hand, merely extending his own for Nekhlyudov to shake when Nekhlyudov greeted him.

13

THE fire had burnt up and the stove was warm; the tea was made and poured out into mugs and tumblers, and milk added; and cracknel biscuits, fresh rye- and wheat-bread, hard-boiled eggs, butter and calves-head and calves-feet were spread out. Everyone moved towards the bunk which was used as a table, and began eating, drinking and talking. Rantseva sat on a wooden box pouring out the tea. The others all crowded round her, except Kryltsov, who had taken off his wet coat and was lying on his bunk wrapped in the rug which had dried, talking to Nekhlyudov.

After the cold damp march, and the dirt and mess they had found here, and the efforts they had spent to tidy up the place, the hot tea and the food put them in the best and happiest of spirits.

The tread of feet, the shouting and cursing that came from the convicts on the other side of the wall, reminding them, as it were, of their surroundings, only increased their sensation of personal comfort. As though they were on a tiny island in the middle of the sea, these people for a brief space no longer felt themselves submerged under the humiliations and misery surrounding them, and consequently they were elated and excited. They talked about everything except their own predicament and what awaited them. Moreover, as always happens with young men and women, especially when forced together by circumstances as all these people were, currents of sympathy or antipathy, curiously blended, had sprung up between them. Nearly all of them were in love. Novodvorov was in love with the pretty, smiling Grabetz, a young woman student very little given to reflection and completely indifferent to revolutionary ideas. But, swayed by the influences of the time, she had in some way compromised herself and been sentenced to exile. When she was free her chief interest in life had been her success with men, and it was the same through her trial, in prison and in exile. Now, on the journey, she found consolation in Novodvorov's infatuation for her, and herself fell in love with him. Vera Bogodoukhovskaya, who fell in love very easily and did not so easily arouse love in others but was always hopeful of reciprocation, loved Nabatov and Novodvorov alternately. Kryltsov could be said to have lost his heart to Marya Pavlovna. He loved her as men love women, but knowing her ideas about love he cleverly concealed his feeling under the guise of friendship and gratitude for her exceptionally tender care of him. Nabatov and Rantseva were united by a very complex bond of affection. Just as Marya Pavlovna was a perfectly chaste virgin, so Rantseva was the most chaste of wives.

She was still a schoolgirl of sixteen when she fell in love with Rantsev, who was studying at Petersburg University, and at nineteen, while he was still a student, she married him. In his fourth year at the university her husband got mixed up in some student disturbances, was sent away from Petersburg, and turned revolutionary. She abandoned the medical course she was attending, followed him and herself became a revolutionary. If she had not considered her husband to be the cleverest and best man in the world she would not have fallen in love with him, and, not loving him, she would not have married him. But once having fallen in love with and married – as she was quite convinced – the best and cleverest man in the world she naturally saw life and its purpose through the eyes of the best and cleverest man in the world. At first he believed that life was for studying, and she thought so too. He became a revolutionary, and so she became a revolutionary. She could argue very capably that the existing order of things was impossible, and that it was everyone's duty to fight it and endeavour to establish a political and economic structure in which the individual should be free to develop, and so on. And it seemed to her that those actually were her ideas and feelings, whereas in point of fact she was merely sure that everything her husband thought – was the absolute truth. She had but one desire – perfect concord, perfect identification of her own soul with his, which alone could give her full moral satisfaction.

The parting from her husband and their child (whom her mother took) had been unspeakably painful. But she bore the separation bravely and without a murmur, knowing it was for her husband's sake and for a cause which was unquestionably the true one, since he served it. She was always with her husband in thought, and could not love anyone else now, any more than she could when with him. But Nabatov's pure and devoted love touched and disturbed her. Being an upright man of strong character and a friend of her husband's, he tried to treat her like a sister, but something more kept creeping into his relations with her, and this something more alarmed them both and at the same time lent colour to their life of hardship.

Marya Pavlovna and Kondratyev were thus the only ones in the group not involved in any love affair.

14

EXPECTING to have a private talk with Katusha, as usual, after they had all drunk tea and had supper together, Nekhlyudov sat beside Kryltsov and talked to him. Among other things, he spoke about the request Makar had made to him, and told him the story of his crime. Kryltsov listened attentively, his sparkling eyes fixed on Nekhlyudov.

'Yes,' he said suddenly, 'I often think that here we are, marching side by side with *them* – but who are *they*? The very people on account of whom we are going into exile. And yet we not only do not know them – we do not even wish to know them. And they are worse still – they hate us and look upon us as their enemies. That is what's so terrible.'

'There is nothing terrible in that,' said Novodvorov, who was listening to the conversation. 'The masses always worship power, and power alone,' he said in his rasping voice. 'The Government has the power now and they worship it and detest us; tomorrow we shall be in power – and they will worship us . . .'

Just then a volley of abuse came from the other side of the wall and they heard a dull thud of bodies flung against it, the clanking of chains, shouts and screeching. Someone was being hit, and there was a cry of 'Murder! Help!'

'Listen to those animals! What contact can there be between them and ourselves?' Novodvorov remarked placidly.

'You call them animals? And only a few minutes ago Nekhlyudov here was telling me of an act –' Kryltsov said angrily, and went on to relate the story of Makar, who was risking his life to save a countryman of his. 'That is not the action of a brute beast: it's heroism.'

'Sentimentality, you mean,' retorted Novodvorov sarcastically. 'It is difficult for us to understand either the emotions of these people or their motives for what they do. What you take for nobility of feeling may be merely envy of the other convict.'

'Why is it you never want to see anything good in people?' Marya Pavlovna exclaimed, suddenly flaring up.

'I can't see what isn't there.'

'Of course it's there when a man takes the risk of a terrible death.'

'I think,' said Novodvorov, 'that if we want to achieve anything, the first condition is' – here Kondratyev put down the book he was reading by the lamp, and began to listen attentively to his mentor – 'that we should not let our imagination run away with us but look at things as they are. We ought to do all we can for the masses and expect nothing from them in return; we are working for the masses, but they cannot collaborate with us so long as they remain in their present state of inertia,' he began, as though addressing a meeting. 'Therefore it is quite illusory to expect help from them before the process of development – which we are preparing them for – has taken place.'

'And what process of development is that?' put in Kryltsov, going red in the face. 'We say that we are against arbitrary rule and despotism, and yet isn't that the most appalling despotism?'

'Not at all,' Novodvorov calmly replied. 'I am only saying

that I know the path that the people must travel, and can show them that path.'

'But how can you be sure the path you indicate is the right one? Isn't yours the same kind of despotism that produced the Inquisition and the executions of the French Revolution? They too, knew, in the light of science, the one true path.'

'The fact that they went wrong does not prove that I have too. And besides, there is a vast difference between the ravings of ideologists and the findings of scientific political economy.'

Novodvorov's voice filled the room. He was the only speaker, all the others were silent.

'These everlasting disputes,' said Marya Pavlovna, when he paused for a moment.

'And you yourself, what is your opinion?' Nekhlyudov asked her.

'I think Kryltsov is right, that we should not force our views on the people.'

'What about you, Katusha?' asked Nekhlyudov with a smile, and waited nervously for her answer, fearing that she might say something out of place.

'I think that the common people are wronged,' she said, blushing scarlet. 'Dreadfully wronged, they are.'

'Quite right, Maslova, quite right,' cried Nabatov. 'The people are shamefully wronged. And this must be stopped. Therein lies our whole task.'

'A curious conception of the object of a revolution,' said Novodvorov, and fell to smoking angrily in silence.

'I cannot talk to him,' Kryltsov said in a whisper, and abandoned the discussion.

'And it's much better not to,' said Nekhlyudov.

15

ALTHOUGH Novodvorov was very much respected by all the revolutionaries, and though he was very learned and passed for being very clever, Nekhlyudov counted him among those revolutionaries who, falling below the average moral level, were very far below it. The mental ability of the man – his numerator – was high; but his opinion of himself – his denominator – was incommensurably enormous and had long outgrown his mental powers.

His spiritual disposition was diametrically the opposite of Simonson's. Simonson belonged to the predominantly masculine type whose actions follow the dictates of their reason and are determined by it. Novodvorov, on the other hand, pertained to the feminine category where mental activity is directed partly to the realization of aims inspired by feelings.

The whole of Novodvorov's revolutionary activity, though he could explain it so eloquently and convincingly, appeared to Nekhlyudov to be founded on nothing more than vanity, on a desire to be a leader among men. To begin with, his talent for assimilating and expressing clearly the thoughts of others had brought him to the top – at school and at the university, where this sort of ability is highly prized – and he was well pleased with himself. But when he had received his diploma and finished his studies and his period of supremacy was over he suddenly completely altered his views, in order to gain power in another sphere (so Kryltsov, who did not like him, told Nekhlyudov), and from being a moderate liberal he became a rabid adherent of the People's Freedom party. Being devoid of aesthetic and moral principles (so frequently the cause of doubt and hesitation), he very soon acquired a position in the revolutionary world – that of leader of a party – which satisfied his ambition. His course once chosen, he never again doubted or wavered, and was therefore certain that he never made a mistake. Everything seemed to him extraordinarily simple, clear, incontrovertible. And indeed, given the narrowness and one-sidedness of his views, everything *was* quite simple and clear, and all that was necessary, as he said, was to be logical. His self-confidence was so great that it could only repel people or bring them to heel. And as his activity was displayed among very young people, who mistook his boundless self-assurance for depth and wisdom, the majority fell under his influence and he had great success in revolutionary circles. He was engaged at that time in preparing an insurrection during which he proposed to seize the reins of government and call a popular parliament, to consider the programme he had composed. And he was perfectly certain that this programme went into every problem and that there could be no question of not carrying it out.

His boldness and determination won the respect of his comrades, but not their love. Nor was he fond of anyone. He looked upon all talented men as rivals; if he could, he would have liked to treat them as male-monkeys treat the young ones. He would have snatched away all their powers and all their ability, to avoid being eclipsed by them. He only liked those who bowed before him. Thus now on the journey he was gracious to Kondratyev, who had swallowed his propaganda and become his disciple, to Vera Bogodoukhovskaya and to pretty little Grabetz, both of whom were in love with him. Though in theory he believed in equality for women, at the bottom of his heart he considered all women stupid and insignificant, with the exception of those with whom he happened to be sentimentally in love (as he was at present with Grabetz), and then he thought them exceptional women, whose worth he alone was capable of appreciating.

The question of relations between the sexes, like all other questions, seemed very simple and clear to him, the recognition of free love being the complete answer.

He had one woman who was known as his wife, and one real wife, from whom he had parted, having come to the conclusion that there was no true love between them, and now he was thinking of contracting another free marriage with Grabetz.

Nekhlyudov he despised for 'acting a part', as he called it, with Maslova, and particularly for daring to think about the defects of the existing system and ways of correcting those defects, not only not word for word as he, Novodvorov, did, but in a special fashion of his own, as a prince – that is, as a fool. Nekhlyudov was aware of Novodvorov's attitude towards him, and to his chagrin felt that, despite his general state on this journey of goodwill to all men, he could not help returning dislike for dislike and was quite unable to overcome his strong antipathy for the man.

16

COMMANDING voices were heard from the next cell, then silence, and immediately afterwards the sergeant entered with two convoy soldiers. It was the roll-call. The sergeant counted everyone, pointing his finger at each in turn. When he came to Nekhlyudov he said with good-natured familiarity:

'Now, prince, you can't stay after roll-call. It's time for you to go.'

Knowing what this meant, Nekhlyudov went up to him and slipped a three-rouble note, which he had ready, into his hand.

'Ah, well, what can I do with you? Stay a bit longer if you like.'

As he was going out another sergeant came in, followed by a tall thin convict with a bruise under his eye and a scant beard.

'I've come to see about the little girl,' he said.

'There's Daddy!' cried a clear small voice, and a flaxen head appeared from behind Rantseva, who, with Katusha's and Marya Pavlovna's help was making a new frock for the child out of a skirt Rantseva had provided.

'Yes, little one, here I am,' said Buzovkin tenderly.

'She is quite happy here,' said Marya Pavlovna, looking with pity at Buzovkin's bruised face. 'Let her stay with us.'

'The ladies are making me new clothes,' said the child, pointing to Rantseva's sewing. 'A fine wed fwock,' she lisped.

'Would you like to sleep here with us tonight?' Rantseva asked, caressing the little girl.

'Yes, I would. And Daddy, too.'

A smile lit up Rantseva's face.

'No, Daddy can't. We'll keep her, then,' she said, turning to the father.

'All right, you may leave her,' said the sergeant, pausing in the doorway before he went out with the other sergeant.

As soon as the guards had gone Nabatov went up to Buzovkin and tapping him on the shoulder asked:

'I say, old man, is it true that Karmanov wants to change places?'

Buzovkin's kindly gentle face suddenly grew sad and his eyes clouded.

'We have not heard. I should hardly think so,' he said, and, his eyes still dim, added: 'Well, Aksyutka, it seems you're to hold court with the ladies,' and hurriedly went out.

'He knows quite well it's true about the exchange,' said Nabatov. 'What will you do about it?'

'I will inform the commanding officer in the next town. I know both prisoners by sight,' said Nekhlyudov.

No one spoke, afraid apparently that the controversy might flare up again.

Simonson, who had remained silent all the evening, lying in a corner with his hands behind his head, rose with a look of determination and, carefully walking round the others who were sitting on the benches, went up to Nekhlyudov.

'May I have a talk with you now?'

'Certainly,' said Nekhlyudov, and rose to follow him.

Looking at Nekhlyudov as he was getting up, and her eyes meeting his, Katusha blushed and shook her head as though at a loss.

'What I want to speak to you about is this,' Simonson began when they were outside in the passage, where the drone of voices and sudden shouts among the criminal prisoners were particularly audible. Nekhlyudov frowned, but the noise did not seem to disturb Simonson. 'Knowing of your friendship with Katusha Maslova,' he went on in an earnest straightforward way, his kind eyes looking directly into Nekhlyudov's, 'I consider it my duty –' he continued, but had to stop because two voices were heard quarrelling and shouting, both at once, at the other side of the door.

'I tell you, you fool, they're not mine!' shouted one voice.

'I hope you choke, you devil!' the other wheezed back.

At this point Marya Pavlovna came out into the passage.

'You can't talk here,' she said. 'Go in there. There's no one but Vera there.' And she led the way through a nearby door into a tiny room, evidently meant for a solitary cell and now set aside for the women political prisoners. Vera Bogodou-khovskaya was lying on a bunk, a blanket drawn over her head.

'She's got a sick headache, and is asleep, so she can't hear you; and I'll go away,' said Marya Pavlovna.

'On the contrary, please stay,' said Simonson. 'I have no secrets from anyone, and least of all from you.'

'Very well,' said Marya Pavlovna, and moving her whole body from side to side, the way a child does, to get farther back on the bunk, she settled down to listen, her beautiful lamb-like eyes gazing in front of her.

'Well, then, this is what I have to say,' Simonson repeated. 'Knowing your friendship with Katusha Maslova, I consider it my duty to inform you of my own relationship with her.'

'What do you mean?' asked Nekhlyudov, who could not help admiring the simple frankness with which Simonson spoke to him.

'I mean that I should like to marry Katusha Maslova –'

'Amazing!' said Marya Pavlovna, fixing her eyes on Simonson.

'. . . and I have made up my mind to ask her to be my wife,' Simonson continued.

'But what can I do? It depends on her,' said Nekhlyudov.

'Yes, but she will not come to any decision without you.'

'Why not?'

'Because so long as the question of your relations with her is not finally settled she cannot make up her mind on anything.'

'It is definitely settled so far as I am concerned. I wanted to do what I regarded as my duty, and I also wanted to make life easier for her. But I would not, on any account, stand in her way.'

'That may be, but she does not want your sacrifice.'

'It is no sacrifice.'

'That decision of hers is final, I know.'

'Well, then, what is it you are talking to me about?' said Nekhlyudov.

'She must be sure that you feel as she does.'

'But how can I say that I ought not to perform a duty when I know I ought to? All I can say is that I am not a free agent but she is.'

Simonson was silent, plunged in thought.

'Very well, I'll tell her. Don't imagine that I am infatuated with her,' he continued. 'I respect and admire her as a splendid unique human being who has suffered much. I need nothing from her, but I long with all my heart to help her, to lighten her bur –'

Nekhlyudov was surprised to hear the tremor in Simonson's voice.

'To lighten her burden,' Simonson went on. 'If she is unwilling to accept your help, let her accept mine. If she agreed, I would petition to be exiled to the same place with her. Four years are not an eternity. I would stay near her and perhaps I could make her lot easier. . . .' Again he stopped, too agitated to continue.

'What can I say?' said Nekhlyudov. 'I am glad she has found someone like you to protect her . . .'

'That is exactly what I wanted to know,' interrupted Simonson. 'I was anxious to know whether, loving her as you do and wanting her happiness, you would consider our marriage a good thing?'

'Oh yes,' Nekhlyudov replied emphatically.

'I am concerned only about her. I only long to give her rest from her sufferings,' said Simonson, gazing at Nekhlyudov with an expression of childlike tenderness, totally unexpected in a man who looked so morose.

Simonson got to his feet, took Nekhlyudov's hand, put his face close to him and, with a shy smile, embraced him.

'I shall tell her,' he said, and went away.

17

'WHAT do you think of that?' said Marya Pavlovna. 'He's in love – head over heels in love. Why, I'd never have expected Vladimir Simonson to fall in love just like a silly boy. Astonishing! And, to tell you the truth, painful, too,' she concluded with a sigh.

'But what about Katusha? How do you think she looks at it?' asked Nekhlyudov.

'Katusha?' Marya Pavlovna paused, evidently wishing to give as exact an answer as possible. 'You see, in spite of her past, she is by nature a highly moral person, and of such good feeling. . . . She loves you, loves you in the right way, and it makes her happy to think she can do you even the negative service of preventing you from entangling yourself with her. Marriage with you would seem to her to be a terrible falling off, far worse than everything that happened before, and that is why she will never agree to it. And at the same time your presence agitates her.'

'What am I to do, then – vanish from the scene?' said Nekhlyudov.

Marya Pavlovna smiled her sweet childlike smile.

'Yes, partly.'

'And how does one disappear partly?'

'I've been talking nonsense; but what I meant to say about her was that no doubt she sees the absurdity of that sort of ecstatic love of his (he has never spoken of it to her), and while it flatters her it also scares her. You know, I am no authority in such matters, but it seems to me that it is nothing else than ordinary sexual feeling on his part, although it is masked. He says that this love inspires him with energy, and that it is a platonic love. But I know this much – that even if it is an exceptional love, there must be something nasty underneath. Just as there is with Novodvorov and Grabetz.'

Marya Pavlovna had wandered from the main question, having struck her favourite theme.

'But what am I to do?' asked Nekhlyudov.

'I think you ought to tell her. It is always better to have everything clear. Talk to her. I'll call her, shall I?'

'Yes, if you please,' said Nekhlyudov, and Marya Pavlovna went from the room.

A strange feeling came over Nekhlyudov when he was left alone in the little cell, listening to Vera Bogodoukhovskaya's soft breathing, broken every now and then by moans, and to the incessant din from the criminal quarters, two doors beyond.

What Simonson had told him, freed him from the self-imposed obligation which had seemed hard and strange to him in moments of weakness, and yet at the same time he was conscious of a disagreeable, even painful sensation. He had a feeling, too, that Simonson's proposition destroyed the exceptional character of his own action, impairing in his own eyes and in those of others the value of the sacrifice he was prepared to make: if such a good man as Simonson, who was not bound to her by any kind of tie, was anxious to join his fate to hers, then his own sacrifice could never have been so great after all. Plain jealousy entered into it also, perhaps: he had grown so used to her loving him that he could not admit that she could love another. Then, too, it ruled out his plan to remain near her while she served her punishment. If she married Simonson his presence would become unnecessary and he would have to make new plans. Before he could finish investigating his feelings the hum of voices from the criminals' quarters (where something unusual seemed to be happening that day) burst in louder than ever as Katusha opened the door and walked up to him with quick steps.

'Marya Pavlovna sent me,' she said, stopping close to him.

'Yes, I want a talk with you. But sit down. Simonson has been speaking to me.'

She sat down, folding her hands in her lap, and seemed quite calm, but hardly had Nekhlyudov mentioned Simonson's name than she flushed crimson.

'What has he been saying to you?' she asked.

'He told me he wanted to marry you.'

Her face suddenly puckered up with pain. She said nothing and only lowered her eyes.

'He asked for my consent, or my advice. I told him that it depended entirely on you. You must decide for yourself.'

'Oh, what is this? Why must I decide?' she muttered, and looked into his eyes with the peculiar squinting glance that always so strangely affected him. For several seconds they stared silently into each other's eyes. And the glance they exchanged made many things clear to both of them.

'You must decide,' repeated Nekhlyudov.

'What am I to decide? It was all decided long ago.'

'No, you must decide whether you will accept Simonson's proposal,' said Nekhlyudov.

'What sort of a wife would I make? A convict like me! Why should I ruin him, too?' she said, frowning.

'Yes, but supposing your sentence is remitted?'

'Oh, let me alone! There is nothing more to be said,' she exclaimed, and, rising, left the room.

18

WHEN Nekhlyudov followed Katusha into the men's cell he found everyone there in a state of great excitement. Nabatov, who went about all over the place, got to know everybody and noticed everything, had just brought back a piece of news which startled them all. The news was that he had discovered on a wall a note written by Petlin, a revolutionary sentenced to hard labour. Everyone supposed that Petlin had reached Kara long ago, but now it appeared that he had passed this way quite recently, the only political prisoner among criminal convicts.

'On the 17th of August,' so ran the note, 'I was sent off alone with the criminal prisoners. Neverov was with me, but he hanged himself in the lunatic asylum at Kazan. I am well and in good spirits and hope for the best.'

They all fell to discussing Petlin's position and the possible causes of Neverov's suicide. Only Kryltsov sat silent and thoughtful, his brilliant eyes staring fixedly in front of him.

'My husband told me that Neverov saw a ghost when he was in the St Peter and St Paul Fortress,' said Rantseva.

'Yes, he was a poet, a dreamer,' said Novodvorov. 'People like that cannot stand solitary confinement. Now when I was in solitary confinement I never let my imagination run away with me but arranged my time in the most systematic manner. That's why I could always endure it so well.'

'Why not? Very often I was quite simply glad to be locked up,' said Nabatov briskly, evidently wishing to dispel the general gloom. 'One minute you're afraid of everything – of getting arrested, or entangling your friends and harming the cause – but once you're locked up, your responsibility ends. Then you can rest. All you have to do is to sit quiet and smoke.'

'You knew him well?' asked Marya Pavlovna, looking uneasily at Kryltsov's altered haggard face.

'Neverov a dreamer?' Kryltsov suddenly began in a strangled voice, as though he had been shouting or singing for a long time. 'Neverov was a man "the like of whom earth seldom bears," as our doorkeeper often said. . . . Yes, he was crystal clear, you could see right into him. Yes . . . he not only could not tell a lie – he couldn't even dissemble. It wasn't that he had a thin skin – he was flayed, as it were, and all his nerves laid bare. Yes, his was a rich and complex nature, not like . . . But what's the use of talking! . . .' He paused. 'We spend our time arguing whether we ought first to educate the people and then change the general conditions of life,' he said with an angry frown, 'or whether we had better begin by changing the conditions of life; and then we discuss methods – is it to be peaceful propaganda or terrorism? Yes, we go on discussing. But *they* never discuss. *They* know their business and we do not care whether dozens or hundreds of men perish. And what men! It's the other way about with them – their purpose is best served when the best men perish. Yes, Herzen used to say that when the Decembrists were withdrawn from society the general level was lowered. I should think it was lowered! Then Herzen himself was eliminated, and his contemporaries. Now the Neverovs . . .'

'They can't exterminate us all,' said Nabatov in his cheerful tones. 'There will always be enough left to propagate the breed.'

'No, there won't, if we continue to spare *them*,' said Kryltsov, raising his voice and refusing to be interrupted. 'Give me a cigarette.'

'Oh, Anatoly, it's not good for you,' said Marya Pavlovna. 'Please don't smoke.'

'Oh, leave me alone,' he exclaimed irritably, and lit the cigarette. But he at once began to cough and looked as though he were going to vomit. Having expectorated, he continued: 'We have not been doing the right thing. Instead of wasting our time on discussion we ought to have banded together and exterminated *them*. Yes, that's it.'

'But they are human beings, too,' said Nekhlyudov.

'No, they are not. Men who can do what they are doing. . . . No . . . I've heard that bombs and balloons have been invented. Well, we ought to go up in a balloon and sprinkle them with bombs, as though they were lice, till they are all exterminated. Yes. Because . . .' he was just beginning when he went red in the face and coughed so violently that the blood gushed from his mouth.

Nabatov ran to get some snow. Marya Pavlovna brought out some valerian drops and offered them to him, but gasping and breathing heavily, his eyes closed, he pushed away her thin white hand. When the snow and cold water had eased him a little and they had put him to bed for the night, Nekhlyudov bade them all good-bye and left with the sergeant, who had come for him and had been waiting for some time.

The criminal convicts had settled down now and most of them were asleep. Though the inmates of the cells were lying on the bunks and under the bunks, and in the spaces in between, there was still not room for all and some were lying on the floor of the passage with their heads on their sacks and their damp cloaks thrown over them. Through the doors of the cells and along the corridor came the sound of snoring, of groans and sleepy muttering. Everywhere lay human bodies, bunched up and wrapped in prison cloaks. Only a few were still awake in the unmarried men's quarters, sitting in a corner near a lighted candle-end (which they blew out when they saw the sergeant approaching); and an old man who sat naked under the lamp in the passage picking vermin off his shirt. The foul air of the political prisoners' rooms seemed fresh compared with the close stench here. The smoking lamp shone dimly as through a mist, and it was difficult to breathe. In order to pass along the corridor without stepping on or tripping over a sleeping figure, one had to look carefully for an empty space, and, having put one foot down, a place had to be found for the other. Three men who apparently had not been able to find room even in the corridor had disposed themselves in the vestibule right by the stinking leaking tub. One of them was an old imbecile whom Nekhlyudov had frequently noticed marching with the gang. Another was a boy of about ten: he lay between two convicts with his hand under his cheek and his head on the leg of one of them.

When he got out of the gate Nekhlyudov stood still and,

expanding his chest to the full capacity of his lungs, inhaled deep draughts of the frosty air.

19

THE sky was studded with stars. Returning to the inn over the mud, iron-hard except for an occasional spot where it gave, Nekhlyudov knocked at a dark window, and the broad-shouldered servant in his bare feet opened the door for him and let him in. The carters asleep in the back room on the right were snoring loudly; out through the door beyond, in the yard, a great number of horses could be heard crunching their oats. On the left a door led to a clean guest-room. The clean guest-room smelled of wormwood and sweat, and someone with mighty lungs was rhythmically snoring and making sucking noises behind a partition. A red lamp was burning in front of the ikons. Nekhlyudov undressed, spread his rug on the oilcloth sofa, arranged his leather pillow and lay down, thinking over all he had heard and seen that day. The most terrible spectacle of all for him had been the small boy sleeping in the liquid that oozed from the stinking tub, his head resting on the convict's leg.

Unexpected and important though his conversation with Simonson and Katusha that evening had been, he did not dwell on it: his relation to the matter was too complex and at the same time so uncertain that he drove the thought of it from his mind. But the picture of those unfortunate creatures stifling in the putrid air, lying in the liquid oozing from the stinking tub, and especially the innocent face of the little boy asleep against the leg of a criminal, was all the more vivid and he could not get it out of his head.

To know that somewhere, far away, one set of people are torturing another set by subjecting them to every kind of humiliation, inhuman degradation and suffering; and for three months to have been a constant eye-witness of that de-filement and agony inflicted on one set of people by another

– are two very different things. And Nekhlyudov was experiencing this. More than once during the last three months he had asked himself: Am I mad, that I see what others do not see, or are they mad who are responsible for all that I see? Yet the people (and there were so many of them) who did the things that so bewildered and horrified him behaved with such calm assurance – not only that what they were doing was necessary but that it was highly important and valuable work – that it was difficult to believe them all to be mad. Nor could he admit that he was mad himself, for he was conscious of the clearness of his thoughts. Consequently, he found himself in a continual state of perplexity.

What he had seen during the past three months had left him with the impression that from the whole population living in freedom the government in conjunction with the courts picked out the most highly strung, mettlesome and excitable individuals, the most gifted and the strongest – but less crafty and cautious than other people – and these, who were not one whit more guilty or more dangerous to society than those who were left at liberty, were locked up in gaols, halting-stations, hard-labour camps, where they were confined for months and years in utter idleness, material security, and exile from nature, from their families and from useful work. In other words, they were forced outside all the conditions required for a normal and moral human existence. This was the first conclusion that Nekhlyudov drew from his observations.

Secondly, these people were subjected to all sorts of unnecessary degradation in these establishments – chains, shaven heads and infamous prison clothing; that is, they were deprived of the main inducements which encourage weak people to lead good lives: regard for public opinion, a sense of shame and a consciousness of human dignity.

Thirdly, with their lives in continual danger from the infectious diseases common in places of confinement, from physical exhaustion and from beatings (to say nothing of exceptional occurrences such as sunstroke, drowning and fire), these people lived continually in circumstances in which the best and most moral of men are led by the instinct of self-preservation to commit (and to condone in others) the most terribly cruel actions.

Fourthly, these people were forced to associate with men singularly corrupted by life (and by these very institutions, especially) – with murderers and wrong-doers who acted like leaven in dough on those not yet corrupted by the means employed.

And fifthly and finally, all the people subject to these influences were instilled in the most effective manner possible – namely, by every imaginable form of inhuman treatment practised upon themselves, by means of the suffering inflicted on children, women and old men, by beatings and floggings with rods and whips, by the offering of rewards for bringing a fugitive back, dead or alive, by the separation of husbands from wives and putting them to cohabit with other partners, by shootings and hangings – it was instilled into them in the most effective manner possible that all sorts of violence, cruelty and inhumanity were not only tolerated but even sanctioned by the government when it suited its purpose, and were therefore all the more permissible to those who found themselves under duress, in misery and want.

All these institutions seemed to have been devised for the express purpose of producing a concretion of depravity and vice, such as could not be achieved in any other conditions, with the ultimate idea of disseminating this concretion of depravity and vice among the whole population. 'It is just as if the problem had been set: to find the best and surest means of corrupting the greatest number of people,' thought Nekhlyudov, as he tried to penetrate to the heart of what happened in gaols and halting-stations. Every year hundreds and thousands of people were brought to the utmost pitch of depravity and, when completely corrupted, they were set free to spread up and down the country the corruption they had learned in prison.

In the prisons of Tumen, Ekaterinburg, Tomsk, and at the halting-stations on the way, Nekhlyudov saw how successfully the objects society seemed to have set itself were attained. Simple ordinary men brought up in the tenets of Russian social, Christian, peasant morality abandoned these principles and acquired new prison ideas, founded mainly on the theory that any outrage to or violation of the human personality, any destruction of the same, is permissible if profitable. In the light of what was done to them, people who had been in prison came to see and realize with every fibre of their being that all the moral laws of respect and compassion for man preached by religious and moral teachers were set aside in real life, and that therefore there was no need for them to adhere to them either. Nekhlyudov noticed evidence of this in all the convicts he knew: in Fedorov, Makar, even in Tarass, who after two months with the convicts had shocked Nekhlyudov by the lack of morality in his arguments. During the journey Nekhlyudov had discovered that tramps who escaped into the marshes would incite comrades to escape with them, and then murder them and eat their flesh. He saw a live man who had been accused of this and had admitted it. And the most appalling thing was that these were not isolated instances but cases that recurred continually.

Only by the special cultivation of vice such as was carried on in these establishments could a Russian be brought to the state of these tramps who (anticipating Nietzsche's doctrine) considered everything permissible and nothing forbidden, and spread this teaching first among the convicts and then among the people in general.

The only explanation of all that was done was that it aimed at the prevention of crime, at inspiring fear, at correcting offenders and at dealing out to them 'natural punishment', as the books expressed it. But in reality nothing of the sort was achieved. Crime, instead of being prevented, was extended. Offenders, instead of being frightened, were encouraged, and many of them – the tramps, for example – had gone to gaol of their own accord. Instead of the correction of the vicious, there was a systematic dissemination of all the vices, while the need for punishment, far from being softened by the measures taken by the government, nurtured a spirit of revenge among the masses where it did not exist before.

'Then why do they persist in what they are doing?' Nekhlyudov asked himself, and found no answer.

And what surprised him most was that none of all this had happened accidentally, by mistake, once only, but that it had been going on for centuries, with the single difference that in the old days men had had their nostrils slit and their ears cut off; then a time came when they were branded and fastened to iron rods; and now they were manacled, and transported by steam instead of in carts.

The official argument that the conditions which excited his indignation arose from the imperfection of the arrangements at the places of confinement and deportation, and could all be improved as soon as prisons were built in accordance with modern methods, did not satisfy Nekhlyudov, because he felt that the things which aroused his indignation were not caused by more or less perfect arrangements at the places of detention. He had read of model prisons with electric bells, where executions were done by electricity as recommended by Tarde, and this perfected system of violence revolted him still more.

What revolted Nekhlyudov most of all was that there were men in the law-courts and in the ministries who received large salaries taken from the people for referring to books written by other officials like themselves, actuated by like motives, fitting to this or that statute actions that infringed the laws which they themselves had framed, and in accordance with these statutes of theirs went on sending people to places where they would never see them again and where those people were completely at the mercy of cruel, hardened inspectors, gaolers and convoy soldiers, and where they perished, body and soul, by the million.

Now that he had a closer acquaintance with prisons and

halting-stations, Nekhlyudov saw that all the vices which developed among the convicts – drunkenness, gambling, brutality and all the dreadful crimes committed by the inmates of the prisons, and even cannibalism itself – were neither accidents nor signs of mental or physical degeneration (as certain obtuse scientists have declared, to the satisfaction of the government) but that they were the inevitable result of the incredible delusion that one group of human beings has the right to punish another. Nekhlyudov saw that cannibalism began, not in the Siberian marshes but in ministerial offices and government departments: it only found consummation in the marshes. He saw that his brother-in-law, for instance, and in fact all the lawyers and functionaries from usher to minister were not in the least concerned about justice or the good of the people, about which they talked: all they cared about were the roubles they were paid for doing the things that caused all this degradation and misery. That was quite evident.

'Can it be, then, that all this simply springs from a misunderstanding? I wonder, could anything be done to secure their salaries to all these bureaucrats, even to pay them a premium, to leave off doing all that they are doing now?' thought Nekhlyudov. And with these thoughts in his head, after the cocks had crowed for the second time he fell into a sound sleep, in spite of the fleas that spurted around him like water from a fountain every time he stirred.

20

THE carters had left the inn long before Nekhlyudov awoke. The landlady had had her tea, and came in, mopping her fat perspiring neck with a handkerchief, to say that a soldier from the halting-station had brought a note. The note was from Marya Pavlovna. She wrote that Kryltsov's attack had proved more serious than they had supposed. 'At one time we wanted him to stay here and for us to remain with him, but this is not allowed, and we will take him along, but we fear the worst. Try to arrange it so that if we have to leave him in the next town one of us can stay with him. If it were necessary for this that I should marry him, I am, of course, willing to do so.'

Nekhlyudov sent the lad to the posting-station to order horses, and began to pack in great haste. Before he had drunk his second tumbler of tea the three-horsed post-cart drove up to the porch with bells jingling and wheels rattling on the frozen mud as if on cobblestones. Having settled his bill with the fat-necked landlady, Nekhlyudov hurried out, got into the cart and told the driver to go as fast as possible in order to catch up with the party. Just beyond the gates of the common pasture ground he came up with the carts, laden with sacks and sick prisoners, rumbling along over the frozen mud that was beginning to be worn smooth. The officer was not there; he had gone on in front. The soldiers, who had clearly been drinking, followed behind and at the sides of the road, chatting cheerfully. There were a great many carts. In each of the front carts half a dozen of the ailing criminals sat huddled together. Three of the carts at the back held three political prisoners each. In the very last one sat Novodvorov, Grabetz and Kondratyev; the second from the rear carried Rantseva, Nabatov and the feeble rheumatic woman to whom Marya Pavlovna had given up her place. On the cart in front of them Kryltsov, supported by pillows, was lying on a heap of hay. Marya Pavlovna sat on the driver's seat by his side. Nekhlyudov stopped his driver near Kryltsov and went over to him. One of the tipsy soldiers waved his hand to warn him off, but Nekhlyudov, paying no attention, went up to the cart and walked alongside with one hand on it. Kryltsov, in a sheepskin coat and fur cap, a scarf tied over his mouth, seemed paler and thinner than ever. His beautiful eyes looked particularly large and brilliant. Shaken from side to side by the bumping of the cart on the rough surface of the road, he lay with his gaze fixed on Nekhlyudov, and when asked how he felt only closed his eyes and angrily shook his head. He was needing all his energy, apparently, to bear the jolting of the cart. Marya Pavlovna was sitting on the farther side. She exchanged a meaning glance with Nekhlyudov which expressed all her anxiety about Kryltsov's condition, and then began to speak in a cheerful manner.

'It looks as if the officer is ashamed of himself,' she shouted, so as to be heard above the clatter of the wheels. 'Buzovkin's manacles have been removed. He is carrying his little girl himself, and Katusha and Simonson are with them, and Vera – she's taking my place.'

Kryltsov said something that could not be heard, pointing to Marya Pavlovna, and shook his head, frowning in the effort to repress his cough. Nekhlyudov bent over him, trying to hear what he was saying. Then Kryltsov freed his mouth from the scarf and whispered:

'Much better now. Only I mustn't catch cold.'

Nekhlyudov nodded agreement and exchanged glances with Marya Pavlovna.

'Well, how about the problem of the three bodies?' Kryltsov whispered, smiling painfully. 'It's a puzzle, isn't it?'

Nekhlyudov did not understand, but Marya Pavlovna explained that he meant the well-known mathematical problem concerning the relative position of the three heavenly bodies, the sun, the moon and the earth, and that Kryltsov had jestingly applied the comparison in relation to Nekhlyudov, Katusha and Simonson. Kryltsov nodded to show that Marya Pavlovna had explained his little joke correctly.

'The solution does not lie with me,' said Nekhlyudov.

'Did you get my note? Will you do it?' asked Marya Pavlovna.

'Certainly,' Nekhlyudov replied, and, noticing a shade of annoyance on Kryltsov's face, went back to his own cart, climbed into its sagging wicker body and, holding on to the sides of the conveyance as it jolted over the ruts on the rough road, started overtaking the party of prisoners in their grey prison cloaks and sheepskins, fettered and handcuffed together in pairs, stretching for three-quarters of a mile along the road. On the far side of the road he espied Katusha's blue kerchief, Vera Bogodoukhovskaya's black coat and Simonson in his short jacket and crocheted cap, his white woollen stockings laced up with leather thongs like sandals. He was walking beside the women, talking to them earnestly.

When they caught sight of Nekhlyudov the women nodded to him, and Simonson solemnly raised his cap. Nekhlyudov had nothing he wanted to say and, not stopping his driver, was soon ahead of them. Back in the middle of the road again, where it was not so rough, the driver drove still faster; but they were continually forced off the smooth part of the road in order to pass the strings of wagons that were moving along the highway in both directions.

The road, deeply grooved everywhere by cart-ruts, ran through a dark forest of pine-trees, enlivened on both sides by the bright sand-yellow leaves still clinging to the branches of birches and larches. When they were about half-way to the next halting-station the forest ended, fields opened on either side and the gilded crosses and cupolas of a monastery appeared in the distance. The day had turned quite fine, the clouds had dispersed, the sun had risen above the forest, and the wet leaves, the puddles, the cupolas and the crosses of the church glistened bright in its rays. In the blue-grey distance ahead on the right there was a gleam of white mountains. The vehicle entered a large village lying on the outskirts of a town. The village street was crowded with people, Russians from European Russia and natives in strange caps and cloaks. Men and women, some tipsy, some sober, swarmed about screaming at one another round booths, eating-houses, taverns and carts. The nearness to a town was in the air.

Giving a pull and a lash of the whip to the horse on the right, the driver turned sideways on his seat so that the reins fell to the right, and, evidently trying to show off, drove down the street at a brisk trot, and without reining in the horses, arrived at the river, which was to be crossed by a ferry. The raft was in the middle of the fast-running river and was coming from the opposite bank. On the near side a score of carts were waiting to cross. Nekhlyudov did not have to wait long. The raft, which had been taken high upstream against the current, was now carried swiftly down towards the planks of the landing-stage.

The tall, silent, broad-shouldered, muscular ferrymen, in sheepskins and Siberian boots, threw the cables and fastened them round the posts with quick, practised hands, and drawing the bolts back allowed the carts on board to drive ashore. Then they began loading again, packing the ferry with wagons and horses that shied at the sight of the water. The swift broad river slapped against the sides of the ferryboats, straining the cables. When the raft was full and Nekhlyudov's cart, with the horses taken out of it, stood hemmed in all round by other wagons, on one side of the boat, the ferrymen put up the bars and, paying no heed to the entreaties of those who had not found room, unfastened the ropes and got under way. All was quiet on the raft, except for the tramp of the ferrymen's boots and the horses' hooves knocking against the wooden boards as they shifted from foot to foot.

21

NEKHLYUDOV stood at the edge of the raft, gazing at the broad fast-flowing river. Two images in turn kept rising in his mind: the jolting head of angry, dying Kryltsov, and Katusha vigorously stepping out at the side of the road with Simonson. The one impression, that of Kryltsov dying and unprepared for death, was distressing and sad. But the other – of Katusha, hale and hearty, who had found the love of a man like Simonson and was now set on the firm straight path of virtue – should have been pleasant. But for Nekhlyudov it, too, was a painful one, and he could not shake off a feeling of depression.

The boom and metallic tremor of a large brass bell was

borne across the water from the town. The driver standing beside Nekhlyudov and all the other drivers one after another took off their caps and crossed themselves. Only a short shaggy-haired old man who was standing nearest to the rail, and whom Nekhlyudov had not noticed before, did not cross himself but, raising his head, stared at Nekhlyudov. The old man wore a patched coat, cloth trousers and patched, down-at-heel shoes. A small wallet was slung over his shoulder and on his head he had a tall fur cap much the worse for wear.

'Why ain't you saying your prayers, old man?' asked Nekhlyudov's driver, as he replaced and straightened his cap. 'Or bain't you a baptized Christian?'

'Who is there to pray to?' riposted the tattered old man in a determinedly aggressive tone, pronouncing each word distinctly.

''Oo? God, a' course,' the driver retorted witheringly.

'An' you just show me where He be, that God of yours.'

There was something so earnest and unhesitating in the old man's expression that the driver, feeling he had a hard customer to deal with, was a bit abashed, but did not show it, and, trying not to be silenced and put to shame before the crowd that was listening to them, he replied quickly:

'Where 'E be? Everyone knows that – in 'eaven.'

'You been there?'

'Whether I 'ave or not, we all knows we got to pray to God.'

'But no one has seen God anywhere. The only begotten Son, in the bosom of the Father, He hath declared Him,' said the old man in the same rapid manner, and with a severe frown on his face.

'I see you bain't no Christian. You be one of them as prays to an empty 'ole,' said the driver, thrusting his whip into his belt and adjusting the trace-horse's breech-band.

Someone laughed.

'What is your faith, grandad?' asked a middle-aged man standing by his cart near the edge of the raft.

'I haven't got a faith. On account of I don't believe in no one, no one but meself,' replied the old man as quickly and decidedly as before.

'But how can one believe in oneself?' said Nekhlyudov, entering into the conversation. 'One might be mistaken.'

'Not on your life,' the old man replied firmly, with a shake of his head.

'Then why is it there are different religions?' asked Nekhlyudov.

'There be different religions just because people believe in other people, and don't believe in themselves. When I used to believe in other men I wandered about like I was in a swamp. I got so lost, I never thought I'd find me way out. There be Old Believers, an' New Believers, an' Sabbatarians, an' Sectarians, an' them as 'as parsons an' them as don't, an' Austrians, an' Malakans, an' them as castrates themselves. Every faith praises itself up only. An' so they all crawl about in different directions like blind puppies. Many faiths there be, but the Spirit is one. In you, an' in me, an' in 'im. That means, if every man of us believes in the Spirit within 'im, us'll all be united. Let everyone be 'imself, and us'll all be as one.'

The old man spoke in a loud voice and kept looking round, evidently wishing to be heard by as many people as possible.

'And have you thought like this for a long time?' Nekhlyudov asked him.

'Me? Aye, a goodish while now. Been persecuting me nigh on twenty-three years, they 'ave.'

'In what way?'

'Like they persecuted Christ, so they persecute me, too. Grab me an' take me to court, an' drag me before the priests – before the scribes and Pharisees. 'Ad me in the madhouse, they did. But they can't do nought to me because I be a free man. "What's your name?" they ask. They thinks I'm going to call meself by a name of me own. But I don't give meself no name. Renounced everything, I 'ave: got no name, no home, no country – no nothing. I am just me. "What do they call you?" – "Man." – "And how old are you?" I tell 'em I don't count the years, and anyway 'twould be impossible, on account of I always was an' I always shall be. "Who be your father and mother?" says they. "Ain't got no father nor mother, 'cept God an' Mother Earth," I says. "God is me father, an' the earth me mother." – "And the Tsar? Do you recognize the Tsar?" — "Why shouldn't I recognize 'im? 'E's a Tsar unto 'imself, an' I be a Tsar unto meself." – "Oh, what's the good of talking to you!" they says, and I reply, "I never asked you to talk to me, did I?" That's the way they plague me.'

'And where are you going now?' asked Nekhlyudov.

'Where God leads me. I works when I can, and when there ain't no work, I begs,' concluded the old man, noticing that the raft was nearing the other bank and casting a victorious glance on all those who had been listening to him.

The ferryboat fastened up on the other bank. Nekhlyudov got out his purse and offered the old man some coins. The old man refused them.

'I don't take money. Bread I do take,' he said.

'Then forgive me.'

'Bain't nothing to forgive. You 'aven't offended me. Nobody can offend me,' said the old man, hoisting the wallet back on to his shoulder. Meanwhile the post-cart had been landed and the horses put in.

'I wonder you talked to the likes of 'im, sir,' said the driver when Nekhlyudov, having tipped the brawny ferrymen, climbed into the cart again. 'A good-for-nothing old tramp like that.'

22

At the top of the hill the driver turned round to Nekhlyudov.

'Where shall I take you, sir?'

'Which is the best hotel?'

'What could be better than the Sibirsk? But Dukov's is good, too.'

'Whichever you like.'

The driver seated himself sideways again and increased the horses' pace. The town was like all other towns: the same sort of houses with dormer windows and green roofs, the same kind of cathedral, the same little stores and shops in the main street and even the same policemen. Only the houses were mostly of wood and the streets were not paved. In one of the busier streets the driver stopped at the entrance to a hotel. But there were no rooms to be had in that hotel, so they were obliged to drive on to another. Here there was one unoccupied room, and for the first time in two months Nekhlyudov found himself in surroundings such as he was accustomed to, so far as cleanliness and comfort went. Though the room he was shown to was far from luxurious, he felt a sense of well-being after post-carts, country inns and halting-stations. His first business was to clean himself from the lice, which he had never managed quite to get rid of after his visits at the halting-stations. The moment he had unpacked he drove to the bath-house, and thence, having donned his city clothes – a starched shirt, trousers somewhat crumpled from long packing, a frock coat and an overcoat – went to the governor of the district. The cabby, who had been called by the hotel porter, had a big sleek Kirghiz horse harnessed to a rattling four-wheeler. He took Nekhlyudov to a large handsome building guarded by sentries and a policeman. There was a garden in front of the house and at the back, where the leafless branches of aspen and birch stood stark against the dense dark green of firs, pines and spruces.

The general was indisposed and not receiving. Nekhlyudov, nevertheless, asked the footman to take in his card, and presently the man returned with a favourable message:

'You are to come in, please.'

The hall, the footman, the orderly, the staircase, the parlour with its polished parquet floor – all reminded him of Petersburg, only that it was slightly dirtier and more pretentious. Nekhlyudov was shown into the study.

The general, a bloated potato-nosed man of sanguine temperament, with large bumps on his forehead, bags under his eyes and a bald head, sat wrapped in a Tartar-silk dressing-gown, smoking a cigarette and sipping his tea out of a tumbler in a silver holder.

'Good morning, my dear sir. Excuse the dressing-gown, but it's better to receive you in a dressing-gown than not at all,' he said, pulling the dressing-gown closer round the fat wrinkled nape of his neck. 'I am not feeling very well and am keeping to the house. What on earth has brought you to this out-of-the-way place?'

'I have been travelling with a party of prisoners, among whom there is a person who is very dear to me,' said Nekhlyudov, 'and now I have come to petition Your Excellency partly in respect of this person, and partly on another matter.'

The general took a puff at his cigarette, and a sip of tea, stubbed the cigarette out in a malachite ashtray, and, fixing his narrow, bloated beady eyes on Nekhlyudov, listened attentively to what he had to say, only interrupting him once to ask whether he wouldn't like to smoke.

The general belonged to the educated type of military man who believe it possible to reconcile liberalism and humanitarianism with their profession. But being by nature a kind and intelligent man he very soon recognized the impossibility of such a combination and in order not to see the inconsistencies of the life he was leading he had given himself more and more to the habit, so prevalent in military circles, of drinking a great deal of wine, and grew so addicted that after thirty-five years' army service he had become what the doctors term an 'alcoholic'. He was literally saturated with alcohol. It was enough for him to drink any kind of liquid to feel intoxicated. But wine had become such a necessity for him that he could not exist without it, and every day towards evening he was quite drunk; but he had grown so used to being in this state that he did not reel about or talk any special nonsense. Or if he did say something silly now and then it was received as a piece of wisdom, so important was the post he occupied. It was only in the morning – just at the time Nekhlyudov came to see him – that he was something like a reasonable being, able to understand what was said to him, and provide a personal illustration, more or less successful, of the proverb he was fond of repeating: 'If you can drink and be clever, then you are two up for ever.' The higher authorities knew he was a drunkard, but he had had a better education than the other men available – although his education had stopped at the point where his fondness for drink began – he was vigorous, adroit and of imposing appearance, and could behave with discretion even when tipsy, and therefore they had appointed him to, and allowed him to retain, his prominent and responsible position.

Nekhlyudov told him that the person he was interested in was a woman, that she had been wrongfully convicted and that a petition on her behalf had been sent to His Majesty.

'Yes, I see,' said the general. 'Well?'

'I was promised in Petersburg that the decision concerning the fate of this woman would be forwarded to me here some time this month . . .'

Without taking his eyes off Nekhlyudov the general reached out his hand with its stumpy fingers towards the table and rang the bell, and continued to listen in silence, puffing at his cigarette and noisily clearing his throat.

'So I came to ask you, if possible, to allow this woman to remain here until we receive the answer to her petition.'

A servant, an orderly in uniform, came in.

'Find out if Her Excellency is up,' the general said to him, 'and bring some more tea. And the other thing?' he asked, turning to Nekhlyudov.

'My other request concerns a political prisoner in the same party.'

'Indeed!' said the general, with a significant shake of his head.

'He is seriously ill – dying – and will probably be left in the hospital here. So one of the women political prisoners would like to stay behind with him.'

'She is no relation of his?'

'No, but she is willing to marry him if that is the only way she could stay with him.'

The general went on smoking and listening in silence, his keen eyes fixed on Nekhlyudov, with an evident wish to embarrass him.

When Nekhlyudov had finished, the general took a book from the table and, moistening his fingers and quickly leafing through the pages, found the statute relating to marriage and read it.

'What is her sentence?' he asked, looking up from the book.

'Hard labour.'

'In that case the circumstances of the sick man wouldn't be improved by such a marriage.'

'Yes, but –'

'Allow me – Even if a free man were to marry her she would still be obliged to serve her term. The question is, which of them has the heavier sentence – he or she?'

'They are both sentenced to hard labour.'

'Well, they are quits, then,' said the general, with a laugh. 'Both in the same boat. Only he can be left here if he is ill, and of course everything would be done to make things easier for him; but so far as she is concerned, even if she married him she would not be allowed to remain here.'

'Her Excellency is having coffee,' announced the orderly.

The general nodded and went on.

'Still, I will think the matter over. What are their names? Write them down here, will you.'

Nekhlyudov wrote down their names.

'No, I couldn't do that, either,' said the general, when Nekhlyudov asked for permission to see the sick man. 'I do not suspect you, of course, but you are interested in him and in the others, and you have money. Here with us, money can buy anything. They tell me to put down bribery. But how can

I hope to, when there isn't anyone who won't take a bribe? And the lower their rank the easier they are to bribe. How am I to keep an eye on a man who is three thousand miles away? Out there every official is as much a little tsar as I am here,' and he laughed. 'Now I'm sure you've been seeing these political prisoners: you gave some money and they let you in,' he said with a smile. 'Isn't that so?'

'Yes, it's true.'

'I quite understand that you had to do it. You want to see a political prisoner: you are sorry for him. And the inspector or a convoy soldier accepts your bribe because he earns tuppence ha'penny a week and has a family to support, and he can't help taking it. If I were in his place, or in yours, I don't doubt that I should behave in exactly the same way. But in my position I cannot allow myself to deviate from the strict letter of the law, just because I am a human being and liable to be influenced by pity. I am a member of the executive and I have been placed in a position of trust on certain conditions, and I must justify that trust. So there you are. Now tell me what is going on in the metropolis?'

And the general talked and asked questions, obviously wishing at the same time to hear the news and to display his own importance and humanity.

23

'By the way, where are you staying?' asked the general, seeing Nekhlyudov off. 'At Dukov's? It's just as bad there as anywhere else. Come and dine with us. We dine at five. Do you speak English?'

'Yes, I do.'

'Splendid. We have an English traveller here, don't you see. He is making a study of the exile system and prison in Siberia. We are expecting him to dinner this evening, and you must come, too. Don't forget, we dine at five and my wife insists on punctuality. By that time I shall be able to give you an answer about the woman and also about the man who is ill. Maybe it will be possible to let someone stay behind with him.'

After taking leave of the general, Nekhlyudov, feeling exhilarated and full of energy, went to the post-office.

The post-office was a low vaulted room. Clerks seated at desks were serving a crowd of people. One official, with his head on one side, was stamping letters, slipping the envelopes quickly and dexterously under the die. Nekhlyudov did not have to wait long: as soon as they heard his name quite a large bundle of correspondence was handed over to him – money, letters, books and the latest number of the *European Messenger*. Having received his post, Nekhlyudov went over to a wooden bench, where a soldier was sitting with a book in his hand waiting for something, and sat down by his side to look through his letters. Among them was one registered letter in a stout envelope with a clean impression on the bright red sealing-wax. He broke the seal and seeing a letter from Selyenin enclosing an official communication he felt the blood rush to his face and his heart stood still. It was the decision in Katusha's case. What would the answer be? Surely not a rejection? Nekhlyudov glanced hurriedly through the letter, written in an illegibly small, firm, cramped hand, and breathed a sigh of relief. The answer was a favourable one.

'My dear friend,' wrote Selyenin,

Our last conversation made a deep impression on me. You were right about Maslova. I went over the case carefully and saw that a shocking injustice had been done her. It could be remedied only by the Appeals' Committee where you entered an appeal. I succeeded in influencing the decision and am now sending you a copy of the mitigation of sentence to the address given me by your aunt, Countess Katerina Ivanovna. The original document has been dispatched to the place of Maslova's confinement during the trial, and, no doubt, will be forwarded at once to the Siberian Central Office. I hasten to communicate this glad news to you.

Yours ever,

Selyenin.

The contents of the document itself ran as follows:

His Imperial Majesty's Office for the Reception of Appeals addressed to the Sovereign. Case No. So-and-so. Division No. Such and such. Reference No. — Such and such a date and year. By order of the Chief of His Majesty's Office for the Reception of Appeals addressed to His Imperial Majesty – Citizen Katerina Maslova is hereby informed that in consequence of the most humble report made to him, His Imperial Majesty deigns to grant the request of the said Maslova and graciously commands that her sentence to hard labour be commuted to one of exile to some less remote region of Siberia.

It was indeed joyful and important news: everything that Nekhlyudov could have hoped for for Katusha, and for himself as well, had come to pass. True, the change in her circumstances brought new complications to his relations with her. While she was a convict the marriage he offered her could be one in name only and would have had no meaning except that he would be in a position to alleviate her condition. But now there was nothing to prevent their living together. And for this Nekhlyudov was unprepared. Besides, what about her relations with Simonson? What did those words she had spoken yesterday really mean? And supposing she were to consent to marry Simonson, would that be a good thing or a bad thing? He was completely unable to unravel all these conundrums, so he gave up thinking about them. 'It will all clear itself up later on,' he said to himself. 'Now I must try and see her as soon as possible and tell her the glad news and have her set free.' He imagined that the copy he had in his hands would suffice for that. And leaving the post-office he told the cabby to drive him to the prison.

Although he had received no permit from the general to visit the prison that morning, Nekhlyudov knew by experience that what the higher authorities categorically refuse can often be obtained very easily from their subordinates, so he decided that he would at all events make an attempt to get into the prison to give Katusha the joyful news, and perhaps have her set free. At the same time he could find out how

Kryltsov was and tell him and Marya Pavlovna what the general had said.

The superintendent of the prison was a very tall stout imposing-looking man with moustaches and side-whiskers that curved round towards the corners of his mouth. His manner was stern in the extreme, and he at once informed Nekhlyudov flatly that he could not grant an outsider permission to interview the prisoners without a special order from his chief. To Nekhlyudov's remark that he had been allowed to even in the capitals he answered:

'Very likely, but I do not allow it,' and his tone implied, 'You city gentlemen think you can awe and disconcert us; but even if we do live in Eastern Siberia we know the rules and regulations and can teach you a thing or two!'

Nor did the copy of a document straight from the Private Chancery of His Imperial Majesty have any effect on the superintendent. He categorically refused to allow Nekhlyudov inside the prison walls. And to Nekhlyudov's naïve supposition that Maslova might be liberated upon presentation of the said copy he merely smiled contemptuously, remarking that a direct order from his immediate superior would be needed before anyone could be set free. All that he would promise was to inform Maslova of the mitigation of her sentence, and not detain her for a single hour after the order for her release was received.

He likewise refused to give any information concerning Kryltsov's condition, declaring that he could not even say whether there was a convict of that name in the prison. And so, with nothing accomplished, Nekhlyudov returned to his cabby and drove back to the hotel.

The severity of the superintendent was mainly due to the fact that an epidemic of typhus had broken out in the prison, which was overcrowded to double its normal capacity. The cabby told Nekhlyudov as they drove along that 'people were dying like flies in the prison. Some sort of sickness it was. Burying up to twenty or more a day, they were.'

24

IN spite of his failure at the prison Nekhlyudov, his energy and confidence unabated, drove to the governor's office to inquire whether the order for Maslova's pardon had been received there. It had not, and so, returning to the hotel, and without waiting, Nekhlyudov made haste to write at once to Selyenin and the lawyer. When both letters were written he looked at his watch and saw that it was time to go to dinner at the general's.

On the way he again began wondering how Katusha would receive her pardon. Where would they exile her? How should he live with her? What about Simonson? What were her feelings towards him? He remembered the change that had come over her, and this reminded him of her past.

'That must be forgotten, blotted out for ever,' he said to himself, and again hastened to drive her out of his mind. 'When the time comes I shall know what to do,' he told himself, and began to think of what he was going to say to the general.

The dinner at the general's, served with all the luxury Nekhlyudov had been used to, and as is customary among the wealthy and the higher ranks of officialdom, was extremely enjoyable to Nekhlyudov, who had been deprived for so long not only of luxury but even of the most primitive amenities of civilization.

The hostess was a Petersburg *grande dame* of the old school, who had been a maid of honour at the court of Nicholas I. She spoke French naturally and Russian unnaturally. She held herself very erect, and when she made a gesture with her hands she always kept her elbows close to her waist. Her attitude towards her husband was one of quiet and somewhat melancholy deference. Towards her guests she was exceedingly gracious and attentive, though in a degree which varied with their social status. Nekhlyudov she received as if he were one of themselves, with that subtle, unostentatious, peculiar flattery that made him once again aware of his virtues, and afforded him a pleasurable sense of satisfaction. She made him feel that she knew of the honourable if rather singular purpose which had brought him to Siberia, and that she regarded him as an exceptional person. This delicate flattery, together with the elegance and luxury of the general's house, had the effect of making Nekhlyudov succumb to the enjoyment of the beautiful surroundings, the appetizing food and the pleasure of associating with well-bred men and women of his own class. It seemed as though the circumstances and surroundings he had known during these last months had been only a dream from which he had now awakened to reality.

Besides the general's household – his daughter, her husband and the aide-de-camp – there were three guests: the Englishman, a merchant interested in gold mines, and the governor of a distant Siberian town. Nekhlyudov liked all these people.

The Englishman, who had healthy red cheeks, spoke very bad French, but had an excellent command of his own language and used it like an orator. He had travelled widely, and what he had to say about America, India, Japan and Siberia was very interesting.

The young gold merchant, the son of a peasant, wore a dinner jacket made in London, and diamond cuff-links. He possessed an extensive library, contributed generously to charity and held liberal European ideas. He pleased and interested Nekhlyudov because he represented an entirely new and attractive example of the civilized grafting of European culture on healthy peasant stock.

The governor of the remote Siberian town was that same ex-director of a government department about whom there had been so much talk when Nekhlyudov was in Petersburg. He was a plump pudgy man with scant curling hair, soft blue eyes, carefully tended white hands adorned with rings, and an agreeable smile. He was very thick round the lower part of the body. The host had a sincere respect for this governor because, surrounded by bribe-takers, he was the only one who refused to take a bribe; while the mistress of the house, who was very fond of music and herself an excellent pianist, esteemed him because he was a fine musician and could play duets with her. Nekhlyudov was in such high good humour that day that he found it impossible to dislike even this man.

The jolly, lively aide-de-camp, with his clean-shaven bluish chin, who was continually offering his services to everybody, was likeable for his obvious good nature.

But it was the charming young couple, the general's daughter and her husband, that Nekhlyudov found the most delightful. The daughter was a plain, artless young woman entirely absorbed in her two children; the husband, whom she had fallen in love with and had married after a long struggle with her parents, was a graduate, a liberal, of Moscow University, a modest and intelligent young man in government service, occupied with statistics, and more particularly with the native tribes, of whom he had made a study, for he liked them and was trying to save them from extinction.

Not only were all these people attentive and amiable to Nekhlyudov – they obviously enjoyed his company, finding him an original and interesting personality. The general, who came in to dinner in uniform, wearing the White Cross, greeted Nekhlyudov like an old friend, and immediately invited his guests to the side-table to partake of hors d'œuvres and vodka. When the general inquired what he had been doing since leaving him Nekhlyudov told him that he had been to the post-office and collected a letter informing him that a pardon had been granted to the person he had spoken about that morning, and again asked for a permit to visit the prison.

The general, evidently displeased that business should be mentioned at dinner, frowned and said nothing.

'Will you have a glass of vodka?' he asked in French to the Englishman who had just come up to the table. The Englishman accepted a glass of vodka and told them that he had been to see the cathedral and the factory, but would very much like to visit the great Transportation Prison.

'An excellent idea!' said the general, turning to Nekhlyudov. 'You can go together. Give them a pass,' he said to the adjutant.

'When would you like to go?' Nekhlyudov asked the Englishman.

'I always prefer to visit prisons in the evening. Everybody is indoors then, no preparations are made, so one sees things as they really are,' replied the Englishman.

'Aha, he wants to see it in all its glory! Let him, let him! When I wrote about the state of affairs they paid no attention to me. Now let them hear about it from the foreign press,' and the general went over to the dinner-table, where the hostess was showing the guests their places.

Nekhlyudov sat between the hostess and the Englishman. Opposite him was the general's daughter and the ex-director of a government department.

The conversation during dinner proceeded by fits and starts: now it was the Englishman talking about India, then it was the Tonkin Expedition, which the general strongly disapproved of, followed by the bribery and corruption widespread in Siberia. None of these topics interested Nekhlyudov very much.

But in the drawing-room after dinner, over their coffee, Nekhlyudov, the Englishman and their hostess began a most absorbing conversation about Gladstone, in the course of which it seemed to Nekhlyudov that he made more than one clever remark not lost on the others. And after the good dinner, and the wine, sitting in a comfortable arm-chair sipping coffee and surrounded by affable well-bred people, Nekhlyudov felt more and more content and at peace with the world. And when the hostess, at the Englishman's request, went up to the piano with the ex-director of a department, and they began to play Beethoven's Fifth Symphony, which they had practised together assiduously, Nekhlyudov fell into a state of perfect harmony with himself, such as he had not known for a long time, as if he had just found out what a good man he was.

The piano was a splendid grand, and the symphony well played. At least Nekhlyudov thought so, and he knew and liked that symphony. As he listened to the beautiful *andante* he felt a tickling in his nose, so moved was he by the contemplation of himself and all his virtues.

Thanking his hostess for the great pleasure he had so long been deprived of, Nekhlyudov was about to say good-bye and go, when the general's daughter, blushing but determined, walked over to him and said:

'You were asking about my children. Would you like to see them?'

'She thinks everybody is interested in seeing her children,' said her mother, smiling at her daughter's charming artlessness. 'The prince is not in the least interested in children.'

'On the contrary, I am very interested indeed,' said Nekhlyudov, touched by this ebullient display of happy mother-love. 'Please let me see them.'

'She is taking the prince to see her infants,' the general called with a laugh from the card-table, where he sat with his son-in-law, the gold-miner and the aide-de-camp. 'Go along, now, and pay your tribute.'

The young woman, obviously excited at the thought that her children were about to be submitted to the critical eye of a stranger, walked quickly towards the inner apartments, followed by Nekhlyudov. In the third room, which had a high ceiling and white wallpaper, and was lit by a small lamp with a dark shade over it, two cots stood side by side. Between the cots sat a nurse with a white cape on her shoulders; she had a good-natured face and the high cheek-bones of a Siberian. She rose and bowed. The mother bent over the first cot, where a little two-year-old girl lay peacefully sleeping with her lips parted and her long curly hair tumbled over the pillow.

'This is my Katya,' said the mother, straightening the

crocheted blue-and-white-striped coverlet, from beneath which a tiny white foot peeped out. 'Isn't she a darling? She is only two, you know.'

'Sweet!'

'And this is Vassuk, as his grandfather calls him. Quite a different type. A real Siberian, don't you think so?'

'A fine little chap,' said Nekhlyudov, bending to look at the chubby youngster lying fast asleep on his stomach.

'You really think so?' said the mother with a meaningful smile.

Nekhlyudov thought of the chains, the shaven heads, the brawls, the debauchery, the dying Kryltsov, Katusha with all her past; and he felt envious and longed for just such pure and refined happiness as this now seemed to him to be.

Having praised the children again and again, and thereby at least partially satisfying their mother, who eagerly drank in his expressions of admiration, Nekhlyudov followed her back to the drawing-room, where the Englishman was waiting for him to go to the prison as they had arranged. Nekhlyudov took leave of his hosts, old and young, and together with the Englishman went out on to the porch of the general's house.

The weather had changed. Snow was falling in heavy flakes and already lay thick on the road, the roof, the trees in the garden and the steps of the porch, and the top of the cab and the horse's back were white. The Englishman had his own carriage, so Nekhlyudov told the coachman to drive to the prison and then seated himself alone in his own vehicle and, with a heavy sense of having to fulfil an unpleasant duty, followed them over the soft snow through which the wheels churned slowly and with difficulty.

25

IN spite of the white mantle which now lay over everything – porch, roof and walls – the gloomy prison building with the sentry, and the lantern hanging over the gate, and the long rows of lighted windows made an even more dismal impression than it had in the morning.

The imposing superintendent came out to the gate and, after reading by the light of the lantern the pass that had been given to Nekhlyudov and the Englishman, shrugged his powerful shoulders in surprise; but in obedience to the order he invited the visitors to follow him. He led them first across the courtyard to a door on the right, then up a staircase into the office. Offering them seats, he asked what he could do for them, and when he heard that Nekhlyudov would like to see Maslova at once he sent a warder to fetch her, and got ready to answer the questions which the Englishman, with Nekhlyudov acting as interpreter, immediately began to put to him.

'How many persons is the prison built to hold?' asked the Englishman. 'How many are here now? How many of them are men, how many women and how many children? How many are sentenced to the mines? How many to exile? How many are following the prisoners of their own free will? How many are sick?'

Nekhlyudov translated the questions and the replies, without entering into their meaning, so agitated was he at the thought of the impending interview. (His agitation was totally unexpected.) In the middle of a sentence which he was translating to the Englishman, he heard approaching steps, and the office door opened. As had happened many times before, a gaoler came in followed by Katusha, in a prison jacket with a kerchief on her head – and at the sight of her his heart felt heavy as lead.

'I want to live. I want a family, children of my own. I want to live like other men,' flashed through his mind as she walked into the room with rapid steps and downcast eyes.

He rose and advanced to meet her, and her face appeared hard and disagreeable. It was the expression he remembered when she reproached him. She flushed and turned pale, her fingers nervously twisting the edge of her jacket, and she alternately looked into his face and lowered her eyes.

'You know that a mitigation of your sentence has been granted?'

'Yes, the gaoler told me.'

'So when the document arrives you will be able to come away and settle where you like. We will think it over –'

She interrupted him hurriedly.

'There's nothing to think over. I shall follow Simonson wherever he goes.'

In spite of her excitement she raised her eyes to Nekhlyudov's and spoke quickly and distinctly, as though she had prepared what she would say in advance.

'I see,' said Nekhlyudov.

'Why not, Dmitri Ivanovich, if he wants me to live with him' – she stopped, abashed, and corrected herself – 'wants me to be with him, what more could I wish for? I must consider myself lucky. What else is there for me? . . .'

'It's one of two things,' thought Nekhlyudov. 'Either she loves Simonson and has no use for the sacrifice I imagined I was making; or she still loves me and is refusing me for my own sake, and is burning her bridges by uniting her lot with Simonson.' And he felt mortified, and knew that he was blushing.

'Of course, if you love him –' he said.

'What does it matter whether I do or don't love him? I have given up all that, and besides Simonson is quite different.'

'Yes, of course,' began Nekhlyudov. 'He is a fine man, and I think –'

She interrupted him again, as though she feared that he might say too much, or that she would not have a chance to say everything.

'You must forgive me, Dmitri Ivanovich, if I am not doing what you want,' she said, looking into his eyes with her mysterious squinting glance. 'But this is how it had to be. And you have your own life to live.'

She was only telling him what he himself had just been saying to himself, but now he was no longer thinking this – he was thinking and feeling something quite different. It was not just that he felt mortified: he was regretting all that he would lose when he lost her.

'I did not expect this,' he said.

'Why should you live here and be wretched? You have suffered enough,' she said, with a strange smile.

'I have not suffered: I have been happy, and I should like to go on looking after you if I could.'

'We' – as she said 'we' she glanced up at Nekhlyudov – 'we do not need anything. You have done so much for me as it is. If it hadn't been for you –' She was about to say something, but her voice quivered.

'I am the last person you should thank,' said Nekhlyudov.

'What's the use of trying to weigh up what we owe one another? God will make up our accounts,' she said, and her black eyes glistened with the tears that welled up into them.

'What a good woman you are!' he said.

'Me, a good woman?' she said through her tears, and a pitiful smile lit up her face.

'Are you ready?'[1] the Englishman interrupted them.

'Directly,'[1] replied Nekhlyudov, and asked her about Kryltsov.

She pulled herself together and quietly told him what she knew: Kryltsov had become very weak on the road, and been sent straight to the infirmary. Marya Pavlovna was very anxious about him and had asked to be taken on as a nurse, but permission had not been granted.

'Had I better go now?' she asked, noticing that the Englishman was waiting.

'I will not say good-bye, I shall see you again,' said Nekhlyudov.

'Forgive me,' she whispered, almost inaudibly. Their eyes met, and by her peculiar squinting look, her pathetic smile and the tone of her voice when she said, not 'Good-bye' but 'Forgive

1. [Tolstoy's English.]

me,' Nekhlyudov understood that his second supposition as to the cause of her decision was the real one: she loved him and thought that by uniting herself to him she would be spoiling his life, but that by staying with Simonson she was setting Nekhlyudov free, and while rejoicing that she had done what she meant to do she found it painful to part from him.

She pressed his hand, turned quickly and left the room.

Nekhlyudov was now ready to go, but glancing at the Englishman he saw that he was writing something down in his notebook. Not wishing to disturb him, he sat down on a wooden seat by the wall and was suddenly overcome by a great weariness. It was not the weariness one feels after a sleepless night, a journey or some strong emotion – he felt terribly tired of living. He leaned back against the back of the bench, closed his eyes and instantly fell into a deep slumber.

'Well, would you like to see the cells now?' the superintendent asked.

Nekhlyudov awoke and wondered where he was. The Englishman had finished his notes and wished to see the cells. Tired and listless, Nekhlyudov followed them.

26

PASSING through the ante-room and a corridor which smelt quite nauseatingly, and where to their astonishment they saw two prisoners urinating on the floor, the superintendent, the Englishman and Nekhlyudov, accompanied by warders, entered the first part of the prison, which housed those sentenced to hard labour. In this cell the prisoners were already lying on their bunks, which ran down the centre of the ward. They numbered around seventy. They lay head to head and side by side. When the visitors came in all the prisoners sprang up, and clanking their chains stood beside their bunks, their half-shaven heads shining in the light. Only two remained lying on their bunks: a young man with a flushed face, obviously running a high temperature, and an old fellow who groaned incessantly.

The Englishman asked if the young man had been ill long. The superintendent said that he had been taken ill that morning, but that the old man had had stomach trouble for a long time, only there was nowhere to put him, as the infirmary had been overcrowded for months. The Englishman shook his head in disapproval, and said that he would like to say a few words to these people, and asked Nekhlyudov to translate for him. It appeared that besides his professed object in making the journey – to investigate the prisons and places of exile in Siberia – he also had another end in view: to preach salvation by faith and atonement.

'Tell them,' he said, 'that Christ pities and loves them, and died for them. If they believe this they will be saved.' While he was speaking, all the prisoners stood silent beside their bunks, with their arms at their sides. 'Tell them that it is all in this book,' he concluded. 'Can any of them read?'

It turned out that above a score of them could. The Englishman took some bound copies of the New Testament out of his bag, and several strong muscular hands with horny blackened finger-nails were stretched out from under the sleeves of their coarse shirts, trying to push one another away. He left two Testaments in this ward and went into the next.

In the next cell it was the same. There was the same close atmosphere and stench; just as in the first cell an ikon hung between the two windows, a tub stood to the left of the door, and again the prisoners lay packed closely side by side, and they all sprang up and stood motionless beside their bunks – all but three, two of whom sat up, while one remained lying and did not even look at the visitors. They were the ill prisoners. The Englishman repeated his speech and again left two Testaments.

Shouting and uproar were heard in the third cell. The superintendent knocked and called for quiet. When the door opened, all those in the room stood to attention again, except for the few who were ill and the two who were fighting, their faces distorted with anger as they clutched each other by the hair and beard. They only let go of one another when a warder ran up to them. One of them had a smashed nose, now all snivel, slobber and blood, which he wiped with the sleeve of his tunic; the other was picking out the hairs torn loose from his beard.

'Head man!' shouted the superintendent sternly.

A handsome powerful-looking man stepped forward.

'There was no stopping them, Your Excellency,' he said, his eyes sparkling merrily.

'I'll stop them all right,' said the superintendent, frowning.

'What did they fight for?'[1] asked the Englishman.

Nekhlyudov asked the head man what the fighting had been about.

'Over a row: he interfered in someone else's row,' said the head man, continuing to smile. 'One of 'em got a shove, and the other gave him what for.'

Nekhlyudov told the Englishman.

'I should like to say a few words to them,' observed the Englishman, turning to the superintendent.

Nekhlyudov translated. The superintendent gave permission, and the Englishman got out his New Testament in its leather binding.

'Will you translate this, please,' he said to Nekhlyudov. 'You have been quarrelling and fighting, but Christ, Who died for us, gave us another way of settling our quarrels. Ask them if they know how, according to Christ's commandment, we should behave with a person who offends us.'

Nekhlyudov translated what the Englishman said, and his question.

'Complain to the authorities so they can sort it out?' hazarded one, glancing sideways at the majestic figure of the superintendent.

1. [Tolstoy's English.]

'Give 'im a 'iding, 'e won't offend no more,' said another.

A number of approving chuckles were heard. Nekhlyudov translated their answers to the Englishman.

'Tell them that Christ's commandment would have us do just the opposite: if a man strike you on one cheek, offer him the other,' said the Englishman, putting his own cheek forward.

Nekhlyudov translated.

'He'd better try it himself,' said a voice.

'And what if you get a sock on the other jaw, what d'you offer then?' inquired one of those who were lying down ill.

'That's the way 'e sloshes you to pieces.'

'Come on, 'ave a go,' said someone at the back, and broke into a ringing laugh. The whole cell was shaken by an irrepressible burst of laughter; even the convict with the smashed nose laughed through the blood and slobber. Those who were ill laughed, too.

The Englishman was not put out of countenance but requested Nekhlyudov to convey to them that what seems impossible becomes possible and easy for the faithful.

'Ask them now – do they drink?'

'Don't we just!' said a voice, and at once there was more chuckling and another burst of laughter.

In this cell four men were ill. When the Englishman asked why the sick were not all together in one ward the superintendent replied that they did not wish it themselves. Their diseases were not infectious, and the doctor's assistant looked after them and did what was necessary.

'He hasn't shown up here for a fortnight,' said a voice.

The superintendent did not answer, and led the visitors into the next cell. As before, when the doors were unlocked, all the convicts rose and stood in silence, and again the Englishman distributed Testaments. It was the same in the fifth and sixth cells, to the right and to the left, on both sides.

From those sentenced to hard labour they went on to the exportation prisoners. From the exiles to those banished by

557

their communes, and then to those who were following voluntarily. Everywhere it was the same: everywhere the same cold, hungry, idle, diseased, degraded men under lock and key, exhibited like wild beasts.

When he had distributed an appointed number of Testaments the Englishman gave away no more and even made no more speeches. The depressing sights and especially the stifling atmosphere apparently undermined even his energy, and he went from cell to cell, merely remarking 'I see' to anything the superintendent said about the prisoners in each. Nekhlyudov walked with them as if in a dream, lacking the strength to excuse himself and go away, and with the same feeling of weariness and hopelessness.

27

IN one of the cells, among the exiles, Nekhlyudov recognized, to his surprise, the strange old man he had met on the ferry that morning. All wrinkled, tattered and barefoot, his only garments a dirty ash-grey shirt and trousers, the shirt torn on one shoulder, the old fellow was sitting on the floor beside his bunk and looking sternly and inquiringly at the newcomers. His emaciated body, visible through the rents in his grimy shirt, looked feeble and wretched, but the expression on his face was even more concentratedly serious and animated than on the ferry. As in the other cells, all the prisoners jumped up and stood to attention when the superintendent entered, but the old man remained sitting on the floor. His eyes glittered and he frowned wrathfully.

'Stand up!' the superintendent shouted at him.

The old man did not move, and only smiled disdainfully.

'Thy servants stand before thee, but I am not thy servant. Thou bearest the seal . . .' muttered the old man, pointing to the superintendent's forehead.

'Wh-a-a-t?' roared the superintendent threateningly, and took a step towards him.

'I know this man,' Nekhlyudov hastened to say. 'Why is he here?'

'The police sent him in for having no identity papers. We ask them not to, but they will send them in,' said the superintendent, looking savagely at the old man out of the corner of his eye.

'So you, too, it seems, are of the legion of Antichrist?' said the old man, addressing Nekhlyudov.

'No, I am only a visitor.'

'You have come, then, to marvel how Antichrist tortures people? All right, take your fill of it. He's captured them, locked them up in a cage, a whole army of them. In the sweat of their faces people ought to eat bread, and he has shut them up with no work to do, feeds them like swine, that they may become brute beasts.'

'What is he saying?' asked the Englishman.

Nekhlyudov told him that the old man was blaming the superintendent for keeping men in prison.

'Ask him what he thinks ought to be done with those who refuse to obey the law,' said the Englishman.

The old man broke into an odd laugh, displaying two rows of sound teeth.

'The law!' he repeated contemptuously. 'First *he* robbed everybody, taking for himself all the land and all the wealth that belonged to the people – converted it all to his own use – killed all those who resisted him, and then wrote laws forbidding men to rob and kill. He should have made the laws first.'

Nekhlyudov translated. The Englishman smiled.

'Still, ask him what is to be done with thieves and murderers now?'

Again Nekhlyudov translated the question. The old man knitted his brows fiercely.

'You tell him to cast off the seal of Antichrist from himself, then he won't have either thieves or murderers. Tell him so.'

'He is crazy,'[1] said the Englishman when Nekhlyudov had translated the old man's words; and shrugging his shoulders he left the cell.

'You get on with your own business and leave other people alone. Every man is his own master. The Lord knows who should be punished and who should be pardoned, but we do not,' said the old man. 'Be your own master and you will need no other. Go, go,' he added, scowling and flashing his eyes at Nekhlyudov, who was lingering in the cell. 'You have gazed enough on how the servants of Antichrist feed lice with the bodies of men. Go, go!'

Nekhlyudov stepped out into the passage and found the Englishman and the superintendent standing by the open door of an empty cell. The Englishman was asking what the cell was for. The superintendent explained that it was the mortuary.

'Oh!' said the Englishman, when Nekhlyudov had translated for him, and expressed a wish to go in.

The mortuary was an ordinary, not very large cell. A small lamp hung on the wall and dimly lit up some sacks and logs that were piled in one corner, and on bunks to the right – four dead bodies. The first of these, clothed in a coarse home-spun shirt and a pair of trousers, was that of a tall man with a little pointed beard and a half-shaven head. The body had already stiffened; the bluish hands had evidently been crossed on the breast, but had now fallen apart; the bare legs had parted, too, and the feet pointed in different directions. Next to him lay a barefooted and bareheaded old woman in a white petti-coat and blouse. She had a tiny, wrinkled, yellow face, a sharp little nose and a short scanty braid of hair. Beyond her was the body of another man, clothed in some mauve garment. The colour reminded Nekhlyudov of something.

He went nearer and began to look at the body.

The little pointed beard turned upward, the firm hand-some nose, the high white forehead, the thin curling hair –

1. [Tolstoy's English.]

he recognized the familiar features and could scarcely believe his own eyes. Yesterday he had seen this face angry, excited, full of suffering. Now it was quiet, motionless and terribly beautiful.

Yes, it was Kryltsov – or, at any rate, all that remained of Kryltsov's material existence.

'Why had he suffered? Why had he lived? Does he understand now what it's all for?' thought Nekhlyudov, and it seemed to him that there was no answer, that there was nothing but death, and he felt faint.

Without a word of farewell to the Englishman, Nekhlyudov asked the warder to show him the way to the courtyard, and, feeling the absolute necessity of being alone to think over all he had seen and heard that evening, he drove back to the hotel.

28

NEKHLYUDOV did not go to bed but for a long time paced up and down his room. The Katusha business was over and done with. She did not need him, and it made him feel sad as well as mortified. But this was not what troubled him now. The other business on which he had embarked was not only unfinished but worried him more than ever, and required all his energy.

All the horrible evil he had seen and heard about over the last months, and today particularly, at that awful prison – all the evil that had destroyed that dear Kryltsov – ruled triumphant, and he could discern no possibility of conquering it or even of knowing how to conquer it.

In his imagination he beheld hundreds and thousands of degraded human beings locked up in noisome prisons by indifferent generals, prosecuting attorneys and superintendents; he recalled the strange defiant old man who denounced the authorities and was considered mad; and then among the bodies the beautiful waxen face of Kryltsov, who had died in anger. And the question he had asked himself before – was he, Nekhlyudov, mad, or was it the people who considered themselves wise and did all these things, who were mad? – arose in his mind with renewed force and demanded an answer.

Tired of pacing to and fro, tired of thinking, he sat down on the sofa near the lamp and mechanically opened the copy of the New Testament the Englishman had given him as a souvenir and which he had thrown on the table when he emptied his pockets. 'They say one can find an answer to everything here,' he said to himself, and opening it at random he began reading Matthew, chapter xviii:

1 At the same time came the disciples unto Jesus, saying, Who is the greatest in the kingdom of heaven?

2 And Jesus called a little child unto him, and set him in the midst of them.

3 And said, Verily I say unto you, Except ye be converted, and become as little children, ye shall not enter into the kingdom of heaven.

4 Whosoever therefore shall humble himself as this little child, the same is greatest in the kingdom of heaven.

'Yes, yes, that is true,' he thought, remembering how he himself had experienced peace and joy of life only to the extent to which he had humbled himself.

5 And whoso shall receive one such little child in my name receiveth me.

6 But whoso shall offend one of these little ones which believe in me, it were better for him that a millstone were hanged about his neck, and that he were drowned in the depth of the sea.

'I wonder what that means – "Whoso shall receive"? And receive where? And what does "in my name" mean?' he asked himself, feeling that the words told him nothing. 'And why a millstone round his neck and the deeps of the sea? No, there must be something wrong here: it is vague, obscure,' he thought, recalling how more than once in his life he had set himself to read the Gospels and every time been discouraged by the obscurity of such passages. He went on to read the seventh, eighth, ninth and tenth verses about offences, and how it must needs be that they come into the world, about punishment by means of hell-fire into which people will be cast, and angels belonging to the little children who behold the face of the Father which is in heaven. 'What a pity it's all so incoherent,' he thought, 'for one feels there is something right about it.'

11 For the Son of man is come to save that which was lost – *he continued to read.*

12 How think ye? if a man have an hundred sheep, and one of them be gone astray, doth he not leave the ninety and nine, and goeth into the mountains, and seeketh that which is gone astray?

13 And if so be that he find it, verily I say unto you, he rejoiceth more of that sheep, than of the ninety and nine which went not astray.

14 Even so it is not the will of your Father which is in heaven, that one of these little ones should perish.

'No, it was not the will of the Father that they should perish, and here they are perishing in their hundreds and thousands. And no means of saving them,' he reflected.

21 Then came Peter to him, and said, Lord, how oft shall my brother sin against me, and I forgive him? till seven times?

22 Jesus saith unto him, I say not unto thee, Until seven times: but, Until seventy times seven.

23 Therefore is the kingdom of heaven likened unto a certain king, which would take account of his servants.

24 And when he had begun to reckon, one was brought unto him, which owed him ten thousand talents.

25 But forasmuch as he had not to pay, his lord commanded him to be sold, and his wife, and children, and all that he had, and payment to be made.

26 The servant therefore fell down, and worshipped him, saying, Lord, have patience with me, and I will pay thee all.

27 Then the lord of that servant was moved with compassion, and loosed him, and forgave him the debt.

28 But the same servant went out, and found one of his fellow-

servants, which owed him an hundred pence: and he laid hands on him, and took him by the throat, saying, Pay me that thou owest.

29 And his fellowservant fell down at his feet, and besought him, saying, Have patience with me, and I will pay thee all.

30 And he would not: but went and cast him into prison, till he should pay the debt.

31 So when his fellowservants saw what was done, they were very sorry, and came and told unto their lord all that was done.

32 Then his lord, after that he had called him, said unto him, O thou wicked servant, I forgave thee all that debt, because thou desiredst me:

33 Shouldest not thou also have had compassion on thy fellow-servant, even as I had pity on thee?

'And can that be the whole answer?' Nekhlyudov suddenly exclaimed aloud. And the inner voice of his whole being said, 'Yes, that is all.'

And it happened to Nekhlyudov as it often happens to people living a spiritual life. The thought that at first had appeared so strange, so paradoxical, laughable even, ever more frequently finding confirmation in life, suddenly appeared to him as the simplest, incontrovertible truth. Thus he realized quite clearly that the only sure means of salvation from the terrible wrongs which mankind endures is for every men to acknowledge himself a sinner before God and therefore unfitted either to punish or reform others. It now became clear to him that all the dreadful evil of which he had been a witness in gaols and halting-places, and the calm self-assurance of those who committed it, resulted from the attempt by men to perform the impossible: being evil themselves they presumed to correct evil. Vicious men undertook to reform other vicious men and thought they could do it by mechanical means. But the only thing that came of it all was that needy and covetous men, having made a profession of so-called punishment and correction, themselves became utterly corrupt, and continually corrupted their victims. Now he knew the cause of all the horrors he had seen, and what ought to be done to put an end to them. The answer he had been unable to find was the same that Christ gave to Peter: to forgive everyone always, forgive an endless number of times, because there was no man living who was guiltless and therefore able to punish or reform.

'But surely it cannot be so simple?' Nekhlyudov said to himself, and yet he saw beyond any doubt that, strange as it had seemed to him at first, used as he was to the opposite, it was certainly not only a theoretical but also the most practical solution of the problem. The age-old question of what to do with wrong-doers – surely not let them go unpunished? – no longer perplexed him. The argument might have some meaning if it had ever been shown that punishment diminished crime or improved the criminal; but when exactly the contrary has been proved – when it has become an established fact that it is not within the power of one set of men to correct others – then the only sensible thing to do is to abandon methods which are not only useless but harmful, immoral and cruel. 'For many centuries criminals have been executed. Well, and are they extinct? Not at all. Far from being extinct, their numbers have been greatly increased by the addition of those criminals who have been demoralized by punishment and those other criminals – the judges, prosecutors, magistrates and gaolers – who judge and punish men.' Now Nekhlyudov understood that society and order generally speaking existed, not thanks to those legalized criminals who judge and punish other men, but because in spite of their depraving influence people still pity and love one another.

Hoping to find a confirmation of this idea in the same Gospel according to St Matthew, Nekhlyudov began it at the beginning. After reading the Sermon on the Mount, which he had always found moving, he saw in it today for the first time, not beautiful abstract thoughts, presenting for the most part exaggerated and impossible demands, but simple, clear, practical commandments, which if obeyed (and this was quite feasible) would establish a completely new order of human society, in which the violence that filled Nekhlyudov with such indignation would not only cease of itself but the greatest blessing man can hope for – the kingdom of heaven on earth – would be attained.

There were five of these commandments.

The first commandment (Matthew v. 21–6) was that man should not only not kill: he must not even be angry with his brother, or call him a fool, and if he should quarrel with anyone, he must be reconciled with him before offering his gift to God, that is, before praying.

The second commandment (Matthew v. 27–32) says that a man must not only refrain from committing adultery: he must avoid the enjoyment of a woman's beauty, and if he has once come together with a woman he should never be faithless to her.

The third commandment (Matthew v. 33–7) says that we must not seal a promise with an oath.

The fourth commandment (Matthew v. 38–42) enjoins us not to demand an eye for an eye but to offer the other cheek when we are smitten on one; tells us that we must forgive injuries and bear them with humility, and never refuse anyone a service he desires of us.

The fifth commandment (Matthew v. 43–8) enjoins us not merely not to hate our enemies or fight them but to love, help and serve them.

Nekhlyudov sat staring at the light of the lamp that had burned low, and his heart stopped beating. Recalling all the monstrous confusion of the life we lead, he pictured to himself what this life might be like if people were taught to obey these commandments, and his soul was swept by an ecstasy such as he had not felt for many a day. It was as though, after long pining and suffering, he had suddenly found peace and liberation.

He did not sleep that night, and as happens to vast numbers who read the Gospels, he understood for the first time the full meaning of words read and passed over innumerable times in the past. Like a sponge soaking up water he drank in all the vital, important and joyous news which the book revealed to him. And everything he read seemed familiar to him, confirming and making real what he had long known but had never fully understood nor really believed. But now he understood and believed.

But he not only realized and believed that if men would obey these commandments they would attain the highest good possible to them: he also realized and believed that it is man's sole duty to fulfil these commandments, that in this lies the only reasonable meaning of life, that every deviation from these laws is a mistake bringing immediate retribution in its wake. This flowed from the whole teaching, and was particularly strongly and clearly expressed in the parable of the vineyard. The husbandmen imagined that the vineyard into which the Master had sent them to work was their own; that everything in it was made for them and that all they had to do was to enjoy life in it, ignoring the Master and killing those who would remind them of him and of their obligations to him.

'We do the same,' thought Nekhlyudov. 'We live in the absurd conviction that we are masters of our lives, that life is given to us for our enjoyment. But this is obviously absurd. If we have been sent into this world, it must be by someone's will and for some purpose. Yet we have made up our minds that we live only for our own enjoyment, and of course things go ill with us, as they do with the husbandman who does not fulfil the will of his master. Now the will of the Master is expressed in these commandments. If men will but fulfil these commandments, the kingdom of heaven will be established here on earth, and they will attain the greatest good possible to them.

'*Seek ye first the kingdom of God, and his righteousness; and all these things shall be added unto you.* But we seek "all these things" and obviously fail to attain them.

'This, then, must be my life's work. One task is completed and another is ready to my hand.'

That night an entirely new life began for Nekhlyudov, not so much because he had entered into new conditions of life but because everything that happened to him from that time on was endowed with an entirely different meaning for him. How this new chapter of his life will end, the future will show.

1899

GORKY

My Childhood

My Childhood, which appeared in 1913, is the first part of Maxim Gorky's autobiographical trilogy. The ordinary experiences of a Russian boy in the nineteenth century are recalled by an altogether extraordinary man, whose gift for recapturing the world of a child is uncanny. Across the vision of the boy above the stove the Russian contrasts flicker – barbaric gaiety and deep gloom, satanic cruelty and saintly forbearance, clownish knaves and holy fools. A shutter in the mind closes: thirty years later the pictures develop, as fresh, as vivid, as exotic as when they were snapped.

This volume is translated by Ronald Wilks.

DOSTOYEVSKY

The Gambler
Bobok
A Nasty Story

Dostoyevsky wrote *The Gambler* in three weeks in 1866 (whilst at work on *Crime and Punishment*) to fulfil a contract and raise the wind. No great writer has ever been so obsessed with the despairing possibilities of roulette and the details of the story are entirely authentic. It also records his passion for Apollinario Suslova, whose cruelty had totally subdued his imagination.

There were other morbid strands in Dostoyevsky's genius: *Bobok* is a macabre, satirical conversation-piece in a graveyard, and *A Nasty Story*, one of his earliest and best, is a nightmare of good intentions gone bad.

This volume is translated by Jessie Coulson.

DOSTOYEVSKY

The Brothers Karamazov
(In two volumes)

The Brothers Karamazov, the culmination of Dostoyevsky's work, was completed in 1880, shortly before his death. A simple story of parricide and fraternal jealousy profoundly involves the questions of anarchism, atheism, and the existence of God.

The first volume in David Magarshack's excellent modern translation introduces Fyodor Karamazov, a mean and disreputable Russian land-owner, and his three legitimate sons: Dmitry, a profligate army officer; Ivan, a writer with revolutionary ideas; and Alexey, a religious novice. They meet to resolve a family dispute in the presence of the monk Zossima.

In the second volume Dmitry Karamazov is apprehended at the height of a wild orgy with his mistress and charged with the murder of his father, who has been robbed and killed by night. At the subsequent trial Ivan, his brother, throws the court into confusion, and the verdict which follows carries little conviction.

ALSO AVAILABLE:

Crime and Punishment
The Devils
The Idiot
Notes from Underground and
The Double

TOLSTOY

Anna Karenin

Tolstoy began to write *Anna Karenin* in 1875, six years after he had finished *War and Peace*, and it is considered by many to be the greater of the two. It is the story of Anna, one of the most admired women of fashionable Moscow and St Petersburg society, who gives up her husband, her son, and her position for a passion which finally drives her to suicide. And in contrast there is the story of Levin, which reflects the apparent peace of Tolstoy's own marriage. On the surface he lives a happy and contented country existence, and yet within is tormented by an intense need to discover the meaning of life without which he can see no purpose in living. In the end this is revealed to him by the simple words of a peasant – a conclusion which mitigates the horror of Anna's death.

TOLSTOY

War and Peace Vols 1 and 2

Few would dispute the claim of *War and Peace* to be regarded
as the greatest novel in any language. This massive chronicle,
to which Leo Tolstoy (1828–1910) devoted five whole years
shortly after his marriage, portrays Russian family life during
and after the Napoleonic War. Tolstoy's faith in life and his
piercing insight lend universality to a work which holds the
mirror up to nature as truly as Shakespeare or Homer.

The first volume of Rosemary Edmonds's modern translation takes the story as far as the appearance of the celebrated
comet before Napoleon's crossing of the Niemen.

The second volume describes Napoleon's Russian campaign of 1812 and the retreat from Moscow.

ALSO AVAILABLE:

Childhood, Boyhood, Youth
The Cossacks Ivan Ilyich, Happy Ever After